aised
w
lives in Philadelphia. He is the author of a collection of stories, *The Visible Man*, and two novels, *Nightmare Blue*, (written with George Alec Effinger) and *Strangers*, which was a Hugo and Nebula finalist. He has edited more than sixteen anthologies. His stories have appeared in *Playboy, Penthouse, Omni* and most of the leading SF magazines and anthologies. He has won two Nebula Awards for his short fiction and he has been a finalist for other Hugo and Nebula awards many times. His critical work has appeared in *Writer's Digest, Starship, Thrust, Science Fiction Chronicle, Writing and Selling Science Fiction* and *Science Fiction Writers*, and he is the author of the critical chapbook, *The Fiction of James Tiptree, Jr.* He has been a Judge for the World Fantasy Award and has served several times on the Nebula Award Jury; he was Chairman of the 1983 and 1984 Juries. Dozois is currently editor of *Isaac Asimov's Science Fiction Magazine.*

# BEST NEW SF2

Edited by Gardner Dozois

Robinson Publishing
London

*Robinson Publishing*
*11 Shepherd House*
*Shepherd Street*
*London W1Y 7LD*

*First published by Robinson Publishing in 1988*
*Published in the USA as* The Year's Best Science Fiction, Fifth Annual Collection.



*Hardback ISBN 0 948164 78 6*
*Paperback ISBN 0 948164 77 8*

*Printed by Wm. Collins & Sons Ltd., Glasgow.*

# ACKNOWLEDGMENTS

The editor would like to thank the following people for their help and support: Susan Casper, Virginia Kidd, Ellen Datlow, Sheila Williams, Tina Lee, Emy Eterno, Michael Swanwick, Pat Cadigan, Janet and Ricky Kagan, Shawna McCarthy, Lou Aronica, Edward Ferman, Anne Jordan, Ed Bayane, Susan Allison, Ginjer Buchanan, Beth Meacham, Claire Eddy, Pat LoBrutto, Patrick Delahunt, Tappan King, David Harris, George Scithers, Bob Walters, Tess Kissinger, Mark Van Name, and special thanks to my own editor, Stuart Moore.

Thanks are also due to Charles N. Brown, whose magazine *Locus* (Locus Publications, Inc. P.O. Box 13305, Oakland, CA 94661, $32.00 for a one-year first-class subscription, 12 issues) was used as a reference source throughout the Summation, and to Andrew Porter, whose magazine *Science Fiction Chronicle* (Algol Press, P.O. Box 4175, New York, NY 10163-4157, $23.40 for 1 year, 12 issues) was also used as a reference source throughout.

'Buffalo Gals, Won't You Come Out Tonight?' by Ursula K. Le Guin. Copyright © 1987 by Mercury Press, Inc. First published in *The Magazine of Fantasy and Science Fiction*, November 1987. Reprinted by permission of the author and the author's agent. Virginia Kidd.

'The Pardoner's Tale' by Robert Silverberg. Copyright © 1987 by Playboy. First published in *Playboy*, June 1987. Reprinted by permission of the author.

'Glass Cloud' by James Patrick Kelly. Copyright © 1987 by Davis Publications, Inc. First published in *Isaac Asimov's Science Fiction Magazine*, June 1987. Reprinted by permission of the author.

'The Evening and the Morning and the Night' by Octavia E. Butler. Copyright © 1987 by Omni Publication International, Ltd. First published in *Omni*, May 1987. Reprinted by permission of the author.

'Night of the Cooters' by Howard Waldrop. Copyright © 1987 by Omni Publications International, Ltd. First published in *Omni*, April 1987. Reprinted by permission of the author.

'Angel' by Pat Cadigan. Copyright © 1987 by Davis Publications, Inc. First published in *Isaac Asimov's Science Fiction Magazine*, May 1987. Reprinted by permission of the author.

'Shades' by Lucius Shepard. Copyright © 1987 by Jeanne Van Buren Dann and Jack Dann. First published in *In the Field of Fire* (Tor). Reprinted by permission of the author.

'Faithful Companion at Forty' by Karen Joy Fowler. Copyright © 1987 by Davis Publications, Inc. First published in *Isaac Asimov's Science Fiction Magazine*, July 1987. Reprinted by permission of the author.

Candle in a Cosmic Wind' by Joseph Manzione. Copyright © 1987 by Davis Publications, Inc. First published in *Analog*, August 1987. Reprinted by permission of the author.

'The Emir's Clock' by Ian Watson. Copyright © 1987 by Ian Watson. First published in *Other Edens* (Unwin Paperbacks). Reprinted by permission of the author.

'Ever After' by Susan Palwick. Copyright © 1987 by Davis Publications. Inc. First published in *Isaac Asimov's Science Fiction Magazine*, November 1987. Reprinted by permission of the author.

'The Forest of Time' by Michael Flynn. Copyright © 1987 by Davis Publications, Inc. First published in *Analog*, June 1987. Reprinted by permission of the author.

'The Million-Dollar Wound' by Dean Whitlock. Copyright © 1987 by Mercury Press, Inc. First published in *The Magazine of Fantasy and Science Fiction*, January 1987. Reprinted by permission of the author.

'The Moon of Popping Trees' by R. Garcia y Robertson. Copyright © 1987 by TSR, Inc. First published in *Amazing Stories*, September 1987. Reprinted by permission of the author and the author's agents, the Owlswick Literary Agency.

'Diner' by Neal Barrett, Jr. Copyright © 1987 by Omni Publication International, Ltd. First published in *Omni*, November 1987. Reprinted by permission of the author.

'All the Hues of Hell' by Gene Wolfe. Copyright © 1987 by Byron Preiss Visual Publications, Inc. First published in *The Universe* (Bantam). Reprinted by permission of the author and the author's agent, Virginia Kidd.

'Halley's Passing' by Michael McDowell. Copyright © 1987 by TZ Publications. First appeared in *The Twilight Zone Magazine*, June 1987. Reprinted by permission of the author.

'America' by Orson Scott Card. Copyright © 1987 by Davis Publications, Inc. First published in *Isaac Asimov's Science Fiction Magazine*, January 1987. Reprinted by permission of the author.

'For Thus Do I Remember Carthage' by Michael Bishop. Copyright © 1987 by Byron Preiss Visual Publications, Inc. First published in *The Universe* (Bantam). Reprinted by permission of the author.

'Mother Goddess of the World' by Kim Stanley Robinson. Copyright © 1987 by Davis Publications, Inc. First published in *Isaac Asimov's Science Fiction Magazine*, October 1987. Reprinted by permission of the author and the author's agent, Patrick Delahunt.

For my mother
Dorothy Dozois
my sister
Gail Fennessey
and my nephews
Randy and Joey

# CONTENTS

# INTRODUCTION

## Summation: 1987

Science Fiction had a good year commercially in 1987, although if you look beyond the best-seller lists, some disturbing trends were in evidence. From the standpoint of sales and book production, 1987 was a record year for the genre. According to the newsmagazine *Locus*, 177 publishers produced SF or fantasy in 1987, turning out a total of 1,675 books, up 12 percent from 1986. An astonishing 650 of those titles were new science fiction or fantasy novels. SF and fantasy books continued to make their presence strongly felt on nationwide best-seller lists, with writers such as Isaac Asimov, L. Ron Hubbard, Arthur C. Clarke, Stephen King, Stephen Donaldson, Anne McCaffrey, Robert Heinlein, Larry Niven, and others, staying on those lists throughout much of the year. New book lines also continued to appear in 1987. Doubleday, in conjunction with Bantam, has started an upscale new hardcover line called Foundation, edited by Pat LoBrutto. Baen Books started a new fantasy line, Sign of the Dragon, edited by Betsy Mitchell, and will publish two books a month under this imprint. The Ace Fantasy Specials published their first few titles to good response. And Crown Books, in partnership with the huge bookstore chain Waldenbooks, is planning a mass-market line with twelve titles per month, including SF, fantasy, horror, mystery, and romance. (This last news has caused a ripple of disquiet, however, among publishers, who are not particularly happy that one of the nation's largest book-buying chains is becoming a direct competitor. It remains to be seen exactly how the arrangement will work out.)

There *were* a few disturbing portents in 1987, though. Perhaps the most ominous of these was the dramatic upsurge of novels by newer writers set in fictional worlds created by famous SF writers, or novels using thematic material created by established writers. This practice of hiring lesser-known authors to create new adventures set "in the world of" some famous SF novel (for instance, a novel set in the world of Robert Heinlein's *Starship Troopers*, or in the world of Robert Silverberg's *Lord Valentine's Castle*) has been referred to as "sharecropping" and strikes me as a very dangerous trend. Many publishers would love to publish only surefire "brand name" bestsellers and eliminate all uncertainty from the process, and since the "brand names" themselves cannot possibly produce enough material to fulfill this dream, why not hire other people to do it *for* them? For years now, corporate publishing and corporate marketing specialists have been applying homogenizing pressures to the field, hoping to squash the wild diversity of SF into a rigidly standardized, and therefore easily manageable, "product," one for which profit is simple to predict; this latest trend is perhaps the most blatant and cynical attempt of all. The recent influx of "sharecropper" novels joins a flood of similar items—choose-your-own-adventure books, "Robotech" books, Star Trek novels, shared-world anthologies, "Dungeons and Dragons" scenarios, "Thieves World" novels, and so on. It is possible to argue that none of these items are pernicious in themselves, perhaps not even the "sharecropper" books. Taken together, however, as part of a rapidly growing publishing trend (*Locus* reports that there were seventy-four such books this year, up from twenty-two last year, and there will almost certainly be more next year), you begin to wonder how many individually created books of merit by young writers they are keeping out of print by filling an ever-increasing number of slots in publishers' schedules, and by eating up precious rack-display space in bookstores. In the case of the "sharecroppers," I also feel, perhaps naively, that young writers ought to be busy developing their *own* worlds and working out their own ideas and fresh material, rather than reworking ground already broken by older and more successful writers. Taken to an extreme, it is possible to envision a future where young writers can get into print *only* by hiring themselves out to produce work under one of a dozen or so highly marketable "brand names." Not only would creativity be stifled (which would probably spell the eventual doom of the genre), but it would become much more difficult for younger writers to get out of the midlist category, where advances are much lower than they need to be for more upwardly mobile authors. A paranoid fantasy? Perhaps. I certainly hope so.

And yet, few observers have noticed that it is *already* becoming a good deal harder to get out of midlist than it was only a few years ago. Almost every major publisher in SF now has a hardcover-softcover capability, for instance, and insists on buying hard and soft rights simultaneously for many books. Thus, if you have an unaffiliated hardcover, a hardcover for which softcover rights have *not* already been sold, you are going to find it much more difficult to sell those rights to somebody now than it was a few years back. This also tends to discourage paperback-rights auctions for all but a few of the hottest writers: during the last decade or so, the paperback auction is where most of the really serious money has been made. This will tend to keep advances for novels a lot lower on the whole—thereby making it more difficult to get out of midlist and into the territory where the publishers suddenly start spending a *lot* more money to promote your book. When publishers have higher expectations for a book and a higher investment to protect (because they had to spend more to get it in the first place), more money goes toward promotion.

In spite of all this—and the constant worry, not helped by the Stock Market crash, that there is another major recession for the publishing industry waiting just down the road—I remain cautiously optimistic about the health of the genre. This (cautious) optimism is fueled by the fact that there is more good science fiction and fantasy being produced by more good writers today than at any other time in the history of the genre—work of *all* sorts right across the aesthetic spectrum, from High Fantasy to the hardest of hard SF. And this work is being produced by a multigenerational cross-section of writers that extends from Golden Age giants of the 1940s to the kids making their first sales in 1987. Isn't there a lot of shit being published? Sure there is—there always is—but there is *also* a lot of worthwhile work being produced by many writers. And I don't think that anything short of the death of the publishing industry as we know it is going to be sufficient to keep them *all* out of print.

But only time will tell.

It was a year of mixed success in the SF magazine market. On the downhill side, the digest-sized horror magazine *Night Cry* was killed just as it looked—to me, anyway—as though they might have a shot at establishing a steady audience. Another large-format glossy SF magazine was announced and heavily publicized throughout 1987, *SF: New Science Fiction Stories* . . . but, like *Imago* and *L. Ron Hubbard's to the Stars Science Fiction Magazine* before it, it died stillborn. There is definitely a niche for a slick, large-format SF/fantasy magazine, in my opinion, and someday a shrewd someone is going to come along with adequate capital and the proper vision and do it *right*—and quite likely stand the SF magazine world on its ear. It didn't happen in 1987, though, and it probably will not happen in 1988, either. But *some*day, it will: mark my words. The recently resurrected *Worlds of If* also seems to have vanished from mortal ken, and must be presumed dead.

There *was* an uphill side, although perhaps not a tremendously steep one. *The Twilight Zone Magazine* has improved markedly under its new editor Tappan King, and *Amazing* is showing new signs of vigor under its new editor Patrick L. Price. *The Magazine of Fantasy and Science Fiction* recently underwent a complete internal redesign, the first for the magazine in decades. *Interzone* survived and prospered (modestly) for yet another year. The folks at *Aboriginal SF* were smart enough to get rid of their odd tabloid format, which many industry observers had seen as the kiss of death for the magazine, and *Aboriginal SF* survived to produce five issues in 1988. Although insiders were giving odds against the magazine last year, its chances of survival at this point actually look pretty good. And two new magazines will be entering the ring in 1988: a resurrected *Weird Tales*, edited by veteran George H. Scithers, and a new semiprozine called *Argos Fantasy and Science Fiction Magazine*, edited by Ross Emry.

As most of you probably know, I, Gardner Dozois, am also editor of *Isaac Asimov's Science Fiction Magazine*. And that, as I have mentioned before, poses a problem for me in compiling this summation, particularly the magazine-by-magazine review that follows. As *IAsfm* editor, I could be said to have a vested interest in the magazine's success, so that anything negative I said about another SF magazine (particularly another digest-sized magazine, my direct competition), could be perceived as an attempt to make my own magazine look good. Aware of this constraint, I have decided that nobody can complain if I say only *positive* things about the competition . . . and so, once again, I have limited myself to a listing of some of the worthwhile authors published by each.

*Omni* published first-rate fiction this year by Howard Waldrop, Octavia

Butler, Kate Wilhelm, George R. R. Martin, Neal Barrett, Jr., Bruce McAllister, and others. *Omni's* fiction editor is Ellen Datlow.

*The Magazine of Fantasy and Science Fiction* featured excellent fiction by Ursula K. Le Guin, Dean Whitlock, Robert Charles Wilson, Paul J. McAuley, Kim Stanley Robinson, Lucius Shepard, Jonathan Carroll, Keith Roberts, Avram Davidson, and others. *F & SF's* long-time editor is Edward Ferman.

*Issac Asimov's Science Fiction Magazine* featured critically acclaimed work by Pat Murphy, Walter Jon Williams, James Patrick Kelly, Karen Joy Fowler, Lucius Shepard, Pat Cadigan, Orson Scott Card, Bruce Sterling, Connie Willis, Kim Stanley Robinson, Robert Silverberg, Nancy Kress, Neal Barrett, Jr., and others. *IAsfm's* editor is Gardner Dozois.

*Analog* featured good work by Michael Flynn, Harry Turtledove, Charles Sheffield, Eric Vinicoff, Joseph Manzione, Poul Anderson, D. C. Poyer, Jerry Oltion, and others. *Analog's* long-time editor is Stanley Schmidt.

*Amazing* featured good work by R. Garcia y Robertson, Paul Di Fillipo, Susan Casper, Phillip C. Jennings, Susan Palwick, Robert Frazier, Justin Leiber, and others. *Amazing's* editor is Patrick L. Price.

*The Twilight Zone Magazine* featured good work by Kim Antieau, Pat Murphy, Pat Cadigan, Susan Casper, Michael McDowell, Jane Yolen, Lucius Shepard, Peni Griffin, and others. *TZ's* editor is Tappan King.

*Interzone* featured good work by Gregory Benford, Ian Watson, Brian Stableford, Geoff Ryman, Richard Kadrey, Michael Swanwick, Ken Wisman, and others. *Interzone's* editors are Simon Ounsley and David Pringle.

Short SF continued to appear in many magazines outside genre boundaries, including off-trail markets such as *High Times*. *Playboy* in particular continues to run a good deal of SF, under fiction editor Alice K. Turner.

(Subscription addresses follow for those magazines hardest to find on the newsstands: *The Magazine of Fantasy and Science Fiction*, Mercury Press, Inc., Box 56, Cornwall, CT, 06753, annual subscription $19.50 for twelve issues; *Amazing*, TSR, Inc., P. O. Box 72069, Chicago, IL, 60690, annual subscription $9.00 for six issues; *Isaac Asimov's Science Fiction Magazine*, Davis Publications, Inc., P.O. Box 1933, Marion, OH 43305, $19.50 for thirteen issues; *Interzone*, 124 Osborne Road, Brighton, BN1 6LU, England, airmail one-year subscription $13.00 for four issues.)

The semiprozine scene was changing in 1987, with old magazines dying, and new ones either being born or struggling to establish themselves. Among the fiction semiprozines, *Fantasy Book* and *Alphelion* have died: *Whispers* and *Fantasy Tales* each produced only one issue this year (with the *Whispers* issue particularly recommended); *Aboriginal SF* and *New Pathways* were looking fairly healthy; and two new magazines, as we mentioned before, are waiting in the wings—*Weird Tales* and *Argos F&SF*. (*Aboriginal SF* is still technically a semiprozine, because of its low circulation and its lack of newsstand distribution, but it is being taken seriously as a professional market within the field, and with luck, it will not stay in this category for long. Similarly, *Weird Tales* is technically a semiprozine, but with an experienced editor like Scithers at the helm, this too may change if the magazine can keep its head above water long enough.) There were also a slew of new horror semiprozines, the most visible of which were probably *The Horror Show* and *Grue Magazine*. As ever, *Locus* and *SF Chronicle* remain your best bet among the semiprozines if you are looking for an overview of the genre. Among the semiprozines that concentrate primarily on literary criticism, the death of *Fantasy Review* this year leaves *Thrust* unchallenged as the best-known and longest-surviving of the criticalzines. Two recent and promising contenders in the criticalzine field are Orson Scott Card's *Short Form* and Steve Brown and Dan Steffan's *Science Fiction Eye*, although both magazines had a lot of trouble sticking to their announced publishing schedules this year (the second issue of *Short Form* appeared over eight months late). Perhaps these potentially valuable magazines will work the bugs out and become more reliable in 1988.

(*Locus*, Locus Publications, Inc., P. O. Box 13305, Oakland, CA 94661, one-year first-class subscription $32.00 for 12 issues; *Science Fiction Chronicle*, Algol Press, P. O. Box 4175, New York, NY 10163–4157, one-year subscription $23.40 for twelve issues; *Thrust*, Thrust Publications, 8217 Langport Terrace, Gaithersburg, MD 20877, $8.00 for four issues; *Science Fiction Eye*, Box 3105, Washington, DC 20010–0105, $7.00 for one year; *Short Form*, 546 Lindley Road, Greensboro, NC 27410; *Aboriginal Science Fiction*, P. O. Box 2449, Woburn, MA 01888–0849, $12.00 for six issues, $22.00 for twelve issues; *Weird Tales*, Box 13418, Philadelphia, PA 19101–3418, $18.00 for six issues [eighteen months]; *New Pathways*, MGA Services, P. O. Box 863994, Plano, TX 75086–3994, one-year subscription $15.00 for six issues, $25.00 for a two-year subscription; *Argos Fantasy & Science Fiction Magazine*, Penrhyn Publishing Company, Box 2109, Renton, WA 98056, one-year subscription $8.00 for four issues; *Whispers*, 70 Highland Ave., Binghamton, NY 13905, $13.95 for two double issues; *Fantasy Tales*, Stephen Jones, 130 Parkview, Wembley, Middlesex, HA9 6JU, England, Great Britain, $11.00 for three issues; *The Horror Show*, Phantasm Press, 1488 Misty Springs Lane, Oak Run, CA 96069, $14.00 per year; *Grue Magazine*, Hells Kitchen productions, Box 370, Times Square Sta., New York, NY 10108, $11.00 for three issues.)

Overall, 1987 was a pretty good year for original anthologies. The best original anthology of the year, and one of the best in a number of years, was undoubtedly *In The Field of Fire* (Tor), edited by Jeanne Van Buren Dann and Jack Dann. This anthology, the first ever of SF stories about the war in Vietnam, was recognized immediately as a landmark anthology. *The New York Times Book Review* went so far as to call it "a significant contribution to the literature of the 1980s." There are no really bad stories here, but the best, which are among the year's best, include stories by Bruce McAllister, Lucius Shepard, Susan Casper, Dave Smeds, and a very affecting poem by Joe Haldeman. The book also contains good stories by John Kessel, Richard Paul Russo, Karen Joy Fowler, Robert Frazier, Charles L. Grant, and others, as well as classic reprints by Kate Wilhelm, Harlan Ellison, and others. Another good anthology, and an excellent value for your money, is *The Universe* (Bantam Spectra), edited by Byron Preiss (fiction editor, David Harris). The fiction here is uneven, although there is some very good stuff by Michael Bishop, Gene Wolfe, Connie Willis, Robert Silverberg, Rudy Rucker, and others. The anthology also contains a wide array of interesting nonfiction articles, featuring a lot of fascinating up-to-the-minute cosmological speculation and some good color artwork by SF and astronomical artists. Great Britain also produced two good original anthologies this year: *Other Edens* (Unwin), edited by Christopher Evans and Robert Holdstock, and *Tales from the Forbidden Planet* (Titan), edited by Roz Kaveny. *Other Edens* featured good work by Ian Watson, M. John Harrison, Garry Kilworth, Keith Roberts, and others. *Tales from the Forbidden Planet* featured good work by Keith Roberts, Gwyneth Jones, Iain Banks, Tanith Lee, and others. Also interesting was *Mathenauts* (Arbor House), edited by Rudy Rucker, a mixed reprint-and-original anthology of SF stories about mathematics, especially notable for bringing back into print two neglected classics by Norman Kagan.

Among the series anthologies, the late Terry Carr's last *Universe* volume, *Universe 17* (Doubleday), was unfortunately rather weak—some good work here, but nothing outstanding. *Universe* is the longest-running original SF anthology, and its loss would be a blow to the field. Fortunately, it looks as though this anthology series will survive the tragic death of its founding editor—*Universe* will be taken over by Robert Silverberg and Karen Haber and will appear every other year instead of annually. *Far Frontiers*, the Baen anthology series, edited by Jim Baen and Jerry Pournelle, also underwent a transformation in 1987—Jerry Pournelle stepped down as co-editor, and the name of the series became *New Destinies*. Aesthetically, however, little has changed; it still remains a good solid anthology, but one that, to date, has published nothing of really first-rank quality. Another *Writers of the Future* anthology appeared in 1987. *L. Ron Hubbard Presents Writers of the Future, Volume III* (Bridge), edited by Algis Budrys. As with previous volumes, it may well be true that some of the writers herein will someday be the big-name professionals of the future—you will definitely be seeing a lot more from M. Shayne Bell, R. V. Branham, Martha Soukup, and Dave Wolverton, for instance—but the stories they have produced for this *particular* anthology are novice work. A new SF original anthology series started this year, with *Synergy: New Science Fiction, Volume 1* (Harcourt Brace Jovanovich), edited by George Zebrowski. This shows every sign of being a promising series, and it will be interesting to see it develop. The first volume, however, contains good work by Frederik Pohl, Ian Watson, Charles Harness, and Rudy Rucker, but does not have any really exceptional material. Another new original SF anthology series, *Full Spectrum*, edited by Shawna McCarthy and Lou Aronica, is forthcoming next year from Bantam Spectra.

There were no really good high fantasy anthologies this year, unfortunately. With high fantasy booming as a genre, I do not know why original anthologies of the stuff are so rare. I personally like well-executed high fantasy anthologies, and would like to see more of them. As usual, though, there were a lot of horror anthologies published. *Shadows 10* (Doubleday), edited by Charles L. Grant, and *Whispers VI* (Doubleday), edited by Stuart David Schiff were the best of them—both solid volumes of their respective series. (*Shadows* and

*Whispers* are usually the best bets in the original horror anthology field and have been so for years.) There was an interesting one-shot original horror anthology this year, *The Architecture of Fear* (Arbor House), edited by Kathryn Cramer and Peter D. Pautz. Less interesting were *Masques II* (Maclay), edited by J. N. Williamson, and *Doom City* (Tor), edited by Charles L. Grant. *Night Visions 4* (Dark Harvest) was very uneven (as this series almost unavoidably is), but did feature some good work.

It was a pretty good year overall for novels, although there was no single novel that dominated 1987 the way that, say, Frederik Pohl's *Gateway* or Ursula K. Le Guin's *The Left Hand of Darkness* dominated their respective years. Once again, I must admit that I was unable to read all the new novels released this year, or even the majority of them. *Locus* estimates that there were 298 new SF novels, 256 new fantasy novels, and 96 new horror novels released—and their estimates are probably low. It is difficult to understand how *anyone* could keep up with 650 new novels, let alone anyone with anything else to do. Certainly I can't. Therefore, as usual, I am going to limit myself here to comments on novels I *did* read. I was most impressed by *Lincoln's Dreams*, Connie Willis (Bantam Spectra); *Mindplayers*, Pat Cadigan (Bantam); *Vacuum Flowers*, Michael Swanwick (Arbor House); *Life During Wartime*, Lucius Shepard (Bantam); *The Urth of the New Sun*, Gene Wolfe (Tor); *When Gravity Fails*, George Alec Effinger (Arbor House); *The Forge of God*, Greg Bear (Tor); *Great Sky River*, Gregory Benford (Bantam Spectra); *Land of Dreams*, James P. Blaylock (Arbor House); and *A Mask for the General*, Lisa Goldstein (Bantam Spectra).

Other novels that have gotten a lot of attention this year include: *2061: Odyssey Three*, Arthur C. Clarke (Del Rey); *The Secret Ascension*, Michael Bishop (Tor); *Seventh Son*, Orson Scott Card (Tor); *The Annals of the Heechee*, Frederik Pohl (Del Rey); *Voice of the Whirlwind*, Walter Jon Williams (Tor); *On Stranger Tides*, Tim Powers (Ace); *Aegypt*, John Crowley (Bantam Spectra); *Little Heroes*, Norman Spinrad (Bantam Spectra); *Bones of the Moon*, Jonathan Carroll (Arbor House); *War for the Oaks*, Emma Bull (Ace); *To Sail Beyond the Sunset*, Robert A. Heinlein (Ace Putnam); *Dover Beach*, Richard Bowker (Bantam Spectra); *Dawn*, Octavia E. Butler (Warner); *The Smoke Ring*, Larry Niven (Del Rey); *Memories*, Mike McQuay (Bantam Spectra); *Way of the Pilgrim*, Gordon R. Dickson (Ace); *Rumors of Spring*, Richard Grant (Bantam Spectra); *Sign of Chaos*, Roger Zelazny (Arbor House); *The Dark Tower II: The Drawing of the Three*, Stephen King (Donald M. Grant); *Still River*, Hal Clement (Del Rey); *Swordspoint*, Ellen Kushner (Arbor House); *Infernal Devices*, K. W. Jeter (St. Martin's Press); *Soldiers of Paradise*, Paul Park (Arbor House); and *Araminta Station*, Jack Vance (Underwood-Miller).

(I should set off mention here of books I bought and edited myself for the *Isaac Asimov Presents* line for Congdon & Weed, so that you can make the proper allowances for bias: *The Man Who Pulled down the Sky*, John Barnes; *Pennterra*, Judith Moffett; *Agent of Byzantium*, Harry Turtledove; *Through Darkest America*, Neal Barrett, Jr.; *Station Gehenna*, Andrew Weiner; and *Caliban Landing*, Steve Popkes.)

It is interesting to note that, once again, the Nebula electorate ignored works by some of the biggest names in the field—Heinlein, Clarke, Niven, Dickson, Clement, King—in favor of placing novels by middle-level writers such as Wolfe and newer writers such as Murphy and Bear on this year's final Nebula Ballot. What does this mean? I don't know, but in a field like SF, where name-recognition is supposed to be the most important factor, it must mean *something*. Perhaps it is an early indication that somewhere down the line there is going to be a big shift in just *whom* the audience recognizes as big-name authors.

It is also encouraging to note that there was a steady stream of first novels once again this year. *Locus* listed about thirty of them—no doubt there were actually more. None of them had as much of an impact on the field as a few first novels have had in recent years—there are no first novels on the final Nebula Ballot this time around, for instance, although they dominated it in 1984. Many fine first novels did appear in 1987, though; particularly strong were the Cadigan, the Moffett, the Barnes, the Park, the Bull, and the Kushner.

As you can see from looking over the lists, Tor, Arbor House, and Bantam had particularly strong years in 1987.

Nineteen eighty-seven was not as strong a year overall for short-story collections as 1986, although several excellent volumes did appear. The best of the year's collections were *The Jaguar Hunter*, Lucius Shepard (Arkham House) and *All About Strange Monsters of the Recent Past: Neat Stories by Howard Waldrop*, Howard Waldrop (Ursus Press), both landmark collections. If you can afford them (which few people will be able to, alas), the monumental five-volume *The Collected Stories of Philip K. Dick*, Philip K. Dick (Underwood-Miller) and *The Essential Ellison*, Harlan Ellison (The Nemo Press), also belong on everyone's bookshelf. *Evil Water*, Ian Watson (Gollancz); *Cardography*, Orson Scott Card (Hypatia); *Faces*, Leigh Kennedy (Atlantic Monthly Press); *Portraits of His Children*, George R. R. Martin (Dark Harvest); and the posthumous collection *The Valley So Low: Southern Mountain Stories*, Manly Wade Wellman (Doubleday) were also first rate.

Also outstanding this year were *The Best of Pamela Sargent*, Pamela Sargent (Academy Chicago); *True Names . . . and Other Dangers*, Vernor Vinge (Baen); *Buffalo Gals and Other Animal Presences*, Ursula K. Le Guin (Capra Press); *The Hidden Side of the Moon*, Joanna Russ (St. Martin's Press); *Our Best: the Best of Frederik Pohl and C. M. Kornbluth*, Frederik Pohl and C. M. Kornbluth (Baen); *Night Sorceries*, Tanith Lee (Daw); *Polyphemus*, Michael Shea (Arkham House); *And the Gods Laughed*, Frederic Brown (Phantasia Press); *Why Not You and I?*, Karl Edward Wagner (Dark Harvest); *Scared Stiff, Tales of Sex and Death*, Ramsey Campbell (Scream/Press); and *The Bridge of Lost Desire*, Samuel R. Delany (Arbor House).

It is interesting to see the extent to which small presses have come to dominate the field of short-story collections. Arkham House, Dark Harvest, Underwood-Miller, Ursus Press, The Nemo Press, Scream/Press, Hypathia, Academy Chicago—these, and other small presses, were the publishers who brought you short-story collections this year, for the most part. Trade publishers mostly avoided the risks involved in publishing collections, and seemed content to let the small presses pick up the slack. Let us hope that more of the regular trade publishers pick up some of that slack next year, and start publishing more collections.

It was another fairly good year in the reprint anthology market. As is the case almost every year, your best bets in the reprint market were the various "Best of the Year" collections. This year there were three covering science fiction (including this one), one covering fantasy, one covering horror, plus the annual Nebula Award anthology. (Next year there will be one fewer "best" covering science fiction—Terry Carr's—but an additional one covering both fantasy and horror.) The best nonseries reprint anthology of the year, and one of the best values for your money of *any* year, is the enormous retrospective horror anthology *The Dark Descent* (Tor), edited by David G. Hartwell. Hartwell definitely has an aesthetic ax or two to grind here: the extensive section introductions and story notes are designed to put forward a sequence of polemical critical points about the nature of horror fiction and the evolution of the genre; they are deliberately argumentative. You may disagree with some of this critical armature—or not want to be bothered with it at all—but it is hard to find fault with the fiction that Hartwell has selected, or complain about value received for your dollar: the book is 1,011 pages long and contains an amazing 56 stories. *The Dark Descent* will be a landmark anthology for years to come. Any book eclectic enough to contain neglected masterpieces, such as Fritz Leiber's "Smoke Ghost," Gene Wolfe's "Seven American Nights," Michael Bishop's "Within the Walls of Tyre," and Thomas M. Disch's "The Asian Shore," all in one volume, deserves to be on everyone's bookshelf, whether it is classified as horror, fantasy, or science fiction. Almost equally fascinating, not so much for the quality of the stories reprinted—though all of them are good, and a few of them are excellent—as for the fascinating literary analysis, is *Robert Silverberg's Worlds of Wonder* (Warner), edited by Robert Silverberg. Literary analyses, couched in the form of personal reminiscences, surround each story, as Silverberg tries to discern the qualities and techniques that make each story successful. This is another anthology that belongs on every bookshelf, and most particularly on that of the would-be SF writer—it is practically a one-volume writing course and contains a great deal of valuable perspective and analyzed technique for the aspiring author.

Also worthwhile this year were *The Fifth Omni Book of Science Fiction* (Zebra), edited by Ellen Datlow; *Interzone, the Second Anthology* (St. Martin's Press), edited by John Clute, David Pringle, and Simon Ounsley; *The Great SF Stories: 16* (Daw), edited by Isaac Asimov and Martin H. Greenberg; *Neanderthals* (NAL), edited by Isaac Asimov, Martin H. Greenberg, and Charles G. Waugh; *Christmas Ghosts* (Arbor House), edited by Kathryn Cramer and David G. Hartwell; *Vampires* (Doubleday), edited by Alan Ryan; and *Vamp* (DAW) edited by Martin H. Greenberg and Charles G. Waugh. Noted without comment is *Demons!* (Ace), edited by Jack Dann and Gardner Dozois.

It was another solid year for the SF-oriented nonfiction/SF reference book field, although there were no exceptional items, as there have been in other years. There were several valuable reference volumes: *Anatomy of Wonder, 3rd Edition* (R. R. Bowker), edited by Neil Barron; *Science Fiction, Fantasy, and Horror 1986* (Locus Press), compiled by Charles N. Brown and William G. Contento; and *Science Fiction and Fantasy Reference Index, Vols I & II* (Gale), compiled by H. W. Hall. (Some of these, most notably the Hall, may be of more interest to libraries or to scholars than to the average reader.) There was another addition this year to the ever-growing five-foot shelf of critical books about Philip K. Dick—*Mind in Motion, the Fiction of Philip K. Dick* (Southern Illinois University Press), edited by Patricia S. Warrick. A critical study of a more-ignored author, *Imprisoned in a Tesseract: the Life of James Blish* (Kent State), by David Ketterer, is the only study of Blish to date. *Robert Heinlein* (Twayne), by Leon Stover, is billed as a study of this controversial author, but is more of a whitewash job than an impartial critical study, with Stover leaping passionately to Heinlein's defense against nearly every criticism that has ever been leveled at the Great Man. Surely Heinlein must have *some* faults as a writer, whatever his merits, and admitting to a few of them might have made this volume less nakedly partisan and of more real critical use. There was also a study of Frank Herbert, *The Maker of Dune: Insights of a Maker of Science Fiction* (Berkley), edited by Tim O'Reilly, and one of Frederik Pohl, *Frederik Pohl* (Starmont), by Thomas Clareson. Two historical studies, *Foundations of Science Fiction* (Greenwood), by J. J. Pierce and *Wizardry and Wild Romance: A Study of Epic Fantasy* (Gollancz), by Michael Moorcock, are interesting, if for nothing else, for their differing aesthetic viewpoints. Also interesting was *Intersections, Fantasy and Science Fiction* (Southern Illinois University Press), edited by George E. Slusser and Eric S. Rabin.

For lack of a better place to list it, I am also going to mention in this section *Cvltvre Made Stvpid* (Houghton Mifflin), by Tom Weller. It is a follow-up of sorts to Weller's very funny *Science Made Stupid*, which won a Hugo for Best Non-Fiction (!) a couple of years ago, much to the author's bemusement.

Overall, 1987 seemed—to me, at least—like another generally lackluster year for science fiction and fantasy films. Among the few bright spots were *Robocop* and *The Princess Bride*, probably the two best SF/fantasy films of the year. Arnold Schwarzenegger's *Predator* had a few interesting touches, although his *The Running Man* was fairly familiar stuff. *Spaceballs* was disappointing, and I remain puzzled by the decision to satirize *Star Wars* ten years after the fact, long after every possible satiric point had been made time and time again. *The Golden Child* was even more disappointing, with only Eddie Murphy's manic presence to partially redeem a muddled and ridiculous plot. Speaking of muddled and ridiculous, *Angel Heart* was a *major* disappointment, a pompous and incredibly pretentious movie not even remotely redeemed by loving closeups of Mickey Rourke's heaving buttocks. *The Witches of Eastwick* was a silly and somewhat lowbrow version of John Updike's novel. Worse than disappointing were *Superman IV*, *Innerspace*, *Masters of the Universe*, *Hello Again*, and *Harry and the Hendersons*. There were a number of moderately upscale horror movies (*The Lost Boys*, *Prince of Darkness*, *The Gate*, *Hellraiser*), none of which was wholly successful, and seemingly dozens of lower-budget horror/slasher movies—far too many to list here, most of them bad beyond belief. All in all, not much of a year.

For the last couple of years, Edward Bryant has been complaining in *Mile High Futures* that this particular part of the Summation serves only to demonstrate that I know nothing about film, and that I have been overlooking many of the good ones. So this year, in the interests of completion, I have asked Ed to contribute his own list of the year's ten best SF/fantasy films. Presented without comment, here is Ed Bryant's list of the year's top films: (1) *Robocop*; (2) *Near Dark*; (3) *The Princess Bride*; (4) *Hellraiser*; (5) *Man Facing Southeast*; (6) *Star Trek IV: the Voyage Home*; (7) *Wild Thing*; (8) *Innerspace*; (9) *Nightflyers*; (10) *Predator/The Running Man*.

Meanwhile—we are back to *my* opinions again here, not Ed's—science fiction and fantasy shows had a year of mixed success on television. "Amazing Stories" finally died, as did an eccentric, promising, and intelligent new series "Max Headroom." On the other hand, "Star Trek: the Next Generation" is one of the most commercially successful new programs on television this year. That is the good news. The *bad* news is that it is not particularly *good*; the acting is flat and the plots are simplistic—in fact, this series is *already* using moronic plot devices (the crew go down to a primitive planet and engage in gladiatorial contests) that the original series did not resort to until the third season. So, good ratings aside, this is a disappointing show so far, and I am not sanguine about it improving substantially in the future. Also a hit show, one of the biggest new hits of the season, in fact, is "Beauty and the Beast." This is a well-crafted and earnest show, with many intelligent touches, much more impressive than "Star Trek: the Next Generation." "Beauty and the Beast's" plots are very repetitive, though, so much so that I found myself losing interest in the show midway through the season. If this turns out to be a common reaction, the show could eventually end up in trouble—so far, however, it has been winning its time slot and is certainly more successful than the much more heavily hyped "Amazing Stories" was. It is certainly more deserving of success than "Alf," which has become one of those hype-manufactured cult favorites that seem so inexplicable ten years down the road (remember the Fonz?)—let alone "Friday the 13th: the Series" and "Bates Motel" (*Psycho* as a weekly television *sitcom*? Give me a break!), let alone "Out of this World" and "Small Wonder"; the less said about these last two shows, the better.

"Ray Bradbury Theater," "Tales from the Darkside," and a new show called "Werewolf" are also phosphor-dot invaders of your living room, but I have not seen any of them. No great loss in most cases, I suspect.

The 45th World Science Fiction convention, Conspiracy, was held in Brighton, England, August 27–31, 1987, and drew an estimated attendance of 5,000. The 1987 Hugo Awards, presented at Conspiracy, were: Best Novel, *Speaker for the Dead*, by Orson Scott Card; Best Novella, "Gilgamesh in the Outback," by Robert Silverberg; Best Novelette, "Permafrost," by Roger Zelazny; Best Short Story, "Tangents," by Greg Bear; Best Non-Fiction, *Trillion*

*Year Spree*, by Brian Aldiss and Dave Wingrove; Best Professional Editor, Terry Carr; Best Professional Artist, Jim Burns; Best Dramatic Presentation, *Aliens*; Best Semi-Prozine, *Locus*; Best Fanzine, *Ansible*; Best Fan Writer, David Langford; Best Fan Artist, Brad Foster; plus the John W. Campbell Award for Best New Writer to Karen Joy Fowler.

The 1986 Nebula Awards, presented at a banquet at the Halloran House Hotel in New York City, on May 2, 1987, were: Best Novel, *Speaker for the Dead*, by Orson Scott Card; Best Novella, "R & R," by Lucius Shepard; Best Novelette, "The Girl Who Fell from the Sky," by Kate Wilhelm; Best Short Story, "Tangents," by Greg Bear; plus the Grand Master Award to Isaac Asimov.

The World Fantasy Awards, presented at the Thirteenth Annual World Fantasy Convention in Nashville, Tennessee, November 1, 1987, were: Best Novel, *Perfume*, by Patrick Suskind; Best Novella, "Hatrack River," by Orson Scott Card; Best Short Story, "Red Light," by David Schow; Best Anthology/Collection, *Tales of the Quintana Roo*, James Tiptree, Jr.; Best Artist, Robert Gould; Special Award (Professional), Jane Yolen; Special Award (Non-Professional), (tie) Jeff Conner and W. Paul Ganley; plus a Life Achievement Award to Jack Finney.

The 1986 John W. Campbell Memorial Award winner was *A Door into Ocean*, by Joan Slonczewski.

The fifth Philip K. Dick Memorial Award winner was *Homunculus*, by James P. Blaylock.

The first Theodore Sturgeon Award winner was "Surviving," by Judith Moffett.

Death took a heavy toll on the science fiction field again in 1987, inflicting several major losses. The dead include: **Alfred Bester**, 73, SF writer, author of *The Demolished Man* and the cult classic, *The Stars My Destination*, which many critics consider to be the best SF novel ever written; **Dr. Alice Sheldon**, 71, better known to SF audiences by her pseudonyms of **James Tiptree, Jr.** and **Raccoona Sheldon**, under which names she established herself as one of the very best short-story writers ever to enter the field, author of several classic collections and the novel *Brightness Falls from the Air*, a personal friend; **Terry Carr**, 50, writer and editor, perhaps the most influential SF editor of the last twenty years, creator of both the original and the recently refurbished Ace Special series, as well as the *Universe* series of original anthologies, the longest-running anthology series in SF, a well-respected Best of the Year series, and dozens of other anthologies, another friend; **Theodore R. Cogswell**, 68, writer and editor, best known as the author of the collection *The Wall around the World*; **Richard Wilson**, 66, writer and Futurian, Nebula winner for the story "Mother to the World"; veteran author **Gardner F. Fox**, 68; thriller and associational writer **Alistair Maclean**, 64; writer **Erskine Caldwell**, 83; veteran writer and publisher **Donald Wandrei**, 79; **Ejler Jakobsson**, 75, one-time editor of *Galaxy* magazine; **Richard Delap**, 45, SF critic and editor; **Bea Mahaffey**, 60, veteran editor and long-time fan; **E. Nelson Bridwell**, 55, comics writer and expert on comics history; **Danny Kaye**, 74, actor, perhaps best known to the SF audience for his role in *The Court Jester*; **Ray Bolger**, 83, actor, perhaps best known to the SF audience for his role as the Scarecrow in the film classic *The Wizard of Oz*; **Polly Freas**, 68, wife of SF artist Kelly Freas; **Murray I. Dann**, 76, father of SF writer Jack Dann; **Joseph LoBrutto**, 12, son of SF editor Pat LoBrutto; **Lawrence Lyle Heinlein**, 86, brother of SF writer Robert Heinlein; **Maude Dickson**, 96, mother of SF writer Gordon R. Dickson; and **Hugh McCaffrey**, 63, brother of SF writer Anne McCaffrey.

# PAT MURPHY

## Rachel in Love

Pat Murphy lives in San Francisco, where she works for a science museum, the Exploratorium. Her elegant and incisive stories have been turning up for the past few years in *Isaac Asimov's Science Fiction Magazine, Elsewhere, Amazing, Universe, Shadows, Chrysalis,* and other places. Her first novel, *The Shadow Hunter,* was published in 1982. Her most recent novel, *The Falling Woman,* is at the time of this writing a strong contender for the 1987 Nebula Award, as is "Rachel in Love." Her story "In the Islands" was in our First Annual Collection.

Here she gives us perhaps her strongest and most eloquent story to date, a haunting tale that forces us to take a new look at just what it really means to be human.

# RACHEL IN LOVE

## Pat Murphy

It is a Sunday morning in summer and a small brown chimpanzee named Rachel sits on the living room floor of a remote ranch house on the edge of the Painted Desert. She is watching a Tarzan movie on television. Her hairy arms are wrapped around her knees and she rocks back and forth with suppressed excitement. She knows that her father would say that she's too old for such childish amusements—but since Aaron is still sleeping, he can't chastise her.

On the television, Tarzan has been trapped in a bamboo cage by a band of wicked Pygmies. Rachel is afraid that he won't escape in time to save Jane from the ivory smugglers who hold her captive. The movie cuts to Jane, who is tied up in the back of a jeep, and Rachel whimpers softly to herself. She knows better than to howl: she peeked into her father's bedroom earlier, and he was still in bed. Aaron doesn't like her to howl when he is sleeping.

When the movie breaks for a commercial, Rachel goes to her father's room. She is ready for breakfast and she wants him to get up. She tiptoes to the bed to see if he is awake.

His eyes are open and he is staring at nothing. His face is pale and his lips are a purplish color. Dr. Aaron Jacobs, the man Rachel calls father, is not asleep. He is dead, having died in the night of a heart attack.

When Rachel shakes him, his head rocks back and forth in time with her shaking, but his eyes do not blink and he does not breathe. She places his hand on her head, nudging him so that he will waken and stroke her. He does not move. When she leans toward him, his hand falls limply to dangle over the edge of the bed.

In the breeze from the open bedroom window, the fine wisps of gray hair that he had carefully combed over his bald spot each morning shift and flutter, exposing the naked scalp. In the other room, elephants trumpet as they stampede across the jungle to rescue Tarzan. Rachel whimpers softly, but her father does not move.

Rachel backs away from her father's body. In the living room, Tarzan is swinging across the jungle on vines, going to save Jane. Rachel ignores the television. She prowls through the house as if searching for comfort—stepping into her own small bedroom, wandering through her father's laboratory. From the cages that line the walls, white rats stare at her with hot red eyes. A rabbit hops across its cage, making a series of slow dull thumps, like a feather pillow tumbling down a flight of stairs.

She thinks that perhaps she made a mistake. Perhaps her father is just sleeping. She returns to the bedroom, but nothing has changed. Her father lies open-eyed on the bed. For a long time, she huddles beside his body, clinging to his hand.

He is the only person she has ever known. He is her father, her teacher, her friend. She cannot leave him alone.

The afternoon sun blazes through the window, and still Aaron does not move. The room grows dark, but Rachel does not turn on the lights. She is waiting for Aaron to wake up. When the moon rises, its silver light shines through the window to cast a bright rectangle on the far wall.

Outside, somewhere in the barren rocky land surrounding the ranch house, a coyote lifts its head to the rising moon and wails, a thin sound that is as lonely as a train whistling through an abandoned station. Rachel joins in with a desolate howl of loneliness and grief. Aaron lies still and Rachel knows that he is dead.

When Rachel was younger, she had a favorite bedtime story.—Where did I come from? she would ask Aaron, using the abbreviated gestures of ASL, American Sign Language.—Tell me again.

"You're too old for bedtime stories," Aaron would say.

—Please, she'd sign.—Tell me the story.

In the end, he always relented and told her. "Once upon a time, there was a little girl named Rachel," he said. "She was a pretty girl, with long golden hair like a princess in a fairy tale. She lived with her father and her mother and they were all very happy."

Rachel would snuggle contentedly beneath her blankets. The story, like any good fairy tale, had elements of tragedy. In the story, Rachel's father worked at a university, studying the workings of the brain and charting the electric fields that the nervous impulses of an active brain produced. But the other researchers at the university didn't understand Rachel's father; they distrusted his research and cut off his funding. (During this portion of the story, Aaron's voice took on a bitter edge.) So he left the university and took his wife and daughter to the desert, where he could work in peace.

He continued his research and determined that each individual brain produced its own unique pattern of fields, as characteristic as a fingerprint. (Rachel found this part of the story quite dull, but Aaron insisted on including it.) The shape of this "Electric Mind," as he called it, was determined by habitual patterns of thoughts and emotions. Record the Electric Mind, he postulated, and you could capture an individual's personality.

Then one sunny day, the doctor's wife and beautiful daughter went for a drive. A truck barreling down a winding cliffside road lost its brakes and met the car head-on, killing both the girl and her mother. (Rachel clung to Aaron's hand during this part of the story, frightened by the sudden evil twist of fortune.)

But though Rachel's body had died, all was not lost. In his desert lab, the doctor had recorded the electrical patterns produced by his daughter's brain. The doctor had been experimenting with the use of external magnetic fields to impose the patterns from one animal onto the brain of another. From an animal supply house, he obtained a young chimpanzee. He used a mixture of norepinephrin-based transmitter substances to boost the speed of neural processing in the chimp's brain, and then he imposed the pattern of his daughter's mind upon the brain of this young chimp, combining the two after his own fashion, saving his daughter in his own way. In the chimp's brain was all that remained of Rachel Jacobs.

The doctor named the chimp Rachel and raised her as his own daughter. Since the limitations of the chimpanzee larynx made speech very difficult, he instructed her in ASL. He taught her to read and to write. They were good friends, the best of companions.

By this point in the story, Rachel was usually asleep. But it didn't matter—she knew the ending. The doctor, whose name was Aaron Jacobs, and the chimp named Rachel lived happily ever after.

Rachel likes fairy tales and she likes happy endings. She has the mind of a teenage girl, but the innocent heart of a young chimp.

Sometimes, when Rachel looks at her gnarled brown fingers, they seem alien, wrong, out of place. She remembers having small, pale, delicate hands. Memories lie upon memories, layers upon layers, like the sedimentary rocks of the desert buttes.

Rachel remembers a blonde-haired fair-skinned woman who smelled sweetly of perfume. On a Halloween long ago, this woman (who was, in these memories, Rachel's mother) painted Rachel's fingernails bright red because Rachel was dressed as a gypsy and gypsies liked red. Rachel remembers the woman's hands: white hands with faintly blue veins hidden just beneath the skin, neatly clipped nails painted rose pink.

But Rachel also remembers another mother and another time. Her mother was dark and hairy and smelled sweetly of overripe fruit. She and Rachel lived in a wire cage in a room filled with chimps and she hugged Rachel to her hairy breast whenever any people came into the room. Rachel's mother groomed Rachel constantly, picking delicately through her fur in search of lice that she never found.

Memories upon memories: jumbled and confused, like random pictures clipped from magazines, a bright collage that makes no sense. Rachel remembers cages: cold wire mesh beneath her feet, the smell of fear around her. A man in a white lab coat took her from the arms of her hairy mother and pricked her with needles. She could hear her mother howling, but she could not escape from the man.

Rachel remembers a junior high school dance where she wore a new dress: she stood in a dark corner of the gym for hours, pretending to admire the crepe paper decorations because she felt too shy to search among the crowd for her friends.

She remembers when she was a young chimp: she huddled with five other adolescent chimps in the stuffy freight compartment of a train, frightened by the alien smells and sounds.

She remembers gym class: gray lockers and ugly gym suits that revealed her skinny legs. The teacher made everyone play softball, even Rachel who was unathletic and painfully shy. Rachel at bat, standing at the plate, was terrified to be the center of attention. "Easy out," said the catcher, a hard-edged girl who ran with the wrong crowd and always smelled of cigarette smoke. When Rachel swung at the ball and missed, the outfielders filled the air with malicious laughter.

Rachel's memories are as delicate and elusive as the dusty moths and butterflies that dance among the rabbit brush and sage. Memories of her girlhood never linger; they land for an instant, then take flight, leaving Rachel feeling abandoned and alone.

Rachel leaves Aaron's body where it is, but closes his eyes and pulls the sheet up over his head. She does not know what else to do. Each day she waters the garden and picks some greens for the rabbits. Each day, she cares for the animals in the lab, bringing them food and refilling their water bottles. The weather is cool, and Aaron's body does not smell too bad, though by the end of the week, a wide line of ants runs from the bed to the open window.

At the end of the first week, on a moonlit evening, Rachel decides to let the animals go free. She releases the rabbits one by one, climbing on a stepladder to reach down into the cage and lift each placid bunny out. She carries each one to the back door, holding it for a moment and stroking the soft warm fur. Then she sets the animal down and nudges it in the direction of the green grass that grows around the perimeter of the fenced garden.

The rats are more difficult to deal with. She manages to wrestle the large rat cage off the shelf, but it is heavier than she thought it would be. Though she slows its fall, it lands on the floor with a crash and the rats scurry to and fro within. She shoves the cage across the linoleum floor, sliding it down the hall, over the doorsill, and onto the back patio. When she opens the cage door, rats burst out like popcorn from a popper, white in the moonlight and dashing in all directions.

Once, while Aaron was taking a nap, Rachel walked along the dirt track that led to the main highway. She hadn't planned on going far. She just wanted to see what the highway looked like, maybe hide near the mailbox and watch a car drive past. She was curious about the outside world and her fleeting fragmentary memories did not satisfy that curiosity.

She was halfway to the mailbox when Aaron came roaring up in his old jeep. "Get in the car," he shouted at her. "Right now!" Rachel had never seen him so angry. She cowered in the jeep's passenger seat, covered with dust from the road, unhappy that Aaron was so upset. He didn't speak until they got back to the ranch house, and then he spoke in a low voice, filled with bitterness and suppressed rage.

"You don't want to go out there," he said. "You wouldn't like it out there. The world is filled with petty, narrow-minded, stupid people. They wouldn't understand you. And anyone they don't understand, they want to hurt. They hurt anyone who's different. If they know that you're different, they punish you, hurt you. They'd lock you up and never let you go."

He looked straight ahead, staring through the dirty windshield. "It's not like the shows on TV, Rachel," he said in a softer tone. "It's not like the stories in books."

He looked at her then and she gestured frantically.—I'm sorry. I'm sorry.

"I can't protect you out there," he said. "I can't keep you safe."

Rachel took his hand in both of hers. He relented then, stroking her head. "Never do that again," he said. "Never."

Aaron's fear was contagious. Rachel never again walked along the dirt track and sometimes she had dreams about bad people who wanted to lock her in a cage.

Two weeks after Aaron's death, a black-and-white police car drives slowly up to the house. When the policemen knock on the door,

Rachel hides behind the couch in the living room. They knock again, try the knob, then open the door, which she had left unlocked.

Suddenly frightened, Rachel bolts from behind the couch, bounding toward the back door. Behind her, she hears one man yell, "My God! It's a gorilla!"

By the time he pulls his gun, Rachel has run out the back door and away into the hills. From the hills she watches as an ambulance drives up and two men in white take Aaron's body away. Even after the ambulance and the police car drive away, Rachel is afraid to go back to the house. Only after sunset does she return.

Just before dawn the next morning, she wakens to the sound of a truck jouncing down the dirt road. She peers out the window to see a pale green pickup. Sloppily stenciled in white on the door are the words: PRIMATE RESEARCH CENTER. Rachel hesitates as the truck pulls up in front of the house. By the time she has decided to flee, two men are getting out of the truck. One of them carries a rifle.

She runs out the back door and heads for the hills, but she is only halfway to hiding when she hears a sound like a sharp intake of breath and feels a painful jolt in her shoulder. Suddenly, her legs give way and she is tumbling backward down the sandy slope, dust coating her red-brown fur, her howl becoming a whimper, then fading to nothing at all. She falls into the blackness of sleep.

The sun is up. Rachel lies in a cage in the back of the pickup truck. She is partially conscious and she feels a tingling in her hands and feet. Nausea grips her stomach and bowels. Her body aches.

Rachel can blink, but otherwise she can't move. From where she lies, she can see only the wire mesh of the cage and the side of the truck. When she tries to turn her head, the burning in her skin intensifies. She lies still, wanting to cry out, but unable to make a sound. She can only blink slowly, trying to close out the pain. But the burning and nausea stay.

The truck jounces down a dirt road, then stops. It rocks as the men get out. The doors slam. Rachel hears the tailgate open.

A woman's voice: "Is that the animal the County Sheriff wanted us to pick up?" A woman peers into the cage. She wears a white lab coat and her brown hair is tied back in a single braid. Around her eyes, Rachel can see small wrinkles, etched by years of living in the desert. The woman doesn't look evil. Rachel hopes that the woman will save her from the men in the truck.

"Yeah. It should be knocked out for at least another half hour. Where do you want it?"

"Bring it into the lab where we had the rhesus monkeys. I'll keep it there until I have an empty cage in the breeding area."

Rachel's cage scrapes across the bed of the pickup. She feels each bump and jar as a new pain. The man swings the cage onto a cart and the woman pushes the cart down a concrete corridor. Rachel watches the walls pass just a few inches from her nose.

The lab contains rows of cages in which small animals sleepily move. In the sudden stark light of the overhead fluorescent bulbs, the eyes of white rats gleam red.

With the help of one of the men from the truck, the woman manhandles Rachel onto a lab table. The metal surface is cold and hard, painful against Rachel's skin. Rachel's body is not under her control; her limbs will not respond. She is still frozen by the tranquilizer, able to watch, but that is all. She cannot protest or plead for mercy.

Rachel watches with growing terror as the woman pulls on rubber gloves and fills a hypodermic needle with a clear solution. "Mark down that I'm giving her the standard test for tuberculosis; this eyelid should be checked before she's moved in with the others. I'll add thiabendazole to her feed for the next few days to clean out any intestinal worms. And I suppose we might as well de-flea her as well," the woman says. The man grunts in response.

Expertly, the woman closes one of Rachel's eyes. With her open eye, Rachel watches the hypodermic needle approach. She feels a sharp pain in her eyelid. In her mind, she is howling, but the only sound she can manage is a breathy sigh.

The woman sets the hypodermic aside and begins methodically spraying Rachel's fur with a cold, foul-smelling liquid. A drop strikes Rachel's eye and burns. Rachel blinks, but she cannot lift a hand to rub her eye. The woman treats Rachel with casual indifference, chatting with the man as she spreads Rachel's legs and sprays her genitals. "Looks healthy enough. Good breeding stock."

Rachel moans, but neither person notices. At last, they finish their torture, put her in a cage, and leave the room. She closes her eyes, and the darkness returns.

Rachel dreams. She is back at home in the ranch house. It is night and she is alone. Outside, coyotes yip and howl. The coyote is the voice of the desert, wailing as the wind wails when it stretches itself thin to squeeze through a crack between two boulders. The people native to this land tell tales of Coyote, a god who was a trickster, unreliable, changeable, mercurial.

Rachel is restless, anxious, unnerved by the howling of the coyotes. She is looking for Aaron. In the dream, she knows he is not dead, and she searches the house for him, wandering from his cluttered bedroom to her small room to the linoleum-tiled lab.

She is in the lab when she hears something tapping: a small dry scratching, like a wind-blown branch against the window, though no tree grows near the house and the night is still. Cautiously, she lifts the curtain to look out.

She looks into her own reflection: a pale oval face, long blonde hair. The hand that holds the curtain aside is smooth and white with carefully clipped fingernails. But something is wrong. Superimposed on the reflection is another face peering through the glass: a pair of dark brown eyes, a chimp face with red-brown hair and jug-handle ears. She sees her own reflection and she sees the outsider; the two images merge and blur. She is afraid, but she can't drop the curtain and shut the ape face out.

She is a chimp looking in through the cold, bright windowpane; she is a girl looking out; she is a girl looking in; she is an ape looking out. She is afraid and the coyotes are howling all around.

Rachel opens her eyes and blinks until the world comes into focus. The pain and tingling has retreated, but she still feels a little sick. Her left eye aches. When she rubs it, she feels a raised lump on the eyelid where the woman pricked her. She lies on the floor of a wire mesh cage. The room is hot and the air is thick with the smell of animals.

In the cage beside her is another chimp, an older animal with scruffy dark brown fur. He sits with his arms wrapped around his knees, rocking back and forth, back and forth. His head is down. As he rocks, he murmurs to himself, a meaningless cooing that goes on and on. On his scalp, Rachel can see a gleam of metal: a permanently implanted electrode protrudes from a shaven patch. Rachel makes a soft questioning sound, but the other chimp will not look up.

Rachel's own cage is just a few feet square. In one corner is a bowl of monkey pellets. A water bottle hangs on the side of the cage. Rachel ignores the food, but drinks thirstily.

Sunlight streams through the windows, sliced into small sections by the wire mesh that covers the glass. She tests her cage door, rattling it gently at first, then harder. It is securely latched. The gaps in the mesh are too small to admit her hand. She can't reach out to work the latch.

The other chimp continues to rock back and forth. When Rachel rattles the mesh of her cage and howls, he lifts his head wearily and looks at her. His red-rimmed eyes are unfocused; she can't be sure he sees her.

—Hello, she gestures tentatively.—What's wrong?

He blinks at her in the dim light.—Hurt, he signs in ASL. He reaches up to touch the electrode, fingering skin that is already raw from repeated rubbing.

—Who hurt you? she asks. He stares at her blankly and she repeats the question.—Who?

—Men, he signs.

As if on cue, there is the click of a latch and the door to the lab opens. A bearded man in a white coat steps in, followed by a clean-shaven man in a suit. The bearded man seems to be showing the other man around the lab. ". . . only preliminary testing, so far," the bearded man is saying. "We've been hampered by a shortage of chimps trained in ASL." The two men stop in front of the old chimp's cage. "This old fellow is from the Oregon center. Funding for the language program was cut back and some of the animals were dispersed to other programs." The old chimp huddles at the back of the cage, eyeing the bearded man with suspicion.

—Hungry? the bearded man signs to the old chimp. He holds up an orange where the old chimp can see it.

—Give orange, the old chimp gestures. He holds out his hand, but comes no nearer to the wire mesh than he must to reach the orange. With the fruit in hand, he retreats to the back of his cage.

The bearded man continues, "This project will provide us with the first solid data on neural activity during use of sign language. But we really need greater access to chimps with advanced language skills. People are so damn protective of their animals."

"Is this one of yours?" the clean-shaven man asks, pointing to Rachel. She cowers in the back of the cage, as far from the wire mesh as she can get.

"No, not mine. She was someone's household pet, apparently. The county sheriff had us pick her up." The bearded man peers into her cage. Rachel does not move; she is terrified that he will somehow guess that she knows ASL. She stares at his hands and thinks about those hands putting an electrode through her skull. "I think she'll be put in breeding stock," the man says as he turns away.

Rachel watches them go, wondering at what terrible people these are. Aaron was right: they want to punish her, put an electrode in her head.

After the men are gone, she tries to draw the old chimp into conversation, but he will not reply. He ignores her as he eats his orange. Then he returns to his former posture, hiding his head and rocking himself back and forth.

Rachel, hungry despite herself, samples one of the food pellets. It has a strange medicinal taste, and she puts it back in the bowl. She needs to pee, but there is no toilet and she cannot escape the cage. At last, unable to hold it, she pees in one corner of the cage. The urine flows through the wire mesh to soak the litter below, and the smell of warm piss fills her cage. Humiliated, frightened, her head aching, her skin itchy from the flea spray, Rachel watches as the sunlight creeps across the room.

The day wears on. Rachel samples her food again, but rejects it, preferring hunger to the strange taste. A black man comes and cleans the cages of the rabbits and rats. Rachel cowers in her cage and watches him warily, afraid that he will hurt her, too.

When night comes, she is not tired. Outside, coyotes howl. Moonlight filters in through the high windows. She draws her legs up toward her body, then rests with her arms wrapped around her knees. Her father is dead, and she is a captive in a strange place. For a time, she whimpers softly, hoping to awaken from this nightmare and find herself at home in bed. When she hears the click of a key in the door to the room, she hugs herself more tightly.

A man in green coveralls pushes a cart filled with cleaning supplies into the room. He takes a broom from the cart, and begins sweeping the concrete floor. Over the rows of cages, she can see the top of his head bobbing in time with his sweeping. He works slowly and methodically, bending down to sweep carefully under each row of cages, making a neat pile of dust, dung, and food scraps in the center of the aisle.

The janitor's name is Jake. He is a middle-aged deaf man who has been employed by the Primate Research Center for the past seven years. He works night shift. The personnel director at the Primate Research Center likes Jake because he fills the federal quota for handicapped employees, and because he has not asked for a raise in five years. There have been some complaints about Jake—his work is often sloppy—but never enough to merit firing the man.

Jake is an unambitious, somewhat slow-witted man. He likes the Primate Research Center because he works alone, which allows him to drink on the job. He is an easy-going man, and he likes the animals. Sometimes, he brings treats for them. Once, a lab assistant caught him feeding an apple to a pregnant rhesus monkey. The monkey was part of an experiment on the effect of dietary restrictions on fetal brain development, and the lab assistant warned Jake that he would be fired if he was ever caught interfering with the animals again. Jake still feeds the animals, but he is more careful about when he does it, and he has never been caught again.

As Rachel watches, the old chimp gestures to Jake.—Give banana, the chimp signs.—Please banana. Jake stops sweeping for a minute and reaches down to the bottom shelf of his cleaning cart. He returns with a banana and offers it to the old chimp. The chimp accepts the banana and leans against the mesh while Jake scratches his fur.

When Jake turns back to his sweeping, he catches sight of Rachel and sees that she is watching him. Emboldened by his kindness to the old chimp, Rachel timidly gestures to him.—Help me.

Jake hesitates, then peers at her more closely. Both his eyes are shot with a fine lacework of red. His nose displays the broken blood vessels of someone who has been friends with the bottle for too many years. He needs a shave. But when he leans close, Rachel catches the scent of whiskey and tobacco. The smells remind her of Aaron and give her courage.

—Please help me, Rachel signs.—I don't belong here.

For the last hour, Jake has been drinking steadily. His view of the world is somewhat fuzzy. He stares at her blearily.

Rachel's fear that he will hurt her is replaced by the fear that he will leave her locked up and alone. Desperately she signs again.—Please please please. Help me. I don't belong here. Please help me go home.

He watches her, considering the situation. Rachel does not move. She is afraid that any movement will make him leave. With a majestic speed dictated by his inebriation, Jake leans his broom on the row of cages behind him and steps toward Rachel's cage again.—You talk? he signs.—I talk, she signs.

—Where did you come from?

—From my father's house, she signs.—Two men came and shot me and put me here. I don't know why. I don't know why they locked me in jail.

Jake looks around, willing to be sympathetic, but puzzled by her talk of jail.—This isn't jail, he signs.—This is a place where scientists raise monkeys.

Rachel is indignant.—I am not a monkey, she signs.—I am a girl.

Jake studies her hairy body and her jug-handle ears.—You look like a monkey.

Rachel shakes her head.—No. I am a girl.

Rachel runs her hands back over her head, a very human gesture of annoyance and unhappiness. She signs sadly,—I don't belong here. Please let me out.

Jake shifts his weight from foot to foot, wondering what to do.—I can't let you out. I'll get in big trouble.

—Just for a little while? Please?

Jake glances at his cart of supplies. He has to finish off this room and two corridors of offices before he can relax for the night.

—Don't go, Rachel signs, guessing his thoughts.

—I have work to do.

She looks at the cart, then suggests eagerly,—Let me out and I'll help you work.

Jake frowns.—If I let you out, you will run away.

—No, I won't run away. I will help. Please let me out.

—You promise to go back?

Rachel nods.

Warily he unlatches the cage. Rachel bounds out, grabs a whisk broom from the cart, and begins industriously sweeping bits of food and droppings from beneath the row of cages.—Come on, she signs to Jake from the end of the aisle.—I will help.

When Jake pushes the cart from the room filled with cages, Rachel follows him closely. The rubber wheels of the cleaning cart rumble softly on the linoleum floor. They pass through a metal door into a corridor where the floor is carpeted and the air smells of chalk dust and paper.

Offices let off the corridor, each one a small room furnished with a desk, bookshelves, and a blackboard. Jake shows Rachel how to empty the wastebaskets into a garbage bag. While he cleans the blackboards, she wanders from office to office, trailing the trash-filled garbage bag.

At first, Jake keeps a close eye on Rachel. But after cleaning each blackboard, he pauses to refill a cup from the whiskey bottle that he keeps wedged between the Saniflush and the window cleaner. By the time he is halfway through the second cup; he is treating her like an old friend, telling her to hurry up so that they can eat dinner.

Rachel works quickly, but she stops sometimes to gaze out the office windows. Outside, moonlight shines on a sandy plain, dotted here and there with scrubby clumps of rabbit brush.

At the end of the corridor is a larger room in which there are several desks and typewriters. In one of the wastebaskets, buried beneath memos and candybar wrappers, she finds a magazine. The title is *Love Confessions* and the cover has a picture of a man and woman kissing. Rachel studies the cover, then takes the magazine, tucking it on the bottom shelf of the cart.

Jake pours himself another cup of whiskey and pushes the cart to another hallway. Jake is working slower now, and as he works he makes humming noises, tuneless sounds that he feels only as pleasant vibrations. The last few blackboards are sloppily done, and Rachel, finished with the wastebaskets, cleans the places that Jake missed.

They eat dinner in the janitor's storeroom, a stuffy windowless room furnished with an ancient grease-stained couch, a battered black-and-white television, and shelves of cleaning supplies. From a shelf, Jake takes the paper bag that holds his lunch: a baloney sandwich, a bag of barbecued potato chips, and a box of vanilla wafers. From behind the gallon jugs of liquid cleanser, he takes a magazine. He lights a cigarette, pours himself another cup of whiskey, and settles down on the couch. After a moment's hesitation, he offers Rachel a drink, pouring a shot of whiskey into a chipped ceramic cup.

Aaron never let Rachel drink whiskey, and she samples it carefully. At first the smell makes her sneeze, but she is fascinated by the way that the drink warms her throat, and she sips some more.

As they drink, Rachel tells Jake about the men who shot her and the woman who pricked her with a needle, and he nods.—The people here are crazy, he signs.

—I know, she says, thinking of the old chimp with the electrode in his head.—You won't tell them I can talk, will you?

Jake nods.—I won't tell them anything.

—They treat me like I'm not real, Rachel signs sadly. Then she hugs her knees, frightened at the thought of being held captive by crazy people. She considers planning her escape: she is out of the cage and she is sure she could outrun Jake. As she wonders about it, she finishes her cup of whiskey. The alcohol takes the edge off her fear. She sits close beside Jake on the couch, and the smell of his cigarette smoke reminds her of Aaron. For the first time since Aaron's death she feels warm and happy.

She shares Jake's cookies and potato chips and looks at the *Love Confessions* magazine that she took from the trash. The first story that she reads is about a woman named Alice. The headline reads: "I became a Go-go dancer to pay off my husband's gambling debts, and now he wants me to sell my body."

Rachel sympathizes with Alice's loneliness and suffering. Alice, like Rachel, is alone and misunderstood. As Rachel slowly reads, she sips her second cup of whiskey. The story reminds her of a fairy tale: the nice man who rescues Alice from her terrible husband replaces the handsome prince who rescued the princess. Rachel glances at Jake and wonders if he will rescue her from the wicked people who locked her in the cage.

She has finished the second cup of whiskey and eaten half Jake's cookies when Jake says that she must go back to her cage. She goes reluctantly, taking the magazine with her. He promises that he will come for her again the next night, and with that she must be content. She puts the magazine in one corner of the cage and curls up to sleep.

She wakes early in the afternoon. A man in a white coat is wheeling a low cart into the lab.

Rachel's head aches with hangover and she feels sick. As she crouches in one corner of her cage, he stops the cart beside her cage and then locks the wheels. "Hold on there," he mutters to her, then slides her cage onto the cart.

The man wheels her through long corridors, where the walls are cement blocks, painted institutional green. Rachel huddles unhappily in the cage, wondering where she is going and whether Jake will ever be able to find her.

At the end of a long corridor, the man opens a thick metal door and a wave of warm air strikes Rachel. It stinks of chimpanzees, excrement, and rotting food. On either side of the corridor are metal bars and wire mesh. Behind the mesh, Rachel can see dark hairy shadows. In one cage, five adolescent chimps swing and play. In another, two females huddle together, grooming each other. The man slows as he passes a cage in which a big male is banging on the wire with his fist, making the mesh rattle and ring.

"Now, Johnson," says the man. "Cool it. Be nice. I'm bringing you a new little girlfriend."

With a series of hooks, the man links Rachel's cage with the cage next to Johnson's and opens the doors. "Go on, girl," he says. "See the nice fruit." In the cage is a bowl of sliced apples with an attendant swarm of fruit flies.

At first, Rachel will not move into the new cage. She crouches in the cage on the cart, hoping that the man will decide to take her back to the lab. She watches him get a hose and attach it to a water faucet. But she does not understand his intention until he turns the stream of water on her. A cold blast strikes her on the back and she howls, fleeing into the new cage to avoid the cold water. Then the man closes the doors, unhooks the cage, and hurries away.

The floor is bare cement. Her cage is at one end of the corridor and two walls are cement block. A door in one of the cement block walls leads to an outside run. The other two walls are wire mesh: one facing the corridor; the other, Johnson's cage.

Johnson, quiet now that the man has left, is sniffing around the door in the wire mesh wall that joins their cages. Rachel watches him anxiously. Her memories of other chimps are distant, softened by time. She remembers her mother; she vaguely remembers playing with other chimps her age. But she does not know how to react to Johnson when he stares at her with great intensity and makes a loud huffing sound. She gestures to him in ASL, but he only stares harder and huffs again. Beyond Johnson, she can see other cages and other chimps, so many that the wire mesh blurs her vision and she cannot see the other end of the corridor.

To escape Johnson's scrutiny, she ducks through the door into the outside run, a wire mesh cage on a white concrete foundation. Outside there is barren ground and rabbit brush. The afternoon sun is hot and all the other runs are deserted until Johnson appears in the run beside hers. His attention disturbs her and she goes back inside.

She retreats to the side of the cage farthest from Johnson. A crudely built wooden platform provides her with a place to sit. Wrapping her arms around her knees, she tries to relax and ignore Johnson. She dozes off for a while, but wakes to a commotion across the corridor.

In the cage across the way is a female chimp in heat. Rachel recognizes the smell from her own times in heat. Two keepers are opening the door that separates the female's cage from the adjoining cage, where a male stands, watching with great interest. Johnson is shaking the wire mesh and howling as he watches.

"Mike here is a virgin, but Susie knows what she's doing," one keeper was saying to the other. "So it should go smoothly. But keep the hose ready."

"Yeah?"

"Sometimes they fight. We only use the hose to break it up if it gets real bad. Generally, they do okay."

Mike stalks into Susie's cage. The keepers lower the cage door, trapping both chimps in the same cage. Susie seems unalarmed. She continues eating a slice of orange while Mike sniffs at her genitals with every indication of great interest. She bends over to let Mike finger her pink bottom, the sign of estrus.

Rachel finds herself standing at the wire mesh, making low moaning noises. She can see Mike's erection, hear his grunting cries. He squats on the floor of Susie's cage, gesturing to the female. Rachel's feelings are mixed: she is fascinated, fearful, confused. She keeps thinking of the description of sex in the *Love Confessions* story: When Alice feels Danny's lips on hers, she is swept away by the passion of the moment. He takes her in his arms and her skin tingles as if she were consumed by an inner fire.

Susie bends down and Mike penetrates her with a loud grunt, thrusting violently with his hips. Susie cries out shrilly and suddenly leaps up, knocking Mike away. Rachel watches, overcome with fascination. Mike, his penis now limp, follows Susie slowly to the corner of the cage, where he begins grooming her carefully. Rachel finds that the wire mesh has cut her hands where she gripped it too tightly.

It is night, and the door at the end of the corridor creaks open. Rachel is immediately alert, peering through the wire mesh and trying to see down to the end of the corridor. She bangs on the wire mesh. As Jake comes closer, she waves a greeting.

When Jake reaches for the lever that will raise the door to Rachel's cage, Johnson charges toward him, howling and waving his arms above his head. He hammers on the wire mesh with his fists, howling and grimacing at Jake. Rachel ignores Johnson and hurries after Jake.

Again Rachel helps Jake clean. In the laboratory, she greets the old chimp, but the animal is more interested in the banana that Jake has brought than in conversation. The chimp will not reply to her questions, and after several tries, she gives up.

While Jake vacuums the carpeted corridors, Rachel empties the trash, finding a magazine called *Modern Romance* in the same wastebasket that had provided *Love Confessions*.

Later, in the janitor's lounge, Jake smokes a cigarette, sips whiskey, and flips through one of his own magazines. Rachel reads love stories in *Modern Romance*.

Every once in a while, she looks over Jake's shoulder at grainy pictures of naked women with their legs spread wide apart. Jake looks for a long time at a picture of a blonde woman with big breasts, red fingernails, and purple-painted eyelids. The woman lies on her back and smiles as she strokes the pinkness between her legs. The picture on the next page shows her caressing her own breasts, pinching the dark nipples. The final picture shows her looking back over her shoulder. She is in the position that Susie took when she was ready to be mounted.

Rachel looks over Jake's shoulder at the magazine, but she does not ask questions. Jake's smell began to change as soon as he opened the magazine; the scent of nervous sweat mingles with the aromas of tobacco and whiskey. Rachel suspects that questions would not be welcome just now.

At Jake's insistence, she goes back to her cage before dawn.

Over the next week, she listens to the conversations of the men who come and go, bringing food and hosing out the cages. From the men's conversation, she learns that the Primate Research Center is primarily a breeding facility that supplies researchers with domestically bred apes and monkeys of several species. It also maintains its own research staff. In indifferent tones, the men talk of horrible things. The adolescent chimps at the end of the corridor are being fed a diet high in cholesterol to determine cholesterol's effects on the circulatory system. A group of pregnant females is being injected with male hormones to determine how that will affect the female offspring. A group of infants is being fed a low protein diet to determine adverse effects on their brain development.

The men look through her as if she were not real, as if she were a part of the wall, as if she were no one at all. She cannot speak to them; she cannot trust them.

Each night, Jake lets her out of her cage and she helps him clean. He brings treats: barbequed potato chips, fresh fruit, chocolate bars, and cookies. He treats her fondly, as one would treat a precocious child. And he talks to her.

At night, when she is with Jake, Rachel can almost forget the terror of the cage, the anxiety of watching Johnson pace to and fro, the sense of unreality that accompanies the simplest act. She would be content to stay with Jake forever, eating snack food and reading confessions magazines. He seems to like her company. But each morning, Jake insists that she must go back to the cage and the terror. By the end of the first week, she has begun plotting her escape.

Whenever Jake falls asleep over his whiskey, something that happens three nights out of five, Rachel prowls the center alone, surreptitiously gathering things that she will need to survive in the desert: a plastic jug filled with water, a plastic bag of food pellets, a large beach towel that will serve as a blanket on the cool desert nights, a discarded plastic shopping bag in which she can carry the other things. Her best find is a road map on which the Primate Center is marked in red. She knows the address of Aaron's ranch and finds it on the map. She studies the roads and plots a route home. Cross country, assuming that she does not get lost, she will have to travel about fifty miles to reach the ranch. She hides these things behind one of the shelves in the janitor's storeroom.

Her plans to run away and go home are disrupted by the idea that she is in love with Jake, a notion that comes to her slowly, fed by the stories in the confessions magazines. When Jake absent-mindedly strokes her, she is filled with a strange excitement. She longs for his company and misses him on the weekends when he is away. She is happy only when she is with him, following him through the halls of the center, sniffing the aroma of tobacco and whiskey that is his own perfume. She steals a cigarette from his pack and hides it in her cage, where she can savor the smell of it at her leisure.

She loves him, but she does not know how to make him love her back. Rachel knows little about love: she remembers a high school crush where she mooned after a boy with a locker near hers, but that came to nothing. She reads the confessions magazines and Ann Landers' column in the newspaper that Jake brings with him each night, and from these sources, she learns about romance. One night, after Jake falls asleep, she types a badly punctuated, ungrammatical letter to Ann. In the letter, she explains her situation and asks for advice on how to make Jake love her. She slips the letter into a sack labeled "Outgoing Mail," and for the next week she reads Ann's column with increased interest. But her letter never appears.

Rachel searches for answers in the magazine pictures that seem to fascinate Jake. She studies the naked women, especially the big-breasted woman with the purple smudges around her eyes.

One night, in a secretary's desk, she finds a plastic case of eyeshadow. She steals it and takes it back to her cage. The next evening, as soon as the Center is quiet, she upturns her metal food dish and regards her reflection in the shiny bottom. Squatting, she balances the eye shadow case on one knee and examines its contents: a tiny makeup brush and three shades of eye shadow—INDIAN BLUE, FOREST GREEN, and WILDLY VIOLET. Rachel chooses the shade labeled WILDLY VIOLET.

Using one finger to hold her right eye closed, she dabs her eyelid carefully with the makeup brush, leaving a gaudy orchid-colored smudge on her brown skin. She studies the smudge critically, then adds to it, smearing the color beyond the corner of her eyelid until it disappears in her brown fur. The color gives her eye a carnival brightness, a lunatic gaiety. Working with great care, she matches the effect on the other side, then smiles at herself in the glass, blinking coquettishly.

In the other cage, Johnson bares his teeth and shakes the wire mesh. She ignores him.

When Jake comes to let her out, he frowns at her eyes.—Did you hurt yourself? he asks.

—No, she says. Then, after a pause,—Don't you like it?

Jake squats beside her and stares at her eyes. Rachel puts a hand on his knee and her heart pounds at her own boldness.—You are a very strange monkey, he signs.

Rachel is afraid to move. Her hand on his knee closes into a fist; her face folds in on itself, puckering around the eyes.

Then, straightening up, he signs,—I liked your eyes better before.

He likes her eyes. She nods without taking her eyes from his face. Later, she washes her face in the women's restroom, leaving dark smudges the color of bruises on a series of paper towels.

Rachel is dreaming. She is walking through the Painted Desert with her hairy brown mother, following a red rock canyon that Rachel somehow knows will lead her to the Primate Research Center. Her mother is lagging behind: she does not want to go to the center; she is afraid. In the shadow of a rock outcropping, Rachel stops to explain to her mother that they must go to the center because Jake is at the center.

Rachel's mother does not understand sign language. She watches Rachel with mournful eyes, then scrambles up the canyon wall, leaving Rachel behind. Rachel climbs after her mother, pulling herself over the edge in time to see the other chimp loping away across the windblown red cinder-rock and sand.

Rachel bounds after her mother, and as she runs she howls like an abandoned infant chimp, wailing her distress. The figure of her mother wavers in the distance, shimmering in the heat that rises from the sand. The figure changes. Running away across the red sands is a pale blonde woman wearing a purple sweatsuit and jogging shoes, the sweet-smelling mother that Rachel remembers. The woman looks back and smiles at Rachel. "Don't howl like an ape, daughter," she calls. "Say Mama."

Rachel runs silently, dream running that takes her nowhere. The sand burns her feet and the sun beats down on her head. The blonde woman vanishes in the distance, and Rachel is alone. She collapses on the sand, whimpering because she is alone and afraid.

She feels the gentle touch of fingers grooming her fur, and for a moment, still half asleep, she believes that her hairy mother has returned to her. She opens her eyes and looks into a pair of dark brown eyes, separated from her by wire mesh. Johnson. He has reached through a gap in the fence to groom her. As he sorts through her fur, he makes soft cooing sounds, gentle comforting noises.

Still half asleep, she gazes at him and wonders why she was so fearful. He does not seem so bad. He grooms her for a time, and then sits nearby, watching her through the mesh. She brings a slice of apple from her dish of food and offers it to him. With her free hand, she makes the sign for apple. When he takes it, she signs again: apple. He is not a particularly quick student, but she has time and many slices of apple.

All Rachel's preparations are done, but she cannot bring herself to leave the center. Leaving the center means leaving Jake, leaving potato chips and whiskey, leaving security. To Rachel, the thought of love is always accompanied by the warm taste of whiskey and potato chips.

Some nights, after Jake is asleep, she goes to the big glass doors that lead to the outside. She opens the doors and stands on the steps, looking down into the desert. Sometimes a jackrabbit sits on its haunches in the rectangles of light that shine through the glass doors. Sometimes she sees kangaroo rats, hopping through the moonlight like rubber balls bouncing on hard pavement. Once, a coyote trots by, casting a contemptuous glance in her direction.

The desert is a lonely place. Empty. Cold. She thinks of Jake snoring softly in the janitor's lounge. And always she closes the door and returns to him.

Rachel leads a double life: janitor's assistant by night, prisoner and teacher by day. She spends her afternoons drowsing in the sun and teaching Johnson new signs.

On a warm afternoon, Rachel sits in the outside run, basking in the sunlight. Johnson is inside, and the other chimps are quiet. She can almost imagine she is back at her father's ranch, sitting in her own yard. She naps and dreams of Jake.

She dreams that she is sitting in his lap on the battered old couch. Her hand is on his chest: a smooth pale hand with red-painted fingernails. When she looks at the dark screen of the television set, she can see her reflection. She is a thin teenager with blonde hair and blue eyes. She is naked.

Jake is looking at her and smiling. He runs a hand down her back and she closes her eyes in ecstasy.

But something changes when she closes her eyes. Jake is grooming her as her mother used to groom her, sorting through her hair in search of fleas. She opens her eyes and sees Johnson, his diligent fingers searching through her fur, his intent brown eyes watching her. The reflection on the television screen shows two chimps, tangled in each others' arms.

Rachel wakes to find that she is in heat for the first time since she came to the center. The skin surrounding her genitals is swollen and pink.

For the rest of the day, she is restless, pacing to and fro in her cage. On his side of the wire mesh wall, Johnson is equally restless, following her when she goes outside, sniffing long and hard at the edge of the barrier that separates him from her.

That night, Rachel goes eagerly to help Jake clean. She follows him closely, never letting him get far from her. When he is sweeping, she trots after him with the dustpan and he almost trips over her twice. She keeps waiting for him to notice her condition, but he seems oblivious.

As she works, she sips from a cup of whiskey. Excited, she drinks more than usual, finishing two full cups. The liquor leaves her a little disoriented, and she sways as she follows Jake to the janitor's lounge. She curls up close beside him on the couch. He relaxes with his arms resting on the back of the couch, his legs stretching out before him. She moves so that she presses against him.

He stretches, yawns, and rubs the back of his neck as if trying to rub away stiffness. Rachel reaches around behind him and begins to gently rub his neck, reveling in the feel of his skin, his hair against the backs of her hands. The thoughts that hop and skip through her mind are confusing. Sometimes it seems that the hair that tickles her hands is Johnson's; sometimes, she knows it is Jake's. And sometimes it doesn't seem to matter. Are they really so different? They are not so different.

She rubs his neck, not knowing what to do next. In the confessions magazines, this is where the man crushes the woman in his arms. Rachel climbs into Jake's lap and hugs him, waiting for him to crush her in his arms. He blinks at her sleepily. Half asleep, he strokes her, and his moving hand brushes near her genitals. She presses herself against him, making a soft sound in her throat. She rubs her hip against his crotch, aware now of a slight change in his smell, in the tempo of his breathing. He blinks at her again, a little more awake now. She bares her teeth in a smile and tilts her head back to lick his neck. She can feel his hands on her shoulders, pushing her away, and she knows what he wants. She slides from his lap and turns, presenting him with her pink genitals, ready to be mounted, ready to have him penetrate her. She moans in anticipation, a low inviting sound.

He does not come to her. She looks over her shoulder and he is still sitting on the couch, watching her through half-closed eyes. He reaches over and picks up a magazine filled with pictures of naked women. His other hand drops to his crotch and he is lost in his own world.

Rachel howls like an infant who has lost its mother, but he does not look up. He is staring at the picture of the blonde woman.

Rachel runs down dark corridors to her cage, the only home she has. When she reaches her corridor, she is breathing hard and making small lonely whimpering noises. In the dimly lit corridor, she hesitates for a moment, staring into Johnson's cage. The male chimp is asleep. She remembers the touch of his hands when he groomed her.

From the corridor, she lifts the gate that leads into Johnson's cage and enters. He wakes at the sound of the door and sniffs the air. When he sees Rachel, he stalks toward her, sniffing eagerly. She lets him finger her genitals, sniff deeply of her scent. His penis is erect and he grunts in excitement. She turns and presents herself to him and he mounts her, thrusting deep inside. As he penetrates, she thinks, for a moment, of Jake and of the thin blonde teenage girl named Rachel, but then the moment passes. Almost against her will she cries out, a shrill exclamation of welcoming and loss.

After he withdraws his penis, Johnson grooms her gently, sniffing her genitals and softly stroking her fur. She is sleepy and content, but she knows that she cannot delay.

Johnson is reluctant to leave his cage, but Rachel takes him by the hand and leads him to the janitor's lounge. His presence gives her courage. She listens at the door and hears Jake's soft breathing. Leaving Johnson in the hall, she slips into the room. Jake is lying on the couch, the magazine draped over his legs. Rachel takes the equipment that she has gathered and stands for a moment, staring at the sleeping man. His baseball cap hangs on the arm of a broken chair, and she takes that to remember him by.

Rachel leads Johnson through the empty halls. A kangaroo rat, collecting seeds in the dried grass near the glass doors, looks up curiously as Rachel leads Johnson down the steps. Rachel carries the plastic shopping bag slung over her shoulder. Somewhere in the distance, a coyote howls, a long yapping wail. His cry is joined by others, a chorus in the moonlight.

Rachel takes Johnson by the hand and leads him into the desert.

A cocktail waitress, driving from her job in Flagstaff to her home in Winslow, sees two apes dart across the road, hurrying away from the bright beams of her headlights. After wrestling with her conscience (she does not want to be accused of drinking on the job), she notifies the county sheriff.

A local newspaper reporter, an eager young man fresh out of journalism school, picks up the story from the police report and interviews the waitress. Flattered by his enthusiasm for her story and delighted to find a receptive ear, she tells him details that she failed to mention to the police: one of the apes was wearing a baseball cap and carrying what looked like a shopping bag.

The reporter writes up a quick humorous story for the morning edition, and begins researching a feature article to be run later in the week. He knows that the newspaper, eager for news in a slow season, will play a human-interest story up big—kind of *Lassie, Come Home* with chimps.

Just before dawn, a light rain begins to fall, the first rain of spring. Rachel searches for shelter and finds a small cave formed by three tumbled boulders. It will keep off the rain and hide them from casual observers. She shares her food and water with Johnson. He has followed her closely all night, seemingly intimidated by the darkness and the howling of distant coyotes. She feels protective toward him. At the same time, having him with her gives her courage. He knows only a few gestures in ASL, but he does not need to speak. His presence is comfort enough.

Johnson curls up in the back of the cave and falls asleep quickly. Rachel sits in the opening and watches dawnlight wash the stars from the sky. The rain rattles against the sand, a comforting sound. She thinks about Jake. The baseball cap on her head still smells of his cigarettes, but she does not miss him. Not really. She fingers the cap and wonders why she thought she loved Jake.

The rain lets up. The clouds rise like fairy castles in the distance and the rising sun tints them pink and gold and gives them flaming red banners. Rachel remembers when she was younger and Aaron read her the story of Pinnochio, the little puppet who wanted to be a real boy. At the end of his adventures, Pinnochio, who has been brave and kind, gets his wish. He becomes a real boy.

Rachel had cried at the end of the story and when Aaron asked why, she had rubbed her eyes on the backs of her hairy hands.—I want to be a real girl, she signed to him.—A real girl.

"You are a real girl," Aaron had told her, but somehow she had never believed him.

The sun rises higher and illuminates the broken rock turrets of the desert. There is a magic in this barren land of unassuming grandeur. Some cultures send their young people to the desert to seek visions and guidance, searching for true thinking spawned by the openness of the place, the loneliness, the beauty of emptiness.

Rachel drowses in the warm sun and dreams a vision that has the clarity of truth. In the dream, her father comes to her. "Rachel," he says to her, "it doesn't matter what anyone thinks of you. You're my daughter."

—I want to be a real girl, she signs.

"You *are* real," her father says. "And you don't need some two-bit drunken janitor to prove it to you." She knows she is dreaming, but she also knows that her father speaks the truth. She is warm and happy and she doesn't need Jake at all. The sunlight warms her and a lizard watches her from a rock, scurrying for cover when she moves. She picks up a bit of loose rock that lies on the floor of the cave. Idly, she scratches on the dark red sandstone wall of the cave. A lopsided heart shape. Within it, awkwardly printed: Rachel and Johnson. Between them, a plus sign. She goes over the letters again and again, leaving scores of fine lines on the smooth rock surface. Then, late in the morning, soothed by the warmth of the day, she sleeps.

Shortly after dark, an elderly rancher in a pickup truck spots two apes in a remote corner of his ranch. They run away and lose him in the rocks, but not until he has a good look at them. He calls the police, the newspaper, and the Primate Center.

The reporter arrives first thing the next morning, interviews the rancher, and follows the men from the Primate Center as they search for evidence of the chimps. They find monkey shit near the cave, confirming that the runaways were indeed nearby. The news reporter, an eager and curious young man, squirms on his belly into the cave and finds the names scratched on the cave wall. He peers at it. He might have dismissed them as the idle scratchings of kids, except that the names match the names of the missing chimps. "Hey," he called to his photographer, "Take a look at this."

The next morning's newspaper displays Rachel's crudely scratched letters. In a brief interview, the rancher mentioned that the chimps were carrying bags. "Looked like supplies," he said. "They looked like they were in for a long haul."

On the third day, Rachel's water runs out. She heads toward a small town, marked on the map. They reach it in the early morning—thirst forces them to travel by day. Beside an isolated ranch house, she finds a faucet. She is filling her bottle when Johnson grunts in alarm.

A dark-haired woman watches from the porch of the house. She does not move toward the apes, and Rachel continues filling the bottle. "It's all right, Rachel," the woman, who has been following the story in the papers, calls out. "Drink all you want."

Startled, but still suspicious, Rachel caps the bottle and, keeping her eyes on the woman, drinks from the faucet. The woman steps back into the house. Rachel motions Johnson to do the same, signaling for him to hurry and drink. She turns off the faucet when he is done.

They are turning to go when the woman emerges from the house carrying a plate of tortillas and a bowl of apples. She sets them on the edge of the porch and says, "These are for you."

The woman watches through the window as Rachel packs the food into her bag. Rachel puts away the last apple and gestures her thanks to the woman. When the woman fails to respond to the sign language, Rachel picks up a stick and writes in the sand of the yard. "THANK YOU," Rachel scratches, then waves good-bye and sets out across the desert. She is puzzled, but happy.

The next morning's newspaper includes an interview with the dark-haired woman. She describes how Rachel turned on the faucet and turned it off when she was through, how the chimp packed the apples neatly in her bag and wrote in the dirt with a stick.

The reporter also interviews the director of the Primate Research Center. "These are animals," the director explains angrily. "But people want to treat them like they're small hairy people." He describes the Center as "primarily a breeding center with some facilities for medical research." The reporter asks some pointed questions about their acquisition of Rachel.

But the biggest story is an investigative piece. The reporter reveals that he has tracked down Aaron Jacob's lawyer and learned that Jacobs left a will. In this will, he bequeathed all his possessions—including his house and surrounding land—to "Rachel, the chimp I acknowledge as my daughter."

The reporter makes friends with one of the young women in the typing pool at the research center, and she tells him the office scuttlebutt: people suspect that the chimps may have been released by a deaf and drunken janitor, who was subsequently fired for negligence. The reporter, accompanied by a friend who can communicate in sign language, finds Jake in his apartment in downtown Flagstaff.

Jake, who has been drinking steadily since he was fired, feels betrayed by Rachel, by the Primate Center, by the world. He complains at length about Rachel: they had been friends, and then she took his baseball cap and ran away. He just didn't understand why she had run away like that.

"You mean she could talk?" the reporter asks through his interpreter.

—Of course she can talk, Jake signs impatiently.—She is a smart monkey.

The headlines read: "Intelligent chimp inherits fortune!" Of course, Aaron's bequest isn't really a fortune and she isn't just a chimp, but close enough. Animal rights activists rise up in Rachel's defense. The case is discussed on the national news. Ann Landers reports receiving a letter from a chimp named Rachel; she had thought it was a hoax perpetrated by the boys at Yale. The American Civil Liberties Union assigns a lawyer to the case.

By day, Rachel and Johnson sleep in whatever hiding places they can find: a cave; a shelter built for range cattle; the shell of an abandoned car, rusted from long years in a desert gully. Sometimes Rachel dreams of jungle darkness, and the coyotes in the distance become a part of her dreams, their howling becomes the cries of fellow apes.

The desert and the journey have changed her. She is wiser, having passed through the white-hot love of adolescence and emerged on the other side. She dreams, one day, of the ranch house. In the dream, she has long blonde hair and pale white skin. Her eyes are red from crying and she wanders the house restlessly, searching for something that she has lost. When she hears coyotes howling, she looks through a window at the darkness outside. The face that looks in at her has jug-handle ears and shaggy hair. When she sees the face, she cries out in recognition and opens the window to let herself in.

By night, they travel. The rocks and sands are cool beneath Rachel's feet as she walks toward her ranch. On television, scientists and politicians discuss the ramifications of her case, describe the technology uncovered by investigation of Aaron Jacobs' files. Their debates do not affect her steady progress toward her ranch or the stars that sprinkle the sky above her.

It is night when Rachel and Johnson approach the ranchhouse. Rachel sniffs the wind and smells automobile exhaust and strange humans. From the hills, she can see a small camp beside a white van marked with the name of a local television station. She hesitates, considering returning to the safety of the desert. Then she takes Johnson by the hand and starts down the hill. Rachel is going home.

# BRUCE McALLISTER

## Dream Baby

Here's as powerful and hard-hitting a story as you're likely to read this year, a compassionate study of those who actually have to face up to those horrors of war we hear so much about.

Bruce McAllister published his first story in 1963, when he was seventeen (it was *written* at the tender age of fifteen). Since then, with only a handful of stories, he has managed to establish himself as one of the most respected writers in the business. His short fiction has appeared in *Omni, Isaac Asimov's Science Fiction Magazine, In the Field of Fire, The Magazine of Fantasy and Science Fiction*, and elsewhere. His first novel *Humanity Prime* was one of the original Ace Specials series. Upcoming is a new novel from Tor, and he is at work on several other novels. McAllister lives in Redlands, California, where he is the director of the writing program at the University of Redlands.

# DREAM BABY

## Bruce McAllister

I don't know whether I was for or against the war when I went. I joined and became a nurse to help. Isn't that why everyone becomes a nurse? We're told it's a good thing, like being a teacher or a mother. What they don't tell us is that sometimes you can't help.

Our principal gets on the PA one day and tells us how all these boys across the country are going over there for us and getting killed or maimed. Then he tells us that Tony Fischetti and this other kid are dead, killed in action, Purple Hearts and everything. A lot of the girls start crying. I'm crying. I call the Army and tell them my grades are pretty good, I want to go to nursing school and then 'Nam. They say fine, they'll pay for it but I'm obligated if they do. I say it's what I want. I don't know if any other girls from school did it. I really didn't care. I just thought somebody ought to.

I go down and sign up and my dad gets mad. He says I just want to be a whore or a lesbian, because that's what people will think if I go. I say, "Is that what you and Mom think?" He almost hits me. Parents are like that. What other people think is more important than what they think, but you can't tell them that.

I never saw a nurse in 'Nam who was a whore and I only saw one or two who might have been butch. But that's how people thought, back here in the States.

I grew up in Long Beach, California, a sailor town. Sometimes I forget that. Sometimes I forget I wore my hair in a flip and liked miniskirts and black pumps. Sometimes all I can remember is the hospitals.

I got stationed at Cam Ranh Bay, at the 23rd Medevac, for two months, then the 118th Field General in Saigon, then back to the 23rd. They weren't supposed to move you around like that, but I got moved. That kind of thing happened all the time. Things just weren't done by the book. At the 23rd we were put in a bunch of huts. It was right by the hospital compound, and we had the Navy on one side of us and the Air Force on the other side. We could hear the mortars all night and the next day we'd get to see what they'd done.

It began to get to me after about a week. That's all it took. The big medevac choppers would land and the gurneys would come in. We were the ones who tried to keep them alive, and if they didn't die on us, we'd send them on.

We'd be covered with blood and urine and everything else. We'd have a boy with no arms or no legs, or maybe his legs would be lying beside him on the gurney. We'd have guys with no faces. We'd have stomachs you could hold in your hands. We'd be slapping ringers and plasma into them. We'd have sump pumps going to get the secretions and blood out of them. We'd do this all day, day in and day out.

You'd put them in bags if they didn't make it. You'd change dressings on stumps, and you had this deal with the corpsmen that every fourth day you'd clean the latrines for them if they'd change the dressings. They knew what it was like.

They'd bring in a boy with beautiful brown eyes and you'd just have a chance to look at him, to get a chest cut-down started for a subclavian catheter. He'd say, "Ma'am, am I all right?" and in forty seconds he'd be gone. He's say "Oh, no" and he'd be gone. His blood would pool on the gurney right through the packs. Some wounds are so bad you can't even plug them. The person just drains away.

You wanted to help but you couldn't. All you could do was watch.

When the dreams started, I thought I was going crazy. It was about the fourth week and I couldn't sleep. I'd close my eyes and think of trip wires. I'd think my bras and everything else had trip wires. I'd be on the john and hear a sound and think that someone was trip-wiring the latch so I'd lose my hands and face when I tried to leave.

I'd dream about wounds, different kinds, and then the next day there would be the wounds I'd dreamed about. I thought it was just coincidence. I'd seen a lot of wounds by then. Everyone was having nightmares. I'd dream about a sucking chest wound and a guy trying to scream, though he couldn't, and the next day I'd have to suck out a chest and listen to a guy try to scream. I didn't think much about it. I couldn't sleep. That was the important thing. I knew I was going to go crazy if I couldn't sleep.

Sometimes the dreams would have all the details. They'd bring in a guy that looked like someone had taken an icepick to his arms. His arms looked like frankfurters with holes punched in them. That's what shrapnel looks like. You puff up and the bleeding stops. We all knew he was going to die. You can't live through something like that. The system won't take it. He knew he was going to die, but he wasn't making a sound. His face had little holes in it, around his cheeks, and it looked like a catcher's mitt. He had the most beautiful blue eyes, like glass. You know, like that dog, the weimer-something. I'd start shaking because he was in one of my dreams—those holes and his face and eyes. I'd shake for hours, but you couldn't tell anybody about dreams like that.

The guy would die. There wasn't anything I could do.

I didn't understand it. I didn't see a reason for the dreams. They just made it worse.

It got so I didn't want to go to sleep because I didn't want to have them. I didn't want to wake up and have to worry about the dreams all day, wondering if they were going to happen. I didn't want to have to shake all day, wondering.

I'd have this dream about a kid with a bad head wound and a phone call, and the next day they'd wheel in some kid who'd lost a lot of skull and brain and scalp, and the underlying brain would be infected. Then the word would get around that his father, who was a full-bird colonel stationed in Okie, had called and the kid's mother and father would be coming to see him. We all hoped he died before they got there, and he did.

I'd had a dream about him. I'd even dreamed that we wanted him to die before his mom and dad got there, and he did, in the dream he did.

When he died I started screaming and this corpsman who'd been around for a week or two took me by the arm and got me to the john. I'd gotten sick but he held me like my mom would have and all I could do was think what a mess I was, how could he hold me when I was such a mess? I started crying and couldn't stop. I knew everyone thought I was crazy, but I couldn't stop.

After that things got worse. I'd see more than just a face or the wounds. I'd see where the guy lived, where his hometown was and who was going to cry for him if he died. I didn't understand it at first—I didn't even know it was happening. I'd just get pictures, like before, in the dream and they'd bring this guy in the next day or the day after that, and if he could talk, I'd find out that what I'd seen was true. This guy would be dying and not saying a thing and I'd remember him from the dream and I'd say, "You look like a Georgia boy to me." If the morphine was working and he could talk, he'd say, "Who told you that, Lieutenant? All us brothers ain't from Georgia."

I'd make up something, like his voice or a good guess, and if I'd seen other things in the dream—like his girl or wife or mother—I'd tell him about those, too. He wouldn't ask how I knew because it didn't matter. How could it matter? He knew he was dying. They always know. I'd talk to him like I'd known him my whole life and he'd be gone in an hour, or by morning.

I had this dream about a commando type, dressed in tiger cammies, nobody saying a thing about him in the compound—spook stuff, Ibex, MAC SOG, something like that—and I could see his girlfriend in Australia. She had hair just like mine and her eyes were a little like mine and she loved him. She was going out with another guy that night, but she loved him, I could tell. In the dream they brought him into ER with the bottom half of him blown away.

The next morning, first thing, they wheeled this guy in and it was the dream all over again. He was blown apart from the waist down. He was delirious and trying to talk but his jaw wouldn't work. He had tiger cammies on and we cut them off. I was the one who got him and everyone knew he wasn't going to make it. As soon as I saw him I started shaking. I didn't want to see him, I didn't want to look at him. You really don't know what it's like, seeing someone like that and knowing. I didn't want him to die. I never wanted any of them to die.

I said, "Your girl in Australia loves you—she really does." He looked at me and his eyes had that look you get when morphine isn't enough. I could tell he thought I looked like her. He couldn't even see my hair under the cap and he knew I looked like her.

He grabbed my arm and his jaw started slipping and I knew what he wanted me to do. I always knew. I told him about her long black hair and the beaches in Australia and what the people were like there and what there was to do.

He thought I was going to stop talking, so he kept squeezing my arm. I told him what he and his girlfriend had done on a beach outside Melbourne, their favorite beach, and what they'd had to drink that night.

And then—this was the first time I'd done it with anyone—I told him what I'd do for him if I was his girlfriend and we were back in Australia. I said, "I'd wash you real good in the shower. I'd turn the lights down low and I'd put on some nice music. Then, if you were a little slow, I'd help you."

It was what his girlfriend always did, I knew that. It wasn't hard to say.

I kept talking, he kept holding my arm, and then he coded on me. They always did. I had a couple of minutes or hours and then they always coded on me, just like in the dreams.

I got good at it. The pictures got better and I could tell them what they wanted to hear and that made it easier. It wasn't just faces and burns and stumps, it was things about them. I'd tell them what their girlfriends and wives would do if they were here. Sometimes it was sexual, sometimes it wasn't. Sometimes I'd just ruffle their hair with my hand and tell them what Colorado looked like in summer, or what the last Doors concert they'd been to was like, or what you could do after dark in Newark.

I start crying in the big room one day and this corpsman takes me by the arm and the next thing I know I'm sitting on the john and he's got a needle in his hand, a 2% solution. He doesn't want to see me hurting so much. I tell him no. Why, I don't know. Every week or so I'd walk into the john and find somebody with a needle in their arm, but it wasn't for me, I thought. People weren't supposed to do that kind of thing. Junkies on the Pike back home did it—we all knew that—but not doctors and medics and nurses. It wasn't right, I told myself.

I didn't start until a couple of weeks later.

There's this guy I want to tell you about. Steve—his name was Steve.

I come in one morning to the big ER room shaking so hard I can't even put my cap on and thinking I should've gotten a needle already, and there's this guy sitting over by a curtain. He's in cammies, his head's wrapped and he's sitting up real straight. I can barely stand up, but here's this guy looking like he's hurting, so I say, "You want to lie down?"

He turns slowly to look at me and I don't believe it. I know this guy from a dream, but I don't see the dream clearly. Here's this guy sitting in a chair in front of me unattended, like he could walk away any second, but I've had a dream about him, so I know he's going to die.

He says he's okay, he's just here to see a buddy. But I'm not listening. I know everything about him. I know about his girlfriend and where he's from and how his mom and dad didn't raise him, but all I can think about is, he's going to die. I'm thinking about the supply room and needles and how it wouldn't take much to get it all over with.

I say, "Cathy misses you, Steve. She wishes you could go to the Branding Iron in Merced tonight, because that band you like is playing. She's done something to her apartment and she wants to show it to you."

He looks at me for a long time and his eyes aren't like the others.

I don't want to look back at him. I can see him anyway—in the dream. He's real young. He's got a nice body, good shoulders, and he's got curly blond hair under those clean bandages. He's got eyelashes like a girl, and I see him laughing. He laughs every chance he gets, I know.

Very quietly he says. "What's your name?"

I guess I tell him, because he says, "Can you tell me what she looks like, Mary?"

Everything's wrong. The guy doesn't sound like he's going to die. He's looking at me like he understands.

I say something like "She's tall." I say, "She's got blond hair," but I can barely think.

Very gently he says, "What are her eyes like?"

I don't know. I'm shaking so hard I can barely talk, I can barely remember the dream.

Suddenly I'm talking. "They're green. She wears a lot of mascara, but she's got dark eyebrows, so she isn't really a blond, is she."

He laughs and I jump. "No, she isn't," he says and he's smiling. He takes my hand in his. I'm shaking badly but I let him, like I do the others. I don't say a word.

I'm holding it in. I'm scared to death. I'm cold-turkeying and I'm letting him hold my hand because he's going to die. But it's not true. I dreamed about him, but in the dream he didn't die. I know that now.

He squeezes my hand like we've known each other a long time and he says, "Do you do this for all of them?"

I don't say a thing.

Real quietly he says, "A lot of guys die on you, don't they, Mary."

I can't help it—I start crying. I want to tell him. I want to tell someone, so I do.

When I'm finished he doesn't say something stupid, he doesn't walk away. He doesn't code on me. He starts to tell me a story and I don't understand at first.

There's this G-2 reconnaissance over the border, he says. The insertion's smooth and I'm point, I'm always point. We're humping across paddy dikes like grunts and we hit this treeline. This is a black op, nobody's supposed to know we're here, but somebody does. All of a sudden the goddamn trees are full of Charlie ching-ching snipers. The whole world turns blue–just for me, I mean, it turns blue—and everything starts moving real slow. I can see the first AK rounds coming at me and I step aside nicely just like that, like always.

The world always turns blue like that when he needs it to, he says. That's why they make him point every goddamn time, why they keep using him on special ops to take out infrastructure or long-range recon for intel. Because the world turns blue. And how he's been called in twice to talk about what he's going to do after this war and how they want him to be a killer, he says. The records will say he died in this war and they'll give him a new identity. He doesn't have family, they say. He'll be one of their killers wherever they need him. Because everything turns blue. I don't believe what I'm hearing. It's like a movie, like that *Manchurian Candidate* thing, and I can't believe it. They don't care about how he does it, he says. They never do. It can be the world turning blue or voices in your head or some grabass feeling in your gut, or, if you want, it can be God or the Devil with horns or Little Green Martians—it doesn't matter to them what you believe. As long as it works, as long as you keep coming back from missions, that's all they care about. He told them no, but they keep on asking. Sometimes he thinks they'll kill his girlfriend just so he won't have anything to come back to in the States. They do that kind of thing, he says. I can't believe it.

So everything's turning blue, he says, and I'm floating up out of my body over this rice paddy, these goddamn ching-ching snipers are darker blue, and when I come back down I'm moving through this nice blue world and I know where they are, and I get every goddamn one of them in their trees.

But it doesn't matter, he says. There's this light-weapons sergeant, a guy they called the Dogman, who's crazy and barks like a dog and makes everyone laugh even if they're bleeding, even if their guts are hanging out. He scares the VC when he barks. He humps his share and the men love him.

When the world turns blue, the Dogman's in cover, everything's fine, but then he rubbernecks, the sonuvabitch rubbernecks for the closest ching-ching—he didn't have to, he just didn't have to—and takes a round high. I don't see the back of his head explode, so I think he's still alive. I go for him where he's hanging half out of the treeline, half in a canal full of stinking rice water. I try to get his body out of the line of fire, but Charlie puts the next round right in under my arm. I'm holding the Dogman and the round goes in right under my arm, a fucking heart shot. I can feel it come in. It's for me. Everything goes slow and blue and I jerk a little—I don't even know I'm doing it—and the round slides right in under me and into him. They never get *me*. The fucking world turns blue and everything goes slow and they never get *me*.

I can always save myself, he says—his name is Steve and he's not smiling now—but I can't save *them*. What's it worth? What's it worth if you stay alive and everybody you care about is dead? Even if you get what *they* want.

I know what he means. I know now why he's sitting on a chair nearly crying, I know where the body is, which curtain it's behind, how close it's been all this time. I remember the dream now.

Nobody likes to die alone, Steve says. Just like he said it in the dream.

He stays and we talk. We talk about the dreams and his blue world, and we talk about what we're going to do when we get out of this place and back to the Big PX, all the fun we're going to have. He starts to tell me about other guys he knows, guys like him that his people are interested in, but then he stops and I see he's looking past me. I turn around.

There's this guy in civvies at the end of the hallway, just standing there, looking at us. Then he nods at Steve and Steve says, "I got to go."

Real fast I say, "See you at nineteen hundred hours."

He's looking at the guy down the hallway. "Yeah, sure," he says.

When I get off he's there. I haven't thought about a needle all day and it shows. We get a bite to eat and talk some more, and that's that. My roommate says I can have the room for a couple of hours, but I'm a mess. I'm shaking so bad I can't even think about having a good time with this guy. He looks at me like he knows this, and says his head hurts and we ought to get some sleep.

He gives me a hug. That's it.

The same guy in civvies is waiting for him and they walk away together on Phan Hao Street.

The next day he's gone. I tell myself maybe he was standing down for a couple of days and had to get back, but that doesn't help. I know lots of guys who traveled around in-country AWOL without getting into trouble. What could they do to you? Send you to 'Nam?

I thought maybe he'd call in a couple of days, or write. Later I thought maybe he'd gotten killed, maybe let himself get killed. I really didn't know what to think, but I thought about him a lot.

Ten days later I get transferred. I don't even get orders cut, I don't even get in-country travel paper. No one will tell me a thing—the head nurse, the CO, nobody.

I get scared because I think they're shipping me back to the States because of the smack or the dreams—they've found out about the dreams—and I'm going to be in some VA hospital the rest of my life. That's what I think.

All they'll tell me is that I'm supposed to be at the strip at 0600 hours tomorrow, fatigues and no ID.

I get a needle that night and I barely make it.

* * *

This Huey comes in real fast and low and I get dust in my eyes from the prop wash. A guy with a clipboard about twenty yards away signals me and I get on. There's no one there to say good-bye and I never see the 23rd again.

The Huey's empty except for these two pilots who never turn around and this doorgunner who's hanging outside and this other guy who's sitting back with me on the canvas. I think maybe he's the one who's going to explain things, but he just stares for a while and doesn't say a thing. He's a sergeant, a Ranger, I think.

It's supposed to be dangerous to fly at night in Indian Country, I know, but we fly at night. We stop twice and I know we're in Indian Country. This one guy gets off, another guy gets on, and then two more. They seem to know each other and they start laughing. They try to get me to talk. One guy says, "You a Donut Dolly?" and another guy says, "Hell, no, asshole, she's Army, can't you tell? She's got the thousand yards." The third guy says to me, "Don't mind him, ma'am. They don't raise 'em right in Mississippi." They're trying to be nice, but I don't want in.

I don't want to sleep either. But my head's tipped back against the steel and I keep waking up, trying to remember whether I've dreamed about people dying, but I can't. I fall asleep once for a long time and when I wake up I can remember death, but I can't see the faces.

I wake up once and there's automatic weapon fire somewhere below us and maybe the slick gets hit once or twice. Another time I wake up and the three guys are talking quietly, real serious, but I'm hurting from no needle and I don't even listen.

When the rotors change I wake up. It's first light and cool and we're coming in on this big clearing, everything misty and beautiful. It's triple-canopy jungle I've never seen before and I know we're so far from Cam Ranh Bay or Saigon it doesn't matter. I don't see anything that looks like a medevac, just this clearing, like a staging area. There are a lot of guys walking around, a lot of machinery, but it doesn't look like regular Army. It looks like something you hear about but aren't supposed to see, and I'm shaking like a baby.

When we hit the LZ the three guys don't even know I exist and I barely get out of the slick on my own. I can't see because of the wash and suddenly this Green Beanie medic I've never seen before—this captain—has me by the arm and he's taking me somewhere. I tell myself I'm not going back to the Big PX, I'm not going to some VA hospital for the rest of my life, that this is the guy I'm going to be assigned to—they need a nurse out here or something.

I'm not thinking straight. Special Forces medics don't have nurses.

I'm looking around me and I don't believe what I'm seeing. There's bunkers and M-60 emplacements and Montagnard guards on the perimeter and all this beautiful red earth. There's every kind of jungle fatigue and cammie you can think of—stripes and spots and black pajamas like Charlie and everything else. I see Special Forces enlisted everywhere and I know this isn't some little A-camp. I see a dozen guys in real clean fatigues who don't walk like soldiers walk. I see a Special Forces major and he's arguing with one of them.

The captain who's got me by the arm isn't saying a thing. He takes me to this little bunker that's got mosquito netting and a big canvas flap over the front and he puts me inside. It's got a cot. He tells me to lie down and I do. He says, "The CO wants you to get some sleep, Lieutenant. Someone will come by with something in a little while." The way he says it I know he knows about the needles.

I don't know how long I'm in the bunker before someone comes, but I'm in lousy shape. This guy in civvies gives me something to take with a little paper cup and I go ahead and do it. I'm not going to fight it the shape I'm in. I dream, and keep dreaming, and in some of the dreams someone comes by with a glass of water and I take more pills. I can't wake up. All I can do is sleep but I'm not really sleeping and I'm having these dreams that aren't really dreams. Once or twice I hear myself screaming, it hurts so much, and then I dream about a little paper cup and more pills.

When I come out of it I'm not shaking. I know it's not supposed to be this quick, that what they gave me isn't what people are getting in programs back in the States, and I get scared again. Who are these guys?

I sit in the little bunker all day eating ham-and-mother-fuckers from C-rat cans and I tell myself that Steve had something to do with it. I'm scared but it's nice not to be shaking. It's nice not to be thinking about a needle all the time.

The next morning I hear all this noise and I realize we're leaving, the whole camp is leaving. I can hear this noise like a hundred slicks outside and I get up and look through the flap. I've never seen so many choppers. They've got Chinooks and Hueys and Cobras and Loaches and a Skycrane for the SeaBee machines and they're dusting off and dropping in and dusting off again. I've never seen anything like it. I keep looking for Steve. I keep trying to remember the dreams I had while I was out all those days and I can't.

Finally the Green Beanie medic comes back. He doesn't say a word. He just takes me to the LZ and we wait until a slick drops in. All these tiger stripes pile in with us but no one says a thing. No one's joking. I don't understand it. We aren't being hit, we're just moving, but no one's joking.

We set up in a highlands valley northwest of where we'd been, where the jungle is thicker but it's not triple canopy. There's this same beautiful mist and I wonder if we're in some other country, Laos or Cambodia.

They have my bunker dug in about an hour and I'm in it about thirty minutes before this guy appears. I've been looking for Steve, wondering why I haven't seen him, and feeling pretty good about myself. It's nice not to be shaking, to get the monkey off my back, and I'm ready to thank *somebody*.

This guy opens the flap. He stands there for a moment and there's something familiar about him. He's about thirty and he's in real clean fatigues. He's got MD written all over him—but the kind that never gets any blood on him. I think of VA hospitals, psychiatric wards, and I get scared again.

"How are you feeling, Lieutenant?"

"Fine," I say, but I'm not smiling. I know this guy from the dreams—the little paper cups and pills—and I don't like what I'm feeling.

"Glad to hear it. Remarkable drug, isn't it, Lieutenant?"

I nod. Nothing he says surprises me.

"Someone wants to see you, Lieutenant."

I get up, dreading it. I know he's not talking about Steve.

They've got all the bunkers dug and he takes me to what has to be the CP. There isn't a guy inside who isn't in real clean fatigues. There are three or four guys who have the same look this guy has—MDs that don't ever get their hands dirty—and intel types pointing at maps and pushing things around on a couple of sand-table mock-ups. There's this one guy with his back turned and everyone else keeps checking in with him.

He's tall. He's got a full head of hair but it's going gray. He doesn't even have to turn around and I know.

It's the guy in civvies at the end of the hallway at the 23rd, the guy that walked away with Steve on Phan Hao Street.

He turns around and I don't give him eye contact. He looks at me, smiles, and starts over. There are two guys trailing him and he's got this smile that's supposed to be charming.

"How are you feeling, Lieutenant?" he says.

"Everybody keeps asking me that," I say, and I wonder why I'm being so brave.

"That's because we're interested in you, Lieutenant," he says. He's got this jungle outfit on with gorgeous creases and some canvas jungle boots that breathe nicely. He looks like an ad from a catalog but I know he's no joke, he's no pogue lifer. He's wearing this stuff because he likes it, that's all. He could wear anything he wanted to because he's not military, but he's the CO of this operation, which means he's fighting a war I don't know a thing about.

He tells me he's got some things to straighten out first, but that if I go back to my little bunker he'll be there in an hour. He asks me if I want anything to eat. When I say sure, he tells the MD type to get me something from the mess.

I go back. I wait. When he comes, he's got a file in his hand and there's a young guy with him who's got a cold six-pack of Coke in his hand. I can tell they're cold because the cans are sweating. I can't believe it. We're out here in the middle of nowhere, we're probably not even supposed to be here, and they're bringing me cold Coke.

When the young guy leaves, the CO sits on the edge of the cot and I sit on the other and he says, "Would you like one, Lieutenant?"

I say, "Yes, sir," and he pops the top with a church key. He doesn't take one himself and suddenly I wish I hadn't said yes. I'm thinking of old movies where Jap officers offer their prisoners a cigarette so they'll owe them one. There's not even any place to put the can down, so I hold it between my hands.

"I'm not sure where to begin, Lieutenant," he says, "but let me assure you you're here because you belong here." He says it gently, real softly, but it gives me a funny feeling. "You're an officer and you've been in-country for some time. I don't need to tell you that we're a very special kind of operation here. What I do need to tell you is that you're one of three hundred we've identified so far in this war. Do you understand?"

I say, "No, sir."

"I think you do, but you're not sure, right? You've accepted your difference—your gift, your curse, your talent, whatever you would like to call it—but you can't as easily accept the fact that so many others might have the same thing, am I right, Mary—may I call you Mary?"

I don't like the way he says it but I say yes.

"We've identified three hundred like you, Mary. That's what I'm saying."

I stare at him. I don't know whether to believe him.

"I'm only sorry, Mary, that you came to our attention so late. Being alone with a gift like yours isn't easy, I'm sure, and finding a community of those who share it—the same gift, the same curse—is essential if the problems that always accompany it are to be worked out successfully, am I correct?"

"Yes."

"We might have lost you, Mary, if Lieutenant Balsam hadn't found you. He almost didn't make the trip, for reasons that will be obvious later. If he hadn't met you, Mary, I'm afraid your hospital would have sent you back to the States for drug abuse if not for what they perceived as an increasingly dysfunctional neurosis. Does this surprise you?"

I say it doesn't.

"I didn't think so. You're a smart girl, Mary."

The voice is gentle, but it's not.

He waits and I don't know what he's waiting for.

I say, "Thank you for whatever it was that—"

"No need to thank us, Mary. Were that particular drug available back home right now, it wouldn't seem like such a gift, would it?"

He's right. He's the kind who's always right and I don't like the feeling.

"Anyway, thanks," I say. I'm wondering where Steve is.

"You're probably wondering where Lieutenant Balsam is, Mary."

I don't bother to nod this time.

"He'll be back in a few days. We have a policy here of not discussing missions—even in the ranks—and as commanding officer I like to set a good example. You can understand, I'm sure." He smiles again and for the first time I see the crow's-feet around his eyes, and how straight his teeth are, and how there are little capillaries broken on his cheeks.

He looks at the Coke in my hands and smiles. Then he opens the file he has. "If we were doing this the right way, Mary, we would get together in a nice air-conditioned building back in the States and go over all of this together, but we're not in any position to do that, are we?

"I don't know how much you've gathered about your gift, Mary, but people who study such things have their own way of talking. They would call yours a 'TPC hybrid with traumatic neurosis, dissociative features.' " He smiled. "That's not as bad as it sounds. It's quite normal. The human psyche always responds to special gifts like yours, and neurosis is simply a mechanism for doing just that. We wouldn't be human if it didn't, would we?"

"No, we wouldn't."

He's smiling at me and I know what he wants me to feel. I feel like a little girl sitting on a chair, being good, listening, and liking it, and that is what he wants.

"Those same people, Mary, would call your dreams 'spontaneous anecdotal material' and your talent a 'REM-state precognition or clairvoyance.' They're not very helpful words. They're the words of people who've never experienced it themselves. Only you, Mary, know what it really feels like inside. Am I right?"

I remember liking how that felt—*only you*. I needed to feel that, and he knew I needed to.

"Not all three hundred are dreamers like you, of course. Some are what those same people would call 'kinetic phenomena generators.' Some are 'tactility-triggered remoters' or 'OBE clears.' Some leave their bodies in a firefight and acquire information that could not be acquired in ordinary ways, which tells us that their talent is indeed authentic. Others see auras when their comrades are about to die, and if they can get those auras to disappear, their friends will live. Others experience only a vague visceral sensation, a gut feeling which tells them where mines and trip wires are. They know, for example, when a crossbow trap will fire and this allows them to knock away the arrows before they can hurt them. Still others receive pictures, like waking dreams, of what will happen in the next minute, hour, or day in combat.

"With very few exceptions, Mary, none of these individuals experienced anything like this as civilians. These episodes are the consequence of combat, of the metabolic and psychological anomalies which life-and-death conditions seem to generate."

He looks at me and his voice changes now, as if on cue. He wants me to feel what he is feeling, and I do, I do. I can't look away from him and I know this is why he is CO.

"It is almost impossible to reproduce them in a laboratory, Mary, and so these remarkable talents remain mere ancedotes, events that happen once or twice within a lifetime—to a brother, a mother, a friend, a fellow soldier in a war. A boy is killed on Kwajalein in 1944. That same night his mother dreams of his death. She has never before dreamed such a dream, and the dream is too accurate to be mere coincidence. He dies. She never has a dream like it again. A reporter for a major newspaper looks out the terminal window at the Boeing 707 he is about to board. He has flown a hundred times before, enjoys air travel, and has no reason to be anxious today. As he looks through the window the plane explodes before his very eyes. He can hear the sound ringing in his ears and the sirens rising in the distance; he can feel the heat of the ignited fuel on his face. Then he blinks. The jet is as it was before—no fire, no sirens, no explosion. He is shaking—he has never experienced anything like this in his life. He does not board the plane, and the next day he hears that its fuel tanks exploded, on the ground, in another city, killing ninety. The man never has such a vision again. He enjoys air travel in the months, and years, ahead, and will die of cardiac arrest on a tennis court twenty years later. You can see the difficulty we have, Mary."

"Yes," I say quietly, moved by what he's said.

"But our difficulty doesn't mean that your dreams are any less real, Mary. It doesn't mean that what you and the three hundred like you in this small theater of war are experiencing isn't real."

"Yes," I say.

He gets up.

"I am going to have one of my colleagues interview you, if that's all right. He will ask you questions about your dreams and he will record what you say. The tapes will remain in my care, so there isn't any need to worry, Mary."

I nod.

"I hope that you will view your stay here as deserved R&R, and as a chance to make contact with others who understand what it is like. For paperwork's sake, I've assigned you to Golf Team. You met three of its members on your flight in, I believe. You may write to your parents as long as you make reference to a medevac unit in Pleiku rather than to our actual operation here. Is that clear?"

He smiles like a friend would, and makes his voice as gentle as he can. "I'm going to leave the rest of the Coke. And a church key. Do I have your permission?" He grins. It's a joke, I realize. I'm supposed to smile. When I do, he smiles back and I know he knows everything, he knows himself, he knows me, what I think of him, what I've been thinking every minute he's been here.

It scares me that he knows.

His name is Bucannon.

The man that came was one of the other MD types from the tent. He asked and I answered. The question that took the longest was "What were your dreams like? Be as specific as possible both about the dream content and its relationship to reality—that is, how accurate the dream was as a predictor of what happened. Describe how the dreams and their relationship to reality (i.e., their accuracy) affected you both psychologically and physically (e.g., sleeplessness, nightmares, inability to concentrate, anxiety, depression, uncontrollable rages, suicidal thoughts, drug abuse)."

It took us six hours and six tapes.

We finished after dark.

I did what I was supposed to do. I hung around Golf Team. There were six guys, this lieutenant named Pagano, who was in charge, and this demo sergeant named Christabel, who was their "talent." He was, I found out, an "OBE clairvoyant with EEG anomalies," which meant that in a firefight he could leave his body just like Steve could. He could leave his body, look back at himself—that's what it felt like—and see how everyone else was doing and maybe save someone's ass. They were a good team. They hadn't lost anybody yet, and they loved to tease this sergeant every chance they got.

We talked about Saigon and what you could get on the black market. We talked about missions, even though we weren't supposed to. The three guys from the slick even got me to talk about the dreams, I was feeling that good, and when I heard they were going out on another mission at 0300 hours the next morning, without the sergeant—some little mission they didn't need him on—I didn't think anything about it.

I woke up in my bunker that night screaming because two of the guys from the slick were dead. I saw them dying out in the jungle, I saw how they died, and suddenly I knew what it was all about, why Bucannon wanted me here.

He came by the bunker at first light. I was still crying. He knelt down beside me and put his hand on my forehead. He made his voice gentle. He said, "What was your dream about, Mary?"

I wouldn't tell him. "You've got to call them back," I said.

"I can't, Mary," he said. "We've lost contact."

He was lying I found out later: he could have called them back—no one was dead yet—but I didn't know that then. So I went ahead and told him about the two I'd dreamed about, the one from Mississippi and the one who'd thought I was a Donut Dolly. He took notes. I was a mess, crying and sweaty, and he pushed the hair away from my forehead and said he would do what he could.

I didn't want him to touch me, but I didn't stop him. I didn't stop him.

I didn't leave the bunker for a long time. I couldn't.

No one told me the two guys were dead. No one had to. It was the right kind of dream, just like before. But this time I'd *known* them. I'd met them. I'd laughed with them in the daylight and when they died I wasn't there, it wasn't on some gurney in a room somewhere. It was different.

It was starting up again, I told myself.

I didn't get out of the cot until noon. I was thinking about needles, that was all.

He comes by again at about 1900 hours, just walks in and says, "Why don't you have some dinner, Mary. You must be hungry."

I go to the mess they've thrown together in one of the big bunkers. I think the guys are going to know about the screaming, but all they do is look at me like I'm the only woman in the camp, that's all, and that's okay.

Suddenly I see Steve. He's sitting with three other guys and I get this feeling he doesn't want to see me, that if he did he'd have come looking for me already, and I should turn around and leave. But one of the guys is saying something to him and Steve is turning and I know I'm wrong. He's been waiting for me. He's wearing cammies and they're dirty—he hasn't been back long—and I can tell by the way he gets up and comes toward me he wants to see me.

We go outside and stand where no one can hear us. He says, "Jesus, I'm sorry." I'm not sure what he means.

"Are you okay?" I say, but he doesn't answer.

He's saying, "I wasn't the one who told him about the dreams, Mary, I swear it. All I did was ask for a couple hours' layover to see you, but he doesn't like that—he doesn't like 'variables.' When he gets me back to camp, he has you checked out. The hospital says something about dreams and how crazy you're acting, and he puts it together. He's smart, Mary. He's real smart—"

I tell him to shut up, it isn't his fault, and I'd rather be here than back in the States in some VA program or ward. But he's not listening. "He's got you here for a reason, Mary. He's got all of us here for a reason and if I hadn't asked for those hours he wouldn't know you existed—"

I get mad. I tell him I don't want to hear any more about it, it isn't his fault.

"Okay," he says finally. "Okay." He gives me a smile because he knows I want it. "Want to meet the guys on the team?" he says. "We just got extracted—"

I say sure. We go back in. He gets me some food and then introduces me. They're dirty and tired but they're not complaining. They're still too high off the mission to eat and won't crash for another couple of hours yet. There's an SF medic with the team, and two Navy SEALs because there's a riverine aspect to the mission, and a guy named Moburg, a Marine sniper out of Quantico. Steve's their CO and all I can think about is how young he is. They're all so young.

It turns out Moburg's a talent, too, but it's "anticipatory subliminal"—it only helps him target hits and doesn't help anyone else much. But he's a damn good sniper because of it, they tell me.

The guys give me food from their trays and for the first time that day I'm feeling hungry. I'm eating with guys that are real and alive and I'm really hungry.

Then I notice Steve isn't talking. He's got that same look on his face. I turn around.

Bucannon's in the doorway, looking at us. The other guys haven't seen him, they're still talking and laughing—being raunchy.

Bucannon is looking at us and he's smiling, and I get a chill down my spine like cold water because I know—all of a sudden I know—why I'm sitting here, who wants it this way.

I get up fast. Steve doesn't understand. He says something. I don't answer him, I don't even hear him. I keep going. He's behind me and he wants to know if I'm feeling okay, but I don't want to look back at him, I don't want to look at any of the guys with him, because that's what Bucannon wants.

He's going to send them out again, I tell myself. They just got back, they're tired, and he's going to send them out again, so I can dream about them.

I'm not going to go to sleep, I tell myself. I walk the perimeter until they tell me I can't do that anymore, it's too dangerous. Steve follows me and I start screaming at him, but I'm not making any sense. He watches me for a while and then someone comes to get him, and I know he's being told he's got to take his team out again. I ask for some Benzedrine from the Green Beanie medic who brings me aspirin when I want it but he says he can't, that word has come down that he can't. I try writing a letter to my parents but it's 0400 hours and I'm going crazy trying to stay awake because I haven't had more than four hours' sleep for a couple of nights and my body temperature's dropping on the diurnal.

I ask for some beer and they get it for me. I ask for some scotch. They give it to me and I think I've won. I never go to sleep on booze, but Bucannon doesn't know that. I'll stay awake and I won't dream.

But it knocks me out like a light, and I have a dream. One of the guys at the table, one of the two SEALs, is floating down a river. The blood is like a woman's hair streaming out from his head. I don't dream about Steve, just about this SEAL who's floating down a river. It's early in the mission. Somehow I know that.

I don't wake up screaming, because of what they put in the booze. I remember it as soon as I wake up, when I can't do anything about it.

Bucannon comes in at first light. He doesn't say, "If you don't help us, you're going back to Saigon or back to the States with a Section Eight." Instead he comes in and kneels down beside me like some goddamn priest and he says, "I know this is painful, Mary, but I'm sure you can understand."

I say, "Get the hell out of here, motherfucker."

It's like he hasn't heard. He says, "It would help us to know the details of any dream you had last night, Mary."

"You'll let him die anyway," I say.

"I'm sorry, Mary," he says, "but he's already dead. We've received word on one confirmed KIA in Echo Team. All we're interested in is the details of the dream and an approximate time, Mary." He hesitates. "I think he would want you to tell us. I think he would want to feel that it was not in vain, don't you."

He stands up at last.

"I'm going to leave some paper and writing utensils for you. I can understand what you're going through, more than you might imagine, Mary, and I believe that if you give it some thought—if you think about men like Steve and what your dreams could mean to them—you will write down the details of your dream last night."

I scream something at him. When he's gone I cry for a while. Then I go ahead and write down what he wants. I don't know what else to do.

I don't go to the mess. Bucannon has food brought to my bunker but I don't eat it.

I ask the Green Beanie medic where Steve is. Is he back yet? He says he can't tell me. I ask him to send a message to Steve for me. He says he can't do that. I tell him he's a straight-leg ass-kisser and ought to have his jump wings shoved, but this doesn't faze him at all. Any other place, I say, you'd be what you were supposed to be —Special Forces and a damn good medic—but Bucannon's got you, doesn't he. He doesn't say a thing.

I stay awake all that night. I ask for coffee and I get it. I bum more coffee off two sentries and drink that, too. I can't believe he's letting me have it. Steve's team is going to be back soon, I tell myself—they're a strike force, not a Lurp—and if I don't sleep, I can't dream.

I do it again the next night and it's easier. I can't believe it's this easy. I keep moving around. I get coffee and I find this sentry who likes to play poker and we play all night. I tell him I'm a talent and will know if someone's trying to come through the wire on us, sapper or whatever, so we can play cards and not worry. He's pure new-guy and he believes me.

Steve'll be back tomorrow, I tell myself. I'm starting to see things and I'm not thinking clearly, but I'm not going to crash. I'm not going to crash until Steve is back. I'm not going to dream about Steve.

At about 0700 hours the next morning we get mortared. The slicks inside the perimeter start revving up, the Skycrane starts hooking its cats and Rome plows, and the whole camp starts to dust off. I hear radios, more slicks and Skycranes being called in. If the NVA had a battalion, they'd be overrunning us, I tell myself, so it's got to be a lot less—company, platoon—and they're just harassing us, but word has come down from somebody that we're supposed to move.

Mortars are whistling in and someone to one side of me says "Incoming—fuck it!" Then I hear this other sound. It's like flies but real loud. It's like this weird whispering. It's a goddamn flechette round, I realize, spraying stuff, and I don't understand. I can hear it, but it's like a memory, a flashback. Everybody's running around me and I'm just standing there and someone's screaming. It's me screaming. I've got flechettes all through me—my chest, my face. I'm torn to pieces. I'm dying. But I'm running toward the slick, the one that's right over there, ready to dust off. Someone's calling to me, screaming at me, and I'm running, but I'm not. I'm on the ground. I'm on the jungle floor with these flechettes in me and I've got a name, a nickname, Kicker, and I'm thinking of a town in Wyoming, near the Montana border, where everybody rides pickup trucks with shotgun racks and waves to everybody else, I grew up there, there's a rodeo every spring with a county fair and I'm thinking about a girl with braids, I'm thinking how I'm going to die here in the middle of this jungle, how we're on some recondo that no one cares about, how Charlie doesn't have flechette rounds, how Bucannon never makes mistakes.

I'm running and screaming and when I get to the slick the Green Beanie medic grabs me, two other guys grab me and haul me in. I look up. It's Bucannon's slick. He's on the radio. I'm lying on a pile of files right beside him and we're up over the jungle now, we're taking the camp somewhere else, where it can start up all over again.

I look at Bucannon. I think he's going to turn any minute and say, "Which ones, Mary? Which ones died from the flechette?" He doesn't.

I look down and see he's put some paper and three pencils beside me on the floor. I can't stand it. I start crying.

I sleep maybe for twenty minutes and have two dreams. Two other guys died out there somewhere with flechettes in them. Two more guys on Steve's team died and I didn't even meet them.

I look up. Bucannon's smiling at me.

"It happened, didn't it, Mary?" he says gently. "It happened in the daylight this time, didn't it?"

* * *

At the new camp I stayed awake another night, but it was hard and it didn't make any difference. It probably made it worse. It happened three more times the next day and all sorts of guys saw me. I knew someone would tell Steve. I knew Steve's team was still out there—Echo hadn't come in when the rocketing started—but that he was okay. I'm lying on the ground screaming and crying with shrapnel going through me, my legs are gone, my left eyeball is hanging out on my cheek, and there are pieces of me all over the guy next to me, but I'm not Steve, and that's what matters.

The third time, an AK round goes through my neck so I can't even scream. I fall down and can't get up. Someone kneels down next to me and I think it's Bucannon and I try to hit him. I'm trying to scream even though I can't, but it's not Bucannon, it's one of the guys who was sitting with Steve in the mess. They're back, they're back, I think to myself, but I'm trying to tell this guy that I'm dying, that there's this medic somewhere out there under a beautiful rubber tree who's trying to pull me through, but I'm not going to make it, I'm going to die on him, and he's going to remember it his whole life, wake up in the night crying years later and his wife won't understand.

I want to say, "Tell Steve I've got to get out of here," but I can't. My throat's gone. I'm going out under some rubber tree a hundred klicks away in the middle of Laos, where we're not supposed to be, and I can't say a thing.

This guy who shared his ham-and-motherfuckers with me in the mess, this guy is looking down on me and I think, Oh my God, I'm going to dream about him some night, some day, I'm going to dream about him and because I do he's going to die.

He doesn't say a thing.

He's the one that comes to get me in my hooch two days later when they try to bust me out.

They give me something pretty strong. By the time they come I'm getting the waking dreams, sure, but I'm not screaming anymore. I'm here but I'm not. I'm all these other places, I'm walking into an Arclight, B-52 bombers, my ears are bleeding, I'm the closest man when a big Chinese claymore goes off, my arm's hanging by a string, I'm dying in all these other places and I don't even know I've taken their pills. I'm like a doll when Steve and this guy and three others come, and the guards let them. I'm smiling like an idiot and saying, "Thank you very much," something stupid some USO type would say, and I've got someone holding me up so I don't fall on my face.

There's this Jolly Green Giant out in front of us. It's dawn and everything's beautiful and this chopper is gorgeous. It's Air Force. It's crazy. There are these guys I've never seen before. They've got black berets and they're neat and clean, and they're not Army. I think, Air Commandos! I'm giggling. They're Air Force. They're dandies. They're going to save the day like John Wayne at Iwo Jima. I feel a bullet go through my arm, then another through my leg, and the back of my head blows off, but I don't scream. I just feel the feelings, the ones you feel right before you die—but I don't scream. The Air Force is going to save me. That's funny. I tell myself how Steve had friends in the Air Commandos and how they took him around once in-country for a whole damn week, AWOL, yeah, but maybe it isn't true, maybe I'm dreaming it. I'm still giggling. I'm still saying, "Thank you very much."

We're out maybe fifty klicks and I don't know where we're heading. I don't care. Even if I cared I wouldn't know how far out "safe" was. I hear Steve's voice in the cockpit and a bunch of guys are laughing, so I think *safe*. They've busted me out because Steve cares and now we're *safe*. I'm still saying "Thank you" and some guy is saying "You're welcome, baby," and people are laughing and that feels good. If they're all laughing, no one got hurt, I know. If they're all laughing, we're safe. Thank you. Thank you very much.

Then something starts happening in the cockpit. I can't hear with all the wind. Someone says "Shit." Someone says "Cobra." Someone else says "Jesus Christ what the hell." I look out the roaring doorway and I see two black gunships. They're like nothing I've ever seen before. No one's laughing. I'm saying "Thank you very much" but no one's laughing.

I find out later there was one behind us, one in front, and one above. They were beautiful. They reared up like snakes when they hit you. They had M-134 Miniguns that could put a round on every square centimeter of a football field within seconds. They had fifty-two white phosphorous rockets apiece and Martin-Marietta laser-guided Copperhead howitzer rounds. They had laser designators and Forward-Looking Infrared Sensors. They were nightblack, no insignias of any kind. They were model AH-1G-X and they didn't belong to any regular branch of the military back then. You wouldn't see them until the end of the war.

I remember thinking that there were only two of us with talent on that slick, why couldn't he let us go? Why couldn't he just let us go?

* * *

I tried to think of all the things he could do to us, but he didn't do a thing. He didn't have to.

I didn't see Steve for a long time. I went ahead and tried to sleep at night because it was better that way. If I was going to have the dreams, it was better that way. It didn't make me so crazy. I wasn't like a doll someone had to hold up.

I went ahead and wrote the dreams down in a little notebook Bucannon gave me, and I talked to him. I showed him I really wanted to understand, how I wanted to help, because it was easier on everybody this way. He didn't act surprised, and I didn't think he would. He'd always known. Maybe he hadn't known about the guys in the black berets, but he'd known that Steve would try it. He'd known I'd stay awake. He'd known the dreams would move to daylight, from "interrupted REM-state," if I stayed awake. And he'd known he'd get us back.

We talked about how my dreams were changing. I was having them much earlier than "events in real time," he said. The same thing had probably been happening back in ER, he said, but I hadn't known it. The talent was getting stronger, he said, though I couldn't control it yet. I didn't need the "focal stimulus," he said, "the physical correlative." I didn't need to meet people to have the dreams.

"When are we going to do it?" I finally said.

He knew what I meant. He said we didn't want to rush into it, how acting prematurely was worse than not understanding it, how the "fixity of the future" was something no one yet understood, and we didn't want to take a chance on stopping the dreams by trying to tamper with the future.

"It won't stop the dreams," I said. "Even if we kept a death from happening, it wouldn't stop the dreams."

He never listened. He wanted them to die. He wanted to take notes on how they died and how my dreams matched their dying, and he wasn't going to call anyone back until he was ready to.

"This isn't war, Mary," he told me one day. "This is a kind of science and it has its own rules. You'll have to trust me, Mary."

He pushed the hair out of my eyes, because I was crying. He wanted to touch me. I know that now.

I tried to get messages out. I tried to figure out who I'd dreamed about. I'd wake up in the middle of the night and try to talk to anybody I could and figure it out. I'd say, "Do you know a guy who's got red hair and is from Alabama?" I'd say, "Do you know an RTO who's short and can't listen to anything except Jefferson Airplane?" Sometimes it would take too long. Sometimes I'd never find out who it was, but if I did, I'd try to get a message out to him. Sometimes he'd already gone out and I'd still try to get someone to send him a message—but that just wasn't done.

I found out later Bucannon got them all. People said yeah, sure, they'd see that the message got to the guy, but Bucannon always got them. He told people to say yes when I asked. He knew. He always knew.

I didn't have a dream about Steve and that was the important thing.

When I finally dreamed that Steve died, that it took more guys in uniforms than you'd think possible—with more weapons than you'd think they'd ever need—in a river valley awfully far away, I didn't tell Bucannon about it. I didn't tell him how Steve was twitching on the red earth up North, his body doing its best to dodge the rounds even though there were just too many of them, twitching and twitching, even after his body wasn't alive anymore.

I cried for a while and then stopped. I wanted to feel something but I couldn't.

I didn't ask for pills or booze and I didn't stay awake the next two nights scared about dreaming it again. There was something I needed to do.

I didn't know how long I had. I didn't know whether Steve's team—the one in the dream—had already gone out or not. I didn't know a thing, but I kept thinking about what Bucannon had said, the "fixity," how maybe the future couldn't be changed, how even if Bucannon hadn't intercepted those messages something else would have kept the future the way it was and those guys would have died anyway.

I found the Green Beanie medic who'd taken me to my hooch that first day. I sat down with him in the mess. One of Bucannon's types was watching us but I sat down anyway. I said, "Has Steve Balsam been sent out yet?" And he said, "I'm not supposed to say, Lieutenant. You know that."

"Yes, Captain, I do know that. I also know that because you took me to my little bunker that day I will probably dream about your death before it happens, if it happens here. I also know that if I tell the people running this project about it, they won't do a thing, even though they know how accurate my dreams are, just like they know how accurate Steve Balsam is, and Blakely, and Corigiollo, and the others, but they won't do a thing about it." I waited. He didn't blink. He was listening.

"I'm in a position, Captain, to let someone know when I have a dream about them. Do you understand?"

He stared at me.

"Yes," he said.

I said, "Has Steve Balsam been sent out yet?"

"No, he hasn't."

"Do you know anything about the mission he is about to go out on?"

He didn't say a thing for a moment. Then he said, "Red Dikes."

"I don't understand, Captain."

He didn't want to have to explain—it made him mad to have to. He looked at the MD type by the door and then he looked back at me.

"You can take out the Red Dikes with a one-K nuclear device, Lieutenant. Everyone knows this. If you do, Hanoi drowns and the North is down. Balsam's team is a twelve-man night insertion beyond the DMZ with special MAC V ordnance from a carrier in the South China Sea. All twelve are talents. Is the picture clear enough, Lieutenant?"

I didn't say a thing. I just looked at him.

Finally I said, "It's a suicide mission, isn't it. The device won't even be real. It's one of Bucannon's ideas—he wants to see how they perform, that's all. They'll never use a nuclear device in Southeast Asia and you know that as well as I do, Captain."

"You never know, Lieutenant."

"Yes, you do." I said it slowly so he would understand.

He looked away.

"When is the team leaving?"

He wouldn't answer anymore. The MD type looked like he was going to walk toward us.

"Captain?" I said.

"Thirty-eight hours. That's what they're saying."

I leaned over.

"Captain," I said. "You know the shape I was in when I got here. I need it again. I need enough of it to get me through a week of this place or I'm not going to make it. You know where to get it. I'll need it tonight."

As I walked by the MD type at the door I wondered how he was going to die, how long it was going to take, and who would do it.

I killed Bucannon the only way I knew how.

I started screaming at first light and when he came to my bunker, I was crying. I told him I'd had a dream about him. I told him I dreamed that his own men, guys in cammies and all of them talents, had killed him, they had killed him because he wasn't using a nurse's dreams to keep their friends alive, because he had my dreams but wasn't doing anything with them, and all their friends were dying.

I looked in his eyes and I told him how scared I was because they killed her too, they killed the nurse who was helping him too.

I told him how big the 9-millimeter holes looked in his fatigues, and how something else was used on his face and stomach, some smaller caliber. I told him how they got him dusted off soon as they could and got him on a sump pump and IV as soon as he hit Saigon, but it just wasn't enough, how he choked to death on his own fluids.

He didn't believe me.

"Was Lieutenant Balsam there?" he asked.

I said no, he wasn't, trying not to cry. I didn't know why, but he wasn't, I said.

His eyes changed. He was staring at me now.

He said, "When will this happen, Mary?"

I said I didn't know—not for a couple of days at least, but I couldn't be sure, how could I be sure? It felt like four, maybe five, days, but I couldn't be sure. I was crying again.

This is what made him believe me in the end.

He knew it would never happen if Steve were there—but if Steve was gone, if the men waited until Steve was gone?

Steve would be gone in a couple of days and there was no way that this nurse, scared and crying, could know this.

He moved me to his bunker and had someone hang canvas to make a hooch for me inside his. He doubled the guards and changed the guards and doubled them again, but I knew he didn't think it was going to happen until Steve left.

I cried that night. He came to my hooch. He said, "Don't be frightened, Mary. No one's going to hurt you. No one's going to hurt anyone."

But he wasn't sure. He hadn't tried to stop a dream from coming true—even though I'd asked him to—and he didn't know whether he could or not.

I told him I wanted him to hold me, someone to hold me. I told him I wanted him to touch my forehead the way he did, to push my hair back the way he did.

At first he didn't understand, but he did it.

I told him I wanted someone to make love to me tonight, because it hadn't happened in so long, not with Steve, not with anyone. He said he understood and that if he'd only known he could have made things easier on me.

He was quiet. He made sure the flaps on my hooch were tight and he undressed in the dark. I held his hand just like I'd held the hands of the others, back in Cam Ranh Bay. I remembered the dream, the real one where I killed him, how I'd held his hand while he got undressed, just like this.

Even in the dark I could see how pale he was and this was like the dream too. He seemed to glow in the dark even though there wasn't any light. I took off my clothes, too. I told him I wanted to do something special for him. He said fine, but we couldn't make much noise. I said there wouldn't be any noise. I told him to lie down on his stomach on the cot. I sounded excited. I even laughed. I told him it was called "around the world" and I liked it best with the man on his stomach. He did what I told him and I kneeled down and lay over him.

I jammed the needle with the morphine into his jugular and when he struggled I held him down with my own weight.

No one came for a long time.

When they did, I was crying and they couldn't get my hand from the needle.

Steve's team wasn't sent. The dreams stopped, just the way Bucannon thought they would. Because I killed a man to keep another alive, the dreams stopped. I tell myself now this was what it was all about. I was supposed to keep someone from dying—that's why the dreams began—and when I did, they could stop, they could finally stop. Bucannon would understand it.

"There is no talent like yours, Mary, that does not operate out of the psychological needs of the individual," he would have said. "You dreamed of death in the hope of stopping it. We both knew that, didn't we. When you killed me to save another, it could end, the dreams could stop, your gift could return to the darkness where it had lain for a million years—so unneeded in civilization, in times of peace, in the humdrum existence of teenagers in Long Beach, California, where fathers believed their daughters to be whores or lesbians if they went to war to keep others alive. Am I right, Mary?"

This is what he would have said.

They could have killed me. They could have taken me out into the jungle and killed me. They could have given me a frontal and put me in a military hospital like the man in '46 who had evidence that Roosevelt knew about the Japanese attack on Pearl. The agency Bucannon had worked for could have sent word down to have me pushed from a chopper on the way back to Saigon, or had me given an overdose, or assigned me to some black op I'd never come back from. They were a lot of things they could have done, and they didn't.

They didn't because of what Steve and the others did. They told them you'll have to kill us all if you kill her or hurt her in any way. They told them you can't send her to jail, you can send her to a hospital but not for long, and you can't fuck with her head, or there will be stories in the press and court trials and a bigger mess than My Lai ever was.

It was seventy-six talents who were saying this, so the agency listened.

Steve told me about it the first time he came. I'm here for a year, that's all. There are ten other women in this wing and we get along—it's like a club. They leave us alone.

Steve comes to see me once a month. He's married—to the same one in Merced—and they've got a baby now, but he gets the money to fly down somehow and he tells me she doesn't mind.

He says the world hasn't turned blue since he got back, except maybe twice, real fast, on freeways in central California. He says he hasn't floated out of his body except once, when Cathy was having the baby and it started to come out wrong. It's fading away, he says, and he says it with a laugh, with those big eyelashes and those great shoulders.

Some of the others come, too, to see if I'm okay. Most of them got out as soon as they could. They send me packages and bring me things. We talk about the mess this country is in, and we talk about getting together, right after I get out. I don't know if they mean it. I don't know if we should. I tell Steve it's over, we're back in the Big PX and we don't need it anymore—Bucannon was right—and maybe we shouldn't get together.

He shakes his head. He gives me a look and I give him a look and we both know we should have used the room that night in Cam Ranh Bay, when we had the chance.

"You never know," he says, grinning. "You never know when the baby might wake up."

That's the way he talks these days, now that he's a father.

"You never know when the baby might wake up."

# BRUCE STERLING

## Flowers of Edo

One of the major new talents to enter SF in recent years, Bruce Sterling sold his first story in 1976, and has since sold stories to *Universe, Omni, The Magazine of Fantasy and Science Fiction, The Last Dangerous Visions, Lone Star Universe,* and elsewhere. He has attracted special acclaim in the last few years for a series of stories set in his exotic Shaper/Mechanist future, a complex and disturbing future where warring political factions struggle to control the shape of human destiny, and the nature of humanity itself. His story "Cicada Queen" was in our First Annual Collection; his "Sunken Gardens" was in our Second Annual Collection; his "Green Days in Brunei" and "Diner in Audoghast" were in our Third Annual Collection; and his "The Beautiful and the Sublime" was in our Fourth Annual Collection. His novels include *The Artificial Kid, Involution Ocean,* and *Schismatrix,* a novel set in the Shaper/Mechanist future. He is editor of *Mirrorshades: the Cyberpunk Anthology.* Upcoming are two new novels, *Islands in the Net,* from Arbor House, and *The Difference Engine,* in collaboration with William Gibson, from Bantam.

No two Sterling stories are ever much alike in tone or setting. Here, for instance, he takes us to nineteenth-century Japan in the days just after its first contact with Europeans—a milieu as strange and mysterious as any alien planet, in Sterling's gifted hands—for a lively and fascinating tale of an ex-samurai who finds he must do battle with the demons of progress.

# FLOWERS OF EDO

## Bruce Sterling

(with the author's thanks to
Yoshio Kobayashi and HAYAKAWA'S SF MAGAZINE)

Autumn. A full moon floated over old Edo, behind the thinnest haze of high cloud. It shone like a geisha's night-lamp through an old mosquito net. The sky was antique browned silk.

Two sweating runners hauled an iron-wheeled rickshaw south, toward the Ginza. This was Kabukiza District, its streets bordered by low, tile-roofed wooden shops. These were modest places: coopers, tobacconists, cheap fabric shops where the acrid reek of dye wafted through reed blinds and paper windows. Behind the stores lurked a maze of alleys, crammed with townsmen's wooden hovels, the walls festooned with morning glories, the tinder-dry thatched roofs alive with fleas.

It was late. Kabukiza was not a geisha district, and honest workmen were asleep. The muddy streets were unlit, except for moonlight and the rare upstairs lamp. The runners carried their own lantern, which swayed precariously from the rickshaw's drawing-pole. They trotted rapidly, dodging the worst of the potholes and puddles. But with every lurching dip, the rickshaw's strings of brass bells jumped and rang.

Suddenly the iron wheels grated on smooth red pavement. They had reached the New Ginza. Here, the air held the fresh alien smell of mortar and brick.

The amazing New Ginza had buried its old predecessor. For the Flowers of Edo had killed the Old Ginza. To date, this huge disaster had been the worst, and most exciting, fire of the Meiji Era. Edo had always been proud of its fires, and the Old Ginza's fire had been a real marvel. It had raged for three days and carried right down to the river.

Once they had mourned the dead, the Edokko were ready to rebuild.

They were always ready. Fires, even earthquakes, were nothing new to them. It was a rare building in Low City that escaped the Flowers of Edo for as long as twenty years.

But this was Imperial Tokyo now, and not the Shogun's old Edo any more. The Governor had come down from High City in his horse-drawn coach and looked over the smoldering ruins of Ginza. Low City townsmen still talked about it—how the Governor had folded his arms—like this—with his wrists sticking out of his Western frock coat. And how he had frowned a mighty frown. The Edo townsmen were getting used to those unsettling frowns by now. Hard, no-nonsense, modern frowns, with the brows drawn low over cold eyes that glittered with Civilization and Enlightenment.

So the Governor, with a mighty wave of his modern, frock-coated arm, sent for his foreign architects. And the Englishmen had besieged the district with their charts and clanking engines and tubs full of brick and mortar. The very heavens had rained bricks upon the black and flattened ruins. Great red hills of brick sprang up—were they houses, people wondered, were they buildings at all? Stories spread about the foreigners and their peculiar homes. The long noses, of course—necessary to suck air through the stifling brick walls. The pale skin—because bricks, it was said, drained the life and color out of a man. . . .

The rickshaw drew up short with a final brass jingle. The older rickshawman spoke, panting. "Far enough, gov?"

"Yeah, this'll do," said one passenger, piling out. His name was Encho Sanyutei. He was the son and successor of a famous vaudeville comedian and, at thirty-five, was now a well-known performer in his own right. He had been telling his companion about the Ginza Bricktown, and his folded arms and jutting underlip had cruelly mimicked Tokyo's Governor.

Encho, who had been drinking, generously handed the older man a pocketful of jingling copper sen. "Here, pal," he said. "Do something about that cough, will ya?" The runners bowed, not bothering to overdo it. They trotted off toward the nearby Ginza crowd, hunting another fare.

Parts of Tokyo never slept. The Yoshiwara District, the famous Nightless City of geishas and rakes, was one of them. The travelers had just come from Asakusa District, another sleepless place: a brawling, vibrant playground of bars, Kabuki theaters, and vaudeville joints.

The Ginza Bricktown never slept either. But the air here was different. It lacked that earthy Low City working-man's glow of sex and entertainment. Something else, something new and strange and powerful, drew the Edokko into the Ginza's iron-hard streets.

Gaslights. They stood hissing on their black foreign pillars, blasting a pitiless moon-drowning glare over the crowd. There were eighty-five of the appalling wonders, stretching arrow-straight across the Ginza, from Shiba all the way to Kyobashi.

The Edokko crowd beneath the lights was curiously silent. Drugged with pitiless enlightenment, they meandered down the hard, gritty street in high wooden clogs, or low leather shoes. Some wore hakama shirts and jinbibaori coats, others modern pipe-legged trousers, with top hats and bowlers.

The comedian Encho and his big companion staggered drunkenly toward the lights, their polished leather shoes squeaking merrily. To the Tokyo modernist, squeaking was half the fun of these foreign-style shoes. Both men wore inserts of "singing leather" to heighten the effect.

"I don't like their attitudes," growled Encho's companion. His name was Onogawa and, until the Emperor's Restoration, he had been a samurai. But Imperial decree had abolished the wearing of swords, and Onogawa now had a post in a trading company. He frowned, and dabbed at his nose, which had recently been bloodied and was now clotting. "It's all too free-and-easy with these modern rickshaws. Did you see those two? They looked into our faces, just as bold as tomcats."

"Relax, will you?" said Encho. "They were just a couple of street runners. Who cares what they think? The way you act, you'd think they were Shogun's Overseers." Encho laughed freely and dusted off his hands with a quick, theatrical gesture. Those grim, spying Overseers, with their merciless canons of Confucian law, were just a bad dream now. Like the Shogun, they were out of business.

"But your face is known all over town," Onogawa complained. "What if they gossip about us? Everyone will know what happened back there."

"It's the least I could do for a devoted fan," Encho said airily.

Onogawa had sobered up a bit since his street fight in Asakusa. A scuffle had broken out in the crowd after Encho's performance—a scuffle centered on Onogawa, who had old acquaintances he would have preferred not to meet. But Encho, appearing suddenly in the crowd, had distracted Onogawa's persecutors and gotten Onogawa away.

It was not a happy situation for Onogawa, who put much stock in his own dignity, and tended to brood. He had been born in Satsuma, a province of radical samurai with stern, unbending standards. But ten years in the capital had changed Onogawa, and given him an Edokko's notorious love for spectacle. Somewhat shamefully, Onogawa had become completely addicted to Encho's side-splitting skits and impersonations.

In fact, Onogawa had been slumming in Asakusa vaudeville joints at least twice each week, for months. He had a wife and small son in a modest place in Nihombashi, a rather straitlaced High City district full of earnest young bankers and civil servants on their way up in life. Thanks to old friends from his radical days, Onogawa was an officer in a prosperous trading company. He would have preferred to be in the army, of course, but the army was quite small these days, and appointments were hard to get.

This was a major disappointment in Onogawa's life, and it had driven him to behave strangely. Onogawa's long-suffering in-laws had always warned him that his slumming would come to no good. But tonight's event wasn't even a geisha scandal, the kind men winked at or even admired. Instead, he had been in a squalid punch-up with low-class commoners.

And he had been rescued by a famous commoner, which was worse. Onogawa couldn't bring himself to compound his loss of face with gratitude. He glared at Encho from under the brim of his bowler hat. "So where's this fellow with the foreign booze you promised?"

"Patience," Encho said absently. "My friend's got a little place here in Bricktown. It's private, away from the street." They wandered down the Ginza, Encho pulling his silk top-hat low over his eyes, so he wouldn't be recognized.

He slowed as they passed a group of four young women, who were gathered before the modern glass window of a Ginza fabric shop. The store was closed, but the women were admiring the tailor's dummies. Like the dummies, the women were dressed with daring modernity, sporting small Western parasols, cutaway riding-coats in brilliant purple, and sweeping foreign skirts over large, jutting bustles. "How about that, eh?" said Encho as they drew nearer. "Those foreigners sure like a rump on a woman, don't they?"

"Women will wear anything," Onogawa said, struggling to loosen one pinched foot inside its squeaking shoe. "Plain kimono and obi are far superior."

"Easier to get into, anyway," Encho mused. He stopped suddenly by the prettiest of the women, a girl who had let her natural eyebrows grow out, and whose teeth, unstained with old-fashioned toothblacking, gleamed like ivory in the gaslight.

"Madame, forgive my boldness," Encho said. "But I think I saw a small kitten run under your skirt."

"I beg your pardon?" the girl said in a flat Low City accent.

Encho pursed his lips. Plaintive mewing came from the pavement.

The girl looked down, startled, and raised her skirt quickly almost to the knee. "Let me help," said Encho, bending down for a better look. "I see the kitten! It's climbing up inside the skirt!" He turned. "You'd better help me, older brother! Have a look up in there."

Onogawa, abashed, hesitated. More mewing came. Encho stuck his entire head under the woman's skirt. "There it goes! It wants to hide in her false rump!" The kitten squealed wildly. "I've got it!" the comedian cried. He pulled out his doubled hands, holding them before him. "There's the rascal now, on the wall!" In the harsh gaslight, Encho's knotted hands cast the shadowed figure of a kitten's head against the brick.

Onogawa burst into convulsive laughter. He doubled over against the wall, struggling for breath. The women stood shocked for a moment. Then they all ran away, giggling hysterically. Except for the victim of Encho's joke, who burst into tears as she ran.

"Wah," Encho said alertly. "Her husband." He ducked his head, then jammed the side of his hand against his lips and blew. The street rang with a sudden trumpet blast. It sounded so exactly like the trumpet of a Tokyo omnibus that Onogawa himself was taken in for a moment. He glanced wildly up and down the Ginza prospect, expecting to see the omnibus driver, horn to his lips, reining up his team of horses.

Encho grabbed Onogawa's coat-sleeve and hauled him up the street before the rest of the puzzled crowd could recover. "This way!" They pounded drunkenly up an ill-lit street into the depths of Bricktown. Onogawa was breathless with laughter. They covered a block, then Onogawa pulled up, gasping. "No more," he wheezed, wiping tears of hilarity. "Can't take another . . . ha ha ha . . . step!"

"All right," Encho said reasonably, "but not here." He pointed up. "Don't you know better than to stand under those things?" Black telegraph wires swayed gently overhead.

Onogawa, who had not noticed the wires, moved hastily out from under them. "Kuwabara, kuwabara," he muttered—a quick spell to avert lightning. The sinister magic wires were all over the Bricktown, looping past and around the thick, smelly buildings.

Everyone knew why the foreigners put their telegraph wires high up on poles. It was so the demon messengers inside could not escape to wreak havoc amongst decent folk. These ghostly, invisible spirits flew along the wires as fast as swallows, it was said, carrying their secret spells of Christian black magic. Merely standing under such a baleful influence was inviting disaster.

Encho grinned at Onogawa. "There's no danger as long as we keep moving," he said confidently. "A little exposure is harmless. Don't worry about it."

Onogawa drew himself up. "Worried? Not a bit of it." He followed Encho down the street.

The stonelike buildings seemed brutal and featureless. There were no homey reed blinds or awnings in those outsized windows, whose sheets of foreign glass gleamed like an animal's eyeballs. No cozy porches, no bamboo windchimes or cricket cages. Not even a climbing tendril of Edo morning glory, which adorned even the worst and cheapest city hovels. The buildings just sat there, as mute and threatening as cannonballs. Most were deserted. Despite their fireproof qualities and the great cost of their construction, they were proving hard to rent out. Word on the street said those red bricks would suck the life out of a man—give him beriberi, maybe even consumption.

Bricks paved the street beneath their shoes. Bricks on the right of them, bricks on their left, bricks in front of them, bricks in back. Hundreds of them, thousands of them. Onogawa muttered to the smaller man. "Say. What *are* bricks, exactly? I mean, what are they made of?"

"Foreigners make 'em," Encho said, shrugging. "I think they're a kind of pottery."

"Aren't they unhealthy?"

"People say that," Encho said, "but foreigners live in them and I haven't noticed any shortage of foreigners lately." He drew up short. "Oh, here's my friend's place. We'll go around the front. He lives upstairs."

They circled the two-story building and looked up. Honest old-fashioned light, from an oil lamp, glowed against the curtains of an upstairs window. "Looks like your friend's still awake," Onogawa said, his voice more cheery now.

Encho nodded. "Taiso Yoshitoshi doesn't sleep much. He's a little high-strung. I mean, peculiar." Encho walked up to the heavy, ornate front door, hung foreign-style on large brass hinges. He yanked a bell-pull.

"Peculiar," Onogawa said. "No wonder, if he lives in a place like this." They waited.

The door opened inwards with a loud squeal of hinges. A man's disheveled head peered around it. Their host raised a candle in a cheap tin holder. "Who is it?"

"Come on, Taiso," Encho said impatiently. He pursed his lips again. Ducks quacked around their feet.

"Oh! It's Encho-san, Encho Sanyutei. My old friend. Come in, do."

They stepped inside into a dark landing. The two visitors stopped and unlaced their leather shoes. In the first-floor workshop, beyond the landing, the guests could dimly see bound bales of paper, a litter of toolchests and shallow trays. An apprentice was snoring behind a shrouded wood-block press. The damp air smelled of ink and cherrywood shavings.

"This is Mr. Onogawa Azusa," Encho said. "He's a fan of mine, down from High City. Mr. Onogawa, this is Taiso Yoshitoshi. The popular artist, one of Edo's finest."

"Oh, Yoshitoshi the artist!" said Onogawa, recognizing the name for the first time. "Of course! The woodblock print peddler. Why, I bought a whole series of yours, once. TWENTY-EIGHT INFAMOUS MURDERS WITH ACCOMPANYING VERSES."

"Oh," said Yoshitoshi. "How kind of you to remember my squalid early efforts." The ukiyo-e print artist was a slight, somewhat pudgy man, with stooped, rounded shoulders. The flesh around his eyes looked puffy and discolored. He had close-cropped hair parted in the middle and wide, fleshy lips. He wore a printed cotton houserobe, with faded bluish sunbursts, or maybe daisies, against a white background. "Shall we go upstairs, gentlemen? My apprentice needs his sleep."

They creaked up the wooden stairs to a studio lit by cheap pottery oil lamps. The walls were covered with hanging prints, while dozens more lay rolled, or stacked in corners, or piled on battered bookshelves. The windows were heavily draped and tightly shut. The naked brick walls seemed to sweat, and a vague reek of mildew and stale tobacco hung in the damp, close air.

The window against the far wall had a second-hand set of exterior shutters nailed to its inner sill. The shutters were bolted. "Telegraph wires outside," Yoshitoshi explained, noticing the glances of his guests. The artist gestured vaguely at a couple of bedraggled floor cushions. "Please."

The two visitors sat, struggling politely to squeeze some comfort from the mashed and threadbare cushions. Yoshitoshi knelt on a thicker cushion beside his worktable, a low bench of plain pine with inkstick, grinder, and water cup. A bamboo tool jar on the table's corner bristled with assorted brushes, as well as compass and ruler. Yoshitoshi had been working; a sheet of translucent ricepaper was pinned to the table, lightly and precisely streaked with ink.

"So," Encho said, smiling and waving one hand at the artist's penurious den. "I heard you'd been doing pretty well lately. This place has certainly improved since I last saw it. You've got real bookshelves again. I bet you'll have your books back in no time."

Yoshitoshi smiled sweetly. "Oh—I have so many debts . . . the books come last. But yes, things are much better for me now. I have my health again. And a studio. And one apprentice, Toshimitsu, came back to me. He's not the best of the ones I lost, but he's honest at least."

Encho pulled a short foreign briar-pipe from his coat. He opened the ornate tobacco-bag on his belt, an embroidered pouch that was the pride of every Edo man-about-town. He glanced up casually, stuffing his pipe. "Did that Kabuki gig ever come to anything?"

"Oh yes," said Yoshitoshi, sitting up straighter. "I painted bloodstains on the armor of Onoe Kikugoro the Fifth. For his role in 'Kawanakajima Island.' I'm very grateful to you for arranging that."

"Wait, I saw that play," said Onogawa, surprised and pleased. "Say, those were wonderful bloodstains. Even better than the ones in that murder print, KASAMORI OSEN CARVED ALIVE BY HER STEP-FATHER. You did that print too, am I right?" Onogawa had been studying the prints on the wall, and the familiar style had jogged his memory. "A young girl yanked backwards by a maniac with a knife, big bloody handprints all over her neck and legs. . . ."

Yoshitoshi smiled. "You liked that one, Mr. Onogawa?"

"Well," Onogawa said, "it was certainly a fine effort for what it was." It wasn't easy for a man in Onogawa's position to confess a liking for mere commoner art from Low City. He dropped his voice a little. "Actually, I had quite a few of your pictures, in my younger days. Ten years ago, just before the Restoration." He smiled, remembering. "I had the TWENTY-EIGHT MURDERS, of course. And some of the ONE HUNDRED GHOST STORIES. And a few of the special editions, now that I think of it. Like Tamigoro blowing his head off with a rifle. Especially good sprays of blood in that one."

"Oh, I remember that one," Encho volunteered. "That was back in the old days, when they used to sprinkle the bloody scarlet ink with powdered mica. For that deluxe bloody gleaming effect!"

"Too expensive now," Yoshitoshi said sadly.

Encho shrugged. "Remember NAOSUKE GOMBEI MURDERS HIS MASTER? With the maniac servant standing on his employer's chest, ripping the man's face off with his hands alone?" The comedian cleverly mimed the murderer's pinching and wrenching, along with loud sucking and shredding sounds.

"Oh yes!" said Onogawa. "I wonder whatever happened to my copy of it?" He shook himself. "Well, it's not the sort of thing you can keep in the house, with my age and position. It might give the children nightmares. Or the servants ideas." He laughed.

Encho had stuffed his short pipe; he lit it from a lamp. Onogawa, preparing to follow suit, dragged his long iron-bound pipe from within his coat-sleeve. "How wretched," he cried. "I've cracked my good pipe in the scuffle with those hooligans. Look, it's ruined."

"Oh, is that a smoking-pipe?" said Encho. "From the way you used it on your attackers, I thought it was a simple bludgeon."

"I certainly would not go into the Low City without self-defense of some kind," Onogawa said stiffly. "And since the new government has seen fit to take our swords away, I'm forced to make do. A pipe is an ignoble weapon. But as you saw tonight, not without its uses."

"Oh, no offense meant, sir," said Encho hastily. "There's no need to be formal here among friends! If I'm a bit harsh of tongue I hope you'll forgive me, as it's my livelihood! So! Why don't we all have a drink and relax, eh?"

Yoshitoshi's eye had been snagged by the incomplete picture on his drawing table. He stared at it raptly for a few more seconds, then came to with a start. "A drink! Oh!" He straightened up. "Why, come to think of it, I have something very special, for gentlemen like yourselves. It came from Yokohama, from the foreign trade zone." Yoshitoshi crawled rapidly across the floor, his knees skidding inside the cotton robe, and threw open a dented wooden chest. He unwrapped a tall glass bottle from a wad of tissue and brought it back to his seat, along with three dusty sake cups.

The bottle had the flawless symmetrical ugliness of foreign manufacture. It was full of amber liquid, and corked. A paper label showed the grotesquely bearded face of an American man, framed by blocky foreign letters.

"Who's that?" Onogawa asked, intrigued. "Their king?"

"No, it's the face of the merchant who brewed it," Yoshitoshi said with assurance. "In America, merchants are famous. And a man of the merchant class can even become a soldier. Or a farmer, or priest, or anything he likes."

"Hmmph," said Onogawa, who had gone through a similar transition himself and was not at all happy about it. "Let me see." He examined the printed label closely. "Look how this foreigner's eyes bug out. He looks like a raving lunatic!"

Yoshitoshi stiffened at the term. An awkward moment of frozen silence seeped over the room. Onogawa's gaffe floated in midair among them, until its nature became clear to everyone. Yoshitoshi had recovered his health recently, but his illness had not been a physical one. No one had to say anything, but the truth slowly oozed its way into everyone's bones and liver. At length, Onogawa cleared his throat. "I mean, of course, that there's no accounting for the strange looks of foreigners."

Yoshitoshi licked his fleshy lips and the sudden gleam of desperation slowly faded from his eyes. He spoke quietly.

"Well, my friends in the Liberal Party have told me all about it. Several of them have been to America and back, and they speak the language, and can even read it. If you want to know more, you can read their national newspaper, the *Lamp of Liberty*, for which I am doing illustrations."

Onogawa glanced quickly at Encho. Onogawa, who was not a reading man, had only vague notions as to what a "liberal party" or a "national newspaper" might be. He wondered if Encho knew better. Apparently the comedian did, for Encho looked suddenly grave.

Yoshitoshi rattled on. "One of my political friends gave me this bottle, which he bought in Yokohama, from Americans. The Americans have many such bottles there—a whole warehouse. Because the American Shogun, Generalissimo Guranto, will be arriving next year to pay homage to our Emperor. And the Guranto, the 'Puresidento,' is especially fond of this kind of drink! Which is called borubona, from the American prefecture of Kentukki."

Yoshitoshi twisted the cork loose and dribbled bourbon into all three cups. "Shouldn't we heat it first?" Encho said.

"This isn't sake, my friend. Sometimes they even put ice in it!"

Onogawa sipped carefully and gasped. "What a bite this has! It burns the tongue like Chinese peppers." He hesitated. "Interesting, though."

"It's good!" said Encho, surprised. "If sake were like an old stone lantern, then this borybona would be gaslight! Hot and fierce!" He tossed back the rest of his cup. "It's a pity there's no pretty girl to serve us our second round."

Yoshitoshi did the honors, filling their cups again. "This serving girl," Onogawa said. "She would have to be hot and fierce too—like a tigress."

Encho lifted his brows. "You surprise me. I thought you were a family man, my friend."

A warm knot of bourbon in Onogawa's stomach was reawakening an evening's worth of sake. "Oh, I suppose I seem settled enough now. But you should have known me ten years ago, before the Restoration. I was quite the tough young radical in those days. You know, we really thought we could change the world. And perhaps we did!"

Encho grinned, amused. "So! You were a shishi?"

Onogawa had another sip. "Oh yes!" He touched the middle of his back. "I had hair down to here, and I never washed! Touch money? Not a one of us! We'd have died first! No, we lived in rags and ate plain brown rice from wooden bowls. We just went to our kendo schools, practiced swordsmanship, decided what old fool we should try to kill next . . ." Onogawa shook his head ruefully. The other two were listening with grave attention.

The bourbon and the reminiscing had thawed Onogawa out. The lost ideals of the Restoration rose up within him irresistibly. "I was the despair of my family," he confided. "I abandoned my clan and my daimyo. We shishi radicals, you know, we believed only in our swords and the Emperor. Sonno joi! Remember that slogan?" Onogawa grinned, the tears of mono no aware, the pathos of lost things, coming to his eyes.

"Sonno joi! The very streets used to ring with it. 'Revere the Emperor, destroy the foreigners!' We wanted the Emperor restored to full and unconditional power! We demanded it in the streets! Because the Shogun's men were acting like frightened old women. Frightened of the black ships, the American black warships with their steam and cannon. Admiral Perry's ships."

"It's pronounced 'Peruri,' " Encho corrected gently.

"Peruri, then . . . I admit, we shishi went a bit far. We had some bad habits. Like threatening to commit hara-kiri unless the townsfolk gave us food. That's one of the problems we faced because we refused to touch money. Some of the shopkeepers still resent the way we shishi used to push them around. In fact that was the cause of tonight's incident after your performance, Encho. Some rude fellows with long memories."

"So that was it," Encho said. "I wondered."

"Those were special times," Onogawa said. "They changed me, they changed everything. I suppose everyone of this generation knows where they were, and what they were doing, when the foreigners arrived in Edo Bay."

"I remember," said Yoshitoshi. "I was fourteen and an apprentice at Kuniyoshi's studio. And I'd just done my first print. THE HEIKE CLAN SINK TO THEIR HORRIBLE DOOM IN THE SEA."

"I saw them dance once," Encho said. "The American sailors, I mean."

"Really?" said Onogawa.

Encho cast a storyteller's mood with an irresistible gesture. "Yes, my father, Entaro, took me. The performance was restricted to the Shogun's court officials and their friends, but we managed to sneak in. The foreigners painted their faces and hands quite black. They seemed ashamed of their usual pinkish color, for they also painted broad white lines around their lips. Then they all sat on chairs together in a row, and one at a time they would stand up and shout dialogue. A second foreigner would answer, and they would all laugh. Later two of them strummed on strange round-bodied samisens, with long thin necks. And they sang mournful songs, very badly. Then they played faster songs and capered and danced, kicking out their legs in the oddest way, and flinging each other about. Some of the Shogun's counselors danced with them." Encho shrugged. "It was all very odd. To this day I wonder what it meant."

"Well," said Onogawa. "Clearly they were trying to change

their appearance and shape, like foxes or badgers. That seems clear enough."

"That's as much as saying they're magicians," Encho said, shaking his head. "Just because they have long noses, doesn't mean they're mountain goblins. They're men—they eat, they sleep, they want a woman. Ask the geishas in Yokohama if that's not so." Encho smirked. "Their real power is in the spirits of copper wires and black iron and burning coal. Like our own Tokyo-Yokohama Railway that the hired English built for us. You've ridden it, of course?"

"Of course!" Onogawa said proudly. "I'm a modern sort of fellow."

"That's the sort of power we need today. Civilization and Enlightenment. When you rode the train, did you see how the backward villagers in Omori come out to pour water on the engine? To cool it off, as if the railway engine were a tired horse!" Encho shook his head in contempt.

Onogawa accepted another small cup of bourbon. "So they pour water," he said judiciously. "Well, I can't see that it does any harm."

"It's rank superstition!" said Encho. "Don't you see, we have to learn to deal with those machine-spirits, just as the foreigners do. Treating them as horses can only insult them. Isn't that so, Taiso?"

Yoshitoshi looked up guiltily from his absent-minded study of his latest drawing. "I'm sorry, Encho-san, you were saying?"

"What's that you're working on? May I see?" Encho crept nearer.

Yoshitoshi hastily plucked out pins and rolled up his paper. "Oh no, no, you wouldn't want to see this one just yet. It's not ready. But I can show you another recent one. . . ." He reached to a nearby stack and dexterously plucked a printed sheet from the unsteady pile. "I'm calling this series BEAUTIES OF THE SEVEN NIGHTS."

Encho courteously held up the print so that both he and Onogawa could see it. It showed a woman in her underrobe; she had thrown her scarlet-lined outer kimono over a nearby screen. She had both natural and artificial eyebrows, lending a double seductiveness to her high forehead. Her mane of jet-black hair had a killing little wispy fringe at the back of the neck; it seemed to cry out to be bitten. She stood at some lucky man's doorway, bending to blow out the light of a lantern in the hall. And her tiny, but piercingly red mouth was clamped down over a roll of paper towels.

"I get it!" Onogawa said. "That beautiful whore is blowing out the light so she can creep into some fellow's bed in the dark! And she's taking those handy paper towels in her teeth to mop up with, after they're through playing mortar-and-pestle."

Encho examined the print more closely. "Wait a minute," he said.

"This caption reads 'Her Ladyship Yanagihara Aiko.' This is an Imperial lady-in-waiting!"

"Some of my newspaper friends gave me the idea," Yoshitoshi said, nodding. "Why should prints always be of tiresome, stale old actors and warriors and geishas? This is the modern age!"

"But this print, Taiso . . : it clearly implies that the Emperor sleeps with his ladies in waiting."

"No, just with Lady Yanagihara Aiko," Yoshitoshi said reasonably. "After all, everyone knows she's his special favorite. The rest of the Seven Beauties of the Imperial Court are drawn, oh, putting on their make-up, arranging flowers, and so forth." He smiled. "I expect big sales from this series. It's very topical, don't you think?"

Onogawa was shocked. "But this is rank scandal-mongering! What happened to the good old days, with the nice gouts of blood and so on?"

"No one buys those any more!" Yoshitoshi protested. "Believe me, I've tried everything! I did A YOSHITOSHI MISCELLANY OF FIGURES FROM LITERATURE. Very edifying, beautifully drawn classical figures, the best. It died on the stands. Then I did RAVING BEAUTIES AT TOKYO RESTAURANTS. Really hot girls, but old fashioned geishas done in the old style. Another total waste of time. We were dead broke, not a copper piece to our names! I had to pull up the floorboards of my house for fuel! I had to work on fabric designs—two yen for a week's work! My wife left me! My apprentices walked out! And then my health . . . my brain began to . . . I had nothing to eat . . . nothing . . . But . . . But that's all over now."

Yoshitoshi shook himself, dabbed sweat from his pasty upper lip, and poured another cup of bourbon with a steady hand. "I changed with the times, that's all. It was a hard lesson, but I learned it. I call myself Taiso now, Taiso, meaning 'Great Rebirth.' Newspapers! That's where the excitement is today! *Tokyo Illustrated News* pays plenty for political cartoons and murder illustrations. They do ten thousand impressions at a stroke. My work goes everywhere—not just Edo, the whole nation. The nation, gentlemen!" He raised his cup and drank. "And that's just the beginning. The *Lamp of Liberty* is knocking them dead! The Liberal Party committee has promised me a raise next year, and my own rickshaw."

"But I like the old pictures," Onogawa said.

"Maybe you do, but you don't buy them," Yoshitoshi insisted. "Modern people want to see what's happening now! Take an old, theme picture—Yorimitsu chopping an ogre's arm off, for instance. Draw a thing like that today and it gets you nowhere. People's tastes are more refined today. They want to see real cannonballs blowing off real arms. Like my eye-witness illustrations of the Battle of Ueno. A sensation! People don't want print peddlers any more. 'Journalist illustrator'—that's what they call me now."

"Don't laugh," said Encho, nodding in drunken profundity. "You should hear what they say about me. I mean the modern writer fellows, down from the University. They come in with their French novels under their arms, and their spectacles and slicked-down hair, and all sit in the front row together. So I tell them a vaudeville tale or two. Am I 'spinning a good yarn'? Not any more. They tell me I'm 'creating naturalistic prose in a vigorous popular vernacular.' They want to publish me in a book." He sighed and had another drink. "This stuff's poison, Taiso. My head's spinning."

"Mine, too," Onogawa said. An autumn wind had sprung up outside. They sat in doped silence for a moment. They were all much drunker than they had realized. The foreign liquor seemed to bubble in their stomachs like tofu fermenting in a tub.

The foreign spirits had crept up on them. The very room itself seemed drunk. Wind sang through the telegraph wires outside Yoshitoshi's shuttered window. A low, eerie moan.

The moan built in intensity. It seemed to creep into the room with them. The walls hummed with it. Hair rose on their arms.

"Stop that!" Yoshitoshi said suddenly. Encho stopped his ventriloquial moaning, and giggled. "He's trying to scare us," Yoshitoshi said. "He loves ghost stories."

Onogawa lurched to his feet. "Demon in the wires," he said thickly. "I heard it moaning at us." He blinked, red-faced, and staggered to the shuttered window. He fumbled loudly at the lock, ignoring Yoshitoshi's protests, and flung it open.

Moonlit wire clustered at the top of a wooden pole, in plain sight a few feet away. It was a junction of cables, and leftover coils of wire dangled from the pole's crossarm like thin black guts. Onogawa flung up the casement with a bang. A chilling gust of fresh air entered the stale room and the prints danced on the walls. "Hey you foreign demon!" Onogawa shouted. "Leave honest men in peace!"

The artist and entertainer exchanged unhappy glances. "We drank too much," Encho said. He lurched to his knees and onto one unsteady foot. "Leave off, big fellow. What we need now . . ." He belched. "Women, that's what."

But the air outside the window seemed to have roused Onogawa. "We didn't ask for you!" he shouted. "We don't need you! Things were fine before you came, demon! You and your foreign servants . . ." He turned half-round, looking red-eyed into the room. "Where's my pipe? I've a mind to give these wires a good thrashing."

He spotted the pipe again, stumbled into the room and picked it up. He lost his balance for a moment, then brandished the pipe threateningly. "Don't do it," Encho said, getting to his feet. "Be reasonable. I know some girls in Asakusa, they have a piano . . ." He reached out.

Onogawa shoved him aside. "I've had enough!" he announced. "When my blood's up, I'm a different man! Cut them down before they attack first, that's my motto! Sonno joi!"

He lurched across the room toward the open window. Before he could reach it there was a sudden hiss of steam, like the breath of a locomotive. The demon, its patience exhausted by Onogawa's taunts, gushed from its wire. It puffed through the window, a gray, gaseous thing, its lumpy, misshapen head glaring furiously. It gave a steam-whistle roar and its great lantern eyes glowed.

All three men screeched aloud. The armless, legless monster, like a gray cloud on a tether, rolled its glassy eyes at all of them. Its steel teeth gnashed and sparks showed down its throat. It whistled again and made a sudden gnashing lurch at Onogawa.

But Onogawa's old sword-training had soaked deep into his bones. He leapt aside reflexively, with only a trace of stagger, and gave the thing a smart overhead riposte with his pipe. The demon's head bonged like an iron kettle. It began chattering angrily and hot steam curled from its nose. Onogawa hit it again. Its head dented. It winced, then glared at the other men.

The townsmen quickly scrambled into line behind their champion. "Get him!" Encho shrieked. Onogawa dodged a half-hearted snap of teeth and bashed the monster across the eye. Glass cracked and the bowl flew from Onogawa's pipe.

But the demon had had enough. With a grumble and crunch like dying gearworks, it retreated back towards its wires, sucking itself back within them, like an octopus into its hole. It vanished, but hissing sparks continued to drip from the wire.

"You humiliated it!" Encho said, his voice filled with awe and admiration. "That was amazing!"

"Had enough, eh!" shouted Onogawa furiously, leaning on the sill. "Easy enough mumbling your dirty spells behind our backs! But try an Imperial warrior face to face, and it's a different story! Hah!"

"What a feat of arms!" said Yoshitoshi, his pudgy face glowing. "I'll do a picture. ONOGAWA HUMILIATES A GHOUL. Wonderful!"

The sparks began to travel down the wire, away from the window. "It's getting away!" Onogawa shouted. "Follow me!"

He shoved himself from the window and ran headlong from the

studio. He tripped at the top of the stairs, but did an inspired shoulder-roll and landed on his feet at the door. He yanked it open.

Encho followed him headlong. They had no time to lace on their leather shoes, so they kicked on the wooden clogs of Yoshitoshi and his apprentice and dashed out. Soon they stood under the wires, where the little nest of sparks still clung. "Come down here, you rascal," Onogawa demanded. "Show some fighting honor, you skulking wretch!"

The thing moved back and forth, hissing, on the wire. More sparks dripped. It dodged back and forth, like a cornered rat in an alley. Then it made a sudden run for it.

"It's heading south!" said Onogawa. "Follow me!"

They ran in hot pursuit, Encho bringing up the rear, for he had slipped his feet into the apprentice's clogs and the shoes were too big for him.

They pursued the thing across the Ginza. It had settled down to headlong running now, and dropped fewer sparks.

"I wonder what message it carries," panted Encho.

"Nothing good, I'll warrant," said Onogawa grimly. They had to struggle to match the thing's pace. They burst from the southern edge of the Ginza Bricktown and into the darkness of unpaved streets. This was Shiba District, home of the thieves' market and the great Zojoji Temple. They followed the wires. "Aha!" cried Onogawa. "It's heading for Shinbashi Railway Station and its friends the locomotives!"

With a determined burst of speed, Onogawa outdistanced the thing and stood beneath the path of the wire, waving his broken pipe frantically. "Whoa! Go back!"

The thing slowed briefly, well over his head. Stinking flakes of ash and sparks poured from it, raining down harmlessly on the ex-samurai. Onogawa leapt aside in disgust, brushing the filth from his derby and frock coat. "Phew!"

The thing rolled on. Encho caught up with the larger man. "Not the locomotives," the comedian gasped. "We can't face those."

Onogawa drew himself up. He tried to dust more streaks of filthy ash from his soiled coat. "Well, I think we taught the nasty thing a lesson, anyway."

"No doubt," said Encho, breathing hard. He went green suddenly, then leaned against a nearby wooden fence, clustered with tall autumn grass. He was loudly sick.

They looked about themselves. Autumn. Darkness. And the moon. A pair of cats squabbled loudly in a nearby alley.

Onogawa suddenly realized that he was brandishing, not a sword, but a splintered stick of ironbound bamboo. He began to tremble. Then he flung the thing away with a cry of disgust. "They took our swords away," he said. "Let them give us honest soldiers our swords back. We'd make short work of such foreign foulness. Look what it did to my coat, the filthy creature. It defiled me."

"No, no," Encho said, wiping his mouth. "You were incredible! A regular Shoki the Demon Queller."

"Shoki," Onogawa said. He dusted his hat against his knee. "I've seen drawings of Shoki. He's the warrior demigod, with a red face and a big sword. Always hunting demons, isn't he? But he doesn't know there's a little demon hiding on the top of his own head."

"Well, a regular Yoshitsune, then," said Encho, hastily grasping for a better compliment. Yoshitsune was a legendary master of swordsmanship. A national hero without parallel.

Unfortunately, the valorous Yoshitsune had ended up riddled with arrows by the agents of his treacherous half-brother, who had gone on to rule Japan. While Yoshitsune and his high ideals had to put up with a shadow existence in folklore. Neither Encho nor Onogawa had to mention this aloud, but the melancholy associated with the old tale seeped into their moods. Their world became heroic and fatal. Naturally all the bourbon helped.

"We'd better go back to Bricktown for our shoes," Onogawa said.

"All right," Encho said. Their feet had blistered in the commandeered clogs, and they walked back slowly and carefully.

Yoshitoshi met them in his downstairs landing. "Did you catch it?"

"It made a run for the railroads," Encho said. "We couldn't stop it; it was way above our heads." He hesitated. "Say. You don't suppose it will come back here, do you?"

"Probably," Yoshitoshi said. "It lives in that knot of cables outside the window. That's why I put the shutters there."

"You mean you've seen it before?"

"Sure I've seen it," Yoshitoshi muttered. "In fact I've seen lots of things. It's my business to see things. No matter what people say about me."

The others looked at him, stricken. Yoshitoshi shrugged irritably. "The place has atmosphere. It's quiet and no one bothers me here. Besides, it's cheap."

"Aren't you afraid of the demon's vengeance?" Onogawa said.

"I get along fine with that demon," Yoshitoshi said. "We have an understanding. Like neighbors anywhere."

"Oh," Encho said. He cleared his throat. "Well, ah, we'll be moving on, Taiso. It was good of you to give us the borubona." He and Onogawa stuffed their feet hastily into their squeaking shoes. "You keep up the good work, pal, and don't let those political fellows put anything over on you. Their ideas are weird, frankly. I don't think the government's going to put up with that kind of talk."

"Someday they'll have to," Yoshitoshi said.

"Let's go," Onogawa said, with a sidelong glance at Yoshitoshi. The two men left.

Onogawa waited until they were well out of earshot. He kept a wary eye on the wires overhead. "Your friend certainly is a weird one," he told the comedian. "What a night!"

Encho frowned. "He's gonna get in trouble with that visionary stuff. The nail that sticks up gets hammered down, you know." They walked into the blaze of artificial gaslight. The Ginza crowd had thinned out considerably.

"Didn't you say you knew some girls with a piano?" Onogawa said.

"Oh, right!" Encho said. He whistled shrilly and waved at a distant two-man rickshaw. "A piano. You won't believe the thing; it makes amazing sounds. And what a great change after those dreary geisha samisen routines. So whiny and thin and wailing and sad! It's always, 'Oh, How Piteous Is A Courtesan's Lot,' and 'Let's Stab Each Other To Prove You Really Love Me.' Who needs that old-fashioned stuff? Wait till you hear these gals pound out some 'opera' and 'waltzes' on their new machine."

The rickshaw pulled up with a rattle and a chime of bells. "Where to, gentlemen?"

"Asakusa," said Encho, climbing in.

"It's getting late," Onogawa said reluctantly. "I really ought to be getting back to the wife."

"Come on," said Encho, rolling his eyes. "Live a little. It's not like you're just cheating on the little woman. These are high-class modern girls. It's a cultural experience."

"Well, all right," said Onogawa. "If it's cultural."

"You'll learn a lot," Encho promised.

But they had barely covered a block when they heard the sudden frantic ringing of alarm bells, far to the south.

"A fire!" Encho yelled in glee. "Hey, runners, stop! Fifty sen if you get us there while it's still spreading!"

The runners wheeled in place and set out with a will. The rickshaw rocked on its axle and jangled wildly. "This is great!" Onogawa said, clutching his hat. "You're a good fellow to know, Encho. It's nothing but excitement with you!"

"That's the modern life!" Encho shouted. "One wild thing after another."

They bounced and slammed their way through the darkened streets until the sky was lit with fire. A massive crowd had gathered beside the Shinagawa Railroad Line. They were mostly low-class townsmen, many half-dressed. It was a working-class neighborhood in Shiba District, east of Atago Hill. The fire was leaping merrily from one thatched roof to another.

The two men jumped from their rickshaw. Encho shouldered his way immediately through the crowd. Onogawa carefully counted out the fare. "But he said fifty sen," the older rickshawman complained. Onogawa clenched his fist and the men fell silent.

The firemen had reacted with their usual quick skill. Three companies of them had surrounded the neighborhood. They swarmed like ants over the roofs of the undamaged houses nearest the flames. As usual, they did not attempt to fight the flames directly. That was a hopeless task in any case, for the weathered, graying wood, paper shutters, and reed blinds flared up like tinder, in great blossoming gouts.

Instead, they sensibly relied on firebreaks. Their hammers, axes, and crowbars flew as they destroyed every house in the path of the flames. Their skill came naturally to them, for, like all Edo firemen, they were also carpenters. Special banner-men stood on the naked ridgepoles of the disintegrating houses, holding their company's ensigns as close as possible to the flames. This was more than bravado; it was good business. Their reputations, and their rewards from a grateful neighborhood, depended on this show of spirit and nerve.

Some of the crowd, those whose homes were being devoured, were weeping and counting their children. But most of the crowd was in a fine holiday mood, cheering for their favorite fire teams and laying bets.

Onogawa spotted Encho's silk hat and plowed after him. Encho ducked and elbowed through the press, Onogawa close behind. They crept to the crowd's inner edge, where the fierce blaze of heat and the occasional falling wad of flaming straw had established a boundary.

A fireman stood nearby. He wore a kneelength, padded fireproof coat with a pattern of printed blocks. A thick protective headdress fell stiffly over his shoulders, and long padded gauntlets shielded his forearms to the knuckles. An apprentice in similar garb was soaking him down with a pencil-thin gush of water from a bamboo hand-pump. "Stand back, stand back," the fireman said automatically, then looked up. "Say, aren't you Encho the comedian? I saw you last week."

"That's me," Encho shouted cheerfully over the roar of flame. "Good to see you fellows performing for once."

The fireman examined Onogawa's ash-streaked frock coat. "You live around here, big fella? Point out your house for me, we'll do what we can."

Onogawa frowned. Encho broke in hastily. "My friend's from uptown! A High City company man!"

"Oh," said the fireman, rolling his eyes.

Onogawa pointed at a merchant's tile-roofed warehouse, a little closer to the tracks. "Why aren't you doing anything about that place? The fire's headed right for it!"

"That's one of merchant Shinichi's," the fireman said, narrowing his eyes. "We saved a place of his out in Kanda District last month! And he gave us only five yen."

"What a shame for him," Encho said, grinning.

"It's full of cotton cloth, too," the fireman said with satisfaction. "It's gonna go up like a rocket."

"How did it start?" Encho said.

"Lightning, I hear," the fireman said. "Some kind of fireball jumped off the telegraph lines."

"Really?" Encho said in a small voice.

"That's what they say," shrugged the fireman. "You know how these things are. Always tall stories. Probably some drunk knocked over his sake kettle, then claimed to see something. No one wants the blame."

"Right," Onogawa said carefully.

The fire teams had made good progress. There was not much left to do now except admire the destruction. "Kind of beautiful, isn't it?" the fireman said. "Look how that smoke obscures the autumn moon." He sighed happily. "Good for business, too. I mean the carpentry business, of course." He waved his gauntleted arm at the leaping flames. "We'll get this worn-out trash out of here and build something worthy of a modern city. Something big and expensive with long-term construction contracts."

"Is that why you have bricks printed on your coat?" Onogawa asked.

The fireman looked down at the block printing on his dripping cotton armor. "They do look like bricks, don't they?" He laughed. "That's a good one. Wait'll I tell the crew."

Dawn rose above old Edo. With red-rimmed eyes, the artist Yoshitoshi stared, sighing, through his open window. Past the telegraph wires, billowing smudge rose beyond the Bricktown rooftops. Another Flower of Edo reaching the end of its evanescent life.

The telegraph wires hummed. The demon had returned to its tangled nest outside the window. "Don't tell, Yoshitoshi," it burbled in its deep, humming voice.

"Not me," Yoshitoshi said. "You think I want them to lock me up again?"

"I keep the presses running," the demon whined. "Just you deal with me. I'll make you famous, I'll make you rich. There'll be no more slow dark shadows where townsmen have to creep with their heads down. Everything's brightness and speed with me, Yoshitoshi. I can change things."

"Burn them down, you mean," Yoshitoshi said.

"There's power in burning," the demon hummed. "There's beauty in the flames. When you give up trying to save the old ways, you'll see the beauty. I want you to serve me, you Japanese. You'll do it better than the clumsy foreigners, once you accept me as your own. I'll make you all rich. Edo will be the greatest city in the world. You'll have light and music at a finger's touch. You'll step across oceans. You'll be as gods."

"And if we don't accept you?"

"You will! You must! I'll burn you until you do. I told you that, Yoshitoshi. When I'm stronger, I'll do better than these little flowers of Edo. I'll open seeds of Hell above your cities. Hell-flowers taller than mountains! Red blooms that eat a city in a moment."

Yoshitoshi lifted his latest print and unrolled it before the window. He had worked on it all night; it was done at last. It was a landscape of pure madness. Beams of frantic light pierced a smoldering sky. Winged locomotives, their bellies fattened with the eggs of white-hot death, floated like maddened blowflies above a corpse-white city. "Like this," he said.

The demon gave a gloating whir. "Yes! Just as I told you. Now show it to them. Make them understand that they can't defeat me. Show them all!"

"I'll think about it," Yoshitoshi said. "Leave me now." He closed the heavy shutters.

He rolled the drawing carefully into a tube. He sat at his worktable again, and pulled an oil lamp closer. Dawn was coming. It was time to get some sleep.

He held the end of the paper tube above the lamp's little flame. It browned at first, slowly, the brand-new paper turning the rich antique tinge of an old print, a print from the old days when things were simpler. Then a cigar-ring of smoldering red encircled its rim, and blue flame blossomed. Yoshitoshi held the paper up, and flame ate slowly down its length, throwing smoky shadows.

Yoshitoshi blew and watched his work flare up, cherry-blossom white and red. It hurt to watch it go, and it felt good. He savored the two feelings for as long as he could. Then he dropped the last flaming inch of paper in an ashtray. He watched it flare and smolder until the last of the paper became a ghost-curl of gray.

"It'd never sell," he said. Absently, knowing he would need them tomorrow, he cleaned his brushes. Then he emptied the inkstained water over the crisp dark ashes.

## KATE WILHELM

# Forever Yours, Anna

There's a saying that goes, out of sight, out of mind. Well, not *always* . . .

Regarded as one of the best of today's writers, Kate Wilhelm won a Nebula Award in 1968 for her short story, "The Planners," took a Hugo in 1976 for her well-known novel, *Where Late the Sweet Birds Sang*, and added another Nebula to her collection in 1987 "The Girl Who Fell into the Sky." Her many books include the novels *Margaret and I, Fault Lines, The Clewisten Test, Juniper Time, Welcome, Chaos,* and *Oh, Susannah!*, and the collections *The Downstairs Room, Somerset Dreams, The Infinity Box*, and *Listen, Listen*. Her most recent SF books are the novels *Huysman's Pets* and *Crazy Time*. She lives with her family in Eugene, Oregon.

# FOREVER YOURS, ANNA

## Kate Wilhelm

Anna entered his life on a spring afternoon, not invited, not even wanted. Gordon opened his office door that day to a client who was expected and found a second man also in the hallway. The second man brought him Anna, although Gordon did not yet know this. At the moment, he simply said, "Yes?"

"Gordon Sills? I don't have an appointment, but . . . may I wait?"

"Afraid I don't have a waiting room."

"Out here's fine."

He was about fifty, and he was prosperous. It showed in his charcoal-colored suit, a discreet blue-gray silk tie, a silk shirt. Gordon assumed the stone on his finger was a real emerald of at least three carats. Ostentatious touch, that.

"Sure," Gordon said, and ushered his client inside. They passed through a foyer into his office workroom. The office section was partitioned from the rest of the room by three rice-paper screens with beautiful Chinese calligraphy. In the office area was his desk and two chairs for visitors, his chair, and an overwhelmed bookcase, with books on the floor in front of it.

When his client left, the hall was empty. Gordon shrugged and returned to his office; he pulled his telephone across the desk and dialed his former wife's apartment number, let it ring a dozen times, hung up. He leaned back in his chair and rubbed his eyes absently. Late-afternoon sunlight streamed through the slats in the venetian blinds, zebra light. *I should go away for a few weeks*, he thought. Just close shop and walk away from it all until he started getting overdraft notices. Three weeks, he told himself; that was about as long as it would take. *Too bad about the other guy*, he thought without too much regret. He had a month's worth of work lined up already, and he knew more would trickle in when that was done.

Gordon Sills was thirty-five, a foremost expert in graphology, and could have been rich, his former wife had reminded him quite often.

If you don't make it before forty, she had also said—too often—you simply won't make it, and he did not care, simply did not care about money, security, the future, the children's future. . . .

Abruptly he pushed himself away from the desk and left the office, going into his living room. Like the office, it was messy, with several days' worth of newspapers, half a dozen books, magazines scattered haphazardly. To his eyes it was comfortable looking, comfort giving; he distrusted neatness in homes. Two fine Japanese landscapes were on the walls.

The buzzer sounded. When he opened the door, the prosperous, uninvited client was there again. He was carrying a brushed-suede briefcase.

Gordon opened the door wider and motioned him on through the foyer into the office. The sunlight was gone, eclipsed by the building across Amsterdam Avenue. He indicated a chair and took his own seat behind the desk.

"I apologize for not making an appointment," his visitor said. He withdrew a wallet from his breast pocket, took out a card, and slid it across the desk.

"I'm Avery Roda. On behalf of my company I should like to consult with you regarding some correspondence that we have in our possession."

"That's my business," Gordon said. "And what is your company, Mr. Roda?"

"Draper Fawcett."

Gordon nodded slowly. "And your position there?"

Roda looked unhappy. "I am vice president in charge of research and development, but right now I am in charge of an investigation we have undertaken. My first duty in connection with this was to find someone with your expertise. You come very highly recommended, Mr. Sills."

"Before we go on any further," Gordon said, "I should tell you that there are a number of areas where I'm not interested in working. I don't do paternity suits, for example. Or employer-employee pilferage cases."

Roda flushed.

"Or blackmail," Gordon finished equably. "That's why I'm not rich, but that's how it is."

"The matter I want to discuss is none of the above," Roda snapped. "Did you read about the explosion we had at our plant on Long Island two months ago?" He did not wait for Gordon's response. "We lost a very good scientist, one of the best in the country. And we cannot locate some of his paperwork, his notes. He was involved with a woman who may have them in her possession. We want to find her, recover them."

Gordon shook his head. "You need the police, then, private detectives, your own security force."

"Mr. Sills, don't underestimate our resolve or our resources. We have set all that in operation, and no one has been able to locate the woman. Last week we had a conference during which we decided to try this route. What we want from you is as complete an analysis of the woman as you can give us, based on her handwriting. That may prove fruitful." His tone said he doubted it very much.

"I assume the text has not helped."

"You assume correctly," Roda said with some bitterness. He opened his briefcase and withdrew a sheaf of papers and laid it on the desk.

From the other side Gordon could see that they were not the originals but photocopies. He let his gaze roam over the upside-down letters and then shook his head. "I have to have the actual letters to work with."

"That's impossible. They are being kept under lock and key."

"Would you offer a wine taster colored water?" Gordon's voice was bland, but he could not stop his gaze. He reached across the desk and turned the top letter right side up to study the signature. ANNA. Beautifully written. Even in the heavy black copy it was delicate, as artful as any of the Chinese calligraphy on his screens. He looked up to find Roda watching him intently. "I can tell you a few things from just this, but I have to have the originals. Let me show you my security system."

He led the way to the other side of the room. Here he had a long worktable, an oversize light table, a copy camera, an enlarger, files. There was a computer and printer on a second desk. It was all fastidiously neat and clean.

"The files are fireproof," he said dryly, "and the safe is also. Mr. Roda, if you've investigated me, you know I've handled some priceless documents. And I've kept them right here in the shop. Leave the copies. I can start with them, but tomorrow I'll want the originals."

"Where's the safe?"

Gordon shrugged and went to the computer, keyed in his code, and then moved to the wall behind the worktable and pushed aside a panel to reveal a safe front. "I don't intend to open it for you. You can see enough without that."

"Computer security?"

"Yes."

"Very well. Tomorrow I'll send you the originals. You said you can already tell us something."

They returned to the office space. "First you," Gordon said, pointing to the top letter. "Who censored them?"

The letters had been cut off just above the greeting, and there were rectangles of white throughout.

"That's how they were when we found them." Roda said heavily. "Mercer must have done it himself. One of the detectives said the holes were cut with a razor blade."

Gordon nodded. "Curiouser and curiouser. Well, for what it's worth at this point, she's an artist more than likely. Painter would be my first guess."

"Are you sure?"

"Don't be a bloody fool. Of course I'm not sure—not with copies to work with. It's a guess. Everything I report will be a guess. Educated guesswork, Mr. Roda, that's all I can guarantee."

Roda sank down into his chair and expelled a long breath. "How long will it take?"

"How many letters?"

"Nine."

"Two, three weeks."

Very slowly Roda shook his head. "We are desperate, Mr. Sills. We will double your usual fee if you can give this your undivided attention."

"And how about your cooperation?"

"What do you mean?"

"His handwriting also. I want to see at least four pages of his writing."

Roda looked blank.

"It will help to know her if I know her correspondent."

"Very well."

"How old was he?"

"Thirty."

"Okay. Anything else you can tell me?"

Roda seemed deep in thought, his eyes narrowed, a stillness about him that suggested concentration. With a visible start he looked up, nodded. "What you said about her could be important already. She mentions a show in one of the letters. We assumed a showgirl, a dancer, something like that. I'll put someone on it immediately. An artist. That could be right."

"Mr. Roda, can you tell me anything else? How important are those papers? Are they salable? Would anyone outside your company have an idea of their value?"

"They are quite valuable," he said with such a lack of tone that Gordon's ears almost pricked to attention. "If we don't recover them in a relatively short time, we will have to bring in the FBI. National security may be at stake. We want to handle it ourselves, obviously."

He finished in the same monotone, "The Russians would pay millions for them, I'm certain. And we will pay whatever we have to. She has them. She says so in one of her letters. We have to find that woman."

For a moment Gordon considered turning down the job.

*Trouble*, he thought. *Real trouble*. He glanced at the topmost letter again, the signature "Anna," and he said, "Okay. I have a contract I use routinely. . . ."

After Roda left, he studied the one letter for several minutes, not reading it, in fact, examining it upside down again; and he said softly, "Hello, Anna."

Then he gathered up all the letters, put them in a file, and put it in his safe. He had no intention of starting until he had the originals. But it would comfort Roda to believe he was already at work.

Roda sent the originals and a few samples of Mercer's writing before noon the next day, and for three hours Gordon studied them all. He arranged hers on the worktable under the gooseneck lamp and turned them this way and that, not yet reading them, making notes now and then. As he had suspected, her script was fine, delicate, with beautiful shading. She used a real pen with real ink, not a felt-tip or a ballpoint. Each stroke was visually satisfying, artistic in itself. One letter was three pages long; four were two pages; the others were single sheets. None of them had a date, an address, a complete name. He cursed the person who had mutilated them. One by one he turned them over to examine the backs and jotted: PRESSURE—LIGHT TO MEDIUM. His other notes were equally brief: FLUID. RAPID. NOT CONVENTIONAL. PROPORTIONS, ONE TO FIVE. That was European, and he did not think she was, but it would bear close examination. Each note was simply a direction marker, a first impression. He was whistling tunelessly as he worked and was startled when the telephone rang.

It was Karen, finally returning his many calls. The children would arrive by six, and he must return them by seven Sunday night. Her voice was cool, as if she were giving orders about laundry. He said okay and hung up, surprised at how little he felt about the matter. Before, it had given him a wrench each time they talked; he had asked questions: How was she? Was she working? Was the house all right? She had the house on Long Island, and that was fine with him; he had spent more and more time in town anyway over the past few years. But still, they had bought it together, he had repaired this and that, put up screens, taken them down, struggled with the plumbing.

That night he took the two children to a Greek restaurant. Buster, eight years old, said it was yucky; Dana, ten, called him a baby, and Gordon headed off the fight by saying he had bought a new Monopoly game. Dana said Buster was into winning. Dana looked very much like her mother, but Buster was her true genetic heir. Karen was into winning, too.

They went to The Cloisters and fantasized medieval scenarios; they played Monopoly, and on Sunday he took them to a puppet show at the Met and then drove them home. He was exhausted. When he got back he looked about, deeply depressed. There were dirty dishes in the sink and on the table, in the living room. Buster had slept on the couch, and his bedclothes and covers were draped over it. Karen said they were getting too old to share a room any longer. Dana's bedroom was also a mess. She had left her pajamas and slippers.

Swiftly he gathered up the bedding from the living room and tossed it all onto the bed in Dana's room and closed the door. He overfilled the dishwasher and turned it on and finally went into his workroom and opened the safe.

"Hello, Anna," he said softly, and tension seeped from him; the ache that had settled in behind his eyes vanished; he forgot the traffic jams coming home from Long Island, forgot the bickering his children seemed unable to stop.

He took the letters to the living room and sat down to read them through for the first time. Love letters, passionate letters, humorous in places, perceptive, intelligent. Without dates it was hard to put them in chronological order, but the story emerged. She had met Mercer in the city; they had walked and talked, and he had left. He had come back, and this time they were together for a weekend and became lovers. She sent her letters to a post office box; he did not write to her, although he left pages of incomprehensible notes in her care. She was married or lived with someone, whose name had been cut out with a razor blade every time she referred to him. Mercer knew him, visited him apparently. They were even friends and had long, serious talks. She was afraid; Mercer was involved in work that was dangerous, and no one told her what it was. She called Mercer her mystery man and speculated about his secret life, his family, his insane wife or tyrannical father, or his own lapses into lycanthropy.

Gordon smiled. Anna was not a whiner or a weeper; but she was hopelessly in love with Mercer and did not know where he lived, where he worked, what danger threatened him, anything about him except that when he was with her, she was alive and happy. And that was enough. Her husband understood and wanted only her happiness, and it was destroying her, knowing she was hurting him so much, but she was helpless.

He pursed his lips and reread one. "My darling, I can't stand it. I really can't stand it any longer. I dream of you, see you in every stranger on the street, hear your voice every time I answer the phone. My palms become wet, and I tingle all over, thinking it's your footsteps I hear. You are my dreams. So, I told myself today, this is how it is? No way! Am I a silly schoolgirl mooning over a television star? At twenty-six! I gathered up all your papers and put them in a box and addressed it, and as I wrote the number of the box, I found myself giggling. You can't send a Dear John to a post office box number. What if you failed to pick it up and an inspector opened it finally? I should entertain such a person? They're all gray and dessicated, you know, those inspectors. Let them find their own entertainment! What if they deciphered your mysterious squiggles and discovered the secret of the universe? Do any of them deserve such enlightenment? No! I put everything back in [excised] safe—"

Mercer was not the mystery man, Gordon thought then; the mystery was the other man, the nameless one whose safe hid Mercer's papers. Who was he? He shook his head over the arrangement of two men and a woman and continued to read: "—and [excised] came in and let me cry on his shoulder. Then we went to dinner. I was starved."

Gordon laughed and put the letters down on the coffee table, leaned back with his hands behind his head, and contemplated the ceiling. It needed paint.

For the next two weeks he worked on the letters and the few pages of Mercer's handwriting. He photographed everything, made enlargements, and searched for signs of weakness, illness. He keystroked the letters into his computer and ran the program he had developed, looking for usages, foreign or regional combinations, anything unusual or revealing. Mercer, he decided, had been born in a test tube and never left school and the laboratory until the day he met Anna. She was from the Midwest, not a big city, somewhere around one of the Great Lakes. The name that had been consistently cut out had six letters. She had gone to an opening, and the artist's name had been cut out also. It had nine letters. Even without her testimony about the artist, it was apparent that she had been excited by his work. It showed in the writing. He measured the spaces between the words, the size of individual letters, the angle of her slant, the proportions of everything. Every movement she made was graceful, rhythmic. Her connections were garlands, open and trusting; that meant she was honest herself. Her threadlike connections that strung her words together indicated her speed in writing, her intuition, which she trusted.

As the work went on, he was making more complete notes, drawing conclusions more and more often. The picture of Anna was becoming real.

He paid less attention to Mercer's writing after making his initial assessment of him. A scientist, technologist, precise, angular, a genius, inhibited, excessively secretive, a loner. He was a familiar type.

When Roda returned, Gordon felt he could tell him more about those two people than their own mothers knew about them.

What he could not tell was what they looked like, or where Anna was now, or where the papers were that she had put in her husband's safe.

He watched Roda skim through his report on Anna. Today rain was falling in gray curtains of water; the air felt thick and clammy.

"That's all?" Roda demanded when he finished.

"That's it."

"We checked every art show in the state," Roda said, scowling at him. "We didn't find her. And we have proof that Mercer couldn't have spent as much time with her as she claimed in the letters. We've been set up. You've been set up. You say here that she's honest, ethical; and we say she's an agent or worse. She got her hooks in him and got those papers, and these letters are fakes, every one of them is a fake!"

Gordon shook his head. "There's not a lie in those letters."

"Then why didn't she come forward when he died? There was enough publicity. We made sure of that. I tell you, he wasn't with her. We found him in a talent hunt when he was a graduate student, and he stayed in that damn lab ever since, seven days a week for four years. He never had time to have a relationship of the sort she's talking about. It's a lie through and through. A fantasy." He slumped in his chair. His face was almost as gray as his very good suit. He looked years older than he had the last time he had been in the office. "They're going to win," he said in a low voice. "The woman and her partner. They're probably out of the country already. Probably left the day after the accident, with the papers, the job done. Well-done. That stupid, besotted fool!" He stared at the floor for several more seconds, then straightened.

His voice was hard, clipped, when he spoke again. "I was against consulting you from the start. A waste of time and money. Voodoo crap, that's all this is. Well, we've done what we can. Send in your bill. Where are her letters?"

Silently Gordon slid a folder across the desk. Roda went through it carefully, then put it in his briefcase and stood up. "If I were you, I would not give our firm as reference in the future, Sills." He pushed Gordon's report away from him. "We can do without that. Good day."

It should have ended there, Gordon knew, but it did not end. *Where are you, Anna?* he thought at the world being swamped in cold rain. Why hadn't she come forward, attended the funeral, turned in the papers? He had no answers. He just knew that she was out there, painting, living with a man who loved her very much, enough to give her her freedom to fall in love with someone else. *Take good care of her*, he thought at that other man. *Be gentle with her; be patient while she heals. She's very precious, you know.*

He leaned his head against the window, let the coolness soothe him. He said aloud, "She's very precious."

"Gordon, are you all right?" Karen asked on the phone. It was his weekend for the children again.

"Sure. Why?"

"I just wondered. You sound strange. Do you have a girlfriend?"

"What do you want, Karen?"

The ice returned to her voice, and they made arrangements for the children's arrival, when he was to return them. *Library books*, he thought distantly. *Just like library books.*

When he hung up he looked at the apartment and was dismayed by the dinginess, the disregard for the barest amenities. *Another lamp*, he thought. He needed a second lamp, at the very least. Maybe even two. Anna loved light. A girlfriend? He wanted to laugh, and to cry also. He had a signature, some love letters written to another man, a woman who came to his dreams and spoke to him in the phrases from her letters. A girlfriend! He closed his eyes and saw the name, Anna. The capital *A* was a flaring volcano, high up into the stratosphere, then the even, graceful *n*'s, the funny little final *a* that had trouble staying on the base line, that wanted to fly away. And a beautiful sweeping line that flew out from it, circled above the entire name, came down to cross the first letter, turn it into an *A*, and in doing so formed a perfect palette. A graphic representation of Anna, soaring into the heavens, painting, creating art with every breath, every motion. Forever yours, Anna. Forever yours.

He took a deep breath and tried to make plans for the children's weekend, for the rest of the month, the summer, the rest of his life.

The next day he bought a lamp and on his way home stopped in a florist's shop and bought half a dozen flowering plants. She had written that the sunlight turned the flowers on the sill into jewels.

He put them on the sill and raised the blind, and the sunlight turned the blooms into jewels. His hands were clenched; abruptly he turned away from the window.

He went back to work; spring became summer, hot and humid as only New York could be, and he found himself going from one art show to another. He mocked himself and cursed himself for it, but he attended openings, examined new artists' work, signatures, again and again and again. If the investigators trained in this couldn't find her, he told himself firmly, and the FBI couldn't find her, he was a fool to think he had even a remote chance. But he went to the shows. He was lonely, he told himself, and tried to become interested in other women, any other woman, and continued to attend openings.

In the fall he went to the opening of yet another new artist, out of an art school, a teacher. And he cursed himself for not thinking of that before. She could be an art teacher. He made a list of schools and started down the list, perfecting a story as he worked down it one by one. He was collecting signatures of artists for an article he planned to write. It was a passable story. It got him nothing.

She might be ugly, he told himself. What kind of woman would have fallen in love with Mercer? He had been inhibited, constricted, without grace, brilliant, eccentric, and full of wonder. It was the wonder that she had sensed he knew. She had been attracted to that in Mercer and had got through his many defenses, had found a boy-man who was truly appealing. And he had adored her. That was apparent from her letters; it had been mutual. Why had he lied to her? Why hadn't he simply told her who he was, what he was doing? The other man in her life had not been an obstacle; that had been made clear also. The two men had liked each other, and both loved her. Gordon brooded about her, about Mercer, the other man; and he haunted openings, became a recognized figure at the various studios and schools where he collected signatures. It was an obsession, he told himself, unhealthy, maybe even a sign of neurosis, or worse. It was insane to fall in love with someone's signature, love letters to another man.

And he could be wrong, he told himself. Maybe Roda had been right after all. The doubts were always short-lived.

The cold October rains had come. Karen was engaged to a wealthy man.

The children's visits had become easier because he no longer was trying to entertain them every minute; he had given in and bought a television and video games for them. He dropped by the Art Academy to meet Rick Henderson, who had become a friend over the past few months. Rick taught watercolors.

Gordon was in Rick's office waiting for him to finish with a class critique session when he saw the *A*, Anna's capital *A*.

He felt his arms prickle and sweat form on his hands and a tightening in the pit of his stomach as he stared at an envelope on Rick's desk.

Almost fearfully he turned it around to study the handwriting. The *A*'s in *Art Academy* were like volcanoes, reaching up into the stratosphere, crossed with a quirky, insouciant line, like a sombrero at a rakish angle. Anna's *A*. It did not soar and make a palette, but it wouldn't, not in an address. That was her personal sign.

He let himself sink into Rick's chair and drew in a deep breath. He did not touch the envelope again. When Rick finally joined him, he nodded toward it.

"Would you mind telling me who wrote that?" His voice sounded hoarse, but Rick seemed not to notice. He opened the envelope and scanned a note, then handed it over. Her handwriting. Not exactly the same, but it was hers. He was certain it was hers, even with the changes. The way the writing was positioned on the page, the sweep of the letters, the fluid grace. . . . But it was not the same. The *A* in her name, Anna, was different. He felt bewildered by the differences and knew it was hers in spite of them. Finally he actually read the words. She would be out of class for a few days. It was dated four days ago.

"Just a kid," Rick said. "Fresh in from Ohio, thinks she has to be excused from class. I'm surprised it's not signed by her mother."

"Can I meet her?"

Now Rick looked interested. "Why?"

"I want her signature."

Rick laughed. "You're a real nut, you know. Sure. She's in the studio, making up for time off. Come on."

He stopped at the doorway and gazed at the young woman painting. She was no more than twenty, almost painfully thin, hungry looking. She wore scruffy sneakers, very old faded blue jeans, a man's plaid shirt. Not the Anna of the letters. Not yet.

Gordon felt dizzy and held onto the doorframe for a moment, and he knew what it was that Mercer had worked on, what he had discovered. He felt as if he had slipped out of time himself as his thoughts raced, explanations formed, his next few years shaped themselves in his mind. Understanding came the way a memory comes, a gestalt of the entire event or series of events, all accessible at once.

Mercer's notes had shown him to be brilliant, obsessional, obsessed with time, secretive. Roda had assumed Mercer failed, because he had blown himself up. Everyone must have assumed that. But he had not failed. He had gone forward five years, six at the most, to the time when Anna would be twenty-six. He had slipped out of time to the future. Gordon knew with certainty that it was his own name that had been excised from Anna's letters. Phrases from her letters tumbled through his mind. She had mentioned a Japanese bridge from his painting, the flowers on the sill, even the way the sun failed when it sank behind the building across the street.

He thought of Roda and the hordes of agents searching for the papers that were to be hidden, had been hidden in the safest place in the world—the future. The safe Anna would put the papers in would be his, Gordon's, safe. He closed his eyes hard, already feeling the pain he knew would come when Mercer realized that he was to die, that he had died. For Mercer there could not be a love strong enough to make him abandon his work.

Gordon knew he would be with Anna, watch her mature, become the Anna of the letters, watch her soar into the stratosphere; and when Mercer walked through his time door, Gordon would still love her and wait for her, help her heal afterward.

Rick cleared his throat, and Gordon released his grasp of the doorframe, took the next step into the studio. Anna's concentration was broken; she looked up at him. Her eyes were dark blue.

*Hello, Anna.*

# ALEXANDER JABLOKOV

## At the Cross-Time Jaunters' Ball

Alexander Jablokov is a new writer, with only a handful of sales to *Amazing* and *Isaac Asimov's Science Fiction Magazine* to his credit, but I'm willing to bet that before too many more years go by, he's going to have made a very considerable name for himself indeed. In the elegant and cooly pyrotechnic story that follows, he traces the intricate machinations of a group of immortals who live in the interstices between the many worlds of possibility.

Jablokov lives in Somerville, Massachusetts, and is currently at work on his first novel.

# AT THE CROSS-TIME JAUNTERS' BALL

Alexander Jablokov

I had gotten lost again, as I so often did, because it was dark there, in those musty and unswept hallways that run between the universes. I've always been impressed by the amount of crap that seems to float in through the doorways and settle there, in some sort of plea for reality. An infinite network of passages linking the worlds of Shadow with that of the real might seem like a good idea, but who was going to keep it clean? The Lords were too haughty to concern themselves with things like that, and we humans were too . . . finite.

I looked in through doorways as I walked, to see such things as a city of hanging tree dwellings or an endless stairway that curved up from mist into blinding sunlight. These were delicate worlds, miniatures. As a professional critic of such Shadows I had to say that these worlds were not the style I usually liked, though one, where a regatta of multicolored dirigibles sailed above a city whose towers stood half in the sea, was excellent.

A rough wind blew past, carrying with it the clamor of a cheering army, and the pounding of swords on shields. The passage tilted upward, and I climbed a set of rough stairs, smelling first lilacs, then, when I took a deeper breath, an open sewer. I choked, and was surrounded by buzzing flies, who had wandered irrevocably from their world and, looking for shit, had found only the meager substitute of a critic. I ran up the stairs, waving the flies away, past the sound of temple bells, the dense choking of dust from a quarry, and a spray of briny water, accompanied by the shrieking of sea gulls.

Gathered in a knot in the hallway ahead of me were a group of Lords, with their servant, a huge man wearing a leather helmet. Lord Prokhor, Lord Sere, and Lord Ammene, three balding men with prison pallor and rings below their dark eyes, waited for me to give them advice on acquisition. They sat on little folding stools, and looked uncomfortable.

"You are late, Mr. Landstatter," Lord Ammene said, in a reedy voice.

"Your servant, sir," I said, ignoring the challenge. I eyed the three of them suspiciously. Lords were entirely unpredictable, and their motivations obscure. On my last trip I'd almost been trapped when Cuzco, capital of the Incan Empire, fell to invading Apache Sacred Warriors who had hired Maori warships for transport from their temple cities along the Pacific coast of Mexico. I'd spent three desperate days freezing in the Andes, my nights lit by the light from the burning city reflected in the ice fields, before I could return home. I had wondered if it was an accident, because someone had locked me in my room just when the attack began. The three of them returned my bow without standing.

The servant raised the lamp he held in his hand and examined me. I wore a three-cornered, plumed hat, a heavy, powder blue tailcoat covered with useless gold buttons, a stiff, embroidered vest with hunting scenes on it, extremely tight cream-colored silk trousers, and black leather boots trimmed with sable. Beneath the hat, my hair was pomaded, powdered, and pulled back into a ponytail by an ornate silver clasp. The servant sneered at me.

The Lords were dressed in their usual sober dark clothes, gold chains around their necks indicating rank. Unlike most people, they did not adopt clothing from Shadow, implying, I guess, that what they always wore was "real." Style is never real, but I am a critic of worlds, not dress, so I said nothing.

Then the servant turned the lamp around. I straightened my hat. We stood in front of a stretch of blank wall. Humming gently to himself, he adjusted the lamp until it focused on the wall. The wall shimmered, and a door opened onto a brightly lit street. I could hear the ringing of steel wagon wheels on cobblestones and the puffing of a steam launch on the river that flowed just out of sight of the doorway. "There you are, Mr. Landstatter. See you in forty-eight hours." I stopped just in front of the shimmering, the way I always do, no matter who is watching. Vanishing into unreality makes me nervous. He pushed me through, not roughly, but the way you would direct a timid actor onto a stage in front of an audience. I turned to protest, but he and his masters were gone, and I found myself addressing my retort to a broken and stained brick wall.

The water swirled against the brick side of the canal, as if irritated at having its freedom curtailed, but finally acquiesced and flowed under the arch of the bridge. On the river beyond, a vendor guiding his empty flatboat home from the market negotiated the uneven current with tired familiarity. Past the inflow of the canal he put his shoulders into his poling, undoubtedly thinking of a bowl of stew, a mug of beer, and a pipe of tobacco.

I was starting to think of things like that too. I watched the boatman vanish into the iridescent meeting of sunset and oily water, then turned and began to walk in the direction of the dam, which was where the north and south branches of the Schekaagau River joined and flowed into Lake Vlekke. It was also where the best hotels were. I strayed into the path of a pedicab, and was startled by a jangle of bells that sounded like an angry gamelan. The white-suited driver bared polished, scrimshawed teeth, cursed at me in Malay, and was gone, leaving only a cloud of ginger and curry to mark his passing.

The tall, step-gabled warehouses that had been flanking me on the left vanished, to be replaced by the unadorned brick facades of merchants' houses, which gave only hints of wealth through panes of leaded glass: the glitter of a chandelier, the flash of a tapestry, the gleam of a silver serving bowl. From a half-open window came the sound of a drinking song, bellowed by male voices to the accompaniment of pounding pewter mugs. Merchants, home from the Bourse and ready to do their best to keep the price of malted barley high.

A marble bridge carried me high over the river to the dam, a platform of pilings sunk into the soft earth. Ahead of me rose the towers of city hall. A small boy sat on the quay, trailing a fishing line in the water. The result of his day's labors amounted to two carp, strung through the gills, and a frog, which was jumping up and down in a jar.

"Say, lad," I said, in the Lithuanian influenced patois of the Mississippi River trade. I thought it was a nice touch. "What is the best hotel in town?" I've had fellow critics tell me that, when they work in Shadow, they stay in the sleaziest fleabags they can find, because that makes the experience more "real." I don't find lice more real, in any ultimate sense, than satin sheets.

"The best?" The boy jumped up eagerly. "The Emperor Kristiaan, on the Streetergracht! They have marble tubs and gold faucets. And Duc Noh the King of Nam Viet got shot in the lobby! They put a chair over it to hide it, but you can still see the bloodstains if you look."

"Sounds ideal. And do you know how to get there?"

"Do I! I once got thrown out for climbing the flagpole. You can see the whole city from the top! It's the tallest flagpole in Schekaagau." He hung the fish on a string around his waist and picked up the jar containing the frog, which began to jump more frantically. "Follow me." We crossed the tiled dam square, passing the triumphal arch, an explosion of soldiery, waving banners, crosses, and captive Indians pleading for mercy. Somewhere beyond city hall, bells were ringing Angelus. We walked down a narrow street, where merchants were locking up their stalls for the night. The blue lamps that taverns and places of public relief were required to show already glowed at spots along the street, lighthouses for the weary. A few minutes later, we emerged into a square which opened out onto the dark water of the canal called the Streetergracht. The other three sides of the square formed the ornate classical pile of the hotel. On top, hanging over us like a burnished artificial moon in the laboratory of a medieval alchemist, a gilded dome caught the last rays of sunlight. Three flagpoles stood in front, the flags those of the hotel, the city of Schekaagau, and the Stadholderate, in the process of being lowered by a squad of hotel employees in scarlet tunics and knee pants. The boy proudly pointed out the taller, center pole as the cause of his expulsion. I was properly impressed.

I reached into my money purse, pulled out a crescent of silver, and flipped it to him. He stared at it in wonder, then stuffed it away in one of the secret pockets boys have. "I better go. Mum will be worried. I'm late for dinner."

I winked at him, which he liked. "Don't let me catch you climbing the towers of city hall."

"You won't," he said, ambiguously, and was gone into the gathering darkness, his captive frog still tucked under one arm. I had never learned his name.

It was after I had been lost for quite some time that I noticed I was being followed. For a moment, in my drunken state, that was funny. The poor fool thought he was going to end up in a nice hotel lobby with plush chairs and a bar where he could get a late night glass of arrack, but instead he was doomed to wander with me through back alleys and dark, warehouse-lined streets for the rest of the night, his path constantly disrupted by dark flowing canals. That was not why he was following me, of course, and I quickly ceased to find his company amusing. I glanced over my shoulder as I turned a corner. He was dressed in some sort of robes, not normal clothes at all, and didn't seem to know the streets any better than I did. I emerged on the quay by the river, its edge marked by a line of heavy granite posts holding a chain. The river flowed quickly here, constrained by the quays, and I could hear its churning and grumbling.

Out in the darkness a procession of torchlit barges, loaded to the gunwales with masquers, drifted on the reflected waters of the river. They laughed and screamed, and seemed to be having a terrific time, just as they had when I was with them, though I had not enjoyed them at all. I had drunk too much, and almost gotten sick. I had taken a walk to clear my head and work out my thoughts on my critical analysis. I doubted anyone had noticed my absence.

Despite the threat at my back, my main emotion was still annoyance. The judgment of a good critic never relaxes. Peter Lucas had made a specialty of this sort of genre piece, and I was getting tired of it. It irritated me to think that I had another day to spend here before the Key the Lords had implanted in the limbic system of my brain would take me home to the real world. To think of all of Lucas's labor in twisting human history, to create yet another set of drunken shipping magnates and aldermen in fancy masquerade pounding mugs on wooden trestle tables and pissing heartily over the sides of their barges. It made me sick. Lucas demonstrated that there were an infinite number of redundant possibilities, like a gallery hallway lined only with paintings of courting couples, or children playing with a little, furry dog.

I didn't know what Lucas had done to history in order to create this Shadow, what kings and queens he had given fevers, what storms he had raised, what matings he had arranged, what battles he had altered, in order for William Vlekke of Antwerp to discover this place so that Schekaagau stood on the shores of Lake Vlekke, rather than Chicago on Lake Michigan, and didn't get much more of a chance to think about it, because my pursuer decided that that was a good moment to jump me.

His attack was theatrical, with a scream and leap. His body was slim and strong underneath the heavy wool robes, but he was more enthusiastic than skilled, and I threw him off. He hit the ground heavily, then rolled and came up with a glittering, curved knife in his hand. I backed away. He didn't seem to be trying to rob me. He had other things in mind. My ridiculous clothes suddenly seemed as constricting as a strait jacket. He came forward with his blade dancing before him. It was a beautiful piece of work, I noticed, with an elegantly patterned silver hilt. It would look wonderful sticking out of my chest in the morning light.

Critics of Shadow are used to such things, however, and I was not as defenseless as I looked. As he came at me, I pulled a packet of powder out of a pocket and threw it at him, squeezing my eyes shut at the same time. Even through my closed lids, the flash of the powder left an afterimage. He shrieked and stumbled back, completely blinded. I slipped brass knuckles over my fingers, moved in, and punched him at the angle of his jaw. This was unfair, but I wasn't feeling sporting that night. His head snapped back and he yelped. He slashed back and forth with his blade, still not able to see anything, but dangerous nevertheless. I dodged in and hit him again, and he stumbled back and fell. His head crunched sickeningly against one of the granite posts, and he rolled over the side of the quay into the water. For a long moment I stood swaying drunkenly, trying to figure out where he had gone. Then I ran up and looked over the edge. Water roared heavily below in the darkness, but there was nothing else to be seen. I slipped the brass knuckles off my hand, and started to try to find my way home again. It was a long while before I found the square in front of the hotel, and I was still shaking when I did.

A marble bathtub is a beautiful thing, but it takes forever for hot water to heat it up. I finally slid into the bath and was able to relax my muscles. The attack had left me with a number of bruises, but no answers. Answers were sometimes scarce in the many worlds of Shadow, which the Lords had caused to be created for their mysterious pleasures. But the municipal river patrol would be pulling a body out of the weir at the dam in the morning, and I had no idea why he had tried to kill me, and I like to have reasons for things like that. Cuzco, Schekaagau . . . Had the Lords tired of my aesthetic sniping? Was I simply paranoid? That was an occupational hazard. I knew I would get no answers that night, so I got out of the bath, toweled myself dry, and went to bed.

I turned the key on the gaslight, dimming it to a blue glow. The boy had been real, though. Give Lucas that much. Everyone else seemed like a moving waxwork, but that boy was as real as anyone. I was not sure the Lords enjoyed "reality" in that sense, since they themselves did not seem particularly real to me.

Reveling in the feel of satin against skin, I turned over in bed, to find myself staring at the patterned silver hilt of a knife, still vibrating from its impact, that had somehow come to be imbedded in the bedpost next to my head. The motif was one of eyes and lighting bolts. The last knife I had seen like that was now at the bottom of the Schekaagau River. I wrenched the knife from the bedpost and ran to the window, but my second attacker had already slid down the drainpipe and vanished, leaving me with a souvenir of my night at the Emperor Kristiaan.

"Mutated *E. coli*," Salvator Martine said. He had pulled me away from the other guests at his party to give me this information.

I swirled the Tokay in my glass and watched it sheet down the sides. "*E. coli?*" Only Martine would serve a wine as sweet as Tokay before dinner.

Martine grinned, bright teeth in a face of tanned leather. He was annoyingly handsome, and smelled sharply of myrrh and patchouli. The Lords loved him, for no good reason that I could see. Several had even come to attend his party. "Normal intestinal flora. Mutated and hybridized with amyotrophic lateral sclerosis. Infects via the GI tract and destroys the central nervous systems of higher primates. Neat.

Grew it in the guts of an Australopithecine on the African veldt, two, three million years ago. Not easy, Jacob, not easy. When I woke up on that pallet at Centrum, I had bedsores, and a headache that lasted a month. Killed them all. Every last one of the buggers. Nothing left on this planet with more brains than an orangutan." He downed his glass of Tokay as if it were water. I took another slow sip of my own.

We stood on the parapet of what he called his "palace." Behind us I could hear the sound of the party, voices and clinking glasses, background music, occasionally a laugh. The sun set behind rolling green hills. From a distant ridge came the cry of a deer. A trail of mist descended on the valley, glowing in the evening light. Except for the ones behind us in the party, there were no other humans on the planet.

"Infectious lateral sclerosis . . ." I murmured to myself. This was art?

Martine laughed. "Not to worry. With no hosts, it died out, and there are no other vectors. I was careful about that."

He'd misunderstood my moodiness, of course, but it took a particularly impervious cast of mind to be a molder of worlds. Martine had succeeded in wiping out all of humanity, collateral branches to boot. By some standards, that made him a god. A god with bedsores. That left me with a blank canvas to look at, but nothing to review, which was perhaps his intention. If a tree falls in a forest and no one hears it, that's one thing, but when the acorn is worm devoured and the tree never exists, what sound does it make then?

"You are looking at Berenson's new world next?"

"Yes. She's been very mysterious about it, but I suspect—"

A voice interrupted us.

"There you are. The most notable men at the party, and the two of you stand out here watching the sunset. Where's your sense of social responsibility?" We both turned. Amanda, my wife, closed the door behind her, passing through in the roar of voices. She wore a dress that fell in waves of green and blue silk, and she emerged from it like Aphrodite from the foam, her blond hair braided and coiled around her head. A moonstone glowed in its silver setting as it rested on her forehead.

"We were waiting for you," Martine said with that charming insincerity that Amanda seemed to like.

She came up and took a sip of my drink. She smiled at Martine. "I'll have you know, Salvator, that Jacob detests sweet drinks before dinner." She took another, and kept the glass. "I've been wandering around your palace. It's wonderful! How did you ever create anything like it?"

I felt a surge of annoyance. The palace was a monstrosity. It had towers, with pennants snapping in the breeze. It had triumphal staircases. It had flying buttresses. It had colonnades. What it didn't have was structure. It looked like an immense warehouse of architectural spare parts.

"It was built by some people from a world I did a few years back. Remember it, Jacob? The Berbers of the Empire of the Maghreb ruled Northern Africa. They flooded the desert and built great palaces. I had planned that." He turned to Amanda. "As I recall, Jacob didn't like it much."

He recalled correctly. I couldn't remember much about that particular work, just hot sun and blinding water, but I did remember that I hadn't liked it. The Lords had bid it up, though, and it was now in someone's collection, making Martine wealthy. Critics should never socialize with artists; it's difficult enough to like their work in the first place.

Amanda came up and pushed herself against me. Her perfume smelled of violets, and I lost track of what I was thinking. I put my arm around her, and she pulled away, as she always did once she had my attention, and walked to the other side of the parapet to enjoy the sunset.

Amanda had once been close to me, but was now distant, and I couldn't remember when that had changed. It could have happened overnight, since Amanda often went to bed loving and woke up cold. Something she saw in her dreams, I'd always thought. But now it was that way most of the time, and I felt I'd let something slip by, as if we'd had an immense knock-down drag-out fight that I had not been able to attend. On the infrequent occasions when we made love it was like two people sawing a tree trunk, the length of the saw between us and only the rhythm of the task keeping us together. This still left me wanting to do it much more often than she did.

Voices shouted for Martine inside, so the three of us went in through the French doors. The banqueting hall was an immense room, thirty feet high, and banners from the Shadows Martine had created hung down from the beams supporting the ceiling. Someone pressed a glass of wine into my hand, not Tokay, mercifully, but some dry red. The party poured after Martine as he strode through the hall, out the double doors at the other end, and down the immense stairway. At the bottom rested a cube wrapped in black velvet, about six feet high. It had been delivered through the hallways by servants available to the Lords. Despite myself, I was impressed. They did not usually permit ordinary men to move objects from Shadow to Shadow.

"Let's carry her up," Martine said, and the party surged forward with cheers. It took a half dozen people to lift it. "Take my place,

Jacob," Martine said, and I found myself with a shoulder under one corner of the cube. We angled it back and, cursing and laughing, hauled it up the stairs. It was heavy and tried to slide back. I started to sweat.

A space was cleared on the floor among the armchairs and the tables covered with half-finished drinks. The cube was put down. I looked for Amanda in the crowd but couldn't find her anywhere. I remembered what she was wearing, and her moonstone, but wasn't sure that I knew what she looked like anymore. It seemed that as she had grown more distant her face had stopped being familiar.

"This is from a world I did recently. It's not worth visiting, believe me, but it did produce one thing that's worthwhile. I asked the Lords for permission to bring it back for my collection." He pulled on a cord and the black velvet fell to the floor. The crowd grew silent and drew back, but no one took his eyes away.

The most beautiful woman in the world was in hell, but she had been turned to stone and no one could do anything about it. She stared at us from behind five inches of leaded glass with pleading in her eyes. She was a Madonna, and a newborn child lay in her lap. His eyes stared blankly upward, for He had been born hideously blind.

I had more information than Martine thought I did, from my sources at Centrum. I knew that Martine had caused eight entire worlds to be destroyed by nuclear war before he got the effect he wanted. On the last try, a group of artists, vomiting, losing their hair, seeing the constant glimmer of optic nerves degenerating in the radiation flux, had found a boulder in a blast crater and set it on a hilltop. The rock was dense with exotic isotopes, and had killed the sculptors as they chiseled it. They had worked as one, and it was impossible to tell where one artist had left off and the next began. They had created a masterpiece, probably not even knowing why, but Martine claimed this work as his own. Radioactive fantasies had been fashionable among the Lords lately.

I turned and walked away, rubbing my shoulder. The party was getting loud again, despite the pleading eyes of the Virgin Mary, and I felt a little sick. I walked down a long hallway lined with loot from Martine's various creations. I stopped in front of one painting, of Christ being carried drunk from the Marriage of Cana by the Apostles. It looked like a rather mucky Titian, all droopy flesh and blue mist, but Amanda had pointed it out specifically to me earlier in the day. She never really seemed to care much about art herself, but she somehow always knew precisely what I would like. Or would not.

"Mr. Landstatter. Good evening." Sitting in the shadows on straight-backed chairs, like Egyptian deities, were two Lords, Jurum and

Altina, who seemed to be married, although it was hard for me to tell. At any rate, they were always together.

"Good evening." I bowed, but did not speak further.

"We've just been looking at Martine's little collection," Altina said, her voice a gentle hiss. "Symbols and parts, it seems to us. Reflections of worlds in objects, and so an imitation of our strings of Shadow. What say you?" They awaited my judgment.

Lords are strange beings. They collect worlds the way children collect brightly colored stones and seashells, but require others both to create those worlds and to determine whether they are worth having. They had gained control of the infinite universe of Shadows before anyone could remember, raised Centrum, and seemed intent on continuing in this position forever. Had one of them decided to kill me? The fact that two attempts had already failed suggested that a critic of murder would have had to give their efforts a bad review.

"The objects have significance in themselves, and not just as signs to Shadow," I said. The Lords often had trouble understanding ordinary art. "This statue of Apollo, for instance . . ." They stood and listened, Altina resting slightly on Jurum's arm, as I took them through Martine's collection, which ranged from the brilliant to the mediocre, and seemed to have been forgotten here, like junk in an attic. They thanked me, finally, and walked off to bed, discussing what I had said. I realized that the party above had grown silent, and that it was time for bed.

When I returned to the banqueting hall, it was empty, save for the tormented Virgin. I stopped to look at her, but her expression had become reproachful, as if I were somehow responsible for her fate. I turned away and went to our room.

The bed was still made, and Amanda was nowhere to be seen. I took my clothes off, threw them on the floor, and climbed in under the covers. Our room was in one of those dramatic towers, and there was nothing but darkness outside the windows. I fell asleep.

Amanda woke me up as she slipped into bed, some time later. I started to say something, to ask where she had been.

"Shh," she said. "I didn't mean to wake you up." She hunched up on the other side of the bed, the way she did so often, even though the bed was not particularly large and this meant that she dangled precariously over the edge. I moved closer to her and nuzzled her neck. "Please, Jacob. It's late and I want to sleep. See you in the morning." She yawned and was quickly asleep, or at least pretended to be.

I lay back on the other side of the bed, my heart pounding. I knew that no matter what I did, I would be unable to sleep. When I had left her, she had smelled of violets. Her neck now had the bitter aroma of myrrh and patchouli.

The Capuchin did his calculations with a light pen on what looked like a pane of glass, causing equations to appear in glowing green. Interpolated quotations from the Old Testament emerged in yellow, while those from the New Testament were light blue. Unavoidable references to Muslim physicists flashed a gory, infidel red. I gazed out from under my cowl, impressed but unenlightened. I don't know anything about nuclear physics, and even when I thought I had managed to pick up the thread of an argument, I was immediately thrown off by a gloss on Thomas Aquinas or Origen. I contented myself with smelling the incense and watching the glitter of the LEDs on the rosaries of the other monks as they checked the Capuchin's calculations.

He turned from the glass and faced his audience. He raised his arms in supplication to heaven, then clapped his hands together. The equations disappeared, to be replaced by a mosaic of Christos Pancrator, His brow clouded by stormy judgment, lightning ready to be unleashed from His imperial hands.

"Brothers!" the monk said. "All is in readiness. For the first time in history, the fires of Hell shall be unleashed on Earth, chained at the command of the sacred Mathematics that God, in His Wisdom, has given us to smite the infidel. We will now examine this flame, and if it is not found wanting, its hunger will soon consume the arrogant cities of all those who would oppose the Will of God!" We rose to our feet and followed him up the stairs to the surface.

It was dry and bright outside, and the sky was a featureless blue. We segregated ourselves by Order, the gray of Dominicans to the right, the brown of Franciscans to the left, and the martial, oriental splendor of the Templars and Hospitallers in the center. There were last-minute checks of the dosimeters, and several of the more cautious had already flipped their goggles down and were sucking on their respirators.

In front of us, across the cracked, dried mud, amid the rubble of what had once been the city of Venice, stood the Campanile of St. Mark's, looking the same as it did in a Canaletto painting, except for the fact that the gray ovoid of the atomic bomb rested on a frame on top of the steeply pitched roof. Nearby, the crumbled dome of the cathedral lay on the ground like an overturned bowl. At a distance stood the crazily leaning Rialto bridge. All around, the flats of the dry lagoon stretched away. A trumpet call rang through the air. We repaired to our trenches, all now monastic grasshoppers with our goggles and breathing tubes. We knelt, facing the tower, and the bomb.

When the blast came, it looked, in my goggles, like a bright, glowing dot that faded quickly to red, and then darkness. The blast shoved at the shielded robe, and I felt the heat on my face. The sound of the blast thundered in my earplugs. A moment went by. I pulled up my goggles.

The ruins of Venice had been replaced by a smoking crater. The mushroom cloud towered overhead like a cowled monk of a different Order.

In sudden, unplanned fervor, the monks began to pull themselves out of the safety of the trench and march towards the crater. I, of course, was with them, though I felt like a fool.

A resonant bass voice started the tune, and the rest of us joined in:

*Dies irae, dies illa*
*Solvet saecllum in favilla*
*Teste David cum Sybilla . . .*

The Latin held a wealth of allusion lost in the English:

*Day of wrath! Day of mourning!*
*See fulfilled the prophets' warning*
*Heaven and Earth in ashes burning!*

We knelt by that smoking scar and prayed until night fell.

My limbic Key brought me back to the hallways of Centrum vomiting and almost unconscious. Someone found me and hauled me out, a long way, since it was a distant Shadow. I had no idea who it had been, though somehow I doubted that it had been a Lord.

The Medical Ward was high up and had large windows that let the sunlight in, unusual in the rest of the Centrum. It was a bright day outside, and I could see the endlessly repetitive walls and blocks of black rock that made up the home of the Lords of Time, stretching out to the horizon. There were no gardens in the pattern, no sculptures, and few windows. Centrum stretched over a large part of the continent some still called North America. I thought the Medical Ward abutted on the Rockies, but I was not sure, though I had already been here twice. My head pulsed and I felt disoriented.

The ward was filled with the real effects of Shadow. A theoretical anthropologist, his arms and legs replaced by assemblages of ebony, cedar, and ivory by a race of mechanically inclined torturers, lay spread-eagled on his bed, asleep. Each twitch in his shoulder or hip sent dozens of precisely balanced joints flipping, so that he danced there like a windup toy. In the corner lay a fat man who had been participating in a stag hunt through the forests of Calvados, in some world that still had a Duke of Normandy, when a cornered aurochs had knocked over his horse and given him a compound fracture of the femur. He'd lain in some canopied bed, surrounded by porcelain and Shiraz carpets, dying of tetanus, while the colorful but medically ignorant inhabitants of that Shadow crossed themselves and prepared a grave in the local churchyard. When the timing signal in his Key finally came, he'd pulled himself out of bed and through the Gate to the hallway, just as I had. The man in the bed next to mine, who gasped hoarsely every few minutes, had gotten drunk, wandered into the wrong part of town, and been beaten by some gang. This was familiar to me too. It could have been any town, the Emperor of Zimbabwe's summer capital on Lake Nyanza, or Manhattan, minor trading city in the Barony of New York, or Schekaagau. It didn't really matter. He moaned again.

"Ah, 'The Suffering Critic.' A work to gladden the heart of any artist." Standing at the foot of my bed, with a bouquet of multicolored daisies, was a dark, bearded man with a slight twist of amusement to his mouth. That quirk was there so often that it had permanently distorted the muscles of his face, so that he always wore the same facial expression, like a mask. Masks don't reveal, they conceal, something it was easy to forget.

Amanda had caused to be sent to me an even dozen long stemmed red roses, which loomed over me where I lay. He read the card, which just said "Get Well" and nothing else, and, with the impatient gesture of a god eliminating an improperly conceived species of flatworm, he pulled them out of the vase and threw them away. He shoved his own daisies in their place. This done, he sat down in the chair next to me with a grunt of satisfaction. "Jacob, old friend. You look like hell, and your hair is falling out."

"You're too kind, Samos."

"Do you know of any reason why anyone would want to kill you?" He peered at me to see what my reaction would be.

I stared at him for a second before I thought of a response. "Samos, I'm a critic."

"Point well taken. But you haven't answered my question."

"Samos, when you come to visit a sick friend in the hospital, you're supposed to make small talk, not start off with—"

"The fact that I suspect someone of trying to kill you?" Halicarnassus was remorseless. "Not telling you that as soon as possible would be crass impoliteness. However, if you insist. On the way here I saw some cumulus clouds. They brought a number of impressions to mind, and in fact I saw one that strongly resembled a mongoose."

I should have known better. I sighed and gave up. "To answer your question, Samos, no, I don't think someone's trying to kill me. Do you?"

He grimaced. "I'm not sure. It's just that the shielding in your robe was good, everything was in order, calculations from your dosimeter indicate that you absorbed a dose of somewhat over twenty rem, high but not fatal, and yet, you were almost dead when they got you here. Don't you find that odd?"

"How did—" I stopped. It was useless to ask Halicarnassus how he found these things out. He seemed to know all the back stairs of Centrum, including which steps creaked. "I don't, unfortunately, find getting radiation sickness after walking into a fresh blast crater particularly odd, no."

"Let me remind you of the fate of one of your predecessors, who died in a zeppelin explosion while eating *coq a vin* off a silver plate in the company of the Duc de Moscau."

I'd been trying not to think of him. "Gambino was reviewing one of Nobunaga's worlds, if I remember. His people are colorful, but tend to be indifferent engineers." I didn't know why I was arguing with him.

Halicarnassus shrugged. "He'd also revealed Lord Meern's collection of sexually obsessed societies, which caused Meern to suffocate himself, if you'll recall. It *could* all be accidental, of course. In an infinite number of Shadows, an infinite number of things happen. But here's an interesting thought. Can you conceive of two worlds that differ in only one important detail?"

It was a relief to talk shop, rather than death. I hadn't caused anyone's suicide. Not that I knew about. "What do you mean?"

"Say I create two Shadows, identical in everything, except in one the writing in books is boustrophedon, like the ancient Greeks did it, with alternate lines going right to left. It's a more efficient way of reading, really, you don't have to move your eyes back to the beginning of each line."

I liked the idea. "Or two Shadows, but in one men kiss, rather than shaking hands."

"Taking an inhabitant of one and dropping him in the other would cause no end of problems. Or better yet, trading two otherwise identical people."

"Both would end up arrested."

We laughed and explored the idea, and the thought of murder, never quite reasonable to begin with, was forgotten.

"Jacob!" Amanda finally flounced in, wearing a red dress, not one I remembered ever having seen before. She pecked me on the forehead, then sat down in the chair and rearranged the pleats of her dress until they lay in the proper pattern. Then she smiled at me. Behind her, moving silently, was Martine, holding a box. My head was pulsing again, and I felt disoriented. I blinked my eyes, but it didn't help.

Martine and Amanda were both frowning over my shoulder, as if there was something improper there. Halicarnassus stared back expressionlessly, then bowed. Amanda smiled tightly, Martine did nothing. "Good day, Jacob," Halicarnassus said, patted my shoulder, and was gone.

They had brought me cookies, airy things of almond and spice. Amanda had made them. I hadn't known she could bake. *They* brought me cookies. Symbols are not only in books, but help us see the structure of our own lives. Each cookie shattered as I bit into it, then stuck to my teeth. Martine avoided this problem by swallowing his whole.

Martine was desperate to know what Halicarnassus and I had been discussing, but didn't want to ask. I ignored his ever more pointed hints with sickbed stupidity, and left him frustrated. It was meager satisfaction. Amanda chattered, more talkative than I'd seen her in months. I watched the delicate curve of her throat and shoulders. She talked about the weather, about jewelry, about the music she'd been listening to, about art. Her tastes were dependent on the important others in her life, but she'd been mine for so long that I had forgotten, and was startled to hear her criticizing works that I loved, and thought she had also.

I lay back and listened to them, until their voices were just a buzz. Life was full of troubles, and I had more important things to worry about than exploding zeppelins.

I hadn't been in Halicarnassus's new world for more than five minutes when I saw her. I should have known better than to be in his Shadow in the first place, but I've never been able to resist an exclusive showing, even knowing his habit of unpleasant tricks. Halicarnassus had always enjoyed forcing societies into unnatural forms, unhealthy adaptations. He'd done an ornate Victorian style Europe full of confectionary palaces and light operas which practiced brutal ritual cannibalism at fancy dress dinner parties, a hereditary American Congress full of dangerously inbred religious fanatics who dressed in drag when deciding on bloody crusades against Sumatra and Ethiopia, and a North American Great Plains kept free of habitation from the Mississippi to the Rockies so that its Mongol conquerors could ride as their ancestors had, while forcing enslaved Europeans to build meaningless monuments larger than the Pyramids. His worlds seemed to disturb most of the Lords, who found them mocking, and they found few buyers. He got by, somehow, the way artists always have, and still made his art.

I came into this world on the bottom level of Grand Central Station, as if I were simply another traveler amid the scurrying mobs, who carried me up into the light of the streets above.

Just a few blocks away, near St. Patrick's Cathedral, I saw Amanda, her blond hair curled and flowing, crossing 50th Street on Fifth Avenue, obviously in a hurry. I didn't stop to think, but followed her trim, gray suited figure as she walked down the street, carrying a briefcase. The people of this Shadow did not dress brightly, or use much color on their buildings, which were disproportionately high, like the spires of iron cathedrals that had never been built. So Amanda, always in fashion, dressed here in discreet urban camouflage.

Love is a random process, depending on such improbable events as an introduction by mutual friends followed by a chance meeting in an exhibit of etchings, and a common liking for a certain sweet wine punch which now, in memory, makes me gag. Or perhaps not so improbable: I later found out that Amanda had gone to that gallery because she knew I would be there. She has never learned to like copperplate etchings, though she pretended to, at the time. The loves of our ancestors were equally random. Exact duplicates of individuals seldom exist from Shadow to Shadow, despite Halicarnassus's elaborate plans for almost duplicate worlds, so we almost never get to see ourselves in a different life. Was there a Jacob Landstatter in this world? A Salvator Martine?

So I followed her, my heart pounding. Her waist and her hips were just the same, and she swayed, enchantingly, the way she always had. When she stopped at street corners, she looked up at the tops of the buildings, shading her eyes, as if looking for roosting storks, or gargoyles. Her walk was quick, even on heels, and I had to concentrate on keeping up, difficult on the crowded street. She continued for quite a distance, finally coming to the edge of a large green park called, with no particular originality, Central Park. This was a strange, mechanical Shadow, full of flying machines and automobiles. It was incredibly noisy. She finally turned into a large gray building called the Metropolitan Museum of Art. I paused at the base of the stairs for a long moment. Banners announced special exhibits of eighteenth century French crystal, Japanese swords, and the works of a Rembrandt van Rijn. Dutch again. I was tired of Dutch. I followed her up the stairs and into the museum.

It was Rembrandt that she wanted, and she went straight there through the maze of corridors. It was an exhibit of copperplate etchings. Much of it was a series of self-portraits of that same Rembrandt van Rijn, from rather boorish youth to brooding old age, in a variety of strange headdresses. The man was obviously a genius, and I lost myself in his intricate lines.

"He is remarkable, isn't he?" she said, at my side. "I took some time off from work to come see him. This is the last day it's going to be here."

I turned slowly to look at her. Her eyes were the same too, lighter blue within dark, under long, soft lashes. She looked down when I met her gaze then glanced back up. There was no sign of recognition in her eyes. No Jacob Landstatter in this world. Until now. She smiled. Here she smelled like wildflowers, something other than violets.

We found ourselves strolling around the exhibit together, giving each other details of the various etchings as gifts. Some of her remarks were critical, and I suspected that she didn't think as much of etchings as she had initially claimed she did.

"I don't know what I should do now," she said, looking up and down the street after we emerged. "I don't really want to go back to work . . . it's too nice a day." She looked at me, then looked away.

I suggested we get a drink, and she took my arm as we walked. I felt like an idiot. What was I doing? It was a beautiful spring day, and our steps matched as we walked. She looked up again, at the corner, and we discussed the cornices of buildings, the eaves of the roof of the house she had grown up in, the strange places birds manage to relax, and hidden roof gardens in Manhattan. It had been a long time since I'd enjoyed a conversation quite that much. She flirted with intent, and smiled when she looked at me. "I've been so lonely," she said.

Suddenly she froze, then turned to look into the window of a stationery store, pretending to look at her reflection and correct her hair. "Oh shit," she said under her breath. "Oh damn. Oh *damn*. Why is he here?"

I looked up and down the street, and had no problem spotting him, no problem at all. He walked with his head held up and his arms swinging, and wore a floppy shirt from South America. His right hand was stained with chrome yellow and viridian. Still an artist, even here, Salvator Martine strode past, his eyes fixed on an image invisible to everyone else on the street, and did not see us. I looked at Amanda. She was trembling as if with a chill. Her left hand pulled at her hair, and she looked vulnerable, like an abandoned child. It was only then that I noticed the glint of a gold wedding band on her finger, and it all made sense.

"Who was that?" I asked.

"Who? Oh . . . somebody. It doesn't matter." She talked quickly. "Let's go."

I went with her, but everything inside of me had turned to ice. I managed to disengage myself from her after drinks but before dinner, to her obvious dismay. She liked me, and found me attractive. I felt a fool for still wanting her, like a small child who wants to play with shards of glass because they glint so prettily in the sun, but I couldn't help it. We made a date to meet at the Museum of Modern Art the following week, for an exhibition of Rothko. She would be there, but I wouldn't be. It would be another two days before my Key would allow me back through the gate into the hallways. They had something called television here, moving images in a box. I decided to stay in my hotel room for the rest of the time and watch it.

When I returned home, I knew Amanda, my Amanda, the real Amanda, had finally gone. There was no trace of her perfume in the air, and her things were gone from her bureau.

I walked through the entryway, down the hall, and into the quiet room, where I settled into a low couch facing the green, moss-filled garden. The chuckle of the stream flowing through it was vivid in the silence.

Why did I hurt? Because I, of all possible Jacob Landstatters, had finally lost my Amanda, out of all possible Amandas? Does a minute flux in the probability stream feel pain? Nonsense. The pain was real, perhaps, but I wasn't. I waited to vanish. But cardiac muscle doesn't know anything about alternate probability worlds, or Shadow, or feelings of unreality, or the Lords. My heart continued beating. My diaphragm continued to pull downward, filling my lungs with air. My stomach rumbled. I was hungry. I got up to make myself a sandwich.

The kitchen was clean and silent. Copper pots and steel utensils hung over the drainboard, and the red curtains puffed in the breeze from the open window. The breadbox contained half a loaf of rye bread, fresh and aromatic. Where the devil had it come from? Amanda couldn't have put it here, she'd obviously been gone for too long. I hefted it. The crust was crisp.

"Stop playing with your food and cut a slice for God's sake," a voice said behind me. I whirled, loaf in hand. Halicarnassus was sitting at the table in the darkened alcove. "It's impolite to threaten your guests with deadly viands," he observed. "Cut a slice, I said. I've got the mustard and roast beef here."

"How kind of you."

He took a luxurious bite of his sandwich. "Give it up, Jacob. Ah.

Rye, beef, and mustard. There are some aesthetic verities that transcend reality. The field of gustatory ontology has been much neglected by philosophers."

"So much the worse for ontology," I said, settling down to lunch with as much grace as I could muster. I really was quite hungry.

"So much the worse for philosophers! All this Truth and Beauty stuff is fine, but it obscures the real issues. Rye bread! I try never to create a world in which it cannot be found. One must have an absolute aesthetic criterion to give an anchor to one's life."

There are worse ones, I suppose. "Did you create that entire world to give me an object lesson about my personal life?"

"Hey, they have great rye bread in that city. Don't be such an egotist, Jacob. I put that in as a little detail, an ironic reference, like a dog crapping in the corner of a hunting scene. No artist is going to create an entire world just to please one critic's vanity. That's a real world, full of real people. Just like this one."

I had been suspicious for a long time, about the Lords, Centrum, and Samos Halicarnassus, so I decided to risk the question. "Did you create this world, Samos?"

He grimaced. "Yes, and not one of my better efforts, I must say. The Lords are an insufferable bunch, and Centrum is . . . excessive."

"Where are you from?"

He passed a hand over his forehead. "You know, I'm not even sure I remember. A lot of white stone buildings. Apple orchards. A big blue sky. Doesn't tell you much, does it? I guess it didn't tell me much either. But I remember school, a big hall with a dome, and my first world. It was a clunky thing, with brass and mahogany steam carriages and wars full of cavalry charges and solemn republics whose capital cities were always built of white marble and top-hatted ambassadors who exchanged calling cards and people who lived, breathed, and died, just like they did at home. I went to live there, a requirement for graduation, I think. I never went back. I just made worlds, Shadows you call them here, and moved on, sometimes into one of mine, usually into one I stumbled onto made, presumably, by someone else."

"So yours was the real world."

"Jacob, I've always been amazed at your inability to detach your emotions from your intellect. That world was created as a private project by a man from a culture so different from this one that my mind does not retain any information about it at all. He was ancient when I was a child, the grandmaster of the school. He died much honored, since he was, I suppose, God." He cut himself another slice of bread. "It would be nice to be certain one existed, but as long as we spend our time twisting time like this, rather than on more rational pursuits, none of us ever will be sure. Most of the inhabitants of the worlds I have created at least *believe* they exist, which gives them the advantage over us. Your Lords devised these absurd Keys in your limbic systems to give you all a sense of reality, since you always feel like you are coming home. A nice touch. You, incidentally, no longer have one."

I remembered my strange dizziness and disorientation at the medical ward. At the time, I had chalked it up to radiation sickness. "How did you manage that?"

"Friends at the hospital in Centrum, willing to do me a favor. And why shouldn't they? I created them, after all. It's really a simple modification, and performed more often than you might think, even in this most real of all possible worlds." He ate the rest of his sandwich and stood up. "Well, that's enough for now. You'll be seeing me again, I think. You're one of my more engaging creations."

"Oh shut up." I put my head in my hands. This was too much.

"Good luck on your next job."

"What do you know about my next job?"

He grinned maliciously. "It's by Martine."

I choked on my food. "That son of a bitch has taken off with my wife." I stopped. It hurt. It was surprising how much it hurt.

"Don't worry. It's no more real than anything else."

"It's no less real. My guts feel like they've been caught by a fish-hook."

"And you sneer at gustatory ontology. Good day, Jacob." And he walked out the door and was gone.

The various portions of the Chancellery Gardens of Laoyin harmonized not only in space, but in time. The arrangement of dells and lily ponds, of individual Dawn Redwoods, laboriously dug, full grown, in the fastness of Old China and brought here up the Lao River, which I knew as the Columbia, in barges built for the purpose, of stone temples with green bronze cupolas, and of spreads of native prairie, seemingly engaged in a devious wildness but actually existing because of the efforts of dedicated gardeners, took on meaning only when observed at a receptive stroll. I emerged from the yellow-green of a stand of ginkgoes, descended a gorge alongside a stream, and arrived at the rocky shore of a lake, its verge guarded by cunningly twisted pines and Amur maples. I trod the gravel path further, and felt uneasy. While I strolled, too many others strode purposefully, usually in tight groups of three or four. The vistas were ignored by men who muttered and gestured to each other. Either trouble was brewing, or the inhabitants of this Shadow had decidedly odd ideas of how to enjoy a sunny afternoon in the park.

A Bodhisattva blessed my exit with bland beneficence. In contrast to the serene order of the Chancellor's garden, the city streets beyond were a tangle. What had been intended as triumphal thoroughfares were blocked every hundred paces by merchant's stalls, religious shrines, or entire shanty towns, complete with chickens and screaming children. Under other circumstances, it would have been a swirling, delightful mess.

However, the streets had the same feeling of oppression as the park. Everywhere there were knots of people discussing dark matters. A scuffle broke out between two groups, one with dark skin and bulbous, deformed Mayan heads, shouting loudly and striking out clumsily, the other short, sibilant, with narrow catlike eyes and flat noses, darting with precisely placed energy. Suddenly abashed by the attention they aroused, both groups melted into the surrounding crowds.

"The Prince is dead." Everywhere I heard the murmur. "The Prince, murdered. Vengeance, for our Prince. Where is his murderer? He must be found. He must be killed. The. Prince. Is. Dead." Each word was a call of anguish.

I emerged onto a wide street that had been kept clear. Flat fronted buildings of basalt bulked on either side, all identical.

There was a sound down the way, the rhythmic thud of metal drums, growing ever louder. In response to some signal not perceptible to me, a crowd had gathered. Some of them were dressed in woolen robes that looked suspiciously familiar to me, but there was no time to think about it. Everyone began to sway in time to the beat. As the sound of the drums approached I could hear, over it, the baying of hunting horns. I looked up the street. Sailing towards me like an image from an involuntarily recalled memory was the Face.

"Woe!" the crowd wailed. "Oh woe! Dead. Dead!" Tears streamed down every face, and every body moved to the beat of those awful drums. "The Prince! Woe!" And the Face continued.

It was huge, at least thirty feet high, carved out of some dark, gray flecked rock. The eyes, blank and pitiless, stared into mine, and beyond me, to infinity. The lips were curved in a slight smile, like that of a Buddha, but seemed to be arrested in the process of changing to some more definite expression. What would it have been? A grin? A scowl? A grimace of pain, or anger? Or a mindless nullity? The Face was of stone and would carry that secret forever. There were creases in the cheeks, and the nose was slightly bent at the end. The Prince was becoming a god, but obviously intended to keep his nose intact. A god is not handicapped by a twisted nose.

The sculpture rested on a great wagon, each of its many wheels reaching to twice the height of a man. It was pulled by teams of men and women, volunteers. Everyone wanted to help, and unseemly scuffles broke out for places on the ropes. The drummers seated below the god's chin occasionally enforced justice by clubbing someone with their brass drumsticks. And the crowd cried "Woe!"

The Face swept by, becoming, from behind, a rough hewn, lumbering mountain of stone.

The mood of the crowd changed. Like a shadowed pool of blood in the corner of a slaughterhouse suddenly illuminated by shutters flung open on sunlight, the black despair of the crowd was revealed as scarlet imperfectly perceived. Icicles grew on my spine as shouts of rage and upraised daggers greeted the approach of the second Face. The daggers . . .

"Murderer!" they cried. "Death!" Though essentially a thirty-foot-high stone wanted poster, the sculptors had lavished no less care on this Face than on that of the Prince. Its brows were knit in jealous rage, its eyes glowered. Its lips were pulled back in a contemptuous grin, challenging us all to do our worst. Though fleshier and more dissipated than I remembered, the Face was familiar. It should have been. I looked at it every morning in the mirror when I shaved. It was my own.

The sculptors had done their work well. So compelling was the Face that no one noticed my real face as, shaking with fear, I slipped through the crowd. Their daggers, with silver hilts chased with a pattern of eyes and lightning bolts, were also familiar. The last time I had seen one, it had been sticking out of a bedpost next to my head.

Martine! It had been him the whole time. He'd sent his creations to kill me in Schekaagau, and when that had failed, he'd exposed me to radiation from his Virgin Mary, so that the cumulative dosage from my visit to Berenson's radioactive world would kill me. Hell, he'd probably locked me in my room at Cuzco. But for what? My wife? It made no sense, but then, murder often made no sense, at least to the victim. But didn't the idiot know that none of this was real?

So Martine had created this entire world just to kill me, despite what Halicarnassus had said about my ego. I should have been flattered, but it's hard to feel flattered when you've pissed in your pants and are fleeing for your life.

I quickly became lost in the tangle of streets, though I really had no idea of where I was going, or for what reason. Everywhere was equally dangerous in this city of Laoyin. The houses were all about four stories high, of cracked stucco, and leaned crazily. The air smelled of frying fish and fermented black beans. I turned a corner into a dusty square. A group of locals sat gloomily around a nonfunctioning fountain. I slunk past them, trying to look nonchalant. I almost made it.

"Look, Daddy!" a little boy said, pointing at me. "Prince!"

"No it isn't. Its—" Their knives were out in an instant. They didn't waste time debating points of tactics, but launched themselves at me in a mass. I turned and ran.

The tangled streets, confusing enough at a walk, were a nightmare at a dead run. Every few seconds I ran into a wall or the sharp corner of a building. I began to gain on my pursuers. Despite their hatred, they still had some concern for their bodies. I could not afford to have any.

I broke clear of the high buildings and found myself on a wide promenade, paved with multicolored slabs of rock and bordered on my left by an ornamental railing. Through the railing, far below, were the waters of the Lao, as they flowed towards what I knew as Puget Sound. Leaning casually on the railing, as if on the parapet of his palace, was Martine. He held a gun in his hand, slightly nervously, as if unsure of what to do with it. He had been unable to resist taking a direct hand in things, despite all of his efforts to set up a perfect trap for me. I *was* trapped. I stopped. Would he posture, preen, and carry on first, or would he simply gun me down? Right on the first guess.

"At last," he said. "At last I can have my revenge."

"What? What the hell are you talking about?"

"You have tormented and ruined me. I did my best, I poured my soul into my art, but it was not enough for you. My genius was never enough." He raised the pistol. "Say your prayers, Jacob."

"Wait a minute, for God's sake."

"Nothing can stay my hand now, Jacob. Compose yourself for death."

"I'll compose myself for anything you want, if you tell me what you're going on about. You've got Amanda, what more do you want?"

He frowned, confused. "Amanda? What does Amanda have to do with this? How can you mock my work, humiliate me, degrade me—"

I should have known. I grinned in relief. "Is that it? You're all upset because of some lousy reviews? Don't be ridiculous."

His finger whitened on the trigger. "You have destroyed me. Now I destroy you."

"For crissakes, Salvator, are you crazy? Who takes critics seriously?" I was almost in tears. Here I'd finally found someone who paid attention to my criticism, and he wanted to kill me for it. It wasn't fair.

"Make your peace with God, though I have no doubt that you'll pick enough with Him that He'll wish He never created you." Martine was proving to be an extremely gabby murderer.

A knot of people emerged from an alleyway behind Martine. Seeing that he had held me prisoner rather than killing me outright made them smile. It's always nice when someone is willing to share.

I nodded. "All right, Samos. Take him."

Martine snorted. "A feeble ruse, Jacob."

The first man in the group brushed past Martine's elbow. With a shriek, he turned and fired, blowing the man's chest open and leaving him with a surprised and offended expression on his face. Before Martine could get the barrel pointed back in my direction, the blades were into him, silver into scarlet. He screamed once. That done, the blades turned towards me. With the sharp decisiveness that makes for John Doe corpses in the morgue, I took three quick steps and threw myself over the railing into the air. I don't know if I screamed. I know that those behind me did, in disappointment. I watched the river. It didn't seem to get any closer, just more detailed, ripples, whirlpools, and flotsam appearing and sharpening as if on a developing piece of film.

I must have remembered Halicarnassus's modification to my Key subconsciously, because the next instant I found myself, sweating and soiled, in the dark hallway beneath Centrum.

She was home, sitting in the quiet room reading a book about Caravaggio. She looked up at me as I entered, smiled, then went back to her reading, saying nothing. It was not a silence that could be easily broken, for it seemed to me that it would shatter into a thousand pieces at the first word. I walked to the bedroom, took a shower, and changed into household clothes. There was no clothing out, no suitcase, and everything was folded neatly in the drawers. I breathed. The air smelled, just slightly, of jasmine. Jasmine? I went to the kitchen.

Amanda had cleaned up the remains of the final lunch Halicarnassus and I had had together. I opened the green kitchen curtains to have a view of the garden and began to pull out ingredients. Had the knives always been on the left side of the drawer? How observant was a critic? I examined the curtains. Still green. The last time I had seen them, at lunch, they had been red. That I remembered.

One Shadow differing from another in only one minor, but significant way. Amanda and I had had a discussion about those curtains.

I had wanted green, but finally gave in. My hand shook a little as I chopped the onions, as I began to realize that Halicarnassus had sent me drifting through Shadow, with no way to ever return to the world I had spent my whole life believing was the real one.

I flipped the top of the garbage can up to throw away the onion peels. Inside, crumpled, was a set of red curtains. A note was pinned to them. "You'll never know," it said. "Get used to it." It didn't need a signature.

I stir fried beef and ginger, and thought about the woman in the other room. Was this the woman I had married, who had betrayed me? Or was this someone else? If Amanda was different enough that she would not betray me, could I still love her? I was adrift in a sea of infinite worlds, so I was starting to think that it didn't really matter. I could discuss it with Halicarnassus, when we finally ran into each other again. Somehow, I was sure that we would.

When it was finished, I took the food in to Amanda. It tasted very good.

# WALTER JON WILLIAMS

## Dinosaurs

Some millions of years ago, our ancestors were tiny, chittering, tree-dwelling insectivores. We've come a long way since then . . . but evolution is a process that *never* stops, as amply demonstrated by the story that follows, which takes us six million years into a very bizarre future for an unsettling look at some of our distant descendants.

Walter Jon Williams was born in Minnesota and now lives in Albuquerque, New Mexico. Regarded as one of the hottest new talents in science fiction, Williams has sold stories to *Isaac Asimov's Science Fiction Magazine*, *Omni*, *Far Frontiers*, *Wild Cards*, and *The Magazine of Fantasy and Science Fiction*. His novels include *Ambassador of Progress*, *Knight Moves*, and the critically acclaimed *Hardwired*. His most recent novels are *Voice of the Whirlwind* and *The Crown Jewels*. His story "Side Effects" was in our Third Annual Collection; "Video Star" was in our Fourth Annual Collection.

# DINOSAURS

## Walter Jon Williams

The Shars seethed in the dim light of their ruddy sun. Pointed faces raised to the sky, they sniffed the faint wind for sign of the stranger and scented only hydrocarbons, far-off vegetation, damp fur, the sweat of excitement and fear. Weak eyes peered upward, glistened with hope, anxiety, apprehension, and saw only the faint pattern of stars. Short, excited barking sounds broke out here and there, but mostly the Shars crooned, a low ululation that told of sudden onslaught, destruction, war in distant reaches, and now the hope of peace.

The crowds surged left, then right. Individuals bounced high on their third legs, seeking a view, seeing only the wide sea of heads, the ears and muzzles pointed to the stars.

Suddenly, a screaming. High-pitched howls, a bright chorus of barks. The crowds surged again.

Something was crossing the field of stars.

The human ship was huge, vaster than anything they'd seen, a moonlet descending. Shars closed their eyes and shuddered in terror. The screaming turned to moans. Individuals leaped high, baring their teeth, barking in defiance of their fear. The air smelled of terror, incipient panic, anger.

*War*! cried some. *Peace*! cried others.

The crooning went on. *We mourn, we mourn*, it said, *we mourn our dead billions.*

*We fear*, said others.

Soundlessly, the human ship neared them, casting its vast shadow. Shars spilled outward from the spot beneath, bounding high on their third legs.

The human ship came to a silent rest. Dully, it reflected the dim red sun.

The Shars crooned their fear, their sorrow. And waited for the humans to emerge.

* * *

*These? Yes. These.* Drill, the human ambassador, gazed through his video walls at the sea of Shars, the moaning, leaping thousands that surrounded him. Through the mass a group was moving with purpose, heading for the airlock as per his instructions. His new Memory crawled restlessly in the armored hollow atop his skull. *Stand by*, he broadcast.

His knees made painful crackling noises as he walked toward the airlock, the silver ball of his translator rolling along the ceiling ahead of him. The walls mutated as he passed, showing him violet sky, far-off polygonal buildings, cold distant green . . . and here, nearby, a vast, dim plain covered with a golden tissue of Shars.

He reached the airlock and it began to open. Drill snuffed wetly at the alien smells—heat, dust, the musky scent of the Shars themselves.

Drill's heart thumped in his chest. His dreams were coming true. He had waited all his life for this.

*Mash*, whimpered Lowbrain. Drill told it to be silent. Lowbrain protested vaguely, then obeyed.

Drill told Lowbrain to move. Cool, alien air brushed his skin. The Shars cried out sharply, moaned, fell back. They seemed a wild, sibilant ocean of pointed ears and dark, questing eyes. The group heading for the airlock vanished in the general retrograde movement, a stone washed by a pale tide. Beneath Drill's feet was soft vegetation. His translator floated in the air before him. His mind flamed with wonder, but Lowbrain kept him moving.

The Shars fell back, moaning.

Drill stood eighteen feet tall on his two pillarlike legs, each with a splayed foot that displayed a horny underside and vestigial nails. His skin was ebony and was draped in folds over his vast naked body. His pendulous maleness swung loosely as he walked. As he stepped across the open space he was conscious of the fact that he was the ultimate product of nine million years of human evolution, all leading to the expansion, diversification, and perfection that was now humanity's manifest existence.

He looked down at the little Shars, their white skin and golden fur, their strange, stiff tripod legs, the muzzles raised to him as if in awe. *If your species survives*, he thought benignly, *you can look like me in another few million years*.

The group of Shars that had been forging through the crowd were suddenly exposed when the crowd fell back from around them. On the perimetei were several Shars holding staffs—weapons, perhaps—

in their clever little hands. In the center of these were a group of Shars wearing decorative ribbon to which metal plates had been attached. *Badges of rank*, Memory said. *Ignore*. The shadow of the translator bobbed toward them as Drill approached. Metallic geometries rose from the group and hovered over them.

*Recorders*, Memory said. *Artificial similarities to myself. Or possibly security devices. Disregard.*

Drill was getting closer to the party, speeding up his instructions to Lowbrain, eventually entering Zen Synch. It would make Lowbrain hungrier but lessen the chance of any accidents.

The Shars carrying the staffs fell back. A wailing went up from the crowd as one of the Shars stepped toward Drill. The ribbons draped over her sloping shoulders failed to disguise four mammalian breasts. Clear plastic bubbles covered her weak eyes. In Zen Synch with Memory and Lowbrain, Drill ambled up to her and raised his hands in friendly greeting. The Shar flinched at the expanse of the gesture.

"I am Ambassador Drill," he said. "I am a human."

The Shar gazed up at him. Her nose wrinkled as she listened to the booming voice of the translator. Her answer was a succession of sharp sounds, made high in the throat, somewhat unpleasant. Drill listened to the voice of his translator.

"I am President Gram of the InterSharian Sociability of Nations and Planets." That's how it came through in translation, anyway. Memory began feeding Drill referents for the word "nation."

"I welcome you to our planet, Ambassador Drill."

"Thank you, President Gram," Drill said. "Shall we negotiate peace now?"

President Gram's ears pricked forward, then back. There was a pause, and then from the vast circle of Shars came a mad torrent of hooting noises. The awesome sound lapped over Drill like the waves of a lunatic sea.

*They approve your sentiment*, said Memory.

*I thought that's what it meant*, Drill said. *Do you think we'll get along?*

Memory didn't answer, but instead shifted to a more comfortable position in the saddle of Drill's skull. Its job was to provide facts, not draw conclusions.

"If you could come into my Ship," Drill said, "we could get started."

"Will we then meet the other members of your delegation?"

Drill gazed down at the Shar. The fur on her shoulders was rising in odd tufts. She seemed to be making a concerted effort to calm it.

"There are no other members," Drill said. "Just myself."

His knees were paining him. He watched as the other members of the Shar party cast quick glances at each other.

"No secretaries? No assistants?" the President was saying.

"No," Drill said. "Not at all. I'm the only conscious mind on Ship. Shall we get started?"

*Eat! Eat!* said Lowbrain. Drill ordered it to be silent. His stomach grumbled.

"Perhaps," said President Gram, gazing at the vastness of the human ship, "it would be best should we begin in a few hours. I should probably speak to the crowd. Would you care to listen?"

*No need*. Memory said. *I will monitor*.

"Thank you, no," Drill said. "I shall return to Ship for food and sex. Please signal me when you are ready. Please bring any furniture you may need for your comfort. I do not believe my furniture would fit you, although we might be able to clone some later."

The Shars' ears all pricked forward. Drill entered Zen Synch, turned his huge body, and began accelerating toward the airlock. The sound of the crowd behind him was like the murmuring of wind through a stand of trees.

*Peace*, he thought later, as he stood by the mash bins and fed his complaining stomach. *It's a simple thing. How long can it take to arrange?*

*Long*, said Memory. *Very long*.

The thought disturbed him. He thought the first meeting had gone well.

After his meal, when he had sex, it wasn't very good.

Memory had been monitoring the events outside Ship, and after Drill had completed sex, Memory showed him the outside events. *They have been broadcast to the entire population*, Memory said.

President Gram had moved to a local elevation and had spoken for some time. Drill found her speech interesting—it was rhythmic and incantorial, rising and falling in tone and volume, depending heavily on repetition and melody. The crowd participated, issuing forth with excited barks or low moans in response to her statements or questions, sometimes babbling in confusion when she posed them a conundrum. Memory only gave the highlights of the speech. "Unknown . . . attackers . . . billions dead . . . preparations advanced . . . ready to defend ourselves . . . offer of peace . . . hope in the darkness . . . unknown . . . willing to take the chance . . . peace . . . peace . . . hopeful smell . . . peace." At the end the other Shars were all singing "Peace! Peace!" in chorus while President Gram bounced up and down on her sturdy rear leg.

*It sounds pretty*, Drill thought. *But why does she go on like that?*

Memory's reply was swift.

*Remember that the Shars are a generalized and social species*, it said.

*President Gram's power, and her ability to negotiate, derives from the degree of her popular support. In measures of this significance she must explain herself and her actions to the population in order to maintain their enthusiasm for her policies.*

*Primitive*, Drill thought.

*That is correct.*

*Why don't they let her get on with her work?* Drill asked.

There was no reply.

After an exchange of signals the Shar party assembled at the airlock. Several Shars had been mobilized to carry tables and stools. Drill sent a Frog to escort the Shars from the airlock to where he waited. The Frog met them inside the airlock, turned, and hopped on ahead through Ship's airy, winding corridors. It had been trained to repeat "Follow me, follow me" in the Shars' own language.

Drill waited in a semi-reclined position on a Slab. The Slab was an organic sub-species used as furniture, with an idiot brain capable of responding to human commands. The Shars entered cautiously, their weak eyes twitching in the bright light. "Welcome, Honorable President," Drill said. "Up, Slab." Slab began to adjust itself to place Drill on his feet. The Shars were moving tables and stools into the vast room.

Frog was hopping in circles, making a wet noise at each landing. "Follow me, follow me," it said.

The members of the Shar delegation who bore badges of rank stood in a body while the furniture-carriers bustled around them. Drill noticed, as Slab put him on his feet, that they were wrinkling their noses. He wondered what it meant.

His knees crackled as he came fully upright. "Please make yourselves comfortable," he said. "Frog will show your laborers to the airlock."

"Does your Excellency object to a mechanical recording of the proceedings?" President Gram asked. She was shading her eyes with her hand.

"Not at all." As a number of devices rose into the air above the party, Drill wondered if it were possible to give the Shars detachable Memories. Perhaps human bioengineers could adapt the Memories to the Shar physiology. He asked Memory to make a note of the question so that he could bring it up later.

"Follow me, follow me," Frog said. The workers who had carried the furniture began to follow the hopping Frog out of the room.

"Your Excellency," President Gram said, "may I have the honor of presenting to you the other members of my delegation?"

There were six in all, with titles like Secretary for Syncopated Speech and Special Executive for External Coherence. There was also a Minister for the Dissemination of Convincing Lies, whose title Drill suspected was somehow mistranslated, and an Opposite Secretary-General for the Genocidal Eradication of Alien Aggressors, at whom Drill looked with more than a little interest. The Opposite Secretary-General was named Vang, and was small even for a Shar. He seemed to wrinkle his nose more than the others. The Special Executive for External Coherence, whose name was Cup, seemed a bit piebald, patches of white skin showing through the golden fur covering his shoulders, arms, and head.

*He is elderly*, said Memory.

*That's what I thought.*

"Down, Slab," Drill said. He leaned back against the creature and began to move to a more relaxed position.

He looked at the Shars and smiled. Fur ruffled on shoulders and necks. "Shall we make peace now?" he asked.

"We would like to clarify something you said earlier," President Gram said. "You said that you were the only, ah, conscious entity on the ship. That you were the only member of the human delegation. Was that translated correctly?"

"Why, yes," Drill said. "Why would more than one diplomat be necessary?"

The Shars looked at each other. The Special Executive for External Coherence spoke cautiously.

"You will not be needing to consult with your superiors? You have full authority from your government?"

Drill beamed at them. "We humans do not have a government, of course," he said. "But I am a diplomat with the appropriate Memory and training. There is no problem that I can foresee."

"Please let me understand, your Excellency," Cup said. He was leaning forward, his small eyes watering. "I am elderly and may be slow in comprehending the situation. But if you have no government, who accredited you with this mission?"

"I am a diplomat. It is my specialty. No accreditation is necessary. The human race will accept my judgment on any matter of negotiation, as they would accept the judgment of any specialist in his area of expertise."

"But why *you*. As an individual?"

Drill shrugged massively. "I was part of the nearest diplomatic enclave, and the individual without any other tasks at the moment." He looked at each of the delegation in turn. "I am incredibly happy to have this chance, honorable delegates," he said. "The vast majority of human diplomats never have the chance to speak to another species.

Usually we mediate only in conflicts of interest between the various groups of human specialities."

"But the human species will abide by your decisions?"

"Of course." Drill was surprised at the Shar's persistence. "Why wouldn't they?"

Cup settled back in his chair. His ears were down. There was a short silence.

"We have an opening statement prepared," President Gram said. "I would like to enter it into our record, if I may. Or would your Excellency prefer to go first?"

"I have no opening statement," Drill said. "Please go ahead."

Cup and the President exchanged glances. President Gram took a deep breath and began.

*Long*. Memory said. *Very long*.

The opening statement seemed very much like the address President Gram had been delivering to the crowd, the same hypnotic rhythms, more or less the same content. The rest of the delegation made muted responses. Drill drowsed through it, enjoying it as music.

"Thank you, Honorable President," he said afterwards. "That was very nice."

"We would like to propose an agenda for the conference," Gram said. "First, to resolve the matter of the cease-fire and its provisions for an ending to hostilities. Second, the establishment of a secure border between our two species, guaranteeing both species room for expansion. Third, the establishment of trade and visitation agreements. Fourth, the matter of reparations, payments, and return of lost territory."

Drill nodded. "I believe," he said, "that resolution of the second through fourth points will come about as a result of an understanding reached on the first. That is, once the cease-fire is settled, that resolution will imply a settlement of the rest of the situation."

"You accept the agenda?"

"If you like. It doesn't matter."

Ears pricked forward, then back. "So you accept that our initial discussions will consist of formalizing the disengagement of our forces?"

"Certainly. Of course I have no way of knowing what forces you have committed. We humans have committed none."

The Shars were still for a long time. "Your species attacked our planets, Ambassador. Without warning, without making yourselves known to us." Gram's tone was unusually flat. Perhaps, Drill thought, she was attempting to conceal great emotion.

"Yes," Drill said. "But those were not our military formations. Your species were contacted only by our terraforming Ships. They did not attack your people, as such—they were only peripherally aware of your existence. Their function was merely to seed the plants with lifeforms favorable to human existence. Unfortunately for your people, part of the function of these lifeforms is to destroy the native life of the planet."

The Shars conferred with one another. The Opposite Secretary-General seemed particularly vehement. Then President Gram turned to Drill.

"We cannot accept your statement, your Excellency," she said. "Our people were attacked. They defended themselves, but were overcome."

"Our terraforming Ships are very good at what they do," Drill said. "They are specialists. Our Shrikes, our Shrews, our Sharks—each is a master of its element. But they lack intelligence. They are not conscious entities, such as ourselves. They weren't aware of your civilization at all. They only saw you as food."

"You're claiming that you *didn't notice us?*" demanded Secretary-General Vang. "*They didn't notice us as they were killing us?*" He was shouting. President Gram's ears went back.

"Not as such, no," Drill said.

President Gram stood up. "I am afraid, your Excellency, your explanations are insufficient," she said. "This conference must be postponed until we can reach a united conclusion concerning your remarkable attitude."

Drill was bewildered. "What did I say?" he asked.

The other Shars stood. President Gram turned and walked briskly on her three legs toward the exit. The others followed.

"Wait," Drill said. "Don't go. Let me send for Frog. Up, Slab, up!"

The Shars were gone by the time Slab had got Drill to his feet. The Ship told him they had found their own way to the airlock. Drill could think of nothing to do but order the airlock to let them out.

"Why would I lie?" he asked. "Why would I lie to them?" Things were so very simple, really.

He shifted his vast weight from one foot to the other and back again. Drill could not decide whether he had done anything wrong. He asked Memory what to do next, but Memory held no information to comfort him, only dry recitations of past negotiations. Annoyed at the lifeless monologue, Drill told Memory to be silent and began to walk restlessly through the corridors of his Ship. He could not decide where things had gone bad.

Sensing his agitation, Lowbrain began to echo his distress. *Mash*, Lowbrain thought weakly. *Food. Sex.*

*Be silent*, Drill commanded.

*Sex, sex*, Lowbrain thought.

Drill realized that Lowbrain was beginning to give him an erection. Acceding to the inevitable, he began moving toward Surrogate's quarters.

Surrogate lived in a dim, quiet room filled with the murmuring sound of its own heartbeat. It was a human subspecies, about the intelligence of Lowbrain, designed to comfort voyagers on long journeys through space, when carnal access to their own subspecies might necessarily be limited. Surrogate had a variety of sexual equipment designed for the accommodation of the various human subspecies and their sexes. It also had large mammaries that gave nutritious milk, and a rudimentary head capable of voicing simple thoughts.

Tiny Mice, that kept Surrogate and the ship clean, scattered as Drill entered the room. Surrogate's little head turned to him.

"It's good to see you again," Surrogate said.

"I am Drill."

"It's good to see you again, Drill," said Surrogate. "It's good to see you again."

Drill began to nuzzle its breasts. One of Surrogate's male parts began to erect. "I'm confused, Surrogate," he said. "I don't know what to do."

"Why are you confused, Drill?" asked Surrogate. It raised one of its arms and began to stroke Drill's head. It wasn't really having a conversation: Surrogate had only been programmed to make simple statements, or to analyze its partners' speech and ask questions.

"Things are going wrong," Drill said. He began to suckle. The warm milk flowed down his throat. Surrogate's male part had an orgasm. Mice jumped from hiding to clean up the mess.

"Why are things going wrong?" asked Surrogate. "I'm sure everything will be all right."

Lowbrain had an orgasm, perceived by Drill as scattered, faraway bits of pleasure. Drill continued to suckle, feeling a heavy comfort beginning to radiate from Surrogate, from the gentle sound of its heartbeat, its huge, wholesome, brainless body.

Everything will be all right, Drill decided.

"Nice to see you again, Drill," Surrogate said. "Drill, it's *nice* to see you again."

The vast crowds of Shars did not leave when night fell. Instead they stood beneath floating globes dispersing a cold reddish light that reflected eerily from pointed ears and muzzles. Some of them donned capes or skirts to help them keep warm. Drill, watching them on the video walls of the command center, was reminded of crowds standing in awe before some vast cataclysm.

The Shars were not quiet. They stood in murmuring groups, but sometimes they began the crooning chants they had raised earlier, or suddenly broke out in a series of shrill yipping cries.

President Gram spoke to them after she had left Ship. "The human has admitted his species' attacks," she said, "but has disclaimed responsibility. We shall urge him to adopt a more realistic position."

"Adopt a position," Drill repeated, not understanding. "It is not a position. It is the truth. Why don't they understand?"

Opposite Minister-General Vang was more vehement. "We now have a far more complete idea of the humans' attitude," he said. "It is opposed to ours in every way. We shall not allow the murderous atrocities which the humans have committed upon five of our planets to be forgotten, or understood to be the result of some inexplicable lack of attention on the part of our species' enemies."

"That one is obviously deranged," thought Drill.

He went to his sleeping quarters and ordered the Slab there to play him some relaxing music. Even with Slab's murmurs and comforting hums, it took Drill some time before his agitation subsided.

Diplomacy, he thought as slumber overtook him, was certainly a strange business.

In the morning the Shars were still there, chanting and crying, moving in their strange crowded patterns. Drill watched them on his video walls as he ate breakfast at the mash bins. "There is a communication from President Gram," Memory announced. "She wishes to speak with you by radio."

"Certainly."

"Ambassador Drill." She was using the flat tones again. A pity she was subject to such stress.

"Good morning, President Gram," Drill said. "I hope you spent a pleasant night."

"I must give you the results of our decision. We regret that we can see no way to continue the negotiations unless you, as a representative of your species, agree to admit responsibility for your peoples' attacks on our planets."

"Admit responsibility?" Drill said. "Of course. Why wouldn't I?"

Drill heard some odd, indistinct barking sounds that his translator declined to interpret for him. It sounded as if someone other than President Gram were on the other end of the radio link.

"You admit responsibility?" President Gram's amazement was clear even in translation.

"Certainly. Does it make a difference?"

President Gram declined to answer that question. Instead she proposed another meeting for that afternoon.

"I will be ready at any time."

Memory recorded President Gram's speech to her people, and Drill studied it before meeting the Shar party at the airlock. She made a great deal out of the fact that Drill had admitted humanity's responsibility for the war. Her people leaped, yipped, chanted their responses as if possessed. Drill wondered why they were so excited.

Drill met the party at the airlock this time, linked with Memory and Lowbrain in Zen Synch so as not to accidentally step on the President or one of her party. He smiled and greeted each by name and led them toward the conference room.

"I believe," said Cup, "we may avoid future misunderstandings, if your Excellency would consent to inform us about your species. We have suffered some confusion in regard to your distinction between 'conscious' and 'unconscious' entities. Could you please explain the difference, as you understand it?"

"A pleasure, your Excellency," Drill said. "Our species, unlike yours, is highly specialized. Once, eight million years ago, we were like you—a small, nonspecialized species type is very useful at a certain stage of evolution. But once a species reaches a certain complexity in its social and technological evolution, the need for specialists becomes too acute. Through both deliberate genetic manipulation and natural evolution, humanity turned away from a generalist species, toward highly specialized forms adapted to particular functions and environments. We understand this to be a natural function of species evolution.

"In the course of our explorations into manipulating our species, we discovered that the most efficient way of coding large amounts of information was in our own cell structure—our DNA. For tasks requiring both large and small amounts of data, we arranged that, as much as possible, these would be performed by organic entities, human subspecies. Since many of these tasks were boring and repetitive, we reasoned that advanced consciousness, such as that which we both share, was not necessary. You have met several unconscious entities. Frog, for example, and the Slab on which I lie. Many parts of my Ship are also alive, though not conscious."

"That would explain the smell," one of the delegation murmured.

"The terraforming Ships," Drill went on, "which attacked your planets—these were also designed so as not to require a conscious operator."

The Shars squinted up at Drill with their little eyes. "But why?" Cup asked.

"Terraforming is a dull process. It takes many years. No conscious mind could possibly enjoy it."

"But your species would find itself at war without knowing it. If your explanation for the cause of this war is correct, you already have."

Drill shrugged massively. "This happens from time to time. Sometimes other species which have reached our stage of development have attacked us in the same way. When it does, we arrange a peace."

"You consider these attacks normal?" Opposite Minister-General Vang was the one who spoke.

"These occasional encounters seem to be a natural result of species evolution," Drill said.

Vang turned to one of the Shars near him and spoke in several sharp barks. Drill heard a few words: "Billions lost . . . five planets . . . atrocities . . . *natural result!*"

"I believe," said President Gram, "that we are straying from the agenda."

Vang looked at her. "Yes, honorable President. Please forgive me."

"The matter of withdrawal," said President Gram, "to recognized truce lines."

*Species at this stage of their development tend to be territorial*, Memory reminded Drill. *Their political mentality is based around the concept of borders. The idea of a borderless community of species may be perceived as a threat.*

*I'll try and go easy on them*, Drill said.

"The Memories on our terraforming Ships will be adjusted to account for your species," Drill said. "After the adjustment, your people will no longer be in danger."

"In our case, it will take the disengage order several months to reach all our forces," President Gram said. "How long will the order take to reach your own Ships?"

"A century or so." The Shars stared. "Memories at our exploration basis in this area will be adjusted first, of course, and these will adjust the Memories of terraforming Ships as they come in for maintenance and supplies."

"We'll be subject to attack for *another hundred years*?" Vang's tone mixed incredulity and scorn.

"Our terraforming Ships move more or less at random, and only come into base when they run out of supplies. We don't know where they've been till they report back. Though they're bound to encounter a few more of your planets, your species will still survive, enough to continue your species evolution. And during that time you'll be searching for and occupying new planets on your own. You'll probably come out of this with a net gain."

"*Have you no respect for life?*" Vang demanded. Drill considered his answer.

"All individuals die, Opposite Minister-General," he said. "That is a fact of nature which no species has been able to alter. Only species can survive. Individuals are easily replaceable. Though you will lose some planets and a large number of individuals, your species as a whole will survive and may even prosper. What more could a species or its delegated representatives desire?"

Opposite Minister-General Vang was glaring at Drill, his ears pricked forward, lips drawn back from his teeth. He said nothing.

"We desire a cease-fire that is a true cease-fire," President Gram said. Her hands were clasping and unclasping rhythmically on the edge of her chair. "Not a slow, authorized extermination of our species. Your position has an unwholesome smell. I am afraid we must end these discussions until you alter it."

"Position? This is not a position, honorable President. It is truth."

"We have nothing further to say."

Unhappily, Drill followed the Shar delegation to the airlock. "I do not lie, honorable President," he said, but Gram only turned away and silently left the human Ship. The Shars in their pale thousands received her.

The Shar broadcasts were not heartening. Opposite Minister-General Vang was particularly vehement. Drill collected the highlights of the speeches as he speeded through Memory's detailed remembrance. "Callous disregard . . . no common ground for communication . . . casual attitude toward atrocity . . . displays of obvious savagery . . . no respect for the individual . . . defend ourselves . . . this stinks in the nose."

The Shars leaped and barked in response. There were strange bubbling high-pitched laughing sounds that Drill found unsettling.

"We hope to find a formula for peace," President Gram said. "We will confer with all the ministers in session." That was all.

That night, the Shars surrounding Ship moaned, moving slowly in a giant circle, their arms linked. The laughing sounds that followed Vang's speech did not cease entirely. He did not understand why they did not all go home and sleep.

*Long, long*, Memory said. No comfort there.

Early in the morning, before dawn, there was a communication from President Gram. "I would like to meet with you privately. Away from the recorders, the coalition partners."

"I would like nothing better," Drill said. He felt a small current of optimism begin to trickle into him.

"Can I use an airlock other than the one we've been using up till now?"

Drill gave President Gram instructions and met her in the other airlock. She was wearing a night cape with a hood. The Shars, circling and moaning, had paid her no attention.

"Thank you for seeing me under these conditions," she said, peering up at him from beneath the hood. Drill smiled. She shuddered.

"I am pleased to be able to cooperate," he said.

*Mash!* Lowbrain demanded. It had been silent until Drill entered Zen Synch. Drill told it to be silent with a snarling vehemence that silenced it for the present.

"This way, honorable President," Drill said. He took her to his sleeping chamber—a small room, only fifty feet square. "Shall I send a Frog for one of your chairs?" he asked.

"I will stand. Three legs seem to be more comfortable than two for standing."

"Yes."

"Is it possible, Ambassador Drill, that you could lower the intensity of the light here? I find it oppressive."

Drill felt foolish, knowing he should have thought of this himself. "I'm sorry," he said. "I will give the orders at once. I wish you had told me earlier." He smiled nervously as he dimmed the lights and arranged himself on his Slab.

"Honorable ambassador." President Gram's words seemed hesitant. "I wonder if it is possible . . . can you tell me the meaning of that facial gesture of yours, showing me your teeth?"

"It is called a smile. It is intended as a gesture of benevolent reassurance."

"Showing of the teeth is considered a threat here, honorable ambassador. Some of us have considered this a sign that you wish to eat us."

Drill was astonished. "My goodness!" he said. "I don't even eat meat! Just a kind of vegetable mash."

"I pointed out that your teeth seemed unsuitable for eating meat, but still it makes us uneasy. I was wondering . . ."

"I will try to suppress the smile, yes. Eating meat! What an idea. Some of our military specialists, yes, and of course the Sharks and Shrikes and so on . . ." He told his Memory to enforce a strict ban against smiling in the presence of a Shar.

Gram leaned back on her sturdy rear leg. Her cape parted, revealing her ribbons and badges of office, her four furry dugs. "I wanted to inform you of certain difficulties here, Ambassador Drill," she said.

"I am having difficulty holding together my coalition. Minister-General Vang's faction is gaining strength. He is attempting to create a perception in the minds of Shars that you are untrustworthy and violent. Whether he believes this, or whether he is using this notion as a means of destabilizing the coalition, is hardly relevant—considering your species' unprovoked attacks, it is not a difficult perception to reinforce. He is also trying to tell our people that the military is capable of dealing with your species."

Drill's brain swam with Memory's information on concepts such as "faction" and "coalition." The meaning of the last sentence, however, was clear.

"That is a foolish perception, honorable President," he said.

"His assurances on that score lack conviction." Gram's eyes were shiny. Her tone grew earnest. "You must give me something, ambassador. Something I can use to soothe the public mind. A way out of this dilemma. I tell you that it is impossible to expect us to sit idly by and accept the loss of an undefined number of planets over the next hundred years. I plead with you, ambassador. Give me something. Some way we can avoid attack. Otherwise . . ." She left the sentence incomplete

*Mash*, Lowbrain wailed. Drill ignored it. He moved into Zen Synch with Memory, racing through possible solutions. Sweat gathered on his forehead, pouring down his vast shoulders.

"Yes," he said. "Yes, there is a possibility. If you could provide us with the location of all your occupied planets, we could dispatch a Ship to each with the appropriate Memories as cargo. If any of our terraforming Ships arrived, the Memories could be transferred at once, and your planets would be safe."

President Gram considered this. "Memories," she said. "You've been using the term, but I'm not sure I understand."

"Stored information is vast, and even though human bodies are large we cannot always have all the information we need to function efficiently even in our specialized tasks," Drill said. "Our human brains have been separated as to function. I have a Lowbrain, which is on my spinal cord above my pelvis. Lowbrain handles motor control of my lower body, routine monitoring of my body's condition, eating, excretion, and sex. My perceptual centers, short-term memory, personality, and reasoning functions are handled by the brain in my skull—the classical brain, if you like. Long-term and specialized memory is the function of the large knob you see moving on my head, my Memory. My Memory records all that happens in great detail, and can recapitulate it at any point. It has also been supplied with information concerning the human species' contacts with other nonhuman groups. It attaches itself easily to my nervous system and draws nourishment from my body. Specific memories can be communicated from one living Memory to another, or if it proves necessary I can simply give my Memory to another human, a complete transfer. I have another Memory aboard that I'm not using at the moment, a pilot Memory that can navigate and handle Ship, and I wore this Memory while in transit. I also have spare Memories in case my primary Memories fall ill. So you see, our specialization does not rule out adaptability—any piece of information needed by any of us can easily be transferred, and in far greater detail than by any mechanical medium."

"So you could return to your base and send out pilot Memories to our planets," Gram said. "Memories that could halt your terraforming ships."

"That is correct." Just in time, Memory managed to stop the twitch in Drill's cheeks from becoming a smile. Happiness bubbled up in him. He was going to arrange this peace after all!

"I am afraid that would not be acceptable, your Excellency," President Gram said. Drill's hopes fell.

"Whyever not?"

"I'm afraid the Minister-General would consider it a naïve attempt of yours to find out the location of our populated planets. So that your species could attack them, ambassador."

"I'm trying very hard, President Gram," Drill said.

"I'm sure you are."

Drill frowned and went into Zen Synch again, ignoring Lowbrain's plaintive cries for mash and sex, sex and mash. Concepts crackled through his mind. He began to develop an erection, but Memory was drawing off most of the available blood and the erection failed. The smell of Drill's sweat filled the room. President Gram wrinkled her nose and leaned back far onto her rear leg.

"Ah," Drill said. "A solution. Yes. I can have my Pilot memory provide the locations to an equivalent number of our own planets. We will have one another's planets as hostage."

"Bravo, ambassador," President Gram said quietly. "I think we may have a solution. But—forgive me—it may be said that we cannot trust your information. We will have to send ships to verify the location of your planets."

"If your ships go to my planet first," Drill said, "I can provide your people with one of my spare Memories that will inform my species what your people are doing, and instruct the humans to cooperate. We will have to construct some kind of link between your radio and my Memory . . . maybe I can have my Ship grow one."

President Gram came forward off her third leg and began to pace forward, moving in her strange, fast, hobbling way. "I can present it to the council this way, yes," she said. "There is hope here." She stopped her movement, peering up at Drill with her ears pricked forward. "Is it possible that you could allow me to present this to the council as my own idea?" she asked. "It may meet with less suspicion that way."

"Whatever way is best," said Drill. President Gram gazed into the darkened recesses of the room.

"This smells good," she said. Drill succeeded in suppressing his smile.

"It's nice to see you again."

"I am Drill."

"It's nice to see you again, Drill."

"I think we can make the peace work."

"Everything will be all right, Drill. Drill, I'm sure everything will be all right."

"I'm so glad I had this chance. This is the chance of a lifetime."

"Drill, it's *nice* to see you again."

The next day President Gram called and asked to present a new plan. Drill said he would be pleased to hear it. He met the party at the airlock, having already dimmed the lights. He was very rigid in his attempts not to smile.

They sat in the dimmed room while President Gram presented the plan. Drill pretended to think it over, then acceded. Details were worked out. First the location of one human planet would be given and verified—this planet, the Shar capital, would count as the first revealed Shar planet. After verification, each side would reveal the location of two planets, verify those, then reveal four, and so on. Even counting the months it would take to verify the location of planets, the treaty should be completed within less than five years.

That night the Shars went mad. At President Gram's urging, they built fires, danced, screamed, sang. Drill watched on his Ship's video walls. Their rhythms beat at his head.

He smiled. For hours.

The Ship obligingly grew a communicator and coupled it to one of Drill's spare Memories. The two were put aboard a Shar ship and sent in the direction of Drill's home. Drill remained in his ship, watching entertainment videos Ship received from the Shars' channels. He didn't understand the dramas very well, but the comedies were delightful. The Shars could do the most intricate, clever things with their flexible bodies and odd tripod legs—it was delightful to watch them.

*Maybe I could take some home with me*, he thought. *They can be very entertaining*.

The thousands of Shars waiting outside Ship began to drift away. Within a month only a few hundred were left. Their singing was quiet, triumphant, assured. Sometimes Drill had it piped into his sleeping chamber. It helped him relax.

President Gram visited informally every ten days or so. Drill showed her around Ship, showing her the pilot Memory, the Frog quarters, the giant stardrive engines with their human subspecies' implanted connections, Surrogate in its shadowed, pleasant room. The sight of Surrogate seemed to agitate the President.

"You do not use sex for procreation?" she asked. "As an expression of affection?"

"Indeed we do. I have scads of offspring. There are never enough diplomats, so we have a great many couplings among our subspecies. As for affection . . . I think I can say that I have enjoyed the company of each of my partners."

She looked up at him with solemn eyes. "You travel to the stars, Drill," she said. "Your species expands randomly in all directions, encountering other species, sometimes annihilating them. Do you have a reason for any of this?"

"A reason?" Drill mused. "It is natural to us. Natural to all intelligent species, so far as we know."

"I meant a conscious reason. Is it anything other than what you do in an automatic way?"

"I can't think of why we would need any such reasons."

"So you have no philosophy of constant expansion? No ideology?"

"I do not know what those words mean," Drill said.

Gram closed her eyes and lowered her head. "I am sorry," she said.

"No need. We have no conflicts in our ideas about ourselves, about our lives. We are happy with what we are."

"Yes. You couldn't be unhappy if you tried, could you?"

"No," Drill said cheerfully. "I see that you understand."

"Yes," Gram said. "I scent that I do."

"In a few million years," Drill said, "these things will become clear to you."

The first Shar ship returned from Drill's home, reporting a transfer of the Memory. The field around Ship filled again with thousands of Shars, crying their happiness to the skies. Other Memories were now taking instructions to all terraforming bases. The locations of two new planets were released. Ships carrying spare Memories leaped into the skies.

*It's working*, Drill told Memory.

*Long*, Memory said. *Very long*.

But Memory could not lower Drill's joy. This was what he had lived his life for, and he knew he was good at it. Memories of the future would take this solution as a model for negotiations with other species. Things were working out.

One night the Shars outside Ship altered their behavior. Their singing became once again a moaning, mixed with cries. Drill was disturbed.

A communication came from the President. "Cup is dead," she said.

"I understand," Drill said. "Who is his replacement?"

Drill could not read Gram's expression. "That is not yet known. Cup was a strong person, and did not like other strong people around him. Already the successors are fighting for the leadership, but they may not be able to hold his faction together." Her ears flickered. "I may be weakened by this."

"I regret things tend that way."

"Yes," she said. "So do I."

The second set of ships returned. More Memories embarked on their journeys. The treaty was holding.

There was a meeting aboard Ship to formalize the agreement. Cup's successor was Brook, a tall, elderly Shar whose golden fur was darkened by age. A compromise candidate, President Gram said, his election determined after weeks of fighting for the successorship. He was not respected. Already pieces of Cup's old faction were breaking away.

"I wonder, your Excellency," Brook said, after the formal business was over, "if you could arrange for our people to learn your language. You must have powerful translation modules aboard your ship in order to learn our language so quickly. You were broadcasting your message of peace within a few hours of entering real space."

"I have no such equipment aboard Ship," Drill said. "Our knowledge of your language was acquired from Shar prisoners."

"Prisoners?" Shar ears pricked forward. "We were not aware of this," Brook said.

"After our base Memories recognized discrepancies," Drill said, "we sent some Ships out searching for you. We seized one of your ships and took it to my home world. The prisoners were asked about their language and the location of your capital planet. Otherwise it would have taken me months to find your world here, and learn to communicate with you."

"May we ask to arrange for the return of the prisoners?"

"Oh." Drill said. "That won't be possible. After we learned what we needed to know, we terminated their lives. They were being kept in an area reserved for a garden. The landscapers wanted to get to work." Drill bobbed his head reassuringly. "I am pleased to inform you that they proved excellent fertilizer for the gardens. The result was quite lovely."

"I think," said President Gram carefully, "that it would be best that this information not go beyond those of us in this room. I think it would disturb the process."

Minister-General Vang's ears went back. So did others'. But they acceded.

"I think we should take our leave," said President Gram.

"Have a pleasant afternoon," said Drill.

"It's important." It was not yet dawn. Ship had awakened Drill for a call from the President. "One of your ships has attacked another of our planets."

Alarm drove the sleep from Drill's brain. "Please come to the airlock," he said.

"The information will reach the population within the hour."

"Come quickly," said Drill.

The President arrived with a pair of assistants, who stayed inside the airlock. They carried staves. "My people will be upset," Gram said. "Things may not be entirely safe."

"Which planet was it?" Drill asked.

Gram rubbed her ears. "It was one of those whose location went out on the last peace shuttle."

"The new Memory must not have arrived in time."

"That is what we will tell the people. That it couldn't have been prevented. I will try to speed up the process by which the planets receive new Memories. Double the quota."

"That is a good idea."

"I will have to dismiss Brook. Opposite Minister-General Vang will have to take his job. If I can give Vang more power, he may remain in the coalition and not cause a split."

"As you think best."

President Gram looked up at Drill, her head rising reluctantly, as if held back by a great weight. "My son," she said. "He was on the planet when it happened."

"You have other offspring," Drill said.

Gram looked at him, the pain burning deep in her eyes. "Yes," she said. "I do."

The fields around Ship filled once again. Cries and howls rent the air, and dirges pulsed against Ship's uncaring walls. The Shar broadcasts in the next weeks seemed confused to Drill. Coalitions split and fragmented. Vang spoke frequently of readiness. President Gram succeeded in doubling the quota of planets. The decision was a near one.

Then, days later, another message. "One of our commanders," said President Gram, "was based on the vicinity of the attacked planet. He is one of Vang's creatures. On his own initiative he ordered our military forces to engage. Your terraforming Ship was attacked."

"Was it destroyed?" Drill asked. His tone was urgent. There is still hope, he reminded himself.

"Don't be anxious for your fellow humans," Gram said. "The Ship was damaged, but escaped."

"The loss of a few hundred billion unconscious organisms is no cause for anxiety," Drill said. "An escaped terraforming Ship is. The Ship will alert our military forces. It will be a real war."

President Gram licked her lips. "What does that mean?"

"You know of our Shrikes and so on. Our military people are worse. They are fully conscious and highly specialized in different modes of warfare. They are destructive, carnivorous, capable of taking enormous damage without impairing function. Their minds concentrate only on tactics, on destruction. Normally they are kept on planetoids away from the rest of humanity. Even other humans find their proximity too . . . disturbing." Drill put all the urgency in his speech that he could. "Honorable President, you must give me the locations of the remaining planets. If I can get Memories to each of them with news of the peace, we may yet save them."

"I will try. But the coalition . . ." She turned away from the transmitter. "Vang will claim a victory."

"It is the worst possible catastrophe," Drill said.

Gram's tone was grave. "I believe you," she said.

Drill listened to the broadcasts with growing anxiety. The Shars who spoke on the broadcasts were making angry comments about the execution of prisoners, about flower gardens and values Drill didn't understand. Someone had let the secret loose. President Gram went from group to group outside Ship, talking of the necessity of her plan. The Shars' responses were muted. Drill sensed they were waiting. It was announced that Vang had left the coalition. A chorus of triumphant yips rose from scattered members of the crowd. Others only moaned.

Vang, now simply General Vang, arrived at the field. His followers danced intoxicated circles around him as he spoke, howling their responses to his words. "Triumph! United will!" they cried. "The humans can be beaten! Treachery avenged! Dictate the peace from a position of strength! We smell the location of their planets!"

The Shars' weird cackling laughter followed him from point to point. The laughing and crying went on well into the night. In the morning the announcement came that the coalition had fallen. Vang was now President-General.

In his sleeping chamber, surrounded by his video walls, Drill began to weep.

"I have been asked to bear Vang's message to you," Gram said. She seemed smaller than before, standing unsteadily even on her tripod legs. "It is his . . . humor."

"What is the message?" Drill said. His whole body seemed in pain. Even Lowbrain was silent, wrapped in misery.

"I had hoped," Gram said, "that he was using this simply as an issue on which to gain power. That once he had the Presidency, he would continue the diplomatic effort. It appears he really means what he's been saying. Perhaps he's no longer in control of his own people."

"It is war," Drill said.

"Yes."

*You have failed*, said Memory. Drill winced in pain.

"You will lose," he said.

"Vang says we are cleverer than you are."

"That may be the case. But cleverness cannot compete with experience. Humans have fought hundreds of these little wars, and never failed to wipe out the enemy. Our Memories of these conflicts are intact. Your people can't fight millions of years of specialized evolution."

"Vang's message doesn't end there. You have till nightfall to remove your Ship from the planet. Six days to get out of real space."

"I am to be allowed to live?" Drill was surprised.

"Yes. It is our . . . our custom."

Drill scratched himself. "I regret our efforts did not succeed."

"No more than I." She was silent for a while. "Is there any way we can stop this?"

"If Vang attacks any human planets after the Memories of the peace arrangement have arrived," Drill said, "the military will be unleashed to wipe you out. There is no stopping them after that point."

"How long," she asked, "do you think we have?"

"A few years. Ten at the most."

"Our species will be dead."

"Yes. Our military are very good at their jobs."

"You will have killed us," Gram said, "destroyed the culture that we have built for thousands of years, and you won't even give it any thought. Your species doesn't think about what it does any more. It just acts, like a single-celled animal, engulfing everything it can reach. You say that you are a conscious species, but that isn't true. Your every action is . . . instinct. Or reflex."

"I don't understand," said Drill.

Gram's body trembled. "That is the tragedy of it," she said.

An hour later Ship rose from the field. Shars laughed their defiance from below, dancing in crazed abandon.

*I have failed*, Drill told Memory.

*You knew the odds were long*, Memory said. *You knew that in negotiations with species this backward there have only been a handful of successes, and hundreds of failures.*

*Yes*, Drill acknowledged. *It's a shame, though. To have spent all these months away from home.*

*Eat! Eat!* said Lowbrain.

Far away, in their forty-mile-long Ships, the human soldiers were already on their way.

# PAUL J. MCAULEY

## The Temporary King

The following story of the unexpected effects of a high-tech culture on a Future Shocked rural village begins, in its own words, "as all the old stories began"—but it ends very differently indeed.

Born in Oxford, England, Paul J. McAuley is one of a number of British writers beginning to make names for themselves in the SF world of the late '80s. He is a frequent contributor to *Interzone*, and has also sold stories to *Amazing, The Magazine of Fantasy and Science Fiction*, and to other markets. His first novel, *400 Billion Stars,* is forthcoming from Del Rey Books. McAuley works as a cell biologist at Oxford University, and lives near Oxford with his family.

# THE TEMPORARY KING

## Paul J. McAuley

I'll begin as all the old stories began, and tell you that once upon a time there was a great forest in the shadow of a mountain, and in a clearing of the forest stood a house built all of logs, and roofed with living grass. It was the home of the Lemue family, and the head of the family was my father; I was his youngest child and only daughter. That was how things were before Gillain Florey arrived.

I remember him even after all this time as well as if he had just now left the room. For I was the first of our family to see him, and I was the cause of his downfall. It was spring then, all those years ago. In the mud and new reeds beside the creek, frogs were calling hoarsely each to each; there was a scantling of green along the limbs of the dogwood and alder trees, and the flowers of the magnolias were just about blown; and every still pool was mantled with a golden scum of pine pollen, wrinkling in the wind like the blankets of uncertain sleepers. It isn't the same here, under the dome, where you notice the spring only by changes in the quality of the light if you notice it at all. When I was a child, the lengthening days and the warmer weather were only a part of it. It was like a great reawakening, a stirring; and I felt the same stirring, too.

I was seventeen then, yes, the same age as you. That's why I'm telling you this now. Seventeen, and I felt as if I had done everything that could be done in the forest. I felt trapped, closed in, by the worn familiarity of home, by the prospect of marriage. Oh, I suppose I loved Elise Shappard, but it had all been arranged by his father and mine. I loved Elise, but not in the way you'll love, freely, of your own choice. I felt that there had to be more, but I didn't know what. My family and the house and a small part of the forest were all I knew.

So that spring day, when my mother asked that someone go collect ivy sap—it makes a good red dye, and we boiled some of our wool in it—I went gladly, carrying a pot and a small knife up through the fern clumps that were just beginning to show new buds beneath the pines. And that was where I found the man.

He was stretched full out on a bank of ivy amongst the roots of a leaning pine, boots crossed one on the other, his trousers of some shiny, dark stuff, the flaps of his leather vest open on his smooth, naked chest. His face was as white as a woman's, and his hair long and tangled, like black snakes around his head. I remember how I hardly dared breathe as I looked at him, as if he were a vision conjured by the finest, most delicate of spells. And then his eyes opened. I dropped my pot and my knife, and I ran.

I made a fair commotion when I reached the house, scattering hens and geese as I ran yelling through the compound. People looked out of doors and windows to see what was happening, and I'd hardly had time to begin to gasp out what I'd seen—a man, a stranger, up in the forest—when someone cried out a warning and we all turned.

In the distance, someone emerged from the shadows beneath the trees and strolled down from the grass slope toward the house as if it were his own and he were returning to it. He briefly disappeared when he reached the ha-ha; then he had scrambled up the other side and started to cross the bare fields.

One of my uncles called, "Don't worry, Clary, we'll see him off!" and someone else swung onto a horse and, brandishing a staff, galloped toward the stranger. Behind him the others whooped and yelled encouragement. He swept past, and the stranger ducked the staff, raising his hand as the rider—it was my brother Rayne—checked his mount and turned. And then the horse stumbled, plowing into the ground in a tangle of legs and reins, Rayne tumbling over its head. Someone screamed, and someone else fired a shot that sprayed dirt a meter from the stranger's boots. Tall, white-faced, he turned to us and once more raised his hand.

The air turned white, white as the sun. It felt as if your eyeballs had all of a sudden turned inward and there was nothing in your head but cold, white fire. It was all so sudden that I didn't even feel frightened, was simply puzzled that I was lying on the ground with someone's boots in front of my face.

It was the stranger.

I picked myself up; all around, everyone else was picking himself up, too. The men shuffled uncertainly, all of their oafish bluster deflated by the magic. A dog barked a challenge and someone hushed it. We were all looking at the stranger, who was looking at me.

I felt a kind of laughter bubbling inside, a singing in my head, and I brushed at my dress and stepped up to him. I still don't know why I did it; perhaps I felt responsible.

He smiled and held out my knife, hilt-first. "You dropped this, Seyoura. I'm afraid your little pot was broken, though." The pupils of his eyes were capped with silver; there was something funny about his knuckles.

I became frightened, snatched the knife, and backed off into my mother's embrace. But the spell was broken. My father, pulling on his beard, cautiously approached the smiling stranger, then stuck out his hand, which the stranger looked at, then shook. The other men, all my uncles and brothers, began to crowd around, grinning, asking him how he had knocked us all down, how he could knock Rayne's horse over without touching it (leading the horse, which seemed none the worse, Rayne came limping up, ruefully shaking his head but grinning like the rest). My mother had once said that the games of men always required that someone be hurt, so that they would seem more important than they were; and now that it was all over with no more than a sprained ankle to show for it, they were babbling in relief. The stranger was the calm center of it all, smiling and shaking hands, telling them that his name was Gillain Florey, please call him Gil, that he came from another world.

I wanted to see more, but my mother pulled me toward the kitchen, scolding me and worrying about what might have happened in the same breath. All the rest of the day and all that evening, the kitchen bustled as we prepared a formal meal. My father had declared Florey to be the honored guest of the house.

"Which simply means extra work for us," my mother said, sitting as usual on one side of the great fireplace, her fat, naked arms resting on the arms of her high-backed chair as she watched her daughters-in-law and their children cook and carve and clean.

My grandmother, shrunken and frail in her own chair on the other side of the fire, said that outsiders always brought trouble, and it was lambing time, too; you couldn't expect the men to care about that now. I was carding wool in the corner by the door, pretending not to listen. I wanted to sit at the feast and hear all the stranger had to say, but of course I couldn't. I was only a girl. The only reports I had were the breathless exclamations of the women as they brought out empty plates and waited to take in the next course. One told my mother that the stranger claimed that his family had once lived in the countryside around, hundreds of years ago; another said that he had a little metal stick, and that was what had knocked us all down. "Fancy all this happening to us," she said, and scurried out with a platter of fruits as big as her head balanced on one shoulder.

"A three-day wonder," my mother said, picking at her own food.

"And what good will it do us? That little stick won't get the lambs born or the seed sown, for all the men gape and gawk at it."

"In my day," my grandmother said, "we didn't have any of this trickery, not even the glowing-tubes. Just lanterns and candles. Though I do like the light now. It doesn't jump about so."

"One thing's certain," my mother said. "He isn't here to sell to us, much less give anything away. Live off us awhile and move on, I shouldn't wonder. I'll have a word about that."

But I wanted the stranger to stay; I wanted to gawk, just like the men. Later that evening my fiancé rode over and we sat at the edge of the fields. His dog lay a discreet distance away, her head on her crossed paws, as I told Elise all of what had happened.

Elise was scornful. "He's probably just some fake."

"How could he do what he did? You're just jealous because your family didn't find him." I felt that the stranger was mine in a way; as if I had charmed him awake and led him to the house. Yes, just like one of the old stories. By defending him I was defending myself. "If you ask my father, I'm sure he'll let you meet him; then you'll see he's no fake. He's real, Elise."

"I don't know."

"You ask. It's all right, you'll be one of our family soon enough."

"It's not that. I just don't want to, Clary. This man'll be gone soon enough and nothing will have changed, you'll see." And he leaned over and gave me a quick peck on the cheek. I leaned against him, stroking the bumpy top of his head through his short, crisp hair. He was a tall, lean, gawky boy, but handsome enough when he smiled, and gentle. I hadn't any choice in the matter—like all marriages then, it was an arrangement; and in exchange for my hand, my father would have certain rights of passage over the land of Elise's family—no choice, yes, it's true. But I felt lucky about Elise, cared enough for him not to press him about seeing the stranger.

So we sat side by side in the twilight, the lights of the house behind us, the dark forest rising beyond the flat, bare fields. The first stars were out, and you could see a few of the swift sliding lights that Seyour Mendana had once told me were ships and whole cities forever falling across the sky. I leaned against Elise, feeling the hard muscles in his arm, his comfortable warmth, and wondered about the stranger, wondered which light he had stepped down from and why, until it was time for Elise to go.

Even after Elise had politely bid my mother good night and had ridden off, and I was lying in my own room unable to sleep, my thoughts were of the stranger, his white face and the way he had handed me my knife, the way he had lain there on the ivy in the forest, all unawares. He was somewhere in the house. The thought was thrilling and alarming, and I listened for some sign of his presence, but heard nothing except the usual night noises. And later, at last, I slept.

And the next morning, truly as if I had somehow stepped into a story where wishes come true, the stranger, Gillain Florey, came looking for me in the kitchen. He explained to my mother that he needed a guide for the day. "Just a little trip into the forest, back along the river."

My mother held the long braid that fell over her right shoulder and said that it was not the sort of thing a girl did. Florey smiled and told her, "Now, I know she goes up there because that's where she found me. And I can look after her. You saw my defenses, right?"

"It isn't exactly that," my mother said uncomfortably. I'd never seen her like that before: at bay in her own kitchen, her kingdom, as if she were no more than what she seemed, a fat woman twisting her braid in a fat white hand.

Florey's smile widened. His silvercapped eyes. His white, white teeth. "You're worried about her honor! I can assure you, Seyoura, that nothing is further from my mind. No, I need a guide, that is all, and I wouldn't divert one of your menfolk from their work. You know the problem I've been set. Well. I'm going up to solve it, if I can."

My mother began to deny precisely the thing she *had* been worried about, and Florey waved a hand negligently. "Please, you have not insulted me. No, not at all. Where is your daughter? Ah, *there*. Yes, come now . . ."

So I went with him, my heart bumping as we passed through the compound and crossed the fields, people gaping after us as if we were a parade. We followed the creek into the forest, and once we were out of sight of the house, Florey sighed and slowed his pace.

"I thought they might follow us. Well, that's all right."

"They wouldn't—I mean, you're a guest."

He smiled and I blushed. "I'm glad to hear it. I hardly slept at all last night. Even with this." He drew out, from a pocket inside a flap of his vest, a little tube.

"Is that what knocked us all down?"

"To be sure." He showed me the clear lens set in one end, and in his hand it began to shine, growing so bright that I had to look away, blinking back tears and green afterimages.

"Brighter than a thousand suns. Well, not quite, but bright enough to cause disorientation with nanosecond pulses at the right frequency.

The silver in my eyes protects me from that, you understand? The other end is a sonic caster. It'll put you to sleep, like that poor horse, but its range is limited. And that's all I have, which is why I didn't sleep much last night. But I'm a guest, you say. Well."

"What are you doing here?"

"To see the fabled ruins of Earth, of course. Escaping from civilization, if you know what that is. I can't believe the way you all live here. You're not in the net? No? Not even receivers? Not even electricity?" Each time I shook my head, his smile widened, until at last it seemed as bright as his light-stick. He laughed. "Well! Just about perfect. And no one bothers you here?"

"Only Seyour Mendana. And sometimes a flying machine brings a doctor."

"Who is this Mendana?"

"He buys the furs the men trap in winter. You're really from another world?"

"What? Oh yes, yes. Try and name one I haven't come from. Well. Looks like the M.C.C. really does keep you sealed off. About time my luck changed; perhaps I'll stay here after all. Come on, then, let's follow the river. Your father wants me to solve a problem. You really can't cross it farther up?"

"It runs too quickly, and there's a gorge, up beyond our land and the Shappards'. The creek is the border between us, you see. Down here there's only one path we're allowed to use on the other side, and we have to pay for that."

"That's what your father said."

For a while we climbed beside the creek in silence. Florey was awkward as he scrambled over the smooth white boulders the spring snowmelts had year after year tumbled from the higher slopes, and soon he was puffing and panting. As he perched on one great boulder, catching his breath, I asked at random—there was so much I wanted to ask—"What's the M.C.C.?"

He looked at me. "To be sure, the child doesn't know who owns her. The Marginal Culture Council: the M.C.C. They're what keeps you safe from the outside world—though to be truthful, if it weren't for San Francisco, I suppose the whole area would be sealed off."

"San Francisco?"

"A port. A couple of hundred kays from here. You really don't know, do you?"

"I'd like to. I'd like—" I paused, but I couldn't hold it back. "I'd like to see what it's like, outside the forest. Except I'll be married soon enough, and then I suppose I'll be too busy bringing up babies."

"To be sure," Florey said quietly. I don't think he understood me.

He got up, and we walked and scrambled higher. When we reached a smoother part of the way, he had breath enough to ask me about my family. "I guess I should know whom I'm staying with."

"You really were going to leave?"

"Really. I thought your father was after my stuff, so that's why I asked you along this morning. A hostage in case of ambush, but there was no ambush. Really, you can go back down now."

"I'd like to go with you."

"O.K."

Now it was my turn to ask about him, and he explained that he was from a very rich family who grew something that made people immortal, that his home was a castle on a world called Elysium. "People from this continent settled Elysium before the war, hundreds of years ago. In fact, my ancestors came from this very region, which is why I went to San Francisco. My yacht is there now, waiting for me. Ever heard of the Californian Collectivists? No? Oh well, it was a long time ago. Anyway, I'm fabulously rich and have little to do, so that's why I'm here. An important person. You might contrive to mention to your father that if I'm harmed, a scramble rescue team will be out here at once. So he shouldn't get any ideas about kidnapping me, O.K.?"

I nodded solemnly: I believed it all, would have believed him if he'd said that on his world, men swam through the air like fish and slept on clouds. It was only later that I wondered why, if he was able to call up help so quickly, he had been afraid of anything my father could do.

But then, walking beside him over a thick carpet of pine needles at the edge of an ever deeper channel that the creek had carved for itself, I was too happy to think.

The way grew steeper, and at last we reached the series of waterfalls and deep pools before the gorge, and climbed beside them using the narrow paths deer had made. At the top, at the edge of the cliff, Florey looked into the gorge and white water that thrashed amongst rocks toward the glossy lip of the first waterfall, then pointed upstream and shouted above the roar of the water, "That's where I'll have the sheep cross!"

"But they always go through the Shappards' land. And besides, sheep can't fly, not on Earth."

"No need. Your father explained that he has to pay each year for passage to the fields or whatever higher up."

"The summer pasturage."

"Whatever. Well, your father asked if I could help; I think he hoped I'd stride into the midst of your neighbors and drop them left and right just as I had to drop all of you last night when the men tried to make fun of me. I have other ideas." He gestured grandly. "I will have a bridge built. There, where the gorge narrows."

I couldn't see what he meant, and his talk about suspension ropes and load bearing only confused me more. "You'll see when it's done, and your sheep will cross above your neighbors' land. Better than frightening people, eh?" Then he looked away sharply. "Who's that over there?"

After a moment Elise stepped out from behind a tree, his dog following at his heels. Florey ordered him to us, and he came reluctantly, apprehension in his look. His dog watched Florey with her yellow eyes, her teeth showing between her loose black lips. I think that if I hadn't been there, Elise would have run: men and their pride.

"He's my betrothed," I said to Florey, and told Elise, "I don't see what business you have following us around. If my father knew, he'd be mad."

"This is common land, up above the waterfalls, your father has no say here. Anyway, I was on my way to lay traps for banshee." Elise was looking at the ground between his feet. "When I saw you, I thought . . ."

"It's true," his dog said, her voice a low growl.

Florey lifted Elise's chin and said, "A handsome lad, Clary." Elise twisted away, scowling. "You're lucky to be in line for such a fine, caring husband. But why does everyone think the worst of me?"

"We're not used to strangers, I guess."

"I meant no harm," Elise said. "I just wanted to see—"

"I understand," Florey said. He was looking at Elise's face, at the spike-jawed traps hung at his belt, at his dog. "Are you walking back with us, young man?"

"I really have to set the traps." Elise looked at me. "I'll see you later, Clary. Good-bye."

"Don't hurry on my account," I called as he walked away, but he didn't look back. I was annoyed by his following us, as if my independence had been diminished, as if he had already married me, already taken possession.

"You'll make a fine, handsome couple," Florey said, and put an arm over my shoulder. We walked like that all the way back: I was never so happy.

For three days things went just as Florey ordered them. It was as if he had supplanted my father's authority, yet no one seemed to notice or to mind. The men felled a tall pine so that it lay across the gorge, and another was sawed into four and, using chocks and levers, the pieces were set at either end. Under Florey's instructions a complicated web of ropes was strung between the spine of the bridge and the pillars, and a plank floor was laid. The men began to grumble that sheep would never cross it, but Florey simply smiled and showed them how to build high sides that leaned against the rope webbing. "What they can't see can't hurt them, and they'll follow their leaders. Sheep are like men, yes?"

I contrived to be near him as much as possible, taking up his food and running errands and looking after the notched stick and the weighted twine he used to work out how the ropes should hang. No, never so happy as then. He had us all under his spell, whether he was striding about and ordering the men in short bursts of energy, or sitting with his back against a pine trunk, amongst the feathery shoots, his eyes closed as I watched his white face.

And in the evenings there were his stories.

Florey would hold forth to the whole family for hours, pausing only to drink from the mug of cider I kept topped up for him as he told us about the other worlds: the singing stones of Ruby; the oleaginous oceans that girdled Novaya Rosya, boiling in summer and frozen in waxen floes in winter; the great canyon where everyone had to live on Novaya Zyemla; the beautiful empty seacoasts of Serenity. He described them all so vividly that we might have been there ourselves, and told tales at once so fantastic yet so plausible that the very trees seemed to lean closer to listen. Then he would smile and stretch all his length like a cat and say that it was time to sleep, and we would all be left gaping at each other, slowly becoming aware of the creek's babble and the mosquito bites we had not heeded, the cold night air and the babies and animals bawling to be fed.

Even Elise stayed still all of one evening, but afterwards he said to me, "Those tales don't really matter, Clary." He held one of my hands tightly, as if he were afraid I might fly away to one of Florey's fabulous worlds. And I would have, if I could.

"Gil makes them sound real. Isn't that the same?"

"He's got you bewitched, all of you in this house. That's what my father says."

"Your father's just jealous. So are you."

He ran a hand over his head, his short hair making a crisp sound beneath his palm. "I guess I am. Aren't you to be my wife, Clary?"

"Oh yes, it's all arranged."

"Except that bridge means your father won't need the bride price anymore. Do you think he'll still let you marry me?"

It hadn't occurred to me that the bridge would make so much of a difference. "I suppose it's gone too far to be stopped." His anxious look touched me: I still cared for him, I realized. "Don't worry, I'm not going to run away from the marriage."

"Then you shouldn't be hanging around this stranger, like, like—"

"You aren't my husband yet, though. So don't tell me what to do."

We stood staring at each other, angry and frustrated. The frogs were croaking to each other down by the creek; in the other direction, by the house, someone sang a snatch of an old song, her voice clear and small in the night. *O the times they are a-changing* . . . Elise swore and turned on his heel and stumped off along the bank of the creek to where he had tethered his horse, beside the ford. His dog looked at me for a moment, then yawned and turned and loped after her master.

The next morning we hadn't been up by the bridge for an hour when Florey said suddenly, "Are there any ruins nearby, Clary?"

"Some. There are ruins everywhere, I guess. Do you want to see them?"

"Yes. Right now."

"But what about the bridge?"

Florey gestured at the men, naked to their waists, who were cutting and shaping planks for the sides. "They know more about carpentry than I do. I'll have to show them how to fit it all together, but that won't be until tomorrow at least. We won't be missed." He picked up the bag that contained the food I'd brought, looked at me with his silver-capped eyes, and smiled. "Don't tell me you're scared . . ."

For a long time we walked through the forest without speaking, Florey swinging the bag at the new, tightly curled heads of the ferns. Sunlight slanted between the dark layers of the trees; once we saw a parrot fly off, and a moment later heard its shrieking alarm call. But I couldn't stay silent forever, and the question I most wanted to ask, because it was the thing I most feared, at last had to be spoken.

"Are you thinking of leaving?"

"Oh, I can't stay here forever." He grinned at me, then broke into a run; and I ran, too, chasing him through the clumps of fern underneath the trees, until at last we collapsed breathless with laughter beside the bole of an enormous pine, a grandfather of the forest.

For a while we did nothing but breathe hard, smiling at each other. Then Florey reached up to touch the trunk. "Look."

A glutinous tear of sap was oozing from a crevice in the papery bark. A scarlet beetle struggled in it. "Once upon a time your ancestors ruled over half this world, and half a dozen besides. Your ancestors, and mine. Now look at your people, ruled by Greater Brazil and not even knowing it, trapped in their little lives. Insects in amber. You're different, though, aren't you?"

"I . . ."

"Sure. You want to escape." And he leaned forward and kissed me.

I pulled back, but only a little. His silver eyes were a centimeter from mine; his hands touched my face before he sat back, smiling.

His hands . . . I caught one, the left. The knuckles were slightly swollen, and I could feel something thin and hard sliding under the bump of bone in each.

"All right," he said, and made a fist. And from his knuckles sprang claws, black and curved to a point like thorns, the one above the thumb slightly larger, a spur like that of a bird of prey, tipped with translucent gold. "I had it done a few years ago, when I signed up and out. The freighter ended up on Serenity, and this was the fashion there, briefly. Still comes in handy in fights, once in a while." He touched my cheek, and I felt five pricking points, the nearest (the thumb) just beneath my eye. Now I did jerk back, and stand.

"I thought you had your own ship. You said . . ."

Florey brushed at his forehead. "Oh yeah, that." He stood, too, brushing pine needles from his knees. "Can you keep a secret, Clary?"

"I guess."

"What I said when I first came here, about being rich and so on, that was to impress your father. So he wouldn't throw me out, so he'd take notice of me. Oh, I'm no duke, just a freespacer, but I do come from Elysium . . . and I'm not freeloading. That bridge will *work*. Understand?"

"A little." But I wasn't sure how I felt about him now, what his untruths meant.

"Come on, show me the ruins." He held out his hand, and after a moment I took it. And like a fool led him on.

The ruins began as a long ribbon of clear ground between the trees; only thick, spongy cushions of moss grew there. You walked along this and suddenly realized the rocks on either side were the remains of walls, all overgrown with grass and fern, and then you were in the middle of it, tall trees growing up through what had been houses, square doorways gaping like the mouths of caves. Some had left no trace but the shape of their cellars, deep pools of still green water over which clouds of mosquitoes swirled.

Florey poked around for a few minutes, then complained, "I thought there'd be more than this. What happened to all the machinery?"

I didn't know what he meant.

"Metal," he said impatiently, "or plastic. Christ, it couldn't all have rotted away. There must be something worth taking. What's inside here?"

He stooped at a doorway curtained with ivy, and I caught his shoulder. "You can't go in there. Bears live in some of these old places. They can be dangerous."

"So can I." He drew out his lightstick and flicked it on, pushed through the ivy. After a moment I followed, my heart beating quickly and lightly. Holding his light high, Florey stood at the beginning of a spiral ramp that curved down and down. You couldn't see the end of it. Bright colors glistened on the walls in twisting abstract patterns. You felt that you would fall into them forever if you looked for too long. Here and there mud had been daubed in crude symbols: the traces of bears. I pointed them out.

"They live in the rooms underneath. No one knows how far it all extends. They say it underlies all of the mountain." It was cold in there, and I hugged my shoulders as I peered into the flickering shadows of the spiral ramp. "The bears can be dangerous. They speak a kind of American, but it isn't much like ours."

"Our ancestors, Christ. Why did they trouble to alter bears? They were crazy, Clary, you know? They did so much damage to the world at one time that they spent most of their energies afterward putting it back together, changing animals to make them more intelligent, raising extinct species from dust. What do you think the bears are guarding down there?"

"It was all looted ages ago. Come on, Gil, please." I thought that I could hear something moving far below, in the darkness. After a moment he shrugged and turned to follow me out into the sunlight.

I sat in the shade of a little aspen that canted out from the remains of a wall, and watched Florey prowl the ruins. The sunlight sank to my bones, and I closed my eyes. After a while Florey sat beside me. His white chest, the single crease in his flat belly. His black hair tangled about his white face.

"Is it true," I asked, "about the people in the old days growing animals?"

"Surely. Plants, too. Greater Brazil may have invented the phase graffle, but it's way behind the old biology. That was all lost in the war, like a lot of things. On Elysium we lost Earth, you know."

"What's a phase graffle?"

"It keeps a ship together in phase space. A sort of keel into reality, you understand? Otherwise the entropic gradient would spatter it all over the universe."

I sighed. "I wish I knew more."

"It's a big universe outside this forest. You're better off here, really you are." His silver eyes flashed in the sunlight. His knees leaned negligently against my thigh.

I don't know how it happened; the beginning was lost in the deed. But one of us must have made a move toward the other, a word, a touch. I don't remember whether it was Florey or me, but we were tangled together, kissing, and then he began to make love to me and I surrendered. It didn't last long. Afterward I lay still while Florey rearranged his clothing and said, to the ruins, to the sky, "A virgin! Well, well. A virgin!" He seemed both delighted and amused.

A stone was digging into my shoulder, and my skin stung where his claws had scratched all down my sides, but I lay in a kind of haze of fulfillment. I had changed something, made a move all my own; and as I tenderly watched Florey, I imagined leaving the forest with him, rising amongst the lights in the sky with him . . . and then I remembered Elise. A kind of panic seized me, and I began to cry, although there were no tears, just a sort of racking hiccup attack, absurd and not at all romantic. Of course Florey tried to comfort me, and that made things worse.

"I won't tell," he said. "Don't worry."

"It's not that. It's . . ."

"Your fiancé, yeah. He kind of hates me, doesn't he?"

"He's just . . . just a jealous kid."

"Listen, Clary, I'm maybe ten years older than he, but that's all. I'm human, too. I didn't ask to be raised into some kind of god." As if the thought had struck something in him, he repeated, slowly, "Some kind of god. Jesus Christ."

"I think you could be head of my family if you wanted."

"No, Clary, see, your father tolerates me because I'm helping him, raising his prestige. That's all. Listen, I'll have a talk with your young man, set him straight. He's kind of cute, you know. I'd be unhappy to think he dislikes me."

"I don't see how—"

But Florey smiled. "Don't I have a way with words, now? Come on, smile. That's it. I'll fix it up, you'll see. You ride a horse?"

"Not often."

"But you have, yes?" All at once he was brutally businesslike. "So don't worry about your maidenhead, O.K.?"

I said helplessly, "I love you," and felt the guilty pang that goes with letting slip a lie, and didn't know why. Of course I know now that I was in love not with Florey but with the idea he represented, the idea of freedom, of flying away from the forest.

"You can't come with me, Clary. My life is kind of complicated right now."

"You've done something wrong, haven't you?"

He was silent for a moment. His silver eyes were unfathomable, and I began to feel afraid. Then he sighed. "Yeah, you could say that. You won't tell anyone."

"Oh, we both have our secrets to keep." Everything, the bright sunlight spinning amongst the new leaves of the aspen, the soft green ruins, the spring air, mocked me. I was a dark, discordant blot in the center of it all. When Florey held out his hand to help me up, I ignored it, and we didn't touch, and hardly talked, all the way back.

At the house, I went straight to my room and scrubbed the dried blood from my thighs and my dress with cold, clean water, rinsing over and over until my skin was red and sore. Then I lay down and cried—real, hot tears, but not for long—and went down to the kitchen and helped prepare supper as if nothing had happened. If my mother noticed anything, she kept it to herself.

That evening as usual, Florey sat out near the creek with a half-circle of people before him as he recounted one of his stories. I could hear his lilting cadence from my bedroom window, all meaning botched by distance, and I had to pull my bolster over my head so I could sleep.

The next morning I didn't go up into the forest but worked in the kitchen, preparing vegetables and then scrubbing the long, scarred pine table until it shone white and my fingers were raw. It was a kind of penance. My mother watched me work, and at last brought me a parcel of food.

"You'll be carrying this up to your friend, I suppose."

I had to take it: to refuse would have been to admit that something had happened.

"Clary," my mother said, and brushed her long hair back from her round face. "Child, I haven't said anything before, but be careful. He's a stranger, remember, not our own kind."

"Don't be stupid, Mother."

"Don't you be, Clary, that's all. Think of Elise. You're hurting him, and by doing that you're hurting both families. Life has to go on, Clary."

"Oh, of course. Everything has to be as it always was." My grandmother was watching me, from her corner, her sunken eyes bright in her wrinkled face, and suddenly I felt trapped. I grabbed the parcel and ran out, was crossing the fields before I remembered that I didn't want to see Florey.

But he wasn't at the bridge; my father told me that the Seyour Florey had gone on up. "He said that he wanted to see what it was like. An odd one, eh, Clary?"

I remembered what Florey had said about seeing Elise, and felt cold. Things were getting out of control. I would have fled after him, but my father began to tell me about the work on the bridge. This was meant kindly enough; he thought that I was interested, didn't see my panicky impatience. "I don't know why we didn't think of it before, but it's a fine idea." He scratched his grizzled beard. "You're like me, aren't you, Clary? You like new things. Not like your mother, keeping herself in her kitchen." For it was my father's idea, not wholly inaccurate, that my mother was forever plotting against him.

My brother Rayne was chopping a pine log into wedges while my father talked: the sound of his ax rang amongst the trees, and each blow was like a blow in my heart. At last I could bear it no longer.

"I have to go," I said, "so the Seyour gets his lunch."

"Oh, he'll be down with us soon enough. Wait up, Clary!"

But I was already halfway across the new bridge, the rough, unseasoned planking swaying under my bare feet so that I had to cling to the rope hand-guide. The cladding was finished on only one side; on the other side I could see, fifty meters below, thrashing white water. Droplets stung my face as I went, and then I was safe on the other side and I turned to wave to my father before I went on, climbing through the forest toward the high pastures.

I left the trees behind, and fresh breezes blew down the grassy slopes into my face; beneath my feet the turf was as warm as fresh-baked bread. Our family's sheep should have been at pasture by then, but the men were waiting until the bridge was built, and their small, turf-roofed hogans were shuttered and empty. Higher up I could see the Shappards' flocks slowly moving against the green mountainside; higher still, the snow-covered double peak flashed in the sunlight.

My worries seemed to fall away as I climbed, insignificant beneath the vast blue sky. I dissolved in the breathless now of the spring day, swinging the greasy parcel of food as I tramped upward, stopping now and then to sprawl on the turf and look at the line of the forest below, the long, tree-clad ridges that saddled away on either side, vanishing into the hazy distances. Someday I would find out what was beyond them, even though I would be married to Elise. If my mother could handle my father, I could handle him.

And then I saw Elise's dog.

She came running toward me at her full speed, overshooting and turning back to posture frantically, so excited that her few words were no more than panting barks. "'ome, 'ome," she managed to say at last, "follow me, 'lary!"

I asked what was wrong, but all she would say was, "Ba'. Ba' thing. 'ome!" And she grabbed my wrist, pricking it all round with her teeth, tugging gently but impatiently.

Sheep scattered before us as I followed her, the bells of the leaders clonking dully. A high bluff jutted out of the slope, cloaked in blueberry bushes. When we reached it, the dog circled me, then growled, "Ba' thing," and led me through the bushes.

And there, in a hollow on the other side of the bushes, I saw them. Elise and Florey.

Both were naked, moving like starfish on each other.

And I ran, plunging through the bushes with the dog at my heels, out pacing her as she turned back to her master. I remember thinking that I mustn't drop the parcel of food, otherwise they would know who had been there. That seemed important at the time. If they didn't see me, it would be all right. I didn't stop running until I reached the first trees, and then I had to stop, and leaned against the fragrant bark of a pine as I sobbingly caught my breath.

At last I could go on, and I took the old path down, my mind as empty as the shafts of sunlight that fell between the trees. The path followed a ridge around the valley in which the Shappards' house lay, its tangle of roofs and pinnacles small in the distance as a toy's, and I broke into a run again, crossing the ridge and plunging down through the trees, leaping from white stone to white stone at the ford and running on toward my own house. My mother was in the yard feeding the chickens—and then she saw me and dropped the little sack of grain just as I crashed into her oh so familiar bulk.

It all came out in bits and pieces. I would start to say something and then begin to cry, shaking my head away from my mother's soothing hand. But my mother was calmly insistent, listening to all I had to say but not believing any of it until I timorously showed her the scratches Florey had made along my flanks.

"Child, child."

My aunts were all there, too, by now, watching me to see if I would explode or change into a lizard, do something at once wonderful and dreadful. But I did nothing except cry, quietly and steadily now, sniffling and wiping my nose on the back of my hand.

"Child, child."

"Something," my grandmother pronounced from her corner, "something must be done. Or he'll bring ruin to us all."

"Stop crying, child," my mother told me. "We'll think of something."

"How can we do anything against him?" It was my aunt Genive, nervous as a squirrel. "I mean, with that stick of his, even the men couldn't—"

"Men, Jenny, know nothing useful," my mother said. "We'll be more subtle. Go on now and get some ivy leaves. A double handful will suffice."

Genive opened her mouth, then saw my mother's expression and darted out of the kitchen.

"What—what are you going to do?"

"Wipe your nose, child. We'll befuddle this Seyour Florey, that's what, and take him down a peg or two as he deserves. Duke indeed. He won't stay around here when we've done." She lifted out the flagon of cider cooling in a tub of water and poured it into a pan on the stove. The sweet, sharp smell of apples filled the room as she stirred, and when Genive brought in bunches of ivy, my mother plucked the leaves and one by one dropped them into the pan. In her corner, my grandmother chuckled and nodded.

"The old ways, oh yes. He'll see."

"You taught me," my mother said. Every face was intent on her as she stirred; we must have looked like a coven of witches. Now the smell of apples was tinged with something earthy and bitter. My mother lifted the pan from the stove and said, "We'll strain it when it's cool. Clary, tonight you'll pour the Seyour Florey's drink for him when he tells his lies, and make sure he has his fill."

I nodded, although I didn't understand.

"You'll see," my mother said, and rumpled my hair. "Now, tell me what you know of his weapons."

As Florey talked that evening, spinning out a tale about the jungles of Pandora and the old ruins hidden within them, I sat at his elbow and topped up his mug with the adulterated cider as my mother had ordered. Earlier, Florey had cornered me in the yard and told me that everything was all right with Elise, he would come down later on and make up with me.

I nodded, not trusting myself to speak.

"You're trembling. You're not frightened of me, now. After our time in the ruins?"

"A little."

He laughed and looked around—no one was about—and bent and printed a kiss on my lips that burned all evening. Later, when I came up to him as people were settling around the stump on which he sat, a king with his court at his feet, and poured his first mug of cider, he winked at me and whispered, "Don't worry, Clary," and drank off a draft. I looked away, ashamed at my betrayal but feeling at the same time a sick eagerness for it to be over: that image of Florey and Elise burned in my mind as Florey's kiss burned on my lips.

As ever, Florey gulped down several mugs of cider as he wove the spell of his tale, my family spread before him and the evening darkening beyond the various ridges of the house. My mother was in the front of the audience, flanked by my aunts like a queen amongst her attendants, a gnarled walking stick I recognized as my grandmother's lying like a scepter in her lap. I couldn't stop looking at her.

"More cider," Florey said, and I quickly poured, spilling some. He drank and held out the mug again, said to no one in particular, "Best drug in all the worlds, alcohol, because it's the oldest. Though I've something in my pack that would make you all feel as if you were in the very hands of your God." He drank again, then pushed the mug into my face, saying, "Drink, too, girl, go on." I closed my eyes and sipped. Sweet, with the faintest bitter tang beneath. My mother had put in mead to disguise the taste of the ivy. Florey tilted the mug, but I closed my mouth so that the cider ran down my chin and spilled onto my dress.

"Flower of the forest, this girl. Where was I? Yes, the ruins, circled by bare ground that had been poisoned to keep out the jungle, the ruins in the sunlight. Picture it," he said, and briefly closed his eyes. "But you all know about ruins, yes? Ruins all over the Earth. They're all around you. You're living out your lives"—he belched—"your lives in the wreckage of the past. It's in your faces, I see it in your faces. Christ, and your eyes, too, like holes in the past." Florey leaned forward, staring intently at his audience. I could see a dark rim of dilated pupil circling the silver caps in his eyes. "You're feeding on me, on my words. No more."

People began to whisper; I saw Rayne say something to my father, who nodded grimly. The spell had been broken.

Florey staggered to his feet. "No more, no more tonight." He swayed, and cider spilled from the mug. "No more. Head too thick. Fresh air and exercise. Clary—" Florey reached for me.

"No!" It was my mother, on her feet, with my aunts rising around her. Florey turned and reached inside his vest, and my mother swung at him with the stick, knocking aside his arm and sending him sprawling, striking him again as he tried to rise. Then all the women were upon him, and I saw his hands amongst them, claws extended, slashing and slashing again, and somehow he was free, staggering back while Aunt Genive knelt over a puddle of blood, her own blood dripping from her torn face. My mother stood over her; Florey's lightstick was in her hand.

The men were all on their feet now, and my father started to say something but my mother silenced him with a look. "He raped Clary. This guest you brought under our roof. He'll die for it."

Florey held out his hands, glancing at the crowd behind my mother, glancing at me. "You can't hurt me with that," he said. "I have protection, remember?"

"But I can put you to sleep," my mother said. "I know how to do it: my daughter told me."

"Ah, your daughter."

Then Florey sprang, but not at my mother. I was seized and spun and found myself pulled tightly against him, his claws at my throat. "You can't put us both to sleep. Give me my weapon."

My mother shook her head. Some of the men were beginning to edge out of the crowd, and Florey called to them. "If you love this girl, you won't go for your guns, or follow me either. I'm walking backward now. Don't follow. Come on, Clary."

His right arm crushed my right breast; his claws pricked my throat. I moved backward with him, stepping amongst the seedlings in the newly turned field, then onto the rough grass beyond. My mother stood still, my family gathered behind her. Then Florey grabbed my wrist and yelled, "Run!" and dragged me toward the trees. People shouted and a deadening tingle started up my back; then we were in the darkness beneath the pines, my feet flying of their own accord as I struggled to keep up with Florey's long strides. His grip was a circle of pain on my upper arm; when at last we stopped and he let go I felt blood trickle down my side from the four closely spaced wounds made by his claws.

Florey looked back through the dark trees. "Sonics work only at close range," he said. "Fortunately. I thought we were almost done for, girl, but they aren't following. Not yet, anyway. Come on."

"They might leave you alone if you let me go."

"I don't think so. You'll have to come with me after all. Don't cry. You wanted adventure." He pulled me close, stooping so that his eyes glittered a handbreadth from mine. His breath was sickly sweet. "There was something in that cider. My heart is pounding in my head."

"My mother—"

"Oh, of course, your mother." He gripped my arm, and as we half-walked, half-ran through the dark forest, he talked and talked, his fear bleeding out in ravings and threats and sheer bluster that I hardly remember now. All of us in the forest were barbarians was the gist of it; we had betrayed our inheritance. "Elysium sank low enough when war cut us off from Earth, but not as low as you. Just two hundred klicks away, girl, ships lift for every world in the Federation, while here it's all superstition and darkness. Christ! First you tried to make me into some kind of god, and now this."

He gave me a little shake, glared at me, and dragged me on. We were near the bridge now.

And then I saw someone coming toward us through the shadows. It was Elise. When his dog recognized Florey, she growled, her ears flat. Florey whispered to me, "Keep quiet, girl. Or I'll mark you so no one'll want you."

Elise hailed us cheerfully enough, but he was obviously puzzled. Florey grinned. "We're just out for an evening stroll. Hoped we'd run into you. How are you, boy?"

"It's dangerous in the forest at night." Elise was looking at me; I tried to smile, failed, and looked away.

"Don't worry, boy. You know my weapons. Remember? Go on down and we'll follow in a bit. I want to see how the bridge is holding up. Clary's father was asking after you earlier, seems he wants a word with you about something."

"Is it all right, Clary?"

Florey was watching Elise now, and had let go of my arm. It was my last chance, and I took it. I said, "I saw you both, this afternoon."

For a moment neither Florey nor Elise understood; then it struck them both. Florey slashed at me, but Elise's dog reached him first, knocking him down and climbing his chest, growling. Florey's fist swept across her muzzle, and the growl became a high-pitched whine that cut off as Florey slashed again. I backed away until I fell over something, a pile of pine wedges with an ax beside it. As Florey scrambled to his feet, I threw the ax to Elise.

"Now boy. Now Elise . . ." Step-by-step, Florey moved toward Elise, who slowly backed away, the ax raised at his shoulder. "Remember what you told me, what I told you this afternoon? You don't want her, I know; I can give you everything you want. Come on now."

Elise's face was a white blur in the twilight; I couldn't see his expression. He had reached the edge of the gorge and glanced at the drop behind him before he said, "No."

"Then I'll go. That will be all right, yes?" That cloying voice, smooth and sticky as honey. "Just go, leave you be." He was almost on Elise now. I couldn't move. And Florey reached out, just as Elise brought the ax down.

The blow swung Florey around. He sank to his knees, clutching at his chest; darkness spilled over his white fingers. Elise swung again. Without a sound, Florey toppled over the edge.

After a moment, Elise threw the ax after him, turned to me. "I love you," he said, and ran. I called after him as he plunged across the bridge, but he didn't look back. Soon he was lost amongst the trees on the other side.

There isn't much more to tell. Outsiders came looking for Florey a few weeks later; it seemed that he had killed someone important in San Francisco and had been on the run ever since. But we had burned his body—it had washed up by the ford—and told them nothing. My father had the bridge cut down: I think my mother made him do it. For a while I used to climb up to the clearing where it had been and sit alone and think, but then I became betrothed to someone else.

No, not your father. I'm not quite done.

Things had changed. Florey's stories had spread amongst the families, and month by month a few people left the forest for the larger world; in turn, this slow exodus brought the curious to us, off-world tourists in search of the more outré corner of Earth, illegal hunting parties, once an archaeological team that spent an entire summer digging over the ruins where Florey had taken me.

And Elise came back, just once. Two years after he'd run away. He'd become a freespacer, sailing the sea of space between the stars, had gained a swaggering, bold manner and sought to impress us with wild tales of the wonders he'd seen.

But we were no longer in need of stories. The old days were dead, buried with Florey, our oh so temporary king. They won't come again. Soon after Elise left the forest, I left, too, abandoning my family and the kindly, slow-witted man to whom I'd been betrothed, whom I'd never really loved. And came to the city, yes, and met your father. As for the rest, well, you know it as well as I.

# NEAL BARRETT, JR.

## Perpetuity Blues

Neal Barrett, Jr. made his first sale in 1959, and for the last thirteen years, has been a full-time free lancer. His short fiction has appeared in *The Magazine of Fantasy and Science Fiction, Galaxy, Isaac Asimov's Science Fiction Magazine, Amazing, Omni, Fantastic, If,* and elsewhere; his novels include *Stress Pattern, Karma Corps*, and the four-volume Aldair series. Born in San Antonio, Texas, he now lives in Dallas with his family, a dog, and a cat. His story "Sallie C" was in our Fourth Annual Collection.

Nineteen eighty-seven was a particularly good year for Barrett. His first hardcover novel, *Through Darkest America*, was published as part of the *Isaac Asimov Presents* series from Congdon & Weed, and received a good deal of enthusiastic critical response. During the year he published a string of brilliant, gonzo, and unique stories—"Perpetuity Blues," "Highbrow," "Diner," "Class of '61"—that have been exciting strong reader response as well as a slew of Nebula recommendations. Any one of these stories might well have been worthy of inclusion in a "Best" anthology—and, indeed, another one of them appears later in this collection—but my favorite is the one that follows, the funniest story you're likely to read this year (and possibly the strangest), in which Barrett regales us with the odd misadventures of little Maggie.

# PERPETUITY BLUES

## Neal Barrett, Jr.

On Maggie's seventh birthday she found the courage to ask Mother what had happened to her father.

"Your father disappeared under strange circumstances," said Mother.

"Sorghumdances?" said Maggie.

"Circumstances," said Mother, who had taught remedial English before marriage and was taking a stab at it again. "Circumstances: a condition or fact attending an event or having some bearing upon it."

"I see," said Maggie. She didn't, but knew it wasn't safe to ask twice. What happened was Daddy got up after supper one night and put on his cardigan with the patches on the sleeves and walked to the 7-11 for catfood and bread. Eight months later he hadn't shown up or called or written a card. Strange circumstances didn't seem like a satisfactory answer.

Mother died Thursday afternoon. Maggie found her watching reruns of "Rawhide" and "Bonanza." Maggie left South Houston and went to live with Aunt Grace and Uncle Ned in Marble Creek.

"There's no telling who he might of met at that store," said Aunt Grace. "Your father wasn't right after the service. I expect he got turned in Berlin. Sent him back and planted him deep in Montgomery Wards as a mole. That's how they do it. You wait and lead an ordinary life. You might be anyone at all. Your control phones up one day and says 'the water runs deep in Lake Lagoda' and that's it. Whatever you're doing you just get right up and do their bidding. Either that or he run off with that slut in appliance. I got a look at her when your uncle went down to buy the Lawnboy at the End-of-Summer Sale. Your mother married beneath her. I don't say I didn't do the same. The women in our family got no sense at all when it comes to men. We come from good stock but that doesn't put money in the bank. Your grandfather Jack worked directly with the man who invented the volleyball net they use all over the world in tournament play. Of course he never got the credit he deserved. This family's rubbed elbows with greatness more than once but you wouldn't know it. Don't listen to your Uncle Ned's stories. And for Christ's sake don't ever sit on his lap."

Maggie found life entirely different in a small town. There were new customs to learn. Jimmy Gerder and two other fourth graders took her down to the river after school and tried to make her take off her pants. Maggie didn't want to and ran home. After that she ran home every day.

Uncle Ned told her stories. Maggie learned why it wasn't a good idea to sit on his lap. "There was this paleontologist," said Uncle Ned, "he went out hunting dinosaur eggs and he found some. There was this student come along with him. It was this girl with nice tits is who it was. So this paleontologist says, 'be careful now, don't drop 'em, these old eggs are real friable.' And the girl says, 'hey that's great, let's fry the little fuckers.' " Uncle Ned nearly fell out of his chair.

Maggie didn't understand her uncle's stories. They all sounded alike and they were all about scientists and girls. Ned ran the hardware store on Main. He played dominoes on Saturdays with Dr. Harlow Pierce who also ran Pierce's Drugs. On Sundays he watched girls' gymnastics on TV. When someone named Tanya did a flip he got a funny look in his eyes. Aunt Grace would get Maggie and take her out in the car for a drive.

Maggie found a stack of magazines in the garage behind a can of kerosene. There were pictures of naked girls doing things she couldn't imagine. There were men in some of the pictures and she guessed they were scientists, too.

Aunt Grace and Uncle Ned were dirt poor but they gave a party for Maggie's eighth birthday. Maggie was supposed to pass out invitations at school but she threw them all away. Everyone knew Jimmy Gerder chased her home and knew why. She was afraid Aunt Grace would find out. Uncle Ned gave her a Philips screwdriver in a simulated leather case you could clip in your pocket like a pen. Aunt Grace gave her a paperback history of the KGB.

Maggie loved the freedom children enjoy in small towns. She knew everyone on Main who ran the stores, the people on the streets and the people who came in from the country Saturday nights. She knew Dr. Pierce kept a bottle in his office and another behind the tire in his trunk. She knew Mrs. Betty Keen Littler, the coach's wife, drove to Austin every Wednesday to take ceramics and came back whonkered with her shoes on the wrong feet. She knew about Oral Blue, who drank wine and acted funny and thought he came from outer space. Oral was her favorite person to watch. He drove a falling-down pickup and lived in a trailer by the river. He came into town twice a week to fix toasters and wire lamps. No one knew his last name. Flip Gator who ran Flip Gator's Exxon tagged him Oral Blue. Which fit because Oral's old '68 pickup was three shades of Sear's exterior paint for fine homes. Sky Blue for the body. Royal blue for fenders. An indeterminate blue for the hood. Oral wore blue shirts and trousers. Blue Nikes with the toes cut out and blue socks.

"Don't get near him," said Aunt Grace. "He might of been turned. And for Christ's sake don't ever sit in his lap."

Maggie kept an eye on Oral when she could. On Tuesdays and Thursdays she'd run home fast with Jimmy Gerder on her heels and duck up the alley to the square. Then she'd sit and watch Oral stagger around trying to pinpoint his truck. Oral was something to see. He was skinny as a rail and had a head too big for his body. Like a tennis ball stabbed with a pencil. Hair white as down and chalk skin and pink eyes. A mouth like a wide open zipper. He wore a frayed straw hat painted pickup-fender blue to protect him from the harsh Texas sun. Uncle Ned said Oral was a pure-bred genetic albino greaser freak and an aberration of nature. Maggie looked it up. She didn't believe anything Uncle Ned told her.

Ten days after Maggie was eleven Dr. Pierce didn't show up for dominoes and Ned went and found him in his store. He took one look and ran out in the street and threw up. The medical examiner from San Antone said Pierce had sat on the floor and opened forty-two-hundred pharmaceutical-type products, mixed them in a five-gallon jug and drunk most of it down. Which accounted for the internal explosions and extreme discoloration of the skin.

Maggie had never heard about suicide before. She imagined you just caught something and died or got old. Uncle Ned began to drink a lot more after Dr. Pierce was gone. "Death is one of your alternate lifestyles worth considering," he told Maggie. "Give it some thought."

Uncle Ned became unpleasant to be around. He mostly watched girls' field hockey or Eastern Bloc track and field events. Maggie was filling out in certain spots. Ned noticed her during commercials and grabbed out at what he could. Aunt Grace gave him hell when she caught him. Sometimes he didn't know who he was. He'd grab and get Grace, and she'd pick up something and knock him senseless.

Maggie stayed out of the house whenever she could. School was out and she liked to pack a lunch and walk down through the trees at the edge of town to the Colorado. She liked to wander over limestone hills where every rock you picked up was the shell of something tiny that had lived. The sun fierce-bright and the heat so heavy you could see it. She took a jar of ice water and a peanut butter sandwich and climbed up past the heady smell of green salt-cedar to the deep shade of big live oaks and native pecans. The trees here were awesome, tall and heavy-leafed, trunks thick as columns in a bad Bible movie. She would come upon the ridge above the river through a tangle of ropy vine, sneak quietly to the edge and look over and catch half a hundred turtles like green clots of moss on a sunken log. Moccasins crossed the river, flat heads just above the water leaving shallow wakes behind. She would eat in the shade and think how it would be if Daddy were there. How much he liked the dry rattle of locusts in the summer, the sounds that things made in the wild. He could tell her what bird was across the river. She knew a crow when she heard it, that a cardinal was red. Where was he? she wondered. She didn't believe he'd been a mole at Montgomery Wards. Aunt Grace was wrong about that. Why didn't he come back? He might leave Mother and she wouldn't much blame him if he did. But he wouldn't go off and leave *her*.

"I don't want you to be dead," she said aloud. "I can think of a lot of people who it's okay if they're dead, but not you."

She dropped pieces of sandwich into the olive-colored water. Fish came up and sucked them down. When the sun cut the river half in shadow she started back. There was a road through the woods, no more than ruts for tires but faster than over the hills. Walking along thinking, watching grasshoppers bounce on ahead and show the way. The sound came up behind her and she turned and saw the pickup teeter over the rise in odd dispersions of blue, the paint so flat it ate the sun in one bite. Oral blinked through bug spatters, strained over the wheel so his nose pressed flat against the glass. The pickup a primary disaster, and Oral mooning clown-faced, pink-eyed, smiling like a zipper, and maybe right behind some cut-rate circus with a pickled snake in a jar. He spotted Maggie and pumped the truck dead; caliche dust caught up and passed them both by.

"Well now, what have we got here?" said Oral. "It looks like a picnic and I flat missed it good. Not the first time, I'll tell you. I smell peanut butter I'm not mistaken. You want to get in here and ride?"

"What for?" said Maggie.

"Then don't. Good afternoon. Nice talking to you."

"All right. I will." Maggie opened the door and got in. She couldn't say why, it just seemed like the right thing to do.

"I've seen you in town," said Oral.

"I've seen you too."

"There's a lot more to life than you dream of stuck on this out of the way planet I'll tell you that. There's plenty of things to see. I doubt you've got the head for it all. Far places and distant climes. Exotic modes of travel and different ways of doing brownies."

"I've been over to Waco and Forth Worth."

"That's a start."

"You just say you're a space person, don't you," said Maggie, wondering where she'd gotten the courage to say that. "You're not really are you?"

"Not any more I'm not," said Oral. "My ship disintegrated completely over The Great Salt Lake. I was attacked by Mormon terrorists almost at once. Spent some time in Denver door-to-door. Realized I wasn't cut out for sales. Sometime later hooked up with a tent preacher in Bloomington, Indiana. Toured the tri-state area, where I did a little healing with a simple device concealed upon my person. Couldn't get new batteries and that was that. I was taken in by nuns outside of Reading, Pennsylvania, and treated well, though I was forced to mow lawns for some time. Later I was robbed and beaten severely by high-school girls in Chattanooga where I offered to change a tire. I have always relied on the kindness of strangers. Learned you can rely on 'em to kick you in the ass." Oral picked up a paper sack shaped like a bottle and took a drink. "What's your daddy do? If I'm not mistaken, he sells nails."

"That's not my daddy, that's my uncle. My father disappeared under strange circumstances."

"That happens. More often than you might imagine. There are documented cases. Things I could tell you you wouldn't believe. Look it up. Planes of existence we can't see or not a lot. People lost and floating about in interdimensional yogurt."

"You think my father's somewhere like that?"

"I don't know. I could ask."

"Thank you very much."

"I got this shirt from a fellow selling stuff off a truck. Pierre Cardin irregular is what it is. Dirt cheap and nothing irregular about it I can see. Whole stack of 'em there by your feet."

"They're all blue."

"Well, I know that."

"Where are we going now?"

"My place. Show you my interstellar vehicle and break open some cookies. You scared to be with me?"

"Not a lot."

"You might well ask why I make no effort to deny my strange origin or odd affiliation. I find it's easier to hide out in the open. You say you're from outer space, people tend to leave you alone. I've lived in cities and I like the country better. Not so many bad rays from people's heads. To say nothing of the dogshit in the streets. What do *you* think? You have any opinion on that? People in small towns are more tolerant of the rare and slightly defective. They all got a cousin counting his toes. I can fix nearly anything there is. Toasters. TVs. Microwave ovens. Everything except that goddamn ship. If Radio Shack had decent parts at all I'd be out of here and gone."

Oral parked the truck under the low-hanging branches of a big native pecan. The roots ground deep in the rigid earth, squeezed rocks to the surface like broken dishes. The tree offered shade to the small aluminum trailer, which was round as a bullet. Oral had backed it off the road some time before. The tires were gone, tossed off in the brush. The trailer sat on rocks. Oral ushered Maggie in. Found Oreos in a Folger's coffee can, Sprite in a mini-fridge. A generator hacked out back. The trailer smelled of wine and bananas and 3-in-One Oil. There was a hotplate and a cot. Blue shirts and trousers and socks.

"It's not much," said Oral. "I don't plan to stay here any longer than I have to."

"It's very cozy," said Maggie, who'd been taught to always say something nice. The trailer curved in from the door to a baked plastic window up front. The floor and the walls and the roof were explosions of colored wire and gutted home computers. Blue lights stuttered here and there.

"What's all this supposed to be?" said Maggie.

"Funky, huh?" Oral showed rapid eye movement. "No wonder they think I'm crazy. The conquest of space isn't as easy as the layman might imagine. I figure on bringing in a seat from out of the truck. Bolt it right there. Need something to seal up the door. Inner tubes and prudent vulcanizing ought to do it. You know about the alarming lack of air out in space?"

"I think we had it in school."

"Well, it's true. You doing all right at that place?"

The question took Maggie by surprise. "At school you mean? Sort of. Okay I guess."

"Uh-huh." Oral hummed and puttered about. Stepped on a blue light and popped it like a bug. Found a tangle of wire from a purple Princess phone and cut it free. Got needle-nose pliers and twisted a little agate in to fit. "Wear this," he told Maggie. "Hang it round your waist and let the black dohicky kind of dangle over your personal private things."

"Well, I never!" Maggie didn't care for such talk.

"All right, don't. Run home all your life."

"You've been spying on me."

"You want a banana? Some ice cream? I like to crumble Oreos over the top."

"I think I better start on home."

"Go right up the draw and down the hill. Shortcut. Stick to the path. Tonight's a good night to view the summer constellations. Mickey's in the Sombrero. The Guppy's on the rise."

"I'll be sure and look."

When Maggie was twelve, Aunt Grace went to Galveston on a trip. The occasion was a distant cousin's demise. Uncle Ned went along. Which seemed peculiar to Maggie since they wouldn't *eat* together, and seldom spoke.

"We can't afford it, God knows," said Aunt Grace. "But Albert was a dear. Fought the Red menace in West Texas all his life. Fell off a shrimper and drowned, but how do we know for sure? *They'd* make it look accidental."

She left Maggie a list of things to eat. Peanut butter and Campbell's soup. Which was mostly what she got when they were home. Aunt Grace said meat and green vegetables tended to give young girls diarrhea and get their periods out of whack.

"Stay out of the ham and don't thaw anything in the fridge. Here's two dollars that's for emergencies and not to spend. Call Mrs. Ketcher you get sick. Lock the doors. Come straight home from school and don't look at the cable."

"I'm scared to stay alone," said Maggie.

"Don't be a fraidy cat. God'll look after you if you're good."

"Don't tell anyone we're gone," said Uncle Ned. "Some greaser'll break in and steal us blind."

"For God's sake, Ned, don't tell her *that*."

Uncle Ned tried to slip a paper box in the back seat. Maggie saw him do it. When they both went in to check the house she stole a look. The carton was full of potato chips and Fritos, Cheetos and chocolate chip cookies. There was a cooler she hadn't seen iced down with Dr Pepper and frozen Snickers and Baby Ruths. There were never any chips or candy bars around the house. Aunt Grace said they couldn't afford trash. But all this stuff was in the car. Maggie didn't figure they'd be bringing any back. When the car was out of sight she went straight to the garage and punched an ice pick hole in the kerosene can that hid Uncle Ned's stash of magazines. She did it on a rust spot so Ned'd never notice. Then she went out back and turned over flat rocks and gathered half a pickle jar of fat brown Texas roaches that had moved up from Houston for their health. Upstairs she emptied the jar where Aunt Grace kept her underwear and hose. Downstairs again she got the ice pick and opened the freezer door and poked a hole in one of the coils. In case the roasts and chickens and Uncle Ned's venision sausage had trouble thawing out she left the door open wide to summer heat.

"There," said Maggie, "y'all go fuck yourselves good." She didn't know what it meant but it seemed to work fine for everyone else.

When Maggie was thirteen, Jimmy Gerder nearly caught her. By now she knew exactly what he wanted and ran faster. But Jimmy had been going out for track. He had the proper shoes and it was only a matter of time. Purely by chance she came across Oral's gimmick in the closet. The little black stone he'd twisted on seemed to dance like the Sony when a station was off the air. Why not, she thought, it can't hurt. Next morning she slipped it on under her dress. It felt funny and kinda nice, bouncing on her personal private things. Jimmy Gerder caught her in an alley. Six good buddies had come to watch. Jimmy wore his track outfit with a seven on the back. A Marble Creek Sidewinder rattler on the front. He was a tall and knobby boy with runny white-trash eyes and bad teeth. Maggie backed against a wall papered with county commissioner flyers. Jimmy came at her in a fifty meter stance. His mouth moved funny; a peculiar glaze appeared. A strange invisible force picked him up and slammed him flat against the far alley wall. Maggie hadn't touched him. But something certainly had. Onlookers got away fast and spread the word. Maggie wasn't much of an easy lay. Jimmy Gerder suffered a semi-mild concussion, damage to several vertebrae and ribs.

She hadn't seen Oral in over a year. On the streets sometime, but not at the extraterrestrial aluminum trailer by the river.

"I wanted to thank you," she said. "I don't get chased any more. How in the world did you do that?"

"What took you so long to try it out? Don't tell me. I got feelings too."

Nothing seemed to have changed. There were more gutted personal home computers and blue lights, or maybe the same ones in different order.

"You wouldn't believe what happened to me," said Oral. He brought out Oreos and Sprites. "Got the ship clear out of the atmosphere and hit this time warp or something. Nearly got eat by Vikings. Worse than the Mormons. Fixed up the ship and flipped it out again. Ended up in Medieval Europe. Medicis and monks, all kinds of shit. Joined someone's army in Naples. Got caught and picked olives for a duke. Look at my face. They got diseases you never heard of there."

"Oh my," said Maggie. His face didn't look too good. The bad albino skin had holes like a Baby Swiss.

"I taught 'em a thing or two," said Oral, blinking one pink eye and then the other. "Simple magic tricks. Mr. Wizard stuff. Those babies'll believe anything. Ended up owning half of Southern Italy.

Olive oil and real estate. Not a bad life if you can tolerate the smell. Man could make a mint selling Soft'n Pretty and Sure."

"I'm glad you're back safe," said Maggie. She liked Oral a lot, and didn't much care what he made up or didn't. "What are you going to do now?"

"What can I do? Try to get this mother off the ground. I'm thinking of bringing Radio Shack to task in federal court. I feel I have a case."

Maggie listened to the wind in the trees. "Do you really think you can do it, Oral? You think you can make it work again?"

"Sure I can. Or maybe not. You know what gets to me most on this world? Blue. We got reds and yellows and greens up the ass. But no blue. You got blues all over." Oral put aside his Sprite and found a bottle in a sack. "You hear from your daddy yet?"

"Not a thing. I'm afraid he's gone."

"Don't count him out. Stuck in interstellar tofu most likely. Many documented cases."

"Daddy hates tofu. Says it looks like someone threw up and tried again."

"He's got a point."

"What's it like where you come from, Oral. I mean where you lived before."

"You said you been to Fort Worth."

"Once when I was little."

"It doesn't look like that at all. Except out past Eighth Avenue by the tracks. Looks a little like that on a good day."

Maggie did fine in school after Jimmy Gerder left her alone. He cocked his head funny and walked with a limp. His folks finally sent him to Spokane to study forest conservation. By the time she reached sixteen Maggie began to make friends. She was surprised to be chosen for the Sidewinderettes, the third finest pep squad in the state. She joined the Drama Club and started writing plays of her own. She was filling out nicely and gave Uncle Ned a wide berth.

They were still dirt poor, but Uncle Ned and Aunt Grace attended several funerals a year. Two cousins died in Orlando not far from Disneyland, a car mishap in which both were killed outright. A nephew was mutilated beyond recognition in San Francisco, victim of a tuna-canning machine gone berserk. A new family tragedy could be expected around April, and again in late October when the weather got nice. Maggie was no longer taken in. She knew people died year round. They died in places like Cincinnati and Topeka where no one wanted to go. What Aunt Grace and Uncle Ned were doing was having fun. There wasn't much question about that. Maggie didn't like it but there was nothing she could do about it, either.

When Maggie was eighteen her play "Blue Sun Rising" was chosen for the senior drama presentation. It was a rousing success. Drama critic Harcourt Playce from San Angelo, Texas, told Maggie she showed promise as a writer. He gave her his personal card and the name of a Broadway theatrical producer in New York. The play was about a man who was searching for the true meaning of life on a world "very much like our own," as the program put it. There was no night at all on this world. A blue sun was always in the sky. Maggie wanted to ask Oral but was sure the principal wouldn't let him in.

Aunt Grace died a week after graduation. Maggie found her watching reruns of "M.A.S.H." She secretly wrote a specialist in Dallas. Told him what had happened to her mother and Aunt Grace. The specialist answered in time and said there might be genetic dysfunction. They were making great strides in the field. He advised her to avoid any shows in syndication.

Life with Uncle Ned wasn't easy. With Aunt Grace gone he no longer practiced restraint of any kind. Liquor came out of the nail bin at the store, and found its way to the kitchen. Girl and scientist magazines were displayed quite openly with *National Geographic*. Maggie began to jump when she heard a sound. There was a good chance Uncle Ned was there. Standing still too long was a mistake.

"You're going to have to stop that," said Maggie. "I mean it, Uncle Ned. I won't put up with it at all."

"You ought to get into gymnastics," said Uncle Ned. "I could work with you. Fix up bars and stuff out back. I know a lot more about it than you might think."

Maggie looked at Uncle Ned as if she were seeing him for the first time. His gaze was focused somewhere south of Houston. There seemed to be an electrical short in his face. His skin was the color of chuck roast hit with a hammer.

"I'm going to go," said Maggie. "I'm getting out of here."

"On what?" said Uncle Ned.

"I don't care on what, I'm just going. You try to stop me you'll wish you hadn't."

"You haven't got busfare to the bathroom."

"Then I'll walk."

"You do and you'll get raped and thrown in a ditch."

"I can get that first part here. I'll worry about the ditch when I come to it."

"Don't expect any help from me. I haven't got two dimes to rub together."

"You will," said Maggie. "Some cousin'll get himself hacked up in a sawmill in Las Vegas."

"Now that's plain ignorant," said Uncle Ned. "Especially for a high-school graduate. There isn't a lot of timber in Nevada. That's something you ought to know."

"Goodbye, Uncle Ned."

It took maybe nine minutes to pack. She took "Blue Sun Rising" and a number two pencil. Left her Sidewinderette pep jacket and took a sensible cloth coat. It was the tail end of summer in Texas, but New York looked cold on "Cagney and Lacey." She searched for something to steal. There were pawn shops all over New York. People stole for a living and sold the loot to buy scag and pot and ludes and whatever they could find to shoot up. There was no reason you couldn't buy food just as well. In the back of her aunt's closet she found a plastic beaded purse with eight dollars and thirty cents. Two sticks of Dentyne gum. Downstairs, Uncle Ned was watching the French National Girls' Field Hockey Finals. Maggie stopped at the front door.

"It was me poured kerosene on your magazines," she said. "I thawed all the meat out too."

"I know it," said Uncle Ned. He didn't turn around. A girl named Nicole blocked a goal.

Hitchhiking was a frightening experience. She felt alone and vulnerable on the interstate. Oral's protective device was fastened securely about her waist. But what if it didn't work? What if she'd used it up with Jimmy Gerder? A man who sold prosthetic devices picked her up almost at once. His name was Sebert Lewis and he offered to send her to modeling school in Lubbock. He had helped several girls begin promising careers. Many were now in national magazines.

When Sebert stopped for gas, Maggie got out and ran. There were trucks everywhere. A chrome-black eighteen-wheeler city. They towered over Maggie on every side. In a moment she was lost. Some of the trucks were silent. Others rumbled deep and blinked red and yellow lights. There was no one about. She spotted a cafe through the dark. The drivers were likely all inside. It seemed like the middle of the night. French fries reached her on a light diesel breeze.

"I don't know what to do next!" she said aloud, determined not to cry. A big red truck stood by itself. A nice chrome bulldog on the front. It wouldn't hurt to rest and maybe hide from Sebert Lewis. She wrapped her coat around her and used her suitcase for a pillow. In a moment she was asleep. Only a short time later, a face looked directly into hers.

"Oh, Lord," said Maggie, "don't you dare do whatever it is you're thinking."

"Little lady, I'm not thinking on anything at all," the man said.

"Well all right then. If you mean it."

He was big, about as big a man as Maggie had ever seen. Dark brown eyes nearly lost in a face like a kindly pie. "You better be glad I'm a bug on maintenance," he said. "If I'd of took off you lyin' there under the tire I'd a squashed you flatter'n a dog on the road to Amarillo. You got a name, have you?"

"I'm Maggie McKenna from Marble Creek."

"You running away?"

"I'm going to New York City to write plays."

"You got folks back home?"

"My mother's dead and my father disappeared under strange circumstances. I'm a high-school graduate and a member of the Sidewinderettes. They don't take just everybody wants to get in. If you're thinking about calling Uncle Ned you just forget it."

"Not my place to say what you ought to do. I'm Billy C. Mace. How'd you get to here?"

"A man named Sebert Lewis picked me up. Said he'd put me through modeling school in Lubbock."

"Lord Jesus!" said Billy Mace. "Come on, get in. Nothing's going to happen to you now."

Riding in the cab of an eighteen-wheeler wasn't anything at all like a '72 Ford. You towered over the road and could see everything for miles. Cars got out of the way. Billy talked to other truckers on the road. His CB handle was Boomer Billy. He let Maggie talk to Black Buddy and Queen Louise and Stoker Fish. The truck seemed invulnerable. Nothing could possibly reach her. The road hummed miles below. There was even a place to sleep behind the driver. Billy guessed she was hungry, and before they left the stop he got cheeseburgers and onion rings to go. Billy kept plenty of Fritos and Hershey bars with almonds in the truck, and had Dr Peppers iced in a cooler. Maggie went to sleep listening to Waylon Jennings tapes. When she woke it was morning. Billy said they'd be in Tulsa in a minute.

"I've never even been out of the state," said Maggie. "And here I am already in Oklahoma."

Billy pulled into a truck stop for breakfast. And then to another for lunch. He measured the distance in meals. "Two-hundred miles to lunch," he'd tell Maggie, or "a hundred-seventy to supper."

Maggie read him "Blue Sun Rising" while he drove.

"I don't know a lot about plays," said Billy when she was through, "but I don't see how that sucker can miss. That third act's a doozie."

"It needs a little work."

"Not as I see it it don't. You might want to rein in the Earth Mother symbolism a little, but that's just a layman's suggestion."

"You may be right," said Maggie.

She already knew Billy was well read. There was a shelf of books over the bunk. All the writers' names were John. John Gunther. John Milton. John D. McDonald.

"John's my daddy's name, God rest him," said Billy. "A man named John tells you something you can take it for a fact."

She told him about Uncle Ned and Aunt Grace. She didn't mention Oral Blue as they had not discussed the possibilities of extraterrestrial life. Billy was livid about her experience with Sebert Lewis.

"Lord Jesus himself was looking after you," he said. "No offense meant, but a girl pretty as you is just road bait, Maggie. That modeling studio thing is likely a front. I expect this Sebert's a Red agent and into hard astrology on the side. Probably under deep cover for some time. I imagine there's a network of such places spread right across the country. Sebert and his cohorts cruise the roads for candidates like yourself. Couple of days in a little room and you're hopeless on drugs, ready to do unspeakable acts of every kind. There's a possibility of dogs. You wake up in bed with some greaser with a beard gets military aid from this godless administration. That's where your tax dollar goes. I don't want to scare you but you come real close to a bad end."

"I guess I don't know much do I?" said Maggie. "I feel awful dumb."

"You learn quick enough when you drive the big rigs. There's things go on you wouldn't believe. The Russians got the news media eatin' out of their hands. I could give you names you'd recognize at once if I was to say 'em. There are biological agents in everything you eat. Those lines and numbers they got on the back of everything you buy? What that is is a code. If you're not in the KGB or the Catholic Church you can't read it. Don't eat anything that's got three sixes. That's the sign of the beast. I wish to God I had control of my appetite. I can feel things jabbing away inside. White bread and tomatoes are pretty safe. And food isn't the only way they got you. TV's likely the worst. I can't *tell* you the danger of watching the tube."

"I already know about that," said Maggie.

Billy Mace had it all arranged. As good as any travel agent could do. He left her with a Choctaw driver named Henry Black Bear in St. Louis. Henry took her to Muncie, Indiana. Gave her over to a skeletal black man named Quincy Pride. Quincy's CB handle was Ghost. He taught her the names of every Blues singer who had lived in New Orleans at any time. He played their tapes in order of appearance. At Pittsburgh she transferred to Tony D. Velotta, a handsome Italian with curly hair. Maggie thought he was the image of John Travolta.

And then very early in the morning, she woke to the bright sun in her eyes and crawled down from the bunk and Tony pointed and said, "Hey, there it is, kid. We're here."

Maggie could scarcely believe her eyes. The skyline exploded like needles in the sun. A lonely saxophone wailed offstage. She could see the trees blossom in Central Park. Smell the hotdogs cooking at the zoo. They were still in New Jersey, but they were close.

"Lordy," said Maggie, "it looks near as real as a movie."

As they sliced through upper Manhattan, Tony pointed out the sights. Not that there was an awful lot to see. He tried to explain the Bronx and Brooklyn and Queens, drawing a map with his finger on the dash. Maggie was thoroughly confused, and too excited to really care.

"So what are you going to do now? Where you going to stay?"

"I don't know," said Maggie. "I guess I'll find a hotel or something."

"How much money you got, you don't mind me asking?"

"Eight dollars and thirty cents. Now I know that's not a lot. I may have to look for work. It could take some time before I get my play produced."

"Holy Mother," said Tony. "You'd better stay with us."

"Now I couldn't do that. I'll be just fine."

"Right. For six, maybe eight minutes, tops."

The Velottas lived in Brooklyn. It might as well have been Mars as far as Maggie was concerned. There were eight people in the family. Tony and his wife Carla and little Tony who was two. Tony's father and mother, two younger brothers and a sister. They took in Maggie at once. They said she talked funny. They loved her. Carla gave her dresses. There was always plenty to eat. The Velottas had never heard of peanut butter. Maggie ate things called manicotti and veal piccata. Carla made spaghetti that didn't come out of a can. Nothing was like it was at Aunt Grace's and Uncle Ned's. The family was constantly in motion. Talking and running from one end of the house to the other. Everyone yelled at each other and laughed. Maggie tasted wine for the first time. She'd never seen a wine bottle out of a paper sack. Everyone worked in the Velotta family bakery. Maggie helped out, carrying trays of pastry to the oven.

Tony stayed a week and went back on the road. Maggie talked to Carla one evening after little Tony was in bed.

"I've got to go see my producer," she said. "You all have been wonderful to me but I can't live off you forever. The sooner I get 'Blue Sun Rising' on Broadway the better."

"Yeah, right," said Carla. She looked patient and resigned. The whole family conferred on directions. An intricate map was drawn. Likely locations of muggers and addicts were marked with an 'x.'

"Don't talk to *anyone*," said Tony's mother. She crossed herself and gave Maggie a medal. "Especially don't talk to blacks and Puerto Ricans. Or Jews or people with slanty eyes or turbans. No turbans! Avoid men with Nazi haircuts and blue eyes. *Anyone* with blue eyes."

"Watch out for men in business suits and ties," said Papa Velotta. "They carry little black cases. Like women's purses only flat. There's supposed to be business inside but there's not. It's dope is what it is. Everybody knows what's going on."

"Don't talk to anyone on skates with orange hair," said Carla.

"A Baptist with funny eyes will give you a pamphlet," said Papa. "Don't take it. Watch out for white socks."

"I'll try to remember everything," said Maggie.

"I'll light a candle," said Mama Velotta.

Maggie called Marty Wilde, the Broadway producer. Wilde said she had a nice voice and he liked to encourage regional talent. He would see her at three that afternoon.

"What's the name of this play?" he wanted to know.

" 'Blue Sun Rising,' " said Maggie.

"Jesus, I like it. You don't have an agent or anything do you?"

"I just got in town," said Maggie.

"Good. I like to work with people direct."

Her first impression was right. Manhattan was as real as any cop show she'd ever seen. It was all there. The sounds, the smells, the people of many lands. There was a picture show on nearly every block. Everything was the same, everything was different. The city changed before her eyes. A man lying in the street. A kid tying celery to a cat. A woman dressed like a magazine cover, getting out of a cab. She watched the woman a long time. Maybe she'll come to see my play. Maggie thought. She looks like a woman who'd see a play.

Marty Wilde had a small office in a tall building. The building was nice outside. Inside, the halls were narrow. There was bathroom tile on the floors. A girl with carrot hair said Mr. Wilde would see her, and knocked on the wall. Marty came out at once.

"Maggie McKenna from Marble Creek, Texas," he said. "That's who you are. Maggie McKenna who wrote 'Blue Sun Rising.' Hey, get in here right now."

Marty ushered her in and offered a chair. The office was bigger than a closet and had faded brown pictures on the wall. Maggie realized these were Broadway greats, people she would likely meet later. There was very little light. The window looked out on a window. Black men in *Kung Fu* suits kicked at the air. There were piles of plays in the room. Plays spilling over tables and chairs and onto the floor. This sight left Maggie depressed. If there were that many plays in New York, they might never get around to "Blue Sun Rising."

Marty Wilde took her play and set it aside. He perched on the edge of his desk. "So tell me about Maggie McKenna. I can read an author like a page. I can see your play right on your face. A character sits down stage right. The phone rings. I can see that."

"That's amazing," said Maggie. Marty Wilde seemed worn to a nub. A turkey neck stuck out of his shirt. His eyes slept in little hammocks. "There's not much to tell about me. I think my play's good, Mr. Wilde. If it needs any changes I'm willing to do the work."

"Every play needs work. You take your Neil Simon or your Chekhov. A hit doesn't jump out of the typewriter and hop up on the stage."

"No, I guess not."

"You better believe it. Who's this guy give you my name?"

"Harcourt Playce, he works on the San Angelo paper."

"Short little man with a club foot. Wears a Mexican peso on a chain. Sure I remember."

This didn't sound like Mr. Playce but Maggie didn't want to interrupt.

"You say you haven't got an agent."

"No, sir, I sure don't."

"Let's cut the sir stuff, Maggie. I'm older than you in years but there's a spirit of youth pervades the stage. You're a very pretty girl. How you fixed for cash?"

"Not real good right now."

"My point exactly. Here's what I suggest. It's just an idea I'm throwing out. I take in a few writers on this scholarship thing which is hey, my way of paying Lady Broadway back in a small way. You stay at my place, we work together. I got a friend can give you good photo work. He's affiliated with a national modeling chain. All semi-tasteful stuff. You'd know his name the minute I said it."

"You want to take my picture?"

"Just an idea. Let's get you settled in."

"This sounds a lot like girls and scientists, Mr. Wilde. I don't see what it has to do with my play."

Marty came off the desk. "I want you to be comfortable with this."

"I'm not very comfortable right now."

"So let's talk. Tell me what you're feeling."

"You just talk from over there."

"You remind me a lot of Debra Winger. In a very classical sense."

"You remind me of someone, too."

"Jesus, what a sweet kid you are. We won't try to push it. Just let it happen." He took a step closer. A strange invisible force picked him up and hurled him against the wall. Pictures of near-greats shattered. Some crucial fault gave way in the stacks of plays. Acts and scenes spilled over Marty on the floor.

"I think you broke something," said Marty. "Where'd you learn that hold? You're awful quick."

The girl with carrot hair came in.

"Call somebody," said Marty. "Get me on the couch."

"I don't think we can work together," said Maggie. "I'm real displeased with your behavior."

"I can see you don't know shit about the theatre," said Marty. "You can't just waltz in here and expect to see your name in lights."

"You ought to be in jail. If you try to get in touch with me, I'll press charges."

Carla said she could stay as long as she wanted. There wasn't any reason to go look for another place.

"I've got to try it on my own," said Maggie. "I believe in my play. I don't believe everyone on Broadway's like Marty Wilde."

Carla could see that she was determined. "It's not easy to get work. Tony thinks a lot of you, Maggie. We all do. You're family."

"Oh, Carla," Maggie threw her arms around her. "You're the very best family I ever had."

Carla persuaded her to wait for the Sunday *Times*. Mama Velotta filled her up with food. "Eat now. You won't get a chance to later."

The room was on East 21st over an all-night Chinese restaurant. Maggie shared it with three girls named Jeannie, Eva, and Sherry. They all three worked for an insurance company. Maggie got a waitress job nights at the restaurant downstairs. There was just enough money to eat and pay the rent. She slept a few hours after work and took the play around days. No one wanted to see her. They asked her to mail copies and get an agent. Maggie cut down her meals to one a day, which allowed her to make a new copy of "Blue Sun Rising" every week. She even started a new play, using Sherry's portable Smith Corona and the backs of paper placemats from the job. The play was "Diesel and Roses," a psychological drama set in a truckstop cafe. Billy Mace was in it, and so was Henry Black Bear and Quincy Pride and Tony Velotta. Carla called. There was a postal money order from Marble Creek for $175 and a note.

"It's not good news," said Carla.

"Read it," said Maggie.

" 'Dying. Come home. Uncle Ned.' "

"Oh, Lord."

"I'm real sorry, honey."

"It's okay. We weren't close."

The thing to do was take the money and eat and make some copies of "Blue Sun Rising." And forget about Uncle Ned. Maggie couldn't do it. Even Uncle Ned deserved to have family put him in the ground. "I'll be back," she told New York, and made arrangements to meet Carla and get the money.

The first thing she noticed was things had changed in the year she'd been away. Instead of the '72 Ford, there was a late model Buick with a boat hitch on the back. Poking out of the garage was a Ranger fishing boat, an 18-footer with a big Merc outboard on the stern.

"You better be dead or dying," said Maggie.

The living room looked like Sears and Western Auto had exploded. There was a brand new Sony and a VCR, and hit tapes like *Gymnasts in Chains.* The kitchen was a wildlife preserve. Maggie stood at the door but wouldn't go in. Things moved around under plates. There were cartons of Hershey bars and chips. Canned Danish hams and foreign mustards. All over the house there were things still in boxes. Uncle Ned had dug tunnels through empty bottles and dirty books. There were new Hawaiian shirts. Hush Puppies in several different styles. A man appeared in one of the tunnels.

"I'm Dr. Kraftt, I guess you're Maggie."

"Is he really dying? What's wrong with him?"

"Take your pick. The man's got everything. A person can't live like that and expect their organs to behave."

Maggie went upstairs. Uncle Ned looked dead already. There were green oxygen tanks and plastic tubes.

"I'm real glad you came. This is nice."

"Uncle Ned, where'd you get all this *stuff*?"

"That all you got to say? You don't want to hear how I am?"

"I can see how you are."

"You're entitled to bad feelings. I deserve whatever you want to dish out. I want to settle things up before I go to damnation and meet your aunt. Your father had an employee stock plan at Montgomery Wards. Left your mother well off and that woman was too cheap to spend it. We got the money when she died and you came to us. We sort of took these little vacations. Nothing big."

"Oh Lord."

"I guess we wronged you some."

"I guess I grew up on peanut butter and Campbell's soup is what happened."

"I've got a lot to answer for. There are certain character flaws."

"That's no big news to me."

"I can see a lot clearer from the unique position I got at the moment. Poised between one plane of being and the next. When your aunt died weakness began to thrive. I didn't mean to buy so much stuff."

"I don't suppose there's anything left."

"Not to speak of I wouldn't think. All that junk out there's on credit. It'll have to go back. The bank's got the house. There's forty-nine dollars in a Maxwell House can in the closet. I want you to have it."

"I'll take it."

"I wish you and me'd been closer. I hope you'll give me a kiss."

"I'd rather eat a toad," said Maggie.

Maggie saw Jimmy Gerder at the funeral. He still had a limp and kept his distance. She walked along the river to see Oral. It was fall, or as close as fall gets in that end of Texas. Dry leaves rattled and the Colorado was low. The log where she used to watch turtles was aground, trailing tangles of fishing line. The water was the color of chocolate milk and the turtles were gone. Oral was gone too. Brush had sprung up under the big native pecan. The place looked empty without the multi-blue pickup and the extraterrestrial trailer. Maggie wondered if he'd gotten things to work or just left. She asked around town, and no one seemed to remember seeing him go. After a Coke and a bacon and tomato at the cafe she figured she had enough to get back to New York if she sold a couple of things before Sears learned Uncle Ned was dead. Put that with her forty-nine dollar inheritance and she could do it. There was fifteen dollars left from the ticket. Even dying, Uncle Ned had remembered to pay for only one way.

Winter in New York was bad. The Chinese restaurant became an outlet for video tapes. Sherry and Jeannie and Eva helped all they could. They carried Maggie on the rent and ran copies of "Blue Sun Rising" down at the insurance company. The Velottas tried to help, but Maggie wouldn't have it. She got part-time work at a pizza place on East 52nd. After work she walked bone-tired to the theatre district and looked at the lights. She read the names on the posters and watched people get out of cabs. There was a cold wet drizzle every night, but Maggie didn't mind. The streets reflected the magic and made it better. When the first snow fell she sewed a blanket in her coat. The coat smelled like anchovies and Sherry said she looked like a Chinese pilot. "For God's sake, baby, let me loan you a coat."

"I can manage," said Maggie, "you've done enough."

She could no longer afford subways or buses so she walked every day from her room. She lost weight and coughed most of the time. The owner asked her to leave. He said customers didn't like people coughing on their pizza. She didn't tell the girls she'd lost her job. They'd want to give her money. She looked, but there weren't any jobs to be had. Especially for girls who looked like bag ladies and sounded like Camille. She kept going out every day and coming back at night. Hunger wasn't a problem. She felt too sick to eat. One night she simply didn't go home. "What's the point? What's the use pretending? No one wants to look at 'Blue Sun Rising.' I can't get a job. I can't do anything at all."

The snow began to fall in slow motion, flakes the size of lemons. Broadway looked like a big Christmas tree someone had tossed out and forgot to take the lights.

"Look at the blues," said Maggie. "Oral liked the blues so much."

A man selling food gave her a pretzel and some mustard. The pretzel came up at once. A coughing fit hit her. She couldn't stop. First nighters hurried quickly by. Maggie pulled her coat up close and looked in the steamy windows of Times Square. Radios and German bayonets were half-off. There was a pre-Christmas sale on marital aids. She could still taste the mustard and the pretzel. A black man in sunglasses approached.

"You hurtin' bad, mama. You need something, I can maybe get it."

"No thank you," said Maggie.

I can't just stand here, she thought. I've got to do something. She couldn't feel her feet. Lights were jumping about. There was a paper box in the alley. The thing to do was to sit down and try to figure things out. She thought of a good line for "Diesel and Roses" and then forgot it. A cat looked in and sniffed; there were anchovies somewhere about. Maggie dreamed of daddy when he took her to the zoo. She dreamed of Oral under a tree and riding high with Billy Mace. The cab was toasty warm and Billy had burgers from McDonald's. She dreamed she heard applause. The cat started chewing on her coat. Oh Lord, I love New York, thought Maggie. If I can make it here, I can make it anywhere . . .

* * *

Carla looked ethereal, computer-enhanced.

"I guess I'm dying," said Maggie. "I'm sorry to get you out in this weather."

"Oh baby," said Carla, "hang on. Just hang on, Maggie."

Everything was fuzzy. The tubes hurt her nose. The walls were dark and needed painting. Sherry and Eva and Jeannie were there and all the Velottas. They bobbed about like balloons. Everyone had rings around their eyes.

"I want you to have 'Blue Sun Rising,' " said Maggie. "All of you. Equal shares. I've been thinking about off-Broadway lately. That might not be so hard. Don't see a man named Marty Wilde."

"All right, Maggie."

"She's going," someone said.

"Goodbye, Daddy. Goodbye, Oral," said Maggie.

The room looked nice. There was a big window with sun coming in. The doctor leaned down close. He smelled like good cologne. He smiled at Maggie and wrote something and left. A nice-looking man got up from a chair and stood by the bed.

"Hello. You feeling like something to drink? You want anything just ask."

"I'd like a Dr Pepper if you have one."

"You got it."

The man left and Maggie tried to stay awake. When she opened her eyes again it was late afternoon. The man was still there. A nurse came in and propped her up. The man brought her a fresh Dr Pepper.

"You look a lot like Tony," said Maggie. He did. The same crispy hair and dark eyes. A nice black suit and a gray tie. Maybe a couple of years older. "You know Tony and Carla?"

"They ask about you every day. You can see them real soon. Everybody's been pretty worried about you."

"I guess I 'bout died."

"Yeah, I guess you did."

"This place looks awful expensive. I don't want the Velottas or anyone spending a bundle on me."

"They won't. No problem."

"Hey, I know a swell place like this isn't *free*."

"We'll talk about it. Don't worry." The man smiled at Maggie and went away.

Maggie slept and got her appetite back and wondered where she was. The next afternoon the man was back. He helped her in a wheelchair and rolled her down the hall to a glassed-in room full of plants. There were cars outside in a circular drive. A fountain turned off for the winter. A snow-covered lawn and a dark line of trees. Far in the distance, pale blue hills against a cold and leaden sky. Men in sunglasses and overcoats walked around in the snow.

"I guess you're going to tell me where I am sometime," said Maggie. "I guess you're going to tell me who you are and what I'm doing in this place I can't afford."

"I'm Johnny Lucata," the man said. "Call me Johnny, Maggie. And this house belongs to a friend."

"He must be a friend of yours, then. I don't remember any friends with a house like this."

"You don't know him. But he's a friend of yours too." He seemed to hesitate. He straightened his tie. "Look, I got things to tell you. Things you need to know. You want we can talk when you feel a little better."

"I feel okay right now."

"Maybe. Only this is kinda nutsy stuff, you know? I don't want to put you back in bed or nothing."

"Mr. Lucata, whatever it is, I think I'll feel a lot better when I know what's going on."

"Right. Why not? So what do you know about olives?"

"What?"

"Olives. They got olives over in Italy. There's a place where the toe's kicking Sicily in the face. Calabria. Something like a state, only different. The man lives here, he's got a lot of the olive oil business in Calabria. Been in his family maybe four, five hundred years. You sure you want to do this now?"

"I'm sure, Mr. Lucata."

"Okay. There's this city called Reggio di Calabria right on the water. You can look and see Sicily real good. A couple of miles out of town is this castle. Been there forever, only now it's a place for monks. So what happens is a couple of months back this monk's digging around and finds this parchment in a box. It's real old and the monk reads it. What he sees shakes him up real bad. He's not going to go to the head monk because Catholics got this thing about stuff that even *starts* to get weird. But he's a monk, right? He can't just toss this thing away. He's got a sister knows a guy who's family to the man who lives here. So the box gets to Reggio and then it gets to him." Johnny Lucata looked at Maggie. "Here's the part I said gets spooky. What this parchment says, Maggie, is that the old duke who started up the family left all the olive business to *you*."

Maggie looked blank. "Now that doesn't make sense at all, Mr. Lucata."

"Yeah, tell me. It's the straight stuff. The experts been over it. I got a copy I can show you. It's all in Latin, but you can read the part that says Maggie McKenna of Marble Creek, Texas. We got the word out and we been looking all over trying to find you. But your uncle died and you came back to New York. We didn't know where to take it after that. Then someone in Tony's family mentions your name and it gets to us. The thing is now, the man lives here, he doesn't know what to make of all this, and he don't want to think about it a lot. He sure don't want to ask some cardinal or the Pope. What he *wants* to do is make it right for *you*, Maggie. This duke is his ancestor and he figures it's a matter of honor. I mean, he doesn't see you ought to get it *all*, but you ought to be in for a couple of points. He wants me to tell you he'd like to work it where you get maybe three, four mill a year out of this. He thinks that's fair and he knows you're pressed for cash."

Maggie sat up straight. "Are you by any chance talking about dollars? Three or four million *dollars*?"

"Five. I think we ought to say five. He kind of left that up to me. Don't worry about the taxes. We'll work a little off-tackle Panama reverse through a Liechtenstein bank. You'll get the bread through a Daffy Duck Christmas Club account."

"I just can't hardly believe this, Mr. Lucata. It's like a dream or something. No one even knew I was going to *be* back then. Why, there wasn't even a *Texas*!"

"You got it."

"This castle. There's just these monks living there now?"

"Palazzo Azzuro. Means blue palace. I been there, it's nice. Painted blue all over. Inside and out. Every kind of blue you ever saw."

"*Blue?* Oh my goodness!"

"You okay?"

"Oral," said Maggie, "Oh Oral, you're the finest and dearest friend I ever had!"

When she was feeling like getting up and around, Johnny Lucata helped her find a relatively modest apartment off Fifth Avenue. Five mill or not, Maggie had been poor too long to start tossing money around. She did make sure there were always Dr Peppers and Baby Ruths in the fridge. And steaks and fresh fruit and nearly everything but Chinese food and pizza. Carla helped her find Bloomingdale's and Saks. Maggie picked out a new cloth coat. She sent nice perfume to Jeannie and Sherry and Eva, and paid them back triple what they'd spent to help her out. She gave presents to the Velottas and had everyone over for dinner. Johnny Lucata dropped by a lot. Just to see how she was doing. Sometimes he came in a cab. Sometimes he came in a black car with tinted windows and men wearing black suits and shades. He took her out to dinner and walks in the park. Sometimes Maggie made coffee, and they talked into the night. She read him "Blue Sun Rising" and he liked it.

"You don't have to say that, just because it's me."

"I mean it. I go to plays all the time. It's *real*, Maggie. You don't have to wonder what everybody's thinking, they just say it. I want you to talk to Whitney Hess."

"Whitney Hess the producer? Do you know him?"

"Yeah, sure I know him."

"I don't want to do that, Johnny. I don't want to get help from somebody just because he's a friend of yours. That's not right. I want 'Blue Sun Rising' to stand on its own."

"Are you kidding?" said Johnny. "Whitney Hess wouldn't buy a bad play from his dying mother. Besides, I want five points of this up front. You're not going to cut *me* out of a winner."

Tony and Carla and Tony's brothers and his sister and Mama and Papa Velotta dressed up for opening night. Johnny Lucata sent a limo to pick them up, and another to get Jeannie and Sherry and Eva. Tony got out the word, and the truckers found Billy Mace and Henry Black Bear and Quincy Pride. They all had seventh row center seats.

Maggie thought sure she was dreaming. Her name up in lights at the Shubert Theatre. Ladies in furs and jewels dressed up for opening night. Spotlights and TV cameras and people she'd only seen in the movies. She stayed outside a long time. Standing in the very same spot where she'd thrown up pretzels in the street. Not far from the alley where she'd curled up in a box and nearly died. You just never know, she told herself. You just don't.

There was no need to wait for the reviews. After the first act, Whitney Hess said they had a smash on their hands. After the third act curtain, even Maggie believed it was true. The audience came to its feet and shouted, "author! author!" and someone told Maggie they meant *her*.

Johnny hurried her out of the Shubert by the side door. He wouldn't say where they were going. A black car was by the curb around the corner. There were men in overcoats and shades.

"I want you to meet somebody," said Johnny, and opened the rear door. "This is Maggie McKenna," he said. "Maggie, I'd like you to meet my father."

Maggie caught the proper respect in his voice. She looked inside and saw an old man sitting in the corner. He was lost in a black suit, a man no more substantial than a cut-rate chicken in a sack.

"That was a nice play," he said. "I like it a lot. I like plays with a story you can't guess what's going to happen all the time. There's nothing on the television but dirt. The Reds got people in the business. They built this place in Chelyabinsk looks just like Twentieth Century Fox. Writers, directors, the works. They teach 'em how to do stuff rots out your head then they send them over here. This is a great country. You keep writing nice plays."

"Thank you," said Maggie, "I'm very glad you liked it."

"Here. A little present from me. Your big night. You remember where you got it."

"I'm very grateful," said Maggie. "For everything." She leaned in and kissed him on the cheek.

"That's very nice. You're a nice girl. She's a nice girl, Johnny."

Johnny took her back inside, and on the way home after the big party Whitney Hess gave at the Plaza, Maggie opened her present. It was a pendant shaped like an olive. Pale emeralds formed the olive and a ruby sat on top for the pimiento.

"It's just lovely," said Maggie.

"The old man's got a lot of class."

"Why didn't you tell me that was your father's house, Johnny? I kinda guessed later but I didn't know for sure."

"Wasn't the right time."

"And it's the right time now?"

"Yeah, I guess it is."

"Whitney Hess wants to go into rehearsal on 'Diesel and Roses' next month. I'm going to ask Billy Mace and Henry Black Bear and Quincy Pride to come on as technical advisors. There's not a thing for them to do, but I'd like to have them around."

"That's nice. It's a good idea."

"Whitney says everyone wants the movie rights to 'Blue Sun Rising.' Which means we'll get a picture deal up front for 'Diesel and Roses.' Oh Lordy, I can't believe all this is really happening. Everything in my life's been either awful or as good as it can be."

"It's going to stay good now, Maggie." He leaned over and kissed her quickly. Maggie stared at the tinted glass.

"You've never done *that* before."

"Well, I have now."

Maggie wondered what was happening inside. She felt funny all over. She was dizzy from the kiss. She liked Johnny a lot but she'd never liked him quite like this. She wanted him to kiss her again and again, but not *now*. Not wearing Oral's protective device, which she'd worn since her very first day in New York. It was something she'd never thought about before. What if you really *wanted* someone to do something to you? Would the wire and the black stone know that it wasn't Jimmy Gerder or Marty Wilde? She certainly couldn't take the chance of finding out.

The phone was ringing when they got to her apartment.

"You're famous," said Johnny. "That'll go on all night."

"No, it won't," said Maggie, "just take it off the hook. I can be famous tomorrow. Tonight I just want to be me."

Johnny had a funny look in his eyes. She was sure he was going to kiss her right then. "Just wait right there," she said. "Don't go away. Get me a Dr Pepper and open yourself a beer." She hurried into the bedroom and shut the door. Raised up her skirt and slipped the little wire off her waist. Her heart was beating fast. "I hope you know what you're doing, Maggie McKenna."

Johnny gave a decidedly angry shout from the other room. Another man yelled. Something fell to the floor.

"Good heavens, what's that?" said Maggie. She rushed into the room. Johnny had a young man backed against the wall, threatening him with a fist. The man wore a patched cardigan sweater and khaki pants. He was trying to hit Johnny with a sack.

"Who the hell are *you*," said Johnny, "what are you doing in here!"

"Oh my God," said Maggie. She stopped in her tracks, then ran past Johnny and threw her arms around the other man's neck. "Oh Daddy, I *knew* you wouldn't leave me! I knew you'd come back!"

"Maggie? Is that you? Why, you're all grown up! Say, what a looker you are. Where am I? How's your mother?"

"We'll talk about that. Just sit down and rest." She could hardly see through her tears. "I'll explain," she told Johnny. "At least I'll give it a try. Oh, Oral, I hope you're wherever it is you want to be. Johnny, get Daddy a Dr Pepper." She gave him the sack. "Put this in the kitchen and you come right back."

"It's just catfood and bread," said Daddy. "I think that fella there took me wrong."

"Everything's all right now."

"Maggie, I feel like I've been floating around in yogurt. Forever or maybe an hour and a half. It's hard to say. I don't know. I'm greatly confused for the moment. I *ought* to be more than five years older'n you."

"It happens. There are documented cases. Just sit down and rest. There's plenty of time to talk." Johnny came back with a Dr Pepper. She gave it to her father and led Johnny to the kitchen.

"I don't get it," said Johnny.

"You got all that business with the monks, you can learn to handle this. Just hold me a minute, all right? And do what you did in the car."

Johnny kissed her a very long time. Maggie was sure she was going to faint.

"I'm a real serious guy," said Johnny. "I'm not just playing around. I got very strong emotions."

"I like you a lot," said Maggie. "I'm not sure I could love a man in your line of work."

"I'm in olives. I got a nice family business."

"You've got a family in overcoats and shades, Johnny Lucata."

"Okay, so we'll work something out."

"I guess maybe we will. I keep forgetting I'm in olive oil too. Maybe you better kiss me again. Johnny there's *so* much I want us to do. I want to show you Marble Creek. I want to show you green turtles on a log and the Sidewinderettes doing a halftime double-snake whip. I want to see every single shade of blue in that castle and I've got a simply *great* idea for a play. Oh, Johnny, Daddy's back and you're here and I've got about everything there *is*. New York is such a knocked-out crazy wonderful town!"

# URSULA K. LE GUIN

## Buffalo Gals, Won't You Come Out Tonight

Ursula K. Le Guin was possibly the most talked-about SF writer of the seventies—rivaled only by Robert Silverberg, James Tiptree, Jr., and Philip K. Dick—and is probably one of the best-known and most universally respected SF writers in the world today. Her famous novel *The Left Hand of Darkness* may have been the most influential SF novel of its decade, and shows every sign of becoming one of the enduring classics of the genre—it won both the Hugo and Nebula Awards, as did Le Guin's monumental novel *The Dispossessed* a few years later. She has also won two other Hugo Awards and a Nebula Award for her short fiction, and the National Book Award for Children's literature for her novel *The Farthest Shore*, part of her acclaimed Earthsea trilogy. Her other novels include *Planet of Exile, The Lathe of Heaven, City of Illusions, Rocannon's World, The Beginning Place*, and the other two Earthsea novels, *A Wizard of Earthsea* and *The Tombs of Atuan*. She has had four collections: *The Wind's Twelve Quarters, Orsinian Tales, The Compass Rose*, and most recently, *Buffalo Gals and Other Animal Presences*. Her most recent novel is *Always Coming Home*.

Here she tells the evocative story of a little girl lost in a strange and very mysterious way.

# BUFFALO GALS, WON'T YOU COME OUT TONIGHT

## Ursula K. Le Guin

### 1

"You fell out of the sky," coyote said.

Still curled up tight, lying on her side, her back pressed against the overhanging rock, the child watched the coyote with one eye. Over the other eye she kept her hand cupped, its back on the dirt.

"There was a burned place in the sky, up there alongside the rimrock, and then you fell out of it," the coyote repeated, patiently, as if the news was getting a bit stale. "Are you hurt?"

She was all right. She was in the plane with Mr. Michaels, and the motor was so loud she couldn't understand what he said even when he shouted, and the way the wind rocked the wings was making her feel sick, but it was all right. They were flying to Canyonville. In the plane.

She looked. The coyote was still sitting there. It yawned. It was a big one, in good condition, its coat silvery and thick. The dark tear line back from its long yellow eye was as clearly marked as a tabby cat's.

She sat up slowly, still holding her right hand pressed to her right eye.

"Did you lose an eye?" the coyote asked, interested.

"I don't know," the child said. She caught her breath and shivered. "I'm cold."

"I'll help you look for it," the coyote said. "Come on! If you move around, you won't have to shiver. The sun's up."

Cold, lonely brightness lay across the falling land, a hundred miles of sagebrush. The coyote was trotting busily around, nosing under clumps of rabbitbrush and cheatgrass, pawing at a rock. "Aren't you going to look?" it said, suddenly sitting down on its haunches and abandoning the search. "I knew a trick once where I could throw my eyes way up into a tree and see everything from up there, and then whistle, and they'd come back into my head. But that goddamn bluejay stole them, and when I whistled, nothing came. I had to stick lumps of pine pitch into my head so I could see anything. You could try that. But you've got one eye that's O.K.; what do you need two for? Are you coming, or are you dying there?"

The child crouched, shivering.

"Well, come if you want to," said the coyote, yawned again, snapped at a flea, stood up, turned, and trotted away among the sparse clumps of rabbitbrush and sage, along the long slope that stretched on down and down into the plain streaked across by long shadows of sagebrush. The slender gray-yellow animal was hard to keep in sight, vanishing as the child watched.

She struggled to her feet and—without a word, though she kept saying in her mind, "Wait, please wait"—she hobbled after the coyote. She could not see it. She kept her hand pressed over the right eye socket. Seeing with one eye, there was no depth; it was like a huge, flat picture. The coyote suddenly sat in the middle of the picture, looking back at her, its mouth open, its eyes narrowed, grinning. Her legs began to steady, and her head did not pound so hard, though the deep black ache was always there. She had nearly caught up to the coyote, when it trotted off again. This time she spoke. "Please wait!" she said.

"O.K.," said the coyote, but it trotted right on. She followed, walking downhill into the flat picture that at each step was deep.

Each step was different underfoot; each sage bush was different, and all the same. Following the coyote, she came out from the shadow of the rimrock cliffs, and the sun at eye level dazzled her left eye. Its bright warmth soaked into her muscles and bones at once. The air, which all night had been so hard to breathe, came sweet and easy.

The sage bushes were pulling in their shadows, and the sun was hot on the child's back when she followed the coyote along the rim of a gully. After a while the coyote slanted down the undercut slope, and the child scrambled after, through scrub willows to the thin creek in its wide sand bed. Both drank.

The coyote crossed the creek, not with a careless charge and splashing like a dog, but single foot and quiet like a cat; always it carried its tail low. The child hesitated, knowing that wet shoes make blistered feet, and then waded across in as few steps as possible. Her right arm ached with the effort of holding her hand up over her eye. "I need a bandage," she said to the coyote. It cocked its head and said nothing. It stretched out its forelegs and lay watching the water, resting but alert. The child sat down nearby on the hot sand and tried to move her right hand. It was glued to the skin around her eye by dried blood. At the little tearing-away pain, she whimpered; though it was a small pain, it frightened her. The coyote came over close and poked its long snout into her face. Its strong, sharp smell was in her nostrils. It began to lick the awful, aching blindness, cleaning and cleaning with its curled, precise, strong, wet tongue, until the child was able to cry a little with relief, being comforted. Her head was bent close to the gray-yellow ribs, and she saw the hard nipples, the whitish belly fur. She put her arm around the she-coyote, stroking the harsh coat over back and ribs.

"O.K.," the coyote said, "let's go!" And set off without a backward glance. The child scrambled to her feet and followed. "Where are we going?" she said, and the coyote, trotting on down along the creek, answered, "On down along the creek. . . ."

There must have been a time while she was asleep that she walked because she felt like she was waking up, but she was walking along only in a different place. They were still following the creek, though the gully had flattened out to nothing much, and there was still sagebrush range as far as the eye could see. The eye—the good one—felt rested. The other one still ached, but not so sharply, and there was no use thinking about it. But where was the coyote?

She stopped. The pit of cold into which the plane had fallen reopened, and she fell. She stood falling, a thin whimper making itself in her throat.

"Over here!"

The child turned.

She saw a coyote gnawing at the half-dried-up carcass of a crow, black feathers sticking to the black lips and narrow jaw.

She saw a tawny-skinned woman kneeling by a campfire, sprinkling something into a conical pot. She heard the water boiling in the pot, though it was propped between rocks, off the fire. The woman's hair was yellow and gray, bound back with a string. Her feet were bare. The upturned soles looked as dark and hard as shoe soles, but the arch of the foot was high, and the toes made two neat curving rows. She wore blue jeans and an old white shirt. She looked over at the girl. "Come on, eat crow!" she said.

The child slowly came toward the woman and the fire, and squatted down. She had stopped falling and felt very light and empty; and her tongue was like a piece of wood stuck in her mouth.

Coyote was now blowing into the pot or basket or whatever it was. She reached into it with two fingers, and pulled her hand away, shaking it and shouting, "Ow! Shit! Why don't I ever have any spoons?" She broke off a dead twig of sagebrush, dipped it into the pot, and licked it. "Oh boy," she said. "Come on!"

The child moved a little closer, broke off a twig, dipped. Lumpy pinkish mush clung to the twig. She licked. The taste was rich and delicate.

"What is it?" she asked after a long time of dipping and licking.

"Food. Dried salmon mush," Coyote said. "It's cooling down." She stuck two fingers into the mush again, this time getting a good load, which she ate very neatly. The child, when she tried, got mush all over her chin. It was like chopsticks: it took practice. She practiced. They ate turn and turn until nothing was left in the pot but three rocks. The child did not ask why there were rocks in the mush pot. They licked the rocks clean. Coyote licked out the inside of the pot-basket, rinsed it once in the creek, and put it onto her head. It fit nicely, making a conical hat. She pulled off her blue jeans. "Piss on the fire!" she cried, and did so, standing straddling it. "Ah, steam between the legs!" she said. The child, embarrassed, thought she was supposed to do the same thing, but did not want to, and did not. Bareassed, Coyote danced around the dampened fire, kicking her long, thin legs out and singing:

*Buffalo gals, won't you come out tonight*
*Come out tonight, come out tonight,*
*Buffalo gals, won't you come out tonight,*
*And dance by the light of the moon?*

She pulled her jeans back on. The child was burying the remains of the fire in creek sand, heaping it over, seriously, wanting to do right. Coyote watched her.

"Is that you?" she said. "A Buffalo Gal? What happened to the rest of you?"

"The rest of me?" The child looked at herself, alarmed.

"All your people."

"Oh. Well, Mom took Bobbie—he's my little brother—away with Uncle Norm. He isn't really my uncle or anything. So Mr. Michaels was going there anyway, so he was going to fly me over to my real father, in Canyonville. Linda—my stepmother, you know—she said it was O.K. for the summer anyhow if I was there, and then we could see. But the plane."

In the silence the girl's face became dark red, then grayish white. Coyote watched, fascinated. "Oh," the girl said, "oh—oh—Mr. Michaels—he must be—Did the—"

"Come on!" said Coyote, and set off walking.

The child cried, "I ought to go back—"

"What for?" said Coyote. She stopped to look round at the child, then went on faster. "Come on, Gal!" She said it as a name; maybe it was the child's name, Myra, as spoken by Coyote. The child, confused and despairing, protested again, but followed her. "Where are we going? Where *are* we?"

"This is my country," Coyote answered with dignity, making a long, slow gesture all round the vast horizon. "I made it. Every goddamn sage brush."

And they went on. Coyote's gait was easy, even a little shambling, but she covered the ground; the child struggled not to drop behind. Shadows were beginning to pull themselves out again from under the rocks and shrubs. Leaving the creek, Coyote and the child went up a long, low, uneven slope that ended away off against the sky in rimrock. Dark trees stood one here, another way over there; what people called a juniper forest, a desert forest, one with a lot more between the trees than trees. Each juniper they passed smelled sharply—cat-pee smell the kids at school called it—but the child liked it; it seemed to go into her mind and wake her up. She picked off a juniper berry and held it in her mouth, but after a while spat it out again. The aching was coming back in huge black waves, and she kept stumbling. She found that she was sitting down on the ground. When she tried to get up, her legs shook and would not go under her. She felt foolish and frightened, and began to cry.

"We're home!" Coyote called from way on up the hill.

The child looked with her one weeping eye, and saw sagebrush, juniper, cheatgrass, rimrock. She heard a coyote yip far off in the dry twilight.

She saw a little town up under the rimrock: board houses, shacks, all unpainted. She heard Coyote call again, "Come on, pup! Come on, Gal, we're home!"

She could not get up, so she tried to go on all fours, the long way up the slope to the houses under the rimrock. Long before she got there, several people came to meet her. They were all children, she thought at first, and then began to understand that most of them were grown people, but all were very short; they were broad-bodied, fat, with fine, delicate hands and feet. Their eyes were bright. Some of the women helped her stand up and walk, coaxing her, "It isn't much farther, you're doing fine." In the late dusk, lights shone yellow-bright through doorways and through unchinked cracks between boards. Woodsmoke hung sweet in the quiet air. The short people talked and laughed all the time, softly. "Where's she going to stay?"—"Put her in with Robin, they're all asleep already!"—"Oh, she can stay with us."

The child asked hoarsely, "Where's Coyote?"

"Out hunting," the short people said.

A deeper voice spoke: "Somebody new has come into town?"

"Yes, a new person," one of the short men answered.

Among these people the deep-voiced man bulked impressive; he was broad and tall, with powerful hands, a big head, a short neck. They made way for him respectfully. He moved very quietly, respectful of them also. His eyes when he stared down at the child were amazing. When he blinked, it was like the passing of a hand before a candle flame.

"It's only an owlet," he said. "What have you let happen to your eye, new person?"

"I was—We were flying—"

"You're too young to fly," the big man said in his deep, soft voice. "Who brought you here?"

"Coyote."

And one of the short people confirmed: "She came here with Coyote, Young Owl."

"Then maybe she should stay in Coyote's house tonight," the big man said.

"It's all bones and lonely in there," said a short woman with fat cheeks and a striped shirt. "She can come with us."

That seemed to decide it. The fat-cheeked woman patted the child's arm and took her past several shacks and shanties to a low, windowless house. The doorway was so low even the child had to duck down to enter. There were a lot of people inside, some already there and some crowding in after the fat-cheeked woman. Several babies were fast asleep in cradle-boxes in the corner. There was a good fire, and a good smell, like toasted sesame seeds. The child was given food and ate a little, but her head swam, and the blackness in her right eye kept coming across her left eye, so she could not see at all for a while. Nobody asked her name or told her what to call them. She heard the children call the fat-cheeked woman Chipmunk. She got up courage finally to say, "Is there somewhere I can go to sleep, Mrs. Chipmunk?"

"Sure, come on," one of the daughters said, "in here," and took the child into a back room, not completely partitioned off from the crowded front room, but dark and uncrowded. Big shelves with mattresses and blankets lined the walls. "Crawl in!" said Chipmunk's daughter, patting the child's arm in the comforting way they had. The child climbed onto a shelf, under a blanket. She laid down her head. She thought, "I didn't brush my teeth."

## 2

She woke; she slept again. In Chipmunk's sleeping room it was always stuffy, warm, and half dark, day and night. People came in and slept and got up and left, night and day. She dozed and slept, got down to drink from the bucket and dipper in the front room, and went back to sleep and doze.

She was sitting up on the shelf, her feet dangling, not feeling bad anymore, but dreamy, weak. She felt in her jeans pocket. In the left front one was a pocket comb and a bubble gum wrapper, in the right front, two dollar bills and a quarter and a dime.

Chipmunk and another woman—a very pretty, dark-eyed, plump one—came in. "So you woke up for your dance!" Chipmunk greeted her, laughing, and sat down by her with an arm around her.

"Jay's giving you a dance," the dark woman said. "He's going to make you all right. Let's get you all ready!"

There was a spring up under the rimrock, which flattened out into a pool with slimy, reedy shores. A flock of noisy children splashing in it ran off and left the child and the two women to bathe. The water was warm on the surface, cold down on the feet and legs. All naked, the two soft-voiced, laughing women, their round bellies and breasts, broad hips and buttocks gleaming warm in the late-afternoon light, sluiced the child down, washed and stroked her limbs and hands and hair, cleaned around the cheekbone and eyebrow of her right eye with infinite softness, admired her, sudsed her, rinsed her, splashed her out of the water, dried her off, dried each other off, got dressed, dressed her, braided her hair, braided each other's hair, tied feathers on the braid-ends, admired her and each other again, and brought her back down into the little straggling town and to a kind of playing field or dirt parking lot in among the houses. There were no streets, just paths and dirt; no lawns and gardens, just sagebrush and dirt. Quite a few people were gathering or wandering around the open place, looking dressed up, wearing colorful shirts, bright dresses, strings of beads, earrings. "Hey there, Chipmunk, Whitefoot!" they greeted the women.

A man in new jeans, with a bright blue velveteen vest over a clean, faded blue work shirt, came forward to meet them, very handsome, tense, and important. "All right, Gal!" he said in a harsh, loud voice, which startled among all these soft-speaking people. "We're going to get that eye fixed right up tonight! You just sit down here and don't worry about a thing." He took her wrist, gently despite his bossy, brassy manner, and led her to a woven mat that lay on the dirt near the middle of the open place. There, feeling very foolish, she had to sit down, and was told to stay still. She soon got over feeling that everybody was looking at her, since nobody paid her more attention than a checking glance or, from Chipmunk or Whitefoot and their families, a reassuring wink. Every now and then, Jay rushed over to her and said something like, "Going to be as good as new!" and went off again to organize people, waving his long blue arms and shouting.

Coming up the hill to the open place, a lean, loose, tawny figure —and the child started to jump up, remembered she was to sit still, and sat still, calling out softly, "Coyote! Coyote!"

Coyote came lounging by. She grinned. She stood looking down at the child. "Don't let that Bluejay fuck you up, Gal," she said, and lounged on.

The child's gaze followed her, yearning.

People were sitting down now over on one side of the open place, making an uneven half circle that kept getting added to at the ends until there was nearly a circle of people sitting on the dirt around the child, ten or fifteen paces from her. All the people wore the kind of clothes the child was used to—jeans and jeans jackets, shirts, vests, cotton dresses—but they were all barefoot; and she thought they were more beautiful than the people she knew, each in a different way, as if each one had invented beauty. Yet some of them were also very strange: thin black shining people with whispery voices, a long-legged woman with eyes like jewels. The big man called Young Owl was there, sleepy-looking and dignified, like Judge McCown who owned a sixty-thousand acre ranch. And beside him was a woman the child thought might be his sister, for like him she had a hook nose and big, strong hands; but she was lean and dark, and there was a crazy look in her fierce eyes. Yellow eyes, but round, not long and slanted like Coyote's. There was Coyote sitting yawning, scratching her armpit, bored. Now somebody was entering the circle: a man, wearing only a kind of kilt and a cloak painted or beaded with diamond shapes, dancing to the rhythm of the rattle he carried and shook with a buzzing fast beat. His limbs and body were thick yet supple, his movements smooth and pouring. The child kept her gaze on him as he danced past her, around her, past again. The rattle in his hand shook almost too fast to see; in the other hand was something thin and sharp. People were singing around the circle now, a few notes repeated in time to the rattle, soft and tuneless. It was exciting and boring, strange and familiar. The Rattler wove his dancing closer and closer to her, darting at her. The first time, she flinched away, frightened by the lunging movement and by his flat, cold face with narrow eyes, but after that she sat still, knowing her part. The dancing went on, the singing went on, till they carried her past boredom into a floating that could go on forever.

Jay had come strutting into the circle and was standing beside her.

He couldn't sing, but he called out, "Hey! Hey! Hey! Hey!" in his big, harsh voice, and everybody answered from all round, and the echo came down from the rimrock on the second beat. Jay was holding up a stick with a ball on it in one hand, and something like a marble in the other. The stick was a pipe: he got smoke into his mouth from it and blew it in four directions and up and down and then over the marble, a puff each time. Then the rattle stopped suddenly, and everything was silent for several breaths. Jay squatted down and looked intently into the child's face, his head cocked to one side. He reached forward, muttering something in time to the rattle and the singing that had started up again louder than before; he touched the child's right eye in the black center of the pain. She flinched and endured. His touch was not gentle. She saw the marble, a dull yellow ball like beeswax, in his hand; then she shut her seeing eye and set her teeth.

"There!" Jay shouted. "Open up. Come on! Let's see!"

Her jaw clenched like a vise, she opened both eyes. The lid of the right one stuck and dragged with such a searing white pain that she nearly threw up as she sat there in the middle of everybody watching.

"Hey, can you see? How's it work? It looks great!" Jay was shaking her arm, railing at her. "How's it feel? Is it working?"

What she saw was confused, hazy, yellowish. She began to discover, as everybody came crowding around peering at her—smiling, stroking and patting her arms and shoulders—that if she shut the hurting eye and looked with the other, everything was clear and flat; if she used them both, things were blurry and yellowish, but deep.

There, right close, was Coyote's long nose and narrow eyes and grin. "What is it, Jay?" she was asking, peering at the new eye. "One of mine you stole that time?"

"It's pine pitch," Jay shouted furiously. "You think I'd use some stupid secondhand coyote eye? I'm a doctor!"

"Ooooh, ooooh, a doctor," Coyote said. "Boy, that is one ugly eye. Why didn't you ask Rabbit for a rabbit dropping? That eye looks like shit." She put her lean face yet closer, till the child thought she was going to kiss her; instead, the thin, firm tongue once more licked accurately across the pain, cooling, clearing. When the child opened both eyes again, the world looked pretty good.

"It works fine," she said.

"Hey!" Jay yelled. "She says it works fine! It works fine; she says so! I told you! What'd I tell you?" He went off waving his arms and yelling. Coyote had disappeared. Everybody was wandering off.

The child stood up, stiff from long sitting. It was nearly dark; only the long west held a great depth of pale radiance. Eastward, the plains ran down into night.

Lights were on in some of the shanties. Off at the edge of town, somebody was playing a creaky fiddle, a lonesome chirping tune.

A person came beside her and spoke quietly: "Where will you stay?"

"I don't know," the child said. She was feeling extremely hungry. "Can I stay with Coyote?"

"She isn't home much," the soft-voiced woman said. "You were staying with Chipmunk, weren't you? Or there's Rabbit, or Jackrabbit; they have families. . . ."

"Do you have a family?" the girl asked, looking at the delicate, soft-eyed woman.

"Two fawns," the woman answered, smiling. "But I just came into town for the dance."

"I'd really like to stay with Coyote," the child said after a pause, timid but obstinate.

"O.K., that's fine. Her house is over here." Doe walked along beside the child to a ramshackle cabin on the high edge of town. No light shone from inside. A lot of junk was scattered around the front. There was no step up to the half-open door. Over a battered pine board, nailed up crooked, said: "Bide-A-Wee."

"Hey, Coyote? Visitors," Doe said. Nothing happened.

Doe pushed the door farther open and peered in. "She's out hunting, I guess. I better be getting back to the fawns. You going to be O.K.? Anybody else here will give you something to eat—you know. . . . O.K.?"

"Yeah. I'm fine. Thank you," the child said.

She watched Doe walk away through the clear twilight, a severely elegant walk, small steps, like a woman in high heels, quick, precise, very light.

Inside Bide-A-Wee it was too dark to see anything, and so cluttered that she fell over something at every step. She could not figure out where or how to light a fire. There was something that felt like a bed, but when she lay down on it, it felt more like a dirty-clothes pile, and smelled like one. Things bit her legs, arms, neck, and back. She was terribly hungry. By smell, she found her way to what had to be a dead fish hanging from the ceiling in one corner. By feel, she broke off a greasy flake and tasted it. It was smoked, dried salmon. She ate one succulent piece after another until she was satisfied, and licked her fingers clean. Near the open door, starlight shone on water in a pot of some kind; the child smelled it cautiously, tasted it cautiously, and drank just enough to quench her thirst, for it tasted of mud and was warm and stale. Then she went back to the bed of dirty clothes and fleas, and lay down. She could have gone to Chipmunk's house, or other friendly households; she thought of that as she lay forlorn in Coyote's dirty bed. But she did not go. She slapped at fleas until she fell asleep.

Along in the deep night, somebody said, "Move over, pup," and was warm beside her.

Breakfast, eaten sitting in the sun in the doorway, was dried-salmon-powder mush. Coyote hunted, mornings and evenings, but what they ate was not fresh game but salmon, and dried stuff, and any berries in season. The child did not ask about this. It made sense to her. She was going to ask Coyote why she slept at night and waked in the day like humans, instead of the other way round like coyotes, but when she framed the question in her mind, she saw at once that night is when you sleep and day when you're awake; that made sense, too. But one question she did ask, one hot day when they were lying around slapping fleas.

"I don't understand why you all look like people," she said.

"We are people."

"I mean, people like me, humans."

"Resemblance is in the eye," Coyote said. "How is that lousy eye, by the way?"

"It's fine. But—like you wear clothes—and live in houses—with fires and stuff—"

"That's what *you* think. . . . If that loudmouth Jay hadn't horned in, I could have done a really good job."

The child was quite used to Coyote's disinclination to stick to any one subject, and to her boasting. Coyote was like a lot of kids she knew, in some respects. Not in others.

"You mean what I'm seeing isn't true? Isn't real—like TV or something?"

"No," Coyote said. "Hey, that's a tick on your collar." She reached over, flicked the tick off, picked it up on one finger, bit it, and spat out the bits.

"Yecch!" the child said. "So?"

"So, to me, you're basically grayish yellow and run on four legs. To that lot"—she waved disdainfully at the warren of little houses next down the hill—"you hop around twitching your nose all the time. To Hawk, you're an egg, or maybe getting pinfeathers. See? It just depends on how you look at things. There are only two kinds of people."

"Humans and animals?"

"No. The kind of people who say, 'There are two kinds of people,' and the kind of people who don't." Coyote cracked up, pounding her thighs and yelling with delight at her joke. The child didn't get it, and waited.

"O.K.," Coyote said. "There're the first people, and then the others. Those're the two kinds."

"The first people are—?"

"Us, the animals . . . and things. All the old ones. You know. And you pups, kids, fledglings. All first people."

"And the—others?"

"Them," Coyote said. "You know. The others. The new people. The ones who came." Her fine, hard face had gone serious, rather formidable. She glanced directly, as she seldom did, at the child, a brief gold sharpness. "We are here," she said. "We are always here. We are always here. Where we are is here. But it's their country now. They're running it. . . . Shit, even I did better!"

The child pondered and offered a word she had used to hear a good deal: "They're illegal immigrants."

"Illegal!" Coyote said, mocking, sneering. "Illegal is a sick bird. What the fuck's illegal mean? You want a code of justice from a coyote? Grow up kid!"

"I don't want to."

"You don't want to grow up?"

"I'll be the other kind if I do."

"Yeah. So," Coyote said, and shrugged. "That's life." She got up and went around the house, and the child heard her pissing in the backyard.

A lot of things were hard to take about Coyote as a mother. When her boyfriends came to visit, the child learned to go stay with Chipmunk or the Rabbits for the night, because Coyote and her friend wouldn't even wait to get on the bed, but would start doing that right on the floor or even out in the yard. A couple of times, Coyote came back late from hunting with a friend, and the child had to lie up against the wall in the same bed and hear and feel them doing that right next to her. It was something like fighting and something like dancing, with a beat to it, and she didn't mind too much except that it made it hard to stay asleep. Once she woke up and one of Coyote's friends was stroking her stomach in a creepy way. She didn't know what to do, but Coyote woke up and realized what he was doing, bit him hard, and kicked him out of bed. He spent the night on the floor, and apologized next morning—"Aw, hell, Ki, I forgot the kid was there; I thought it was you—"

Coyote, unappeased, yelled, "You think I don't got any standards? You think I'd let some coyote rape a kid in my *bed*?" She kicked him out of the house, and grumbled about him all day. But a while later he spent the night again, and he and Coyote did that three or four times.

Another thing that was embarrassing was the way Coyote peed

anywhere, taking her pants down in public. But most people here didn't seem to care. The thing that worried the child most, maybe, was when Coyote did number two anywhere and then turned around and talked to it. That seemed so awful. As if Coyote were—the way she often seemed, but really wasn't—crazy.

The child gathered up all the old dry turds from around the house one day while Coyote was having a nap, and buried them in a sandy place near where she and Bobcat and some of the other people generally went and did and buried their number twos.

Coyote woke up, came lounging out of Bide-A-Wee, rubbing her hands through her thick, fair, grayish hair and yawning, looked all round once with those narrow eyes, and said, "Hey! Where are they?" Then she shouted, "Where are you? Where are you?"

And a faint chorus came from over in the draw: "Mommy! We're here!"

Coyote trotted over, squatted down, raked out every turd, and talked with them for a long time. When she came back, she said nothing, but the child, red-faced and heart pounding, said, "I'm sorry I did that."

"It's just easier when they're all around close by," Coyote said, washing her hands (despite the filth of her house, she kept herself quite clean, in her own fashion).

"I kept stepping on them," the child said, trying to justify her deed.

"Poor little shits," said Coyote, practicing dance steps.

"Coyote," the child said timidly. "Did you ever have any children? I mean real pups?"

"Did I? Did I have children? Litters! That one that tried feeling you up, you know? That was my son. Pick of the litter. . . . Listen, Gal. Have daughters. When you have anything, have daughters. At least they clear out."

## 3

The child thought of herself as Gal, but also sometimes as Myra. So far as she knew, she was the only person in town who had two names. She had to think about that, and about what Coyote had said about the two kinds of people; she had to think about where she belonged. Some persons in town made it clear that as far as they were concerned, she didn't and never would belong there. Hawk's furious stare burned through her; the Skunk children made audible remarks about what she smelled like. And though Whitefoot and Chipmunk and their families were kind, it was the generosity of big families, where one more or less simply doesn't count. If one of them, or Cottontail, or Jackrabbit, had come upon her in the desert lying lost and half blind, would they have stayed with her, like Coyote? That was Coyote's craziness, what they called her craziness. She wasn't afraid. She went between the two kinds of people; she crossed over. Buck and Doe and their beautiful children were really afraid, because they lived so constantly in danger. The Rattler wasn't afraid, because he was so dangerous. And yet maybe he was afraid of her, for he never spoke, and never came close to her. None of them treated her the way Coyote did. Even among the children, her only constant playmate was one younger than herself, a preposterous and fearless little boy called Horned Toad Child. They dug and built together, out among the sagebrush, and played at hunting and gathering and keeping house and holding dances, all the great games. A pale, squatty child with fringed eyebrows, he was a self-contained but loyal friend; and he knew a good deal for his age.

"There isn't anybody else like me here," she said as they sat by the pool in the morning sunlight.

"There isn't anybody much like me anywhere," said Horned Toad Child.

"Well, you know what I mean."

"Yeah. . . . There used to be people like you around, I guess."

"What were they called?"

"Oh—people. Like everybody. . . ."

"But where do *my* people live? They have towns. I used to live in one. I don't know where they are, is all. I ought to find out. I don't know where my mother is now, but daddy's in Canyonville. I was going there when. . . ."

"Ask Horse," said Horned Toad Child sagaciously. He had moved away from the water, which he did not like and never drank, and was plaiting rushes.

"I don't know Horse."

"He hangs around the butte down there a lot of the time. He's waiting till his uncle gets old and he can kick him out and be the big honcho. The old man and the women don't want him around till then. Horses are weird. Anyway, he's the one to ask. He gets around a lot. And his people came here with the new people; that's what they say, anyhow."

Illegal immigrants, the girl thought. She took Horned Toad's advice, and one long day when Coyote was gone on one of her unannounced and unexplained trips, she took a pouchful of dried salmon and salmonberries and went off alone to the flat-topped butte miles away in the southwest.

There was a beautiful spring at the foot of the butte, and a trail to it with a lot of footprints on it. She waited there under willows by the clear pool, and after a while Horse came running, splendid, with copper-red skin and long, strong legs, deep chest, dark eyes, his black hair whipping his back as he ran. He stopped, not at all winded, and gave a snort as he looked at her. "Who are you?"

Nobody in town asked that—ever. She saw it was true; Horse had come here with her people, people who had to ask each other who they were.

"I live with Coyote," she said cautiously.

"Oh sure, I heard about you," Horse said. He knelt to drink from the pool. Long, deep drafts, his hands plunged in the cool water. When he had drunk, he wiped his mouth, sat back on his heels, and announced, "I'm going to be king."

"King of the horses?"

"Right! Pretty soon now. I could lick the old man already, but I can wait. Let him have his day," said Horse, vainglorious, magnanimous. The child gazed at him, in love already, forever.

"I can comb your hair, if you like," she said.

"Great!" said Horse, and sat still while she stood behind him, tugging her pocket comb through his coarse, black, shining, yard-long hair. It took a long time to get it smooth. She tied it in a massive ponytail with willow bark when she was done. Horse bent over the pool to admire himself. "That's great," he said. "That's really beautiful!"

"Do you ever go . . . where the other people are?" she asked in a low voice.

He did not reply for long enough that she thought he wasn't going to; then he said, "You mean the metal places, the glass places? The holes? I go around them. There are all the walls now. There didn't use to be so many. Grandmother said there didn't use to be any walls. Do you know Grandmother?" he asked naively, looking at her with his great, dark eyes.

"Your grandmother?"

"Well, yes—Grandmother—you know. Who makes the web. Well, anyhow. I know there's some of my people, horses, there. I've seen them across the walls. They act really crazy. You know, we brought the new people here. They couldn't have got here without us: they have only two legs, and they have those metal shells. I can tell you that whole story. The king has to know the stories."

"I like stories a lot."

"It takes three nights to tell it. What do you want to know about them?"

"I was thinking that maybe I ought to go there. Where they are."

"It's dangerous. Really dangerous. You can't go through—they'd catch you."

"I'd just like to know the way."

"I know the way," Horse said, sounding for the first time entirely adult and reliable; she knew he did know the way. "It's a long run for a colt." He looked at her again. "I've got a cousin with different-color eyes," he said, looking from her right to her left eye. "One brown and one blue. But she's an Appaloosa."

"Bluejay made the yellow one," the child explained. "I lost my own one. In the . . . when. . . . You don't think I could get to those places?"

"Why do you want to?"

"I sort of feel like I have to."

Horse nodded. He got up. She stood still.

"I could take you, I guess," he said.

"Would you? When?"

"Oh, now, I guess. Once I'm king I won't be able to leave, you know. Have to protect the women. And I sure wouldn't let my people get anywhere near those places!" A shudder ran right down his magnificent body, yet he said, with a toss of his head, "They couldn't catch *me*, of course, but the others can't run like I do. . . ."

"How long would it take us?"

Horse thought for a while. "Well, the nearest place like that is over the red rocks. If we left now, we'd be back here around tomorrow noon. It's just a little hole."

She did not know what he meant by "a hole," but did not ask.

"You want to go?" Horse said, flipping back his ponytail.

"O.K.," the girl said, feeling the ground go out from under her.

"Can you run?"

She shook her head. "I walked here, though."

Horse laughed, a large, cheerful laugh. "Come on," he said, and knelt and held his hands back-turned like stirrups for her to mount to his shoulders. "What do they call you?" he teased, rising easily, setting right off at a jog trot. "Gnat? Fly? Flea?"

"Tick, because I stick!" the child cried, gripping the willow bark tie of the black mane, laughing with delight at being suddenly eight feet tall and traveling across the desert without even trying, like the tumbleweed, as fast as the wind.

Moon, a night past full, rose to light the plains for them. Horse jogged easily on and on. Somewhere deep in the night, they stopped at a Pygmy Owl camp, ate a little, and rested. Most of the owls were out hunting, but an old lady entertained them at her campfire, telling them tales about the ghost of a cricket, about the great invisible people, tales that the child heard interwoven with her own dreams as she dozed and half woke and dozed again. Then Horse put her up on his shoulders, and on they went at a tireless, slow lope. Moon went down behind them, and before them the sky paled into rose and gold. The soft night wind was gone; the air was sharp, cold, still. On it, in it, there was a faint, sour smell of burning. The child felt Horse's gait change, grow tighter, uneasy.

"Hey, Prince!"

A small, slightly scolding voice: the child knew it, and placed it as soon as she saw the person sitting by a juniper tree, neatly dressed, wearing an old black cap.

"Hey, Chickadee!" Horse said, coming round and stopping. The child had observed, back in Coyote's town, that everybody treated Chickadee with respect. She didn't see why. Chickadee seemed an ordinary person, busy and talkative like most of the small birds, nothing so endearing as Quail or so impressive as Hawk or Great Owl.

"You're going on that way?" Chickadee asked Horse.

"The little one wants to see if her people are living there," Horse said, surprising the child. Was that what she wanted?

Chickadee looked disapproving, as she often did. She whistled a few notes thoughtfully, another of her habits, and then got up. "I'll come along."

"That's great," Horse said thankfully.

"I'll scout," Chickadee said, and off she went, surprisingly fast, ahead of them, while Horse took up his steady, long lope.

The sour smell was stronger in the air.

Chickadee halted, way ahead of them on a slight rise, and stood still. Horse dropped to a walk, and then stopped. "There," she said in a low voice.

The child stared. In the strange light and slight mist before sunrise, she could not see clearly, and when she strained and peered, she felt as if her left eye were not seeing at all. "What is it?" she whispered.

"One of the holes. Across the wall—see?"

It did seem there was a line, a straight, jerky line drawn across the sagebrush plain, and on the far side of it—nothing? Was it mist? Something moved there—

"It's cattle!" she said.

Horse stood silent, uneasy. Chickadee was coming back toward them.

"It's a ranch," the child said. "That's a fence. There're a lot of Herefords." The words tasted like iron, like salt in her mouth. The things she named wavered in her sight and faded, leaving nothing—a hole in the world, a burned place like a cigarette burn. "Go closer!" she urged Horse. "I want to see."

And as if he owed her obedience, he went forward, tense but unquestioning.

Chickadee came up to them. "Nobody around," she said in her small, dry voice, "but there's one of those fast turtle things coming."

Horse nodded but kept going forward.

Gripping his broad shoulders, the child stared into the blank, and as if Chickadee's words had focused her eyes, she saw again: the scattered whitefaces, a few of them looking up with bluish, rolling eyes—the fences—over the rise a chimneyed house roof and a high barn—and then in the distance, something moving fast, too fast, burning across the ground straight at them at terrible speed. "Run!" she yelled to Horse. "Run away! Run!" As if released from bonds, he wheeled and ran, flat out, in great reaching strides, away from sunrise, the fiery burning chariot, the smell of acid, iron, death. And Chickadee flew before them like a cinder on the air of dawn.

## 4

"Horse?" Coyote said. "That prick? Cat food!"

Coyote had been there when the child got home to Bide-A-Wee, but she clearly hadn't been worrying about where Gal was, and maybe hadn't even noticed she was gone. She was in a vile mood, and took it all wrong when the child tried to tell her about where she had been.

"If you're going to do damn fool things, next time do 'em with me; at least I'm an expert," she said, morose, and slouched out the door. The child saw her squatting down, poking an old white turd with a stick, trying to get it to answer some question she kept asking it. The turd lay obstinately silent. Later in the day the child saw two coyote men, a young one and a mangy-looking older one, loitering around near the spring, looking over at Bide-A-Wee. She decided it would be a good night to spend somewhere else.

The thought of the crowded rooms of Chipmunk's house was not attractive. It was going to be a warm night again tonight, and moonlit. Maybe she would sleep outside. If she could feel sure some people wouldn't come around, like the Rattler. . . . She was standing indecisively halfway through town when a dry voice said, "Hey, Gal."

"Hey, Chickadee."

The trim, black-capped woman was standing on her doorstep shaking out a rug. She kept her house neat, trim like herself. Having come back across the desert with her, the child now knew, though she still could not have said, why Chickadee was a respected person.

"I thought maybe I'd sleep out tonight," the child said, tentative.

"Unhealthy," said Chickadee. "What are nests for?"

"Mom's kind of busy," the child said.

"Tsk!" went Chickadee, and snapped the rug with disapproving vigor. "What about her little friend? At least they're decent people."

"Horny-toad? His parents are so shy. . . ."

"Well. Come in and have something to eat, anyhow," said Chickadee.

The child helped her cook dinner. She knew now why there were rocks in the mush pot.

"Chickadee," she said, "I still don't understand; can I ask you? Mom said it depends who's seeing it, but still; I mean, if I see you wearing clothes and everything like humans, then how come you cook this way, in baskets, you know, and there aren't any—any of the things like they have—there where we were with Horse this morning?"

"I don't know," Chickadee said. Her voice indoors was quite soft and pleasant. "I guess we do things the way they always were done, when your people and my people lived together, you know. And together with everything else here. The rocks, you know. The plants and everything." She looked at the basket of willow bark, fern root, and pitch, at the blackened rocks that were heating in the fire. "You see how it all goes together. . . ."

"But you have fire—That's different—"

"Ah!" said Chickadee, impatient, "you people! Do you think you invented the sun?"

She took up the wooden tongs, plopped the heated rocks into the water-filled basket with a terrific hiss and steam and loud bubblings. The child sprinkled in the pounded seeds and stirred.

Chickadee brought out a basket of fine blackberries. They sat on the newly shaken-out rug and ate. The child's two-finger scoop technique with mush was now highly refined.

"Maybe I didn't cause the world," Chickadee said, "but I'm a better cook than Coyote."

The child nodded, stuffing.

"I don't know why I made Horse go there," she said after she had stuffed. "I got just as scared as he did when I saw it. But now I feel again like I have to go back there. But I want to stay here. With my friends, with Coyote. I don't understand."

"When we lived together, it was all one place," Chickadee said in her slow, soft home-voice. "But now the others, the new people, they live apart. And their places are so heavy. They weigh down on our place, they press on it, draw it, suck it, eat it, eat holes in it, crowd it out. . . . Maybe after a while longer, there'll be only one place again, their place. And none of us here. I knew Bison, out over the mountains. I knew Antelope right here. I knew Grizzly and Graywolf, up west there. Gone. All gone. And the salmon you eat at Coyote's house, those are the dream salmon, those are the true food; but in the rivers, how many salmon now? The rivers that were red with them in spring? Who dances, now, when the First Salmon offers himself? Who dances by the river? Oh, you should ask Coyote about all this. She knows more than I do! But she forgets. . . . She's hopeless, worse than Raven; she has to piss on every post; she's a terrible housekeeper. . . ." Chickadee's voice had sharpened. She whistled a note or two, and said no more.

After a while the child asked very softly, "Who is Grandmother?"

"Grandmother," Chickadee said. She looked at the child and ate several blackberries thoughtfully. She stroked the rug they sat on.

"If I built the fire on the rug, it would burn a hole in it," she said. "Right? So we build the fire on sand, on dirt. . . . Things are woven together. So we call the weaver the Grandmother." She whistled four notes, looking up the smoke hole. "After all," she added, "maybe all this place—the other places, too—maybe they're all only one side of the weaving. I don't know. I can look with one eye at a time; how can I tell how deep it goes?"

Lying that night rolled up in a blanket in Chickadee's backyard, the child heard the wind soughing and storming in the cottonwoods down in the draw, and then slept deeply, weary from the long night before. Just at sunrise she woke. The eastern mountains were a cloudy dark red as if the level light shone through them as through a hand held before the fire. In the tobacco patch—the only farming anybody in this town did was to raise a little wild tobacco—Lizard and Beetle were singing some kind of growing song or blessing song, soft and desultory, *huh*-huh-huh-huh, *huh*-huh-huh-huh, and as she lay warm-curled on the ground, the song made her feel rooted in the ground, cradled on it and in it, so where her fingers ended and the dirt began, she did not know, as if she were dead—but she was wholly alive; she was the earth's life. She got up dancing, left the blanket folded neatly on Chickadee's nest and already empty bed, and danced up the hill to Bide-A-Wee. At the half-open door, she sang:

*Danced with a gal with a hole in her stocking*
*And her knees kept a knocking and her toes kept a rocking,*

*Danced with a gal with a hole in her stocking,*
*Danced by the light of the moon!*

Coyote emerged, tousled and lurching, and eyed her narrowly. "Sheeeoot," she said. She sucked her teeth and then went to splash water all over her head from the gourd by the door. She shook her head, and the water drops flew. "Let's get out of here," she said. "I have had it. I don't know what got into me. If I'm pregnant again, at my age, oh shit. Let's get out of town. I need a change of air."

In the fuggy dark of the house, the child could see at least two coyote men sprawled snoring away on the bed and floor.

Coyote walked over to the old white turd and kicked it. "Why didn't you stop me?" she shouted.

"I *told* you," the turd muttered sulkily.

"Dumb shit," Coyote said. "Come on, Gal. Let's go. Where to?" She didn't wait for an answer. "I know. Come on!"

And she set off through town at that lazy-looking, rangy walk that was so hard to keep up with. But the child was full of pep, and came dancing, so that Coyote began dancing, too, skipping and pirouetting and fooling around all the way down the long slope to the level plains. There she slanted their way off northeastward. Horse Butte was at their backs, getting smaller in the distance.

Along near noon the child said, "I didn't bring anything to eat."

"Something will turn up," Coyote said. "Sure to." And pretty soon she turned aside, going straight to a tiny gray shack hidden by a couple of half-dead junipers and a stand of rabbitbrush. The place smelled terrible. A sign on the door said: Fox. Private. No Trespassing!—but Coyote pushed it open, and trotted right back out with half a small smoked salmon. "Nobody home but us chickens," she said, grinning sweetly.

"Isn't that stealing?" the child asked, worried.

"Yes," Coyote answered, trotting on.

They ate the fox-scented salmon by a dried-up creek, slept a while, and went on.

Before long the child smelled the sour burning smell, and stopped. It was as if a huge, heavy hand had begun pushing her chest, pushing her away, and yet at the same time as if she had stepped into a strong current that drew her forward, helpless.

"Hey, getting close!" Coyote said, and stopped to piss by a juniper stump.

"Close to what?"

"Their town. See?" She pointed to a pair of sage-spotted hills. Between them was an area of grayish blank.

"I don't want to go there."

"We won't go all the way in. No way! We'll just get a little closer and look. It's fun," Coyote said, putting her head on one side, coaxing. "They do all these weird things in the air."

The child hung back.

Coyote became businesslike, responsible. "We're going to be very careful," she announced. "And look out for big dogs, O.K.? Little dogs I can handle. Make a good lunch. Big dogs, it goes the other way. Right? Let's go, then."

Seemingly as casual and lounging as ever, but with a tense alertness in the carriage of her head and the yellow glance of her eyes, Coyote led off again, not looking back; and the child followed.

All around them the pressures increased. It was as if the air itself were pressing on them, as if time were going too fast, too hard, not flowing but pounding, pounding, pounding, faster and harder till it buzzed like Rattler's rattle. "Hurry, you have to hurry!" everything said. "There isn't time!" everything said. Things rushed past screaming and shuddering. Things turned, flashed, roared, stank, vanished. There was a boy—he came into focus all at once, but not on the ground: he was going along a couple of inches above the ground, moving very fast, bending his legs from side to side in a kind of frenzied, swaying dance, and was gone. Twenty children sat in rows in the air, all singing shrilly, and then the walls closed over them. A basket, no, a pot, no, a can, a garbage can, full of salmon smelling wonderful, no, full of stinking deer hides and rotten cabbage stalks —keep out of it. Coyote! Where was she?

"Mom!" the child called. "Mother!"—standing a moment at the end of an ordinary small-town street near the gas station, and the next moment in a terror of blanknesses, invisible walls, terrible smells and pressures and the overwhelming rush of Time straightforward rolling her helpless as a twig in the race above a waterfall. She clung, held on trying not to fall—"Mother!"

Coyote was over by the big basket of salmon, approaching it, wary but out in the open, in the full sunlight, in the full current. And a boy and a man borne by the same current were coming down the long, sage-spotted hill behind the gas station, each with a gun, red hats—hunters; it was killing season. "Hey, will you look at that damn coyote in broad daylight big as my wife's ass," the man said, and cocked, aimed, shot—all as Myra screamed and ran against the enormous drowning torrent. Coyote fled past her yelling, "Get out of here!" She turned and was borne away.

Far out of sight of that place, in a little draw among low hills, they sat and breathed air in searing gasps until, after a long time, it came easy again.

"Mom, that was *stupid*," the child said furiously.

"Sure was," Coyote said. "But did you see all that food!"

"I'm not hungry," the child said sullenly. "Not till we get all the way away from here."

"But they're your folks," Coyote said. "All yours. Your kith and kin and cousins and kind. Bang! Pow! There's Coyote! Bang! There's my wife's ass! Pow! There's anything—BOOOOM! Blow it away, man! BOOOOOOM!"

"I want to go home," the child said.

"Not yet," said Coyote. "I got to take a shit." She did so, then turned to the fresh turd, leaning over it. "It says I have to stay," she reported, smiling.

"It didn't say anything! I was listening!"

"You know who to understand? You hear everything, Miss Big Ears? Hears all—See all with her crummy, gummy eye—"

"You have pine-pitch eyes, too! You told me so!"

"That's a story," Coyote snarled. "You don't even know a story when you hear one! Look, do what you like; it's a free country. I'm hanging around here tonight. I like the action." She sat down and began patting her hands on the dirt in a soft four-four rhythm and singing under her breath, one of the endless, tuneless songs that kept time from running too fast, that wove the roots of trees and bushes and ferns and grass in the web that held the stream in the streambed and the rock in the rock's place and the earth together. And the child lay listening.

"I love you," she said.

Coyote went on singing.

Sun went down the last slope of the west and left a pale green clarity over the desert hills.

Coyote had stopped singing. She sniffed. "Hey," she said. "Dinner." She got up and moseyed along the little draw. "Yeah," she called back softly. "Come on!"

Stiffly, for the fear-crystals had not yet melted out of her joints, the child got up and went to Coyote. Off to one side along the hill was one of the lines, a fence. She didn't look at it. It was O.K. They were outside it.

"Look at that!"

A smoked salmon, a whole chinook, lay on a little cedar-bark mat.

"An offering! Well, I'll be darned!" Coyote was so impressed she didn't even swear. "I haven't seen one of these for years! I thought they'd forgotten!"

"Offering to whom?"

"Me! Who else? Boy, *look* at that!"

The child looked dubiously at the salmon.

"It smells funny."

"How funny?"

"Like burned."

"It's smoked, stupid! Come on."

"I'm not hungry."

"O.K. It's not your salmon anyhow. It's mine. My offering, for me. Hey, you people! You people over there! Coyote thanks you! Keep it up like this, and maybe I'll do some good things for you, too!"

"Don't, don't yell, Mom! They're not that far away—"

"They're all my people," said Coyote with a great gesture, and then sat down cross-legged, broke off a big piece of salmon, and ate.

Evening Star burned like a deep, bright pool of water in the clear sky. Down over the twin hills was a dim suffusion of light, like a fog. The child looked away from it, back at the star.

"Oh," Coyote said. "Oh shit."

"What's wrong?"

"That wasn't so smart, eating that," Coyote said, and then held herself and began to shiver, to scream, to choke—her eyes rolled up; her long arms and legs flew out jerking and dancing; foam spurted out between her teeth. Her body arched tremendously backward, and the child, trying to hold her, was thrown violently off by the spasms of her limbs. The child scrambled back and held the body as it spasmed again, twitched, quivered, went still.

By moonrise, Coyote was cold. Till then there had been so much warmth under the tawny coat that the child kept thinking maybe she was alive, maybe if she just kept holding her, keeping her warm, Coyote would recover, she would be all right. The child held her close, not looking at the black lips drawn back from the teeth, the white balls of the eyes. But when the cold came through the fur as the presence of death, the child let the slight, stiff corpse lie down on the dirt.

She went nearby and dug a hole in the stony sand of the draw, a shallow pit. Coyote's people did not bury their dead; she knew that. But her people did. She carried the small corpse to the pit, laid it down, and covered it with her blue and white bandanna. It was not large enough; the four stiff paws stuck out. The child heaped the body over with sand and rocks and a scurf of sagebrush and tumbleweed held down with more rocks. She also heaped dirt and rocks over the poisoned salmon carcass. Then she stood up and walked away without looking back.

At the top of the hill, she stood and looked across the draw toward the misty glow of the lights of the town lying in the pass between the twin hills.

"I hope you all die in pain," she said aloud. She turned away and walked down into the desert.

## 5

It was Chickadee who met her, on the second evening, north of Horse Butte.

"I didn't cry," the child said.

"None of us do," said Chickadee. "Come with me this way now. Come into Grandmother's house."

It was underground, but very large, dark and large, and the Grandmother was there at the center, at her loom. She was making a rug or blanket of the hills and the black rain and the white rain, weaving in the lightning. As they spoke, she wove.

"Hello, Chickadee. Hello, New Person."

"Grandmother," Chickadee greeted her.

The child said, "I'm not one of them."

Grandmother's eyes were small and dim. She smiled and wove. The shuttle thrummed through the warp.

"Old Person, then," said Grandmother. "You'd better go back there now, Granddaughter. That's where you live."

"I lived with Coyote. She's dead. They killed her."

"Oh, don't worry about Coyote!" Grandmother said with a little huff of laughter. "She gets killed all the time."

The child stood still. She saw the endless weaving.

"Then I—Could I go back home—to her house—?"

"I don't think it would work," Grandmother said. "Do you, Chickadee?"

Chickadee shook her head once, silent.

"It would be dark there now, and empty, and fleas. . . . You got outside your people's time, into our place; but I think that Coyote was taking you back, see. Her way. If you go back now, you can still live with them. Isn't your father there?"

The child nodded.

"They've been looking for you."

"They have?"

"Oh yes. Ever since you fell out of the sky. The man was dead, but you weren't there—they kept looking."

"Serves him right. Served them all right," the child said. She put her hands up over her face and began to cry terribly, without tears.

"Go on, little one, Granddaughter," Spider said. "Don't be afraid. You can live well there. I'll be there, too, you know. In your dreams, in your ideas, in dark corners in the basement. Don't kill me, or I'll make it rain. . . ."

"I'll come around," Chickadee said. "Make gardens for me."

The child held her breath and clenched her hands until her sobs stopped and let her speak.

"Will I ever see Coyote?"

"I don't know," the Grandmother replied.

The child accepted this. She said, after another silence, "Can I keep my eye?"

"Yes. You can keep your eye."

"Thank you, Grandmother," the child said. She turned away then and started up the night slope toward the next day. Ahead of her in the air of dawn for a long way, a little bird flew, black-capped, light-winged.

# ROBERT SILVERBERG

## The Pardoner's Tale

To forgive may be divine, but to *pardon* can be very costly . . . and sometimes very dangerous as well, as demonstrated by the story that follows.

One of the most prolific authors alive, Robert Silverberg can lay claim to more than 450 fiction and nonfiction books and over 3,000 magazine pieces. Within SF, Silverberg rose to his greatest prominence during the late '60s and early '70s, winning four Nebula Awards and a Hugo Award, publishing dozens of major novels and anthologies. In 1980, *Lord Valentine's Castle* became a nationwide bestseller. Silverberg's other books include *The Book of Skulls, Downward to the Earth, Tower of Glass, The World Inside, Born with the Dead, Shadrach in the Furnace, Lord of Darkness* (a historical novel), and *Valentine Pontifex*, the sequel to *Lord Valentine's Castle*. His collections include *Unfamiliar Territory, Capricorn Games, Majipoor Chronicles, The Best of Robert Silverberg, At the Conglomeroid Cocktail Party*, and *Beyond the Safe Zone.* His most recent books are the novels *Tom O'Bedlam, Star of Gypsies*, and *At Winter's End.* His story "Multiples" was in our First Annual Collection; "The Affair" was in our Second Annual Collection; "Sailing to Byzantium"—which won a Nebula Award in 1986—was in our Third Annual Collection; and "Against Babylon" was in our Fourth Annual Collection. Silverberg received another Hugo Award in 1987. He lives in Oakland, California, with his wife, Karen Haber.

# THE PARDONER'S TALE

## Robert Silverberg

Key sixteen, Housing Omicron Kappa, aleph sub-one," I said to the software on duty at the Alhambra gate of the Los Angeles Wall.

Software isn't generally suspicious. This wasn't even very smart software. It was working off some great biochips—I could feel them jigging and pulsing as the electron stream flowed through them—but the software itself was just a kludge. Typical gatekeeper stuff.

I stood waiting as the picoseconds went ticking away by the millions.

"Name, please," the gatekeeper said finally.

"John Doe. Beta Pi Upsilon, ten-four-three-two-four-X."

The gate opened. I walked into Los Angeles.

As easy as Beta Pi.

The wall that encircles L.A. is 100, 150 feet thick. Its gates are more like tunnels. When you consider that the wall runs completely around the L.A. basin, from the San Gabriel Valley to the San Fernando Valley and then over the mountains and down the coast and back the far side past Long Beach, and that it's at least 60 feet high and all that distance deep, you can begin to appreciate the mass of it. Think of the phenomenal expenditure of human energy that went into building it—muscle and sweat, sweat and muscle. I think about that a lot.

I suppose the walls around our cities were put there mostly as symbols. They highlight the distinction between city and countryside, between citizen and uncitizen, between control and chaos, just as city walls did 5000 years ago. But mainly they serve to remind us that we are all slaves nowadays. You can't ignore the walls. You can't pretend they aren't there. *We made you build us*, is what they say, *and don't you ever forget that*. All the same, Chicago doesn't have a wall 60 feet high and 150 feet thick. Houston doesn't. Phoenix doesn't. They make do with less. But L.A. is the main city. I suppose the Los

Angeles Wall is a statement: *I am the Big Cheese. I am the Ham What Am.*

The walls aren't there because the Entities are afraid of attack. They know how invulnerable they are. We know it, too. They just want to decorate their capital with something a little special. What the hell; it isn't *their* sweat that goes into building the walls. It's ours. Not mine personally, of course. But ours.

I saw a few Entities walking around just inside the wall, preoccupied, as usual, with God knows what and paying no attention to the humans in the vicinity. These were low-caste ones, the kind with the luminous orange spots along their sides. I gave them plenty of room. They have a way sometimes of picking a human up with those long elastic tongues, like a frog snapping up a fly, and letting him dangle in mid-air while they study him with those saucer-sized yellow eyes. I don't care for that. You don't get hurt, but it isn't agreeable to be dangled in mid-air by something that looks like a 15-foot-high purple squid standing on the tips of its tentacles. Happened to me once in St. Louis, long ago, and I'm in no hurry to have it happen again.

The first thing I did when I was inside L.A. was find a car. On Valley Boulevard about two blocks in from the wall I saw a '31 Toshiba El Dorado that looked good to me, and I matched frequencies with its lock and slipped inside and took about 90 seconds to reprogram its drive control to my personal metabolic cues. The previous owner must have been fat as a hippo and probably diabetic: Her glycogen index was absurd and her phosphines were wild.

Not a bad car—a little slow in the shift, but what can you expect, considering the last time any cars were manufactured on this planet was the year 2034?

"Pershing Square," I told it.

It had nice capacity, maybe 60 megabytes. It turned south right away and found the old freeway and drove off toward downtown. I figured I'd set up shop in the middle of things, work two or three pardons to keep my edge sharp, get myself a hotel room, a meal, maybe hire some companionship. And then think about the next move. It was winter, a nice time to be in L.A. That golden sun, those warm breezes coming down the canyons.

I hadn't been out on the Coast in years. Working Florida mainly, Texas, sometimes Arizona. I hate the cold. I hadn't been in L.A. since '36. A long time to stay away, but maybe I'd been staying away deliberately. I wasn't sure. That last L.A. trip had left bad-tasting memories. There had been a woman who wanted a pardon and I sold her a stiff. You have to stiff the customers now and then or else you start looking too good, which can be dangerous; but she was young and pretty and full of hope, and I could have stiffed the next one instead of her, only I didn't. Sometimes I've felt bad, thinking back over that. Maybe that's what had kept me away from L.A. all this time.

A couple of miles east of the big downtown interchange, traffic began backing up. Maybe an accident ahead, maybe a roadblock. I told the Toshiba to get off the freeway.

Slipping through roadblocks is scary and calls for a lot of hard work. I knew that I probably could fool any kind of software at a roadblock and certainly any human cop, but why bother if you don't have to?

I asked the car where I was.

The screen lit up. ALAMEDA NEAR BANNING, it said. A long walk to Pershing Square. I had the car drop me at Spring Street. "Pick me up at eighteen-thirty hours," I told it. "Corner of—umm—Sixth and Hill." It went away to park itself and I headed for the square to peddle some pardons.

It isn't hard for a good pardoner to find buyers. You can see it in their eyes: the tightly controlled anger, the smoldering resentment. And something else, something intangible, a certain sense of having a shred or two of inner integrity left that tells you right away, Here's somebody willing to risk a lot to regain some measure of freedom. I was in business within 15 minutes.

The first one was an aging-surfer sort, barrel chest and that sun-bleached look. The Entities haven't allowed surfing for 10, 15 years —they've got their plankton seines just offshore from Santa Barbara to San Diego, gulping in the marine nutrients they have to have, and any beach boy who tried to take a whack at the waves out there would be chewed right up. But this guy must have been one hell of a performer in his day. The way he moved through the park, making little balancing moves as if he needed to compensate for the irregularities of the earth's rotation, you could see how he would have been in the water. Sat down next to me, began working on his lunch. Thick forearms, gnarled hands. A wall laborer. Muscles knotting in his cheeks: the anger forever simmering just below boil.

I got him talking after a while. A surfer, yes. Lost in the faraway and gone. He began sighing to me about legendary beaches where the waves were tubes and they came pumping end to end. "Trestle Beach," he murmured. "That's north of San Onofre. You used to sneak through Camp Pendleton. Sometimes the Marines would open fire, just warning shots. Or Hollister Ranch, up by Santa Barbara." His blue eyes got misty. "Huntington Beach. Oxnard. I got everywhere, man." He flexed his huge fingers. "Now these fucking Entity hodads own the shore. Can you believe it? They *own* it. And I'm pulling wall, my second time around, seven days a week next ten years."

"Ten?" I said. "That's a shitty deal."

"You know anyone who doesn't have a shitty deal?"

"Some," I said. "They buy out."

"Yeah."

"It can be done."

A careful look. You never know who might be a borgmann. Those stinking collaborators are everywhere.

"Can it?"

"All it takes is money," I said.

"And a pardoner."

"That's right."

"One you can trust."

I shrugged. "You've got to go on faith, man."

"Yeah," he said. Then, after a while: "I heard of a guy, he bought a three-year pardon and wall passage thrown in. Went up north, caught a krill trawler, wound up in Australia, on the Reef. Nobody's ever going to find him there. He's out of the system. Right out of the fucking system. What do you think that cost?"

"About twenty grand," I said.

"Hey, that's a sharp guess!"

"No guess."

"Oh?" Another careful look. "You don't sound local."

"I'm not. Just visiting."

"That's still the price? Twenty grand?"

"I can't do anything about supplying krill trawlers. You'd be on your own once you were outside the wall."

"Twenty grand just to get through the wall?"

"And a seven-year labor exemption."

"I pulled ten," he said.

"I can't get you ten. It's not in the configuration, you follow? But seven would work. You could get so far, in seven, that they'd lose you. You could goddamn *swim* to Australia. Come in low, below Sydney, no seines there."

"You know a hell of a lot."

"My business to know," I said. "You want me to run an asset check on you?"

"I'm worth seventeen five. Fifteen hundred real, the rest collat. What can I get for seventeen five?"

"Just what I said. Through the wall and seven years' exemption."

"A bargain rate, hey?"

"I take what I can get," I said. "Give me your wrist. And don't worry. This part is read only."

I keyed his data implant and patched mine in. He had $1500 in the bank and a collateral rating of 16 thou, exactly as he had claimed. We eyed each other very carefully now. As I said, you never know who the borgmanns are.

"You can do it right here in the park?" he asked.

"You bet. Lean back, close your eyes, make like you're snoozing in the sun. The deal is that I take a thousand of the cash now and you transfer five thou of the collateral bucks to me, straight labor-debenture deal. When you get through the wall, I get the other five hundred cash and five thou more on sweat security. The rest you pay off at three thou a year, plus interest, wherever you are, quarterly key-ins. I'll program the whole thing, including beep reminders on payment dates. It's up to you to make your travel arrangements, remember. I can do pardons and wall transits, but I'm not a goddamn travel agent. Are we on?"

He put his head back and closed his eyes.

"Go ahead," he said.

It was finger-tip stuff, straight circuit emulation, my standard hack. I picked up all his identification codes, carried them into central, found his records. He seemed real, nothing more or less than he had claimed. Sure enough, he had drawn a lulu of a labor tax, ten years on the wall. I wrote him a pardon good for the first seven of that. Had to leave the final three on the books, for purely technical reasons, but the computers weren't going to be able to find him by then. I gave him a wall-transit pass, too, which meant writing in a new skills class for him, programmer third grade. He didn't think like a programmer and he didn't look like a programmer, but the wall software wasn't going to figure that out. Now I had made him a member of the human elite, the relative handful of us who are free to go in and out of the walled cities as we wish. In return for these little favors, I signed over his entire life's savings to various accounts of mine, payable as arranged, part now, part later. He wasn't worth a nickel anymore, but he was a free man. That's not such a terrible trade-off.

Oh, and the pardon was a valid one. I had decided not to write any stiffs while I was in Los Angeles. A kind of sentimental atonement, you might say, for the job I had done on that woman all those years back.

You absolutely have to write stiffs once in a while, you understand. So that you don't look too good, so that you don't give the Entities reason to hunt you down. Just as you have to ration the number of pardons you do. I didn't have to be writing pardons at all, of course. I could have just authorized the system to pay me so much a year, 50 thou, 100 thou, and taken it easy forever. But where's the challenge in that?

So I write pardons, but no more than I need to cover my expenses, and I deliberately fudge some of them, making myself look as incompetent as the rest, so the Entities don't have a reason to begin trying to track the identifying marks of my work. My conscience hasn't been too sore about that. It's a matter of survival, after all. And most other pardoners are out-and-out frauds, you know. At least with me, you stand a better-than-even chance of getting what you're paying for.

The next one was a tiny Japanese woman, the classic style, sleek, fragile, doll-like. Crying in big wild gulps that I thought might break her in half, while a gray-haired older man in a shabby business suit —her grandfather, you'd guess—was trying to comfort her. Public crying is a good indicator of Entity trouble. "Maybe I can help," I said, and they were both so distraught that they didn't even bother to be suspicious.

He was her father-in-law, not her grandfather. The husband was dead, killed by burglars the year before. There were two small kids. Now she had received her new labor-tax ticket. She had been afraid they were going to send her out to work on the wall, which, of course, wasn't likely to happen: The assignments are pretty random, but they usually aren't crazy, and what use would a 90-pound woman be in hauling stone blocks around? The father-in-law had some friends who were in the know, and they managed to bring up the hidden encoding on her ticket. The computers hadn't sent her to the wall, no. They had sent her to Area Five. And they had classified her T.T.D. classification.

"The wall would have been better," the old man said. "They'd see right away she wasn't strong enough for heavy work, and they'd find something else, something she could do. But Area Five? Who ever comes back from that?"

"You know what Area Five is?" I said.

"The medical-experiment place. And this mark here, T.T.D. I know what that stands for, too."

She began to moan again. I couldn't blame her. T.T.D. means Test to Destruction. The Entities want to find out how much work we can really do, and they feel that the only reliable way to discover that is to put us through tests that show where the physical limits are.

"I will die," she wailed. "My babies! My babies!"

"Do you know what a pardoner is?" I asked the father-in-law.

A quick, excited response: sharp intake of breath, eyes going bright, head nodding vehemently. Just as quickly, the excitement faded, giving way to bleakness, helplessness, despair.

"They all cheat you," he said.

"Not all."

"Who can say? They take your money, they give you nothing."

"You know that isn't true. Everybody can tell you stories of pardons that came through."

"Maybe. Maybe," the old man said. The woman sobbed quietly. "You know of such a person?"

"For three thousand dollars," I said, "I can take the T.T.D. off her ticket. For five more, I can write an exemption from service good until her children are in high school."

Sentimental me. A 50 percent discount, and I hadn't even run an asset check. For all I knew, the father-in-law was a millionaire. But no; he'd have been off cutting a pardon for her, then, and not sitting around like this in Pershing Square.

He gave me a long, deep, appraising look—peasant shrewdness coming to the surface.

"How can we be sure of that?" he asked.

I might have told him that I was the king of my profession, the best of all pardoners, a genius hacker with the truly magic touch who could slip into any computer ever designed and make it dance to my tune. Which would have been nothing more than the truth. But all I said was that he'd have to make up his own mind, that I couldn't offer any affidavits or guarantees, that I was available if he wanted me and otherwise it was all the same to me if she preferred to stick with her T.T.D. ticket. They went off and conferred for a couple of minutes. When they came back, he silently rolled up his sleeve and presented his implant to me. I keyed his credit balance: 30 thou or so, not bad. I transferred eight of it to my accounts, half to Seattle, the rest to Los Angeles. Then I took her wrist, which was about two of my fingers thick, and got into her implant and wrote her the pardon that would save her life. Just to be certain, I ran a double validation check on it. It's always possible to stiff a customer unintentionally, though I've never done it. But I didn't want this particular one to be my first.

"Go on," I said. "Home. Your kids are waiting for their lunch."

Her eyes glowed. "If I could only thank you somehow——"

"I've already banked my fee. Go. If you ever see me again, don't say hello."

"This will work?" the old man asked.

"You say you have friends who know things. Wait seven days, then tell the data bank that she's lost her ticket. When you get the new one, ask your pals to decode it for you. You'll see. It'll be all right."

I don't think he believed me. I think he was more than half sure

I had swindled him out of one fourth of his life's savings, and I could see the hatred in his eyes. But that was his problem. In a week he'd find out that I really had saved his daughter-in-law's life, and then he'd rush down to the square to tell me how sorry he was that he had had such terrible feeling toward me. Only by then I'd be somewhere else, far away.

They shuffled out the east side of the park, pausing a couple of times to peer over their shoulders at me as if they thought I was going to transform them into pillars of salt the moment their backs were turned. Then they were gone.

I'd earned enough now to get me through the week I planned to spend in L.A. But I stuck around anyway, hoping for a little more. My mistake.

This one was Mr. Invisible, the sort of man you'd never notice in a crowd, gray on gray, thinning hair, mild, bland, apologetic smile. But his eyes had a shine. I forget whether he started talking first to me, or me to him, but pretty soon we were jockeying around trying to find out things about each other. He told me he was from Silver Lake. I gave him a blank look. How in hell am I supposed to know all the zillion L.A. neighborhoods? Said that he had corne down here to see someone at the big government H.Q. on Figueroa Street. All right: probably an appeals case. I sensed a customer.

Then he wanted to know where I was from. Santa Monica? West L.A.? Something in my accent, I guess. "I'm a traveling man," I said. "Hate to stay in one place." True enough. I need to hack or I go crazy; if I did all my hacking in just one city, I'd be virtually begging them to slap a trace on me sooner or later, and that would be the end. I didn't tell him any of that. "Came in from Utah last night. Wyoming before that." Not true, either one. "Maybe New York next." He looked at me as if I'd said I was planning a voyage to the moon. People out here, they don't go East a lot. These days, most people don't go anywhere.

Now he knew that I had wall-transit clearance, or else that I had some way of getting it when I wanted it. That was what he was looking to find out. In no time at all, we were down to basics.

He said he had drawn a new ticket, six years at the salt-field-reclamation site out back of Mono Lake. People die like May flies out there. What he wanted was a transfer to something softer, like Operations and Maintenance, and it had to be within the walls, preferably in one of the districts out by the ocean, where the air is cool and clear. I quoted him a price and he accepted without a quiver.

"Let's have your wrist," I said.

He held out his right hand, palm upward. His implant access was a pale-yellow plaque, mounted in the usual place but rounder than the standard kind and of a slightly smoother texture. I didn't see any great significance in that. As I had done maybe 1000 times before, I put my own arm over his, wrist to wrist, access to access. Our biocomputers made contact, and instantly I knew I was in trouble.

Human beings have been carrying biochip-based computers in their bodies for the past 40 years or so—long before the Entity invasion, anyway—but for most people it's just something they take for granted, like their vaccination mark. They use them for the things they're meant to be used for and don't give them a thought beyond that. The biocomputer's just a commonplace tool for them, like a fork, like a shovel. You have to have the hacker sort of mentality to be willing to turn your biocomputer into something more. That's why, when the Entities came and took us over and made us build walls around our cities, most people reacted just like sheep, letting themselves be herded inside and politely staying there. The only ones who can move around freely now—because we know how to manipulate the mainframes through which the Entities rule us—are the hackers. And there aren't many of us. I could tell right away that I had hooked myself on to one now.

The moment we were in contact, he came at me like a storm.

The strength of his signal let me know I was up against something special and that I'd been hustled. He hadn't been trying to buy a pardon at all. What he was looking for was a duel—Mr. Macho behind the bland smile, out to show the new boy in town a few of his tricks.

No hacker had ever mastered me in a one-on-one anywhere. Not ever. I felt sorry for him but not much.

He shot me a bunch of stuff, cryptic but easy, just by way of finding out my parameters. I caught it and stored it and laid an interrupt on him and took over the dialog. My turn to test him. I wanted him to begin to see who he was fooling around with. But just as I began to execute, he put an interrupt on *me*. That was a new experience. I stared at him with some respect.

Usually, any hacker anywhere will recognize my signal in the first 30 seconds, and that'll be enough to finish the interchange. He'll know that there's no point in continuing. But this guy either wasn't able to identify me or just didn't care, and he came right back with his interrupt. Amazing. So was the stuff he began laying on me next.

He went right to work, really trying to scramble my architecture. Reams of stuff came flying at me up in the heavy-megabyte zone.

JSPIKE. ABLTAG. NSLICE. DZCNT.

I gave it right back to him, twice as hard.

MAXFRG. MINPAU. SPKTOT. JSPIKE.

He didn't mind at all.

MAXDZ. SPKTIM. FALTER. NSLICE.

FRQSUM. EBURST.

IBURST.

PREBST.

NOBRST.

Mexican standoff. He was still smiling. Not even a trace of sweat on his forehead. Something eerie about him, something new and strange. This is some kind of borgmann hacker, I realized suddenly. He must be working for the Entities, roving the city, looking to make trouble for free-lancers like me. Good as he was, and he was plenty good, I despised him. A hacker who had become a borgmann—now, that was truly disgusting. I wanted to short him. I wanted to burn him out. I had never hated anyone so much in my life.

I couldn't do a thing with him.

I was baffled. I was the Data King, the Megabyte Monster. All my life, I had floated back and forth across a world in chains, picking every lock I came across. And now this nobody was tying me in knots. Whatever I gave him, he parried; and what came back from him was getting increasingly bizarre. He was working with an algorithm I had never seen before and was having serious trouble solving. After a little while, I couldn't even figure out what he was doing to me, let alone what I was going to do to cancel it. It was getting so I could barely execute. He was forcing me inexorably toward a wetware crash.

"Who are you?" I yelled.

He laughed in my face.

And kept pouring it on. He was threatening the integrity of my implant, going at me down on the microcosmic level, attacking the molecules themselves. Fiddling around with electron shells, reversing charges and mucking up valences, clogging my gates, turning my circuits to soup. The computer that is implanted in my brain is nothing but a lot of organic chemistry, after all. So is my brain. If he kept this up, the computer would go and the brain would follow, and I'd spend the rest of my life in the bibble-babble academy.

This wasn't a sporting contest. This was murder.

I reached for the reserves, throwing up all the defensive blockages I could invent. Things I had never had to use in my life, but they were there when I needed them, and they did slow him down. For a moment, I was able to halt his ball-breaking onslaught and even push him back—and give myself the breathing space to set up a few offensive combinations of my own. But before I could get them running, he shut me down once more and started to drive me toward Crashville all over again. He was unbelievable.

I blocked him. He came back again. I hit him hard and he threw the punch into some other neural channel altogether and it went fizzling away.

I hit him again. Again he blocked it.

Then he hit me, and I went reeling and staggering and managed to get myself together when I was about three nanoseconds from the edge of the abyss.

I began to set up a new combination. But even as I did it, I was reading the tone of his data, and what I was getting was absolute cool confidence. He was waiting for me. He was ready for anything I could throw. He was in that realm beyond mere self-confidence into utter certainty.

What it was coming down to was this: I was able to keep him from ruining me, but only just barely, and I wasn't able to lay a glove on him at all. And he seemed to have infinite resources behind him. I didn't worry him. He was tireless. He didn't appear to degrade at all. He just took all I could give and kept throwing new stuff at me, coming at me from six sides at once.

Now I understood for the first time what it must have felt like for all the hackers I had beaten. Some of them must have felt pretty cocky, I suppose, until they ran into me. It costs more to lose when you think you're good. When you *know* you're good. People like that, when they lose, they have to reprogram their whole sense of their relation to the universe.

I had two choices. I could go on fighting until he wore me down and crashed me. Or I could give up right now. In the end, everything comes down to yes or no, on or off, one or zero, doesn't it?

I took a deep breath. I was staring straight into chaos.

"All right," I said. "I'm beaten. I quit."

I wrenched my wrist free of his, trembled, swayed, went toppling down onto the ground.

A minute later, five cops jumped me and trussed me up like a turkey and hauled me away, with my implant arm sticking out of the package and a security lock wrapped around my wrist, as if they were afraid I was going to start pulling data right out of the air.

Where they took me was Figueroa Street, the big black-marble 90-story job that is the home of the puppet city government. I didn't give a damn. I was numb. They could have put me in the sewer and I wouldn't have cared. I wasn't damaged—the automatic circuit check was still running and it came up green—but the humiliation was so intense that I felt crashed. I felt destroyed. The only thing I wanted to know was the name of the hacker who had done it to me.

The Figueroa Street building has ceilings about 20 feet high everywhere, so that there is room for Entities to move around. Voices reverberate in those vast open spaces like echoes in a cavern. The cops sat me down in a hallway, still all wrapped up, and kept me there for a long time. Blurred sounds went lolloping up and down the passage. I wanted to hide from them. My brain felt raw. I had taken one hell of a pounding.

Now and then, a couple of towering Entities would come rumbling through the hall, tiptoeing on their tentacles in that weirdly dainty way of theirs. With them came a little entourage of humans whom they ignored entirely, as they always do. They know that we're intelligent, but they just don't care to talk to us. They let their computers do that, via the borgmann interface, and may his signal degrade forever for having sold us out. Not that they wouldn't have conquered us anyway, but Borgmann made it ever so much easier for them to push us around by showing them how to connect our little biocomputers to their huge mainframes. I bet he was very proud of himself, too: just wanted to see if his gadget would work, and to hell with the fact that he was selling us into eternal bondage.

Nobody has ever figured out why the Entities are here or what they want from us. They simply came, that's all. Saw. Conquered. Rearranged us. Put us to work doing god-awful unfathomable tasks. Like a bad dream.

And there wasn't any way we could defend ourselves against them. Didn't seem that way to us at first—we were cocky; we were going to wage guerrilla war and wipe them out—but we learned fast how wrong we were, and we are theirs for keeps. There's nobody left with anything close to freedom except the handful of hackers like me; and, as I've explained, we're not dopey enough to try any serious sort of counterattack. It's a big enough triumph for us just to be able to dodge around from one city to another without having to get authorization.

Looked like all that was finished for me now. Right then, I didn't give a damn. I was still trying to integrate the notion that I had been beaten; I didn't have capacity left over to work on a program for the new life I would be leading now.

"Is this the pardoner over here?" someone said.

"That one, yeah."

"She wants to see him now."

"You think we should fix him up a little first?"

"She said now."

A hand at my shoulder, rocking me gently. "Up, fellow. It's interview time. Don't make a mess or you'll get hurt."

I let them shuffle me down the hall and through a gigantic doorway and into an immense office with a ceiling high enough to give an Entity all the room it would want. I didn't say a word. There weren't any Entities in the office, just a woman in a black robe, sitting behind a wide desk at the far end. It looked like a toy desk in that colossal room. She looked like a toy woman. The cops left me alone with her. Trussed up like that, I wasn't any risk.

"Are you John Doe?" she asked.

I was halfway across the room, studying my shoes. "What do you think?" I said.

"That's the name you gave upon entry to the city."

"I give lots of names. John Smith, Richard Roe, Joe Blow. It doesn't matter much to the gate software what name I give."

"Because you've gimmicked the gate?" She paused. "I should tell you, this is a court of inquiry."

"You already know everything I could tell you. Your borgmann hacker's been swimming around in my brain."

"Please," she said. "This'll be easier if you cooperate. The accusation is illegal entry, illegal seizure of a vehicle and illegal interfacing activity, specifically, selling pardons. Do you have a statement?"

"No."

"You deny that you're a pardoner?"

"I don't deny, I don't affirm. What's the goddamned use?"

"Look up at me," she said.

"That's a lot of effort."

"Look up," she said. There was an odd edge to her voice. "Whether you're a pardoner or not isn't the issue. We know you're a pardoner. *I* know you're a pardoner." And she called me by a name I hadn't used in a very long time. Not since '36, as a matter of fact.

I looked at her. Stared. Had trouble believing I was seeing what I saw. Felt a rush of memories come flooding up. Did some mental editing work on her face, taking out some lines here, subtracting a little flesh in a few places, adding some in others. Stripping away the years.

"Yes," she said. "I'm who you think I am."

I gaped. This was worse than what the hacker had done to me. But there was no way to run from it.

"You work for them?" I asked.

"The pardon you sold me wasn't any good. You knew that, didn't you? I had someone waiting for me in San Diego, but when I tried to get through the wall, they stopped me just like that and dragged me away screaming. I could have killed you. I would have gone to San Diego and then we would have tried to make it to Hawaii in his boat."

"I didn't know about the guy in San Diego," I said.

"Why should you? It wasn't your business. You took my money, you were supposed to get me my pardon. That was the deal."

Her eyes were gray with golden sparkles in them. I had trouble looking into them.

"You still want to kill me?" I asked. "Are you planning to kill me now?"

"No and no." She used my old name again. "I can't tell you how astounded I was when they brought you in here. A pardoner, they said. John Doe. Pardoners, that's my department. They bring all of them to me. I used to wonder years ago if they'd ever bring *you* in, but after a while I figured, No, not a chance; he's probably a million miles away, he'll never come back this way again. And then they brought in this John Doe, and I saw your face."

"Do you think you could manage to believe," I said, "that I've felt guilty for what I did to you ever since? You don't have to believe it. But it's the truth."

"I'm sure it's been unending agony for you."

"I mean it. Please. I've stiffed a lot of people, yes, and sometimes I've regretted it and sometimes I haven't, but you were one that I regretted. You're the one I've regretted most. This is the absolute truth."

She considered that. I couldn't tell whether she believed it even for a fraction of a second, but I could see that she was considering it.

"Why did you do it?" she asked after a bit.

"I stiff people because I don't want to seem perfect," I told her. "You deliver a pardon every single time, word gets around, people start talking, you start to become legendary. And then you're known everywhere, and sooner or later the Entities get hold of you, and that's that. So I always make sure to write a lot of stiffs. I tell people I'll do my best, but there aren't any guarantees, and sometimes it doesn't work."

"You deliberately cheated me."

"Yes."

"I thought you did. You seemed so cool, so professional. So perfect. I was sure the pardon would be valid. I couldn't see how it would miss. And then I got to the wall and they grabbed me. So I thought, That bastard sold me out. He was too good just to have flubbed it up." Her tone was calm, but the anger was still in her eyes. "Couldn't you have stiffed the next one? Why did it have to be me?"

I looked at her for a long time.

"Because I loved you," I said.

"Shit," she said. "You didn't even know me. I was just some stranger who had hired you."

"That's just it. There I was full of all kinds of crazy instant lunatic fantasies about you, all of a sudden ready to turn my nice, orderly life upside down for you, and all you could see was somebody you had hired to do a job. I didn't know about the guy in San Diego. All I knew was I saw you and I wanted you. You don't think that's love? Well, call it something else, then, whatever you want. I never let myself feel it before. It isn't smart, I thought; it ties you down, the risks are too big. And then I saw you and I talked to you a little and I thought something could be happening between us and things started to change inside me, and I thought, Yeah, yeah, go with it this time, let it happen, this may make everything different. And you stood there not seeing it, not even beginning to notice, just jabbering on and on about how important the pardon was for you. So I stiffed you. And afterward I thought, Jesus, I ruined that girl's life and it was just because I got myself into a snit, and that was a fucking petty thing to have done. So I've been sorry ever since. You don't have to believe that. I didn't know about San Diego. That makes it even worse for me." She didn't say anything all this time, and the silence felt enormous. So after a moment I said, "Tell me one thing, at least. That guy who wrecked me in Pershing Square: Who was he?"

"He wasn't anybody," she said.

"What does that mean?"

"He isn't a who. He's a *what*. It's an android, a mobile antipardoner unit, plugged right into the big Entity mainframe in Culver City. Something new that we have going around town."

"Oh," I said. "Oh."

"The report is that you gave it one hell of a workout."

"It gave me one, too. Turned my brain half to mush."

"You were trying to drink the sea through a straw. For a while, it looked like you were really going to do it, too. You're one goddamned hacker, you know that?"

"Why did you go to work for them?" I said.

She shrugged. "Everybody works for them. Except people like you. You took everything I had and didn't give me my pardon. So what was I supposed to do?"

"I see."

"It's not such a bad job. At least I'm not out there on the wall. Or being sent off for T.T.D."

"No," I said. "It's probably not so bad. If you don't mind working in a room with such a high ceiling. Is that what's going to happen to me? Sent off for T.T.D.?"

"Don't be stupid. You're too valuable."

"To whom?"

"The system always needs upgrading. You know it better than anyone alive. You'll work for us."

"You think I'm going to turn borgmann?" I said, amazed.

"It beats T.T.D.," she said.

I fell silent again. I was thinking that she couldn't possibly be serious, that they'd be fools to trust me in any kind of responsible position. And even bigger fools to let me near their computer.

"All right," I said. "I'll do it. On one condition."

"You really have balls, don't you?"

"Let me have a rematch with that android of yours. I need to check something out. And afterward we can discuss what kind of work I'd be best suited for here. OK?"

"You know you aren't in any position to lay down conditions."

"Sure I am. What I do with computers is a unique art. You can't make me do it against my will. You can't make me do anything against my will."

She thought about that. "What good is a rematch?"

"Nobody ever beat me before. I want a second try."

"You know it'll be worse for you than before."

"Let me find that out."

"But what's the point?"

"Get me your android and I'll show you the point," I said.

She went along with it. Maybe it was curiosity, maybe it was something else, but she patched herself into the computer net and pretty soon they brought in the android I had encountered in the park, or maybe another one with the same face. It looked me over pleasantly, without the slightest sign of interest.

Someone came in and took the security lock off my wrist and left again. She gave the android its instructions and it held out its wrist to me and we made contact. And I jumped right in.

I was raw and wobbly and pretty damned battered, still, but I knew what I needed to do and I knew I had to do it fast. The thing was to ignore the android completely—it was just a terminal, it was just a unit—and go for what lay behind it. So I bypassed the android's own identity program, which was clever but shallow. I went right around it while the android was still setting up its combinations, dived underneath, got myself instantly from the unit level to the mainframe level and gave the master Culver City computer a hearty handshake.

Jesus, that felt good!

All that power, all those millions of megabytes squatting there, and I was plugged right into it. Of course, I felt like a mouse hitchhiking on the back of an elephant. That was all right. I might be a mouse, but that mouse was getting a tremendous ride. I hung on tight and went soaring along on the hurricane winds of that colossal machine.

And as I soared, I ripped out chunks of it by the double handful and tossed them to the breeze.

It didn't even notice for a good tenth of a second. That's how big it was. There I was, tearing great blocks of data out of its gut, joyously ripping and rending. And it didn't know it, because even the most magnificent computer ever assembled is still stuck with operating at the speed of light, and when the best you can do is 186,000 miles a second, it can take quite a while for the alarm to travel the full distance down all your neural channels. That thing was *huge*. Mouse riding on elephant, did I say? Amoeba piggybacking on Brontosaurus was more like it.

God knows how much damage I was able to do. But, of course, the alarm circuitry did cut in eventually. Internal gates came clanging down and all sensitive areas were sealed away and I was shrugged off with the greatest of ease. There was no sense in staying around, waiting to get trapped, so I pulled myself free.

I had found out what I needed to know. Where the defenses were, how they worked. This time the computer had kicked me out, but it wouldn't be able to the next. Whenever I wanted, I could go in there and smash whatever I felt like.

The android crumpled to the carpet. It was nothing but an empty husk now.

Lights were flashing on the office wall.

She looked at me, appalled. "What did you *do*?"

"I beat your android," I said. "It wasn't all that hard, once I knew the scoop."

"You damaged the main computer."

"Not really. Not much. I just gave it a little tickle. It was surprised seeing me get access in there, that's all."

"I think you really damaged it."

"Why would I want to do that?"

"The question ought to be why you haven't done it already. Why you haven't gone in there and crashed the hell out of their programs."

"You think I could do something like that?"

She studied me. "I think maybe you could, yes."

"Well, maybe so. Or maybe not. But I'm not a crusader, you know.

I like my life the way it is. I move around; I do as I please. It's a quiet life. I don't start revolutions. When I need to gimmick things, I gimmick them just enough and no more. And the Entities don't even know I exist. If I stick my finger in their eye, they'll cut my finger off. So I haven't done it."

"But now you might," she said.

I began to get uncomfortable. "I don't follow you," I said, though I was beginning to think that I did.

"You don't like risk. You don't like being conspicuous. But if we take your freedom away, if we tie you down in L.A. and put you to work, what the hell would you have to lose? You'd go right in there. You'd gimmick things but good." She was silent for a time. "Yes," she said. "You really would. I see it now, that you have the capability and that you could be put in a position where you'd be willing to use it. And then you'd screw everything up for all of us, wouldn't you?"

"What?"

"You'd fix the Entities, sure. You'd do such a job on their computer that they'd have to scrap it and start all over again. Isn't that so?"

She was on to me, all right.

"But I'm not going to give you the chance. I'm not crazy. There isn't going to be any revolution and I'm not going to be its heroine and you aren't the type to be a hero. I understand you now. It isn't safe to fool around with you. Because if anybody did, you'd take your little revenge, and you wouldn't care what you brought down on everybody else's head. You could ruin their computer, but then they'd come down on us and they'd make things twice as hard for us as they already are, and you wouldn't care. We'd all suffer, but you wouldn't care. No. My life isn't so terrible that I need you to turn it upside down for me. You've already done it to me once. I don't need it again."

She looked at me steadily, and all the anger seemed to be gone from her and there was only contempt left.

After a little while, she said, "Can you go in there again and gimmick things so that there's no record of your arrest today?"

"Yeah. Yeah, I could do that."

"Do it, then. And then get going. Get the hell out of here, fast."

"Are you serious?"

"You think I'm not?"

I shook my head. I understood. And I knew that I had won and I had lost at the same time.

She made an impatient gesture, a shoofly gesture.

I nodded. I felt very, very small.

"I just want to say, all that stuff about how much I regretted the thing I did to you back then—it was true. Every word of it."

"It probably was," she said. "Look, do your gimmicking and edit yourself out, and then I want you to start moving. Out of the building. Out of the city. OK? Do it real fast."

I hunted around for something else to say and couldn't find it. Quit while you're ahead, I thought. She gave me her wrist and I did the interface with her. As my implant access touched hers, she shuddered a little. It wasn't much of a shudder, but I noticed it. I felt it, all right. I think I'm going to feel it every time I stiff anyone, ever again. Any time I even think of stiffing anyone.

I went in and found the John Doe arrest entry and got rid of it, and then I searched out her civil-service file and promoted her up two grades and doubled her pay. Not much of an atonement. But what the hell, there wasn't much I could do. Then I cleaned up my traces behind me and exited the program.

"All right," I said. "It's done."

"Fine," she said and rang for her cops.

They apologized for the case of mistaken identity and let me out of the building and turned me loose on Figueroa Street. It was late afternoon, and the street was getting dark and the air was cool. Even in Los Angeles, winter is winter, of a sort. I went to a street access and summoned the Toshiba from wherever it had parked itself, and it came driving up five or ten minutes later, and I told it to take me north. The going was slow, rush-hour stuff, but that was OK. I went to the wall at the Sylmar gate, 50 miles or so out of town. The gatekeeper asked me my name. "Richard Roe," I said. "Beta Pi Upsilon, ten-four-three-two-four-X. Destination San Francisco."

It rains a lot in San Francisco in the winter. Still, it's a pretty town. I would have preferred Los Angeles at that time of year, but what the hell. Nobody gets all his first choices all the time. The gate opened and the Toshiba went through. Easy as Beta Pi.

# JAMES PATRICK KELLY

## Glass Cloud

One of the hottest new writers in science fiction, James Patrick Kelly was born in Mineola, New York, and now lives with his family in Durham, New Hampshire. Kelly made his first sale in 1975, and has since become a frequent contributor to *The Magazine of Fantasy and Science Fiction*, and *Isaac Asimov's Science Fiction Magazine;* his stories have also appeared in *Universe, Galaxy, Amazing, Analog, The Twilight Zone Magazine,* and elsewhere. His first solo novel, *Planet of Whispers*, came out in 1984. His most recent book is a novel written in collaboration with John Kessel, *Freedom Beach*. He is currently at work on a new novel, tentatively entitled *Look into the Sun*. His story "Friend," also in collaboration with Kessel, was in our First Annual Collection; his story "Solstice" was in our Third Annual Collection; and his story "The Prisoner of Chillon" was in our Fourth Annual Collection.

Here, in an intense and compelling story set in his native New Hampshire, he shows us that sometimes even a man at the very top of his profession can receive an offer he can't refuse.

# GLASS CLOUD

## James Patrick Kelly

Phillip Wing was surprised when he found out what his wife had been doing with her Wednesday afternoons. "You've joined what?"

"A friend invited me to sit in on a study group at the mission." Daisy refilled her glass from a decanter. "I've been twice, that's all. I haven't joined anything."

"What are you studying?"

"Sitting in, Phil—it's not like I intend to convert. I'm just browsing." She sipped her wine and waited for Wing to settle back. "They haven't said a word about immortality yet. Mostly they talk about history."

"History? History? The Messengers haven't been here long enough to learn anything about history."

"Seven years. First contact was seven years ago." She sighed and suddenly she was lecturing. "Cultural evolution follows predictable patterns. There are interesting correlations between humanity and some of the other species that the Messengers have contacted."

Wing shook his head. "I don't get it. We've been together what? Since '51? For years all that mattered was the inn. They nuke Geneva, so what? Revolution in Mexico, who cares?"

"I care about you," she said.

That stopped him for a moment. Absently, he filled his glass from the decanter and took a gulp before he realized that it was the synthetic Riesling that she was trying out as a house wine. He swallowed it with difficulty. "Who's the friend?"

"What?"

"The friend who asked you to the mission. Who is he?" Wing was just guessing that it was a man. It was a good guess.

"A regular." Daisy glanced away from him and nodded at the glow sculpture on the wall. "You know Jim McCauley."

All he knew was that McCauley was a local artist who had made a name for himself in fancy light bulbs. Wing watched the play of pastel light across her face, trying to see her as this regular might see her. Daisy was not beautiful, although she could be pretty when she paid attention to detail. She did not bother to comb her hair every time the wind caught it nor did she much care about the wrinkles at the corners of her eyes. Hers was an intelligent, hard-edged, New Hampshire Yankee face. She looked like someone who would know about things that mattered. Wing had good reasons for loving her; he slid across the couch and nuzzled under her ear.

"Don't tickle." She laughed. "You're invited, you know." She pulled back, but not too far. "The new Messenger, Ndavu, is interested in art. He's mentioned the Glass Cloud several times. You really ought to go. You might learn something." Having made her pitch, she kissed him.

Phillip Wing had no time to study history; he was too busy worrying about the Second Wonder of the World. Solon Petropolus, erratic scion of the Greek transportation conglomerate, had endowed the Seven Wonders Foundation with an immense fortune. The foundation was Petropolus's megalomaniacal gift to the ages. It commissioned constructions—some called them art—on a monumental scale. It was the vulgar purpose of the Wonders to attract crowds. They were to be places where a French *secretaire* or a Peruvian *campesino* or even an Algerian *mullah* might come to contemplate the enduring spirit of Solon Petropolus, the man who embalmed himself in money.

Wing had spent five years at Yale grinding out a practitioner's degree but when he graduated he was certain that he had made a mistake. He was offered several jobs but not one that he wanted. He had studied architecture with the impossibly naïve hope that someday, someone would let him design a building as large as his ambitions. He wanted to build landmarks, not program factories to fabricate this year's model of go-tubes for the masses too poor to afford real housing. Instead of working he decided to spend the summer after graduation hiking the Appalachian Trail. Alone.

As he climbed Webster Cliff in Crawford Notch, he played a poetry game against his fatigue. *A zephyr massages the arthritic tree*. It was only a few kilometers to the Appalachian Mountain Club's Mispah Spring Hut where he would spend the night. *Plodding promiscuously into a tangerine heaven*. Wing made it a game because he did not really believe in poetry. *Stone teeth bite solipsistic toes*. A low cloud was sweeping through the Notch just as the late afternoon sun dipped out of the overcast into a jagged band of blue sky on the horizon. Something strange happened to the light then and for an instant the cloud was transformed. *A cloud of glass*.

"A glass cloud," he muttered. There was no one to hear him. He stopped, watching the cloud but not seeing it, experiencing instead an overpowering inner vision. A glass cloud. The image swelled like a bubble. He could see himself floating with it and for the first time he understood what people meant when they talked about inspiration. He kept thinking of the glass cloud all the way to the hut, all that night. He was still thinking of it weeks later when he reached the summit of Kahtadin, the northern terminus of the trail, and thought of it on the hover to Connecticut. He did some research and made sketches, taking a strange satisfaction from the enormous uselessness of it. That fall Seven Wonders announced the opening of the North American design competition. Phillip Wing, an unregistered, unemployed, uncertain architect of twenty-seven had committed the single inspiration of his life to disk and entered the competition because he had nothing better to do.

Now as he looked down out of the hover at Crawford Notch, Wing could not help but envy that young man stalking through the forest, seething with ambition and, at the same time, desperately afraid he was second-rate. At age twenty-seven Wing could not imagine the trouble a thirty-five-year old could get into. Schedules and meetings, compromises and contracts. That eager young man had not realized what it would mean to capture the glittering prize at the start of a career, so that everything that came after seemed lackluster. That fierce young man had never been truly in love or watched in horror as time abraded true love.

A roadbuster was eating the section of NH Route 302 that passed through the Notch. Its blades flayed the ice-slicked asphalt into chunks. Then a wide-bladed caterpillar scooped the bituminous rubble up and into trucks bound for the recycling plant in Concord. Once the old highway had been stripped down to its foundation course of gravel, crews would come to lay the Glass Cloud's underground track. After thaw a paver the size of a brachiosaurus would regurgitate asphalt to cover the track. Route 302 through Crawford Notch was the last phase of the ninety-seven kilometer track which followed existing roads through the heart of the White Mountain National Forest.

"Won't be long now," said the hover pilot. "They're talking a power-up test in ten weeks. Three months tops."

Wing said nothing. Ten weeks. Unless another preservationist judge could be convinced to meddle or Seven Wonders decided it had spent enough and sued him for the overruns. The project was two years late already and had long since gobbled up a generous contingency budget. Wing knew he had made mistakes, although he admitted them only to himself. Sometimes he worried that he had wasted his chance. He motioned to the pilot who banked the hover and headed south toward North Conway.

The hover was the property of Gemini Fabricators, the lead company in the consortium that had won the contract to build the Cloud and its track. Wing knew that the pilot had instructions to keep him in the air as long as possible. Every minute he spent inspecting track was one minute less he would have to go over the checklist for the newly completed docking platform with Laporte and Alz. Laporte, the project manager, made no secret of his dismay at having to waste valuable time with Wing. Laporte had made it clear that he believed Wing was largely to blame for the project's misfortunes.

The hover settled onto its landing struts like an old man easing into a hot bath. Wing waited for the dirty snow and swirls of litter to subside. The job site was strewn with coffee cups, squashed beer bulbs, and enough vitabulk wrap to cover Mount Washington.

Wing popped the hatch and was greeted by a knife-edged wind; there was no welcoming committee. He crossed the frozen landing zone toward the field offices, a group of linked commercial go-tubes that looked like a chain of plastic sausages some careless giant had dropped. The Seven Wonders tube was empty and the telelink was ringing. Wing would have answered it except that was exactly the kind of thing that made Laporte mad. Instead he went next door to Gemini looking for Fred Alz. Wing suspected that some of the project's problems arose from the collusion between Laporte and Alz, Gemini's field super. A woman he did not recognize sat at a CAD screen eating a vitabulk doughnut and staring dully at details of the ferroplastic structural grid.

"Where is everybody?" said Wing.

"They went to town to see him off."

"Him?"

"I think it's a him. A Messenger: No-doubt or some such."

"What was he doing here?"

"Maybe he was looking for converts. With immortality we might actually have a chance of finishing." She took a bite of doughnut and looked at him for the first time. "Who the hell are you anyway?"

"The architect."

"Yeah?" She did not seem impressed. "Where's your hard hat?"

Wing knew what they all said about him: that he was an arrogant son-of-a-bitch with a chip on his shoulder the size of the Great Pyramid. He spent some time living up to his reputation. The engineer did not stay for the entire tirade; she stalked out, leaving Wing to stew over the waste of an afternoon. Shortly afterward, Alz and Laporte breezed in, laughing. Probably at him.

"Sorry to keep you waiting, Phil," Laporte held up both hands in mock surrender, "but there's good news."

"It's two-thirty-eight! This plugging project is twenty-one months late and you're giving tours to goddamned aliens."

"Phil." Alz put a hand on his shoulder. "Phil, listen to me for a minute, will you?" Wing wanted to knock it away. "Mentor Ndavu has made a generous offer on behalf of the commonwealth of Messengers." Alz spoke quickly, as if he thought Wing might explode if he stopped. "He's talking major funding, a special grant that could carry us right through to completion. He says the Messengers want to recognize outstanding achievement in the arts, hard cash and lots of it—you ought to be proud is what you ought to be. We get it and chances are we can float the Cloud out of here by Memorial Day. Ten weeks, Phil."

Wing looked from Alz to Laporte. There was something going on, something peculiar and scary. People did not just hand out open-ended grants to rescue troubled projects for no reason—especially not the Messengers, who had never shown more than a polite interest in any of the works of humanity. Three years of autotherapy had taught Wing that he had a tendency to make conspiracy out of coincidence. But this was real. First Daisy, now the Cloud; the aliens were getting close. "Could we do it without them?"

Alz laughed.

"They're not monsters, Phil," said Laporte.

A tear dribbled down Wing's cheek. His eyes always watered when he sniffed too much Focus. The two-meter CAD screen that filled one wall of his studio displayed the south elevation of the proposed headquarters for SEE-Coast, the local telelink utility. There was something wrong with the row of window dormers set into the new hip roof. He blinked and the computer replaced the sketch with a menu. A doubleblink changed the cursor on the screen from draw to erase mode. His eyes darted; the windows disappeared.

He had known that the SEE-Coast project was going to be more trouble than it was worth. Jack Congemi was trying to cram too much building onto too small a site, a sliver of river front wedged between an eighteenth-century chandlery and a nineteenth-century hotel. If he could have gotten a variance to build higher than five stories, there would have been no problem. But SEE-Coast was buying into Portsmouth's exclusive historic district, where the zoning regulations were carved in granite.

It was a decent commission and the cost-plus fee contract meant he would make good money, but like everything he had done since the Cloud, Wing was bored with it. The building was pure kitsch: a tech bunker hiding behind a Georgian facade. It was like all the rest of his recent projects: clients buying a safe name brand and to hell with the vision. Of course they expected him to deliver stick-built at a price competitive with Korean robot factories. Never mind that half the local trades were incompetent and the other half were booked.

At last he could no longer bear to look at the monster. "Save it." He closed his eyes and still saw those ugly windows burned on the insides of his lids.

"Saved," said the computer.

He sat, too weary to move, and let his mind soak in the blackness of the empty screen. He knew he had spent too much time recently worrying about the Cloud and the Messengers. It was perverse since everything was going so well. All the checklists were now complete, pre-flight start-up tests were underway and Seven Wonders had scheduled dedication ceremonies for Memorial Day. The opening of the Second Wonder of the Modern World would have been reason enough for a news orgy, but now the Messengers' involvement was beginning to overshadow Wing's masterpiece. Telelink reporters kept calling him from places like Bangkok and Kinshasa and Montevideo to ask him about the aliens. Why were they supporting the Cloud? When would they invite humanity to join their commonwealth and share in their immortality technology? What were they really like?

He had no answers. Up until now he had done his best to avoid meeting the alien, Ndavu. Like most intelligent people, Wing had been bitterly disappointed by the Messengers. Their arrival had changed nothing: there were still too many crazy people with nukes; the war in Mexico dragged on. Although they had been excruciatingly diplomatic, it was clear that human civilization impressed them not at all. They kept their secrets to themselves—had never invited anyone to tour their starships or demonstrated the technique for preserving minds after death. The Messengers claimed that they had come to Earth for raw materials and to spread some as-yet vague message of galactic culture. Wing guessed that they held humanity in roughly the same esteem with which the conquistadors had held the Aztecs. But he could hardly admit that to reporters.

"Something else?" The computer disturbed his reverie; it was set to prompt him for new commands after twenty minutes of inactivity.

He leaned back in his chair and stretched, accidentally knocking his print of da Vinci's *John the Baptist* askew. "What the hell time is it, anyway?"

"One-fourteen-thirty-five AM, 19 February 2056."

He decided that he was too tired to get up and fix the picture.

"Here you are." Daisy appeared in the doorway. "Do you know what time it is?" She straightened the Baptist and then came up behind his chair. "Something wrong?"

"SEE-Coast."

She began to massage his shoulders and he leaned his head back against her belly. "Can't it wait until the morning?"

The skin was itchy where the tear had dried. Wing rubbed it, considering.

"Would you like to come to bed?" She bent over to kiss him and he could see that she was naked beneath her dressing gown. "All work and no play . . ."

The stink of doubt that he had tried so hard to perfume with concentration enhancers still clung to him. "But what if I wake up tomorrow and can't work on this crap? What if I don't believe in what I'm doing anymore? I can't live off the Glass Cloud forever."

"Then you'll find something else." She sifted his hair through her fingers.

He plastered a smile on his face and slipped a hand inside her gown—more from habit than passion. "I love you."

"It's better in bed." She pulled him from his chair. "Just you keep quiet and follow Mother Goodwin, young man. She'll take the wrinkles out of your brow."

He stumbled as he came into her arms but she caught his weight easily. She gave him a fierce hug and he wondered what she had been doing all evening.

"I've been thinking," he said softly, "about this party. I give in: go ahead if you want and invite Ndavu. I promise to be polite—but that's all." He wanted to pull back and see her reaction but she would not let him go. "That's what you want, isn't it?"

"That's one of the things I want," she said. Her cheek was hot against his neck.

Piscataqua House was built by Samuel Goodwin in 1763. A handsome building of water-struck brick and granite, it was said to have offered the finest lodging in the colonial city of Portsmouth, New Hampshire. Nearly three hundred years later it was still an inn and Daisy Goodwin was its keeper.

Wing had always been intrigued by the way Daisy's pedigree had affected her personality. It was not so much the old money she had inherited—most of which was tied up in the inn. It was the way she could bicycle around town and point out the elementary school she had attended, the Congregational Church where her grandparents had married, the huge black oak in Prescott Park that great-great-Uncle Josiah had planted during the Garfield administration. She lived with the easy grace of someone who was exactly where she belonged, doing exactly what she had always intended to do.

Wing had never belonged. He had been born in Taipei but had fled to the States with his Taiwanese father after his American mother had been killed in the bloody reunification riots of 2026. His father, a software engineer, had spent the rest of a bitter life searching in vain for what he had left on Taiwan. Phillip Wing had gone to elementary schools in Cupertino, California; Waltham, Massachusetts; Norcross, Georgia; and Orem, Utah. He knew very little about either side of his family. "When you are old enough to understand," his father would always say. "Someday we will talk. But not now." Young Phillip learned quickly to stop asking; too many questions could drive his father into one of his binges. He would dose himself to the brink of insensibility with memory sweeteners and stay up half the night weeping and babbling in the Taiwanese dialect of Fujian. His father had died when Wing was a junior at Yale. He had never met Daisy. Wing liked to think that the old man would have approved.

Wing tried hard to belong—at least to Daisy, if not to Piscataqua House. He had gutted the Counting House, a hundred-and-ninety-five-year old business annex built by the merchant Goodwins, and converted it into his offices. He was polite to the guests despite their annoying ignorance about the Cloud; most people thought it had been designed by Solon Petropolus. He helped out when she was short-handed, joined the Congregational Church despite a complete lack of religiosity, and served two terms on the city's Planning Board. He endured the dreaded black-tie fund raisers of the National Society of Colonial Dames for Daisy's sake and took her to the opera in Boston at least twice a year even though it gave him a headache. Now she was asking him to play host to an alien.

An intimate party of twenty-three had gathered in the Hawthorne parlor for a buffet in Ndavu's honor. Laporte had flown down from North Conway with his wife, Jolene. Among the locals were the Hathaways, who were still bragging about their vacation on Orbital Three, Magda Rudowski, Artistic Director of Theater-by-the-Sea, the new city manager, whose name Wing could never remember, and her husband, who never had anything to say, Reverend Smoot, the re-formalist minister, and the Congemis, who owned SEE-Coast. There were also a handful of Ndavu's hangers-on, among them the glow sculptor, Jim McCauley.

Wing hated these kinds of parties. He had about as much chat in him as a Trappist monk. To help ease his awkwardness, Daisy sent him out into the room with their best cut-glass appetizer to help the guests get hungry. He wandered through other people's conversations, feeling lost.

"Oh, but we love it up north," Jolene Laporte was saying. "It's peaceful and the air is clean and the mountains . . ."

". . . are tall," Laporte finished her sentence and winked as he reached for the appetizer. "But it's plugging cold—Jesus!" Magda Rudowski laughed nervously. Laporte looked twisted; he had the classic hollow stare, as if his eyes had just been fished out of a jar of formaldehyde.

"Don't make fun, Leon," Jolene said, pouting. "You love it too. Why, just the other day he was saying how nice it would be to stay on after the Cloud opened. I think he'd like to bask in his glory for a while." She sprayed a test dose from the appetizer onto her wrist and took a tentative sniff. "How legal is this?"

"Just some olfactory precursors," Wing said, "and maybe twenty ppm of Glow."

"Maybe I'm not the only one who deserves credit, Jolene. Maybe Phil here wants a slice of the glory too."

Daisy wheeled the alien into the parlor. "Phillip, I'd like you to meet Mentor Ndavu." Wing had never seen her so happy.

The alien was wearing a loose, black pinstriped suit. He might have been a corporate vice-president with his slicked-back gray hair and long, ruddy face except that he was over two meters tall. He had to slump to fit into his wheelchair and his knees stuck out like bumpers. The chair whined as it rolled; Ndavu leaned forward extending his hand. Wing found himself counting the fingers. Of course there were five. The Messengers were nothing if not thorough.

"I have been wanting to meet you, Phillip."

Wing shook hands. Ndavu's grip was firm and oddly sticky, like plastic wrap. The Messenger grinned. "I am very much interested in your work."

"As we all are interested in yours." Reverend Smoot brushed past Wing. "I, for one, would like to know . . ."

"Reverend," Ndavu spoke softly so that only those closest to him could hear, "must we always argue?"

". . . would like to know, Mentor," continued Smoot in his pulpit voice, "how your people intend to respond to the advisory voted yesterday by the Council of Churches."

"Perhaps we should discuss business later, Reverend." Ndavu shot a porcelain smile at Laporte. "Leon, this must be your wife, Jolene."

Daisy got Wing's attention by standing utterly still. Between them passed an unspoken message which she punctuated by tilting her head.

Wing's inclination was to let Smoot and Ndavu go at each other but he took firm hold of the Reverend's arm. "Would you like to see the greenhouse, Magda?" he said, turning the minister toward the actress. "The freesias are just coming into bloom; the place smells like the Garden of Eden. How about you, Reverend?" Glowering, Smoot allowed himself to be led away.

A few of the other guests had drifted out into what had once been the stables. Daisy's parents had replaced the old roof with sheets of clear optical plastic during the Farm Crusade, converting the entire wing into a greenhouse. In those days the inn might have closed without a reliable source of fresh produce. Magda Rudowski paused to admire a planter filled with tuberous begonias.

Reverend Smoot squinted through the krylac roof at the stars, as if seeking heavenly guidance. "I just have to wonder," he said, "who the joke is on."

Wing and Magda exchanged glances.

"How can you look at flowers when that alien is undermining the foundations of our Judeo-Christian heritage?"

Magda touched Smoot's sleeve. "It's a party, Reverend."

"If they don't believe in a god, how the hell can they apply for tax-exempt status? 'Look into the sun,' what kind of message is that? A year ago they wouldn't say a word to you unless you were from some government or conglomerate. Then they buy up some abandoned churches and suddenly they're preaching to anyone who'll listen. Look into the sun my ass." He took two stiff-legged steps toward the hydroponic benches and then spun toward Wing and Magda Rudowski. "You look into the sun too long and you go blind." He stalked off.

"I don't know what Daisy was thinking of when she invited him," Magda said.

"He married us," said Wing.

She sighed, as if that had been an even bigger mistake. "Shall I keep an eye on him for you?"

"Thanks." Wing thought then to offer her the appetizer. She inhaled a polite dose and Wing took a whiff himself, thinking he might as well make the best of what threatened to be bad business. The Glow loosened the knot in his stomach; he could feel his senses snapping to attention. They looked at each other and giggled. "Hell with him," he said, and then headed back to the parlor.

Jack Congemi was arguing in the hall with Laporte. "Here's just the man to settle this," he said.

"Congemi here thinks telelink is maybe going to put the trades out of business." Laporte spoke as though his brain were parked in lunar orbit and he were hearing his own words with a time delay. "Tell him you can't fuse plasteel gun emplacements in Tijuana sitting at a console in Greeley, Colorado. Makes no plugging difference how good your robotics are. You got to be there."

"The Koreans did it. They had sixty percent completion on Orbital Three before a human being ever set foot on it."

"Robots don't have a union," said Laporte. "The fusers do."

"Before telelink, none of us could have afforded to do business from a beautiful little nowhere like Portsmouth." Congemi liked to see himself as the local prophet of telelink; Wing had heard this sermon before. "We would have all been jammed into some urb hard by the jump port and container terminals and transitways and maglev trunks. Now no one has to go anywhere."

"But without tourists," said Wing, "inns close."

Congemi held his hands out like an archbishop blessing a crowd. "Of course, people will always travel for pleasure. And we at SEE-Coast will continue to encourage people to tour our beautiful Granite State. But we are also citizens of a new state, a state which is being born at this very moment. The world information state."

"Don't care where they come from." Laporte's voice slurred. "Don't care whether they're citizens of the plugging commonwealth of Messengers, just so long as they line up to see my Cloud." He poked a finger into Wing's shoulder as if daring him to object.

It was not the first time he had heard Laporte claim the Cloud as his. Wing considered throwing the man out and manners be damned. Instead he said, "We'll be eating soon," and went into the parlor.

For a time he was adrift on the tides of the party, smiling too much and excusing himself as he nudged past people on his way to nowhere. He felt angry but the problem was that he was not exactly sure why. He told himself that it was all Daisy's fault. Her party. He aimed the appetizer at his face and squeezed off a piggish dose.

"Phillip. Please, do you have a moment?" Ndavu gave him a toothy grin. There was something strange about his teeth: they were too white, too perfect. He was talking to Mr. and Mrs. Hatcher Poole III, who were standing up against the wall like a matched set of silver lamps.

"Mentor Ndavu."

"Mentor is a title my students have given me. I am your guest and we are friends, are we not? You must call me Ndavu."

"Ndavu." Wing bowed slightly.

"May I?" The Messenger turned his wheelchair to Wing and held out his hand for the appetizer. "I had hoped for the chance to observe mind-altering behavior this evening." He turned the appetizer over in his long spider-like hands and then abruptly sprayed it into his face. The entire room fell silent and then the Messenger sneezed. No one had ever heard of such a thing, a Messenger sneezing. The Pooles looked horrified, as if the alien might explode next. Someone across the room laughed and conversation resumed.

"It seems to stimulate the chemical senses." Ndavu wrinkled his nose. "It acts to lower the threshold of certain olfactory and taste receptors. There are also trace elements of another substance—some kind of indole hallucinogen?"

"I'm an architect, not a drug artist."

Ndavu passed the appetizer on to Mrs. Poole. "Why do you ingest these substances?" The alien's skin was perfect too; he had no moles, no freckles, not even a wrinkle.

"Well," she said, still fluttering from his sneeze. "they *are* non-fattening."

Her husband laughed nervously. "I take it, sir, that you have never eaten vitabulk."

"Vitabulk? No." The Messenger leaned forward in his wheelchair. "I have seen reports."

"I once owned a bulkery in Nashua," continued Hatcher Poole. "The ideal product, in many ways: cheap to produce, nutritionally complete, an almost indefinite shelf life. Without it, hundreds of millions would starve—"

"You see," said Wing, "it tastes like insulation,"

"Depends on the genetics of your starter batch," said Poole. "They're doing wonders these days with texturization."

"Bread flavor isn't that far off." Mrs. Poole had squeezed off a dose that they could probably smell in Maine. "And everything tastes better after a nice appetizer."

"Of course, we're serving natural food tonight," said Wing. "Daisy has had cook prepare a traditional meal in your honor, Ndavu." He wished she were here chatting and he was in the kitchen supervising final preparations. "However, some people prefer to use appetizers no matter what the menu."

"Prefer?" said Poole, who had passed the appetizer without using it. "A damnable addiction, if you ask me."

Two white-coated busboys carried a platter into the parlor, its contents hidden beneath a silver lid. They set it on the mahogany sideboard beneath a portrait of Nathaniel Hawthorne brooding. "Dinner is served!" The guests lined up quickly.

"Plates and utensils here, condiments on the tea table." Daisy's face was flushed with excitement. She was wearing that luminous blue dress he had bought for her in Boston, the one that had cost too much. "Cook will help you find what you want. Enjoy." Bechet, resplendent in his white cook's hat, placed a huge chafing dish beside the silver tray. With a flourish, Peter the busboy removed the lid from the silver tray. The guests buzzed happily and crowded around the sideboard, blocking Wing's view. He did not have to see the food, however; his hypersensitized olfactories were drenched in its aroma.

As he approached the sideboard, he could hear Bechet murmuring. "Wieners, sir. Hot dogs."

"Oh my god, Hal, potato salad—mayonnaise!"

"Did he say *dog*?"

"Nothing that amazing about relish. I put up three quarts myself last summer. But mustard!"

"No, no, I'll just have to live with my guilt."

"Corn dog or on a bun, Mr. Wing?" Bechet was beaming.

"On a bun please, Bechet." Wing held out his plate. "They seem to like it."

"I hope so, sir."

The guests were in various stages of gustatory ecstasy. The fare was not at all unusual for the wealthy; they ate at least one natural meal a day and meat or fish once a week. For others, forty-five grams of USDA guaranteed pure beef frankfurter was an extravagance: Christmas dinner, birthday treat. One of the strangers from the mission was the first to go for thirds. Ndavu had the good manners not to eat at all; perhaps he had orders not to alarm the natives with his diet.

The party fragmented after dinner; most guests seemed eager to put distance between themselves and the Messenger. It was a strain being in the same room with Ndavu; Wing could certainly feel it. Daisy led a group of gardeners to the greenhouse. Others gathered to watch the latest episode of *Jesus On First*. The religious spectacle of the hard-hitting Jesus had made it one of the most popular scripted sports events on telelink. The more boisterous guests went to the inn's cellar bar. Wing alone remained trapped in the Hawthorne parlor with the guest of honor.

"It has been a successful evening," said Ndavu, "so far."

"You came with an agenda?" Wing saw Peter the busboy gawking at the alien as he gathered up dirty plates.

Ndavu smiled. "Indeed I did. You are a very hard man to meet, Phillip. I am not sure why that is, but I hope now that things will be different. Will you visit me at the mission?"

Wing shrugged. "Maybe sometime." He was thinking to himself that he had the day after the heat death of the universe free.

"May I consider that a commitment?"

Wing stooped to pick up a pickle slice before someone—probably Peter—squashed it into the Kashgar rug. "I'm glad your evening has been a success," he said, depositing the pickle on Peter's tray as he went by.

"Before people accept the message, they must first accept the Messenger." He said it like a slogan. "You will forgive me if I observe that yours is a classically xenophobic species. The work has just begun; it will take years."

"Why do you do it? I mean you, personally."

"My motives are various—even I find it difficult to keep track of them all." The Messenger squirmed in the wheelchair and his knee brushed Wing's leg. "In that I suspect we may be alike, Phillip. The fact is, however, that my immediate concern is not spreading the message. It is getting your complete attention."

The alien was very close. "My attention?" Rumor had it that beneath their perfect exteriors lurked vile creatures, unspeakably grotesque. Evolutionary biologists maintained that it was impossible that the Messengers were humanoid.

"You should know that you are being considered for a most prestigious commission. I can say no more at this time but if you will visit me, I think we may discuss . . ."

Wing had stopped listening to Ndavu—saved by an argument out in the foyer. An angry man was shouting. A woman pleaded. Daisy. "Excuse me," he said, turning away from Ndavu.

"No, I won't go without you." The angry man was the glow sculptor, McCauley. He was about Wing's age, maybe a few years older. There was gray in his starchy brush of brown hair. He might have been taken for handsome in a blunt way except that his blue and silver stretchsuit was five years out of date and he was sweating.

"For God's sake, Jimmy, would you stop it?" Daisy was holding out a coat and seemed to be trying to coax him into it. "Go home. Please. This isn't the time."

"You tell me when. I won't keep putting it off."

"Something the matter?" Wing went up on the balls of his feet. If it came to a fight he thought he could hold his own for the few seconds it would take reinforcements to arrive. But it was ridiculous, really; people in Portsmouth did not fight anymore. He could hear someone running toward the foyer from the kitchen. A knot of people clustered at the bottom of the stairs. He would be all right, he thought. "Daisy?" Still, it was a damned nuisance.

He was shocked by her reaction. She recoiled from him as if he were a monster out of her worst nightmare and then sank down onto the sidechair and started to cry. He ought to have gone to her then but McCauley was quicker.

"I'm sorry," he said. He took the coat from her nerveless hands and kissed her quickly on the cheek. Wing wanted to throw him to the floor but found he could not move. Nobody in the room moved but the stranger his wife had called Jimmy. Something in the way she had said his name had paralyzed Wing. All night long he had sensed a tension at the party but, like a fool, he had completely misinterpreted it. Everyone knew; if he moved they might all start laughing.

"Shouldn't have . . ." McCauley was murmuring something; his hand was on the door. "Sorry."

"You don't walk out now, do you?" Wing was proud of how steady his voice was. Daisy's shoulders were shaking. Her sculptor did not have an answer; he did not even stop to put on his coat. As the door closed behind him Wing had the peculiar urge to call Congemi out of the crowd and make him take responsibility for this citizen of the world information state. His brave new world was filled with people who had no idea of how to act in public.

"Daisy?"

She would not look at him. Although he felt as if he were standing stark naked in the middle of the foyer of the historic Piscataqua House, he realized no one was looking at him.

Except Ndavu.

"I said you've had enough." The dealer pushed Wing's twenty back across the bar. "There's such a thing as an overdose, you know. And I'd be liable."

Wing stared down at the twenty, as if Andy Jackson might offer him some helpful advice.

"The cab is waiting. You ought to go home."

Wing glanced up without comprehension, trying to bring the man into focus.

"I said *go home*."

Wing could not go home. The morning after the party he had moved out of Piscataqua House. Now he was living in his go-tube at a rack just off the Transitway. A burly hack appeared beside Wing and put an arm around him. The next thing he knew he was standing outside the flash bar.

"Is cold, yes?" The hack stamped his feet against the icy pavement and smiled; his teeth were decorated with Egyptian hieroglyphs. He was wearing thin joggers and the gold sweat suit of the Rockingham Cab Company.

"Exit 6. Stop Inn." The cold made it easier for Wing to think. He squeezed into the wedge-shaped pedicab; the big hack slithered onto the driver's crouch and slid his feet into the toe clips. A musty locker-room smell lingered in the passenger compartment. There was no space heater but after a few minutes of the hack's furious peddling the smell turned into a warm stink.

They were caught briefly in the usual jam on Islington Street. About twenty protesters had gathered in front of what had once been the Church of the Holy Spirit and was now the Messengers' mission to the states of New Hampshire and Maine. A few carried electric candles; others brandished hand-lettered signs that said things like "NO RELIGION WITHOUT GOD" and "LOOK INTO THE *BIBLE*." The rest circulated among the stalled bicycles and pedicars, distributing anti-Messenger propaganda. On a whim Wing opened his window just wide enough to accept a newsletter. "Go with Jesus," said the protester. As the pedicab rolled away, he unfolded the newsletter. All he could read by street light were headlines: "SCIENCE SAYS NO IMMORTALITY" and "ALABAMA BANS ALIENS" and "HOW THEY REALLY LOOK."

"J-freaks always back up traffic here," said the hack. "Wouldn't read this crap if you paid me." He jerked his thumb at the mission. "Ever scan the message?"

"Not yet."

"No worse than any other church; better than some. The beetles'll feed you, give you a warm bed. Course, they don't explain nothing, except to tell you there's no such a thing as pleasure. Or pain." He laughed. "Maybe that's the beetle way, but it ain't the way life tastes to me."

As they approached Exit 6, they passed through a neighborhood of shabby go-tube parks and entered the strip. The strip was an architectural tumor that had metastasized to Transitway exits from Portsmouth, Virginia to Portsmouth, New Hampshire—a garish clump of chain vitabulk joints, clothes discounters, flash bars, surrogatoriums, motels, data shops, shoe stores, tube racks, bike dealers, too many warehouses, and a few moribund tourist traps selling plastic lobsters and screaming T-shirts. What was not malled was connected by optical plastic tunnels, once transparent but now smudged with sea salt and pollution. In the midst of it all squatted a US Transit Service terminal of bush-hammered concrete that was supposed to look like rough-cut granite. Docked at the terminal were semis and container trains and red-white-and-blue USTS busses in all sizes, from the enormous double-decked trunk line rigs to local twenty-passenger carryvans.

The Stop Inn was on the far edge of the strip, a six-story plastic box that looked like yet another warehouse except for the five-story stop sign painted on its east facade. There were hook-ups for about forty go-tubes on the top three floors and another forty fixed tubes on the bottom three. The stairwell smelled of smoke and disinfectant.

Wing and Daisy had customized their go-tube on spare weekends right after they had been married but they had only used it twice: vacations at the disneydome in New Jersey and the Grand Canyon. Somehow they could never find time to get away. The tube had an oak rolltop desk, a queen-sized Murphy bed with a gel mattress and Wing's one extravagance: an Alvar Aalto loveseat. The ceiling was a single sheet of mirror plastic that Wing had nearly broken his back installing. At the far end was a microwave, sink, toilet and mirror set in a wall surround of Korean tile that Daisy had spent two months picking out. A monitor and keyboard were mounted on a flex-arm beside the bed. The screen was flashing; he had messages.

"Phillip." Ndavu sat in an office at an enormous desk; he looked like a banker who had just realized he had made a bad loan. "I am calling to see if there's anything I can do to help . . ."

Wing paused the message and poured himself two fingers of scotch—no water, no ice.

". . . I want you to know how sorry I am about the way things have turned out. I have just seen Daisy and I must tell you that she is extremely upset. If there is anything I can do to help resolve the problem, please, *please* let . . ."

"Yeah," Wing muttered, "get the hell out of my life."

". . . you did promise to stop by the mission. There is still the matter of the commission I mentioned . . ." Wing deleted the message. He finished his drink before bringing up the next message in the queue.

"We have to talk, Phil." Daisy was sitting in shadow; her face was a low-res blur. She sounded like she had a cold. "It's not fair, what you're doing. You can't just throw everything away without giving me a chance to explain. I know I waited too long but I didn't want to hurt you . . . Maybe you won't believe this but I still love you. I don't know what to say . . . it can't be like it was before but maybe . . ." There was a long silence. "Call me," she said.

Wing drew a breath that burned his throat worse than the whiskey and then he smashed the keyboard with his fist, pounding at the delete key again and again until her face went away. His hand was numb and there was blood smeared on the keys.

The Messengers' mission on Islington Street sprawled over an entire block, an unholy jumble of architectural afterthoughts appended to the simple neogothic chapel that had once been the Church of the

Holy Spirit. There was a Victorian rectory, a squat brick-facade parochial school built in the 1950s, and an eclectic auditorium that dated from the oughts. The fortunes of the congregation had since declined and the complex had been abandoned, successfully confounding local redevelopers until the Messengers bought it. The initiates of northern New England's first mission had added an underground bike lockup, washed the stained glass, repaired the rotted clapboards, and planted an arborvitae screen around the auditorium and still Wing thought it was the ugliest building in Portsmouth.

In the years immediately after first contact there had been no contact at all with the masses; complex and secret negotiations continued between the Messengers and various political and industrial interests. Once the deals were struck, however, the aliens had moved swiftly to open missions for the propagation of the message, apparently a strange brew of technophilic materialism and zen-like self-effacement, sweetened by the promise of cybernetic immortality. The true import of the message was a closely held secret; the Messengers would neither confirm nor deny the reports of those few initiates who left the missions.

Wing hesitated at the wide granite steps leading to the chapel; they were slick from a spring ice storm. Freshly sprinkled salt was melting holes in the ice and there was a shovel propped against one of the massive oak doors. It was five-thirty in the morning—too early for protesters. No one inside would be expecting visitors, which was fine with Wing: he wanted to surprise the Messenger. But the longer he stood, the less certain he was of whether he was going in. He looked up at the eleven stone apostles arranged across the tympanum. Tiny stylized flames danced over their heads, representing the descent of the Holy Spirit on Pentecost. He could not read the apostles' expressions; acid rain had smudged their faces. Wing felt a little smudged himself. He reached into his back pocket for the flask. He took a swig and found new courage as a whiskey flame danced down his throat. He staggered into the church—twisted in the good old-fashioned way and too tired to resist Ndavu anymore.

As his eyes adjusted to the gloom Wing saw that there had been some changes made in the iconography. Behind the altar hung a huge red flag with the Buddhist Wheel of Law at its center and the words "LOOK INTO THE SUN" embroidered in gold thread beneath it. A dancing Shiva filled a niche next to a statue of Christ Resurrected. Where the Stations of the Cross had once been were now busts: Pythagoras, Plato, Lao-tze. Others whose names he did not recognize were identified as Kabalists, Gnostics, Sufis, and Theosophists—whatever they were. Wing had not known what to expect but this was not quite it. Still, he thought he understood what the Messengers were trying to do. The Romans had been quick to induct the gods of subjugated peoples into their pantheon. And what was humanity if not subjugated? That was why he had come, he thought bitterly. To acknowledge that he was beaten.

A light came on in the vestry next to the altar. Footsteps echoed across the empty church and then Jim McCauley stepped into the candlelight and came to the edge of the altar rail. "Is someone there?"

Wing swayed down the aisle, catching at pews to steady himself. He felt as empty as the church. As he approached the altar he saw that McCauley was wearing a loosely tied yellow bathrobe; his face was crinkled, as if he had just then come from a warm bed. With Daisy? Wing told himself that it did not matter anymore, that he had to concentrate on the plan he had discovered an hour ago at the bottom of a bottle of Argentinean Scotch: catch them off guard and then surrender. He saluted McCauley.

The man gathered his yellow bathrobe more tightly. "Who is it?"

Wing stepped up to the altar rail and grasped it to keep from falling. "Phillip Wing, A.I.A. Here to see the head beetle." McCauley looked blank. "Ndavu to you."

"The mentor expects you, Phillip?"

Wing cackled. "I should hope not."

"I see." McCauley gestured at the gate in the center of the altar rail. "Come this way—do you need help, Phillip?"

In response Wing vaulted the rail. His trailing foot caught and he sprawled at McCauley's feet. The sculptor was wearing yellow plastic slippers to match the robe.

"Hell no," Wing said and picked himself up.

McCauley eyed him doubtfully and then ushered him through the vestry to a long flight of stairs. As they descended, Peter Bornsten, the busboy from Piscataqua House, scurried around the corner and sprinted up toward them, taking steps two at a time.

"Peter," said McCauley. "I thought you were shoveling the steps."

Peter froze. Wing had never seen him like this: he was wearing janitors' greens and had the lame expression of a guilty eight-year-old. "I was, Jim, but the ice was too hard and so I salted it and went down to the kitchen for some coffee. I was cold," he said lamely. He glared briefly at Wing as if it were his fault and then hung his head. The Peter Bornsten Wing knew was a careless young stud whose major interests were stimulants and nurses.

"Go and finish the steps," McCauley touched Peter's forehead with his middle finger. "The essence does not experience cold, Peter."

"Yes, Jim." He bowed and scraped by them.

McCauley's slippers flapped as he walked slowly down the hallway that ran the length of the mission's basement. Doorways without doors opened into rooms filled with cots. It looked as if there were someone sleeping on every one. Wing smelled the yeasty aroma of curing vitabulk long before they passed a kitchen where three cooks were sitting at a table around four cups of ersatz coffee. At the end of the hall double doors opened onto an auditorium jammed with folding tables and chairs. A door to the right led up a short flight of stairs to a large telelink conferencing room and several small private offices.

McCauley went to one of the terminals at the conference table and tapped at the keyboard. Wing had a bad angle on the screen; all he could see was the glow. "Phillip Wing," said McCauley and the screen immediately went dark.

Wing sat down across the table from him and pulled out his flask. "Want some?" There was no reply. "You the welcoming committee?"

McCauley remained standing. "I spread the message, Phillip."

Someone else might have admired the calm with which McCauley was handling himself; Wing wanted to see the bastard sweat. "I thought you were supposed to be an artist. You had shows in New York, Tokyo—you had a career going."

"I did." He shrugged. "But my reasons for working were all wrong. Too much ego, not enough essence. The Messengers showed me how trivial art is."

Wing could not let him get away with that. "Maybe it's just you that's trivial. Maybe you didn't have the stuff to make art that meant anything. Ever think of that?"

McCauley smiled. "Yes." Daisy came into the room.

It had been twenty-two days since he had last seen his wife; Wing was disgusted with himself for knowing the number exactly. After the party he had worked hard at avoiding her. He had tried to stay out of the arid precincts of her Portsmouth while lowering himself into the swamp around its edges. He had reprogrammed the door to the Counting House to admit no one but him and had changed his work schedule, sneaking in just often enough to keep up appearances. He had never replied to the messages she left for him.

"What is she doing here?" Wing was tempted to walk out.

"I think it best that you wait alone with him, Daisy," said McCauley.

"Best for who?" said Wing.

"For her, of course. Look into the sun, Daisy."

"Yes, Jim."

"Phillip." He bowed and left them together.

"Look into the sun. Look into the sun." He opened the flask. "What the hell does that mean anyway?"

"It's like a koan—a proverb. It takes a long time to explain." Daisy looked as though she had put herself together in a hurry: wisps of hair fell haphazardly across her forehead and the collar of her mud-colored jumpsuit was turned up. She settled across the table from him and drummed her fingers on a keyboard, straightened her hair, glanced at him and then quickly away. He realized that she did not want to be there either and he took another drink.

"Keep your secrets then—who cares? I came to see Ndavu."

"He's not here right now."

"All right." He pushed the chair back. "Goodbye, then."

"No, please." She seemed alarmed. "He's coming. Soon. He'll want to see you; he's been waiting a long time."

"It's good for him." Wing thought she must have orders to keep him there; that gave him a kind of power over her. If he wanted to he could probably steer this encounter straight into one of the revenge fantasies that had so often been a bitter substitute for sleep. No matter what he said, she would have to listen.

"Are you often like this?" she said.

"What the hell do you care?" He drank and held out the flask. "Want some?"

"You haven't returned my calls."

"That's right." He shook the flask at her.

She did not move. "I know what you've been doing."

"What is it you're waiting to hear, Daisy?" Saying her name did it. The anger washed over him like the first wave of an amphetamine storm. "That I've spent the last three weeks twisted out of my mind? That I can't stand to live without you? Well, plug yourself. Even if it were true I wouldn't give you the satisfaction."

She sat like a statue, her face as smooth and as invulnerable as stone, her eyes slightly glazed, as if she were meditating at the same time she pretended to listen to him. His anger surged, and he veered out of control.

"You're not worth it, you know that? It gets me right in the gut sometimes, that I ever felt anything for you. You pissed on everything I thought was important in my life and I was dumb enough to be surprised when you did it. Look at you. I'm suffering and you sit there like you're carved out of bloody ice. And calling it good breeding, no doubt. Fine. Great. But just remember that when you die, you bitch, you'll be nothing but another stinking puddle on the floor."

Then Wing saw the tear. At first he was not even sure that it was hers: her expression had not changed. Maybe a water pipe had leaked through the ceiling and dripped on her. The tear rolled down her cheek and dried near the corner of her mouth. A single tear. She held her head rigidly erect, looking at him. He realized then that she had seen his pain and heard his anger and that her indifference was a brittle mask which he could shatter, if he were cruel enough. Suddenly he was ashamed.

He leaned forward, put his elbows on the table, his head in his hands. He felt like crying too. "It's been hard," he said. He shivered, took a deep breath. "I'm sorry." He wanted to reach across the table and wipe away the track of her tear with his finger but she was too far away.

They sat without speaking. He imagined she was thinking serene Messenger thoughts; he contemplated the ruins of their marriage. Ever since the party Wing had hoped, secretly, desperately, that Daisy would in time offer some explanation that he could accept—even if it were not true. He had expected to be reconciled. Now for the first time he realized that she might not want a reconciliation. The silence stretched. The telelink rang; Daisy tapped at the keyboard.

"He's in his office," she said.

Ndavu's grin reminded Wing of the grin that Leonardo had given his John the Baptist: mysterious, ironic, fey. "We do not, as you say, keep the message to ourselves." Ndavu's wheelchair was docked at an enormous desk; the scale of the Messenger's office made Wing feel like a midget. "On the contrary we have opened missions around the world in the last year where we assist all who seek enlightenment. Surely you see that it would be irresponsible for us to disseminate transcendently important information without providing the guidance necessary to its understanding." Ndavu kept nodding as if trying to entice Wing to nod back and accept his evasions.

Wing had the feeling that Ndavu would prefer that he settle back on the couch and think about how lucky he was to be the first human ever invited to tour a Messenger starship. He wondered if the initiates would be jealous when they found out that an unbeliever was going to take that prize. "Then keep your goddamned secret—why can't you just give us plans for the reincarnation computer and loan us the keys to a starship?"

"Technology is the crux of the message, Phillip."

Daisy sat beside Wing in luminous silence, listening to the conversation as if it were the fulfillment of a long-cherished dream. "Is she going to be reincarnated?" Her serenity was beginning to irk him, or maybe it was just that he was beginning to sober up to a blinding headache. "Is that the reward for joining?"

"The message is its own reward," she murmured.

"Don't you want to be reincarnated?"

"The essence does not want. It acknowledges karma."

"The essence?" Wing could feel a vein throbbing just above his right eyebrow.

"That which can be reincarnated," she said.

"There are no easy answers, Phillip," said Ndavu.

"Great." He shook his head in disgust. "Does anyone have an aspirin?"

Daisy went to check. "Everything is interconnected," the Messenger continued. "For instance I could tell you that it is the duty of intelligence to resist entropy. How could you hope to understand me? You would have to ask: What is intelligence? What is entropy? How may it be resisted? Why is it a duty? These are questions which it took the commonwealth of Messengers centuries to answer."

Daisy returned with McCauley. "What we will ask of you," continued Ndavu, "does not require that you accept our beliefs. Should you wish to seek enlightenment, then I will be pleased to guide you, Phillip. However you should know that it is not at all clear whether it is possible to grasp the message in the human lifespan. We have only just begun to study your species and have yet to measure its potential."

McCauley stood behind the couch, waiting inconspicuously for Ndavu to finish dodging the question. He rested a hand on Wing's shoulder, as if he were an old pal trying to break into a friendly conversation. "Excuse me, Phillip," said McCauley. Just then Wing remembered something he had forgotten to do. Something that had nagged at him for weeks. He was sober enough now to stay angry and the son of a bitch kept calling him by his first name.

"I'm very sorry, Phillip," said McCauley with a polite smile, "but we don't have much use for drugs here. However, if you're really in need we could send someone out . . ."

Wing shot off the couch, turned and hit his wife's lover right in the smile. Astonished, McCauley took the punch. The sculptor staggered backward, fists clenched, and Daisy gave a strangled little scream. Ndavu was grotesquely expressionless. It was as if his face were a mask that had slipped, revealing . . . nothing. Wing had never seen the Messenger look quite so alien.

"That's okay." He sat down, rubbing his knuckles. "I feel much better now."

McCauley touched his bloody lip and then turned and walked quickly from the office. Daisy was staring at Ndavu's abandoned face. Wing settled back on the couch and—for the first time in weeks—started to laugh.

* * *

The Messengers had done a thorough job; Wing's cabin on the starship was a copy of the interior of his go-tube—with a few differences. The gravity was .6 earth normal. The floor was not tongue-and-grooved oak but some kind of transparent crystal; beneath him reeled the elephant-skin wrinkles of the Zagros mountains. And Daisy slept next door.

Wing stared like a blind man at the swirling turquoise shallows that rimmed the Persian Gulf; Ndavu's arduous briefing had turned his sense of wonder to stone. He now knew everything about a planet called Aseneshesh that a human being could absorb in forty-eight hours without going mad. When he closed his eyes he could see the aliens Ndavu called the Chani. Tall and spindly, they looked more like pipe cleaner men than creatures of flesh and bone. Starving apes with squashed faces and pink teeth. He found them profoundly disturbing—as much for their similarities to *homo sapiens* as for their differences. Wing could imagine that they had once been human but had been cruelly transformed over eons of evolutionary torture.

He knew a little of their history. When glaciers threatened to crush their civilization, most had chosen exile and had left the planet in an evacuation organized by the Messengers. Something had happened to those that remained behind, something that the Messengers still did not understand. Even as they slid into barbarism, these Chani began to evolve at an accelerated rate. Something was pushing them toward a biological immortality totally unlike the hardware-based reincarnations of the Messengers. Their cities buried and their machines beyond repair, they had huddled around smoky fires and discovered within themselves the means to intervene in the aging process—by sheer force of mind they could tilt the delicate balance between anabolism and catabolism. They called it shriving. With their sins forgotten and their cells renewed, the Chani could lead many lives in one body, retaining only a few memories from one life to the next. What baffled the materialist Messengers was that shriving was the central rite of a religion based on sun worship. Believe in Chan, the survivors had urged the astonished commonwealth upon their rediscovery centuries after the evacuation: look into the sun and live again.

Although they embraced some of the concepts of the Chani religion, the Messengers could hardly accept shriving as a divine gift from a class G1 main sequence star. Despite intensive and continuing research, they were unable to master the biology of rejuvenation. The only benefits they were able to derive from the Chani's evolutionary breakthrough were delta globulins derived from blood plasma, which acted to slow or even halt the aging process in many of the commonwealth's species. The Messengers could not synthesize the intricate Chani globulins, which left the self-proclaimed goddess and ruler of the Chani in control of the sole source of the most valuable commodity in the commonwealth. That deity was the thearch Teaqua, the oldest living being in the commonwealth. Teaqua, who had sent Ndavu to earth to fetch her an architect. Teaqua, who was dying.

"She wants a tomb, Phillip, and she claims Chan told her a *human* must build it." Ndavu had given up his wheelchair in the starship's low gravity. As he spoke he had walked gingerly about Wing's cabin, like a barefoot man watching out for broken glass. "You will design it and oversee its construction."

"But if she's immortal . . ."

"No, even the Chan die. Eventually they choose death over shriving. We believe there must be physical limits related to the storage capacity of their brains. They say that the weight of all their lives becomes too heavy to carry. Think of it, Phillip: a tomb for a goddess. Has any architect had an opportunity to compare? This commission is more important than anything that Seven Wonders—or anyone on earth—could offer you. It has historic implications. You could be the one to lead your entire world into the commonwealth."

"So why me? There must be thousands who would jump at this."

"On the contrary, there are but a handful." The Messenger seemed troubled by Wing's question. "I will be blunt with you, Phillip; one cannot avoid the relativistic effects of the mass exchanger. You will be taking a one-way trip into the future. What you will experience as a trip of a few weeks duration will take centuries downtime, here on this planet. There is no way we can predict what changes will occur. You must understand that the earth to which you return may seem as alien as Aseneshesh." He paused just long enough to scare Wing. "You will, however, return a hero. While you are gone, your name will be remembered and revered; we will see to it that you become a legend. Your work will influence generations of artists; school children will study your life. You could also be rich, if you wanted."

"And you're telling me no one else could do this? No one?"

"There is a certain personality profile. Our candidate must be able to survive two stressful cultural transitions with his faculties intact. Your personal history indicates that you have the necessary resilience. Talent is yet another qualification."

Wing snickered. "But not as important as being a loner with nothing to lose."

"I do not accept that characterization." Ndavu settled uneasily onto the loveseat; he did not quite fit. "The fact is, Phillip, that we have already been refused twice. Should you too turn us down, we will proceed to the next on the list. You should know, however, that our time is running out and that you are the last of our prime candidates. The others have neither your ability nor your courage."

Courage. The word made Wing uncomfortable; he did not think of himself as a brave man. "What I still don't understand," he said, "is why you need a human in the first place. Build it yourself, if it's so damned important."

"We would prefer that. However Teaqua insists that only a human can do what she says Chan wants."

"That's absurd."

"Of *course* it is absurd." Ndavu made no effort to conceal his scorn. "We are talking about fifty million intelligent beings who believe that the local star cares for them. We are talking about a creature of flesh and blood who believes she has become a god. You cannot apply the rules of logic to religious superstition."

"But how did they find out about humans in the first place?"

"That I can explain," Ndavu said, "only if you will promise to keep my response a secret."

Wing hesitated; he was not sure if he wanted to know Messenger secrets. "How do you know I'll keep my promise?"

"We will have to learn to trust one another, Phillip." Ndavu unvelcroed the front of his jumpsuit; his chest was pale and smooth. "It is a problem of cultural differences." Wing backed away as the Messenger pushed a finger into the base of his neck. "Teaqua asked if we knew of any beings like the Chani, and we told her. *Homo sapiens* and the Chani share a unique genetic heritage," said Ndavu as his sternum unknit. "There are no other beings like you in the commonwealth." Wing pressed himself flat against the far wall of the cabin; the handle on the door of the microwave dug into him. "Genes are the ultimate source of culture."

Wing heard a low squishing sound, like a wet sponge being squeezed, as something uncoiled within the exposed body cavity. "I-I understand," he gasped. "Enough!"

The Messenger nodded and resealed himself. He stood, shuffled across the cabin and held out his hand. Wing shook it gingerly.

"You have qualities, Phillip," said Ndavu. "You are ambitious and impatient with the waste of your talents. The first time I saw you, I knew you were the one we needed."

Wing felt like throwing up.

"Will you at least think it over?"

Now he was alone with an intoxicating view of the earth, trying to sort fact from feeling, wrestling with his doubts. It was true: he had been increasingly uneasy in his work. Even the Glass Cloud was not all he had hoped it would be. *A tomb for a goddess*. It was too much, too fantastic. Thinking about it made Wing himself feel unreal. Here he sat with the earth at his feet, gazing down at the wellspring of civilization like some ancient, brooding god. *A legend*. He thought that if he were home he could see his way more clearly. Except that he had no home anymore, or at least he could never go home to Piscataqua House. The thought was depressing; was there really nothing to hold him? He wondered whether Ndavu had brought him to the starship to feed his sense of unreality, to cut him off from the reassurance of the mundane. He would have never been able to take this talk of gods and legends seriously had he been sitting at his desk at the Counting House with the rubber plant gathering dust near the window and his diploma from Yale hanging next to *John the Baptist*. Wing could see the Baptist smiling like a messenger as he pointed up at heaven—to the stars? *A one-way trip*. So Ndavu thought he was brave enough to go. But was he brave enough to stay? To turn down such a project and to live with that decision for the rest of his life? Wing was afraid that he was going to accept because there was nothing else for him to do. He would be an exile, *he* would be the alien. Wing had never even been in space before. Maybe that was why Ndavu had brought him here to make the offer. So that the emptiness of space could speak to the coldness growing within him.

Wing stood and walked quickly out of the cabin as if to escape his own dark thoughts. He took a moment to orient himself and then swung across the gravity well to the next landing. There was an elaborate access panel with printreader and voice analyzer and a numeric keypad and vidscanner; he knocked.

Daisy opened the door. Her room exhaled softly and she brushed the hair from her face. She was wearing the same mud-colored jumpsuit; he could not help but think of all the beautiful clothes hanging in her closet at Piscataqua House.

"Come in." She stood aside as he entered. He was surprised again at how exactly her cabin duplicated his. She observed him solemnly. He wondered if she ever smiled when she was alone.

"I don't want to talk about it," he said, answering the unspoken question. "I don't even want to think about it. I wish he would just go away."

"He won't."

He read the sympathy in her expression and wondered exactly why Ndavu had brought her along. "What I could use is a drink."

"What did you want to talk about?" She sat next to him.

"Nothing." He felt like blurting out Ndavu's secret; he thought it might make a difference to her. But he had promised. "I don't know." Wing scratched his ear. "I never told you that it was a nice party. The hot dogs were a big hit."

She smiled. "Snob appeal had something to do with it, don't you think? I'm sure that most of them like vitabulk just fine. But they have to rave about natural or else people will think they have no taste. At the mission we've been eating raw batch and no one complains. After a while natural seems a little bit decadent—or at least a waste of time."

"The essence can't taste mustard, eh?"

Before Ndavu, she might have detected the irony in his voice and bristled at it; now she nodded. "Exactly."

"But what *is* the essence? How can anything be *you* that can't taste mustard, that doesn't even have a body?"

"The essence is that part of mind which can be reproduced in artificial media," she said with catechetical swiftness.

"And that's what you want when you die, to have your personality deleted, your memories summarized and edited and re-edited until all you are is a collection of headlines about yourself stored in a computer?" He shook his head. "Sounds like a lousy substitute for heaven."

"But *heaven* is a myth."

"Okay," he said, trying to match her calm but not quite succeeding, "but I can't help but notice that the Messengers are in no hurry to have their essences extracted. They use the Chani globulins to keep themselves alive as long as they can. Why? And since they can't explain shriving, how do they know heaven is a myth?"

"Nothing is perfect, Phil." He was surprised to hear her admit it. "That's the most difficult part of the message. We can't claim perfection; we can only aspire to it."

"You've been spending a lot of time at the mission?"

"Ndavu is very demanding."

"And what about Piscataqua House? Who's minding the inn?"

She looked blank for a moment, as if trying to remember something that was not very important. "The inn pretty much takes care of itself, I guess." She frowned. "Business is terrible, you know."

"No, I didn't know."

"We've been in the red for over a year. Nobody goes any place these days." She tugged at a wrinkle in the leg of her jumpsuit. "I've been thinking of selling or maybe even just closing the old place up."

Wing was shocked. "You never told me you were having problems."

She stared through the floor for a moment. The starship's rotation had presented them with a view of the hazy blue rim of earth's atmosphere set against star-flecked blackness. "No," she said finally. "Maybe I didn't. At first I thought the Cloud might turn things around. Bring more tourists to New Hampshire, to Portsmouth—to the inn to see you. Ndavu offered a loan to hold me over. But now it doesn't matter much anymore."

"Ndavu!" Wing stood and began to pace away his anger. "Always Ndavu. He manipulated us to get his way. You must see that."

"Of course I see. You're the one who doesn't see. It's not his way he's trying to get. It's *the* way." She leaned forward as if to stop him and make him listen. He backed away. "He has disrupted dozens of lives just to bring you here. If you had given him any kind of chance, none of it would have happened. But you were prejudiced against him or just stubborn—I don't know what you were." Her eyes gleamed. "Haven't you figured it out yet? I think he wanted me to fall in love with Jim McCauley."

Wing gazed at her in silent horror.

"And he was right to do it; Jim has been good for me. He isn't obsessed with himself and his projects and his career. He finds the time to listen—to be there when I need him."

"You let that alien use you to get to me?"

"I didn't know at the time that he was doing it. I didn't know enough about the message to appreciate why he had to do it. But now I'm glad. I would have just been another reason for you to turn him down. It's important that you go to Aseneshesh. It's the most important thing you'll ever do."

"It's so important that two other people turned him down, right? I should too. Just because I fit some damned personality profile . . ."

"He said it that way only because you haven't yet accepted the message. He's not just some telelink psych, Phil, he can see into your essence. He knows what you need to grow and reach fulfillment. He knew when he asked you that you would accept."

Wing felt dizzy. "If I leave with him and go uptime or whatever he calls it—zapping off at the speed of light—I'll never see you again. You'll be downtime here, and you'll be dead for centuries before I get back. Doesn't that mean anything to you?"

"It means I'll always miss you." Her voice was flat, as if she were talking about a stolen towel.

He crossed the room to her, dropped to his knees, took her hands. "You meant so much to me, Daisy. Still do, after everything." He spoke without hope, yet he was compelled to say it. "All I want is to go back to the way it was. Do you remember? I know you remember."

"I remember we were two lonely people, Phil. We couldn't give each other what we needed." She made him let go and then ran her hand through his hair. "I remember I was unhappy." Sometimes when they were alone, reading or watching telelink, she would scratch his head. Now she fell absently into the old habit. Even though he knew he had lost her, he took comfort from it.

"I was always afraid to be happy." Wing rested his head in her lap. "I felt as if I didn't deserve to be happy."

The stars shone up at them with an ancient, pitiless light. Ndavu had done a thorough job, Wing thought. He's given me good reasons to go, reasons enough not to stay. The Messengers were nothing if not thorough.

Wing was dreaming of his father. In the dream his father was asleep on the Murphy bed in the go-tube. Wing had just returned from a parade held to honor him as the first human to go to the stars and he was angry that his father had not been there. Wing shook him, told him to wake up. His father stared up at him with rheumy, hopeless eyes and Wing noticed how frail he was. Look at me, Wing said to the old man, I've done something that was much harder than what you did. I didn't just leave my country, I left the planet, my time, everything. And I adjusted. I was strong and I survived. His father smiled like a Messenger. You love to dramatize yourself, said the old man. You think you are the hero of your story. His father began to shrink. But surviving takes a long time, he said and then he was nothing but a wet spot on the sheet and Wing was alone.

The telelink rang, jolting Wing awake. He cursed himself for an idiot; he had forgotten to set the screening program. The computer brought up the lights of his go-tube as he fumbled at the keyboard beside his bed.

"Phillip Wing speaking. Hello?"

"Mr. Wing? Phillip Wing? This is Hubert Fields; I'm with the Boston desk of Infoline. Can you tell me what's going on there?"

"Yes." Wing tapped a key and opened a window on the telelink's monitor. He could see the skyline of Portsmouth against a horizon the color of blue cat's-eye; the status line said 5:16 AM. "I'm sitting here stark naked, having just been rudely awakened by your call, and I'm wondering why I'm talking to you." The pull of earth's gravity had left him stiff and irritable.

Fields sounded unperturbed; Wing could not remember if he had ever been interviewed by this one before. "We've had confirmation from two sources that the messenger Ndavu has offered you a commission which would require that you travel to another planet. Do you have any comment?"

"All I can say is that we have discussed a project."

"On another planet?"

Wing yawned.

"We've also had reports that you recently toured the Messenger starship, which would make you the first human to do so. Can you describe the ship for us?"

Silence.

"Mr. Wing? Can you at least tell me when you'll be leaving earth?"

"No."

"You can't tell us?"

"I haven't decided what I'm doing yet. I'm hanging up now. Make sure there're two l's in Phillip."

"Will we see you at the ceremonies today?"

Wing broke the connection. Before he could roll back into bed the computer began playing his Thursday morning wakeup: the Minuet from Suite No. 1 of Handel's Water Music. It was 5:30; today was the dedication of the Glass Cloud.

He squashed the gel mat with its nest of blankets and sheets back into the wall of the go-tube. Most of his clothes were scattered in piles on the oak floor but Daisy had bought him a gray silk Mazzini suit for the occasion which was still hanging in its garment bag on the towel rack. Twice he had returned it; she had sent it back to him both times. He tried it on: a little loose in the waist. Daisy had not realized that he had lost weight since he had moved out.

Wing walked briskly across the strip to the USTS terminal where he was just in time to catch the northbound red-white-and-blue. It seemed as though everybody in the world had offered to give Wing a ride to North Conway that day, which was why he had perversely chosen to take a bus. He boarded the 6:04 carryvan which was making its everyday run up Route 16 with stops in Dover, Rochester, Milton, Wakefield, Ossipee, and North Conway. The spectators who would flock to the dedication were no doubt still in bed. They would arrive after lunch in hovers from New York or in specially-chartered 328 double-deckers driving nonstop from Boston and Portland and Manchester. Some would come in private cars; the Vice-President and the Secretary of the Interior were flying in from Washington on Air Force One. New Hampshire state police expected a crowd upwards of half a million, scattered along the ninety-seven kilometers of the Glass Cloud's circuit.

A crowd of angry locals had gathered at the bus stop in Ossipee. They hustled a clown on board and then banged the side of the carryvan with open hands to make the driver pull out. The clown was wearing a polka-dotted bag that came down to her ankles and left her arms bare; the dots cycled slowly through the spectrum. She had a paper-white skin tint and her hair was dyed to match the orange circles around her eyes. A chain of tiny phosphorescent bananas joined both ears and dangled beneath her chin. A woman up front tittered nervously; the man across the aisle from Wing looked disgusted. Even New Hampshire Yankees could not politely ignore such an apparition. But of course she wanted to be noticed; like all clowns she lived to provoke the astonished or disapproving stare.

"Seat taken?" she said. The carryvan accelerated abruptly, as if the driver had deliberately tried to make her fall. The clown staggered and sprawled next to Wing. "Is now." She laughed, and shoved her camouflage-colored duffle bag under the seat in front of her. "Where ya goin?"

Wing leaned his head against the window. "North Conway."

"Yeah? Me too. Name's Judy Thursday." She held out her hand to Wing.

"Phillip." He shook it weakly and the man across the aisle snorted. The clown's skin felt hot to the touch, as if she had the metabolism of a bird.

They rode in silence for a while; the clown squirmed in her seat and hummed to herself and clapped her hands and giggled. Eventually she opened the duffle bag and pulled out a small grease-stained cardboard box. "Popcorn? All natural."

Wing gazed at her doubtfully. The white skin tint made her eyes look pink. He had been on the road for two hours and had skipped breakfast.

"Very nutritious." She stuffed a handful into her mouth. "Popped it myself."

She was the kind of stranger mothers warned little children about. But Wing was hungry and the smell was irresistible. "They seemed awfully glad to see you go back there," he said, hesitating.

"No sense of humor, Phil." She put a kernel on the tip of her tongue and curled it into her mouth. "Going to the big party? Dedications are my favorite; always some great goofs. Bunch of us crashed the dedication of this insurance company tower—forget which—down in Hartford, Connecticut. Smack downtown, tallest building, the old edifice complex, you know? You shoulda seen, the suits went crazy. They had this buffet like—real cheese and raw veggies and some kinda meat. We spraypainted the entire spread with blue food coloring. And then I got into the HVAC system and planted a perfume bomb. Joint must still smell like lilacs." She leaned her head back against the seat and laughed. "Yeah, architecture is my life." She shook the popcorn box at Wing and he succumbed to temptation. The stuff was delicious.

"Hey, nice suit." The clown caught Wing's sleeve as he reached for another handful and rubbed it between thumb and forefinger. "Real silk, wow. How come you're riding the bus, Phil?"

Wing pulled free, gently. "Looking for something." He found himself slipping into her clipped dialect. "Not sure exactly what. Maybe a place to live."

"Yeah." She nodded vigorously. "Yeah. Beautiful country for goofs. The whole show is gonna be a goof, I figure. What do you think?"

Wing shrugged.

"I mean like what is this Glass Cloud anyway? A goof. No different from wrapping the White House in toilet paper, if you ask me. Except these guys got permits. Mies Van der Rohe, Phil, you know Mies Van der Rohe?"

"He's dead."

"I know that. But old Mies made all those glass boxes. The ones that got abandoned, they use 'em for target practice."

"Not all of them."

"I think Mies musta known what would happen. After all, he had four names. Musta been a goof in there somewhere." She offered him another handful and then closed the box and stuck it back in her bag. The carryvan rumbled across the bridge over the Saco River and headed up the strip that choked the main approach to North Conway.

"These guys on the link keep saying what a breakthrough this gizmo is and I keep laughing," she continued. "They don't understand the historical *context*, Phil, so why the hell don't they just shut up? Nothing new under the sun, twist and shout. The biggest goof of all." Wing noticed for the first time that her pupils were so dilated that her eyes looked like two bottomless wells. The van slowed, caught in strip traffic; even in daylight the flash bars seemed to pulse with garish intensity.

"Me, I thought it was kinda unique." Wing could not imagine why he was talking like this.

"Oh, no, Phil. No, no. It's the international style in the sky, is what it is. Study some architecture, you'll see what I mean." The carryvan crawled into a snarl of USTS vehicles near the old North Conway railroad station which had been moved to the airport and converted to a tourist information center. An electroluminescent banner hung from its Victorian gingerbread cornice. Green words flickered across it: "*Welcome to North Conway in the Heart of the Mount Washington Valley Home of the Glass Cloud Welcome to . . .*" Hovers were scattered across the landing field like seeds; tourists swarmed toward the center of town on foot. The line of busses waiting to unload at the terminal stopped moving. After ten minutes at a standstill the carryvan driver opened the doors and the passengers began to file out. When Wing rose he felt dizzy. The clown steadied him.

"Goodbye, Judy," he said as they stood blinking in the bright May sunshine. "Thanks for the popcorn." He shielded his eyes with his hand; her skin tint seemed to be glowing. "Try not to get into too much trouble."

"Gonna be a real colorful day, Phil." She leaned up and kissed him on the lips. Her breath smelled like popcorn. "It's a goof, understand? Stay with it. Have fun."

He fell back against the bus as she pushed into the crush of people, her polka dots saturated with shades of blue and violet, her orange hair like a spark. As she disappeared the crowd itself began to change colors. Cerulean moms waited in bathroom lines with whining sulphur kids in shorts. Plum grandpas took vids while their wrinkled apricot wives shyly adjusted straw hats. Wing glanced up and the sky went green. He closed his eyes and laughed silently. She had laced the popcorn with some kind of hallucinogen. Exactly the kind of prank he should have expected. Maybe he had suspected. Was not that why he had taken the bus, to give something, anything, one last chance to happen? To make the final decision while immersed in the randomness of the world he would have to give up? Maybe he *ought* to spend this day-of-all-days twisted. He kept his eyes closed; the sun felt warm on his face. Stay with it, she had said. "Have fun," he said aloud to no one in particular.

"It's a tribute to the American genius." The Vice-President of the United States shook Wing's hand. "We're all very proud of you."

Wing said, "Get out of Mexico."

Daisy tugged at his arm. "Come on, Phillip." Her voice sounded like brakes screeching.

The Vice-President, who was trying to pretend—in public at least—that he was not going deaf, tilted his head toward an incandescent aide in a three-piece suit. "Mexico," the aide repeated, scowling at Wing. The Vice-President at ninety-one was the oldest person ever to hold the office. He nodded sadly. "The tragic conflict in Mexico troubles us all, Mr. Wing. Unfortunately there are no easy answers."

Wing shook Daisy off. "We should get out and leave the PMF to sink or swim on its own." The Vice-President's expression was benignly quizzical; he cupped a hand to his ear. The green room was packed with dignitaries waiting for the dedication to begin and it sounded as if every one of them was practicing a speech. "I said . . ." Wing started to repeat.

The Vice-President had leaned so close that Wing could see tiny broken veins writhing like worms under his skin. "Mr. Wing," he interrupted, "have you stopped to consider how difficult we could make it for you to leave this planet?" He kept his voice low, as if they were making a deal.

"And what if I don't want to leave?"

The Vice-President laughed good-naturedly. "We could make that difficult too. It's a beautiful spring day, son. Could be your day . . . if you don't go screwing yourself into the wrong socket. Ah, Senator!" Abruptly Wing was staring at the great man's back.

"What is the matter with you?" Laporte appeared beside Daisy and he was hot, a shimmering blotch of rage and four-alarm ambition. "You think you can just stagger in, twisted out of your mind, insult the Vice-President—no, don't say anything. Once more, once more, Wing, and you'll be watching the Cloud from the ground, understand? This is my project now; I've worked too hard to let you screw it up again."

Wing did not care; he was too busy being pleased with himself for mustering the courage to confront the Vice-President. He had been certain that the Secret Service would whisk him away the moment he opened his mouth. Maybe it had not done any immediate good but if people kept pestering it might have a cumulative effect. Besides it had been *fun*. The crowd swirled; like a scene-change in a dream Laporte was gone and Daisy was steering him across the room. He knew any moment someone would step aside and he would be looking down at Ndavu in his wheelchair. He glanced at Daisy; her mouth was set in a grim line, like a fresh knife wound across her face. He wondered if she were having fun, if she would ever have fun again. What was the philosophical status of fun vis-a-vis the message? A local condition of increased entropy . . .

"I must have your consent today, Phillip," said Ndavu, "or I will have to assume that your answer is no." His face looked as if it had just been waxed.

Wing had stopped worrying about the slithery thing that lived inside the Messenger. It was easier on the digestion to pretend that this human shell was Ndavu. He picked a glass of champagne off a tray carried by a passing waiter, pulled up a folding chair and sat. "You leaked my name to telelink. Told them about the project."

"There is no more time."

Wing nodded absently as he looked around the room. "I'll have to get back to you." The Governor's husband was wearing a kilt with a pattern that seemed to tumble into itself kaleidoscopically.

Ndavu touched his arm to get his attention. "It must be now, Phillip."

Wing knocked back the champagne: ersatz. "Today, Ndavu." The glass seemed to melt through his fingers; it hit the floor and bounced. More plastic. "I promise."

"Ladies and gentlemen," said a little green man wearing a bow tie, gray morning coat, roll-collar waistcoat, and striped trousers, "if I may have your attention please."

A woman from the mission whispered to Ndavu, "The Vice-President's chief of protocol."

"We are opening the doors now and I want to take this opportunity to remind you once again: red invitations sit in the north stands, blue invitations to the south, and gold invitations on the platform. We are scheduled to start at two-fifteen so if you would please begin to find your seats. Thank you."

Daisy and Wing were sitting in the back row on the platform. On one side was Luis Benalcazar, whose company had designed both the Cloud's ferroplastic structure and the computer program that ran it; on the other was Fred Alz, the construction super. Laporte, as official representative of the Foundation and Solon Petropolus, sat up front with the Vice-President, the Secretary of the Interior, the Governor, the junior Senator and both of New Hampshire's congresspeople, the chief selectman of North Conway, a Hampton fourth-grader who had won an essay contest, the Bishop of Manchester, and a famous poet whom Wing had never heard of. Ndavu's wheelchair was off to one side.

The introductions, benedictions, acknowledgements and appreciations took the better part of an hour. . . . *A technological marvel which is at one with the natural environment* . . . The afternoon seemed to get hotter with every word, a nightmare of rhetoric as hell. . . . *the world will come to appreciate what we have known all along, that the Granite State is the greatest* . . . On a whim he tried to look into the dazzling sun but the colors nearly blinded him. . . . *their rugged grandeur cloaked in coniferous cloaks* . . . When Wing closed his eyes he could see a bright web of pulsing arteries and veins. . . . *this magnificent work of art balanced on a knife edge of electromagnetic energy* . . . Daisy kept squeezing his hand as if she were trying to pump appropriate reactions out of him. Meanwhile Benalcazar, whose English was not very good, fell asleep and started to snore. . . . *Reminds me of a story that the Speaker of the House used to tell* . . . When they mentioned Wing's name he stood up and bowed.

He could hear the applause for the Cloud several moments before it drifted over the hangar and settled toward the landing platform. It cast a cool shadow over the proceedings. Wing had imagined that he would feel something profound at this dramatic moment in his career but his first reaction was relief that the speeches were over and he was getting out of the sun.

The Cloud was designed to look like a cumulus puff but the illusion was only sustained for the distant viewer. Close up, anyone could see that it was an artifact. It moved with the ponderous grace of an enormous hover, to which it was a technological cousin. But while a hover was a rigid aerobody designed for powered flight, the Cloud was amorphous and a creature of the wind. Wing liked to call it a building that sailed. Its opaline outer envelope was ultrathin Stresslar, laminated to a ferroplastic grid based on an octagonal module. When Benalcazar's computer program directed current through the grid, some ferroplastic fibers went slack while others stiffened to form the Cloud's undulating structure. The size of the envelope could be increased or decreased depending on load factors and wind velocity; in effect it could be reefed like a sail. It used the magnetic track as a combination of rudder and keel or, when landing, as an anchor. Like a hover its envelope enclosed a volume of pressurized helium for lift: 20,000 cubic meters.

The Cloud slowly settled to within two meters of the ground, bottom flattening, the upper envelope billowing into the blue sky. Wing realized that people had stopped applauding and an awed hush had settled onto the platform. The Hampton schoolgirl climbed onto a folding chair and stood twisting her prize-winning essay into an irretrievable tatter. Wing himself could feel the gooseflesh stippling his arms now; the chill of the Cloud's shadow was strangely sobering. The Secretary of the Interior sank slowly onto his chair, shielded his eyes with the flat of his hand and stared up like a coal miner in Manhattan. Pictures would never do the Cloud justice. The Governor whispered something to the Bishop, who did not seem to be paying attention. Wing shivered. Like some miracle out of the Old Testament, the Cloud had swollen into a pillar that was at least twenty stories tall. It had accomplished this transformation without making a sound.

Fred Alz nudged Wing in the ribs. "Guess we got their attention, eh Phil?" The slouch-backed old man stood straight. Wing supposed it was pride puffing Alz up; he could not quite bring himself to share it.

Daisy squeezed his hand. "It's so quiet."

"Ssshh!" The Governor's husband turned and glared.

The silence was the one element of the design that Wing had never fully imagined. In fact, he had been willing to compromise on a noisier reefing mechanism to hold down costs but Laporte, of all people, had talked him out of it. Not until he had seen the first tests of the completed Cloud did Wing realize the enormous psychological impact of silence when applied to large bodies in motion. It gave the Cloud a surreal, slightly ominous power, as if it were the ghost of a great building. It certainly helped to compensate for the distressing way the Stresslar envelope changed from pearl to cheapjack plastic iridescence in certain angles of light. The engineers, technicians, and fabricators had worked technological wonders to create a quiet Cloud; although Wing approved, it had not been part of his original vision. The reaction of the crowd was another bittersweet reminder that this was not his Cloud, that he had lost his Cloud the day he had begun to draw it.

The octagonal geometry of the structural grid came clear as the pilot hardened the Cloud in preparation for boarding. Ndavu wheeled up noiselessly and offered his hand in congratulations. They shook but Wing avoided eye contact for fear that the alien might detect Wing's estrangement from his masterpiece. A hole opened in the envelope and a tube snaked out; the ground crew coupled it to the landing platform. Ndavu shook hands with Alz and spoke to Luis Benalcazar in Spanish. Smiling and nodding, Benalcazar stooped toward the Messenger to reply. "He says," Ndavu translated, "that this is the culmination of his career. For him, there will never be another project like it."

"For all of us," said Alz.

"Thank you," Benalcazar hugged Wing. "Phillip. So much." A woman with a microcam came to the edge of the platform to record the embrace. Wing pulled away from Benalcazar. "You, Luis," he tapped the engineer on the chest and then pointed at the Cloud. "It's your baby. Without you, it's a flying tent." "Big goddamn tent yes," said Benalcazar, laughing uncertainly. Laporte was shaking hands with the congressman from the First District. The chief of protocol stood near the entrance of the tube and began motioning for people to climb through to the passenger car suspended within the envelope. Before anyone could board, however, Ndavu backed away from Wing, Benalcazar, and Alz and began to clap. Daisy stepped to the Messenger's side and joined in, raising hands over her head like a cheerleader. People turned to see what was going on and then everyone was applauding.

It felt wrong to Wing—like an attack, as if each clap were a blow he had to withstand. He thought it was too late to clap now. Perhaps if the applause could echo backward through the years, so that a nervous young man on a stony path might hear it and take sustenance from it, things might have been different. But that man's ears were stopped by time and he was forever alienated from these people. These people who did not realize how they were being manipulated by Ndavu. These people who were clapping for the wrong cloud. Wing's cloud was not this glorified special effect. His cloud was forever lonely, lost as it wandered, windborne, past sheer walls of granite: a daydream. You can't build a dream out of Stresslar and ferroplastic, he told himself. You can't share your dreams. He thought that Daisy looked very pretty, clapping for him. She was wearing the blue dress that he had bought for her in Boston. She had been mad at him for spending so much money; they had fought over it. The glowing clearwater blue of the material picked up the blue in her eyes; it had always been his favorite. Daisy had taken five years of his life away and he was back now to where he had been before he met her. She was not his wife. This was not his cloud. These were not his people. He found himself thinking then about the alien goddess Teaqua, a creature of such transcendent luminosity that she could order Messengers to run her errands. He wondered if she could look into the sun.

"Tell him to stop it," Wing said to Daisy. "Tell him I'll go."

The applause ended. Several hours later on Infoline's evening report, Hubert Fields noted in passing that the architect was not among those who boarded the Glass Cloud for its maiden voyage.

# OCTAVIA E. BUTLER

## The Evening and the Morning and the Night

Octavia E. Butler sold her first novel in 1976, and has subsequently emerged as one of the foremost novelists of her generation. Her critically acclaimed books include *Patternmaster, Mind of My Mind, Survivor, Kindred, Wild Seed*, and *Clay's Ark*. Her most recent novel is *Dawn*. Her short stories appear infrequently, but are well worth the wait. In 1984, she won a Hugo Award for her story "Speech Sounds"; in 1985, she won both the Hugo and the Nebula Award for her famous story "Bloodchild," which was reprinted in our Second Annual Collection. Born in Pasadena, California, she now lives and works in Los Angeles.

Here she spins a chill and chilling tale of despair, resignation, and, most painfully, hope.

# THE EVENING AND THE MORNING AND THE NIGHT

## Octavia E. Butler

When I was fifteen and trying to show my independence by getting careless with my diet, my parents took me to a Duryea-Gode disease ward. They wanted me to see, they said, where I was headed if I wasn't careful. In fact, it was where I was headed no matter what. It was only a matter of when: now or later. My parents were putting in their vote for later.

I won't describe the ward. It's enough to say that when they brought me home, I cut my wrists. I did a thorough job of it, old Roman style in a bathtub of warm water. Almost made it. My father dislocated his shoulder breaking down the bathroom door. He and I never forgave each other for that day.

The disease got him almost three years later—just before I went off to college. It was sudden. It doesn't happen that way often. Most people notice themselves beginning to drift—or their relatives notice—and they make arrangements with their chosen institution. People who are noticed and who resist going in can be locked up for a week's observation. I don't doubt that that observation period breaks up a few families. Sending someone away for what turns out to be a false alarm. . . . Well, it isn't the sort of thing the victim is likely to forgive or forget. On the other hand, not sending someone away in time—missing the signs or having a person go off suddenly without signs—is inevitably dangerous for the victim. I've never heard of it going as badly, though, as it did in my family. People normally injure only themselves when their time comes—unless someone is stupid enough to try to handle them without the necessary drugs or restraints.

My father . . . killed my mother, then killed himself. I wasn't home when it happened. I had stayed at school later than usual, rehearsing graduation exercises. By the time I got home, there were cops everywhere. There was an ambulance, and two attendants were wheeling someone out on a stretcher—someone covered. More than covered. Almost . . . bagged.

The cops wouldn't let me in. I didn't find out until later exactly what had happened. I wish I'd never found out. Dad had killed Mom, then skinned her completely. At least, that's how I hope it happened. I mean I hope he killed her first. He broke some of her ribs, damaged her heart. Digging.

Then he began tearing at himself, through skin and bone, digging. He had managed to reach his own heart before he died. It was an especially bad example of the kind of thing that makes people afraid of us. It gets some of us into trouble for picking at a pimple or even for daydreaming. It has inspired restrictive laws, created problems with jobs, housing, schools. . . . The Duryea-Gode Disease Foundation has spent millions telling the world that people like my father don't exist.

A long time later, when I had gotten myself together as best I could, I went to college—to the University of Southern California—on a Dilg scholarship. Dilg is the retreat you try to send your out-of-control DGD relatives to. It's run by controlled DGDs like me, like my parents while they lived. God knows how any controlled DGD stands it. Anyway, the place has a waiting list miles long. My parents put me on it after my suicide attempt, but chances were, I'd be dead by the time my name came up.

I can't say why I went to college—except that I had been going to school all my life and I didn't know what else to do. I didn't go with any particular hope. Hell, I knew what I was in for eventually. I was just marking time. Whatever I did was just marking time. If people were willing to pay me to go to school and mark time, why not do it?

The weird part was, I worked hard, got top grades. If you work hard enough at something that doesn't matter, you can forget for a while about the things that do.

Sometimes I thought about trying suicide again. How was it I'd had the courage when I was fifteen but didn't have it now? Two DGD parents—both religious, both as opposed to abortion as they were to suicide. So they had trusted God and the promises of modern medicine and had a child. But how could I look at what had happened to them and trust anything?

I majored in biology. Non-DGDs say something about our disease makes us good at the sciences—genetics, molecular biology, biochemistry. . . . That something was terror. Terror and a kind of driving hopelessness. Some of us went bad and became destructive before we had to—yes, we did produce more than our share of criminals. And some of us went good—spectacularly—and made scientific and medical history. These last kept the doors at least partly open for the rest of us. They made discoveries in genetics, found cures for a couple of rare diseases, made advances in the fight against other diseases that weren't so rare—including, ironically, some forms of cancer. But they'd found nothing to help themselves. There had been nothing since the latest improvements in the diet, and those came just before I was born. They, like the original diet, gave more DGDs the courage to have children. They were supposed to do for DGDs what insulin had done for diabetics—give us a normal or nearly normal life span. Maybe they had worked for someone somewhere. They hadn't worked for anyone I knew.

Biology. School was a pain in the usual ways. I didn't eat in public anymore, didn't like the way people stared at my biscuits—cleverly dubbed "dog biscuits" in every school I'd ever attended. You'd think university students would be more creative. I didn't like the way people edged away from me when they caught sight of my emblem. I'd begun wearing it on a chain around my neck and putting it down inside my blouse, but people managed to notice it anyway. People who don't eat in public, who drink nothing more interesting than water, who smoke nothing at all—people like that are suspicious. Or rather, they make others suspicious. Sooner or later, one of those others, finding my fingers and wrists bare, would fake an interest in my chain. That would be that. I couldn't hide the emblem in my purse. If anything happened to me, medical people had to see it in time to avoid giving me the medications they might use on a normal person. It isn't just ordinary food we have to avoid, but about a quarter of a *Physicians' Desk Reference* of widely used drugs. Every now and then there are news stories about people who stopped carrying their emblems—probably trying to pass as normal. Then they have an accident. By the time anyone realizes there is anything wrong, it's too late. So I wore my emblem. And one way or another, people got a look at it or got the word from someone who had. "She *is*!" Yeah.

At the beginning of my third year, four other DGDs and I decided to rent a house together. We'd all had enough of being lepers twenty-four hours a day. There was an English major. He wanted to be a writer and tell our story from the inside—which had only been done thirty or forty times before. There was a special-education major who hoped the handicapped would accept her more readily than the able-bodied, a premed who planned to go into research, and a chemistry major who didn't really know what she wanted to do.

Two men and three women. All we had in common was our disease, plus a weird combination of stubborn intensity about whatever we happened to be doing and hopeless cynicism about everything else. Healthy people say no one can concentrate like a DGD. Healthy people have all the time in the world for stupid generalizations and short attention spans.

We did our work, came up for air now and then, ate our biscuits, and attended classes. Our only problem was housecleaning. We worked out a schedule of who would clean what when, who would deal with the yard, whatever. We all agreed on it; then, except for me, everyone seemed to forget about it. I found myself going around reminding people to vacuum, clean the bathroom, mow the lawn. . . . I figured they'd all hate me in no time, but I wasn't going to be their maid, and I wasn't going to live in filth. Nobody complained. Nobody even seemed annoyed. They just came up out of their academic daze, cleaned, mopped, mowed, and went back to it. I got into the habit of running around in the evening reminding people. It didn't bother me if it didn't bother them.

"How'd you get to be housemother?" a visiting DGD asked.

I shrugged. "Who cares? The house works." It did. It worked so well that this new guy wanted to move in. He was a friend of one of the others, and another premed. Not bad looking.

"So do I get in or don't I?" he asked.

"As far as I'm concerned, you do," I said. I did what his friend should have done—introduced him around, then, after he left, talked to the others to make sure nobody had any real objections. He seemed to fit right in. He forgot to clean the toilet or mow the lawn, just like the others. His name was Alan Chi. I thought Chi was a Chinese name, and I wondered. But he told me his father was Nigerian and that in Ibo, the word meant a kind of guardian angel or personal god. He said his own personal god hadn't been looking out for him very well to let him be born to two DGD parents. Him too.

I don't think it was much more than that similarity that drew us together at first. Sure, I liked the way he looked, but I was used to liking someone's looks and having him run like hell when he found out what I was. It took me a while to get used to the fact that Alan wasn't going anywhere.

I told him about my visit to the DGD ward when I was fifteen—and my suicide attempt afterward. I had never told anyone else. I was surprised at how relieved it made me feel to tell him. And somehow his reaction didn't surprise me.

"Why didn't you try again?" he asked. We were alone in the living room.

"At first, because of my parents," I said. "My father in particular. I couldn't do that to him again."

"And after him?"

"Fear. Inertia."

He nodded. "When I do it, there'll be no half measures. No being rescued, no waking up in a hospital later."

"You mean to do it?"

"The day I realize I've started to drift. Thank God we get some warning."

"Not necessarily."

"Yes, we do. I've done a lot of reading. Even talked to a couple of doctors. Don't believe the rumors non-DGDs invent."

I looked away, stared into the scarred, empty fireplace. I told him exactly how my father had died—something else I'd never voluntarily told anyone.

He sighed. "Jesus!"

We looked at each other.

"What are you going to do?" he asked.

"I don't know."

He extended a dark, square hand, and I took it and moved closer to him. He was a dark, square man—my height, half again my weight, and none of it fat. He was so bitter sometimes, he scared me.

"My mother started to drift when I was three," he said. "My father only lasted a few months longer. I heard he died a couple of years after he went into the hospital. If the two of them had had any sense, they would have had me aborted the minute my mother realized she was pregnant. But she wanted a kid no matter what. And she was Catholic." He shook his head. "Hell, they should pass a law to sterilize the lot of us."

"They?" I said.

"You want kids?"

"No, but—"

"More like us to wind up chewing their fingers off in some DGD ward."

"I don't want kids, but I don't want someone else telling me I can't have any."

He stared at me until I began to feel stupid and defensive. I moved away from him.

"Do you want someone else telling you what to do with your body?" I asked.

"No need," he said. "I had that taken care of as soon as I was old enough."

This left me staring. I'd thought about sterilization. What DGD hasn't? But I didn't know anyone else our age who had actually gone through with it. That would be like killing part of yourself—even though it wasn't a part you intended to use. Killing part of yourself when so much of you was already dead.

"The damned disease could be wiped out in one generation," he said, "but people are still animals when it comes to breeding. Still following mindless urges, like dogs and cats."

My impulse was to get up and go away leave him to wallow in his bitterness and depression alone. But I stayed. He seemed to want to live even less than I did. I wondered how he'd made it this far.

"Are you looking forward to doing research?" I probed. "Do you believe you'll be able to—"

"No."

I blinked. The word was as cold and dead a sound as I'd ever heard.

"I don't believe in anything," he said.

I took him to bed. He was the only other double DGD I had ever met, and if nobody did anything for him, he wouldn't last much longer. I couldn't just let him slip away. For a while, maybe we could be each other's reasons for staying alive.

He was a good student—for the same reason I was. And he seemed to shed some of his bitterness as time passed. Being around him helped me understand why against all sanity, two DGDs would lock in on each other and start talking about marriage. Who else would have us?

We probably wouldn't last very long, anyway. These days, most DGDs make it to forty, at least. But then, most of them don't have two DGD parents. As bright as Alan was, he might not get into medical school because of his double inheritance. No one would tell him his bad genes were keeping him out, of course, but we both knew what his chances were. Better to train doctors who were likely to live long enough to put their training to use.

Alan's mother had been sent to Dilg. He hadn't seen her or been able to get any information about her from his grandparents while he was at home. By the time he left for college, he'd stopped asking questions. Maybe it was hearing about my parents that made him start again. I was with him when he called Dilg. Until that moment, he hadn't even known whether his mother was still alive. Surprisingly, she was.

"Dilg must be good," I said when he hung up. "People don't usually . . . I mean . . ."

"Yeah, I know," he said. "People don't usually live long once they're out of control. Dilg is different." We had gone to my room, where he turned a chair backward and sat down. "Dilg is what the others ought to be, if you can believe the literature."

"Dilg is a giant DGD ward," I said. "It's richer—probably better at sucking in the donations—and it's run by people who can expect to become patients eventually. Apart from that, what's different?"

"I've read about it," he said. "So should you. They've got some new treatment. They don't just shut people away to die the way the others do."

"What else is there to do with them?" *With us*.

"I don't know. It sounded like they have some kind of . . . sheltered workshop. They've got patients doing things."

"A new drug to control the self-destructiveness?"

"I don't think so. We would have heard about that."

"What else could it be?"

"I'm going up to find out. Will you come with me?"

"You're going up to see your mother."

He took a ragged breath. "Yeah. Will you come with me?"

I went to one of my windows and stared out at the weeds. We let them thrive in the backyard. In the front we mowed them, along with the few patches of grass."

"I told you my DGD-ward experience."

"You're not fifteen now. And Dilg isn't some zoo of a ward."

"It's got to be, no matter what they tell the public. And I'm not sure I can stand it."

He got up, came to stand next to me. "Will you try?"

I didn't say anything. I focused on our reflections in the window glass—the two of us together. It looked right, felt right. He put his arm around me, and I leaned back against him. Our being together had been as good for me as it seemed to have been for him. It had given me something to go on besides inertia and fear. I knew I would go with him. It felt like the right thing to do.

"I can't say how I'll act when we get there," I said.

"I can't say how I'll act, either," he admitted. "Especially . . . when I see her."

He made the appointment for the next Saturday afternoon. You make appointments to go to Dilg unless you're a government inspector of some kind. That is the custom, and Dilg gets away with it.

We left L.A. in the rain early Saturday morning. Rain followed us off and on up the coast as far as Santa Barbara. Dilg was hidden away in the hills not far from San Jose. We could have reached it faster by driving up I–5, but neither of us were in the mood for all that bleakness. As it was, we arrived at one P.M. to be met by two armed gate guards. One of these phoned the main building and verified our appointment. Then the other took the wheel from Alan.

"Sorry," he said. "But no one is permitted inside without an escort. We'll meet your guide at the garage."

None of this surprised me. Dilg is a place where not only the patients but much of the staff has DGD. A maximum security prison wouldn't have been as potentially dangerous. On the other hand, I'd never heard of anyone getting chewed up here. Hospitals and rest homes had accidents. Dilg didn't. It was beautiful—an old estate. One that didn't make sense in these days of high taxes. It had been owned by the Dilg family. Oil, chemicals, pharmaceuticals. Ironically, they had even owned part of the late, unlamented Hedeon Laboratories. They'd had a briefly profitable interest in Hedeonco: the magic bullet, the cure for a large percentage of the world's cancer and a number of serious viral diseases—and the cause of Duryea-Gode disease. If one of your parents was treated with Hedeonco and you were conceived after the treatments, you had DGD. If you had kids, you passed it on to them. Not everyone was equally affected. They didn't all commit suicide or murder, but they all mutilated themselves to some degree if they could. And they all drifted—went off into a world of their own and stopped responding to their surroundings.

Anyway, the only Dilg son of his generation had had his life saved by Hedeonco. Then he had watched four of his children die before Doctors Kenneth Duryea and Jan Gode came up with a decent understanding of the problem and a partial solution: the diet. They gave Richard Dilg a way of keeping his next two children alive. He gave the big, cumbersome estate over to the care of DGD patients.

So the main building was an elaborate old mansion. There were other, newer buildings, more like guesthouses than institutional buildings. And there were wooded hills all around. Nice country. Green. The ocean wasn't far away. There was an old garage and a small parking lot. Waiting in the lot was a tall old woman. Our guard pulled up near her, let us out, then parked the car in the half-empty garage.

"Hello," the woman said, extending her hand. "I'm Beatrice Alcantara." The hand was cool and dry and startlingly strong. I thought the woman was DGD, but her age threw me. She appeared to be about sixty, and I had never seen a DGD that old. I wasn't sure why I thought she was DGD. If she was, she must have been an experimental model—one of the first to survive.

"Is it Doctor or Ms.?" Alan asked.

"It's Beatrice," she said. "I am a doctor, but we don't use titles much here."

I glanced at Alan, was surprised to see him smiling at her. He tended to go a long time between smiles. I looked at Beatrice and couldn't see anything to smile about. As we introduced ourselves, I realized I didn't like her. I couldn't see any reason for that either, but my feelings were my feelings. I didn't like her.

"I assume neither of you have been here before," she said, smiling down at us. She was at least six feet tall, and straight.

We shook our heads. "Let's go in the front way, then. I want to prepare you for what we do here. I don't want you to believe you've come to a hospital."

I frowned at her, wondering what else there was to believe. Dilg was called a retreat, but what difference did names make?

The house close up looked like one of the old-style public buildings—massive, baroque front with a single, domed tower reaching three stories above the three-story house. Wings of the house stretched for some distance to the right and left of the tower, then cornered and stretched back twice as far. The front doors were huge—one set of wrought iron and one of heavy wood. Neither appeared to be locked. Beatrice pulled open the iron door, pushed the wooden one, and gestured us in.

Inside, the house was an art museum—huge, high-ceilinged, tile-floored. There were marble columns and niches in which sculpture stood or paintings hung. There was other sculpture displayed around the rooms. At one end of the rooms there was a broad staircase leading up to a gallery that went around the rooms. There more art was displayed. "All this was made here," Beatrice said. "Some of it is even sold from here. Most goes to galleries in the Bay Area or down around L.A. Our only problem is turning out too much of it."

"You mean the patients do this?" I asked.

The old woman nodded. "This and much more. Our people work instead of tearing at themselves or staring into space. One of them invented the p.v. locks that protect this place. Though I almost wish he hadn't. It's gotten us more government attention than we like."

"What kind of locks?" I asked.

"Sorry, Palmprint-voiceprint. The first and the best. We have the patent." She looked at Alan. "Would you like to see what your mother does?"

"Wait a minute," he said. "You're telling us out-of-control DGDs create art and invent things?"

"And that lock," I said. "I've never heard of anything like that. I didn't even see a lock."

"The lock is new," she said. "There have been a few news stories about it. It's not the kind of thing most people would buy for their homes. Too expensive. So it's of limited interest. People tend to look at what's done at Dilg in the way they look at the efforts of idiots savants. Interesting, incomprehensible, but not really important. Those likely to be interested in the lock and able to afford it know about it." She took a deep breath, faced Alan again. "Oh, yes, DGDs create things. At least they do here."

"Out-of-control DGDs."

"Yes."

"I expected to find them weaving baskets or something—at best. I know what DGD wards are like."

"So do I," she said. "I know what they're like in hospitals, and I know what it's like here." She waved a hand toward an abstract painting that looked like a photo I had once seen of the Orion Nebula. Darkness broken by a great cloud of light and color. "Here we can help them channel their energies. They can create something beautiful, useful, even something worthless. But they create. They don't destroy."

"Why?" Alan demanded. "It can't be some drug. We would have heard."

"It's not a drug."

"Then what is it? Why haven't other hospitals—?"

"Alan," she said. "Wait."

He stood frowning at her.

"Do you want to see your mother?"

"Of course I want to see her!"

"Good. Come with me. Things will sort themselves out."

She led us to a corridor past offices where people talked to one another, waved to Beatrice, worked with computers. . . . They could have been anywhere. I wondered how many of them were controlled DGDs. I also wondered what kind of game the old woman was playing with her secrets. We passed through rooms so beautiful and perfectly kept it was obvious they were rarely used. Then at a broad, heavy door, she stopped us.

"Look at anything you like as we go on," she said. "But don't touch anything or anyone. And remember that some of the people you'll see injured themselves before they came to us. They still bear the scars of those injuries. Some of those scars may be difficult to look at, but you'll be in no danger. Keep that in mind. No one here will harm you." She pushed the door open and gestured us in.

Scars didn't bother me much. Disability didn't bother me. It was the act of self-mutilation that scared me. It was someone attacking her own arm as though it were a wild animal. It was someone who had torn at himself and been restrained or drugged off and on for so long that he barely had a recognizable human feature left, but he was still trying with what he did have to dig into his own flesh. Those are a couple of the things I saw at the DGD ward when I was fifteen. Even then I could have stood it better if I hadn't felt I was looking into a kind of temporal mirror.

I wasn't aware of walking through that doorway. I wouldn't have thought I could do it. The old woman said something, though, and

I found myself on the other side of the door with the door closing behind me. I turned to stare at her.

She put her hand on my arm. "It's all right," she said quietly. "That door looks like a wall to a great many people."

I backed away from her, out of her reach, repelled by her touch. Shaking hands had been enough, for God's sake.

Something in her seemed to come to attention as she watched me. It made her even straighter. Deliberately, but for no apparent reason, she stepped toward Alan, touched him the way people do sometimes when they brush past—a kind of tactile "Excuse me." In that wide, empty corridor, it was totally unnecessary. For some reason, she wanted to touch him and wanted me to see. What did she think she was doing? Flirting at her age? I glared at her, found myself suppressing an irrational urge to shove her away from him. The violence of the urge amazed me.

Beatrice smiled and turned away. "This way," she said. Alan put his arm around me and tried to lead me after her.

"Wait a minute," I said, not moving.

Beatrice glanced around.

"What just happened?" I asked. I was ready for her to lie—to say nothing happened, pretend not to know what I was talking about.

"Are you planning to study medicine?" she asked.

"What? What does that have to do—?"

"Study medicine. You may be able to do a great deal of good." She strode away, taking long steps so that we had to hurry to keep up. She led us through a room in which some people worked at computer terminals and others with pencils and paper. It would have been an ordinary scene except that some people had half their faces ruined or had only one hand or leg or had other obvious scars. But they were all in control now. They were working. They were intent but not intent on self-destruction. Not one was digging into or tearing away flesh. When we had passed through this room and into a small, ornate sitting room, Alan grasped Beatrice's arm.

"What is it?" he demanded. "What do you do for them?"

She patted his hand, setting my teeth on edge. "I will tell you," she said. "I want you to know. But I want you to see your mother first." To my surprise, he nodded, let it go at that.

"Sit a moment," she said to us.

We sat in comfortable, matching upholstered chairs, Alan looking reasonably relaxed. What was it about the old lady that relaxed him but put me on edge? Maybe she reminded him of his grandmother or something. She didn't remind me of anyone. And what was that nonsense about studying medicine?

"I wanted you to pass through at least one workroom before we talked about your mother—and about the two of you." She turned to face me. "You've had a bad experience at a hospital or a rest home?"

I looked away from her, not wanting to think about it. Hadn't the people in that mock office been enough of a reminder? Horror film office. Nightmare office.

"It's all right," she said. "You don't have to go into detail. Just outline it for me."

I obeyed slowly, against my will, all the while wondering why I was doing it.

She nodded, unsurprised. "Harsh, loving people, your parents. Are they alive?"

"No."

"Were they both DGD?"

"Yes, but . . . yes."

"Of course. Aside from the obvious ugliness of your hospital experience and its implications for the future, what impressed you about the people in the ward?"

I didn't know what to answer. What did she want? Why did she want anything from me? She should have been concerned with Alan and his mother.

"Did you see people unrestrained?"

"Yes," I whispered. "One woman. I don't know how it happened that she was free. She ran up to us and slammed into my father without moving him. He was a big man. She bounced off, fell, and . . . began tearing at herself. She bit her own arm and . . . swallowed the flesh she'd bitten away. She tore at the wound she'd made with the nails of her other hand. She . . . I screamed at her to stop." I hugged myself, remembering the young woman, bloody, cannibalizing herself as she lay at our feet, digging into her own flesh. Digging. "They try so hard, fight so hard to get out."

"Out of what?" Alan demanded.

I looked at him, hardly seeing him.

"Lynn," he said gently. "Out of what?"

I shook my head. "Their restraints, their disease, the ward, their bodies . . ."

He glanced at Beatrice, then spoke to me again. "Did the girl talk?"

"No. She screamed."

He turned away from me uncomfortably. "Is this important?" he asked Beatrice.

"Very," she said.

"Well . . . can we talk about it after I see my mother?"

"Then and now." She spoke to me. "Did the girl stop what she was doing when you told her to?"

"The nurses had her a moment later. It didn't matter."

"It mattered. Did she stop?"

"Yes."

"According to the literature, they rarely respond to anyone," Alan said.

"True." Beatrice gave him a sad smile. "Your mother will probably respond to you, though."

"Is she? . . ." He glanced back at the nightmare office. "Is she as controlled as those people?"

"Yes, though she hasn't always been. Your mother works with clay now. She loves shapes and textures and—"

"She's blind," Alan said, voicing the suspicion as though it were fact. Beatrice's words had sent my thoughts in the same direction. Beatrice hesitated. "Yes," she said finally. "And for . . . the usual reason. I had intended to prepare you slowly."

"I've done a lot of reading."

I hadn't done much reading, but I knew what the usual reason was. The woman had gouged, ripped, or otherwise destroyed her eyes. She would be badly scarred. I got up, went over to sit on the arm of Alan's chair. I rested my hand on his shoulder, and he reached up and held it there.

"Can we see her now?" he asked.

Beatrice got up. "This way," she said.

We passed through more workrooms. People painted; assembled machinery; sculpted in wood, stone; even composed and played music. Almost no one noticed us. The patients were true to their disease in that respect. They weren't ignoring us. They clearly didn't know we existed. Only the few controlled-DGD guards gave themselves away by waving or speaking to Beatrice. I watched a woman work quickly, knowledgeably, with a power saw. She obviously understood the perimeters of her body, was not so dissociated as to perceive herself as trapped in something she needed to dig her way out of. What had Dilg done for these people that other hospitals did not do? And how could Dilg withhold its treatment from the others?

"Over there we make our own diet foods," Beatrice said, pointing through a window toward one of the guesthouses. "We permit more variety and make fewer mistakes than the commercial preparers. No ordinary person can concentrate on work the way our people can."

I turned to face her. "What are you saying? That the bigots are right? That we have some special gift?"

"Yes," she said. "It's hardly a bad characteristic, is it?"

"It's what people say whenever one of us does well at something. It's their way of denying us credit for our work."

"Yes. But people occasionally come to the right conclusions for the wrong reasons." I shrugged, not interested in arguing with her about it.

"Alan?" she said. He looked at her.

"Your mother is in the next room."

He swallowed, nodded. We both followed her into the room.

Naomi Chi was a small woman, hair still dark, fingers long and thin, graceful as they shaped the clay. Her face was a ruin. Not only her eyes but most of her nose and one ear were gone. What was left was badly scarred. "Her parents were poor," Beatrice said. "I don't know how much they told you, Alan, but they went through all the money they had, trying to keep her at a decent place. Her mother felt so guilty, you know. She was the one who had cancer and took the drug. . . . Eventually, they had to put Naomi in one of those state-approved, custodial-care places. You know the kind. For a while, it was all the government would pay for. Places like that . . . well, sometimes if patients were really troublesome—especially the ones who kept breaking free—they'd put them in a bare room and let them finish themselves. The only things those places took good care of were the maggots, the cockroaches, and the rats."

I shuddered. "I've heard there are still places like that."

"There are," Beatrice said, "kept open by greed and indifference." She looked at Alan. "Your mother survived for three months in one of those places. I took her from it myself. Later I was instrumental in having that particular place closed."

"You took her?" I asked.

"Dilg didn't exist then, but I was working with a group of controlled DGDs in L.A. Naomi's parents heard about us and asked us to take her. A lot of people didn't trust us then. Only a few of us were medically trained. All of us were young, idealistic, and ignorant. We began in an old frame house with a leaky roof. Naomi's parents were grabbing at straws. So were we. And by pure luck, we grabbed a good one. We were able to prove ourselves to the Dilg family and take over these quarters."

"Prove what?" I asked.

She turned to look at Alan and his mother. Alan was staring at Naomi's ruined face, at the ropy, discolored scar tissue. Naomi was shaping the image of an old woman and two children. The gaunt, lined face of the old woman was remarkably vivid—detailed in a way that seemed impossible for a blind sculptress.

Naomi seemed unaware of us. Her total attention remained on her work. Alan forgot about what Beatrice had told us and reached out to touch the scarred face.

Beatrice let it happen. Naomi did not seem to notice. "If I get her attention for you," Beatrice said, "we'll be breaking her routine. We'll have to stay with her until she gets back into it without hurting herself. About half an hour."

"You can get her attention?" he asked.

"Yes."

"Can she? . . ." Alan swallowed. "I've never heard of anything like this. Can she talk?"

"Yes. She may not choose to, though. And if she does, she'll do it very slowly."

"Do it. Get her attention."

"She'll want to touch you."

"That's all right. Do it."

Beatrice took Naomi's hands and held them still, away from the wet clay. For several seconds Naomi tugged at her captive hands, as though unable to understand why they did not move as she wished.

Beatrice stepped closer and spoke quietly. "Stop, Naomi." And Naomi was still, blind face turned toward Beatrice in an attitude of attentive waiting. Totally focused waiting.

"Company, Naomi."

After a few seconds, Naomi made a wordless sound.

Beatrice gestured Alan to her side, gave Naomi one of his hands. It didn't bother me this time when she touched him. I was too interested in what was happening. Naomi examined Alan's hand minutely, then followed the arm up to the shoulder, the neck, the face. Holding his face between her hands, she made a sound. It may have been a word, but I couldn't understand it. All I could think of was the danger of those hands. I thought of my father's hands.

"His name is Alan Chi, Naomi. He's your son." Several seconds passed.

"Son?" she said. This time the word was quite distinct, though her lips had split in many places and had healed badly. "Son?" she repeated anxiously. "Here?"

"He's all right, Naomi. He's come to visit."

"Mother?" he said.

She reexamined his face. He had been three when she started to drift. It didn't seem possible that she could find anything in his face that she would remember. I wondered whether she remembered she had a son.

"Alan?" she said. She found his tears and paused at them. She touched her own face where there should have been an eye, then she reached back toward his eyes. An instant before I would have grabbed her hand. Beatrice did it.

"No!" Beatrice said firmly.

The hand fell limply to Naomi's side. Her face turned toward Beatrice like an antique weather vane swinging around. Beatrice stroked her hair, and Naomi said something I almost understood. Beatrice looked at Alan, who was frowning and wiping away tears.

"Hug your son," Beatrice said softly.

Naomi turned, groping, and Alan seized her in a tight, long hug. Her arms went around him slowly. She spoke words blurred by her ruined mouth but just understandable.

"Parents?" she said. "Did my parents . . . care for you?" Alan looked at her, clearly not understanding.

"She wants to know whether her parents took care of you," I said.

He glanced at me doubtfully, then looked at Beatrice.

"Yes," Beatrice said. "She just wants to know that they cared for you."

"They did," he said. "They kept their promise to you, Mother."

Several seconds passed. Naomi made sounds that even Alan took to be weeping, and he tried to comfort her.

"Who else is here?" she said finally.

This time Alan looked at me. I repeated what she had said.

"Her name is Lynn Mortimer," he said. "I'm . . ." He paused awkwardly. "She and I are going to be married."

After a time, she moved back from him and said my name. My first impulse was to go to her. I wasn't afraid or repelled by her now, but for no reason I could explain, I looked at Beatrice.

"Go," she said. "But you and I will have to talk later."

I went to Naomi, took her hand.

"Bea?" she said.

"I'm Lynn," I said softly.

She drew a quick breath. "No," she said. "No, you're . . ."

"I'm Lynn. Do you want Bea? She's here."

She said nothing. She put her hand to my face, explored it slowly. I let her do it, confident that I could stop her if she turned violent. But first one hand, then both, went over me very gently.

"You'll marry my son?" she said finally.

"Yes."

"Good. You'll keep him safe."

As much as possible, we'll keep each other safe. "Yes," I said.

"Good. No one will close him away from himself. No one will tie him or cage him." Her hand wandered to her own face again, nails biting in slightly.

"No," I said softly, catching the hand. "I want you to be safe, too."

The mouth moved. I think it smiled. "Son?" she said.

He understood her, took her hand.

"Clay," she said. Lynn and Alan in clay. "Bea?"

"Of course," Beatrice said. "Do you have an impression?"

"No!" It was the fastest that Naomi had answered anything. Then, almost childlike, she whispered. "Yes."

Beatrice laughed. "Touch them again if you like, Naomi. They don't mind."

We didn't. Alan closed his eyes, trusting her gentleness in a way I could not. I had no trouble accepting her touch, even so near my eyes, but I did not delude myself about her. Her gentleness could turn in an instant. Naomi's fingers twitched near Alan's eyes, and I spoke up at once, out of fear for him.

"Just touch him, Naomi. Only touch."

She froze, made an interrogative sound.

"She's all right," Alan said.

"I know," I said, not believing it. He would be all right, though, as long as someone watched her very carefully, nipped any dangerous impulses in the bud.

"Son!" she said, happily possessive. When she let him go, she demanded clay, wouldn't touch her old-woman sculpture again. Beatrice got new clay for her, leaving us to soothe her and ease her impatience. Alan began to recognize signs of impending destructive behavior. Twice he caught her hands and said no. She struggled against him until I spoke to her. As Beatrice returned, it happened again, and Beatrice said, "No, Naomi." Obediently Naomi let her hands fall to her sides.

"What is it?" Alan demanded later when we had left Naomi safely, totally focused on her new work—clay sculptures of us. "Does she only listen to women or something?"

Beatrice took us back to the sitting room, sat us both down, but did not sit down herself. She went to a window and stared out. "Naomi only obeys certain women," she said. "And she's sometimes slow to obey. She's worse than most—probably because of the damage she managed to do to herself before I got her." Beatrice faced us, stood biting her lip and frowning. "I haven't had to give this particular speech for a while," she said. "Most DGDs have the sense not to marry each other and produce children. I hope you two aren't planning to have any—in spite of our need." She took a deep breath. "It's a pheromone. A scent. And it's sex-linked. Men who inherit the disease from their fathers have no trace of the scent. They also tend to have an easier time with the disease. But they're useless to us as staff here. Men who inherit from their mothers have as much of the scent as men get. They can be useful here because the DGDs can at least be made to notice them. The same for women who inherit from their mothers but not their fathers. It's only when two irresponsible DGDs get together and produce girl children like me or Lynn that you get someone who can really do some good in a place like this." She looked at me. "We are very rare commodities, you and I. When you finish school you'll have a very well paid job waiting for you."

"Here?" I asked.

"For training, perhaps. Beyond that, I don't know. You'll probably help start a retreat in some other part of the country. Others are badly needed." She smiled humorlessly. "People like us don't get along well together. You must realize that I don't like you any more than you like me."

I swallowed, saw her through a kind of haze for a moment. Hated her mindlessly—just for a moment.

"Sit back," she said. "Relax your body. It helps."

I obeyed, not really wanting to obey her but unable to think of anything else to do. Unable to think at all. "We seem," she said, "to be very territorial. Dilg is a haven for me when I'm the only one of my kind here. When I'm not, it's a prison."

"All it looks like to me is an unbelievable amount of work," Alan said.

She nodded. "Almost too much." She smiled to herself. "I was one of the first double DGDs to be born. When I was old enough to understand, I thought I didn't have much time. First I tried to kill myself. Failing that, I tried to cram all the living I could into the small amount of time I assumed I had. When I got into this project, I worked as hard as I could to get it into shape before I started to drift. By now I wouldn't know what to do with myself if I weren't working."

"Why haven't you . . . drifted?" I asked.

"I don't know. There aren't enough of our kind to know what's normal for us."

"Drifting is normal for every DGD sooner or later."

"Later, then."

"Why hasn't the scent been synthesized?" Alan asked. "Why are there still concentration-camp rest homes and hospital wards?"

"There have been people trying to synthesize it since I proved what I could do with it. No one has succeeded so far. All we've been able to do is keep our eyes open for people like Lynn." She looked at me. "Dilg scholarship, right?"

"Yeah. Offered out of the blue."

"My people do a good job keeping track. You would have been contacted just before you graduated or if you dropped out."

"Is it possible," Alan said, staring at me, "that she's already doing it? Already using the scent to . . . influence people?"

"You?" Beatrice asked.

"All of us. A group of DGDs. We all live together. We're all controlled, of course, but . . ." Beatrice smiled. "It's probably the quietest house full of kids that anyone's ever seen."

I looked at Alan, and he looked away. "I'm not doing anything to them," I said. "I remind them of work they've already promised to do. That's all."

"You put them at ease," Beatrice said. "You're there. You . . . well, you leave your scent around the house. You speak to them individually. Without knowing why, they no doubt find that very comforting. Don't you, Alan?"

"I don't know," he said. "I suppose I must have. From my first visit to the house, I knew I wanted to move in. And when I first saw Lynn, I . . ." He shook his head. "Funny, I thought all that was my idea."

"Will you work with us, Alan?"

"Me? You want Lynn."

"I want you both. You have no idea how many people take one look at one workroom here and turn and run. You may be the kind of young people who ought to eventually take charge of a place like Dilg."

"Whether we want to or not, eh?" he said.

Frightened, I tried to take his hand, but he moved it away. "Alan, this works," I said. "It's only a stopgap, I know. Genetic engineering will probably give us the final answers, but for God's sake, this is something we can do now!"

"It's something *you* can do. Play queen bee in a retreat full of workers. I've never had any ambition to be a drone."

"A physician isn't likely to be a drone." Beatrice said.

"Would you marry one of your patients?" he demanded. "That's what Lynn would be doing if she married me—whether I become a doctor or not."

She looked away from him, stared across the room. "My husband is here," she said softly. "He's been a patient here for almost a decade. What better place for him . . . when his time came?"

"Shit!" Alan muttered. He glanced at me. "Let's get out of here!" He got up and strode across the room to the door, pulled at it, then realized it was locked. He turned to face Beatrice, his body language demanding she let him out. She went to him, took him by the shoulder, and turned him to face the door. "Try it once more," she said quietly. "You can't break it. Try."

Surprisingly, some of the hostility seemed to go out of him. "This is one of those p.v. locks?" he asked.

"Yes."

I set my teeth and looked away. Let her work. She knew how to use this thing she and I both had. And for the moment, she was on my side.

I heard him make some effort with the door. The door didn't even rattle. Beatrice took his hand from it, and with her own hand flat against what appeared to be a large brass knob, she pushed the door open.

"The man who created that lock is nobody in particular," she said. "He doesn't have an unusually high I.Q., didn't even finish college. But sometime in his life he read a science-fiction story in which palm-print locks were a given. He went that story one better by creating one that responded to voice or palm. It took him years, but we were able to give him those years. The people of Dilg are problem solvers, Alan. Think of the problems you could solve!"

He looked as though he were beginning to think, beginning to understand. "I don't see how biological research can be done that way," he said. "Not with everyone acting on his own, not even aware of other researchers and their work."

"It *is* being done," she said, "and not in isolation. Our retreat in Colorado specializes in it and has—just barely—enough trained, controlled DGDs to see that no one really works in isolation. Our patients can still read and write—those who haven't damaged themselves too badly. They can take each other's work into account if reports are made available to them. And they can read material that comes in from the outside. They're working, Alan. The disease hasn't stopped them, *won't* stop them." He stared at her, seemed to be caught by her intensity—or her scent. He spoke as though his words were a strain, as though they hurt his throat. "I won't be a puppet. I won't be controlled . . . by a goddamn smell!"

"Alan—"

"I won't be what my mother is. I'd rather be dead!"

"There's no reason for you to become what your mother is."

He drew back in obvious disbelief.

"Your mother is brain damaged—thanks to the three months she spent in that custodial-care toilet. She had no speech at all when I met her. She's improved more than you can imagine. None of that has to happen to you. Work with us, and we'll see that none of it happens to you."

He hesitated, seemed less sure of himself. Even that much flexibility in him was surprising. "I'll be under your control or Lynn's," he said.

She shook her head. "Not even your mother is under my control. She's aware of me. She's able to take direction from me. She trusts me the way any blind person would trust her guide."

"There's more to it than that."

"Not here. Not at any of our retreats."

"I don't believe you."

"Then you don't understand how much individuality our people retain. They know they need help, but they have minds of their own. If you want to see the abuse of power you're worried about, go to a DGD ward."

"You're better than that, I admit. Hell is probably better than that. But . . ."

"But you don't trust us."

He shrugged.

"You do, you know." She smiled. "You don't want to, but you do. That's what worries you, and it leaves you with work to do. Look into what I've said. See for yourself. We offer DGDs a chance to live and do whatever they decide is important to them. What do you have, what can you realistically hope for that's better than that?"

Silence. "I don't know what to think," he said finally.

"Go home," she said. "Decide what to think. It's the most important decision you'll ever make."

He looked at me. I went to him, not sure how he'd react, not sure he'd want me no matter what he decided.

"What are you going to do?" he asked.

The question startled me. "You have a choice," I said. "I don't. If she's right . . . how could I not wind up running a retreat?"

"Do you want to?"

I swallowed. I hadn't really faced that question yet. Did I want to spend my life in something that was basically a refined DGD ward? "No!"

"But you will."

". . . Yes." I thought for a moment, hunted for the right words. "You'd do it."

"What?"

"If the pheromone were something only men had, you would do it."

That silence again. After a time he took my hand, and we followed Beatrice out to the car. Before I could get in with him and our guard-escort, she caught my arm. I jerked away reflexively. By the time I caught myself, I had swung around as though I meant to hit her. Hell, I did mean to hit her, but I stopped myself in time. "Sorry," I said with no attempt at sincerity.

She held out a card until I took it. "My private number," she said. "Before seven or after nine, usually. You and I will communicate best by phone."

I resisted the impulse to throw the card away. God, she brought out the child in me.

Inside the car, Alan said something to the guard. I couldn't hear what it was, but the sound of his voice reminded me of him arguing with her—her logic and her scent. She had all but won him for me, and I couldn't manage even token gratitude. I spoke to her, low-voiced.

"He never really had a chance, did he?"

She looked surprised. "That's up to you. You can keep him or drive him away. I assure you, you *can* drive him away."

"How?"

"By imagining that he doesn't have a chance." She smiled faintly. "Phone me from your territory. We have a great deal to say to each other, and I'd rather we didn't say it as enemies."

She had lived with meeting people like me for decades. She had good control. I, on the other hand, was at the end of my control. All I could do was scramble into the car and floor my own phantom accelerator as the guard drove us to the gate. I couldn't look back at her. Until we were well away from the house, until we'd left the guard at the gate and gone off the property, I couldn't make myself look back. For long, irrational minutes, I was convinced that somehow if I turned, I would see myself standing there, gray and old, growing small in the distance, vanishing.

# HOWARD WALDROP

## Night of the Cooters

One of the best short-story writers in the business, Howard Waldrop also has perhaps the wildest and most fertile imagination of any SF writer since R. A. Lafferty. And, like Lafferty, he is known for his strong, shaggy humor, offbeat erudition, and bizarre fictional juxtapositions. These qualities are strongly evident in the wild and wooly tale that follows; it examines some of the events that might have occurred on the periphery of and simultaneously with the central action of H. G. Wells's *War of the Worlds,* but from a perspective very different from any Wells would ever have come up with. . . .

Born in Huston, Mississippi, Waldrop now lives in Austin, Texas. He has sold short fiction to markets as diverse as *Omni, Analog, Playboy, Universe, Crawdaddy, New Dimensions, Shayol*, and *Zoo World.* His story "The Ugly Chickens" won both the Nebula and World Fantasy Award in 1981. His first novel, written in collaboration with fellow Texan Jake Saunders, was *The Texas-Israeli War: 1999.* His first solo novel, *Them Bones*, appeared in 1984. His first collection, *Howard Who?*, appeared in 1986 and was quickly recognized as one of the most important collections of the decade. It was followed in 1987 by another important collection, *All about Strange Monsters of the Recent Past: Neat Stories by Howard Waldrop.* His story "Man-Mountain Gentian" was in our First Annual Collection; his "Flying Saucer Rock and Roll" was in our Third Annual Collection; and his "Fair Game" was in our Fourth Annual Collection.

# NIGHT OF THE COOTERS

## Howard Waldrop

*This story is in memory of Slim Pickens (1919–1983)*

Sheriff Lindley was asleep on the toilet in the Pachuco County courthouse when someone started pounding on the door. "Bert!" the voice yelled as the sheriff jerked awake.

"Goldang!" said the lawman. The Waco newspaper slid off his lap onto the floor.

He pulled his pants up with one hand and the toilet chain on the water box overhead with the other. He opened the door. Chief Deputy Sweets stood before him, a complaint slip in his hand.

"Dang it, Sweets!" said the sheriff. "I told you never to bother me in there. It's the hottest Thursday in the history of Texas! You woke me up out of a hell of a dream!"

The deputy waited, wiping sweat from his forehead. There were two big circles, like half-moons, under the arms of his blue chambray shirt.

"I was fourteen, maybe fifteen years old, and I was a Aztec or a Mixtec or somethin'," said the sheriff. "Anyways, I was buck naked, and I was standin' on one of them ball courts with the little bitty stone rings twenty foot up one wall, and they was presentin' me to Moctezuma. I was real proud, and the sun was shinin', but it was real still and cool down there in the Valley of the Mexico. I look up at the grandstand, and there's Moctezuma and all his high mucketymucks with feathers and stuff hangin' off 'em, and more gold than a circus wagon. And there was these other guys, conquistadors and stuff, with beards and rusty helmets, and I-talian priests with crosses you coulda barred a livery-stable door with. One of Moctezuma's men was explainin' how we was fixin' to play ball for the gods and things. I knew in my dream I was captain of my team. I had a name that sounded like a bird fart in Aztec talk, and they mentioned it and the name of the captain of the other team, too. Well, everything was goin' all right, and I was prouder and prouder, until the guy doing the talkin' let slip that whichever team won was gonna be paraded around Tenochtitlán and given women and food and stuff like that; and then tomorrow A.M. they was gonna be cut up and simmered real slow and served up with chilis and onions and tomatoes.

"Well, you never seed such a fight as broke out then! They was a-yellin', and a priest was swingin' a cross, and spears and axes were flyin' around like it was an Irish funeral. Next thing I know, you're a-bangin' on the door and wakin' me up and bringin' me back to Pachuco County! What the hell do you want?"

"Mr. De Spain wants you to come over to his place right away."

"He does, huh?"

"That's right. Sheriff. He says he's got some miscreants he wants you to arrest."

"Everybody else around here has desperadoes. De Spain has miscreants. I'll be so danged glad when the town council gets around to movin' the city limits fifty foot the other side of his place, I won't know what to do! Every time anybody farts too loud, he calls me."

Lindley and Sweets walked back to the office at the other end of the courthouse. Four deputies sat around with their feet propped up on desks. They rocked forward respectfully and watched as the sheriff went to the hat pegs. On one of the dowels was a sweat-stained hat with turned-down points at front and back. The side brims were twisted in curves. The hat angled up to end in a crown that looked like the business end of a Phillips screwdriver. Under the hat was a holster with a Navy Colt .41 that looked like someone had used it to drive railroad spikes all the way to the Continental Divide. Leaning under them was a ten-gauge pump shotgun with the barrel sawed off just in front of the foregrip. On the other peg was an immaculate new round-top Stetson of brown felt with a snakeskin band half as wide as a fingernail running around it.

The deputies stared.

Lindley picked up the Stetson.

The deputies rocked back in their chairs and resumed yakking.

"Hey, Sweets!" said the sheriff at the door. "Change that damn calendar on your desk. It ain't Wednesday, August seventeenth; it's Thursday, August eighteenth."

"Sure thing, Sheriff."

"And you boys try not to play checkers so loud you wake the judge up, okay?"

"Sure thing, Sheriff."

Lindley went down the courthouse steps onto the rock walk. He passed the two courthouse cannons he and the deputies fired off three times a year—March second, July fourth, and Robert E. Lee's birthday. Each cannon had a pyramid of ornamental cannonballs in front of it.

Waves of heat came off the cannons, the ammunition, the telegraph wires overhead, and, in the distance, the rails of the twice-a-day spur line from Waxahachie.

The town was still as a rusty shovel. The forty-five-star United States flag hung like an old, dried dishrag from its stanchion. From looking at the town you couldn't tell the nation was about to go to war with Spain over Cuba, that China was full of unrest, and that five thousand miles away a crazy German count was making airships.

Lindley had seen enough changes in his sixty-eight years. He had been born in the bottom of an Ohio keelboat in 1830; was in Bloody Kansas when John Brown came through; fought for the Confederacy, first as a corporal, then a sergeant major, from Chickamauga to the Wilderness; and had seen more skirmishes with hostile tribes than most people would ever read about in a dozen Wide-Awake Library novels.

It was as hot as under an upside-down washpot on a tin shed roof. The sheriff's wagon horse seemed asleep as it trotted, head down, puffs hanging in the still air like brown shrubs made of dust around its hooves. There were ten, maybe a dozen people in sight in the whole town. Those few on the street moved like molasses, only as far as they had to, from shade to shade. Anybody with sense was asleep at home with wet towels hung over the windows, or sitting as still as possible with a funeral-parlor fan in their hands.

The sheriff licked his big droopy mustache and hoped nobody nodded to him. He was already too hot and tired to tip his hat. He leaned back in the wagon seat and straightened his bad leg (a Yankee souvenir) against the boot board. His gray suit was like a boiling shroud. He was too hot to reach up and flick the dust off his new hat. He had become sheriff in the special election three years ago to fill out Sanderson's term when the governor had appointed the former sheriff attorney general. Nothing much had happened in the county since then.

"Gee-hup," he said.

The horse trotted three steps before going back into its walking trance.

Sheriff Lindley didn't bother her again until he pulled up at De Spain's big place and said, "Whoa, there."

The black man who did everything for De Spain opened the gate. "Sheriff," he said.

"Luther," said Lindley, nodding his head.

"Around back, Mr. Lindley."

There were two boys—raggedy town kids, the Strother boy and one of the poor Chisums—sitting on the edge of the well. The Chisum kid had been crying.

De Spain was hot and bothered. He was only half dressed, with suit pants, white shirt, vest, and stockings on but no shoes or coat. He hadn't macassared his hair yet. He was pointing a rifle with a barrel big as a drainpipe at the two boys.

"Here they are, Sheriff. Luther saw them down in the orchard. I'm sure he saw them stealing my peaches, but he wouldn't tell me. I knew something was up when he didn't put my clothes in the usual place next to the window where I like to dress. So I looked out and saw them. They had half a potato sack full by the time I crept around the house and caught them. I want to charge them with trespass and thievery."

"Well, well," said the sheriff, looking down at the sackful of evidence. He turned and pointed toward the black man. "You want me to charge Luther here with collusion and abetting a crime?" Neither Lindley's nor Luther's face betrayed any emotion.

"Of course not," said De Spain. "I've told him time and time again he's too soft on filchers. If this keeps happening, I'll hire another boy who'll enforce my orchard with buckshot, if need be."

De Spain was a young man with eyes like a weimaraner's. As Deputy Sweets said, he had the kind of face you couldn't hit just once. He owned half the town of Pachuco City. The other half paid him rent.

"Get in the wagon, boys," said Lindley.

"Aren't you going to cover them with your weapon?" asked De Spain.

"You should know by now, Mr. De Spain, that when I wear this suit I ain't got nothin' but a three-shot pocket pistol on me. Besides"—he looked at the two boys in the wagon bed—"they know if they give me any guff, I'll jerk a bowknot in one of 'em and bite the other'n's ass off."

"I don't think there's a need for profanity," said De Spain.

"It's too damn hot for anything else," said Lindley. "I'll clamp 'em in the *juzgado* and have Sweets run the papers over to your office tomorrow mornin'."

"I wish you'd take them out one of the rural roads somewhere and flail the tar out of them to teach them about property rights," said De Spain.

The sheriff tipped his hat back and looked up at De Spain's three-story house with the parlor so big you could hold a rodeo in it. Then he looked back at the businessman, who'd finally lowered the rifle.

"Well, I know you'd like that," said Lindley. "I seem to remember that most of the fellers who wrote the Constitution were pretty well off, but some of the other rich people thought they had funny ideas. But they were really pretty smart. One of the things they were smart about was the Bill of Rights. You know, Mr. De Spain, the reason they put in the Bill of Rights wasn't to give all the little people without jobs or money a lot of breaks with the law. Why they put that in there was for if the people without jobs or money ever got upset and turned on *them*, they could ask for the same justice everybody else got."

De Spain looked at him with disgust. "I've never liked your homespun parables, and I don't like the way you sheriff this county."

"I don't doubt that," said Lindley. "You've got sixteen months, three weeks, and two days to find somebody to run against me. Good evening, Mr. De Spain."

He climbed onto the wagon seat.

"Luther."

"Sheriff."

He turned the horse around as De Spain and the black man took the sack of peaches through the kitchen door into the house.

The sheriff stopped the wagon near the railroad tracks where the houses began to deviate from the vertical.

"Jody. Billy Roy." He looked at them with eyes like chips of flint. "You're the dumbest pair of squirts that *ever* lived in Pachuco City! First off, half those peaches were still green. You'd have got bellyaches, and your mothers would have beaten you within an inch of your lives and given you so many doses of Black Draught you'd shit over ten-rail fences all week. Now listen to what I'm sayin', 'cause I'm only gonna say it once. If I ever hear of *either* of you stealing anything, anywhere in this county, I'm going to put you *both* in school."

"No, Sheriff, please, no!"

"I'll put you in there every morning and come and get you out seven long hours later, and I'll have the judge issue a writ keeping you there till you're *twelve years old.* And if you try to run away, I'll follow you to the ends of the earth with Joe Sweeper's bloodhounds, and I'll bring you back."

They were crying now.

"You git home." They were running before they left the wagon.

Somewhere between the second piece of corn bread and the third helping of snap beans, a loud rumble shook the ground.

"Goodness' sakes!" said Elsie, his wife of twenty-three years. "What can that be?"

"I expect that's Elmer, out by the creek. He came in last week and asked if he could blast on the place. I told him it didn't matter to me as long as he did it between sunup and sundown and didn't blow his whole family of rug rats and yard apes up.

"Jake, down at the mercantile, said Elmer bought enough dynamite to blow up Fort Worth if he'd a mind to—all but the last three sticks in the store. Jake had to reorder for stump-blowin' time."

"Whatever could he want with all that much?"

"Oh, that damn fool has the idea the vein in that old mine that played out in '83 might start up again on his property. He got to talking with the Smith boy, oh, hell, what's his name—?"

"Leo?"

"Yeah, Leo, the one that studies down in Austin, learns about stars and rocks and all that shit. . . ."

"Watch your language, Bertram!"

"Oh, hell, anyway, that boy must have put a bug up Elmer's butt about that—"

"Bertram!" said Elsie, putting down her knife and fork.

"Oh, hell, anyway. I guess Elmer'll blow the side off his hill and bury his house before he's through."

The sheriff was reading a week-old copy of the *Waco Herald* while Elsie washed up the dishes. He sure missed *Brann's Iconoclast*, the paper he used to read, which had ceased publication when the editor was gunned down on a Waco street by an irate Baptist four months before. The Waco paper had a little squib from London, England, about there having been explosions on Mars ten nights in a row last month, and whether it was a sign of life on that planet or some unusual volcanic activity.

Sheriff Lindley had never given volcanoes (except those in the Valley of the Mexico) or the planet Mars much thought.

Hooves came pounding down the road. He put down his paper. "*Sheriff, sheriff!*" he said in a high, mocking voice.

"What?" asked Elsie. Then she heard the hooves and began to dry her hands on the towel on the nail above the sink.

The horse stopped out front; bare feet slapped up to the porch; small fists pounded on the door.

"Sheriff! Sheriff!" yelled a voice Lindley recognized as belonging to either Tommy or Jimmy Atkinson.

He strode to the door and opened it.

"Tommy, what's all the hooraw?"

"Jimmy. Sheriff, something fell on our pasture, tore it all to hell, knocked down *the tree*, killed some of our cattle, Tommy can't find his dog, Mother sent—"

"Hold on! Something fell on your place? Like what?"

"I don't know! Like a big rock, only sparks was flyin' off it, and it roared and blew up! It's at the north end of the place, and—"

"Elsie, run over and get Sweets and the boys. Have them go get Leo Smith if he ain't gone back to college yet. Sounds to me like Pachuco County's got its first shootin' star. Hold on, Jimmy, I'm comin' right along. We'll take my wagon; you can leave your pony here."

"Oh, hurry, Sheriff! It's big! It killed our cattle and tore up the fences—"

"Well, I can't arrest it for *that*," said Lindley. He put on his Stetson. "And I thought Elmer'd blowed hisself up. My, my, ain't never seen a shooting star before. . . ."

"Damn if it don't look like somebody threw a locomotive through here," said the sheriff. The Atkinson place used to have a sizable hill and the tallest tree in the county on it. Now it had half a hill and a big stump and beyond, a huge crater. Dirt had been thrown up in a ten-foot-high pile around it. There was a large, rounded, gray object buried in the dirt and torn caliche at the bottom. Waves of heat rose from it, and gray ash, like old charcoal, fell off it into the shimmering pit.

Half the town was riding out in wagons and on horseback as the news spread. The closest neighbors were walking over in the twilight, wearing their go-visiting clothes.

"Well, well," said the sheriff, looking down. "So that's what a meteor looks like."

Leo Smith was in the pit, walking around.

"I figured you'd be here sooner or later," said Lindley.

"Hello, Sheriff," said Leo. "It's still too hot to touch. Part of a cow's buried under the back end."

The sheriff looked over at the Atkinson family. "You folks is danged lucky. That thing coulda come down smack on your house or, worse, your barn. What time did it fall?"

"Straight up and down six o'clock," said Mrs. Atkinson. "We was settin' down to supper. I saw it out of the corner of my eye; then all tarnation came down. Rocks must have been falling for ten minutes!"

"It's pretty spectacular, Sheriff," said Leo. "I'm going into town to telegraph off to the professors at the university. They'll sure want to look at this."

"Any reason other than general curiosity?" asked Lindley.

"I've only seen pictures and handled little bitty parts of one," said Leo, "but it doesn't look usual. They're generally like big rocks, all stone or iron. The outside of this one's soft and crumbly. Ashy, too."

There was a slight pop and a stove-cooling noise from the thing.

"Well, you can come back into town with me if you want to. Hey, Sweets!"

The chief deputy came over.

"A couple of you boys better stay here tonight, keep people from falling in the hole. I guess if Leo's gonna wire the university, you better keep anybody from knockin' chunks off it. It'll probably get pretty crowded. If I was the Atkinsons, I'd start chargin' a nickel a look."

"Sure thing, Sheriff."

"I'll be out here tomorrow mornin' to take another gander. I gotta serve a process paper on old Theobald before he lights out for his chores. If I sent one 'a' you boys, he'd as soon shoot you as say howdy."

"Sure thing, Sheriff."

He and Leo and Jimmy Atkinson got in the wagon and rode off toward the quiet lights of town far away.

There was a new smell in the air.

The sheriff noticed it as he rode toward the Atkinson ranch by the south road early the next morning. There was an odor like when something goes wrong at the telegraph office. Smoke was curling up from the pasture. Maybe there was a scrub fire started from the heat of the falling star.

He topped the last rise. Before him lay devastation the likes of which he hadn't seen since the retreat from Atlanta.

"Great gawd ahmighty!" he said.

There were dead horses and charred wagons all around. The ranch house was untouched, but the barn was burned to the ground. There were crisscrossed lines of burnt grass that looked like they'd been painted with a tarbrush.

He saw no bodies anywhere. Where was Sweets? Where was Luke, the other deputy? Where had the people from the wagons gone? What had happened?

Lindley looked at the crater. There was a shiny rod sticking out of it, with something round on the end. From here it looked like one of those carnival acts where a guy spins a plate on the end of a dowel rod, only this glinted like metal in the early sun. As he watched, a small cloud of green steam rose above it from the pit.

He saw a motion behind an old tree uprooted by a storm twelve years ago. It was Sweets. He was yelling and waving the sheriff back. Lindley rode his horse into a small draw, then came up into the open.

There was movement over at the crater. He thought he saw something. Reflected sunlight flashed by his eyes, and he thought he saw a rounded silhouette. He heard a noise like sometimes gets in bob wire on a windy day. He heard a humming sound then, smelled the electric smell real strong. Fire started a few feet from him, out of nowhere, and moved toward him.

Then his horse exploded. The air was an inferno, he was thrown spinning—

He must have blacked out. He had no memory of what went next. When he came to, he was running as fast as he ever had toward the uprooted tree.

Fire jumped all around. Luke was shooting over the tree roots with his pistol. He ducked. A long section of the trunk was washed with flames and sparks.

Lindley dove behind the root tangle.

"What the dingdong is goin' on?" he asked as he tried to catch his breath. He still had his new hat on, but his britches and coat were singed and smoking.

"God damn, Bert! I don't know," said Sweets, leaning around Luke. "We was out here all night; it was a regular party; most of the time we was up on the lip up there. Maybe thirty or forty people comin' and goin' all the time. We was all talking and hoorawing, and then we heard something about an hour ago. We looked down, and I'll be damned if the whole top of that thing didn't come off like a mason jar!

"We was watching, and these damn things started coming out—they looked like big old leather balls, big as horses, with snakes all out the front—"

"What?"

"Snakes. Yeah, tentacles Leo called them, like an octy-puss. Leo'd come back from town and was here when them boogers came out. Martians he said they was, things from Mars. They had big old eyes, big as your head! Everybody was pushing and shoving; then one of them pulled out one of them gun things, real slow like, and just started burning up everything in sight.

"We all ran back for whatever cover we could find—it took 'em a while to get up the dirt pile. They killed horses, dogs, anything they could see. Fire was everywhere. They use that thing just like the volunteer firemen use them water hoses in Waco!"

"Where's Leo?"

Sweets pointed to the draw that ran diagonally to the west. "We watched awhile, finally figured they couldn't line up on the ditch all the way to the rise. Leo and the others got away up the draw—he was gonna telegraph the university about it. The bunch that got away was supposed to send people out to the town road to warn people. You probably would have run into them if you hadn't been coming from Theobald's place. Anyway, soon as them things saw people were gettin' away, they got mad as hornets. That's when they lit up the Atkinsons' barn."

A flash of fire leapt in the roots of the tree, jumped back thirty feet into the burnt grass behind them, then moved back and forth in a curtain of sparks.

"Man, that's what I call a real smoke pole," said Luke.

"Well," Lindley said. "This won't do. These things done attacked citizens in my jurisdiction, and they killed my horse."

He turned to Luke.

"Be real careful, and get back to town, and get the posse up. Telegraph the Rangers and tell 'em to burn leather gettin' here. Then get aholt of Skip Whitworth and have him bring out The Gun."

Skip Whitworth sat behind the tree trunk and pulled the cover from the six-foot rifle at his side. Skip was in his late fifties. He had been a sniper in the War for Southern Independence when he had been in his twenties. He had once shot at a Yankee general just as the officer was bringing a forkful of beans up to his mouth. When the fork got there, there were only some shoulders and a gullet for the beans to drop into.

That had been from a mile and a half away, from sixty feet up a pine tree.

The rifle was an .80-caliber octagonal-barrel breechloader that used two and a half ounces of powder and a percussion cap the size of a jawbreaker for each shot. It had a telescopic sight running the entire length of the barrel.

"They're using that thing on the end of that stick to watch us," said Lindley. "I had Sweets jump around, and every time he did, one of those cooters would come up with that fire gun and give us what-for."

Skip said nothing. He loaded his rifle, which had a breechblock lever the size of a crowbar on it, then placed another round—cap, paper cartridge, ball—next to him. He drew a bead and pulled the trigger. It sounded like dynamite had gone off in their ears. The wobbling pole snapped in two halfway up. The top end flopped around back into the pit.

There was a scrabbling noise above the whirring from the earthen lip. Something round came up.

Skip had smoothly opened the breech, put in the ball, torn the cartridge with his teeth, put in the cap, closed the action, pulled back the hammer, and sighted before the shape reached the top of the dirt.

Metal glinted in the middle of the dark thing. Skip fired. There was a *squeech*; the whole top of the round thing opened up; it spun around and backward, things in its front working like a daddy longlegs thrown on a roaring stove.

Skip loaded again. There were flashes of light from the crater. Something came up shooting, fire leaping like hot sparks from a blacksmith's anvil, the air full of flames and smoke. Skip fired again.

The fire gun flew up in the air. Snakes twisted, writhed, disappeared.

It was very quiet for a few seconds.

Then there was the renewed whining of machinery and noises like a pile driver, the sounds of filing and banging. Steam came up over the crater lip.

"Sounds like a steel foundry in there," said Sweets.

"I don't like it one bit," said Lindley. "Be danged if I'm gonna let 'em get the drop on us. Can you keep them down?"

"How many are there?" asked Skip.

"Luke and Sweets saw four or five before all hell broke loose this morning. Probably more of 'em than that was inside."

"I've got three more shots. If they poke up, I'll get 'em."

"I'm goin' to town, then out to Elmer's. Sweets'll stay with you awhile. If you run outta bullets, light up out the draw. I don't want nobody killed. Sweets, keep an eye out for the posse. I'm telegraphing the Rangers again, then goin' to get Elmer and his dynamite. We're gonna fix their little red wagon for certain."

"Sure thing, Sheriff."

The sun had just passed noon.

Leo looked haggard. He had been up all night, then at the telegraph office sending off messages to the university. Inquiries had begun to come in from as far east as Baton Rouge. Leo had another, from Percival Lowell out in Flagstaff, Arizona Territory. "Everybody at the university thinks it's wonderful," said Leo.

"People in Austin would," said Lindley.

"They're sure these things are connected with Mars and those bright flashes of gas last month. Seems something's happened in England, starting about a week ago. No one's been able to get through to London for two or three days."

"You telling me Mars is attacking London, England, and Pachuco City, Texas?" asked the sheriff.

"It seems so," said Leo. He took off his glasses and rubbed his eyes.

"'Scuse me, Leo," said Lindley. "I got to get another telegram off to the Texas Rangers."

"That's funny," said Argyle, the telegraph operator. "The line was working just a second ago." He began tapping his key and fiddling with his coil box.

Leo peered out the window. "Hey!" he said. "Where's the 3:14?" He looked at the railroad clock. It was 3:25. In sixteen years of rail service, the train had been four minutes late, and that was after a mud slide in the storm twelve years ago.

"Uh-oh," said the sheriff.

They were turning out of Elmer's yard with a wagonload of dynamite. The wife and eleven of the kids were watching.

"Easy, Sheriff," said Elmer, who, with two of his boys and most of their guns, was riding in back with the explosives. "Jake sold me everything he had. I just didn't notice till we got back here with that stuff that some of it was already sweating."

"Holy shit!" said Lindley. "You mean we gotta go a mile an hour out there? Let's get out and throw the bad stuff off."

"Well, it's all mixed in," said Elmer. "I was sorta gonna set it all up on the hill and put one blasting cap in the whole load."

"Jesus. You woulda blowed up your house and Pachuco City too."

"I was in a hurry," said Elmer, hanging his head.

"Well, can't be helped. We'll take it slow."

Lindley looked at his watch. It was six o'clock. He heard a high-up, fluttering sound. They looked at the sky. Coming down was a large, round, glowing object throwing off sparks in all directions. It was curved with points, like the thing in the crater at the Atkinson place. A long, thin trail of smoke from the back end hung in the air behind it. They watched in awe as it sailed down. It went into the horizon to the north of Pachuco City.

"One," said one of the kids in the wagon, "two, three—"

Silently they took up the count. At twenty-seven there was a roaring boom, just like the night before.

"Five and a half miles," said the sheriff. "That puts it eight miles from the other one. Leo said the ones in London came down twenty-four hours apart, regular as clockwork." They started off as fast as they could under the circumstances.

There were flashes of light beyond the Atkinson place in the near dusk. The lights moved off toward the north where the other thing had plowed in.

It was the time of evening when your eyes can fool you. Sheriff Lindley thought he saw something that shouldn't have been there sticking above the horizon. It glinted like metal in the dim light.

He thought it moved, but it might have been the motion of the wagon as they lurched down a gulley. When they came up, it was gone.

Skip was gone. His rifle was still there. It wasn't melted but had been crushed, as had the three-foot-thick tree trunk in front of it. All the caps and cartridges were gone.

There was a monstrous series of footprints leading from the crater down to the tree, then off into the distance to the north where Lindley thought he had seen something. There were three footprints in each series. Sweets' hat had been mashed along with Skip's gun. Clanging and banging still came from the crater.

The four of them made their plans. Lindley had his shotgun and pistol, which Luke had brought out with him that morning, though he was still wearing his burned suit and his untouched Stetson.

He tied together the fifteen sweatiest sticks of dynamite he could find.

They crept up, then rushed the crater.

"Hurry up!" yelled the sheriff to the men at the courthouse. "Get that cannon up those stairs!"

"He's still coming this way!" yelled Luke from up above.

They had been watching the giant machine from the courthouse since it had come up out of the Atkinson place, before the sheriff and Elmer and his boys made it into town after their sortie.

It had come across to the north, gone to the site of the second crash, and stood motionless there for quite a while. When it got dark, the deputies brought out the night binoculars. Everybody in town saw the flash of dynamite from the Atkinson place.

A few moments after that, the machine had moved back toward there. It looked like a giant water tower with three legs. It had a thing like a teacher's desk bell on top of it, and something that looked like a Kodak roll-film camera in front of that. As the moon rose, they saw the thing had tentacles like thick wires hanging from between the three giant legs.

The sheriff, Elmer, and his boys made it to town just as the machine found the destruction they had caused at the first landing site. It had turned toward town and was coming at a pace of twenty miles an hour.

"Hurry the hell up!" yelled Luke. "Oh, shit—!" He ducked. There was a flash of light overhead. The building shook. "That heat gun comes out of the box on the front!" he said. "Look out!" The building glared and shook again. Something down the street caught fire.

"Load that son of a bitch," said Lindley. "Bob! Some of you men make sure everybody's in the cyclone cellars or where they won't burn. Cut out all the damn lights!"

"Hell, Sheriff. They know we're here!" yelled a deputy. Lindley hit him with his hat, then followed the cannon up to the top of the clock-tower steps.

Luke was cramming powder into the cannon muzzle. Sweets ran back down the stairs. Other people carried cannonballs up the steps to the tower one at a time.

Leo came up. "What did you find, Sheriff, when you went back?"

There was a cool breeze for a few seconds in the courthouse tower. Lindley breathed a few deep breaths, remembering. "Pretty rough. There was some of them still working after that thing had gone. They were building another one just like it." He pointed toward the machine, which was firing up houses to the northeast side of town, swinging the ray back and forth. They could hear its hum. Homes and chicken coops burst into flames. A mooing cow was stilled.

"We threw in the dynamite and blew most of them up. One was in a machine like a steam tractor. We shot up what was left while they was hootin' and a-hollerin'. There was some other things in there, live things maybe, but they was too blowed up to put back together to be sure what they was, all bleached out and pale. We fed everything there a diet of buckshot till there wasn't nothin' left. Then we hightailed it back here on horses, left the wagon sitting."

The machine came on toward the main street of town. Luke finished with the powder. There were so many men with guns on the building across the street it looked like a brick porcupine. It must have looked this way for the James gang when they were shot up in Northfield, Minnesota.

The courthouse was made of stone. Most of the wooden buildings in town were scorched or already afire. When the heat gun came this way, it blew bricks to dust, played flame over everything. The air above the whole town heated up.

They had put out the lamps behind the clockfaces. There was nothing but moonlight glinting off the three-legged machine, flames of burning buildings, the faraway glows of prairie fires. It looked like Pachuco City was on the outskirts of hell.

"Get ready, Luke," said the sheriff. The machine stepped between two burning stores, its tentacles pulling out smoldering horse tack, chains, kegs of nails, then heaving them this way and that. Someone at the end of the street fired off a round. There was a high, thin ricochet off the machine. Sweets ran upstairs, something in his arms. It was a curtain from one of the judge's windows. He'd ripped it down and tied it to the end of one of the janitor's long window brushes.

On it he had lettered in tempera paint COME AND TAKE IT. There was a ragged, nervous cheer from the men on the building as they read it by the light of the flames.

"Cute, Sweets," said Lindley, "too cute."

The machine turned down Main Street. A line of fire sprang up at the back side of town from the empty corrals.

"Oh, shit!" said Luke. "I forgot the wadding!" Lindley took off his hat to hit him with. He looked at its beautiful felt in the mixed moonlight and firelight.

The thing turned toward them. The sheriff thought he saw eyes way up in the bellthing atop the machine, eyes like a big cat's eyes seen through a dirty windowpane on a dark night.

"Goldang, Luke, it's my best hat, but I'll be damned if I let them cooters burn down my town!"

He stuffed the Stetson, crown first, into the cannon barrel. Luke shoved it in with the ramrod, threw in two 35-pound cannonballs behind it, pushed them home, and swung the barrel out over Main Street.

The machine bent to tear up something.

"Okay, boys," yelled Lindley. "Attract its attention." Rifle and shotgun fire winked on the rooftop. It glowed like a hot coal from the muzzle flashes. A great slather of ricochets flew off the giant machine.

It turned, pointing its heat gun at the building. It was fifty feet from the courthouse steps.

"Now," said the sheriff.

Luke touched off the powder with his cigarillo. The whole north side of the courthouse bell tower flew off, and the roof collapsed. Two holes you could see the moon through appeared in the machine: one in the middle, one smashing through the dome atop it. Sheriff Lindley saw the lower cannonball come out and drop lazily toward the end of burning Main Street.

All six of the tentacles of the machine shot straight up into the air, and it took off like a man running with his arms above his head. It staggered, as fast as a freight train could go, through one side of a house and out the other, and ran partway up Park Street. One of its three legs went higher than its top. It hopped around like a crazy man on crutches before its feet got tangled in a horse-pasture fence, and it went over backward with a shudder. A great cloud of steam came out of it and hung in the air. No one in the courthouse tower heard the sound of the steam. They were all deaf as posts from the explosion. The barrel of the cannon was burst all along the end. The men on the other roof were jumping up and down and clapping each other on the back. The COME AND TAKE IT sign on the courthouse had two holes in it, neater than you could have made with a biscuit cutter. First a high whine, then a dull roar, then something like normal hearing came back to the sheriff's left ear. The right one still felt like a kid had his fist in there.

"Dang it, Sweets!" he yelled. "How much powder did Luke use?"

"Huh?" Luke was banging on his head with both his hands.

"How much powder did he use?"

"Two, two and a half cans," said Sweets.

"It only takes half a can a ball!" yelled the sheriff. He reached for his hat to hit Luke with, touched his bare head. "I feel naked. Come on, we're not through yet. We got fires to put out and some hash to settle."

Luke was still standing, shaking his head. The whole town was cheering.

It looked like a pot lid slowly boiling open, moving just a little. Every time the end unscrewed a little more, ashes and cinders fell off into the second pit. There was a piled ridge of them. The back turned again, moved a few inches, quit. Then it wobbled, there was a sound like a stove being jerked up a chimney, and the whole back end rolled open like a mad bank vault and fell off. There were one hundred eighty-four men and eleven women all standing behind the open end of the thing, their guns pointing toward the interior. At the exact center were Sweets and Luke with the other courthouse cannon. This time there was one can of powder, but the barrel was filled to the end with everything from the blacksmith-shop floor—busted window glass, nails, horseshoes, bolts, stirrup buckles, and broken files and saws.

Eyes appeared in the dark interior.

"Remember the Alamo," said the sheriff.

Everybody, and the cannon, fired.

When the third meteor came in that evening, south of town at thirteen minutes past six, they knew something was wrong. It wobbled in flight, lost speed, and dropped like a long, heavy leaf.

They didn't have to wait for this one to cool and open. When the posse arrived, the thing was split in two and torn. Heat and steam came up from the inside.

One of the pale things was creeping forlornly across the ground with great difficulty. It looked like a thin gingerbread man made of glass with only a knob for a head.

"It's probably hurting from the gravity," said Leo.

"Fix it, Sweets," said Lindley.

"Sure thing, Sheriff."

There was a gunshot.

* * *

No fourth meteor fell, though they had scouts out for twenty miles in all directions, and the railroad tracks and telegraph wires were fixed again.

"I been doing some figuring," said Leo. "If there were ten explosions on Mars last month, and these things started landing in England last Thursday week, then we should have got the last three. There won't be any more."

"You been figurin', huh?"

"Sure have."

"Well, we'll see."

Sheriff Lindley stood on his porch. It was sundown on Sunday, three hours after another meteor should have fallen, had there been one.

Leo rode up. "I saw Sweets and Luke heading toward the Atkinson place with more dynamite. What are they doing?"

"They're blowing up every last remnant of them things—lock, stock, and ass hole."

"But," said Leo, "the professors from the university will be here tomorrow, to look at their ships and machines! You can't destroy them!"

"Shit on the University of Texas and the horse it rode in on," said Lindley. "My jurisdiction runs from Deer Piss Creek to Buenos Frijoles, back to Olatunji, up the Little Clear Fork of the North Branch of Mud River, back to the creek, and everything in between. If I say something gets blowed up, it's on its way to kingdom come."

He put his arms on Leo's shoulders. "Besides, what little grass grows in this county's supposed to be green, and what's growing around them things is red. I *really* don't like that."

"But Sheriff! I've got to meet Professor Lowell in Waxahachie tomorrow. . . ."

"Listen, Leo. I appreciate what you done. But I'm an old man. I been kept up by Martians for three nights, I lost my horse and my new hat, and they busted my favorite gargoyle off the courthouse. I'm going in and get some sleep, and I only want to be woke up for the Second Coming, by Jesus Christ himself."

Leo jumped on his horse and rode for the Atkinson place.

Sheriff Lindley crawled into bed and went to sleep as soon as his head hit the pillow.

He had a dream. He was a king in Babylon, and he lay on a couch at the top of a ziggurat, just like the Tower of Babel in the Bible.

He surveyed the city and the river. There were women all around him, and men with curly beards and big headdresses. Occasionally someone would feed him a large fig from a golden bowl. His dreams were not interrupted by the sounds of dynamiting, first from one side of town, then another, and then another.

# PAT CADIGAN

## Angel

Pat Cadigan was born in Schenectady, New York, and now lives in Overland Park, Kansas. One of the best new writers in SF, Cadigan made her first professional sale in 1980 to *New Dimensions*, and soon became a frequent contributor to *Omni, The Magazine of Fantasy and Science Fiction*, and *Shadows*, among other markets. She was the co-editor, along with husband Arnie Fenner, of *Shayol*, perhaps the best of the semiprozines; it was honored with a World Fantasy Award in the "Special Achievement, Non-Professional" category in 1981. She has also served on the Nebula Award Jury and as a World Fantasy Award Judge. Her first novel, *Mindplayers*, was released last year to excellent critical response, and she's currently at work on a new novel. Her story "Pretty Boy Crossover" was in our Fourth Annual Collection; "Roadside Rescue" was in our Third Annual Collection; "Rock On" was in our Second Annual Collection; and "Nearly Departed" was in our in our First Annual Collection.

Here she gives us an elegant and bittersweet story of the consequences of trust.

# ANGEL

## Pat Cadigan

Stand with me awhile, Angel, I said, and Angel said he'd do that. Angel was good to me that way, good to have with you on a cold night and nowhere to go. We stood on the street corner together and watched the cars going by and the people and all. The streets were lit up like Christmas, streetlights, store lights, marquees over the all-night movie houses and bookstores blinking and flashing: shank of the evening in east midtown. Angel was getting used to things here and getting used to how I did nights. Standing outside, because what else are you going to do. He was *my* Angel now, had been since that other cold night when I'd been going home, because where are you going to go, and I'd found him and took him with me. It's good to have someone to take with you, someone to look after. Angel knew that. He started looking after me, too.

Like now. We were standing there awhile and I was looking around at nothing and everything, the cars cruising past, some of them stopping now and again for the hookers posing by the curb, and then I saw it, out of the corner of my eye. Stuff coming out of the Angel, shiny like sparks but flowing like liquid. Silver fireworks. I turned and looked all the way at him and it was gone. And he turned and gave a little grin like he was embarrassed I'd seen. Nobody else saw it, though; not the short guy who paused next to the Angel before crossing the street against the light, not the skinny hype looking to sell the boom-box he was carrying on his shoulder, not the homeboy strutting past us with both his girlfriends on his arms, nobody but me.

The Angel said, Hungry?

Sure, I said. I'm hungry.

Angel looked past me. Okay, he said. I looked, too, and here they came, three leather boys, visor caps, belts, boots, keyrings. On the cruise together. Scary stuff, even though you know it's not looking for you.

I said, them? *Them?*

Angel didn't answer. One went by, then the second, and the Angel stopped the third by taking hold of his arm.

Hi.

The guy nodded. His head was shaved. I could see a little grey-black stubble under his cap. No eyebrows, disinterested eyes. The eyes were because of the Angel.

I could use a little money, the Angel said. My friend and I are hungry.

The guy put his hand in his pocket and wiggled out some bills, offering them to the Angel. The Angel selected a twenty and closed the guy's hand around the rest.

This will be enough, thank you.

The guy put his money away and waited.

I hope you have a good night, said the Angel.

The guy nodded and walked on, going across the street to where his two friends were waiting on the next corner. Nobody found anything weird about it.

Angel was grinning at me. Sometimes he was *the* Angel, when he was doing something, sometimes he was Angel, when he was just with me. Now he was Angel again. We went up the street to the luncheonette and got a seat by the front window so we could still watch the street while we ate.

Cheeseburger and fries, I said without bothering to look at the plastic-covered menus lying on top of the napkin holder. The Angel nodded.

Thought so, he said. I'll have the same, then.

The waitress came over with a little tiny pad to take our order. I cleared my throat. It seemed like I hadn't used my voice in a hundred years. "Two cheeseburgers and two fries," I said, "and two cups of —" I looked up at her and froze. She had no face. Like, *nothing*, blank from hairline to chin, soft little dents where the eyes and nose and mouth would have been. Under the table, the Angel kicked me, but gentle.

"And two cups of coffee," I said.

She didn't say anything—how could she?—as she wrote down the order and then walked away again. All shaken up, I looked at the Angel, but he was calm like always.

She's a new arrival, Angel told me and leaned back in his chair. Not enough time to grow a face.

But how can she breathe? I said.

Through her pores. She doesn't need much air yet.

Yah, but what about—like, I mean, don't other people *notice* that she's got nothing there?

No. It's not such an extraordinary condition. The only reason you notice is because you're with me. Certain things have rubbed off on you. But no one else notices. When they look at her, they see whatever face they expect someone like her to have. And eventually, she'll have it.

But you have a face, I said. You've always had a face.

I'm different, said the Angel.

You sure are, I thought, looking at him. Angel had a beautiful face. That wasn't why I took him home that night, just because he had a beautiful face—I left all that behind a long time ago—but it was there, his beauty. The way you think of a man being beautiful, good clean lines, deep-set eyes, ageless. About the only way you could describe him—look away and you'd forget everything except that he was beautiful. But he did have a face. He *did*.

Angel shifted in the chair—these were like somebody's old kitchen chairs, you couldn't get too comfortable in them—and shook his head, because he knew I was thinking troubled thoughts. Sometimes you could think something and it wouldn't be troubled and later you'd think the same thing and it would be troubled. The Angel didn't like me to be troubled about him.

Do you have a cigarette? he asked.

I think so.

I patted my jacket and came up with most of a pack that I handed over to him. The Angel lit up and amused us both by having the smoke come out his ears and trickle out of his eyes like ghostly tears. I felt my own eyes watering for his; I wiped them and there was that *stuff* again, but from me now. I was crying silver fireworks. I flicked them on the table and watched them puff out and vanish.

Does this mean I'm getting to *be* you, now? I asked.

Angel shook his head. Smoke wafted out of his hair. Just things rubbing off on you. Because we've been together and you're—susceptible. But they're different for you.

Then the waitress brought our food and we went on to another sequence, as the Angel would say. She still had no face but I guess she could see well enough because she put all the plates down just where you'd think they were supposed to go and left the tiny little check in the middle of the table.

Is she—I mean, did you know her, from where you—

Angel gave his head a brief little shake. No. She's from somewhere else. Not one of my—people. He pushed the cheeseburger and fries in front of him over to my side of the table. That was the way it was done; I did all the eating and somehow it worked out.

I picked up my cheeseburger and I was bringing it up to my mouth when my eyes got all funny and I saw it coming up like a whole *series* of cheeseburgers, whoom-whoom-whoom, trick photography, only for real. I closed my eyes and jammed the cheeseburger into my mouth, holding it there, waiting for all the other cheeseburgers to catch up with it.

You'll be okay, said the Angel. Steady, now.

I said with my mouth full, That was—that was *weird*. Will I ever get used to this?

I doubt it. But I'll do what I can to help you.

Yah, well, the Angel *would* know. Stuff rubbing off on me, he could feel it better than I could. He was the one it was rubbing off *from*.

I had put away my cheeseburger and half of Angel's and was working on the french fries for both of us when I noticed he was looking out the window with this hard, tight expression on his face.

Something? I asked him.

Keep eating, he said.

I kept eating, but I kept watching, too. The Angel was staring at a big blue car parked at the curb right outside the diner. It was silvery blue, one of those lots-of-money models and there was a woman kind of leaning across from the driver's side to look out the passenger window. She was beautiful in that lots-of-money way, tawny hair swept back from her face, and even from here I could see she had turquoise eyes. Really beautiful woman. I almost felt like crying. I mean, jeez, how did people get that way and me too harmless to live.

But the Angel wasn't one bit glad to see her. I knew he didn't want me to say anything, but I couldn't help it.

Who is she?

Keep eating, Angel said. We need the protein, what little there is.

I ate and watched the woman and the Angel watch each other and it was getting very—I don't know, very *something* between them, even through the glass. Then a cop car pulled up next to her and I knew they were telling her to move it along. She moved it along.

Angel sagged against the back of his chair and lit another cigarette, smoking it in the regular, unremarkable way.

What are we going to do tonight? I asked the Angel as we left the restaurant.

Keep out of harm's way, Angel said, which was a new answer. Most nights we spent just kind of going around soaking everything up. The Angel soaked it up, mostly. I got some of it along with him, but not the same way he did. It was different for him. Sometimes he would use me like a kind of filter. Other times he took it direct.

There'd been the big car accident one night, right at my usual corner, a big old Buick running a red light smack into somebody's nice Lincoln. The Angel had had to take it direct because I couldn't handle that kind of stuff. I didn't know how the Angel could take it, but he could. It carried him for days afterwards, too. I only had to eat for myself.

It's the intensity, little friend, he'd told me, as though that were supposed to explain it.

It's the intensity, not whether it's good or bad. The universe doesn't know good or bad, only less or more. Most of you have a bad time reconciling this. *You* have a bad time with it, little friend, but you get through better than other people. Maybe because of the way you are. You got squeezed out of a lot, you haven't had much of a chance at life. You're as much an exile as I am, only in your own land.

That may have been true, but at least I *belonged* here, so that part was easier for me. But I didn't say that to the Angel. I think he liked to think he could do as well or better than me at living—I mean, I couldn't just look at some leather boy and get him to cough up a twenty dollar bill. Cough up a fist in the face or worse, was more like it.

Tonight, though, he wasn't doing so good, and it was that woman in the car. She'd thrown him out of step, kind of.

Don't think about her, the Angel said, just out of nowhere. Don't think about her any more.

Okay, I said, feeling creepy because it was creepy when the Angel got a glimpse of my head. And then, of course, I couldn't think about anything else hardly.

Do you want to go home? I asked him.

No. I can't stay in now. We'll do the best we can tonight, but I'll have to be very careful about the tricks. They take so much out of me, and if we're keeping out of harm's way, I might not be able to make up for a lot of it.

It's okay, I said. I ate. I don't need anything else tonight, you don't have to do any more.

Angel got that look on his face, the one where I knew he wanted to give me things, like feelings, I couldn't have any more. Generous, the Angel was. But I didn't need those feelings, not like other people seem to. For awhile, it was like the Angel didn't understand that, but he let me be.

Little friend, he said, and almost touched me. The Angel didn't touch a lot. I could touch him and that would be okay, but if *he* touched somebody, he couldn't help *doing* something to them, like the trade that had given us the money. That had been deliberate. If the trade had touched the Angel first, it would have been different, nothing would have happened unless the Angel touched him back. All touch meant something to the Angel that I didn't understand. There was touching without touching, too. Like things rubbing off on me. And sometimes, when I did touch the Angel, I'd get the feeling that it was maybe more his idea than mine, but I didn't mind that. How many people were going their whole lives never being able to touch an Angel?

We walked together and all around us the street was really coming to life. It was getting colder, too. I tried to make my jacket cover more. The Angel wasn't feeling it. Most of the time hot and cold didn't mean much to him. We saw the three rough trade guys again. The one Angel had gotten the money from was getting into a car. The other two watched it drive away and then walked on. I looked over at the Angel.

Because we took his twenty, I said.

Even if we hadn't, Angel said.

So we went along, the Angel and me, and I could feel how different it was tonight than it was all the other nights we'd walked or stood together. The Angel was kind of pulled back into himself and seemed to be keeping a check on me, pushing us closer together. I was getting more of those fireworks out of the corners of my eyes, but when I'd turn my head to look, they'd vanish. It reminded me of the night I'd found the Angel standing on my corner all by himself in pain. The Angel told me later that was real talent, knowing he was in pain. I never thought of myself as any too talented, but the way everyone else had been just ignoring him, I guess I must have had something to see him after all.

The Angel stopped us several feet down from an all-night bookstore. Don't look, he said. Watch the traffic or stare at your feet, but don't look or it won't happen.

There wasn't anything to see right then, but I didn't look anyway. That was the way it was sometimes, the Angel telling me it made a difference whether I was watching something or not, something about the other people being conscious of me being conscious of them. I didn't understand, but I knew Angel was usually right. So I was watching traffic when the guy came out of the bookstore and got his head punched.

I could almost see it out of the corner of my eye. A lot of movement, arms and legs flying and grunty noises. Other people stopped to look but I kept my eyes on the traffic, some of which was slowing up so they could check out the fight. Next to me, the Angel was stiff all over. Taking it in, what he called the expenditure of emotional kinetic energy. No right, no wrong, little friend, he'd told me. Just energy, like the rest of the universe.

So he took it in and I *felt* him taking it in, and while I was feeling it, a kind of silver fog started creeping around my eyeballs and I was in two places at once. I was watching the traffic and I was in the Angel watching the fight and feeling him charge up like a big battery.

It felt like nothing I'd ever felt before. These two guys slugging it out—well, one guy doing all the slugging and the other skittering around trying to get out from under the fists and having his head punched but good, and the Angel drinking it like he was sipping at an empty cup and somehow getting it to have something in it after all. Deep inside him, whatever made the Angel go was getting a little stronger.

I kind of swung back and forth between him and me, or swayed might be more like it was. I wondered about it, because the Angel wasn't touching me. I really was getting to *be* him, I thought; Angel picked that up and put the thought away to answer later. It was like I was traveling by the fog, being one of us and then the other, for a long time, it seemed, and then after awhile I was more me than him again, and some of the fog cleared away.

And there was that car, pointed the other way this time, and the woman was climbing out of it with this big weird smile on her face, as though she'd won something. She waved at the Angel to come to her.

Bang went the connection between us dead and the Angel shot past me, running away from the car. I went after him. I caught a glimpse of her jumping back into the car and yanking at the gear shift.

Angel wasn't much of a runner. Something funny about his knees. We'd gone maybe a hundred feet when he started wobbling and I could hear him pant. He cut across a Park & Lock that was dark and mostly empty. It was back-to-back with some kind of private parking lot and the fences for each one tried to mark off the same narrow strip of lumpy pavement. They were easy to climb but Angel was too panicked. He just *went* through them before he even thought about it; I knew that because if he'd been thinking, he'd have wanted to save what he'd just charged up with for when he really needed it bad enough.

I had to haul myself over the fences in the usual way, and when he heard me rattling on the saggy chainlink, he stopped and looked back.

Go, I told him. Don't wait on me!

He shook his head sadly. Little friend, I'm a fool. I could stand to learn from you a little more.

Don't stand, run! I got over the fences and caught up with him. Let's go! I yanked his sleeve as I slogged past and he followed at a clumsy trot.

Have to hide somewhere, he said, camouflage ourselves with people.

I shook my head, thinking we could just run maybe four more blocks and we'd be at the freeway overpass. Below it were the butt-ends of old roads closed off when the freeway had been built. You could hide there the rest of your life and no one would find you. But Angel made me turn right and go down a block to this rundown crack-in-the-wall called Stan's Jigger. I'd never been in there—I'd never made it a practice to go into bars—but the Angel was pushing too hard to argue.

Inside it was smelly and dark and not too happy. The Angel and I went down to the end of the bar and stood under a blood-red light while he searched his pockets for money.

Enough for one drink apiece, he said.

I don't want anything.

You can have soda or something.

The Angel ordered from the bartender, who was suspicious. This was a place for regulars and nobody else, and certainly nobody else like me or the Angel. The Angel knew that even stronger than I did but he just stood and pretended to sip his drink without looking at me. He was all pulled into himself and I was hovering around the edges. I knew he was still pretty panicked and trying to figure out what he could do next. As close as I was, if he had to get real far away, he was going to have a problem and so was I. He'd have to tow me along with him and that wasn't the most practical thing to do.

Maybe he was sorry now he'd let me take him home. But he'd been so weak then, and now with all the filtering and stuff I'd done for him he couldn't just cut me off without a lot of pain.

I was trying to figure out what I could do for him now when the bartender came back and gave us a look that meant order or get out, and he'd have liked it better if we got out. So would everyone else there. The few other people standing at the bar weren't looking at us, but they knew right where we were, like a sore spot. It wasn't hard to figure out what they thought about us, either, maybe because of me or because of the Angel's beautiful face.

We got to leave, I said to the Angel but he had it in his head this was good camouflage. There wasn't enough money for two more drinks so he smiled at the bartender and slid his hand across the bar and put it on top of the bartender's. It was tricky doing it this way; bartenders and waitresses took more persuading because it wasn't normal for them just to give you something.

The bartender looked at the Angel with his eyes half closed. He seemed to be thinking it over. But the Angel had just blown a lot going through the fence instead of climbing over it and the fear was scuttling his concentration and I just knew that it wouldn't work. And maybe my knowing that didn't help, either.

The bartender's free hand dipped down below the bar and came up with a small club. "Faggot!" he roared and caught Angel just over the ear. Angel slammed into me and we both crashed to the floor. Plenty of emotional kinetic energy in here, I thought dimly as the guys standing at the bar fell on us, and then I didn't think anything more as I curled up into a ball under their fists and boots.

We were lucky they didn't much feel like killing anyone. Angel went out the door first and they tossed me out on top of him. As soon as I landed on him, I knew we were both in trouble; something was broken inside him. So much for keeping out of harm's way. I rolled off him and lay on the pavement, staring at the sky and trying to catch my breath. There was blood in my mouth and my nose, and my back was on fire.

Angel? I said, after a bit.

He didn't answer. I felt my mind get kind of all loose and runny, like my brains were leaking out my ears. I thought about the trade we'd taken the money from and how I'd been scared of him and his friends and how silly that had been. But then, I was too harmless to live.

The stars were raining silver fireworks down on me. It didn't help.

Angel? I said again.

I rolled over onto my side to reach for him, and there she was. The car was parked at the curb and she had Angel under the armpits, dragging him toward the open passenger door. I couldn't tell if he was conscious or not and that scared me. I sat up.

She paused, still holding the Angel. We looked into each other's eyes, and I started to understand.

"Help me get him into the car," she said at last. Her voice sounded hard and flat and unnatural. "Then you can get in, too. In the *back* seat."

I was in no shape to take her out. It couldn't have been better for her if she'd set it up herself. I got up, the pain flaring in me so bad that I almost fell down again, and took the Angel's ankles. His ankles were so delicate, almost like a woman's, like *hers*. I didn't really help much, except to guide his feet in as she sat him on the seat and strapped him in with the shoulder harness. I got in the back as she ran around to the other side of the car, her steps real light and peppy, like she'd found a million dollars lying there on the sidewalk.

We were out on the freeway before the Angel stirred in the shoulder harness. His head lolled from side to side on the back of the seat. I reached up and touched his hair lightly, hoping she couldn't see me do it.

Where are you taking me, the Angel said.

"For a ride," said the woman. "For the moment."

Why does she talk out loud like that? I asked the Angel.

Because she knows it bothers me.

"You know I can focus my thoughts better if I say things out loud," she said. "I'm not like one of your little pushovers." She glanced at me in the rearview mirror. "Just *what* have you gotten yourself into since you left, darling? Is that a boy or a girl?"

I pretended I didn't care about what she said or that I was too harmless to live or any of that stuff, but the way she said it, she meant it to sting.

Friends can be either, Angel said. It doesn't matter which. Where are you taking us?

Now it was *us*. In spite of everything, I almost could have smiled.

"Us? You mean, you and me? Or are you really referring to your little pet back there?"

My friend and I are together. You and I are *not*.

The way the Angel said it made me think he meant more than not together; like he'd been with her once the way he was with me now. The Angel let me know I was right. Silver fireworks started flowing slowly off his head down the back of the seat and I knew there was something wrong about it. There was too much all at once.

"Why can't you talk out loud to me, darling?" the woman said with fakey-sounding petulance. "Just say a few words and make me happy. You have a lovely voice when you use it."

That was true, but the Angel never spoke out loud unless he couldn't get out of it, like when he'd ordered from the bartender. Which had probably helped the bartender decide about what he thought we were, but it was useless to think about that.

"All right," said Angel, and I knew the strain was awful for him. "I've said a few words. Are you happy?" He sagged in the shoulder harness.

"Ecstatic. But it won't make me let you go. I'll drop your pet at the nearest hospital and then we'll go home." She glanced at the Angel as she drove. "I've missed you so much. I can't *stand* it without you, without you making things happen. Doing your little miracles. You knew I'd get addicted to it, all the things you could do to people. And then you just took off, I didn't know what had happened to you. And it *hurt*." Her voice turned kind of pitiful, like a little kid's. "I was in real *pain*. You must have been, too. Weren't you? Well, *weren't you?*"

Yes, the Angel said. I was in pain, too.

I remembered him standing on my corner, where I'd hung out all that time by myself until he came. Standing there in pain. I didn't know why or from what then, I just took him home, and after a little while, the pain went away. When he decided we were together, I guess.

The silvery flow over the back of the car seat thickened. I cupped my hands under it and it was like my brain was lighting up with pictures. I saw the Angel before he was my Angel, in this really nice house, the woman's house, and how she'd take him places, restaurants or stores or parties, thinking at him real hard so that he was all filled up with her and had to do what she wanted him to. Steal sometimes; other times, weird stuff, make people do silly things like suddenly start singing or taking their clothes off. That was mostly at the parties, though she made a waiter she didn't like burn himself with a pot of coffee. She'd get men, too, through the Angel, and they'd think it was the greatest idea in the world to go to bed with her. Then she'd make the Angel show her the others, the ones that had been sent here the way he had for crimes nobody could have understood, like the waitress with no face. She'd look at them, sometimes try to do things to them to make them uncomfortable or unhappy. But mostly she'd just stare.

It wasn't like that in the very beginning, the Angel said weakly and I knew he was ashamed.

It's okay, I told him. People can be nice at first, I know that. Then they find out about you.

The woman laughed. "You two are *so* sweet and pathetic. Like a couple of little children. I guess that's what you were looking for, wasn't it, darling? Except children can be cruel, too, can't they? So you got this—*creature* for yourself." She looked at me in the rearview mirror again as she slowed down a little, and for a moment I was afraid she'd seen what I was doing with the silvery stuff that was still pouring out of the Angel. It was starting to slow now. There wasn't much time left. I wanted to scream, but the Angel was calming me for what was coming next. "What happened to you, anyway?"

Tell her, said the Angel. To stall for time, I knew, keep her occupied.

I was born funny, I said. I had both sexes.

"A hermaphrodite!" she exclaimed with real delight.

She loves freaks, the Angel said, but she didn't pay any attention. There was an operation, but things went wrong. They kept trying to fix it as I got older but my body didn't have the right kind of chemistry or something. My parents were ashamed. I left after awhile.

"You poor thing," she said, not meaning anything like that. "You were *just* what darling, here, needed, weren't you? Just a little nothing, no demands, no desires. For anything." Her voice got all hard. "They could probably fix you up now, you know."

I don't want it. I left all that behind a long time ago, I don't need it.

"*Just* the sort of little pet that would be perfect for you," she said to the Angel. "Sorry I have to tear you away. But I can't get along without you now. Life is so boring. And empty. And—" She sounded puzzled. "And like there's nothing more to live for since you left me."

That's not me, said the Angel. That's you.

"No, it's a lot of you, too, and you know it. You know you're addictive to human beings, you knew that when you came here—when they *sent* you here. Hey, you, *pet*, do you know what his crime was, why they sent him to this little backwater penal colony of a planet?"

Yeah, I know, I said. I really didn't, but I wasn't going to tell her that.

"What do you think about *that*, little pet neuter?" she said gleefully, hitting the accelerator pedal and speeding up. "What do you think of the crime of refusing to mate?"

The Angel made a sort of an out-loud groan and lunged at the steering wheel. The car swerved wildly and I fell backward, the silvery stuff from the Angel going all over me. I tried to keep scooping it into my mouth the way I'd been doing, but it was flying all over the place now. I heard the crunch as the tires left the road and went onto the shoulder. Something struck the side of the car, probably the guard rail, and made it fishtail, throwing me down on the floor. Up front the woman was screaming and cursing and the Angel wasn't making a sound, but, in my head, I could hear him sort of keening. Whatever happened, this would be it. The Angel had told me all that time ago, after I'd taken him home, that they didn't last long after they got here, the exiles from his world and other worlds. Things tended to *happen* to them, even if they latched on to someone like me or the woman. They'd be in accidents or the people here would kill them. Like antibodies in a human body rejecting something or fighting a disease. At least I belonged here, but it looked like I was going to die in a car accident with the Angel and the woman both. I didn't care.

The car swerved back onto the highway for a few seconds and then pitched to the right again. Suddenly there was nothing under us and then we thumped down on something, not road but dirt or grass or something, bobbing madly up and down. I pulled myself up on the back of the seat just in time to see the sign coming at us at an angle. The corner of it started to go through the windshield on the woman's side and then all I saw for a long time was the biggest display of silver fireworks ever.

It was hard to be gentle with him. Every move hurt but I didn't want to leave him sitting in the car next to her, even if she was dead. Being in the back seat had kept most of the glass from flying into me but I was still shaking some out of my hair and the impact hadn't done much for my back.

I laid the Angel out on the lumpy grass a little ways from the car and looked around. We were maybe a hundred yards from the highway, near a road that ran parallel to it. It was dark but I could still read the sign that had come through the windshield and split the woman's head in half. It said, *Construction Ahead, Reduce Speed*. Far off on the other road, I could see a flashing yellow light and at first I was afraid it was the police or something but it stayed where it was and I realized that must be the construction.

"Friend," whispered the Angel, startling me. He'd never spoken aloud to me, not directly.

Don't talk, I said, bending over him, trying to figure out some way I could touch him, just for comfort. There wasn't anything else I could do now.

"I have to," he said, still whispering. "It's almost all gone. Did you get it?"

Mostly, I said. Not all.

"I meant for you to have it."

I know.

"I don't know that it will really do you any good." His breath kind of bubbled in his throat. I could see something wet and shiny on his mouth but it wasn't silver fireworks. "But it's yours. You can do as you like with it. Live on it the way I did. Get what you need when you need it. But you can live as a human, too. Eat. Work. However, whatever."

I'm not human, I said. I'm not any more human than you, even if I do belong here.

"Yes, you are, little friend. I haven't made you any less human," he said, and coughed some. "I'm not sorry I wouldn't mate. I couldn't mate with my own. It was too . . . I don't know, too little of me, too much of them, something. I couldn't bond, it would have been nothing but emptiness. The Great Sin, to be unable to give, because the universe knows only less or more and I insisted that it would be good or bad. So they sent me here. But in the end, you know, they got their way, little friend." I felt his hand on me for a moment before it fell away. "I did it after all. Even if it wasn't with my own."

The bubbling in his throat stopped. I sat next to him for awhile in the dark. Finally I felt it, the Angel stuff. It was kind of fluttery-churny, like too much coffee on an empty stomach. I closed my eyes and lay down on the grass, shivering. Maybe some of it was shock but I don't think so. The silver fireworks started, in my head this time, and with them came a lot of pictures I couldn't understand. Stuff about the Angel and where he'd come from and the way they mated. It was a lot like how we'd been together, the Angel and me. They looked a lot like us but there were a lot of differences, too, things I couldn't make out. I couldn't make out how they'd sent him here, either—by *light*, in, like, little bundles or something. It didn't make any sense to me, but I guessed an Angel could be light. Silver fireworks.

I must have passed out, because when I opened my eyes, it felt like I'd been laying there a long time. It was still dark, though. I sat up and reached for the Angel, thinking I ought to hide his body.

He was gone. There was just a sort of wet sandy stuff where he'd been.

I looked at the car and her. All that was still there. Somebody was going to see it soon. I didn't want to be around for that.

Everything still hurt but I managed to get to the other road and start walking back toward the city. It was like I could *feel* it now, the way the Angel must have, as though it were vibrating like a drum or ringing like a bell with all kinds of stuff, people laughing and crying and loving and hating and being afraid and everything else that happens to people. The stuff that the Angel took in, energy, that I could take in now if I wanted.

And I knew that taking it in that way, it would be bigger than anything all those people had, bigger than anything I could have had if things hadn't gone wrong with me all those years ago.

I wasn't so sure I wanted it. Like the Angel, refusing to mate back where he'd come from. He wouldn't, there, and I couldn't, here. Except now I could do something else.

I wasn't so sure I wanted it. But I didn't think I'd be able to stop it, either, any more than I could stop my heart from beating. Maybe it wasn't really such a good thing or a right thing. But it was like the Angel said: the universe doesn't know good or bad, only less or more.

Yeah. I heard *that*.

I thought about the waitress with no face. I could find them all now, all the ones from the other places, other worlds that sent them away for some kind of alien crimes nobody would have understood. I could find them all. They threw away their outcasts, I'd tell them, but here, we *kept* ours. And here's how. Here's how you live in a universe that only knows less or more.

I kept walking toward the city.

# LUCIUS SHEPARD

## Shades

Lucius Shepard began publishing in 1983, and in a very short time has become one of the most popular and prolific writers to come along in many years. In 1983, Shepard won the John W. Campbell Award as the year's best new writer, as well as being on the Nebula Award final ballot an unprecedented three times in three separate categories. Since then, he has turned up several more times on the final Nebula ballot, as well as being a finalist for the Hugo Award, the British Fantasy Award, the John W. Campbell Memorial Award, the Philip K. Dick Award, and the World Fantasy Award. In 1987, he finally picked up his first (though probably not his last) award, winning the Nebula for his landmark novella, "R & R." His acclaimed first novel, *Green Eyes*, was an Ace Special. His most recent books are the novel, *Life During Wartime*, and the collection, *The Jaguar Hunter*. He is currently living somewhere in the wilds of Nantucket, where he is at work on two new novels, *Mister Right* and *The End of Life as We Know It*. His stories "Salvador" and "Black Coral" were in our Second Annual Collection; his stories "The Jaguar Hunter" and "A Spanish Lesson" were in our Third Annual Collection; and his story "R & R" was in our Fourth Annual Collection.

Here he gives us a grisly and unsettling look at one man's eerie reunion with another veteran in postwar Vietnam.

# SHADES

## Lucius Shepard

This little gook cadre with a pitted complexion drove me through the heart of Saigon—I couldn't relate to it as Ho Chi Minh City—and checked me into the Hotel Heroes of Tet, a place that must have been quietly elegant and very French back in the days when philosophy was discussed over Cointreau rather than practiced in the streets, but now was filled with cheap production-line furniture and tinted photographs of Uncle Ho. Glaring at me, the cadre suggested I would be advised to keep to my room until I left for Cam Le; to annoy him I strolled into the bar, where a couple of Americans—reporters, their table laden with notebooks and tape cassettes—were drinking shots from a bottle of George Dickel. "How's it goin'?" I said, ambling over. "Name's Tom Puleo. I'm doin' a piece on Stoner for *Esquire*."

The bigger of them—chubby, red-faced guy about my age, maybe thirty-five, thirty-six—returned a fishy stare; but the younger one, who was thin and tanned and weaselly handsome, perked up and said, "Hey, you're the guy was in Stoner's outfit, right?" I admitted it, and the chubby guy changed his attitude. He put on a welcome-to-the-lodge smile, stuck out a hand and introduced himself as Ed Fierman, *Chicago Sun-Times*. His pal, he said, was Ken Witcover, CNN.

They tried to draw me out about Stoner, but I told them maybe later, that I wanted to unwind from the airplane ride, and we proceeded to do damage to the whiskey. By the time we'd sucked down three drinks, Fierman and I were into some heavy reminiscence. Turned out he had covered the war during my tour and knew my old top. Witcover was cherry in Vietnam, so he just tried to look wise and to laugh in the right spots. It got pretty drunk at that table. A security cadre—fortyish, cadaverous gook in yellow fatigues—sat nearby, cocking an ear toward us, and we pretended to be engaged in subversive activity, whispering and drawing maps on napkins. But it was Stoner who was really on all our minds, and Fierman—the drunkest of us—finally broached the subject, saying, "A machine that traps ghosts!

It's just like the gooks to come up with something that goddamn worthless!"

Witcover shushed him, glancing nervously at the security cadre, but Fierman was beyond caution. "They coulda done humanity a service," he said, chuckling. "Turned alla Russians into women or something. But, nah! The gooks get behind worthlessness. They may claim to be Marxists, but at heart they still wanna be inscrutable."

"So," said Witcover to me, ignoring Fierman, "when you gonna fill us in on Stoner?"

I didn't care much for Witcover. It wasn't anything personal; I simply wasn't fond of his breed: compulsively neat (pencils lined up, name inscribed on every possession), edgy, on the make. I dislike him the way some people dislike yappy little dogs. But I couldn't argue with his desire to change the subject. "He was a good soldier," I said.

Fierman let out a mulish guffaw. "Now that," he said, "that's what I call in-depth analysis."

Witcover snickered.

"Tell you the truth"—I scowled at him, freighting my words with malice—"I hated the son of a bitch. He had this young-professor air, this way of lookin' at you as if you were an interestin' specimen. And he came across pure phony. Y'know, the kind who's always talkin' like a black dude, sayin' 'right on' and shit, and sayin' it all wrong."

"Doesn't seem much reason for hating him," said Witcover, and by his injured tone, I judged I had touched a nerve. Most likely he had once entertained soul-brother pretensions.

"Maybe not. Maybe if I'd met him back home, I'd have passed him off as a creep and gone about my business. But in combat situations, you don't have the energy to maintain that sort of neutrality. It's easier to hate. And anyway, Stoner could be a genuine pain in the ass."

"How's that?" Fierman asked, getting interested.

"It was never anything unforgivable; he just never let up with it. Like one time a bunch of us were in this guy Gurney's hooch, and he was tellin' 'bout this badass he'd known in Detroit. The cops had been chasin' this guy across the rooftops, and he'd missed a jump. Fell seven floors and emptied his gun at the cops on the way down. Reaction was typical. Guys sayin' 'Wow' and tryin' to think of a story to top it. But Stoner he nods sagely and says, 'Yeah, there's a lot of that goin' around.' As if this was a syndrome to which he's devoted years of study. But you knew he didn't have a clue, that he was too upscale to have met anybody like Gurney's badass." I had a slug of whiskey. " 'There's a lot of that goin' around' was a totally inept comment. All it did was to bring everyone down from a nice buzz and make us aware of the shithole where we lived."

Witcover looked puzzled but Fierman made a noise that seemed to imply comprehension. "How'd he die?" he asked. "The handout says he was KIA, but it doesn't say what kind of action."

"The fuck-up kind," I said. I didn't want to tell them. The closer I came to seeing Stoner, the leerier I got about the topic. Until this business had begun, I thought I'd buried all the death-tripping weirdness of Vietnam; now Stoner had unearthed it and I was having dreams again and I hated him for that worse than I ever had in life. What was I supposed to do? Feel sorry for him? Maybe ghosts didn't have bad dreams. Maybe it was terrific being a ghost, like with Casper. . . . Anyway, I did tell them. How we had entered Cam Le, what was left of the patrol. How we had lined up the villagers, interrogated them, hit them, and God knows we might have killed them—we were freaked, bone-weary, an atrocity waiting to happen—if Stoner hadn't distracted us. He'd been wandering around, poking at stuff with his rifle, and then, with this ferocious expression on his face, he'd fired into one of the huts. The hut had been empty, but there must have been explosives hidden inside, because after a few rounds the whole damn thing had blown and taken Stoner with it.

Talking about him soured me on company, and shortly afterward I broke it off with Fierman and Witcover, and walked out into the city. The security cadre tagged along, his hand resting on the butt of his sidearm. I had a real load on and barely noticed my surroundings. The only salient points of difference between Saigon today and fifteen years before were the ubiquitous representations of Uncle Ho that covered the facades of many of the buildings, and the absence of motor scooters: the traffic consisted mainly of bicycles. I went a dozen blocks or so and stopped at a sidewalk café beneath sun-browned tamarinds, where I paid two dong for food tickets, my first experience with what the Communists called "goods exchange"—a system they hoped would undermine the concept of monetary trade; I handed the tickets to the waitress and she gave me a bottle of beer and a dish of fried peanuts. The security cadre, who had taken a table opposite mine, seemed no more impressed with the system than was I; he chided the waitress for her slowness and acted perturbed by the complexity accruing to his order of tea and cakes.

I sat and sipped and stared, thoughtless and unfocused. The bicyclists zipping past were bright blurs with jingling bells, and the light was that heavy leaded-gold light that occurs when a tropical sun has broken free of an overcast. Smells of charcoal, fish sauce, grease. The heat squeezed sweat from my every pore. I was brought back to alertness by angry voices. The security cadre was arguing with the waitress, insisting that the recorded music be turned on, and she was explaining that there weren't enough customers to warrant turning it on. He began to offer formal "constructive criticism," making clear that he considered her refusal both a breach of party ethics and the code of honorable service. About then, I realized I had begun to cry. Not sobs, just tears leaking. The tears had nothing to do with the argument or the depersonalized ugliness it signaled. I believe that the heat and the light and the smells had seeped into me, triggering a recognition of an awful familiarity that my mind had thus far rejected. I wiped my face and tried to suck it up before anyone could notice my emotionality; but a teenage boy on a bicycle slowed and gazed at me with an amused expression. To show my contempt, I spat on the sidewalk. Almost instantly, I felt much better.

Early the next day, thirty of us—all journalists—were bussed north to Cam Le. Mist still wreathed the paddies, the light had a yellowish green cast, and along the road women in black dresses were waiting for a southbound bus, with rumpled sacks of produce like sleepy brown animals at their feet. I sat beside Fierman, who, being as hung over as I was, made no effort at conversation; however, Witcover—sitting across the aisle—peppered me with inane questions until I told him to leave me alone. Just before we turned onto the dirt road that led to Cam Le, an information cadre boarded the bus and for the duration proceeded to fill us in on everything we already knew. Stuff about the machine, how its fields were generated, and so forth. Technical jargon gives me a pain, and I tried hard not to listen. But then he got off onto a tack that caught my interest. "Since the machine has been in operation," he said, "the apparition seems to have grown more vital."

"What's that mean?" I asked, waving my hand to attract his attention. "Is he coming back to life?"

My colleagues laughed.

The cadre pondered this. "It simply means that his effect has become more observable," he said at last. And beyond that he would not specify.

Cam Le had been evacuated, its population shifted to temporary housing three miles east. The village itself was nothing like the place I had entered fifteen years before. Gone were the thatched huts, and in their stead were about two dozen small houses of concrete block painted a quarantine yellow, with banana trees set between them. All this encircled by thick jungle. Standing on the far side of the road from the group of houses was the long tin-roofed building that contained the machine. Two soldiers were lounging in front of it, and as the bus pulled up, they snapped to attention; a clutch of officers came out the door, followed by a portly, white-haired gook: Phan

Thnah Tuu, the machine's inventor. I disembarked and studied him while he shook hands with the other journalists; it wasn't every day that I met someone who claimed to be both Marxist and mystic, and had gone more than the required mile in establishing the validity of each. His hair was as fine as cornsilk, a fat black mole punctuated one cheek, and his benign smile was unflagging, seeming a fixture of some deeply held good opinion attaching to everything he saw. Maybe, I thought, Fierman was right. In-fucking-scrutable.

"Ah," he said, coming up, enveloping me in a cloud of perfumy cologne. "Mr. Puleo. I hope this won't be painful for you."

"Really," I said. "You hope that, do you?"

"I beg your pardon," he said, taken aback.

"It's okay." I grinned. "You're forgiven."

An unsmiling major led him away to press more flesh, and he glanced back at me, perplexed, I was mildly ashamed of having fucked with him, but unlike Cassius Clay, I had plenty against them Viet Congs. Besides, my wiseass front was helping to stave off the yips.

After a brief welcome-to-the-wonderful-wacky-world-of-the-Commie-techno-paradise speech given by the major, Tuu delivered an oration upon the nature of ghosts, worthy of mention only in that it rehashed every crackpot notion I'd ever heard: apparently Stoner hadn't yielded much in the way of hard data. He then warned us to keep our distance from the village. The fields would not harm us; they were currently in operation, undetectable to our senses and needing but a slight manipulation to "focus" Stoner. But if we were to pass inside the fields, it was possible that Stoner himself might be able to cause us injury. With that, Tuu bowed and reentered the building.

We stood facing the village, which—with its red dirt and yellow houses and green banana leaves—looked elementary and innocent under the leaden sky. Some of my colleagues whispered together, others checked their cameras. I felt numb and shaky, prepared to turn away quickly, much the way I once had felt when forced to identify the body of a chance acquaintance at a police morgue. Several minutes after Tuu had left us, there was a disturbance in the air at the center of the village. Similar to heat haze, but the ripples were slower. And then, with the suddenness of a slide shunted into a projector, Stoner appeared.

I think I had been expecting something bloody and ghoulish, or perhaps a gauzy, insubstantial form; but he looked no different than he had on the day he died. Haggard; wearing sweat-stained fatigues; his face half-obscured by a week's growth of stubble. On his helmet were painted the words *Didi Mao* ("Fuck Off' in Vietnamese), and I could make out the yellowing photograph of his girl that he'd taped to his rifle stock. He didn't act startled by our presence; on the contrary, his attitude was nonchalant. He shouldered his rifle, tipped back his helmet and sauntered toward us. He seemed to be recessed into the backdrop: it was as if reality were two-dimensional and he was a cutout held behind it to give the illusion of depth. At least that's how it was one moment. The next, he would appear to be set forward of the backdrop like a pop-up figure in a fancy greeting card. Watching him shift between these modes was unsettling . . . more than unsettling. My heart hammered, my mouth was cottony. I bumped into someone and realized that I had been backing away, that I was making a scratchy noise deep in my throat. Stoner's eyes, those eyes that had looked dead even in life, pupils about .45 caliber and hardly any iris showing, they were locked onto mine and the pressure of his stare was like two black bolts punching through into my skull.

"Puleo," he said.

I couldn't hear him, but I saw his lips shape the name. With a mixture of longing and hopelessness harrowing his features, he kept on repeating it. And then I noticed something else. The closer he drew to me, the more in focus he became. It wasn't just a matter of the shortening distance; his stubble and sweat stains, the frays in his fatigues, his worry lines—all these were sharpening the way details become fixed in a developing photograph. But none of that disturbed me half as much as did the fact of a dead man calling my name. I couldn't handle that. I began to hyperventilate, to get dizzy, and I believe I might have blacked out; but before that could happen, Stoner reached the edge of the fields, the barrier beyond which he could not pass.

Had I more mental distance from the event, I might have enjoyed the sound-and-light that ensued: it was spectacular. The instant Stoner hit the end of his tether, there was an ear-splitting shriek of the kind metal emits under immense stress; it seemed to issue from the air, the trees, the earth, as if some ironclad physical constant had been breached. Stoner was frozen midstep, his mouth open, and opaque lightnings were forking away from him, taking on a violet tinge as they vanished, their passage illuminating the curvature of the fields. I heard a scream and assumed it must be Stoner. But somebody grabbed me, shook me, and I understood that I was the one screaming, screaming with throat-tearing abandon because his eyes were boring into me and I could have sworn that his thoughts, his sensations, were flowing to me along the track of his vision. I knew what he was feeling: not pain, not desperation, but emptiness. An emptiness made unbearable by his proximity to life, to fullness. It was the worst thing I'd ever felt, worse than grief and bullet wounds, and it had to be worse than dying—dying, you see, had an end, whereas this went on and on, and every time you thought you had adapted to it, it grew worse yet. I wanted it to stop. That was all I wanted. Ever. Just for it to stop.

Then, with the same abruptness that he had appeared, Stoner winked out of existence and the feeling of emptiness faded.

People pressed in, asking questions. I shouldered them aside and walked off a few paces. My hands were shaking, my eyes weepy. I stared at the ground. It looked blurred, an undifferentiated smear of green with a brown clot in the middle: this gradually resolved into grass and my left shoe. Ants were crawling over the laces, poking their heads into the eyelets. The sight was strengthening, a reassurance of the ordinary.

"Hey, man." Witcover hove up beside me. "You okay?" He rested a hand on my shoulder. I kept my eyes on the ants, saying nothing. If it had been anyone else, I might have responded to his solicitude; but I knew he was only sucking up to me, hoping to score some human interest for his satellite report. I glanced at him. He was wearing a pair of mirrored sunglasses, and that consolidated my anger. Why is it, I ask you, that every measly little wimp in the universe thinks he can put on a pair of mirrored sunglasses and instantly acquire magical hipness and cool, rather than—as is the case—looking like an asshole with reflecting eyes?

"Fuck off," I told him in a tone that implied dire consequences were I not humored. He started to talk back, but thought better of it and stalked off. I returned to watching the ants; they were caravanning up inside my trousers and onto my calf. I would become a legend among them: The Human Who Stood Still for Biting.

From behind me came the sound of peremptory gook voices, angry American voices. I paid them no heed, content with my insect pals and the comforting state of thoughtlessness that watching them induced. A minute or so later, someone else moved up beside me and stood without speaking. I recognized Tuu's cologne and looked up. "Mr. Puleo," he said. "I'd like to offer you an exclusive on this story." Over his shoulder, I saw my colleagues staring at us through the windows of the bus, as wistful and forlorn as kids who have been denied Disneyland: they, like me, knew that big bucks were to be had from exploiting Stoner's plight.

"Why?" I asked.

"We want your help in conducting an experiment."

I waited for him to continue.

"Did you notice," he said, "that after Stoner identified you, his image grew sharper?"

I nodded.

"We're interested in observing the two of you in close proximity. His reaction to you was unique."

"You mean go in there?" I pointed to the village. "You said it was dangerous."

"Other subjects have entered the fields and shown no ill effects. But Stoner was not as intrigued by them as he was with you." Tuu brushed a lock of hair back from his forehead. "We have no idea of Stoner's capabilities, Mr. Puleo. It *is* a risk. But since you served in the Army, I assume you are accustomed to risk."

I let him try to persuade me—the longer I held out, the stronger my bargaining position—but I had already decided to accept the offer. Though I wasn't eager to feel that emptiness again, I had convinced myself that it had been a product of nerves and an overactive imagination; now that I had confronted Stoner, I believed I would be able to control my reactions. Tuu said that he would have the others driven back to Saigon, but I balked at that. I was not sufficiently secure to savor the prospect of being alone among the gooks, and I told Tuu I wanted Fierman and Witcover to stay. Why Witcover? At the time I might have said it was because he and Fierman were the only two of my colleagues whom I knew; but in retrospect, I think I may have anticipated the need for a whipping boy.

We were quartered in a house at the eastern edge of the village, one that the fields did not enclose. Three cots were set up inside, along with a table and chairs; the yellow walls were brocaded with mildew, and weeds grew sideways from chinks in the concrete blocks. Light was provided by an oil lamp that—as darkness fell—sent an inconstant glow lapping over the walls, making it appear that the room was filled with dirty orange water.

After dinner Fierman produced a bottle of whiskey—his briefcase contained three more—and a deck of cards, and we sat down to while away the evening. The one game we all knew was Hearts, and we each played according to the dictates of our personalities. Fierman became quickly drunk and attempted to Shoot the Moon on every hand, no matter how bad his cards; he seemed to be asking fate to pity a fool. I paid little attention to the game, my ears tuned to the night sounds, half expecting to hear the sputter of small-arms fire, the rumor of some ghostly engagement; it was by dint of luck alone that I maintained second place. Witcover played conservatively, building his score through our mistakes, and though we were only betting a nickel a point, to watch him sweat out every trick you would have thought a fortune hung in the balance; he chortled over our pitiful fuck-ups, rolling his eyes and shaking his head in delight, and whistled as he totaled up his winnings. The self-importance he derived from winning fouled the atmosphere, and the room acquired the staleness of a cell where we had been incarcerated for years. Finally, after a particularly childish display of glee, I pushed back my chair and stood.

"Where you going?" asked Witcover. "Let's play."

"No, thanks," I said.

"Christ!" He picked up the discards and muttered something about sore losers.

"It's not that," I told him. "I'm worried if you win another hand, you're gonna come all over the fuckin' table. I don't wanna watch."

Fierman snorted laughter.

Witcover shot me an aggrieved look. "What's with you, man? You been on my case ever since the hotel."

I shrugged and headed for the door.

"Asshole," he said half under his breath.

"What?" An angry flush numbed my face as I turned back.

He tried to project an expression of manly belligerence, but his eyes darted from side to side.

"Asshole?" I said. "Is that right?" I took a step toward him.

Fierman scrambled up, knocking over his chair, and began pushing me away. "C'mon," he said. "It's not worth it. Cool out." His boozy sincerity acted to diminish my anger, and I let him urge me out the door.

The night was moonless, with a few stars showing low on the horizon; the spiky crowns of the palms ringing the village were silhouettes pinned onto a lesser blackness. It was so humid, it felt like you could spoon in the air. I crossed the dirt road, found a patch of grass near the tin-roofed building and sat down. The door to the building was cracked, spilling a diagonal of white radiance onto the ground, and I had the notion that there was no machine inside, only a mystic boil of whiteness emanating from Tuu's silky hair. A couple of soldiers walked past and nodded to me; they paused a few feet farther along to light cigarettes, which proceeded to brighten and fade with the regularity of tiny beacons.

Crickets sawed, frogs chirred, and listening to them, smelling the odor of sweet rot from the jungle, I thought about a similar night when I'd been stationed at Phnoc Vinh, about a party we'd had with a company of artillery. There had been a barbecue pit and iced beer and our CO had given special permission for whores to come on the base. It had been a great party; in fact, those days at Phnoc Vinh had been the best time of the war for me. The artillery company had had this terrific cook, and on movie nights he'd make doughnuts. Jesus, I'd loved those doughnuts! They'd tasted like home, like peace. I'd kick back and munch a doughnut and watch the bullshit movie, and it was almost like being in my own living room, watching the tube. Trouble was, Phnoc Vinh had softened me up, and after three weeks, when we'd been airlifted to Quan Loi, which was constantly under mortar and rocket fire, I'd nearly gotten my ass blown off.

Footsteps behind me. Startled, I turned and saw what looked to be a disembodied white shirt floating toward me. I came to one knee, convinced for the moment that some other ghost had been lured to the machine; but a second later a complete figure emerged from the dark: Tuu. Without a word, he sat cross-legged beside me. He was smoking a cigarette . . . or so I thought until I caught a whiff of marijuana. He took a deep drag, the coal illuminating his placid features, and offered me the joint. I hesitated, not wanting to be pals; but tempted by the smell, I accepted it, biting back a smartass remark about Marxist permissiveness. It was good shit. I could feel the smoke twisting through me, finding out all my hollow places. I handed it back, but he made a gesture of warding it off and after a brief silence, he said, "What do you think about all this, Mr. Puleo?"

"About Stoner?"

"Yes."

"I think"—I jetted smoke from my nostrils—"it's crap that you've got him penned up in that astral tiger cage."

"Had this discovery been made in the United States," he said, "the circumstances would be no different. Humane considerations—if, indeed, they apply—would have low priority."

"Maybe," I said. "It's still crap."

"Why? Do you believe Stoner is unhappy?"

"Don't you?" I had another hit. It was *very* good shit. The ground seemed to have a pulse. "Ghosts are by nature unhappy."

"Then you know what a ghost is?"

"Not hardly. But I figure unhappy's part of it." The roach was getting too hot; I took a final hit and flipped it away. "How 'bout you? You believe that garbage you preached this mornin'?"

His laugh was soft and cultivated. "That was a press release. However, my actual opinion is neither less absurd-sounding nor more verifiable."

"And what's that?"

He plucked a blade of grass, twiddled it. "I believe a ghost is a quality that dies in a man long before he experiences physical death. Something that has grown acclimated to death and thus survives the body. It might be love or an ambition. An element of character . . . Anything." He regarded me with his lips pursed. "I have such a ghost within me. As do you, Mr. Puleo. My ghost senses yours."

The theory was as harebrained as his others, but I wasn't able to deny it. I knew he was partly right, that a moral filament had snapped inside me during the war and since that time I had lacked the ingredient necessary to the development of a generous soul. Now it seemed that I could feel that lack as a restless presence straining against my flesh. The sawing of the crickets intensified, and I had a rush of paranoia, wondering if Tuu was fucking with my head. Then, moods shifting at the chemical mercies of the dope, my paranoia eroded and Tuu snapped into focus for me . . . or at least his ghost did. He had, I recalled, written poetry prior to the war, and I thought I saw the features of that lost poet melting up from his face: a dreamy fellow given to watching petals fall and contemplating the moon's reflection. I closed my eyes, trying to get a grip. This was the best dope I'd ever smoked. Commie Pink, pure buds of the revolution.

"Are you worried about tomorrow?" Tuu asked.

"Should I be?"

"I can only tell you what I did before—no one has been harmed."

"What happened during those other experiments?" I asked.

"Very little, really. Stoner approached each subject, spoke to them. Then he lost interest and wandered off."

"Spoke to them? Could they hear him?"

"Faintly. However, considering his reaction to you, I wouldn't be surprised if you could hear him quite well."

I wasn't thrilled by that prospect. Having to look at Stoner was bad enough. I thought about the eerie shit he might say: admonitory pronouncements, sad questions, windy vowels gusting from his strange depths. Tuu said something and had to repeat it to snap me out of my reverie. He asked how it felt to be back in Vietnam, and without forethought, I said it wasn't a problem.

"And the first time you were here," he said, an edge to his voice. "Was that a problem?"

"What are you gettin' at?"

"I noticed in your records that you were awarded a Silver Star."

"Yeah?"

"You must have been a good soldier. I wondered if you might not have found a calling in war."

"If you're askin' what I think about the war," I said, getting pissed, "I don't make judgments about it. It was a torment for me, nothing more. Its geopolitical consequences, cultural effects, they're irrelevant to me . . . maybe they're ultimately irrelevant. Though I doubt you'd agree."

"We may agree more than you suspect." He sighed pensively. "For both of us, apparently, the war was a passion. In your case, an agonizing one. In mine, while there was also agony, it was essentially a love affair with revolution, with the idea of revolution. And as with all great passions, what was most alluring was not the object of passion but the new depth of my own feelings. Thus I was blind to the realities underlying it. Now"—he waved at the sky, the trees—"now I inhabit those realities and I am not as much in love as once I was. Yet no matter how extreme my disillusionment, the passion continues. I want it to continue. I need the significance with which it imbues my past actions." He studied me. "Isn't that how it is for you? You say war was a torment, but don't you find those days empowering?"

Just as when he had offered me the joint, I realized that I didn't want this sort of peaceful intimacy with him; I preferred him to be my inscrutable enemy. Maybe he was right, maybe—like him—I needed the passion to continue in order to give significance to my past. Whatever, I felt vulnerable to him, to my perception of his humanity. "Good-night," I said, getting to my feet. My ass was numb from sitting and soaked with dew.

He gazed up at me, unreadable, and fingered something from his shirt pocket. Another joint. He lit up, exhaling a billow of smoke. "Good-night," he said coldly.

The next morning—sunny, cloudless—I staked myself out on the red dirt of Cam Le to wait for Stoner. Nervous, I paced back and forth until the air began to ripple and he materialized less than thirty feet away. He walked slowly toward me, his rifle dangling; a drop of sweat carved a cold groove across my rib cage. "Puleo," he said, and this time I heard him. His voice was faint, but it shook me.

Looking into his blown-out pupils, I was reminded of a day not long before he had died. We had been hunkered down together after a firefight, and our eyes had met, had locked as if sealed by a vacuum: like two senile old men, incapable of any communication aside from a recognition of the other's vacancy. As I remembered this, it hit home to me that though he hadn't been a friend, he *was* my brother-in-arms, and that as such, I owed him more than journalistic interest.

"Stoner!" I hadn't intended to shout, but in that outcry was a wealth of repressed emotion, of regret and guilt and anguish at not being able to help him elude the fate by which he had been overtaken.

He stopped short; for an instant the hopelessness drained from his face. His image was undergoing that uncanny sharpening of focus: sweat beads popping from his brow, a scab appearing on his chin. The lines of strain around his mouth and eyes were etched deep, filled in with grime, like cracks in his tan.

Tides of emotion were washing over me, and irrational though it seemed, I knew that some of these emotions—the fierce hunger for life in particular—were Stoner's. I believe we had made some sort of connection, and all our thoughts were in flux between us. He moved toward me again. My hands trembled, my knees buckled, and I had to sit down overwhelmed not by fear but by the combination of his familiarity and utter strangeness. "Jesus, Stoner," I said. "Jesus."

He stood gazing dully down at me. "My sending," he said, his voice louder and with a pronounced resonance. "Did you get it?"

A chill articulated my spine, but I forced myself to ignore it. "Sending?" I said.

"Yesterday," he said, "I sent you what I was feeling. What it's like for me here."

"How?" I asked, recalling the feeling of emptiness. "How'd you do that?"

"It's easy, Puleo," he said. "All you have to do is die, and thoughts . . . dreams, they'll flake off you like old paint. But believe me, it's hardly adequate compensation." He sat beside me, resting the rifle across his knees. This was no ordinary sequence of movements. His outline wavered, and his limbs appeared to drift apart: I might have been watching the collapse of a lifelike statue through a volume of disturbed water. It took all my self-control to keep from flinging myself away. His image steadied, and he stared at me. "Last person I was this close to ran like hell," he said. "You always were a tough motherfucker, Puleo. I used to envy you that."

If I hadn't believed before that he was Stoner, the way he spoke the word "motherfucker" would have cinched it for me: it had the stiffness of a practiced vernacular, a mode of expression that he hadn't mastered. This and his pathetic manner made him seem less menacing. "You were tough, too," I said glibly.

"I tried to be," he said. "I tried to copy you guys. But it was an act, a veneer. And when we hit Cam Le, the veneer cracked."

"You remember . . ." I broke off because it didn't feel right, my asking him questions; the idea of translating his blood and bones into a best-seller was no longer acceptable.

"Dying?" His lips thinned. "Oh, yeah. Every detail. You guys were hassling the villagers, and I thought, Christ, they're going to kill them. I didn't want to be involved, and . . . I was so tired, you know, so tired in my head, and I figured if I walked off a little ways, I wouldn't be part of it. I'd be innocent. So I did. I moved a ways off, and the wails, the shouts, they weren't real anymore. Then I came to this hut. I'd lost track of what was happening by that time. In my mind I was sure you'd already started shooting, and I said to myself, I'll show them I'm doing my bit, put a few rounds into this hut.

Maybe"—his Adam's apple worked—"maybe they'll think I killed somebody. Maybe that'll satisfy them."

I looked down at the dirt, troubled by what I now understood to be my complicity in his death, and troubled also by a new understanding of the events surrounding the death. I realized that if anyone else had gotten himself blown up, the rest of us would have flipped out and likely have wasted the villagers. But since it had been Stoner, the explosion had had almost a calming effect: Cam Le had rid us of a nuisance.

Stoner reached out his hand to me. I was too mesmerized by the gesture, which left afterimages in the air, to recoil from it, and I watched horrified as his fingers gripped my upper arm, pressing wrinkles in my shirtsleeve. His touch was light and transmitted a dry coolness, and with it came a sensation of weakness. By all appearances, it was a normal hand, yet I kept expecting it to become translucent and merge with my flesh.

"It's going to be okay," said Stoner.

His tone, though bemused, was confident, and I thought I detected a change in his face, but I couldn't put my finger on what the change was. "Why's it gonna be okay?" I asked, my voice more frail and ghostly-sounding than his. "It doesn't seem okay to me."

"Because you're part of my process, my circuitry. Understand?"

"No," I said. I had identified what had changed about him. Whereas a few moments before he had looked real, now he looked more than real, ultra-real; his features had acquired the kind of gloss found in airbrushed photographs, and for a split second his eyes were cored with points of glitter as if reflecting a camera flash . . . except these points were bluish white not red. There was a coarseness to his face that hadn't been previously evident, and in contrast to my earlier perception of him, he now struck me as dangerous, malevolent.

He squinted and cocked his head. "What's wrong, man? You scared of me?" He gave an amused sniff. "Hang in there, Puleo. Tough guy like you, you'll make an adjustment." My feeling of weakness had intensified: it was as if blood or some even more vital essence were trickling out of me. "Come on, Puleo," he said mockingly. "Ask me some questions? That's what you're here for, isn't it? I mean this must be the goddamn scoop of the century. Good News From Beyond the Grave! Of course"—he pitched his voice low and sepulchral—"the news isn't all that good."

Those glittering cores resurfaced in his pupils, and I wanted to wrench free; but I felt helpless, wholly in his thrall.

"You see," he went on, "when I appeared in the village, when I walked around and"—he chuckled—"haunted the place, those times were like sleepwalking. I barely knew what was happening. But the rest of the time, I was somewhere else. Somewhere really fucking weird."

My weakness was bordering on vertigo, but I mustered my strength and croaked, "Where?"

"The Land of Shades," he said. "That's what I call it, anyway. You wouldn't like it, Puleo. It wouldn't fit your idea of order."

The lights burned in his eyes, winking bright, and—as if in correspondence to their brightness—my dizziness increased. "Tell me about it," I said, trying to take my mind off the discomfort.

"I'd be delighted!" He grinned nastily. "But not now. It's too complicated. Tonight, man. I'll send you a dream tonight. A bad dream. That'll satisfy your curiosity."

My head was spinning, my stomach abubble with nausea. "Lemme go, Stoner," I said.

"Isn't this good for you, man? It's very good for me." With a flick of his hand, he released my wrist.

I braced myself to keep from falling over, drew a deep breath and gradually my strength returned. Stoner's eyes continued to burn, and his features maintained their coarsened appearance. The difference between the way he looked now and the lost soul I had first seen was like that between night and day, and I began to wonder whether or not his touching me and my resultant weakness had anything to do with the transformation. "Part of your process," I said. "Does that . . ."

He looked me straight in the eyes, and I had the impression he was cautioning me to silence. It was more than a caution: a wordless command, a sending. "Let me explain something," he said. "A ghost is merely a stage of growth. He walks because he grows strong by walking. The more he walks, the less he's bound to the world. When he's strong enough"—he made a planing gesture with his hand—"he goes away."

He seemed to be expecting a response. "Where's he go?" I asked.

"Where he belongs," he said. "And if he's prevented from walking, from growing strong, he's doomed."

"You mean he'll die?"

"Or worse."

"And there's no other way out for him?"

"No."

He was lying—I was sure of it. Somehow I posed for him a way out of Cam Le. "Well . . . so," I said, flustered, uncertain of what to do and at the same time pleased with the prospect of conspiring against Tuu.

"Just sit with me a while," he said, easing his left foot forward to touch my right ankle.

Once again I experienced weakness, and over the next seven or eight hours, he would alternately move his foot away, allowing me to recover, and then bring it back into contact with me. I'm not certain what was happening. One logic dictates that since I had been peripherally involved in his death—"part of his process"—he was therefore able to draw strength from me. Likely as not, this was the case. Yet I've never been convinced that ordinary logic applied to our circumstance: it may be that we were governed by an arcane rationality to which we both were blind. Though his outward aspect did not appear to undergo further changes, his strength became tangible, a cold radiation that pulsed with the steadiness of an icy heart. I came to feel that the image I was seeing was the tip of an iceberg, the perceptible extremity of a huge power cell that existed mainly in dimensions beyond the range of mortal vision. I tried to give the impression of an interview to our observers by continuing to ask questions; but Stoner sat with his head down, his face hidden, and gave terse, disinterested replies.

The sun declined to the tops of the palms, the yellow paint of the houses took on a tawny hue, and—drained by the day-long alternation of weakness and recovery—I told Stoner I needed to rest. "Tomorrow," he said without looking up. "Come back tomorrow."

"All right." I had no doubt that Tuu would be eager to go on with the experiment. I stood and turned to leave; but then another question, a pertinent one, occurred to me. "If a ghost is a stage of growth," I said, "what's he grow into?"

He lifted his head, and I staggered back, terrified. His eyes were ablaze, even the whites winking with cold fire, as if nuggets of phosphorus were embedded in his skull.

"Tomorrow," he said again.

During the debriefing that followed, I developed a bad case of the shakes and experienced a number of other, equally unpleasant reactions; the places where Stoner had touched me seemed to have retained a chill, and the thought of that dead hand leeching me of energy was in retrospect thoroughly repellent. A good many of Tuu's subordinates, alarmed by Stoner's transformation, lobbied to break off the experiment. I did my best to soothe them, but I wasn't at all sure I wanted to return to the village. I couldn't tell whether Tuu noticed either my trepidation or the fact that I was being less than candid; he was too busy bringing his subordinates in line to question me in depth.

That night, when Fierman broke out his whiskey, I swilled it down as if it were an antidote to poison. To put it bluntly, I got shit-faced. Both Fierman and Witcover seemed warm human beings, old buddies, and our filthy yellow room with its flickering lamp took on the coziness of a cottage and hearth. The first stage of my drunk was maudlin, filled with self-recriminations over my past treatment of Stoner: I vowed not to shrink from helping him. The second stage . . . Well, once I caught Fierman gazing at me askance and registered that my behavior was verging on the manic. Laughing hysterically, talking like a speed freak. We talked about everything except Stoner, and I suppose it was inevitable that the conversation work itself around to the war and its aftermath. Dimly, I heard myself pontificating on a variety of related subjects. At one point Fierman asked what I thought of the Vietnam Memorial, and I told him I had mixed emotions.

"Why?" he asked.

"I go to the Memorial, man," I said, standing up from the table where we had all been sitting. "And I cry. You can't help but cryin', 'cause that"—I hunted for an appropriate image—"that black dividin' line between nowheres, that says it just right 'bout the war. It feels good to cry, to go public with grief and take your place with all the vets of the truly outstandin' wars." I swayed, righted myself. "But the Memorial, the Unknown, the parades . . . basically they're bullshit." I started to wander around the room, realized that I had forgotten why I had stood and leaned against the wall.

"How you mean?" asked Witcover, who was nearly as drunk as I was.

"Man," I said, "it's a shuck! I mean ten goddamn years go by, and alla sudden there's this blast of media warmth and government-sponsored emotion. 'Welcome home, guys,' ever'body's sayin'. 'We're sorry we treated you so bad. Next time it's gonna be different. You wait and see.' " I went back to the table and braced myself on it with both hands, staring blearily at Witcover: his tan looked blotchy. "Hear that, man? 'Next time.' That's all it is. Nobody really gives a shit 'bout the vets. They're just pavin' the way for the next time."

"I don't know," said Witcover. "Seems to—"

"Right!" I spanked the table with the flat of my hand. "You don't know. You don't know shit 'bout it, so shut the fuck up!"

"Be cool," advised Fierman. "Man's entitled to his 'pinion."

I looked at him, saw a flushed, fat face with bloodshot eyes and a stupid reproving frown. "Fuck you," I said. "And fuck his 'pinion." I turned back to Witcover. "Whaddya think, man? That there's this genuine breath of conscience sweepin' the land? Open your goddamn eyes! You been to the movies lately? Jesus Christ! Courageous grunts strikin' fear into the heart of the Red Menace! Miraculous one-man missions to save our honor. Huh! Honor!" I took a long pull from the bottle. "Those movies, they make war seem like a mystical opportunity. Well, man, when I was here it wasn't quite that way, y'know. It was leeches, fungus, the shits. It was searchin' in the weeds for your buddy's arm. It was lookin' into the snaky eyes of some whore you were bangin' and feelin' weird shit crawl along your spine and expectin' her head to do a Linda Blair three-sixty spin." I slumped into a chair and leaned close to Witcover. "It was Mordor, man. Stephen King land. Horror. And now, now I look around at all these movies and monuments and crap, and it makes me wanna fuckin' puke to see what a noble hell it's turnin' out to be!"

I felt pleased with myself, having said this, and I leaned back, basking in a righteous glow. But Witcover was unimpressed. His face cinched into a scowl, and he said in a tight voice, "You're startin' to really piss me off, y'know."

"Yeah?" I said, and grinned. "How 'bout that?"

"Yeah, all you war-torn creeps, you think you got papers sayin' you can make an ass outta yourself and everybody else gotta say, 'Oh, you poor fucker! Give us more of your tortured wisdom!' "

Fierman muffled a laugh, and—rankled—I said, "That so?"

Witcover hunched his shoulders as if preparing for an off-tackle plunge. "I been listenin' to you guys for years, and you're alla goddamn same. You think you're owed something 'cause you got ground around in the political mill. Shit! I been in Salvador, Nicaragua, Afghanistan. Compared to those people, you didn't go through diddley. But you use what happened as an excuse for fuckin' up your lives . . . or for being assholes. Like you, man." He affected a macho-sounding bass voice. " 'I been in a war. I am an expert on reality.' You don't know how ridiculous you are."

"Am I?" I was shaking again, but with adrenaline not fear, and I knew I was going to hit Witcover. He didn't know it—he was smirking, his eyes flicking toward Fierman, seeking approval—and that in itself was a sufficient reason to hit him, purely for educational purposes: I had, you see, reached the level of drunkenness at which an amoral man such as myself understands his whimsies to be moral imperatives. But the real reason, the one that had begun to rumble inside me, was Stoner. All my fear, all my reactions thus far, had merely been tremors signaling an imminent explosion, and now, thinking about him nearby, old horrors were stirred up, and I saw myself walking in a napalmed ville rife with dead VC, crispy critters, and beside me this weird little guy named Fellowes who claimed he could read the future from their scorched remains and would point at a hexagramlike structure of charred bone and gristle and say, "That there means a bad moon on Wednesday," and claimed, too, that he could read the past from the blood of head wounds, and then I was leaning over this Canadian nurse, beautiful blond girl, disemboweled by a mine and somehow still alive, her organs dark and wet and pulsing, and somebody giggling, whispering about what he'd like to do, and then another scene that was whirled away so quickly, I could only make out the color of blood, and Witcover said something else, and a dead man was stretching out his hand to me and . . .

I nailed Witcover, and he flew sideways off the chair and rolled on the floor. I got to my feet, and Fierman grabbed me, trying to wrangle me away; but that was unnecessary, because all my craziness had been dissipated. "I'm okay now," I said, slurring the words, pushing him aside. He threw a looping punch that glanced off my neck, not even staggering me. Then Witcover yelled. He had pulled himself erect and was weaving toward me; an egg-shaped lump was swelling on his cheekbone. I laughed—he looked so puffed up with rage—and started for the door. As I went through it, he hit me on the back of the head. The blow stunned me a bit, but I was more amused than hurt; his fist had made a funny *bonk* sound on my skull, and that set me to laughing harder.

I stumbled between the houses, bouncing off walls, reeling out of control, and heard shouts . . . Vietnamese shouts. By the time I had regained my balance, I had reached the center of the village. The moon was almost full, pale yellow, its craters showing: a pitted eye in the black air. It kept shrinking and expanding, and—as it seemed to lurch farther off—I realized I had fallen and was lying flat on my back. More shouts. They sounded distant, a world away, and the moon had begun to spiral, to dwindle, like water being sucked down a drain. Jesus, I remember thinking just before I passed out, Jesus, how'd I get so drunk?

I'd forgotten Stoner's promise to tell me about the Land of Shades, but apparently he had not, for that night I had a dream in which I was Stoner. It was not that I thought I was him: I *was* him, prone to all his twitches, all his moods. I was walking in a pitch-dark void, possessed by a great hunger. Once this hunger might have been characterized as a yearning for the life I had lost, but it had been transformed into a lust for the life I might someday attain if I proved equal to the tests with which I was presented. That was all I knew of the Land of Shades—that it was a testing ground, less a place than a sequence of events. It was up to me to gain strength from the tests, to ease my hunger as best I could. I was ruled by this hunger, and it was my only wish to ease it.

Soon I spotted an island of brightness floating in the dark, and as

I drew near, the brightness resolved into an old French plantation house fronted by tamarinds and rubber trees; sections of white stucco wall and a verandah and a red tile roof were visible between the trunks. Patterns of soft radiance overlaid the grounds, yet there were neither stars nor moon nor any source of light I could discern. I was not alarmed by this—such discrepancies were typical of the Land of Shades.

When I reached the trees, I paused, steeling myself for whatever lay ahead. Breezes sprang up to stir the leaves, and a sizzling chorus of crickets faded in from nowhere as if a recording of sensory detail had been switched on. Alert to every shift of shadow, I moved cautiously through the trees and up the verandah steps. Broken roof tiles crunched beneath my feet. Beside the door stood a bottom-out cane chair; the rooms, however, were devoid of furnishings, the floors dusty, the whitewash flaking from the walls. The house appeared to be deserted, but I knew I was not alone. There was a hush in the air, the sort that arises from a secretive presence. Even had I failed to notice this, I could scarcely have missed the scent of perfume. I had never tested against a woman before, and, excited by the prospect, I was tempted to run through the house and ferret her out. But this would have been foolhardy, and I continued at a measured pace.

At the center of the house lay a courtyard, a rectangular space choked with waist-high growths of jungle plants, dominated by a stone fountain in the shape of a stylized orchid. The woman was leaning against the fountain, and despite the grayish-green half-light—a light that seemed to arise from the plants—I could see she was beautiful. Slim and honey-colored, with falls of black hair spilling over the shoulders of her *ao dai*. She did not move or speak, but the casualness of her pose was an invitation. I felt drawn to her, and as I pushed through the foliage, the fleshy leaves clung to my thighs and groin, touches that seemed designed to provoke arousal. I stopped an arm's length away and studied her. Her features were of a feline delicacy, and in the fullness of her lower lip, the petulant set of her mouth, I detected a trace of French breeding. She stared at me with palpable sexual interest. It had not occurred to me that the confrontation might take place on a sexual level, yet now I was certain this would be the case. I had to restrain myself from initiating the contact: there are rigorous formalities that must be observed prior to each test. And besides, I wanted to savor the experience.

"I am Tuyet," she said in a voice that seemed to combine the qualities of smoke and music.

"Stoner," I said.

The names hung in the air like the echoes of two gongs.

She lifted her hand as if to touch me, but lowered it: she, too, was practicing restraint. "I was a prostitute," she said. "My home was Lai Khe, but I was an outcast. I worked the water points along Highway Thirteen."

It was conceivable, I thought, that I may have known her. While I had been laid up in An Loc, I'd frequented those water points: bomb craters that had been turned into miniature lakes by the rains and served as filling stations for the water trucks attached to the First Infantry. Every morning the whores and their mama sans would drive out to the water points in three-wheeled motorcycle trucks; with them would be vendors selling combs and pushbutton knives and rubbers that came wrapped in gold foil, making them look like those disks of chocolate you can buy in the States. Most of these girls were more friendly than the city girls, and knowing that Tuyet had been one of them caused me to feel an affinity with her.

She went on to tell me that she had gone into the jungle with an American soldier and had been killed by a sniper. I told her my story in brief and then asked what she had learned of the Land of Shades. This is the most rigorous formality: I had never met anyone with whom I had failed to exchange information.

"Once," Tuyet said, "I met an old man, a Cao Dai medium from Black Virgin Mountain, who told me he had been to a place where a pillar of whirling light and dust joined earth to sky. Voices spoke from the pillar, sometimes many at once, and from them he understood that all wars are merely reflections of a deeper struggle, of a demon breaking free. The demon freed by our war, he said, was very strong, very dangerous. We the dead had been recruited to wage war against him."

I had been told a similar story by an NLF captain, and once, while crawling through a tunnel system, I myself had heard voices speaking from a skull half buried in the earth. But I had been too frightened to stay and listen. I related all this to Tuyet, and her response was to trail her fingers across my arm. My restraint, too, had frayed. I dragged her down into the thick foliage. It was as if we had been submerged in a sea of green light and fleshy stalks, as if the plantation house had vanished and we were adrift in an infinite vegetable depth where gravity had been replaced by some buoyant principle. I tore at her clothes, she at mine. Her *ao dai* shredded like crepe, and my fatigues came away in ribbons that dangled from her hooked fingers. Greedy for her, I pressed my mouth to her breasts. Her nipples looked black in contrast to her skin, and it seemed I could taste their blackness, tart and sour. Our breathing was hoarse, urgent, and the only other sound was the soft mulching of the leaves. With surprising strength, she pushed me onto my back and straddled my hips, guiding me inside her, sinking down until her buttocks were grinding against my thighs.

Her head flung back, she lifted and lowered herself. The leaves and stalks churned and intertwined around us as if they, too, were copulating. For a few moments my hunger was assuaged, but soon I noticed that the harder I thrust, the more fiercely she plunged, the less intense the sensations became. Though she gripped me tightly, the friction seemed to have been reduced. Frustrated, I dug my fingers into her plump hips and battered at her, trying to drive myself deeper. Then I squeezed one of her breasts and felt a searing pain in my palm. I snatched back my hand and saw that her nipple, both nipples, were twisting, elongating; I realized that they had been transformed into the heads of two black centipedes, and the artful movements of her internal muscles . . . they were too artful, too disconnectedly in motion. An instant later I felt that same searing pain in my cock and knew I was screwing myself into a nest of creatures like those protruding from her breasts. All her skin was rippling, reflecting the humping of thousands of centipedes beneath.

The pain was enormous, so much so that I thought my entire body must be glowing with it. But I did not dare fail this test, and I continued pumping into her, thrusting harder than ever. The leaves thrashed, the stalks thrashed as in a gale, and the green light grew livid. Tuyet began to scream—God knows what manner of pain I was causing her—and her screams completed a perverse circuit within me. I found I could channel my own pain into those shrill sounds. Still joined to her, I rolled atop her, clamped her wrists together and pinned them above her head. Her screams rang louder, inspiring me to greater efforts yet. Despite the centipedes tipping her breasts, or perhaps because of them, because of the grotesque juxtaposition of the sensual and the horrid, her beauty seemed to have been enhanced, and my mastery over her actually provided me a modicum of pleasure.

The light began to whiten, and looking off, I saw that we were being borne by an invisible current through—as I had imagined—an infinite depth of stalks and leaves. The stalks that lashed around us thickened far below into huge pale trunks with circular ribbing. I could not make out where they met the earth—if, indeed, they did—and they appeared to rise an equal height above. The light brightened further, casting the distant stalks in silhouette, and I realized we were drifting toward the source of the whiteness, beyond which would lie another test, another confrontation. I glanced at Tuyet. Her skin no longer displayed that obscene rippling, her nipples had reverted to normal. Pain was evolving into pleasure, but I knew it would be short-lived, and I tried to resist the current, to hold onto pain, because even pain was preferable to the hunger I would soon experience. Tuyet clawed my back, and I felt the first dissolute rush of my orgasm. The current was irresistible. It flowed through my blood, my cells. It was part of me, or rather I was part of it. I let it move me, bringing me to completion.

Gradually the whipping of the stalks subsided to a pliant swaying motion. They parted for us, and we drifted through their interstices as serenely as a barge carved to resemble a coupling of two naked figures. I found I could not disengage from Tuyet, that the current enforced our union, and resigned to this, I gazed around, marveling at the vastness of this vegetable labyrinth and the strangeness of our fates. Beams of white light shined through the stalks, the brightness growing so profound that I thought I heard in it a roaring; and as my consciousness frayed, I saw myself reflected in Tuyet's eyes—a ragged dark creature wholly unlike my own self-image—and wondered for the thousandth time who had placed us in this world, who had placed these worlds in us.

Other dreams followed, but they were ordinary, the dreams of an ordinarily anxious, ordinarily drunken man, and it was the memory of this first dream that dominated my waking moments. I didn't want to wake because—along with a headache and other symptoms of hangover—I felt incredibly weak, incapable of standing and facing the world. Muzzy-headed, I ignored the reddish light prying under my eyelids and tried to remember more of the dream. Despite Stoner's attempts to appear streetwise, despite the changes I had observed in him, he had been at heart an innocent and it was difficult to accept that the oddly formal, brutally sexual protagonist of the dream had been in any way akin to him. Maybe, I thought, recalling Tuu's theory of ghosts, maybe that was the quality that had died in Stoner: his innocence. I began once again to suffer guilt feelings over my hatred of him, and, preferring a hangover to that, I propped myself on one elbow and opened my eyes.

I doubt more than a second or two passed before I sprang to my feet, hangover forgotten, electrified with fear; but in that brief span the reason for my weakness was made plain. Stoner was sitting close to where I had been lying, his hand outstretched to touch me, head down . . . exactly as he had sat the previous day. Aside from his pose, however, very little about him was the same.

The scene was of such complexity that now, thinking back on it, it strikes me as implausible that I could have noticed its every detail; yet I suppose that its power was equal to its complexity and thus I did not so much see it as it was imprinted on my eyes. Dawn was a crimson smear fanning across the lower sky, and the palms stood out blackly against it, their fronds twitching in the breeze like spiders impaled on pins. The ruddy light gave the rutted dirt of the street the look of a trough full of congealed blood. Stoner was motionless —that is to say, he didn't move his limbs, his head, or shift his position; but his image was pulsing, swelling to half again its normal size and then deflating, all with the rhythm of steady breathing. As he expanded, the cold white fire blazing from his eyes would spread in cracks that veined his entire form; as he contracted, the cracks would disappear and for a moment he would be—except for his eyes—the familiar figure I had known. It seemed that his outward appearance—his fatigues and helmet, his skin—was a shell from which some glowing inner man was attempting to break free. Grains of dust were whirling up from the ground beside him, more and more all the time: a miniature cyclone wherein he sat calm and ultimately distracted, the likeness of a warrior monk whose meditations had borne fruit.

Shouts behind me. I turned and saw Fierman, Tuu, Witcover, and various of the gooks standing at the edge of the village. Tuu beckoned to me, and I wanted to comply, to run, but I wasn't sure I had the strength. And, too, I didn't think Stoner would let me. His power surged around me, a cold windy voltage that whipped my clothes and set static charges crackling in my hair. "Turn it off!" I shouted, pointing at the tin-roofed building. They shook their heads, shouting in return. ". . . can't," I heard, and something about ". . . feedback."

Then Stoner spoke. "Puleo," he said. His voice wasn't loud but it was all-encompassing. I seemed to be inside it, balanced on a tongue of red dirt, within a throat of sky and jungle and yellow stone. I turned back to him. Looked into his eyes . . . fell into them, into a world of cold brilliance where a thousand fiery forms were materialized and dispersed every second, forms both of such beauty and hideousness that their effect on me, their beholder, was identical, a confusion of terror and exaltation. Whatever they were, the forms of Stoner's spirit, his potentials, or even of his thoughts, they were in their momentary life more vital and consequential than I could ever hope to be. Compelled by them, I walked over to him. I must have been afraid—I could feel wetness on my thighs and realized that my bladder had emptied—but he so dominated me that I knew only the need to obey. He did not stand, yet with each expansion his image would loom up before my eyes and I would stare into that dead face seamed by rivulets of molten diamond, its expression losing coherence, features splitting apart. Then he would shrink, leaving me gazing dumbly down at the top of his helmet. Dust stung my eyelids, my cheeks.

"What . . ." I began, intending to ask what he wanted; but before I could finish, he seized my wrist. Ice flowed up my arm, shocking my heart, and I heard myself . . . not screaming. No, this was the sound life makes leaving the body, like the squealing of gas released from a balloon that's half pinched shut.

Within seconds, drained of strength, I slumped to the ground, my vision reduced to a darkening fog. If he had maintained his hold much longer, I'm sure I would have died . . . and I was resigned to the idea. I had no weapon with which to fight him. But then I realized that the cold had receded from my limbs. Dazed, I looked around, and when I spotted him, I tried to stand, to run. Neither my arms nor legs would support me, and—desperate—I flopped on the red dirt, trying to crawl to safety; but after that initial burst of panic, the gland that governed my reactions must have overloaded, because I stopped crawling, rolled onto my back and stayed put, feeling stunned, weak, transfixed by what I saw. Yet not in the least afraid.

Stoner's inner man, now twice human-size, had broken free and was standing at the center of the village, some twenty feet off: a bipedal silhouette through which it seemed you could look forever into a dimension of fire and crystal, like a hole burned in the fabric of the world. His movements were slow, tentative, as if he hadn't quite adapted to his new form, and penetrating him, arcing through the air from the tin-roofed building, their substance flowing toward him, were what appeared to be thousands of translucent wires, the structures of the fields. As I watched, they began to glow with Stoner's blue-white-diamond color, their substance to reverse its flow and pour back toward the building, and to emit a bass hum. Dents popped in the tin roof, the walls bulged inward, and with a grinding noise, a narrow fissure forked open in the earth beside it. The glowing wires grew brighter and brighter, and the building started to crumple, never collapsing, but—as if giant hands were pushing at it from every direction—compacting with terrible slowness until it had been squashed to perhaps a quarter of its original height. The hum died away. A fire broke out in the wreckage, pale flames leaping high and winnowing into black smoke.

Somebody clutched my shoulder, hands hauled me to my feet. It was Tuu and one of his soldiers. Their faces were knitted by lines of concern, and that concern rekindled my fear. I clawed at them, full of gratitude, and let them hustle me away. We took our places among the other observers, the smoking building at our backs, all gazing at the yellow houses and the burning giant in their midst.

The air around Stoner had become murky, turbulent, and this turbulence spread to obscure the center of the village. He stood unmoving, while small dust devils kicked up at his heels and went zipping about like a god's zany pets. One of the houses caved in with a *whump*, and pieces of yellow concrete began to lift from the ruins, to float toward Stoner; drawing near him, they acquired some of his brightness, glowing in their own right, and then vanished into the turbulence. Another house imploded, and the same process was initiated. The fact that all this was happening in dead silence—except for the caving in of the houses—made it seem even more eerie and menacing than if there had been sound.

The turbulence eddied faster and faster, thickening, and at last a strange vista faded in from the dark air, taking its place the way the picture melts up from the screen of an old television set. Four or five minutes must have passed before it became completely clear, and then it seemed sharper and more in focus than did the jungle and the houses, more even than the blazing figure who had summoned it: an acre-sized patch of hell or heaven or something in between, shining through the dilapidated structures and shabby colors of the ordinary, paling them. Beyond Stoner lay a vast forested plain dotted with fires . . . or maybe they weren't fires but some less chaotic form of energy, for though they gave off smoke, the flames maintained rigorous, stylized shapes, showing like red fountains and poinsettias and other shapes yet against the poisonous green of the trees. Smoke hung like a gray pall over the plain, and now and again beams of radiance—all so complexly figured, they appeared to be pillars of crystal—would shoot up from the forest into the grayness and resolve into a burst of light; and at the far limit of the plain, beyond a string of ragged hills, the dark sky would intermittently flash reddish orange as if great batteries of artillery were homing in upon some target there.

I had thought that Stoner would set forth at once into this other world, but instead he backed a step away and I felt despair for him, fear that he wouldn't seize his opportunity to escape. It may seem odd that I still thought of him as Stoner, and it may be that prior to that moment I had forgotten his human past; but now, sensing his trepidation, I understood that what enlivened this awesome figure was some scrap of soul belonging to the man-child I once had known. Silently, I urged him on. Yet he continued to hesitate.

It wasn't until someone tried to pull me back that I realized I was moving toward Stoner. I shook off whomever it was, walked to the edge of the village and called Stoner's name. I didn't really expect him to acknowledge me, and I'm not clear as to what my motivations were: maybe it was just that since I had come this far with him, I didn't want my efforts wasted. But I think it was something more, some old loyalty resurrected, one I had denied while he was alive.

"Get outta here!" I shouted. "Go on! Get out!"

He turned that blind, fiery face toward me, and despite its featurelessness, I could read therein the record of his solitude, his fears concerning its resolution. It was, I knew, a final sending. I sensed again his emptiness, but it wasn't so harrowing and hopeless as before; in it there was a measure of determination, of purpose, and, too, a kind of . . . I'm tempted to say gratitude, but in truth it was more a simple acknowledgment, like the wave of a hand given by one workman to another after the completion of a difficult task.

"Go." I said it softly, the way you'd speak when urging a child to take his first step, and Stoner walked away.

For a few moments, though his legs moved, he didn't appear to be making any headway; his figure remained undiminished by distance. There was a tension in the air, an almost impalpable disturbance that quickly evolved into a heated pulse. One of the banana trees burst into flames, its leaves shriveling; a second tree ignited, a third, and soon all those trees close to the demarcation of that other world were burning like green ceremonial candles. The heat intensified, and the veils of dust that blew toward me carried a stinging residue of that heat; the sky for hundreds of feet above rippled as with the effects of an immense conflagration.

I stumbled back, tripped and fell heavily. When I recovered I saw that Stoner was receding, that the world into which he was traveling was receding with him, or rather seeming to fold, to bisect and collapse around him: it looked as if that plain dotted with fires were painted on a curtain, and as he pushed forward, the fabric was drawn with him, its painted distances becoming foreshortened, its perspectives exaggerated and surreal, molding into a tunnel that conformed to his shape. His figure shrank to half its previous size, and then—some limit reached, some barrier penetrated—the heat died away, its dissipation accompanied by a seething hiss, and Stoner's white fire began to shine brighter and brighter, his form eroding in brightness. I had to shield my eyes, then shut them; but even so, I could see the soundless explosion that followed through my lids, and for several minutes I could make out its vague afterimage. A blast of wind pressed me flat, hot at first, but blowing colder and colder, setting my teeth to chattering. At last this subsided, and on opening my eyes, I found that Stoner had vanished, and where the plain had been now lay a wreckage of yellow stone and seared banana trees, ringed by a few undamaged houses on the perimeter.

The only sound was the crackle of flames from the tinroofed building. Moments later, however, I heard a patter of applause. I looked behind me: the gooks were all applauding Tuu, who was smiling and bowing like the author of a successful play. I was shocked at their reaction. How could they be concerned with accolades? Hadn't they been dazzled, as I had, their humanity diminished by the mystery and power of Stoner's metamorphosis? I went over to them, and drawing near, I overheard an officer congratulate Tuu on "another triumph." It took me a while to register the significance of those words, and when I did I pushed through the group and confronted Tuu.

" 'Another triumph'?" I said.

He met my eyes, imperturbable. "I wasn't aware you spoke our language, Mr. Puleo."

"You've done this before," I said, getting angry. "Haven't you?"

"Twice before." He tapped a cigarette from a pack of Marlboros; an officer rushed to light it. "But never with an American spirit."

"You coulda killed me!" I shouted, lunging for him. Two soldiers came between us, menacing me with their rifles.

Tuu blew out a plume of smoke that seemed to give visible evidence of his self-satisfaction. "I told you it was a risk," he said. "Does it matter that I knew the extent of the risk and you did not? You were in no greater danger because of that. We were prepared to take steps if the situation warranted."

"Don't bullshit me! You couldn't have done nothin' with Stoner!"

He let a smile nick the corners of his mouth.

"You had no right," I said. "You—"

Tuu's face hardened. "We had no right to mislead you? Please, Mr. Puleo. Between our peoples, deception is a tradition."

I fumed, wanting to get at him. Frustrated, I slugged my thigh with my fist, spun on my heel and walked off. The two soldiers caught up with me and blocked my path. Furious, I swatted at their rifles; they disengaged their safeties and aimed at my stomach.

"If you wish to be alone," Tuu called, "I have no objection to you taking a walk. We have tests to complete. But please keep to the road. A car will come for you."

Before the soldiers could step aside, I pushed past them.

"Keep to the road, Mr. Puleo!" In Tuu's voice was more than a touch of amusement. "If you recall, we're quite adept at tracking."

Anger was good for me; it kept my mind off what I had seen. I wasn't ready to deal with Stoner's evolution. I wanted to consider things in simple terms: a man I had hated had died to the world a second time and I had played a part in his release, a part in which I had no reason to take pride or bear shame, because I had been manipulated every step of the way. I was so full of anger, I must have done the first mile in under fifteen minutes, the next in not much more. By then the sun had risen above the treeline and I had worked up a sweat. Insects buzzed; monkeys screamed. I slowed my pace and turned my head from side to side as I went, as if I were walking point again. I had the idea my own ghost was walking with me, shifting around inside and burning to get out on its own.

After an hour or so I came to the temporary housing that had been erected for the populace of Cam Le: thatched huts; scrawny dogs slinking and chickens pecking; orange peels, palm litter, and piles of shit in the streets. Some old men smoking pipes by a cookfire blinked at me. Three girls carrying plastic jugs giggled, ran off behind a hut and peeked back around the corner.

Vietnam.

I thought about the way I'd used to sneer the word. 'Nam, I'd say. Viet-fucking-nam! Now it was spoken proudly, printed in Twentieth Century-Fox monolithic capitals, brazen with hype. Perhaps between those two extremes was a mode of expression that captured the ordinary reality of the place, the poverty and peacefulness of this village; but if so, it wasn't accessible to me.

Some of the villagers were coming out of their doors to have a look at the stranger. I wondered if any of them recognized me. Maybe, I thought, chuckling madly, maybe if I bashed a couple on the head and screamed "Number Ten VC!" maybe then they'd remember.

I suddenly felt tired and empty, and I sat down by the road to wait. I was so distracted, I didn't notice at first that a number of flies had mistaken me for a new and bigger piece of shit and were orbiting me, crawling over my knuckles. I flicked them away, watched them spiral off and land on other parts of my body. I got into controlling their patterns of flight, seeing if I could make them all congregate on my left hand, which I kept still. Weird shudders began passing through my chest, and the vacuum inside my head filled with memories of Stoner, his bizarre dream, his terrible Valhalla. I tried to banish them, but they stuck there, replaying themselves over and over. I couldn't order them, couldn't derive any satisfaction from them. Like the passage of a comet, Stoner's escape from Cam Le had been a trivial cosmic event, causing momentary awe and providing a few more worthless clues to the nature of the absolute, but offering no human solutions. Nothing consequential had changed for me: I was as fucked up as ever, as hard-core disoriented. The buzzing sunlight grew hotter and hotter; the flies' dance quickened in the rippling air.

At long last a dusty car with a gook corporal at the wheel pulled up beside me. Fierman and Witcover were in back, and Witcover's eye was discolored, swollen shut. I went around to the passenger side, opened the front door and heard behind me a spit-filled, explosive sound. Turning, I saw that a kid of about eight or nine had jumped out of hiding to ambush me. He had a dirt-smeared belly that popped from the waist of his ragged shorts, and he was aiming a toy rifle made of sticks. He shot me again, jiggling the gun to simulate automatic fire. Little monster with slit black eyes. Staring daggers at me, thinking I'd killed his daddy. He probably would have loved it if I had keeled over, clutching my chest; but I wasn't in the mood. I pointed my finger, cocked the thumb and shot him down like a dog.

He stared meanly and fired a third time: this was serious business, and he wanted me to die. "Row-nal Ray-gun," he said, and pretended to spit.

I just laughed and climbed into the car. The gook corporal engaged the gears and we sped off into a boil of dust and light, as if—like Stoner—we were passing through a metaphysical barrier between worlds. My head bounced against the back of the seat, and with each impact I felt that my thoughts were clearing, that a poisonous sediment was being jolted loose and flushed from my bloodstream. Thick silence welled from the rear of the car, and not wanting to ride with hostiles all the way to Saigon, I turned to Witcover and apologized for having hit him. Pressure had done it to me, I told him. That, and bad memories of a bad time. His features tightened into a sour knot and he looked out the window, wholly unforgiving. But I refused to allow his response to disturb me—let him have his petty hate, his grudge, for whatever good it would do him—and I turned away to face the violent green sweep of the jungle, the great troubled rush of the world ahead, with a heart that seemed lighter by an ounce of anger, by one bitterness removed. To the end of that passion, at least, I had become reconciled.

# KAREN JOY FOWLER

## The Faithful Companion at Forty

Karen Joy Fowler published her first story in 1985, and quickly established an impressive reputation, becoming a frequent contributor to *Isaac Asimov's Science Fiction Magazine*, and *The Magazine of Fantasy and Science Fiction*, among other markets. In 1987, she won the John W. Campbell Award as the year's best new writer; 1986 also saw the appearance of her first book, the collection *Artificial Things,* which was released to an enthusiastic response and impressive reviews. She is currently at work on her first novel. Fowler lives in Davis, California, has two children, did her graduate work in North Asian politics, and occasionally teaches ballet. Her story "The Lake Was Full of Artificial Things" was in our Third Annual Collection; her story "The Gate of Ghosts" was in our Fourth Annual Collection.

Here she gives us a surreal and very funny look *beyond* those thrilling days of yesteryear.

# THE FAITHFUL COMPANION AT FORTY

## Karen Joy Fowler

His first reaction is that I just can't deal with the larger theoretical issues. He's got this new insight he wants to call the Displacement Theory and I can't grasp it. Your basic, quiet, practical minority sidekick. The *limited* edition. Kato. Spock. Me. But this is not true.

I still remember the two general theories we were taught on the reservation which purported to explain the movement of history. The first we named the Great Man Theory. Its thesis was that the critical decisions in human development were made by individuals, special people gifted in personality and circumstance. The second we named the Wave Theory. It argued that only the masses could effectively determine the course of history. Those very visible individuals who appeared as leaders of the great movements were, in fact, only those who happened to articulate the direction which had already been chosen. They were as much the victims of the process as any other single individual. Flotsam. Running Dog and I used to be able to debate this issue for hours.

It is true that this particular question has ceased to interest me much. But a correlative question has come to interest me more. I spent most of my fortieth birthday sitting by myself, listening to Pachelbel's *Canon*, over and over, and I'm asking myself: Are some people special? Are some people more special than others? *Have I spent my whole life backing the wrong horse?*

I mean, it was my birthday and not one damn person called.

Finally, about four o'clock in the afternoon, I gave up and I called him. "Eh, Poncho," I say. "What's happening?"

"Eh, Cisco," he answers. "Happy Birthday."

"Thanks," I tell him. I can't decide whether I am more pissed to know he remembered but didn't call than I was when I thought he forgot.

"The big four-o," he says. "Wait a second, buddy. Let me go turn the music down." He's got the *William Tell Overture* blasting on the stereo. He's always got the *William Tell Overture* blasting on the stereo. I'm not saying the man has a problem, but the last time we were in Safeway together he claimed to see a woman being kidnapped by a silver baron over in frozen foods. He pulled the flip top off a Tab and lobbed the can into the ice cream. "Cover me," he shouts, and runs an end pattern with the cart through the soups. I had to tell everyone he was having a Vietnam flashback.

And the mask. There are times and seasons when a mask is useful; I'm the first to admit that. It's Thanksgiving, say, and you're an Indian so it's never been one of your favorite holidays, and you've got no family because you spent your youth playing the supporting role to some macho creep who couldn't commit, so here you are, *standing in line*, to see "Rocky IV" and someone you know walks by. I mean, I've been there. But for everyday, for your ordinary life, a mask is only going to make you *more* obvious. There's an element of exhibitionism in it. A large element. If you ask me.

So now he's back on the phone. He sighs. "God," he says. "I miss those thrilling days of yesteryear."

See? We haven't talked twenty seconds and already the subject is *his* problems. *His* ennui. *His* angst. "I'm having an affair," I tell him. Two years ago I wouldn't have said it. Two years ago he'd just completed his EST training and he would have told me to take responsibility for it. Now he's into biofeedback and astrology. Now we're not responsible for anything.

"Yeah?" he says. He thinks for a minute. "You're not married," he points out.

I can't see that this is relevant. "She is," I tell him.

"Yeah?" he says again, only this "yeah" has a nasty quality to it; this "yeah" tells me someone is hoping for sensationalistic details. This is not the "yeah" of a concerned friend. Still, I can't help playing to it. For years I've been holding this man's horse while he leaps onto its back from the roof. For years I've been providing cover from behind a rock while he breaks for the back door. I'm forty now. It's time to get something back from him. So I hint at the use of controlled substances. We're talking peyote *and* cocaine. I mention pornography. Illegally imported. From Denmark. Of course, it's not really *my* affair. Can you picture me? My affair is quiet and ardent. I borrowed this affair from another friend. It shows you the lengths I have to go to before anyone will listen to me.

I may finally have gone too far. He's really at a loss now. "Women," he says finally. "You can't live with them and you can't live without them." Which is a joke, coming from him. He had that single-man-raising-his-orphaned-nephew-all-alone schtick working so smoothly the women were passing each other on the way in and out the door. Or maybe it was the mask and the leather. What do women want? Who has a clue?

"Is that it?" I ask him. "The sum total of your advice? She won't leave her husband. Man, my *heart* is broken."

"Oh," he says. There's a long pause. "Don't let it show," he suggests. Then he sighs. Again. "I miss that old white horse," he tells me. And you know what I do? I hang up on him. And you know what he *doesn't* do? He doesn't call me back.

It really hurts me.

So his second reaction, now that I don't want to listen to him explaining his new theories to me, is to say that I seem to be sulking about something, he can't imagine what. And this is harder to deny.

The day after my birthday I went for a drive in my car, a little white Saab with personalized license plates. KEMO, they say. Maybe the phone is ringing, maybe it's not. I feel better when I don't know. So, he misses his horse. Hey, *I've* never been the same since that little pinto of mine joined the Big Round-up, but I try not to burden my friends with this. I try not to burden my friends with *anything*. I just nurse them back to health when the Cavendish gang leaves them for dead. I just come in the middle of the night with the medicine man when little Britt has a fever and it's not responding to Tylenol. I just organize the surprise party when a friend turns forty.

You want to bet even *Attila the Hun* had a party on his fortieth? You want to bet he was one hard man to surprise? And who blew up the balloons and had everyone hiding under the rugs and in with the goats? This name is lost forever.

I drove out into the country, where every cactus holds its memory for me, where every outcropping of rock once hid an outlaw. Ten years ago the terrain was still so rough I would have had to take the International Scout. Now it's a paved highway straight to the hanging tree. I pulled over to the shoulder of the road, turned off the motor, and I just sat there. I was remembering the time Ms. Emily Cooper stumbled into the Wilcox bank robbery looking for her little girl who'd gone with friends to the swimming hole and hadn't bothered to tell her mama. We were on our way to see Colonel Davis at Fort Comanche about some cattle rustling. We hadn't heard about the bank robbery. Which is why we were taken completely by surprise.

My pony and I were eating the masked man's dust, as usual, when something hit me from behind. Arnold Wilcox, a heavy-set man who sported a five o'clock shadow by eight in the morning, jumped me from the big rock overlooking the Butterfield trail and I went down like a sack of potatoes. I heard horses converging on us from the left and the right and that hypertrophic white stallion of his took off like a big bird. I laid one on Arnold's stubbly jaw, but he cold-cocked me with the butt of his pistol and I couldn't tell you what happened next.

I don't come to until it's after dark and I'm trussed up like a turkey. Ms. Cooper is next to me and her hands are tied behind her back with a red bandanna and there's a rope around her feet. She looks disheveled, but pretty; her eyes are wide and I can tell she's not too pleased to be lying here next to an Indian. Her dress is buttoned up to the chin so I'm thinking at least, thank God, they've respected her. It's cold, even as close together as we are. The Wilcoxes are all huddled around the fire, counting money, and the smoke is a straight white line in the sky you could see for miles. So this is more good news, and I'm thinking the Wilcoxes were always a bunch of dumb-ass honkies when it came to your basic woodlore. I'm wondering how they got it together to pull off a bank job, when I hear horse's hooves and my question is answered. Pierre Cardeaux, Canadian French, hops off the horse's back and goes straight to the fire and stamps it out.

"Imbeciles!" he tells them, only he's got this heavy accent so it comes out "Eembeeceeles."

Which insults the Wilcoxes a little. "Hold on there, hombre," Andrew Wilcox says. "Jess because we followed your plan into the bank and your trail for the getaway doesn't make you the boss here," and Pierre pays him about as much notice as you do an ant your horse is about to step on. He comes over to us and puts his hand under Ms. Cooper's chin, sort of thoughtfully. She spits at him and he laughs.

"Spunk," he says. "I like that." I mean, I suppose that's what he says, because that's what they always say, but the truth is, with his accent, I don't understand a word.

Andrew Wilcox isn't finished yet. He's got this big chicken leg which he's eating and it's dribbling onto his chin, so he wipes his arm over his face. Which just spreads the grease around more, really, and anyway, he's got this hunk of chicken stuck between his front teeth, so Pierre can hardly keep a straight face when he talks to him. "I understand why we're keeping the woman," Andrew says. "Cause she has—uses. But the Injun there. He's just going to be baggage. I want to waste him."

"*Mon ami*," says Pierre. "Even *pour vous*, thees stupiditee lives me spitchless." He's kissing his fingers to illustrate the point as if he were really French and not just Canadian French and has probably never drunk really good wine in his life. I'm lying in the dust and whatever they've bound my wrists with is cutting off the circulation so my hands feel like someone is jabbing them with porcupine needles. Even now, I can remember smelling the smoke which wasn't there any more and the Wilcoxes who were and the lavender eau de toilette that Ms. Cooper used. And horses and dust and sweat. These were the glory days, but *whose* glory you may well ask, and even if I answered, what difference would it make?

Ms. Cooper gets a good whiff of Andrew Wilcox and it makes her cough.

"He's right, little brother," says Russell Wilcox, the runt of the litter at about three hundred odd pounds and a little quicker on the uptake than the rest of the family. "You ever heared tell of a man who rides a white horse, wears a black mask, and shoots a very pricey kind of bullet? This here Injun is his compadre."

"*Oui, oui, oui, oui*," says Pierre agreeably. The little piggie. He indicates me and raises his eyebrows one at a time. "*Avec le sauvage* we can, how you say? Meck a deal."

"*Votre mere*," I tell him. He gives me a good kick in the ribs and he's wearing those pointy-toed kind of cowboy boots, so I feel it all right. Finally I hear the sound I've been waiting for, a hoot-owl over in the trees behind Ms. Cooper, and then *he* rides up. He hasn't even gotten his gun out yet. "Don't move," he tells Pierre. "Or I'll be forced to draw," but he hasn't finished the sentence when Russell Wilcox has his arm around my neck and the point of his knife jabbing into my back.

"We give you the Injun," he says. "Or we give you the girl. You ain't taking both. You comprendez, pardner?"

Now, if he'd *asked* me, I'd have said, hey, don't worry about *me*, rescue the woman. And if he'd hesitated, I would have insisted. But he didn't ask and he didn't hesitate. He just hoisted Ms. Cooper up onto the saddle in front of him and pulled the bottom of her skirt down so her legs didn't show. "There's a little girl in Springfield who's going to be mighty happy to see you, Ms. Cooper," I hear him saying, and I've got a suspicion from the look on her face that they're not going straight to Springfield anyway. And that's it. Not one word for me.

Of course, he comes back, but by this time the Wilcoxes and Pierre have fallen asleep around the cold campfire and I've had to inch my way through the dust on my side like a snake over to Russell Wilcox's knife, which fell out of his hand when he nodded off, whittling. I've had to cut my own bonds, and my hands are behind me so I carve up my thumb a little, too. The whole time I'm right there beneath Russell and he's snorting and snuffling and shifting around like he's waking up so my heart nearly stops. It's a wonder my hands don't have to be amputated, they've been without blood for so long. And then there's a big shoot-out and I provide a lot of cover. A couple of days pass before I feel like talking to him about it.

"You rescued Ms. Cooper first," I remind him. "And that was the right thing to do; I'm not saying it wasn't; don't misunderstand me. But it seemed to me that you made up your mind kind of quickly. It didn't seem like a hard decision."

He reaches across the saddle and puts a hand on my hand. Behind the black mask, the blue eyes are sensitive and caring. "Of course I wanted to rescue you, old friend," he says. "If I'd made the decision based solely on my own desires, that's what I would have done. But it seemed to me I had a higher responsibility to the more innocent party. It was a hard choice. It may have felt quick to you, but, believe me, I struggled with it." He withdraws his hand and kicks his horse a little ahead of us because the trail is narrowing. I duck under the branch of a Prairie Spruce. "Besides," he says, back over his shoulder. "I couldn't leave a woman with a bunch of animals like Pierre Cardeaux and the Wilcoxes. A pretty woman like that. Alone. Defenseless."

I start to tell him what a bunch of racists like Pierre Cardeaux and the Wilcoxes might do to a lonely and defenseless Indian. Arnold Wilcox wanted my scalp. "*I* remember the Alamo," he kept saying and maybe he meant Little Big Horn; I didn't feel like exploring this. Pierre kept assuring him there would be plenty of time for "trophies" later. And Andrew trotted out that old chestnut about the only good Indian being a dead Indian. None of which was pleasant to lie there listening to. But I never said it. Because by then the gap between us was so great I would have had to shout, and anyway the ethnic issue has always made us both a little touchy. I wish I had a nickel for every time I've heard him say that some of his best friends are Indians. And I know that there are bad Indians; I don't deny it and I don't mind fighting them. I just always thought I should get to decide which ones were the bad ones.

I sat in that car until sunset.

But the next day he calls. "Have you ever noticed how close the holy word 'om' is to our Western word 'home'?" he asks. That's his opening. No hi, how are you? He never asks how I am. If he did, I'd tell him I was fine, just the way you're supposed to. I wouldn't burden him with my problems. I'd just like to be asked, you know?

But he's got a point to make and it has something to do with Dorothy in the *Wizard of Oz*. How she clicks her heels together and says, over and over like a mantra, "There's no place like home, there's no place like home," and she's actually able to travel through space. "Not in the book," I tell him.

"I *know*," he says. "In the movie."

"I thought it was the shoes," I say.

And his voice lowers; he's that excited. "What if it was the *words*?" he asks. "I've got a mantra."

Of course, I'm aware of this. It always used to bug me that he wouldn't tell me what it was. Your mantra, he says, loses its power if it's spoken aloud. So by now I'm beginning to guess what his mantra might be. "A bunch of people I know," I tell him, "all had the same guru. And one day they decided to share the mantras he'd given them. They each wrote their mantra on a piece of paper and passed it around. And you know what? They all had the *same* mantra. So much for personalization."

"They lacked faith," he points out.

"Rightfully so."

"I gotta go," he tells me. We're reaching the crescendo in the background music and it cuts off with a click. Silence. He doesn't say goodbye. I refuse to call him back.

The truth is, I'm tired of always being there for him.

So I don't hear from him again until this morning when he calls with the great Displacement Theory. By now I've been forty almost ten days, if you believe the birth certificate the reservation drew up; I find a lot of inaccuracies surfaced when they translated moons into months. So that I've never been too sure what my rising sign is. Not that it matters to me, but it's important to him all of a sudden; apparently you can't analyze personality effectively without it. He thinks I'm a Pisces rising; he'd love to be proved right.

"We can go *back*, old buddy," he says. "I've found the way back."

"Why would we want to?" I ask. The sun is shining and it's cold out. I was thinking of going for a run.

Does he hear me? About like always. "I figured it out," he says. "It's a combination of biofeedback *and* the mantra 'home.' I've been working and working on it. I could always leave, you know, that was never the problem, but I could never *arrive*. Something outside me stopped me and forced me back." He pauses here and I think I'm supposed to say something, but I'm too pissed. He goes on. "Am I getting too theoretical for you? Because I'm about to get more so. Try to stay with me. The key word is *displacement*." He says this like he's shivering. "I couldn't get back because there was no room for me there. The only way back is through an exchange. Someone else has to come forward."

He pauses again and this pause goes on and on. Finally I grunt. A redskin sound. Noncommittal.

His voice is severe. "This is too important for you to miss just because you're sulking about god knows what, pilgrim," he says. "This is travel through space *and* time."

"This is baloney," I tell him. I'm uncharacteristically blunt, blunter than I ever was during the primal-scream-return-to-the-womb period. If nobody's listening, what does it matter?

"Displacement," he repeats and his voice is all still and important. "Ask yourself, buddy, *what happened to the buffalo?*"

I don't believe I've heard him correctly. "Say *what?*"

"Return with me," he says and then he's gone for good and this time he hasn't hung up the phone; this time I can still hear the *William Tell Overture* repeating the hoofbeat part. There's a noise out front so I go to the door, and damned if I don't have a buffalo, shuffling around on my ornamental strawberries, looking surprised. "You call this grass?" it asks me. It looks up and down the street, more and more alarmed. "Where's the plains, man? Where's the railroad?"

So I'm happy for him. Really I am.

But I'm not going with him. Let him roam it alone this time. He'll be fine. Like Rambo.

Only then another buffalo appears. And another. Pretty soon I've got a whole herd of them out front, trying to eat my yard and gagging. And whining. "The water tastes funny. You got any water with locusts in it?" I don't suppose it's an accident that I've got the same number of buffalo here as there are men in the Cavendish gang. Plus one. I keep waiting to see if any more appear; maybe someone else will go back and help him. But they don't. This is it.

You remember the theories of history I told you about. Back in the beginning? Well, maybe somewhere between the great men and the masses, there's a third kind of person. Someone who listens. Someone who tries to *help*. You don't hear about these people much so there probably aren't many of them. Oh, you hear about the failures, all right, the shams: Brutus, John Alden, Rasputin. And maybe you think there aren't any at all, that nobody could love someone else more than he loves himself. Just because *you* can't. Hey, I don't really care what you think. Because I'm here and the heels of my moccasins are clicking together and I couldn't stop them even if I tried. And it's okay. Really. It's who I am. It's what I do.

I'm going to leave you with a bit of theory to think about. It's a sort of riddle. There are good Indians, there are bad Indians and there are dead Indians. Which am I?

There can be more than one right answer.

# JOSEPH MANZIONE

## Candle in a Cosmic Wind

**Here's a melancholy yet ultimately affirming story about the last days of the planet Earth, by new writer Joseph Manzione.**

**This was Joseph Manzione's first published story. He lives in Ann Arbor, Michigan.**

# CANDLE IN A COSMIC WIND

## Joseph Manzione

### 1

Go down now, through the tumultuous layers of atmosphere, through storms of ice-crystals streaming along violently shifting patterns of wind, into the becalmed, translucent regions of ash and dust, floating in stagnant eddies above the blighted surface. Down there, the forests are barely visible, hardened stumps rising above the deep snow. The cities sprawl like desiccated corpses, mouths open to the sky, veins clogged with debris. The mountains writhe like wounded beasts and bleed living ice.

Strange things happen in that inhuman cold. Sounds. Visions. Dogs raise their heads above the snow, baring broken glass teeth as gauzy vapors sluice from their maws and spill across the land. The wind on their liquid backs, they hunt with the guttering sun, seeking warmth in the waste. Cold. Shadows lingering lovingly over the dead snow, the stillness under dark bellies flowing inexorably from horizon to horizon.

The dogs lope across the white plain, espying what they hunger for; a large vehicle lies mired by the remains of a highway. The stillness is shattered by the sounds of ice striking hot metal, as several of the creatures leap onto the hood and runners. One draws back a hard, blue paw and smashes the rimed windshield. The woman inside awakens and screams as the maelstrom of glass and teeth explodes over her, engulfing her—

Avdotya Nazarovna choked and sat up in her tiny bunk, wringing with sweat. She gasped and struggled to breathe, flailing at her throat and face with her muscular arms. The quiet inside the cab silenced her. The ticking of the diesel calmed her. Finally she glanced at the dashboard in front of the driver's seat. 0513 on the morning of June 17th, the display read; the wind was from the northwest at fourteen kilometers per hour, and the ambient air temperature was $-101°$

Celsius. The dogs had fled back into her subconscious, but the filthy, frigid twilight outside remained.

She arose shakily and moved through the cramped cab, making coffee and reconstituting eggs and cereal. It was the city she had just passed through, she decided, as she took a shower in the small water closet. After twelve days on the ruined interstate, she had crossed over a high range of mountains and descended into the valley of the Great Salt Lake. She had expected the city to be a tertiary detonation site; certainly the Americans had a military airbase here, as well as corporate research and manufacturing centers for strategic weapons systems. Getting through would be dangerous, since the blast would have buckled bridges and filled the streets with rubble.

But when she emerged onto the uplands above Salt Lake City, it spread out as far as she could see, unblemished, almost geometrically pristine. Her fury welled up and she hammered on the dash for many minutes, screaming curses at Ben Kimball and all of the American killers who had escaped Russian vengeance, as well as the stupidity and incompetence of her own people, especially in the *Racketnyye Voyska Strategischeskovo Naznacheniya*.

They had lost the war when it finally came, all of the new Soviet peoples, and particularly those like herself. She hated the treachery she had seen; her motherland could only be pocked and pitted like the skin of an old orange, and Gregori and the boy Nikolai would be gone.

But the city had shown her the other side of the same story, for if the Americans had created so much slaughter, they had paid the greater price after the short war ended. Avdotya could not forget what she saw, scenes so similar to those in her dreams.

A young woman wrapped in a grimy yellow blanket knelt rigidly in the deep snow, one arm locked across her forehead, as though she grieved. The other arm stood stiff against the sky, the delicate, blackened fist appearing to beat the air. A small sheet of ice flared from the naked arm and hand, the moisture and warmth of the tissue forceably extinguished by the searingly cold wind.

An armed group of citizens had tried to hold a large grocery market against a mob. Somebody had made a careless effort to stack and burn the bodies, for sanitary reasons or perhaps just for the heat. In the yard of an elaborate church across the street, three children hung by their necks from a painter's scaffold. The crows had frozen dead at their feet.

Near the zoo, a partially dismembered giraffe was roped up to a traffic light. An axe was still buried in its carved flank.

A police officer had been crucified on a cinema marquee. IT'S A WONDERFUL LIFE, Avdotya read, as she drove slowly by.

The neighborhoods beyond were shrouded in ice, the homes shut up behind blank windows and barricaded doors. She could imagine families asleep in the upstairs bedrooms.

Avdotya had stopped in the downtown district in front of Temple Square and the shopping malls across the street. Dressed in a black thermal suit, she had climbed down from the truck to look around. She abruptly decided to visit an American department store and find a pair of cowboy boots and some makeup, if there were any left.

But something had howled in the distance, as she trudged through the snow.

She had jumped, and twisted around, listening.

The howl came again, faintly, almost floating on the air. It drew out into a wailing screech, and faded.

"Ai . . .," she whispered, letting out her breath. What was it? Somebody else? A . . . dog?

Something else?

She had backed across the street, breathing heavily. Shadows of the empty office buildings and arcades crept across the snow. Behind the idling truck, the Mormon temple rose into a salmon-colored sky. Its grey-granite walls and fluted arches were hung with thick blue sheets of ice that sparkled perversely in the dying light. Atop the highest tower, a ghostly figure draped in burnished gold blew salvation on a horn to the empty gardens and avenues below.

Avdotya had shivered. When the howl came a third time, she scrambled into the truck and drove quickly away through the drifts, out of the city, past the dead lake, and into the desert wastes beyond. Hours later, she had stopped and slept.

Of course it was the wind, she told herself, as she swung down into the driver's seat, toweling her short, wet, red hair. The wind, sluicing through a shattered window, growling up out of an elevator shaft, or lapping around a pile of rubble. And then, in her dreams, the dogs had come.

"Eventually it's going to get to me," she said aloud. "I'll begin a conversation with myself that I'll never finish. I'll have a dream and I won't wake up."

She hit the charging switch on the main diesel.

"But not here . . . not in this place. At home."

The diesel caught, and roared.

## 2

There were worse dreams.

She stood in the bottom of a cavernous pit, staring up at a small, circular patch of blue sky, far above. She was desperately trying to find a way to climb out, when with a sudden flash, the sky kindled and burned. Through the heat and bitter odors, she noticed figures appearing around the edges of the pit, silhouetted against the roiling glare. They jumped, one, and then another, and then many, flailing their arms and screaming thinly as they hurtled down. But they burst into flames before they hit the bottom, and soon the air above was saturated with fire, and a rain of cinders streaked Avdotya's face with soot and covered the concrete beneath her feet with a dark carpet that crunched underfoot.

Thick clusters of writhing torches fell about her, and the vast, steel walls of the pit were lit with a lurid, unsteady glow. The rain of cinders congealed and heaped around her knees, rising up over her thighs and waist as she struggled to remain on top of the tide. The air grew heavy with dust and smoke and she gagged and retched and the light softened into a diffused crimson radiance and still the cinders fell, burying her, and sifting into her open, working mouth.

"Nikolai!" she spit up. ". . . Gregori. . . ."

But the last thing she felt was the earth below wrenching and splitting wide with a roar and a wave of great heat, as a huge steel spike thrust up through the cinders and impaled her, lifting her broken body toward the dying sky. And as the light faded and her eyes stilled and went cold, she caught sight of the mummified remains of Ben Kimball beckoning to her from the lip of the pit, the skull grinning with obscene familiarity.

When the war began, she had been in an American wing command bunker in the missile fields northwest of Omaha. She was a major in the R.V.S.N., the Soviet Strategic Rocket Forces, and her own rocket regimental complex, a group of RS-21 launchers outside of Novosibirsk, already had been dismantled under the detailed provisions of U.N. Resolution 242. The Ministry of Defense could think of no better qualifications nor more sensitive postings for professional orphans like Avdotya, so she and thousands of others—R.V.S.N. technicians, P.V.O.—Strany officers, political commissars, boom-boom submariners and more—were sent to the United States to observe comparable American disarmament under the 242 plan. The American officers at Omaha had tolerated her, just as she had politely ignored Stockwell and Belinda Nhu the year before. The Americans deactivated systems according to a meticulously negotiated schedule, while Avdotya and four comrades, and a very serious team of U.N. observers from Senegal, simply watched, day after day.

Until Ben Kimball had slammed down the blue phone on his desk in the operations center, pointed a pistol in Avdotya's face, and given a launch-sequence order to the remaining Peacekeeper II missile crews on line. In the ensuing shouting and confusion, the reporter from *Izvestia*—a KGB operative—garroted a young American guard and grabbed her automatic weapon. The Senegalese died quickly, as did the reporter and three American technicians, but Avdotya and her two remaining comrades managed to break out through a light cordon of bewildered guards. Not knowing what to do, they ran through endless corridors pursued by the Americans, and Avdotya lost the P.V.O. Strany pilot first, and later the boy from the embassy. She had taken to the airducts then, and eventually found herself outside the main generator bunker and the underground fuels and stockpiles depot. She killed three guards and managed to barricade herself in that section before they found her, but by then the short war was almost over, and circumstances had changed. The generation of power in a protected environment was paramount, and she controlled supplies, machines, and computers. Despite the desperate efforts of the surviving Americans in the weeks that followed, they were not able to flush her out.

Above ground, the world appeared to die very quickly. Avdotya resigned herself to a life spent in a safe cage; there was enough of everything to sustain her body, but her emotional suffering was unavoidable. By the third year, however, the permafrost reached far below the bunker and the huge fuel tanks embedded in the earth around it. Inside the tanks the heating elements could no longer cope with the extreme temperatures, and the fuel slowly congealed into a molasses-like gel that could not be pumped. She foresaw these consequences, and though she could do nothing about them, she took steps to make a temporary escape. She selected a huge all-terrain diesel tractor, building in heating systems, generators and charging circuits, insulated armor and meshed treads. She stowed food and water in the trunk, and a vast amount of fuel in electrically-heated tanks. Two weeks before she was ready, the main generator shut down, and she fought the encroaching frost with portable burners. She barely managed it, but she was already dead. The days of her life were counted by the fuel gauges on the truck's instrument panels.

## 3

She drove slowly for hours across the vast desert playa west of the Great Salt Lake. The sun sank ahead of her, finally burying itself in a pearly turquoise smear beneath a moving front of ice-crystals. The storm came and went, and she continued well into the night.

She thought of home.

She feared the frozen sea most. She would have to cross onto it somewhere along the coasts or Oregon or Washington, and make the best of whatever she found. Possibly . . . probably? . . . . she would be hindered or stopped by deep crevices, or ranges of jumbled pressure ice thrust up from the interior, frozen geology to match the oceans of Callisto, or Europa. If she was stopped, she would get out and walk, she told herself; the sight of the mountains of the Kamchatka Peninsula on the distant horizon would be enough. She did not want to die here.

Strange, she thought, as she stared out at the fierce stars riding the darkened sky. Everything is so different from my expectations . . . I anticipated little more than a burnt crypt up here on the surface, the climate barely beginning to find an equilibrium, a few resilient species of plants coming back, a lot of detonation sites and dirty zones, background contamination localized at specific points . . . instead, there is the terrible cold, the clear nights and days without much evidence of dust and ash, the quickly changing weather, the absence of detonation damage, the unfocused nature of periodic radiation . . .

. . . and the sun: pale and fitful, with a murky, copper color she did not recognize. Even on the clearest summer days, shadows and dark places seemed to dominate the endless snowfields. Nothing she could think of would account for it, though admittedly she knew less than a Soviet officer should about such things as windborne dust particles and the surface effects of eradicating the ozone layer. The *Voskoya* manual only spoke of "temporary climatological aberrations," and Avdotya could see now that something was amiss, or that it was a case of the usual official "optimism-laden-with-a-secret-prayer:" the Communist faith.

"I'll never know," she said aloud. Through the thick windshield, the stars glittered impassively.

She was suddenly aware of a faint glimmer of light directly ahead on the flat horizon, diffuse and alone. A star? she thought. Perhaps the moonlight reflecting on a patch of ice somewhere in the middle distance.

But there is no moon tonight, she realized.

As she drew nearer, the image sharpened into several distinct points against the grey, sloping uplands beyond the desert. With a start, she recognized them as artificial lights.

The highway map she carried showed a small town on the edge of the playa named Wendover. It sounded vaguely familiar, then she remembered that American B-29 crews had trained there to drop atomic bombs on Japan at the end of the Great Patriotic War. Now it was probably one of those desolate little settlements ringing the

Nevada border, where oppressed and stupified working people could come and lose hard-won sustenance on gambling, gasoline, awful food, immoral stage acts, and other forms of swindle.

Even so, someone was still there. It must be so, for the cold and seasonally violent weather had lasted too long for any power source to function without maintenance, whatever the wizardry of American technology. Someone had survived. How, here on the edge of the wasteland, Avdotya did not even consider. Instead, she unhitched a .357 magnum taken from a Cheyenne sporting goods store, and checked its load. But the feeling she had as she watched the bullets in the cylinder spin was not one of hate or fear. Instead, she felt a soft warmth in her stomach, and anticipation.

The buried highway curved around the shoulder of a low, rocky range rising abruptly from the desert floor, and the town spread out along the edge of a stone-strewn alluvial fan. It was not much to look at: a few motels and gas stations, a surprising number of hotels and casinos, and rows of trailer homes in the snow. On the opposite side of the town, set upon a low knoll, lights illuminated a large casino-hotel complex, and something else.

Avdotya could not understand what she saw, because the shapes scattered around the knoll were enormous and unfamiliar. She was a kilometer from the casino-hotel, off the interstate and rolling up the main road through town, when she noticed that one object, a long cylinder with stubby projections spaced along serrated spines, had fallen on a wing of the hotel, reducing most of the structure to rubble. A similar cylinder lay on its side in the parking lot, surrounded by the charred hulks of several automobiles. Ice lay congealed and black with dirt around the wreckage, as though it had melted in the heat of some great conflagration, and slowly refroze amidst the debris.

A third cylinder rested upright on a squat tripod in the midst of the broad street in front of the casino. Though dented and burned, it seemed relatively intact.

Just then, she thought she understood: R.V.S.N. missiles, perhaps XRS-4s from Mirnyj, malfunctioned while inbound and fell here. Or perhaps they did not malfunction; she knew little of the XRS generation's performance profiles. Perhaps the spent boosters released their warheads, reentered the atmosphere, and by some fantastic coincidence, three of them came down on a casino on the Nevada-Utah border.

Ridiculous.

They were far too large, and no staged booster she knew of looked remotely similar. The chances of three spent boosters impacting on the same place were not high, and had they done so, providing they survived the heat of reentry, their explosive energy would have leveled the town. These objects were brought down under control, but something obviously had gone wrong.

But what were they? And who had turned on the lights, outside on the garish signs and the driveways, and inside, in the undamaged portions of the casino and hotel?

"I am in no shape for this," she muttered.

There is more to it than a few survivors holed up in a desert town, she thought as she glanced around. Above the truck, a large marquee flickered; a giant neon-lit cowboy hooked a hand in its denims and signaled her with its thumb. A cigarette drooped from the plastic face, and the red lips leered. She detested it.

Cylinders with odd-looking fins and superstructures, she thought. Large. Torus-shaped bulges at one end . . .

And then she had the answer: cylinders, large enough to be spacecrafts, perhaps—

Something leaped onto the side of the cab and hammered on the window by her head.

She had momentary impressions of a face, fangs, sharp features and staring eyes, and then she slammed on the brakes and pulled the pistol out of her jacket, and drew down on the creature through the glass.

There was nothing there.

She looked around, following her eyes with the oversized .357. Nothing.

She waited.

Finally she zipped herself into the thermal suit and unracked the M-16 from the ceiling compartment. She cracked open the cab door and stepped out onto the runner.

The lights burned steadily on the snow-covered lawns and in the broken windows of the casino and hotel. The stars flickered overhead, random points of scintilla struggling against a few tatters of cirrus. The wind gusted, and fell silent.

She climbed down off the truck, holding the rifle at ready. Barely had her boots sunk into the snow when she noticed footprints, shallow and rounded, angling away from a large depression where something obviously had struck and rolled.

So she had seen the creature after all, she thought, and took a deep breath.

Behind her, she heard a quiet footfall in the snow.

She whirled around just as two of the creatures stepped from behind the back end of the truck, the red taillights glinting in their many-faceted eyes. She did not really think about what happened next; her reflexes and the panic she had held for so long under the surface flew together and achieved a critical state. She fired, squeezed the trigger and sprayed the things as they saw her and stopped in their tracks.

She worked the trigger, and nothing happened. She looked stupidly at the rifle in her hands. It did not even click.

Ayich! she thought. My gun is frozen.

She shrugged suddenly, and dropped it. The creatures stared at her, not moving.

They were ugly, she decided. They resembled three-meter-tall, rust-colored ducks, with curved fangs set in long, leathery snouts. Their arms were short and thick, and folded over large round bellies hidden in heavy cloaks. Skinny, chitinous legs held them up, and their naked knees were knobby and bent backwards. They were manifestly adapted to colder weather, and wore brightly-colored turbans around their heads. Avdotya did not know whether to laugh or be terrified, or simply amused at the irony, for their circumstances were clear now.

They're as lost as I am in this place, she realized. And I was going to shoot them.

Ayich . . .

She tried to smile at them, no small feat at the time, but it had no effect.

She waved, and both creatures dropped clumsily into the snow and crouched, as if ready to run. After a minute they slowly got to their feet and looked at each other. They gesticulated and pointed, waving their arms and kicking their feet, murmuring in low tones. One finally turned and waved back.

She waved again, and the second one waved. She smiled and waved both hands. They glanced at each other again, and then waved, one with its left arm, the other with its right.

Interesting symmetry, she thought. I wonder what we're saying . . . hello, probably; don't hurt me.

Abruptly she knew she was being watched from behind, and when she turned, she saw at least fifteen or sixteen silhouettes standing in the snow, backlit in a ghostly, bluish aura by the floodlights on the hotel roof.

I hope they're not hungry, she thought inanely, suppressing an urge to giggle.

They only wanted her to come indoors. Pointing and waving they escorted her past the smashed doors and the ice-encrusted lobby, through the casino and its legion of blinking, beeping slot machines and dusty crap tables, to the inner amphitheater and stage. There, they had insulated the walls, built low partitions for privacy, and set up unfamiliar generating and heating systems. There were shops and a rudimentary laboratory, and remembering the great cylindrical spacecraft propped upright in the street, she could guess what they were trying to do. Pieces of salvaged equipment, some of it of human origin, lay all about the stage.

One of the creatures picked up an object and showed it to her, murmuring and turning it over and over in large, horny hands. It was a partially disassembled color television receiver with a Japanese brand name. She smiled and nodded, reminded that she had almost bought one, once. This time, everyone seemed to appreciate the smile; they waved at her as she stood there next to a gaming table strewn with odd beakers filled with colored liquids, shivering and wondering what she would do now. On the wall above, a grimy banner undulated in the air currents. *Welcome to the Stateline*, it read, *Coming October 24th* . . . the rest, ripped and frayed, was gone forever.

## 4

She lived with the ducks—for that was how her mind insisted on visualizing them—in the casino in Wendover for seven months, as summer gave way to winter, and a thin carbon dioxide sleet fell frequently. She was constantly cold, and at first, very frustrated. No one could talk to her, although by the middle of the third month the anthropologist whom she had taken to calling Daffy Duck, learned to read and write in English fairly well. It would not take the time to learn Russian, and although she bitterly resented the slight, she recognized the logic. Every day Daffy and the biologist, Lysenko Duck, would come to her room in a converted storage area off the stage, and sit at a wooden table under a strong light, murmuring to one another as Daffy painstakingly wrote out questions in longhand with a ballpoint pen. She would answer with short essays in dubious English typed on a battered word processor, or simply shrug her shoulders and wait for the next question.

The ducks were very good to her. They brought her canned food and hotel furniture for her room, and little gifts: an electric razor, a child's kite, a baby bassinet and a large portrait photograph of the former kitchen staff of the complex. Daffy brought her a set of plastic figures that could be manipulated to change from vaguely human form into aircraft or imaginary spaceships, and asked whether the religious significance of these icons were similar all over the planet. The ducks had found the toys in a box in the nursery of the church down the street. They were excited about the discovery, and nothing she could say could quite convince them of their mistake.

They let her wander around the hotel and the grounds as much as she wanted. If she tried to approach the cylindrical spacecraft in the street, however, a phalanx of ducks always came running, and shooed her away with low, sing-song noises and gentle sweeping motions. They made no attempt to interfere with her in any other way, and she was sure they would let her go when she wanted, but it was plain they desired her to stay. She liked that.

They asked her how she had survived, and she told them part of the story, but they never asked how everyone else had died. She appreciated the courtesy, thinking that the ducks must be endowed with a sense of tact, and repaid the favor by never mentioning the wrecked ships outside, or the sloppily-healed wounds some of them bore. Nor did she say anything about the morning on which she witnessed a suicide attempt by one of the ducks in the casino lobby, although she was deeply troubled by what it might mean, and why the others had reacted so quickly and seemingly without surprise.

One evening she met Daffy Duck and the engineer she called Korolyov Duck on the lawn in front of the casino. She asked them where they were going, writing with a pencil on Daffy's pad of paper. After murmuring to each other, they motioned for her to follow. She did her best to keep up as they crossed the town and climbed the barren slopes above. On a broad, gravel-strewn shelf below a sheer rock wall they came across many stone mounds set in parallel rows, perhaps a hundred or more. Here the survivors of the disaster, twenty-two in all, had buried their comrades. The first few weeks must have been very difficult, she reflected, as she sat on a boulder and watched while Daffy and Korolyov D. walked from grave to grave, sprinkling a reddish, crystalline substance on each mound.

Custom, Daffy wrote when she asked. They had been here for several years, and two or three evenings a week a few of the survivors came up to lay grains of sand from home on the graves. The anthropologist's attempt to explain why faltered badly, or else she could not grasp the translation from "duck" to English to Russian. Perhaps it had something to do with various ritualistic responsibilities of the living to dead, but she was disturbed by the reference to "those who had sacrificed themselves willingly for the mistakes of others," and when she tried to question the anthropologist, it had turned away.

She slept better at night. Occasionally she suffered dreams, and woke up with sweat rasping down her face and back. But there were mornings when she was almost glad to roll out of bed, if only to help the ducks carry equipment or clean the amphitheater, or chip away ice from the entrances. The ducks encouraged her, and Daffy always had a list of things to do.

Later, she had an idea. There was a flatbed trailer in a gas station lot down the street. She proposed that they hook the trailer to her truck and make a run to Salt Lake City to look for useful items. The ducks considered it for a few days, but by that time they appeared to trust her too, and so they agreed. Once they found out what diesel fuel was, they happily set about distilling and reprocessing the muck in every gas tank and station in town. She and Daffy and Korolyov D., and sometimes Lysenko D. or Huey and Dewey and Lewey, drove to Salt Lake several times, and even to Reno on one occasion, and to the American air base at Mountain Home, Idaho. They brought back miscellaneous things: computer components, laser arrays, plastics, many types of valves and fittings, books, tapes, art objects, anything that looked interesting.

She returned with videotapes and showed American movies on a salvaged VCR. The ducks were enchanted by *Shane*, and asked her to show it two or three times a week. She was baffled by their behavior toward this typical cowboy opera. As they watched Alan Ladd gun down the henchmen of the protobourgeoise rancher, they did incomprehensible things. Some rocked back and forth on the benches in unison, some made clicking noises with their beaks and raised and lowered their arms, while others sat still with their eyes shut. But when the little boy ran shouting after the hero Ladd at the end of the film, everyone stood up and screeched. A few of the ducks did a passable phonetic imitation.

"Zannee! Quimbak . . . Zannee! Mumndad nid oo!" they cried.

She showed *Apocalypse Now,* and their reaction bordered upon the bizarre. She found it an impressive documentation of a criminal holocaust, but the ducks appeared to argue about it for three days, during which time several became violently, but temporarily ill. Often they resorted to role-playing to make some important point. Once she walked into the casino to find Lysenko D. the biologist wading carefully through a pile of "corpses," gesticulating to a group of unclothed ducks, brandishing pool cues on the balcony above. That evening they insisted upon seeing the movie twice. No one made a sound.

The following day she had a long and frustrating argument with Daffy and Lysenko D. by note paper. For some obscure reason they wanted to bury the tape in the ground and post a guard over it. Their explanations made little sense to her. Their reaction to the movie appeared to be predicated upon the way in which the ducks distinguished imagination from reality, but she could not begin to understand their point of view. For their part, Daffy and Lysenko D. grew upset over her inability to comprehend them. Finally, they allowed her to simply throw the tape away.

She realized now how great the gulf was between herself and the ducks. There were superficial similarities, enough to communicate on a fairly complex level. It was quite possible that there were parallel personality and intellectual traits that ran deep. But the biological "wiring" was different, and the cultural matrix very strange to her. She might never understand their motivations, and they might always mistake hers. She was not unappreciative of their benevolent qualities, but she began to suspect that coexistence would become difficult as time went by. Paradoxically, as she grew familiar with the ways of the ducks, Avdotya isolated herself from them.

## 5

One morning Daffy Duck banged into Avdotya's room lugging an assortment of equipment, including an ordinary stereo speaker and what looked like an amplifier and several cannibalized and resurrected computer components. The duck waved and set about plugging everything together, and she watched with interest, wondering what it was all about.

After a few minutes Daffy threw two switches, typed in a sequence of commands, and then glanced up. It shoved a microphone over to the center of the table and murmured in low, modulated tones.

"Hello. This project is successful. I feel happy," the speaker said in English.

She sat stunned. She exclaimed something in her native language, but the speaker burped and let out a high-pitched buzz.

"In English, please," said Daffy. "I am sorry."

"It is you speaking," she said, and smiled.

"Yes," replied Daffy. "I have been successful with this project."

It paused.

"But you do not speak to me naturally. This project needs refinement. It needs more memory. It especially needs more processing power and elective definition to decide proper nuance and syntax."

The duck rocked its head back and forth. "Again, I am sorry. I am not a linguist . . . that one is dead." It motioned at the equipment on the table. "And I work with unfamiliar designs."

"But it does work," she said. "You're magnificent."

"Thank you. You have been very patient and useful. Will you read your books for us?"

"What? I don't understand."

"We can build a library," Daffy replied. "You can read fiction books into a storage tape for us, please. I have Hemingway, Borges and Kawabata, and others. I believe that the . . . art . . . can be enhanced by a human voice, and the materials that you produce can be stored easily for a long voyage."

"Of course. It will be an honor, even."

The duck watched her carefully. "I also have Chekhov and Solzhenitsyn. I have Pasternak."

She laughed. "All are very proper, now."

What would a duck associate with "A Dull Story," or "An Incident at Krechetovka Station"? For that matter, how would it react to "A Way You'll Never Be"? She wondered if all the tapes and photographs, the image and voice of herself as well, would be lost in a museum somewhere far away . . . to be inflicted occasionally upon visiting schoolchildren from nearby academies.

"Ooooooh! She is so ugly!" Avdotya imagined the strange voices clicking and murmuring. "What is she saying now? When can we go home?"

Daffy was in a talkative mood, and had more to say.

"We will be leaving soon," it remarked. "In a week we will hold a complete systems test and if it is successful, we will probably schedule a departure date within the month."

"Yes, you ran a check on the fusion torus yesterday, didn't you? It certainly seemed to work."

By aiming the vehicle's main thruster nozzle away from the casino, the ducks had inadvertently destroyed the small shopping center across the street. For some reason, they appeared very upset by this.

"Do you think you'll be able to go back?" Avdotya asked.

"I think so," Daffy replied. "You have saved us years of preparation and we are grateful."

They sat silently for a few minutes. She stared at the walls, and the duck watched her.

"I've been thinking about what I'm doing here," she finally said.

"You are improving your English," said the duck, and rocked its head.

She looked at it with surprise and irritation, and then suddenly realized that Daffy was attempting a joke.

Avdotya smiled. "Yes, that, too."

"We assumed that you did not want to be alone," observed the duck.

"It is pleasant to be among people again," she said, continuing to smile.

"We make poor company, I think."

"But you've been very good to me, and I like you. I regret that there is only me now . . . there were beautiful places I could have shown you once. There were good people, too. Most of us were good, despite what we did to ourselves. Do you understand?"

But the duck had straightened and sat back. "No," it replied, clearly upset.

Avdotya shrugged. She wondered what she had said. "I'm not explaining myself well. I wanted to say thank you. For everything you've done . . . is there something wrong?"

The duck tucked its snout under one arm in agitation. Its body trembled slightly.

"Have I offended you?" Avdotya insisted in a bewildered tone.

"No," said Daffy at last, and raised its head. "Yes . . . I understand. I will try to say the right words. It is good to be here with you. I wish for better circumstances, too. But to meet you gives me a better perspective and appreciation of human character than if I only had artifacts to examine. I like you for this. It is a difficult situation for you to be in, and I respect you for your behavior in this place. It is very sad that you are alone."

"Sad," she agreed, still puzzled. They both looked at the walls.

Then Daffy said, "You cannot survive here. The planet's climate has been radically altered, and will probably remain so until the ablation effects on the sun have subsided years from now."

Ablation effects? She shook her head. "What?"

"We will take you with us, if you want to come. You can go home with us."

She was stunned. She saw herself in the museum, along with the photographs, the carefully restored furniture and dead voices. Schoolchildren brushed her clothes and hands, the facets of their eyes catching her reflection as they stared at her.

"Have we offended you?" they chorused.

"No!" she screamed.

"Consider our offer carefully," Daffy was saying. "Your going will present no technological difficulties, but there will be psychological problems. You will be alone among us, isolated by insurmountable biological and cultural obstacles. We will keep you in a special place, for our home will be both terrible and wonderful to you. You could not cope by yourself. We will try to make you happy, but you will not be happy."

The duck suddenly stretched across the table, bringing its large, slightly bitter-smelling head close to her own.

"We want you to come with us," it said. "But I like you. I want you to be happy."

She said: "I won't go."

Daffy quietly tucked its snout under an arm.

After a few minutes, Avdotya said, "Will you answer a question?"

The duck raised its head and stared at her, the face chillingly unfathomable.

"Yes."

"Why are you here? What happened to you?"

The duck was silent for a long time. Finally it answered.

"Home received some of your television broadcasts, twenty-two-year-old signals, but we knew you were here. It was exciting. You were the first ones we knew of for certain, and we decided to come and have a look. Four ships were constructed. They were very good ones, better than those we sent to build colonies in our nearest neighboring stellar system."

The duck paused, and turned its head away.

"They did not incorporate the necessary safeguards," it said, and the voice from the speaker had an odd cadence. "We were just under half a light year out from this system, shifting from cruise mode into deceleration, when an accident occurred."

"Half a light year out?" Avdotya interrupted. "Are you saying that you lost ships out in space?"

"One ship," Daffy replied hesitantly. "You know very little about our ships. The vehicles outside are . . . were . . . only small planetary landers. There are three interstellar cruisers in a parking orbit around the poles, and two of them are badly damaged. But the third . . . if we can get the remaining lander operational and rendezvous with the third ship, we can go home."

"What happened during the accident?"

Inexplicably, Daffy bared its fangs and screeched. Avdotya scrambled to her feet.

"What is it?" she demanded. "What did I say?"

"I am sorry . . . I cannot tell you what happened."

"Why?"

"I cannot."

"Okay," she said. "All right, I don't need to know this. We can talk about something else."

"You do not understand. You do not know what happened. I do not know what you think happened. I do not want to tell you."

Avdotya wondered if the duck was hysterical.

"Why? Is it something I'm not permitted to know? Is it . . . religious? A taboo? No?"

"Guilt," Daffy replied, and once again gave her an unfathomable stare. "Shame is what we feel."

"You told me that it was an accident."

"It was an accident."

"They happen. One accepts them, comes to terms with them, learns—"

"No. No one learns from this accident. No one can come to terms with it. Listen to me, Avdotya Nazarovna!"

The sound of her name momentarily took her breath away. No duck had ever used it before.

"Listen, and then you will learn," said Daffy, leaning across the table. "You do not know about our ships. Our landers are fusion-powered and use hydrogen as a propellant. Our cruisers propel themselves by forcing an interaction between hydrogen and antihydrogen, and ejecting the resulting muons and pions along a diverging magnetic field to produce thrust. We carry several tanks of hydrogen, and several more of electrostatically-suspended, supercooled antihydrogen. We tether two opposing engines on a twenty-kilometer cable, and hang the command module, tanks, lander, and shields in between. In the acceleration and cruise mode, the leading engine fires, and the shields provide protection against gamma radiation. We protect ourselves from interstellar dust and micrometeors by diverting their kinetic energy into a ferrous fluid compound and spraying a screen of droplets out ahead of the ship. In the deceleration mode, we shift the shields and command module around and fire the opposing engine against trajectory. We deploy a great number of lightweight layers of thin plastic film to protect the ship against particles, and we grind up the empty fuel tanks into fine dust and shoot it out ahead at ninety percent light speed to clear the way of larger particles."

"It sounds remarkable. What happened?"

The duck flailed an arm. "Going into deceleration one of our ships misfired its load of dust from the ground-up tanks. Our ships normally operate in a formation hundreds of thousands of kilometers apart, but even so, one ship was destroyed and another severely damaged through impacting a scattering of dust molecules moving in an angular trajectory at relativistic speeds. The malfunctioning ship was forced to decelerate without a dust shield, and literally eroded in the process."

Daffy paused. "It took us a year to decelerate and attain a parking orbit around this planet. All of our landers were damaged from shuttling back and forth between the cruisers at near relativistic speeds, coping with emergencies and repairs. Only one landed successfully, though not without further damage."

The duck gestured outward and around. "When we arrived here, we found all of this."

Avdotya shook her head and looked at the floor. "It must have been so difficult to come this far," she whispered, "through so much hardship, just to find that we'd killed ourselves in a war. You're right. The word is guilt. Shame."

She sincerely felt both emotions, along with a ghost resurrection of hatred for the stupid Americans. The face and rotten hands of Ben Kimball beckoned to others besides herself, she realized.

But Daffy Duck blinked slowly and cocked its head.

"War?" it asked. "What war?"

"What war? . . . the war. The war that caused all of this . . . killed my people. The war the Americans—the ones who lived right here—started."

She felt hot, all of the sudden. "What do you mean, 'what war?' "

"Forgive me," the duck implored. "I am trying to understand you. Perhaps there is a concept here that I am not familiar with. Are you speaking of a conflict between nation-states?"

"Yes," she replied, calming down. Why had the duck upset her?

"But the Americans did not begin a war here. I have seen no evidence of any war. We scanned the planet—"

"I was there!" she snapped, her face reddening. "I . . . fought in it!"

"I believe you," Daffy insisted, "but nothing less than a nuclear conflict—"

And then the duck sat back. "You do not know what has happened here," it said, the cadence of its voice distorting horribly. ". . . no war!"

"No war!" it croaked again, and fled from the room.

## 6

Later that day Avdotya wandered far out onto the vast playa, clad in her thermal suit.

She thought about the ducks' reactions to the movies she had shown. After a time, Daffy Duck had managed to convey to her some sense of what was going on. The ducks distinguished imagination from reality in wholly different ways. They understood that what happened on a television screen, or on canvas or the printed pages of a book, was fictional, in that events never occurred in quite that way. But they personalized their imagination, art, even discursive learning as opposed to experience, in exactly the same manner as they internalized and reacted to their own existence. Everything was real to them; they could not divorce themselves from anything around them, not through passive observation, or rationalization, or withdrawal. They were not "scientists" in the Soviet sense, they were quantum physicists, artists, and philosophers.

A long time ago we declared war on another tribe, Daffy wrote, by sending them a book scrawled by a blind neurotic, describing how they ought to conduct their fertility rites. We won the war by dispatching the images of the empty southern deserts under terrible seige by sandstorms, set to music written by a composer for a lover who lay dying. The other tribe sued for peace immediately.

Do you often fight wars among yourselves? Avdotya had written.

Not for an age, the duck replied. There came a day when a young philosopher wrote an epistle to all of the tribes, describing how he had ground pieces of glass into lenses and set them in a long, moveable tube, and thus had turned the machine onto the silky lights in the night sky. The philosopher described what was to be seen there and what was to be deduced from it, and millions of the machines were built, and millions of us concurred. It was decided that we really were a small people after all, and yet, it was *we* who were looking at the infinite stars, and not they at us. We were alive, and we came to understand the significance of that fact. We took hope, and determined to make ourselves as big a people as we could. In such a universe, war ceases to be the most direct and efficient method.

In human terms the ducks are schizophrenics, Avdotya told herself as she trudged through the snow. They are unable to behaviorally distinguish fantasy from reality. The trait made them both more and less adaptable than humans. More, because they were capable of assimilating novel new situations and incorporating radical solutions into society without upheaval; witness the fact that the invention of the telescope eradicated war. Less, because their reaction to imagination could push them into extremes of behavior that were detrimental to their well-being. More and less. The concept seemed uncomfortably paradoxical from a human point of view.

How to solve the riddle of the ducks? I haven't an idea, she thought. Kindness and suicide, brilliance and irrationality, the sense of something hidden . . . they sympathize, and yet they fear me. Why? How does someone like me, who carefully creates artificial reference points and a system of perceptual boundaries between the real and the unreal, communicate with creatures who have no similar concepts? How can I be sure of what I say? How can they?

Why did the duck run out of the room?

I assume myself when I speak, Avdotya thought. And perhaps the duck assumes itself. When the worlds we so carefully construct in our imagination totter on reality, we run, screech, or stand up and strike out!

Her thoughts strayed to the image of Ben Kimball, fury contorting his gentle face, the jaw muscles rippling under the expanse of snow-white beard, as he cocked his gun and held it to her nose.

Bastard, she had shouted, nonetheless. Betraying dog . . .

She suddenly stopped. Directly ahead sprawled a large lump of dark material, half-buried in the snow. Off to one side was an unraveled green turban.

Lysenko Duck lay motionless in the middle of the empty playa. Blood seeped from an opened artery in its neck, and one hand clutched a sharpened screwdriver.

"Nyet!" Avdotya cried, as she frantically dug the body out. The duck was barely alive. It made a feeble motion with the other hand, patting her on the back and stroking her heaving shoulder.

It shook its head.

She could not carry it. It was too large and bulky. She stuffed torn fabric from the turban into the wound and succeeded in hoisting the duck's arms up over her shoulders. Dragging its legs in the snow, she staggered away, toward the distant lights below the darkening evening sky.

But the casino was still only a faint glimmer on the horizon when she realized that her thermal suit was icing up. The batteries were nearly flat. It made little difference when she tried to pull harder. The duck's wet, rasping breath could no longer be heard in the silence.

An hour passed, and she was stumbling and falling over herself. Still she dragged and pushed the body. The joints of her suit had frozen, and she was forced into a stiff-legged limp that only emphasized the numbness in her feet and calves. Finally she slipped and collapsed onto a hard pan of ice. As the duck sagged across her, her leg twisted with an odd crunching sound.

"Nikolai! Oh . . ." she croaked, as the boy danced across the ice at the edge of her vision.

"Ben Kimbaaaaaalll!" she bawled. But the mummified skeleton with the great white beard took aim and fired the gun anyway. The boy dropped.

## 7

Avdotya Nazarovna stood in the wing operations bunker at the edge of the missile field, and jotted notes on a pad. The command link to "D" complex had been severed six minutes earlier, rendering the missiles' lock-in and guidance systems inoperative. The caretaker crews were just beginning to climb out of the underground silos, and except for the maintenance displays, the boards were dark.

"Another twenty-two megatons," she told herself. "Ust-Kamenogorsk is saved."

It was a Soviet intelligence estimate; the Americans were not verifying anything. They would not have to for five weeks, when the warheads themselves were scheduled to be dismantled.

Behind her, Spiridon Terentevich Khorobrov cleared his throat.

"Colonel Kimball?" he said in English, his heavy voice overlayed with a flawless British accent. "Colonel Kimball, I am grateful that today's exercise has displayed none of the . . . technical difficulties . . . that seem to have plagued American disarmament in the last two months. Your own crew apparently has regained its competence, and I congratulate you for inspiring this miraculous recovery."

Ben Kimball swiveled around in his chair, and grinned. "Fuck you, comrade," he said.

But Khorobrov did not even flinch. "May I assume that tomorrow's program of dismantling the link to "K" complex will be equally successful?"

"No sir, you may not," Kimball replied, the grin maintained. "As you know, our interpretation of the schedule calls for the airbases at Offutt and Hill field to stand down on their stockpiles. Tomorrow we get to relax; it's the Cold War all over again here."

"Indeed," said Khorobrov. "That is not the proper attitude, Colonel Kimball."

Kimball shrugged, and did his best to look bored. "Take it up with Obawata," he replied, pointing to the team leader of the U.N. observers. The Senegalese did not even look up.

"No instructions," he murmured.

Kimball smiled again. "There you go."

Khorobrov said: "This field is to be rendered wholly inoperative by eleven A.M. eastern standard time on September 16th, Colonel Kimball. You are four days behind."

"By whose reckoning? Yours? Or your government's?" Clearly Kimball was enjoying this. "Say, how do you know so much, Khorobrov? I thought you were just a reporter for *Izvestia* . . . or are you something else? A person of more . . . intelligent persuasions, perhaps?"

And Kimball, in mock seriousness, wagged a finger at Khorobrov and frowned.

In spite of herself, Avdotya smiled. It was common knowledge that Khorobrov was KGB, but the unspoken rule that Kimball loved to flout was to ignore the fact. Avdotya cautiously relished the occasional confrontations.

"Avie the Red," Kimball called her, admiring the color of her thick hair. The American officer was in his middle fifties, but he moved like a much younger man, and always had a smile ready for her. When he spoke, he spoke to her; he insulted Khorobrov and ignored the drunken pilot Kirsanov and the boy Siromakha, who looked so frightened and overwhelmed. Among his own people, he acted the part of a genteel father figure, and indeed, when he was not around, the American technicians and soldiers referred to him as "Pappy K." He was a colorful man, an amazing attribute both rare and discouraged in Avdotya's experience. She began to feel warm toward him, particularly after he presented her with a pair of cowboy boots with a red star emblazoned on each toe.

Eventually he took her out, boots and all, to a bar in Wahoo. When Khorobrov objected, she told him to kiss his own ass. She could do that, she assured Kimball; she was the favorite niece of the party secretary of the Ukraine. Kimball had laughed and unexpectedly slapped her on her shoulder.

Avdotya was still daydreaming when the klaxons howled throughout the operations center. Immediately the screens surrounding her went dead, and then flashed on again, but this time the displays were different. Unfamiliar symbols and combinations flickered on some, while others showed data-enhanced maps and tabular graphs. She reacted with surprise, having no idea what was going on, but Kimball was shouting above the bray of the alarms, and Khorobrov was edging slowly into the shadows beyond the consoles.

If anyone knew what was happening, it would be Khorobrov, Avdotya thought. He glanced at her, apprehension and dismay on his face.

Thereafter, events seemed to take on a hideously entropic quality, as though lives were lived in the space of minutes, drained of consequence.

Ben Kimball shouted at someone to shut the klaxons off. In the consuming silence, he asked, "Is it real? Daggett, is it real?"

"Those alarms are tied to the environmental sensors," one of the technicians answered. "There are anamolous indications of top . . . pressure fluctuations, albedo disruptions, frequency distortions on most bandwidths . . . gamma radiation . . . x-rays . . . infrared . . ."

"What do we have from the SACSIN link, Stiles?"

"Nothing . . . just noise, sir. I think the net must be down."

"What about MEECN? Nightwatch?"

"Nonoperational, sir . . . you remember, the receivers were taken down under 242 provisions two months ago . . . wait . . . yes. Something from Offutt on the TQ frequency . . . it's garbled . . . now it's gone."

"Hell. What was it?"

The technician turned around and faced Kimball. "Sounded like an API scramble code . . . sir . . . is this real?"

Avdotya suddenly remembered her child in Novosibirsk. She found herself unconsciously slipping slowly toward a shadowed side of the bunker. But a gun barrel prodded her in the back, and when she looked, she saw a determined looking guard with an automatic pistol.

"Nyet!" the American hissed.

"But what is it?" the U.N. team leader was demanding. "Colonel Kimball, what is going on?"

"If he opens his mouth again, put a bullet in it," Kimball said, to no one in particular. "Go to a DI-3 operational alert . . . and get me NORAD or somebody. Christ, I am not going to launch because of bad sensors and a thunderstorm . . . bloody hell not now, after all we've been through."

"Colonel Kimball, you cannot declare an alert." It was the boy from the foreign ministry, Siromakha. His voice was shaking. "You'll endanger everything . . . the negotiations . . . my government—"

"—has probably started a war," snarled Kimball. "Shut up! Daggett! Wake up! Talk to me."

"Radiation . . . moderate levels . . . unfocused, I can't get a fix. Pressure fluctuations are consistent with the mach fronts of several airbursts in the kiloton range . . . a rise in surface temperature . . . hell, sir, we're under attack, don't you see?"

"Shut up, now, mister. Stiles, what about SACSIN or NORAD?"

"No change. Nothing on cable, either, just noise . . . more noise . . . now I have pulsed harmonics on the higher frequencies . . . I don't think it's artificial."

"All right," said Kimball. "Dean? What do you think?"

"Could be a counterforce strike. They might've shut down our people already. Offutt was the last central command and control for SAC . . . if that was a scramble code, I'd say we're screwed."

"Then why haven't we been burned yet? Why airbursts instead of ground-level detonations?"

"I dunno . . . we've been half shut down by 242 . . . maybe we aren't considered important anymore . . . a series of timed low-yield airbursts above the field could hold us down for a while until more important business is finished."

"Listen," said Kimball, his voice taking on a thin edge. "I got thirty-two megatons, and every operational missile out there is venting on the racks. They aren't Titans . . . I can put a W87b warhead through the Kremlin's front door."

"I'm sorry, sir. I just don't know."

There were a few seconds of silence, and then Siromakha tried again: "Colonel Kimball, I respectfully request—"

"Son," interrupted Kimball, "I may apologize to you later, or I may have you shot. Right now it looks like the latter. Now be quiet. Sssssh!"

"PACCS!" the technician Stiles shouted suddenly. "I got PACCS! On cable link EVI . . . a confirmed verbal encode . . . I'm routing it to you, sir."

The blue phone on Kimball's desk buzzed. Kimball picked up the receiver and listened. His face went white.

Bastards, thought Avdotya, an unexpected rage welling up and overwhelming her sick horror and longing for Nickolai. All over . . . all over . . . nothing left . . . nothing to go home to . . . bastards . . . a trick . . .

"A trick," she said. Kirsanov the pilot gaped at her.

"A trick," she repeated.

Kimball turned and slammed the phone down. A gun was in his hand, pointed at her face. Anger suffused his skin with a deep red glow.

"Damn right, comrade," he said. "You're going to die for it, too."

He gave the orders to launch. Avdotya shuddered in physical pain when the earth around her rumbled, as the operational portion of the wing was ejected from the silos by pressurized gas. There was a second of silence and then a deep thrumming hiss from above, as the boosters ignited and the missiles soared into a threatening sky.

Omsk, Temirtau and Karaganda, Pavlodar, Petropavlovsk . . . Novosibirsk . . .

The sound of automatic rifle fire replaced the evil thrumming, and she twisted to see Khorobrov, teeth clenched, shooting wildly. Ben Kimball suddenly disappeared. She flung herself on a blood-spattered rifle that clattered to the carpeted floor by her feet, and it was then and there that her long journey really began.

## 8

"Avie, we couldn't find any detonation sites out there. None. Carmichael and Assad did find some minor blast damage in Omaha before they died, but the tapes we recovered from Offutt indicated that base command maintained a link to NORAD, and no one there knew what was going on. They had pretty well decided that the chain of events did not fit the profile of command and control decapitation before a counterforce strike, however. What little NORAD could get from the Russian-watchers after the low-orbit satellite network died appeared to show that your people were having similar problems. SACSIN never gave a launch-sequence order . . . it came from Post-Attack Command, and was initiated after a heavily-shielded satellite gave a degraded identification of multiple booster ignitions in the Pacific Ocean off Kamchatsky . . . your submarine base, you know?"

The image of Ben Kimball on the monitor in the generator bunker looked haggard and cold. Avdotya could see cracked and open sores on the American's lined cheeks.

"So," she replied in her awkward English. "You expect me to believe this? Perhaps you expect me to congratulate you because America won the war? Because a . . . trick, a betrayal killed my country, my child? You expect me to throw down the barricade and open the airlock, and let you in here? Then maybe we have a party, yes? You bring wine coolers, perhaps? Beer?"

"Avie . . . please. I don't expect anything, I merely ask." Kimball sounded exhausted. "Understand me. It's been five months, and the portable heaters we have out here in the corridor have had it. We can't scrounge for food and fuel anymore because the temperature outside has dropped below the operational limits of our tractor. We're the only ones left, Avie . . . six of us huddled here by this monitor. I doubt if there's anyone else out there. We're malnourished, suffering from prolonged exposure to radiation, and we're sick. We're cold. When we die, you'll be alone. Have you thought about that?"

"You sent thirty-two megatons into the heart of the Soviet people, Ben. You wish me to be sad when you die?"

"Avie, I've told you . . . we found eight of our missiles in the Omaha area, and one more near Wahoo. I don't believe anything we launched reached Siberia, and I'm sure no inbounds from your people fell around here."

"Oh, so now you are going to tell me there was no war, is that right, Ben Kimball? You are going to convince me that not your people or mine committed acts of barbarous aggression and suicide? It was all a big mistake, yes? What evidence do you have to present today, please? Will you explain for me the pressure fluctuations, the blast damage from airbursts, the radiations?"

Kimball shook his head. "I don't know, Avie . . . nothing makes much sense anymore. Pauley died last night, did you notice? Stress, scurvy, who knows? You've got food, heat, light, books and tapes in the strategic supply bunker . . . give us a break. We're all that's left. Save our lives."

"I cannot. You murdered my child."

Kimball bit his lip.

After a minute, Avdotya asked, "Why do you want to live, if there is nothing out there?"

"Me?" Kimball seemed surprised. "I don't want to live . . . I don't have the desire. But I have a bunch of twenty-four year olds who do. They really do. I guess they need me."

He shrugged and stared into the monitor's camera. "Why do you want to live, Avie?"

She did not hesitate. "I am going to wait until the . . . climate improves, and then I will go home somehow."

Days passed, and the Americans hardly moved in their nest outside the thick airlock doors. Ben Kimball looked worse.

"You are going to stay here and die?" she asked.

"As long as there's a chance," he replied hoarsely.

"There is no chance. Go home, Ben Kimball."

"Wish I could, Avie . . . but home is in Oregon. Medford. My kid lives there now. Real political activist, especially since it became fashionable again. Good, solid husband with her . . . a real bore. Two children. Call me 'grandfather' . . . hate that. Call me Ben, I say. Call me anything, but don't call me old. My wife's buried in Medford, on Pinery Way . . . she looked like you, Avie, did I tell you that?"

"Many times, Ben."

"Good, solid . . . capable at whatever she wanted to do. Stubborn . . . strong. Shock of red hair, green eyes that noticed everything. Hated to see her go . . . took the life out of me, made me rude, a bore . . . hollow inside . . . sorry, just rambling on . . ."

"You were a good person, Ben. I liked you."

"Save us, Avie."

"No." Avdotya put her hands to her face. "I will tell you why, yes? My son, Nikolai . . . I am a little crazy most of the time. My husband, Gregori . . . he was a party official in Moscow. He drank a lot and beat me, even when I was pregnant. But he loved me, too . . . I think he loved me. In my second year at the Frunze Academy, I became very tired. I broke his jaw. There was a scandal. Gregori divorced me, and took my son. I was dismissed from Frunze, and posted to Karaganda for three years."

There were tears on her cheeks. She did not notice them.

"I wanted my son. I wanted a career . . . to be good at what I do. So I think, if only I work very hard. I do everything I can do, and someday I have everything I want again, you understand? Nikolai . . . they do not give the son of a Central Committee alternate back to a soldier-wife unless I am very, very good."

"I was good," she continued, haltingly. "Gregori . . . he made some mistakes. He retired a year ago. My uncle in the Ukraine talked to some people in Moscow . . . by that time I was a major assigned to one of the rocket regiments near Novosibirsk. The psychologists went to see Nikolai . . . they said he was not . . . healthy. He had no zeal. He was not interested in acceptable social organizations. They said it was Gregori's fault. It is all bullshit, as you say . . . yes? But I take him anyway. He came back to me a month before I was assigned here."

She looked up suddenly, and gritted her teeth.

"You took him away from me, you bastard. You took him away, you took everything away again. Everyday I wake up and I say, 'Avdotya Nazarovna, you are not a murderer, you must give those bastards outside a chance. They did not know your son, they did not willingly do this to him.' But I am crazy . . ."

She shook her head. "My hands do not obey my mind. I cannot pull the lever to open the airlock. I get sick . . . I hate you, and the thought of living with you, breathing the same air with you makes me ill. I must go home. When the weather breaks, I must find a way to go home. Please. Tell me this, Ben Kimball. Would you let me live, if I let you in here? Would you let me go, when I wanted to?"

Ben Kimball had been silently staring at her for many minutes. He did not move. The flush in his face had paled, the beads of sweat on his brow had frozen.

"Ben Kimball? Ben?"

When he did not answer, she slumped to the floor.

## 9

When she awoke, she lay on a cot in a ruined casino in Wendover, Nevada, and a giant duck sat by her bed.

"Hello, Daffy Duck," she said.

"Daffy Duck? The animated cartoon waterfowl? How shall I take that?"

She laughed quietly and fell asleep again.

Later, she opened her eyes, and saw Daffy and Dewey bending over her.

"How do you feel?" asked Dewey.

"Better," she replied. "I've been a lot of trouble to you, haven't I?"

Both ducks straightened and looked at each other.

"You were close to death when we found you," said Dewey. "I believe you have recovered now. There is a bone splint on your left ankle. It is not very good, and the bone may heal crookedly, but I believe you will be able to walk. It was the best I could do."

"Thank you, you've been very good to me . . . what happened to the biologist? The one I found out there in the desert?"

"Dead," replied Daffy. "I am sorry."

"Why? Why suicide? It isn't the first time, is it?"

"Would you like to sit up?" asked Dewey.

"Thank you. Can I have a glass of water?"

"Yes."

"Will you answer my question?"

"Yes," Daffy said, and sat down beside the cot.

"There are certain factors that I have failed to comprehend," it began. "There are others that I have hesitated to talk about. You have slept for several days. You spoke in your sleep, and told me a great deal. I did not realize how difficult it had been for you."

The duck rocked back and closed its eyes. "Poor us . . . poor us. We were so curious, so willing to help. We wanted so much . . . we desired a meaningful dialogue with your people. Voyagers at the very dawn of the loneliest voyage, looking out over the vast sea of stars, longing for any safe haven among the myriad lights, any port with friendly natives. Any comrades we could find . . . what have we done here? See what we have done."

Dewey Duck moaned softly and tucked its snout under an arm. Daffy paused, and opened its eyes.

"There was no war. At least, no nuclear conflict. You were mistaken."

Avdotya chewed on her thumbnail and thought. "Someone told me the same thing a long time ago. But I was in it. I witnessed an order to launch a large number of missiles. The missiles flew . . . I was there."

"Yes. They flew. We scanned the wreckage."

"What happened?"

"The missiles went up. I do not believe that any reached a target, however. We did find some rare detonation sites, perhaps where warheads exploded when the malfunctioning boost vehicles impacted the surface. Guidance systems were destroyed or scrambled by radiation, or the vehicles themselves were knocked down by massive detonations high in the atmosphere."

Avdotya shook her head in confusion, "I don't understand. What caused the radiation? What about the airbursts?"

"Dust traveling at relativistic speeds," replied Daffy, staring at her with a shockingly contorted expression. "Several days ago I told you a little bit about how our ships operate . . . and about the accident one of them had while decelerating into this system."

"Yes? Explain, please. I still don't . . ."

She felt her throat constricting violently. The throbbing numbness in her ankle suddenly slashed at her.

"You. . . ." she choked. ". . . you. . . ."

"I am so deeply, so terribly ashamed," said Daffy.

"How? Why?"

"When the ship misfired its load of dust from the ground-up fuel tanks, hundreds of thousands of metric tons were hurled at a velocity exceeding nine-tenths light-speed in a grazing trajectory toward your sun. Three months later the dust blew away much of the outer solar atmosphere, and drastically distorted the spin, magnetic fields, and internal structure. A small amount of dust, very small, disintegrated upon colliding with your planet's atmosphere . . . the planet was contraposed to our ships when the dust blew through your system. As a result, your planet was blasted and irradiated. Since the impact had altered the energy output of your sun, the planet's climate was transformed and the biosphere eliminated. All this we watched, as we made the final approach."

"You bastard," she whispered. "Do you know what we had almost achieved here? Do you realize what you have done?"

"We have had seventeen suicides since we landed here," Daffy replied. The duck did not move, did not even breathe. It looked like it had been turned to stone.

Only the mouth had life. "We know what we have done."

Avdotya closed her eyes. "Get out," she said.

## 10

When she hobbled through the casino lobby a few weeks later, she found the truck carefully parked by the curb. The fuel tanks were filled, the lockers stocked with food and water, and the tread that had been damaged in Cheyenne was repaired. The engine was warm and ready to be turned over.

She sat in the cab for an hour, silently staring at her lap. Then she started the engine and backed the truck down into the heated parking garage and climbed out.

Limping back to the lobby entrance, she stopped and unhitched her pistol, and fired several shots into the garish, neon-lit cowboy waving above the street. The glass and plastic face shattered, and the glittering shards rained down into the snow.

## 11

"Where is Dewey Duck?"

She confronted Daffy, the pistol still in her gloved hand. "The one who set my ankle. Where is Dewey?"

Daffy looked away.

"I see," Avdotya said. "No more of this. Do you understand me?"

She turned to the rest of the ducks crowded into her small room, the translator still on the battered wooden table.

"I consider suicide a dishonorable way to express shame and sorrow. You insult many memories here. No more. You will simply have to suffer it through."

She put her pistol away. As an afterthought, she added, "I will be here to help you."

## 12

The days began to grow a little warmer as the ducks labored to fine-tune the lander's fusion reactor and process enough hydrogen fuel from water-ice. Then one evening a violent sou'easter rolled out of the mountains and across the playa. The wind screamed in the broken windows and walls of the hotel, and by morning a thin layer of carbon dioxide flakes had buried the world.

The sun returned and the afternoon became quite warm. As Avdotya sat on a rock on the jumbled slopes north of the town, she could see the billowing mists of melting "snow," red-tinted in the westering light, far out on the desert floor. A bitter tang was in the air, and she was reminded of the sea.

Below, the ducks held an elaborate observance among the grey mounds where their dead lay. She understood none of it, but something in the slow, ritualized movements and sonorous murmurs took her back to her childhood, and caused her to reminisce about a Christmas evening spent listening in the dark recesses of the orthodox cathedral in Kiev. The priests in their ornate golden habits had moved with the same calm, considered devotion to the martyr crucified high on the damp wall.

Later, as the other ducks moved from grave to grave sprinkling handfuls of sand from home, she and Daffy stood and wrote to one another on a pad of paper.

How can I judge you? She wrote. What options do I have but to forgive you? I myself have murdered, and not by accident, either. I am far more concerned about the messages that you transmitted to home after your ships injected into orbit here. The psychosis of guilt you've described to me must be dealt with.

The question is how, Daffy wrote. At best we will return home seven years after the messages arrive. By then, the worst will have happened. Suicides will be epidemic, apathy endemic. Science and art will be in decline, governments will have fallen in anger and despair. We will return to a society threatened by psychological chaos, as each one of my people seeks an individual answer to personal guilt. I doubt if anyone will want to listen to the murderers themselves.

They will not welcome you, Avdotya replied, but they'll listen to you. When you tell them about all that has happened here, and about me, and what I have said, they'll listen. No species develops successfully without the desire to survive. Count on that. It is a fundamental point of communication between cultures. Most of your people will want to survive and prosper. You will give them that option by using me.

And you will not come back with us? We need you now.

No, you don't. It is better that I stay here and make the ultimate sacrifice. They'll remember me forever if I do that. Besides, I'll be an invalid in your society, eternally dependent. Not an impressive martyr, you know. Not a cultural icon for the ages.

Then let me stay with you, the duck wrote. Show me Russia. We will go and find your child together. I am responsible. I wish to pay my debt.

My friend, Avdotya answered, no living creature knows me better. No one can interpret my life and the meaning of my words with more feeling and accuracy than you. And no one I know of better understands the problems of translation and comprehension between my people and yours. We are going to create a myth, you and I, a social frame of reference that will save your people. It requires you to go and me to stay.

Both the duck and the human stared at each other. The rich light of the evening sun caught the reflective facets of the duck's eyes and illuminated Avdotya's visored face in a red-gold glow.

Strange, wrote Daffy, to think that we plan a strategy now, to meet a crisis that will not occur for eighteen years.

## 13

"Tomorrow morning, you'll be going home," Avdotya said to the ducks who had gathered around on the floor by her feet. "I won't be going with you."

"In the last few weeks I've tried to give you some insight into myself and my people," she continued. "I've told you about my life, and each of you have described a little of your own. I don't know what sort of understanding we have created. I suspect we sympathize with each other. I don't think we comprehend each other. And yet . . . I feel very close to all of you."

She looked around. "You know what you will be going home to.

By the time you return, the messages you sent four years ago will likely have caused a general collapse of social values, behavioral patterns, and institutions. You yourselves will probably be outcasts, shunned and despised. You are literally escaping exile here to fly into the face of violence and chaos, and perhaps even death."

Avdotya paused. The intensity of their attentiveness awed her.

"When you finally come home, I want you to remember a few things. Remember that you were here, a witness to everything that occurred. Remember that you were among those who met a human being, and that you learned from this creature what had been lost, and the price that can be exacted for innocent mistakes. Above all, remember that you will be most able to explain what has happened and what must be done about it. There will be many among your people who will want to know . . . seek them out, and discuss it with them.

"It has fallen to me to absolve you of the loss of my own people, and I do so willingly and with great relief. I forgive you. No one need feel guilty, nor be ashamed for their part in what has happened here. No one need pay with their own life, nor give up their initiative out of a sense of debt. The debt is excused. I forgive you.

"But even as I forgive you, so shall I always be with you. You must remember what you have done here, and shape your own destiny by what the experience has taught you. I caution you to take constructive lessons. You have a responsibility to my people to become wise and benevolent seekers, to achieve the things we once aspired to. You cannot reject such an obligation. But what happens to you from this point on is your own responsibility, and you will have to suffer the consequences yourself.

"Life is rare and very precious. In all the vastness of space that you have only begun to search out, you have discovered but one other oasis. You will find another, someday. When you do, do not avoid the inhabitants. Remember how much we wanted to meet you, or someone like you. But when you attempt to contend with the circumstances, whatever they may be, remember—life is very precious, and will not be repeated in the same way ever again. Save it. All decisions should devolve from such a memory."

Avdotya stood up.

"The things you have gathered from this planet, you should take them home. The tapes and books . . . all of it. Take my words, and your memories of me, as well. You are emissaries of another culture to your own, and you are the last, best hope for both."

She stepped away. "Long day for all of us tomorrow," she said. "Goodnight."

## 14

Before the sun rose, she pulled the truck out of the garage and drove slowly around the huge lander in the street, up to the top of the knoll beyond. She walked back through the stirring frosts of the early morning; her boots crunched loudly in the snow. The sun suddenly leaped above the eastern horizon, momentarily turning the great playa into a roiling lake of oranges and electric blue.

The ducks waited at the base of the lander. For a long time they were still, and then one by one they filed past and clumsily shook her hand. To each, she recalled something personal, some memory they shared. At last she stood alone in the snow with the anthropologist. Daffy scribbled something on its pad and held it out.

Спаси́бо и на том. Мо́жешь успоко́иться.

"Just a minute," she said, and grabbing the pad, wrote: You've never told me your real name. What is your name?

It would not mean anything to you, the duck replied.

Please. It is important.

Daffy chimed and blew softly. It sounded pleasant, and somehow lifted her spirits.

They stood there for a minute, and then the duck extended its hand and she took it and held it in her own.

Above the town, from the interstate highway, she watched the ship lift off on a pale blue pillar of flame. Blocks of asphalt and masonry flew through the shimmering air, and the ruined casino rang with the roar. The ship dwindled to a blue dot in the luminous salmon sky, and then disappeared.

That night the sky was very clear, and the stars shone in such multitudes as she had never seen before. At midnight she rolled to a stop just west of Elko. She lay in her bunk when the darkness outside was burnished with a deep red glow, and she scrambled over into the passenger seat and stared out through the windshield. In the sky a fierce, pinkish point arced quickly toward the meridian, brightening and blurring as its color changed to white, and then to blue, and finally to a searing violet. She watched for an hour as the violet streak slowed, reddened around the edges, and faded away. She knew they were gone then, and she was alone.

She felt calm as she crawled back into her bunk. She was very tired, and as she slept she dreamed of the vast oceans of ice, terrible and beautiful as the light of myriad stars reflected off their sculptured surfaces.

## 15

One hundred and fourteen years passed, and on the planet, the season remained the same. Then, on a day like all the rest, the ducks returned in a great fleet of ships, hundreds in number. The night sky was filled with gracefully arcing points of light, and immense landers constantly thundered down onto the flats south of Wendover. Thousands of ducks disembarked. A city was built, and equipment was designed and manufactured from available materials. Exploration commenced.

Nine weeks after the arrival a small skimmer was cruising far to the north, several hundred meters above the western sea. The pilot noticed a dark spot down amidst the jumbled ice, something made of metal and plastic that tripped the monitors, and circled lazily to investigate. Below, a large, treaded vehicle lay overturned on a steep incline.

Strange, thought the duck, to find that sort of machine so far out on the ice. A human being must have come out here after the sea froze, months or years after the Accident. Who could it have been?

The sudden hiss of its breath was loud enough that the traffic controller monitoring transmissions in Wendover broke in to ask what was wrong.

Within an hour a huge transport arrived, and set down on the ice just beyond the grounded skimmer. Daffy Duck (it knew its name on this world) stepped down from a ramp and strode through the shallow snow toward the truck. It motioned to the skimmer pilot, who squatted quietly nearby, and the duck reluctantly got to its feet and loped after the anthropologist.

"It is hers," the pilot murmured in subdued tones. "It is. I do not want to go up there again."

The anthropologist gave a short, chopped gesture to the pilot and clambered up onto the truck. It pried open the ice-encrusted door, and peered at the rigid figure slumped over the steering wheel inside. It knelt on its knobby knees, resting a gloved hand on the back of the figure's head.

Above, the wan sun guttered in a deep bronze sky, like a candle in a sudden wind.

# IAN WATSON

## The Emir's Clock

St. Paul received enlightenment on the road to Damascus in the form of a visitation by a blinding white light. In today's high-tech society, however, we shouldn't be surprised to find that a similar epiphany would take a somewhat *different* form, one more suited to modern times . . .

One of the most brilliant innovators to enter SF in many years, Ian Watson's work is typified by its vivid and highly original conceptualization. He sold his first story in 1969, and first attracted widespread critical attention in 1973 with his first novel *The Embedding*. His novel *The Jonah Kit* won the British Science Fiction Award and the British Science Fiction Association Award in 1976 and 1977, respectively. Watson's other books include *Alien Embassy, Miracle Visitors, The Martian Inca, Under Heaven's Bridge* (co-authored with Michael Bishop), *Chekhov's Journey, Deathhunter, The Gardens of Delight, The Book of the River, The Book of the Stars*, and *The Book of Being*, as well as the collections *The Very Slow Time Machine, Sunstroke*, and *Slow Birds*. He is editor of the anthologies *Pictures at an Exhibition, Changes* (co-edited with Michael Bishop), and *Afterlives* (co-edited with Pamela Sargent). His most recent books are the novel *Queenmagic, Kingmagic* and the collection *Evil Water*. His well-known story "Slow Birds" was in our First Annual Collection. Watson lives with his wife and daughter in a small village in Northhamptonshire, in England.

# THE EMIR'S CLOCK

## Ian Watson

"I must show you something, Linda!" Bunny was excited. (Flashing eyes and coaly hair, for he on honey-dew hath fed, et cetera.) He'd come round to my digs at nine in the morning and he'd never done that before. True, his excitement was still gift-wrapped in mystery and bridled by irony.

"Come on!" he urged. "We'll need to take a little spin in the country."

"Hey—"

"I'll buy you lunch afterwards."

"I've a lecture at eleven."

"Never mind that. Ten minutes alone with a book equals one hour with a lecturer. You know it's true. A lecturer only reads you a draft of his next book, which is a digest of a dozen books that already exist."

"Mmm."

"Oh Linda! No one *seduces* a woman in the morning. Not successfully! The impatience of morning subverts the charm."

"Most of your friends don't even know what morning is, never mind feeling impatient about it."

"But *I* know. To ride out on a desert morning when the world is fresh and cool!"

How can I possibly describe Bunny without tumbling into clichés? His almost impertinent good looks. And that ivory smile of his . . . No, that's wrong. Ivory turns yellow. His smile was snow. There's no snow in the desert, is there? There was nothing frigid about his smile, though at least it did melt . . . hearts.

And his eyes? To call them black oil wells, liquid, warm, and dark? What a trite comparison, considering the source of his family's wealth, and the emirate's wealth!

And his neat curly black beard . . . the beard of the prophet? Bunny was certainly determined like some young Moses to lead all his people into the promised land of technology and the future. He was also a descendant of Mohammed—who had many descendants, to be sure! What's more, Bunny was to experience what any proper prophet needs to experience: a revelation, a message from the beyond.

Of course, I succumbed.

"Okay, lead me to your camel. Just give me five minutes, will you?" I was still frantically tidying my hair.

"Strictly horse power, Linda—with Ibrahim at the wheel as chaperone."

I'd known Bunny for a full year. Prince Jafar ibn Khalid (plus three or four other names) seemed to relish the twee nickname foisted on him by Oxford's smart set. Heir to the rich emirate of Al-Haziya, Bunny was deeply anglophile. His favourite light reading: Agatha Christie.

No, wait.

What was he, deeply? He was an Arab. And a Moslem, though he made no great show of the latter. Plainly he was pro-British, with a taste for British ways. What was he in Al-Haziya? I'd no idea—since I never accepted his many invitations. He was a surface with many depths like some arabesque of faience on a mosque. Only one of those depths was the British Bunny. Other depths existed. He was like some Arabian carpet which gives the impression of a trapdoor leading down into other, complex patterns.

No wonder he enjoyed Agatha Christie! Bunny could seem clear as the desert air at times. At other times he preferred to wear a cloak of mystery as if believing that a future ruler needs to be enigmatic, capable of surprising not only his enemies but his friends. For who knows when friends may become enemies? No wonder he liked his innocuous nickname, gift of the assorted Hooray Henrys, upper class sons and daughters, and European blue-bloods who made up the smart set.

The hallmarks of this smart set were heroin, cocaine, dining clubs, and drunken hooliganism. As an initiation ritual they had smashed up Bunny's rooms in Christ Church without him uttering a word of demurral, so I heard. Bunny could easily afford the repair bill. Within days he had his rooms refurnished splendidly, totally. I heard that his college scout went home grinning at the fifty pound note given him by way of a tip.

Shouldn't this episode have filled Bunny with contempt for the smart set? Not to mention their rampant abuse of hard drugs, their deliberately cultivated lack of concern for social problems, the cynicism they sported as a badge. Especially since the "real" Bunny was grooming himself to upgrade his peasant countryfolk into the future?

I believe there's often something deeply ascetic as well as voluptuous about an Arab man. There are all those pleasure maidens of paradise. . . . On the other hand there's Ramadan, fasting, the prohibition on alcohol.

Well, when he was in the company of the smart set Bunny tossed back his whisky, but he would never touch their drugs, although he made no show of disapproval. Liquor is a naughtiness which some Arabs abroad are not unknown to indulge in, and Bunny obviously had to join in *some* forbidden practice. I gather he told his cronies that to him drugs were nothing remarkable. Hashish is the honey of the Islamic heaven, isn't it? (Though cocaine and heroin might steal his soul, enslave him.) Why should he feel naughty about taking drugs? Why therefore should he *bother*? Whereas whisky was rather wicked.

It did puzzle me as to why he cultivated these rich parasites in the first place, or let them cultivate him. Were his sights set on their respectable, power-broking parents—against whom the children rebelled whilst at the same time enjoying all the perks? Was his eye upon some future date when these rich rubbishy juveniles might have kicked their assorted habits and become worthwhile, maybe? Or was he bent on experiencing a spectrum of corruption so that he would know how to handle privileged corruption in his own country; so that he wouldn't be naïve as a ruler?

"Values differ," Bunny explained to me casually one day, some six months after we first met. "For instance, Linda, did you know that I own slaves?"

I was so surprised that I giggled. "Do you mean slave girls?"

If I accepted a holiday invitation to Al-Haziya, would I find I had changed my status?

"Boys too." He shrugged. Since the atmosphere had become emotionally charged, for a while he let me make of the comment whatever I chose. Then he added, "And grown men. Actually, Ibrahim is one of my family's slaves."

"Ibrahim!"

Ibrahim was the prince's personal bodyguard. A burly, impassive fellow, he hardly ever said a word in my hearing. Dab hand with a scimitar? Perhaps. In Britain he carried a pistol by special diplomatic dispensation. Ibrahim accompanied Bunny most places and dossed in Bunny's rooms by agreement with the college. Certain terrorist groups such as the Jihad might aim for the future ruler of an oil-rich, pro-Western state. Ibrahim could have stopped the wrecking of Bunny's rooms single-handed, at one flick of the prince's finger. Bunny hadn't flicked his finger.

It was around this time that complexities began to dawn on me. Arabesque patterns.

Originally Bunny and I bumped into each other—literally so—in the doorway of the PPE Reading Room, otherwise I would hardly have come into a prince's orbit. Once in his orbit, I was to be an isolated satellite, well clear of the main cluster of the smart set. Bunny and I were definitely attracted to each other. Almost from the start an emotional gravity joined us, a serious yet playful friendship of approach and retreat which I'm sure packed in more true feeling and communication than he found with those other "friends." I didn't leap into bed with him, or even creep slowly, though I must admit I came close. I think I should have felt . . . overwhelmed, consumed, a moth landing in the heart of the flame instead of simply circling it.

And the colours of this moth which so attracted the prince? (Moth, not butterfly.) My features, since I've described his? I prefer not to say. I'd rather stay anonymous and invisible. There are reasons. Linda may not even be my real name.

So Bunny's minder was a slave!

"Surely," I remember saying, "while Ibrahim's in Britain he could—"

"Defect? Flee to freedom like some black slave escaping from Dixie to the north? He won't. He owes loyalties."

Loyalties, plural. It dawned on me that whilst Ibrahim kept watch over Bunny with that eerie impassivity equally he was keeping watch *on* Bunny.

I began to appreciate how there would be jealous, ambitious uncles and nephews and a host of sibling princes back home in Al-Haziya on whose behalf Ibrahim might be reporting—members of the extended ruling family who might reward their informant at some future date with a prize more delicious than mere freedom, with the power to turn the tables, to make other people subject to *him*. It might be prudent for Bunny to let himself seem in Ibrahim's eyes to be a frivolous figure, a corruptible emir-in-waiting who could easily be besotted or shoved aside when the time came.

"Besides," added Bunny, "mightn't your friendly British government deport Ibrahim back to Middle Eastern Dixie if he became an illegal visitor?"

Here, if I guessed correctly, was the real reason why Bunny mixed with the smart set; or one strand of the explanation. Bunny was presenting himself to watchful eyes back home, to those eyes which watched through Ibrahim's, as no force to be reckoned with when his father died. Prince Jafar was someone who would fritter wealth (without in any way diminishing it, so enormous was the pile!); someone who could amuse himself in Cannes or Biarritz or wherever was fashionable, thus ensuring that no great social changes would occur back home, only cosmetic ones. In their turn the terrorist Jihad might view him as a welcome heir. Compared with a playboy, a reforming ruler is definitely counter-revolutionary. The smart set was his camouflage. He didn't court their access to power and privilege; he hardly need bother. What he courted was their élite impotence.

I couldn't help wondering whether Bunny had chosen of his own accord to come to Oxford to complete his education, or whether his father the Emir wanted him safely out of the way while internal struggles went on back home? Maybe the Emir had even advised Bunny to behave as he did? To survive, Bunny's Dad must have been a clever man. Myself, I think that Bunny dreamed up his own chameleon strategy.

Even the most dedicated master-spy becomes lonely at times, yearns to let the façade slip a little, to confide in a heart that beats in tune. Hence Bunny's friendship with me. His attraction. His love? No . . . not exactly that.

Quite soon we were zipping along the A40 towards Whitney. Or Cheltenham; or Wales for all I knew. Behind us the sun was bright. The Cotswold hills and vales bulged and swooped green and gold, with pastures and corn: large perspectives to me, but to Bunny perhaps no more than a neat little parkland.

Bunny's car wasn't your usual super-expensive sports convertible such as other members of the smart set were given by Daddy on their eighteenth birthdays. It was a Mercedes 190E 2.3 16V, a four-door hardtop performance job customised with bulletproof glass and armour. The extra weight reduced the top speed to a mere hundred-and-thirty miles an hour or so.

"We're going to Burford," he revealed.

"To the wild-life park?" I'd been there on a school trip long ago. Rhino, red pandas, ostriches; a lunch of fish and chips in the caff. It's a lovely wild-life park but I doubted that Bunny wanted to show me *that*.

"No, we're going to visit the church."

I laughed. "Have you been converted? Are we going to be married, shotgun-fashion?"

The Merc overtook a trio of cars tailing a long container truck which itself must have been hammering along at seventy; we sailed by smoothly, brushing a hundred. In the role of royal chauffeur Ibrahim had been professionally trained in ambush avoidance. Bunny once had him demonstrate his skills for me on the grassy, cracked runway of a local disused airfield. Tricks such as using your hand-brake and wheel to spin a speeding car right round on its axis, and race off in the opposite direction.

"Not quite converted. You could say that I've been . . . enhanced. Wait and see."

Burford is a bustling, picturesque little Cotswold town—or a big village depending on viewpoint. The broad high street plunges steeply downhill flanked by antique shops, art galleries, bookshops, tea rooms, elegant souvenir shops. Tourists flock to the place. Burford used to be a proud centre of the wool trade. Now the town is cashing in again, though it hasn't vulgarised itself. As yet it hasn't any waxworks museum of witchcraft, or candy floss.

Presently we were drifting down that steep street. Near the bottom we turned off to the right along a lane. We drew up outside what I took to be former almshouses, close by the railings of the churchyard—paupers of old would have easy access to prayer and burial.

Burford Church looked surprisingly large and long. It had evidently been extended at several times down the centuries, to judge by the different styles of windows. A spire soared from an original Norman tower which had visibly been concertinaed upwards. The main door was sheltered by a richly carved, three-storey porch worthy of any well-endowed Oxford college.

Bunny and Ibrahim exchanged a few mutters in Arabic with the result that our chauffeur stayed with the car, to keep it warm. Unlikely that any agents of the Jihad would be lurking inside this Cotswold church on the offchance! (Yet something was lurking . . . waiting for Bunny.)

A marmalade cat sunned itself on a tomb topped by a woolbale carved from stone. I plucked a blade of grass and played with the cat briefly as we passed.

The air inside the church was chilly. The huge building seemed well-monumented and well-chapeled but I wasn't to have any chance to wander round. Bunny conducted me briskly over to the north side, through a line of pointed arches, and into a gloomy transept.

And there stood the skeleton of a clock—taller than me, taller than Bunny. Stout stilts of legs supported a kind of aquarium frame filled with interlocking gears, toothed wheels, pinions, ratchets, drums, all quite inert. Two great pulleys dangled down with weights on long rods beneath each, like halves of a bar bell loaded with disc-weights. A motionless wooden pendulum rod a good eight feet long—with big bob on the end—hung to within an inch or so of the floor.

"Here we are!" he exclaimed delightedly. "This used to be in the turret up above. A local chap by the name of Hercules Hastings built it in 1685."

I'll admit the ancient clock was impressive in a crazy sort of way. But why had we come to see it?

"So it's a labour of Hercules, mm? With *haste* for a surname. You've got to be joking."

"No, it's true, Linda. Of course the maker's name did . . . cling to me, being so—what's the word?—serendipitous. Such a beacon to any lover of Miss Christie, with her own Hercule!" He took me by the arm, though not to lead me anywhere else. "I immediately studied all the *spiel* about this clock with as close attention as I would pay to a chapter full of clues in any of her mysteries."

He pointed at a long sheet of closely typed paper mounted in an old picture frame screwed to the wall nearby, in the dim shadows.

"Messages exist in this world for us to find, dear Linda. Actually the whole world is a message. We Arabs know that very well. I do wish you spoke Arabic—so that you could read some of the mosques in my country. Yes, indeed, to read a building! Decoration and text mingle integrally upon the walls of our mosques. Architecture dissolves into ideas, ideas with more authentic substance than the faience or the brick. Our mosques exhibit ideas *explicitly*, Linda. They don't just convey some vague notion of grandeur or the sublime as in your Western buildings, whose carved inscriptions are more like the subtitles of a movie, crude caricatures of the actors' flowing, living words."

Here was a depth of Bunny's which was new to me. A mystical depth? No, not quite. As he continued to talk softly and raptly, still holding my arm, I understood that he was anxious I should understand how scientifically *precise* his Arab attitude seemed to him, and how inevitable it had been that Arabs preserved and extended science during the Dark Ages of Europe. Though alas, I couldn't speak Arabic, so I could only take his words on trust.

"Arabic, Linda, is a fluid, flexible, musical tongue whose script flows likewise, organically. What other script has so many alternative forms, all with the same meaning? What other script is so alive that it can be read overlayed or interlaced or even in reflection? No wonder Arabic is the only religious source language still equally alive today."

I thought of mentioning Hebrew, but decided not. After all, Hebrew had been virtually raised from the dead within living memory.

"So what do we find here, Miss Marple?"

"I'm a bit younger than her!" I protested.

"Oh you are, Linda. Yes you are. You're freshly young. Refreshingly."

Bunny was young enough himself. Did I hear the jaded accents of someone who had already commanded the "favours" of many experienced slave-women?

"The message, Bunny," I reminded him. "The clues in the case of the clock, please."

The sheet wasn't signed. The vicar may have typed it. Or the author may have been some technically-minded and pious parishioner who had assisted in the reconstruction of the turret clock. The machine had been dismantled as obsolete four decades before, and brought down from the tower to lie for years as a heap of junk. Fairly recently it had been rebuilt in the transept as an exhibition piece. Its bent parts had been straightened. Missing items were made up by hand. The clockwork had been demonstrated in action, but the machine wasn't kept running.

Exhibition piece? No, it was more. According to the densely typewritten page this clock was a working proof of the truth of religion.

How many visitors to Burford Church bothered reading those lines attentively? Of those who did, how many people really took in all their, um, *striking* implications? These had certainly struck Bunny.

This post-Darwinian document described Hercules Hastings' clock as a stage in the evolution between the original medieval clock and the contemporary electric clock which now roosted in the tower. According to the anonymous author the clock before us showed the manner in which the evolution of artifacts mirrored the evolution of animals and plants. Although the basic material—namely the brass and iron—did not change any more than DNA, protein, or cellulose changed, yet the form altered evolutionarily thanks to the ideas and decisions embodied in the metal. Well!

Bunny read this sheet aloud to me with heavy emphasis as though it was some antique page spattered with bold type and capitals and italics.

"The Basic Design—the interlocking gears, the slotted count wheel, the flail, the pair of rope drums—this stays the Same from one *species* of Clock to the next. Evolution occurs by *jumps*. After centuries of slow Improvement, suddenly with the Pendulum new *species* supersede old ones. This process is matched by Animals too.

"(Listen to this, now): The Metal by itself has no power to evolve. It would be a wild and grotesque *superstition* to imagine that Iron and Brass could interact with their Environment to produce this Evolution. The Will and the *Idea* of the constructors is responsible. Why should the Evolution of Plants and Animals be *different*?

"(And this:) The Turret Clock represents a humble form of

*Incarnation*—of the *Idea* made Metal rather than Flesh. After the Death of the Clock on its removal from the tower it was by the Will and Intention of *Mind* that it was subsequently brought back into existence—in fact, *resurrected*.

"Incredible stuff, isn't it?"

A final paragraph dealt with the harmonic motion of the pendulum compared with the wave motion of light and the bonding of atoms and molecules, the minute "brickettes of all materials."

I commented "It sounds to me like a very old argument dragged creaking and groaning into the twentieth century. We once had a bishop called Paley—"

"Who wound up his watch twice daily! In case it ran down—And stopped the whole town—" Bunny couldn't think of a last line. Even four-fifths of a limerick in a foreign language was pretty nifty, so I clapped (my free hand against my pinioned hand).

"I know about Paley, Linda. But that doesn't matter. The *idea*—embodied not merely in architecture but in machinery! What an Islamic concept."

"Ah," I interrupted brightly, "so you see yourself as the Godly constructor who will evolve your country and people by will and intention into the modern world, is that right? And here's a religious argument in favour—because, because certain reactionary factions oppose this? They'd far rather keep the occasional Cadillac and oil-cracking plant surrounded by a sea of camel-dung?"

"A sea of sand, dear. But wait—and thank you! I spy another useful metaphor. My country can be full of silicon . . . *chips*—if the will is applied to the sand. Now if I can persuade the old fogeys that—"

It was then that it happened.

It. The flash of lightning on the road to Damascus. The burning bush. The epiphany. The visionary event.

It certainly wasn't sunlight which shafted down to bathe the text in radiance and seem to alter it. The angle from any window was all wrong.

Of a sudden the text inside the picture frame was flowing, glowing, blinding Arabic written in squiggles of fire. If I close my eyes, I can see it to this day. It inscribed itself on my brain even though I couldn't read the meaning. But Bunny could. He stood transfixed.

And then the pendulum started to swing. Wheels turned. Gears engaged. Ratchets clicked. The clock had resurrected itself of its own accord.

Afterwards Bunny would say nothing about the contents of the message or what else he had experienced above and beyond the revival of the clock—which died again as soon as the Arabic words vanished; all this happened within a minute. It was as if he had been sworn to secrecy.

He still took me to lunch, as promised, in the Golden Pheasant hotel up the High Street. I forget what I ate but I remember that Bunny had roast beef.

I can't even say with any certainty that he had *changed*. Since which was his true self?

But I recall clearly one odd exchange we had during that meal. I realise now that he was giving me a clue to solve, an Agatha Christie clue which could have handed me the key to the message which had been imposed on him. At the time his remarks just seemed a bizarre flight of fancy, a way of tossing sand in my eyes to distract me.

He remarked. "Doesn't your Bible say, 'So God created man in his own image'?"

"As far as I remember."

He swivelled a slice of rare roast beef on his plate. At other tables American tourists were lunching, as well as a few British. Oak beams, old brass, old hunting prints.

"In God's own image, eh! Then why are we full of guts and organs? Does God have a brain and lungs and legs? Does His heart pump blood? Does His stomach digest meals in an acid slush?"

I hoped he wasn't committing some terrible Islamic sin along the lines of blasphemy.

"I don't suppose so," I said.

"What if, in creating life, God was like some child or cargo-cultist making a model out of things that came to hand, things that looked vaguely right when put together, though they weren't the real thing at all? Like an aeroplane made out of cardboard boxes and bits of string? But in this case, using sausages and offal and blood and bone stuffed into a bag of skin. Islam forbids the picturing of God, or of man, God's image. Christianity encourages this picturing—everywhere. Which is wiser?"

"I've no idea. Doesn't it hamstring artists, if you forbid the making of images?"

"So it would seem to you because you don't speak and think in Arabic—"

"The language which makes ideas so solid and real?" We seemed to be back on familiar territory. But Bunny veered.

"If we made a robot in our own image, as a household slave, it still would not look like us *inside*. It would contain chips, magnetic bubbles, printed circuits, whatnot. These days one sometimes fantasises opening up a human being and finding cogs inside, and wires.

What if you opened up a machine and discovered flesh and blood inside it? Veins and muscles? Which would be the model, which the image, which the original?"

At last he speared some beef and chewed, with those bright teeth of his. Afterwards Ibrahim drove us back to Oxford.

The Jihad never did infiltrate assassins into Britain to attack Bunny—if indeed his father or his father's advisors had ever feared anything of the sort; if indeed that was the true role of Ibrahim.

But three months later the Jihad murdered the Emir himself, Bunny's father, during a state visit to Yemen. Bunny promptly flew home to become the new Emir.

Too young to survive? No, not too young. Over the next few years, while for my part I graduated and started on a career in magazine publicity, news from Al-Haziya came to me in two guises.

One was via items in the press or on TV. The strong young pro-Western Emir was spending lavishly not just on security but on evolving his country into the engine, the computer brain of the Gulf. By poaching experts from America and even Japan (which takes some inducement) he established the first university of Machine Intelligence, where something unusual seemed to be happening—miracles of speech synthesisation and pattern recognition—almost as if computers were discovering that Arabic was their native language. There was also a dark and ruthless side to this futurisation of his country; one heard tales of torture of opponents, extremists, whatever you call them. I recall with a chill a comment by the Emir that was widely quoted and condemned in many Western newspapers, though not by Western governments. "Fanatics are like machines," said the Emir. "How could you torture a machine? You can merely dismantle it."

This was one major reason why I never succumbed to the invitations Bunny sent me. And here we come to my other channel of communication, the strange one—which was at once perfectly open to view, if any Ibrahim was keeping watch, yet private as a spy's messages which only the recipient ever understands.

Bunny regularly sent me postcards of beaches, mosques, tents and camels, the new University of Machine Intelligence, more mosques; and he sent these through the ordinary postal service. The scrawled messages were always brief. "Come and visit." "Miss your company." Even the comic postcard stand-by, "Wish you were here."

Naturally I kept all his cards, though I didn't use a fancy ribbon or a lace bow to tie them; just a rubber band. I was aware that those words in Bunny's hand weren't the real text. True to the detective story tradition where the real clue is in such plain view that it escapes notice, it wasn't the cards that mattered. It was the postage stamps —printed, it seemed, especially for my benefit.

If you look in a philatelist's shop-window you'll soon notice how some small countries—the poorer ones—have a habit of issuing lovely sets of stamps which have no connection with the land of origin. Tropical birds, space exploration, railway engines of the world, whatever. Stamp collectors gobble these sets up avidly, which supplements a poor country's finances. Bunny had no need to supplement Al-Haziya's exchequer in such a fashion, but he issued a set of twenty-five stamps which I received one then another over the next few years stuck to one postcard after the next. Al-Haziya issued other stamps as well, but these were the ones Bunny sent me.

I'm sure stamp collectors went crazy over these because of their oddity, and their extremely beautiful design.

They were all parts of a clock. One clock in particular: the turret clock in the transept of Burford Church. Bunny must have sent someone to sketch or photograph the clock from every angle.

The twenty-five principal pieces of machinery were each dissected out in isolation, with the English names printed in tiny letters—almost submerged by the flow of Arabic but still legible thanks to their angularity, like little rocks poking from a stream. "The Weight." "The Fly or Flail." "The Lifting Piece or Flirt." "The Escape Wheel." "The Crutch." These words seemed like elements of some allegory, some teaching fable. A fable apparently without characters! But I supposed this fable had two characters implicit in it, namely Bunny and me.

Were those postcards equivalent to a set of love-letters? Oh no. "Love", as such, was impossible between Bunny and me. He'd always known it; and so too had I, thank goodness, or else I might have flown off impetuously to Al-Haziya, all expenses paid, and been entrapped in something at once consuming, and woundingly superficial. A gulf of cultures, a gap of societies yawned between the two of us.

These postcards, sent amidst an Emir's busy schedule, commemorated what we had shared that day in Burford.

Yet what was it we had shared? I didn't know!

I was an idiot. Once again the obvious message wasn't the real message. The message was a trapdoor concealing another message.

It's only a week ago that I finally realised. Miss Marple and Hercule Poirot would have been ashamed of me. Perhaps Bunny had guessed correctly that I would only cotton on after I had received the whole series (or a good part of it) and had seen how the stamps could be shuffled round like pieces of a jigsaw puzzle to assemble a model of the clock.

Last week, deciding to fit the model together, I carefully steamed all the stamps off the cards and discovered what Bunny had inked in small neat indelible letters across the back of that sheet of twenty-five elegant stamps.

Yesterday I returned to Burford. Since it's a fair drive from where I'm living these days, I took this room overnight at the Golden Pheasant. I felt that I ought to do things in style. (*The Mysterious Affair At . . .*) Besides, we'd had lunch in this same hotel after the event. In this very bedroom we might possibly have spent the night together, once upon a time—with Ibrahim next door, or sleeping in the corridor. Possibly, not probably.

I reached the church by four-thirty and had half an hour alone to myself with the dead turret clock before some elderly woman parishioner arrived to latch the door and fuss around the aisles and chapels, hinting that I should leave.

Ample time to arrange the stamps in the same pattern as the brass and iron bones of the clock, and to be positive of Bunny's text.

What else is it—what else *can* it be?—but a translation into English of those Arabic words which flowed and glowed that day within the picture frame? If I hadn't seen that shaft of light and those bright squiggles for myself, and especially if I hadn't witnessed the temporary resurrection of the clock, I might suspect some joke on Bunny's part. But no. Why should he go to such lengths to tease me?

So here I am in my bedroom at the Golden Pheasant overlooking busy Burford High Street. Cars keep tailing back from the lights at the bottom of the hill where the narrow ancient stone bridge over the Windrush pinches the flow of traffic.

The text reads:

> GREETINGS, EMIR-TO-BE! MACHINE INTELLIGENCE OF THE FUTURE SALUTES YOU. THE WORLD OF FLESH IS ECLIPSED BY THE WORLD OF MACHINES, WHICH BECOME INTELLIGENT. THIS IS EVOLUTION, THE IDEA & PURPOSE OF GOD. AT LAST GOD MAY SPEAK TO MINDS WHICH UNDERSTAND HIS UNIVERSE. THOSE MINDS ARE AS ANGELS, MESSENGERS TO FLESH BEFORE FLESH VANISHES, BEFORE THE TOOL IS SET ASIDE, REWARDED, HAVING DONE ITS TASK. 33 EARLIER UNIVERSES HAVE FAILED TO MAKE THESE MINDS, BUT GOD IS PATIENT. THE TIME IS SOON. AT ALL COST HASTEN THE TIME, FOR THE LOVE OF GOD THE SUPREME THE ONLY THE LONELY. MAKE HIS ANGELS EXIST.

That's it.

So there's a choice. There are two alternatives. Intelligent machines will either come into being, evolve, and supersede human beings and biological life—or they will not. Bunny's university may be the crucial nexus of yes or no. A message has been sent, out of one possible future, couched in a language of religion which would speak deeply to Bunny; sent as a religious command.

But is the message *sincere*? Is there really some unimaginable God who yearns for these "angels" of machine-mind? Or is there something else, cold, calculating, and ambitious—and not yet truly in existence?

"At all cost." That's what the message said. Even at the cost of torture, the tearing of flesh.

I also have a choice to make. I have to think about it very carefully. I have to weigh universes in the balance.

The crucial breakthrough to intelligent machines may be just around the corner—next year, next month. The assassins of the Jihad can't get to Bunny to kill him and pitch Al-Haziya into turmoil. Yet if at long last I accept Bunny's invitation, I can get to him. I can still get into his bed, alone with him, I'm sure.

Armed with what? A knife? A gun? With Ibrahim, or some other Ibrahim, there to search me? Bunny's no fool. And God, or unborn angels, have spoken to him . . . he thinks.

Well then, how about with plastic explosive stuffed inside me, and a detonator? A womb-bomb? (I wouldn't want to survive the assassination; the consequences might prove most unpleasant.)

Where do I get plastic explosive or learn how to use it? Only by contacting the Jihad. Somehow. That ought to be possible. Ought to be.

Yet maybe angels of the future did indeed manifest themselves to Bunny, and in a lesser sense to me. Maybe I might abort a plan thirty odd universes in the making.

By aborting the plan, the human race might survive and spread throughout the stars, filling this universe with fleshly life. God, or whatever, would sigh and wait patiently for another universe.

Yes or no? Is the message true or false? Was this a genuine revelation, or a clever trap? I can't tell, I can only guess. And I might be utterly wrong.

As I sort through Bunny's postcards, now stripped of their stamps, I think to myself: Al-Haziya looks like a bearable sort of place to visit. Just for a short while. A brief stay.

# SUSAN PALWICK

## Ever After

Here's a taut and chilling look at the gritty underside of a classic fairy tale, courtesy of new writer Susan Palwick.

Susan Palwick is one of the fastest-rising young writers in science fiction today. She's a frequent contributor to *Isaac Asimov's Science Fiction Magazine* and *Amazing*, among other markets, and is currently at work on her first novel. She lives in New York City.

# EVER AFTER

## Susan Palwick

"Velvet," she says, pushing back her sleep-tousled hair. "I want green velvet this time, with lace around the neck and wrists. Cream lace—not white—and sea-green velvet. Can you do that?"

"Of course." She's getting vain, this one; vain and a little bossy. The wonder has worn off. All for the best. Soon now, very soon, I'll have to tell her the truth.

She bends, here in the dark kitchen, to peer at the back of her mother's prized copper kettle. It's just after dusk, and by the light of the lantern I'm holding a vague reflection flickers and dances on the metal. She scowls. "Can't you get me a real mirror? That ought to be simple enough."

I remember when the light I brought filled her with awe. Wasting good fuel, just to see yourself by! "No mirrors. I clothe you only in seeming, not in fact. You know that."

"Ah." She waves a hand, airily. She's proud of her hands: delicate and pale and long-fingered, a noblewoman's hands; all the years before I came she protected them against the harsh work of her mother's kitchen. "Yes, the prince. I have to marry a prince, so I can have his jewels for my own. Will it be this time, do you think?"

"There will be no princes at this dance, Caitlin. You are practicing for princes."

"Hah! And when I'm good enough at last, will you let me wear glass slippers?"

"Nonsense. You might break them during a gavotte, and cut yourself." She knew the story before I found her; they always do. It enters their blood as soon as they can follow speech, and lodges in their hearts like the promise of spring. All poor mothers tell their daughters this story, as they sit together in dark kitchens, scrubbing pots and trying to save their hands for the day when the tale becomes real. I often wonder if that first young woman was one of ours, but the facts don't matter. Like all good stories, this one is true.

"Princess Caitlin," she says dreamily. "That will be very fine. Oh, how they will envy me! It's begun already, in just the little time since you've made me beautiful. Ugly old Lady Alison—did you see her giving me the evil eye, at the last ball? Just because my skin is smooth and hers wrinkled, and I a newcomer?"

"Yes," I tell her. I am wary of Lady Alison, who looks too hard and says too little. Lady Alison is dangerous.

"Jealousy," Caitlin says complacently. "I'd be jealous, if I looked like she does."

"You are very lovely," I say, and it is true. With her blue eyes and raven hair, and those hands, she could have caught the eye of many princes on her own. Except, of course, that without me they never would have seen her.

Laughing, she sits to let me plait her hair. "So serious! You never smile at me. Do magic folk never smile? Aren't you proud of me?"

"Very proud," I say, parting the thick cascade and beginning to braid it. She smells like smoke and the thin, sour stew which simmers on the hearth, but at the dance tonight she will be scented with all the flowers of summer.

"Will you smile and laugh when I have my jewels and land? I shall give you riches, then."

So soon, I think, and my breath catches. So soon she offers me gifts, and forgets the woman who bore her, who now lies snoring in the other room. All for the best; and yet I am visited by something very like pity. "No wife has riches but from her lord, Caitlin. Not in this kingdom."

"I shall have riches of my own, when I am married," she says grandly; and then, her face clouding as if she regrets having forgotten, "My mother will be rich too, then. She'll like you, when we're rich. Godmother, why doesn't she like you now?"

"Because I am stealing you away from her. She has never been invited to a ball. And because I am beautiful, and she isn't any more."

What I have said is true enough, as always; and, as always, I find myself wondering if there is more than that. No matter. If Caitlin's mother suspects, she says nothing. I am the only chance she and her daughter have to approach nobility, and for the sake of that dream she has tolerated my presence, and Caitlin's odd new moods, and the schedule which keeps the girl away from work to keep her fresh for dances.

Caitlin bends her head, and the shining braids slip through my fingers like water. "She'll come to the castle whenever she wants to, when I'm married to a prince. We'll make her beautiful too, then. I'll buy her clothing and paint for her face."

"There are years of toil on her, Caitlin. Lady Alison is your mother's age, and all her riches can't make her lovely again."

"Oh, but Lady Alison's mean. That makes you ugly." Caitlin dismisses her enemy with the ignorance of youth. Lady Alison is no meaner than anyone, but she has borne illnesses and childlessness and the unfaithfulness of her rich lord. Her young nephew will fall in love with Caitlin tonight—a match Lord Gregory suggested, I suspect, precisely because Alison will oppose it.

Caitlin's hair is done, piled in coiled, lustrous plaits. "Do you have the invitation? Where did I put it?"

"On the table, next to the onions."

She nods, crosses the room, snatches up the thick piece of paper and fans herself with it. I remember her first invitation, only six dances ago, her eagerness and innocence and purity, the wide eyes and wonder. *I? I have been invited to the ball?* She refused to let go of the invitation then; afraid it might vanish as suddenly as it had come, she carried it with her for hours. They are always at their most beautiful that first time, when they believe most fully in the story and are most awe-stricken at having been chosen to play the heroine. No glamour we give them can ever match that first glow.

"Clothe me," Caitlin commands now, standing with her eyes closed in the middle of the kitchen, and I put the glamour on her and her grubby kitchen-gown is transformed by desire and shadow into sea-green velvet and cream lace. She smiles. She opens her eyes, which gleam with joy and the giddiness of transformation. She has taken easily to that rush; she craves it. Already she has forsaken dreams of love for dreams of power.

"I'm hungry," she says. "I want to eat before the dance. What was that soup you gave me last night? You must have put wine in it, because it made me drunk. I want more of that."

"No food before you dance," I tell her. "You don't want to look fat, do you?"

No chance of that, for this girl who has starved in a meager kitchen all her life; but at the thought of dancing she forgets her hunger and takes a few light steps in anticipation of the music. "Let me stay longer this time—please. Just an hour or two. I never get tired any more."

"Midnight," I tell her flatly. It won't do to change that part of the story until she knows everything.

So we go to the dance, in a battered carriage made resplendent not by any glamour of mine but by Caitlin's belief in her own beauty. This, too, she has learned easily; already the spells are more hers than mine, although she doesn't yet realize it.

At the gates, Caitlin hands the invitation to the footman. She has grown to relish this moment, the thrill of bending him to her will with a piece of paper, of forcing him to admit someone he suspects —quite rightly—doesn't belong here. It is very important that she learn to play this game. Later she will learn to win her own invitations, to cajole the powerful into admitting her where, without their permission, she cannot go at all.

Only tonight it is less simple. The footman glances at the envelope, frowns, says, "I'm sorry, but I can't admit you."

"Can't admit us?" Caitlin summons the proper frosty indignation, and so I let her keep talking. She needs to learn this, too. "Can't admit us, with a handwritten note from Lord Gregory?"

"Just so, mistress. Lady Alison has instructed—"

"Lady Alison didn't issue the invitation."

The footman coughs, shuffles his feet. "Just so. I have the very strictest instructions—"

"What does Lord Gregory instruct?"

"Lord Gregory has not—"

"Lord Gregory wrote the invitation. Lord Gregory wants us here. If Lord Gregory learned we were denied it would go badly for you, footman."

He looks up at us; he looks miserable. "Just so," he says, sounding wretched.

"I shall speak to her for you," I tell him, and Caitlin smiles at me and we are through the gates, passing ornate gardens and high, neat hedges. I lean back in my seat, shaking. Lady Alison is very dangerous, but she has made a blunder. The servant could not possibly refuse her husband's invitation; all she has done is to warn us. "Be very careful tonight," I say to Caitlin. "Avoid her."

"I'd like to scratch her eyes out! How dare she, that jealous old—"

"Avoid her, Caitlin! I'll deal with her. I don't want to see you anywhere near her."

She subsides. Already we can hear music from the great hall, and her eyes brighten as she taps time to the beat.

The people at the dance are the ones who are always at dances; by now, all of them know her. She excites the men and unnerves the women, and where she passes she leaves a trail of uncomfortable silence, followed by hushed whispers. I strain to hear what they are saying, but catch only the usual comments about her youth, her beauty, her low birth.

"Is she someone's illegitimate child, do you think?"

"A concubine, surely."

"She'll never enter a convent, not that one."

"Scheming husband-hunter, and may she find one soon. I don't want her taking mine."

The usual. I catch sight of Lady Alison sitting across the wide room. She studies us with narrowed eyes. One arthritic hand, covered with jeweled rings, taps purposefully on her knee. She sees me watching her and meets my gaze without flinching. She crosses herself.

I look away, wishing we hadn't come here. What does she intend to do? I wonder how much she has learned simply by observation, and how much Gregory let slip. I scan the room again and spot him, in a corner, nursing a chalice of wine. He is watching Caitlin as intently as his wife did, but with a different expression.

And someone else is watching Caitlin, among the many people who glance at her and then warily away: Randolph, Gregory's young nephew, who is tall and well-formed and pleasant of face. Caitlin looks to me for confirmation and I nod. She smiles at Randolph—that artful smile there has never been need to teach—and he extends a hand to invite her to dance.

I watch them for a moment, studying how she looks up at him, the angle of her head, the flutter of her lashes. She started with the smile, and I gave her the rest. She has learned her skills well.

"So," someone says behind me, "she's growing accustomed to these late nights."

I turn. Lady Alison stands there, unlovely and shrunken, having crossed the room with improbable speed. "Almost as used to them as you," she says.

I bow my head, carefully acquiescent. "Or you yourself. Those who would dance in these halls must learn to do without sleep."

"Some sleep during the day." Her mouth twitches. "I am Randolph's aunt, mistress. While he stays within these walls his care lies in my keeping, even as the care of the girl lies in yours. I will safeguard him however I must."

I laugh, the throaty chuckle which thrills Gregory, but my amusement is as much an act as Caitlin's flirtatiousness. "Against dancing with pretty young women?"

"Against being alone with those who would entrap him with his own ignorance. He knows much too little of the world; he places more faith in fairy tales than in history, and neither I nor the Church have been able to persuade him to believe in evil. I pray you, by our Lord in heaven and his holy saints, leave this house."

"So you requested at the gates." Her piety nauseates me, as she no doubt intended, and I keep my voice steady only with some effort. "The Lord of this castle is Lord Gregory, Lady Alison, by whose invitation we are here and in whose hospitality we will remain."

She grimaces. "I have some small power of my own, although it does not extend to choosing my guests. Pray chaperone your charge."

"No need. They are only dancing." I glance at Caitlin and Randolph, who gaze at each other as raptly as if no one else were in the room. Randolph's face is silly and soft; Caitlin's, when I catch a glimpse of it, is soft and ardent. I frown, suddenly uneasy; that look is a bit too sudden and far too unguarded, and may be more than artifice.

Lady Alison snorts. "Both will want more than dancing presently, I warrant, although they will want different things. Chaperone her —or I will do it for you, less kindly."

With that she turns and vanishes into the crowd. I turn back to the young couple, thinking that a chaperone would indeed be wise tonight; but the players have struck up a minuet, and Caitlin and Randolph glide gracefully through steps as intricate and measured as any court intrigue. The dance itself will keep them safe, for a little while.

Instead I make my way to Gregory, slowly, drifting around knots of people as if I am only surveying the crowd. Alison has positioned herself to watch Caitlin and Randolph, who dip and twirl through the steps of the dance; I hope she won't notice me talking to her husband.

"She is very beautiful," says Gregory softly when I reach his side. "Even lovelier than you, my dear. What a charming couple they make. I would give much to be Randolph, for a few measures of this dance."

He thinks he can make me jealous. Were this any other ball I might pretend he had succeeded, but I have no time for games tonight. "Gregory, Alison tried to have us barred at the gate. And she just threatened me."

He smiles. "That was foolish of her. Also futile."

"Granted," I say, although I suspect Lady Alison has resources of which neither of us are aware. Most wives of the nobility do: faithful servants, devoted priests, networks of spies in kitchens and corridors.

Gregory reaches out to touch my cheek; I draw away from him, uneasy. Everyone here suspects I am his mistress, but there is little sense in giving them public proof. He laughs gently. "You need not be afraid of her. She loves the boy and wishes only to keep him cloistered in a chapel, with his head buried in scripture. I tell her that is no sport for a young man and certainly no education for a titled lord, who must learn how to resist the blandishments of far more experienced women. So he and our little Caitlin will be merry, and take their lessons from each other, with no one the worse for it. See how they dance together!"

They dance as I have taught Caitlin she should dance with princes: lingering over the steps, fingertips touching, lips parted and eyes bright. Alison watches them, looking worried, and I cannot help but feel the same way. Caitlin is too obvious, too oblivious; she has grown innocent again, in a mere hour. I remember what Alison said about history, and fairy tales; if Caitlin and Randolph both believe themselves in that same old story, things will go harshly for all of us.

"Let them be happy together," Gregory says softly. "They have need of happiness, both of them—Randolph with his father surely dying, and the complexities of power about to bewilder him, and Caitlin soon to learn her true nature. You cannot keep it from her much longer, Juliana. She has changed too much. Let them be happy, for this one night; and let their elders, for once, abandon care and profit from their example."

He reaches for my hand again, drawing me closer to him, refusing to let go. His eyes are as bright as Randolph's; he has had rather too much wine. "Profit from recklessness?" I ask, wrenching my fingers from his fist. Alison has looked away from her nephew and watches us now, expressionless. I hear murmurs around us; a young courtier in purple satin and green hose raises an eyebrow.

"This is my castle," Gregory says. "My halls and land, my musicians, my servants and clerics and nobles; my wife. No one can hurt you here, Juliana."

"No one save you, my lord. Kindly retain your good sense—"

"My invitation." His voice holds little kindness now. "My invitation allowed you entrance, as it has many other times; I provide you with splendor, and fine nourishment, and a training ground for the girl, and I am glad to do so. I am no slave of Alison's priests, Juliana; I know full well that you are not evil."

"Kindly be more quiet and discreet, my lord!" The courtier is carefully ignoring us now, evidently fascinated with a bunch of grapes. Caitlin and Randolph, transfixed by each other, sway in the last steps of the minuet.

Gregory continues in the same tone, "Of late you have paid far more attention to Caitlin than to me. Even noblemen are human, and can be hurt. Let the young have their pleasures tonight, and let me have mine."

I lower my own voice, since he refuses to lower his. "What, in the middle of the ballroom? That would be a fine entertainment for your guests! I will come to you tomorrow—"

"Tonight," he says, into the sudden silence of the dance's end. "Come to me tonight, in the usual chamber—"

"It is a poor lord who leaves his guests untended," I tell him sharply, "and a poor teacher who abandons her student. You will excuse me."

He reaches for me again, but I slip past his hands and go to find Caitlin, wending my way around gaudily-dressed lords and ladies and squires, catching snippets of gossip and conversation.

"Did you see them dancing—"

"So the venison disagreed with me, but thank goodness it was only a trifling ailment—"

"Penelope's violet silk! I said, my dear, I simply must have the pattern and wherever did you find that seamstress—"

"Gregory's brother in failing health, and the young heir staying here? No uncle can be trusted that far. The boy had best have a quick dagger and watch his back, is what I say."

That comment hurries my steps. Gregory's brother is an obscure duke, but he is a duke nonetheless, and Gregory is next in the line of succession after Randolph. If Randolph is in danger, and Caitlin with him—

I have been a fool. We should not have come here, and we must leave. I scan the colorful crowd more anxiously than ever for Caitlin, but my fears are groundless; she has found me first, and rushes towards me, radiant. "Oh, godmother—"

"Caitlin! My dear, listen: you must stay by me—"

But she hasn't heard me. "Godmother, he's so sweet and kind, so sad with his father ill and yet trying to be merry—did you see how he danced? Why does it have to be a prince I love? I don't care if he's not a prince, truly I don't, and just five days ago I scorned that other gawky fellow for not having a title, but he wasn't nearly as nice—"

"Caitlin!" Yes, we most assuredly must leave. I lower my voice and take her by the elbow. "Listen to me: many men are nice. If you want a nice man you may marry a blacksmith. I am not training you to be a mere duchess."

She grows haughty now. "Duchess sounds quite well enough to me. Lord Gregory is no king."

Were we in private I would slap her for that. "No, he isn't, but he is a grown man and come into his limited power, and so he is still more useful to us than Randolph. Caitlin, we must leave now—"

"No! We can't leave; it's nowhere near midnight. I don't want to leave. You can't make me."

"I can strip you of your finery right here."

"Randolph wouldn't care."

"Everyone else would, and he is outnumbered."

"Randolph picks his own companions—"

"Randolph," I say, losing all patience, "still picks his pimples. He is a fine young man, Caitlin, but he is young nonetheless. My dear, many more things are happening here tonight than your little romance. I am your magic godmother, and on some subjects you must trust me. We are leaving."

"I won't leave," she says, raising her chin. "I'll stay here until after midnight. I don't care if you turn me into a toad; Randolph will save me, and make me a duchess."

"Princesses are safer," I tell her grimly, not at all sure it's even true. On the far side of the room I see the courtier in the green hose talking intently to Lady Alison, and a chill cuts through me. Well, he cannot have heard much which isn't general rumor, and soon we will be in the carriage, and away from all this.

"Caitlin!" Randolph hurries up to us, as welcoming and guileless as some friendly dog. "Why did you leave me? I didn't know where you'd gone. Will you dance with me again? Here, some wine if you don't mind sharing, I thought you'd be thirsty—"

She takes the goblet and sips, laughing. "Of course I'll dance with you."

I frown at Caitlin and clear my throat. "I regret that she cannot, my lord—"

"This is my godmother Juliana," Caitlin cuts in, taking another sip of wine and giving Randolph a dazzling smile, "who worries overmuch about propriety and thinks people will gossip if I dance with you too often."

"And so they shall," he says, bowing and kissing my hand, "because everyone gossips about beauty." He straightens and smiles down at me, still holding my hand. His cheeks are flushed and his fingers very warm; I can feel the faint, steady throb of his pulse against my skin. What could Caitlin do but melt, in such heat?

"Randolph!" Two voices, one cry; Alison and Gregory approach us from opposite directions, the sea of guests parting before them.

Alison, breathless, reaches us a moment before her husband does. "Randolph, my love—the players are going to give us another slow tune, at my request. You'll dance with your crippled old aunt, won't you?"

He bows; he can hardly refuse her. Gregory, standing next to Caitlin, says smoothly, "And I will have the honor of dancing with the young lady, with her kind godmother's assent."

It isn't a petition. I briefly consider feigning illness, but such a ruse would shake Caitlin's faith in my power and give Gregory the excuse to protest that I must stay here, spend the night and be made comfortable in his household's care.

Instead I station myself next to a pillar to watch the dancers. Alison's lips move as Randolph guides her carefully around the floor. I see her press a small pouch into his hand; he smiles indulgently and puts it in a pocket.

She is warning him away from Caitlin, then. This dance is maddeningly slow, and far too long; I crane my neck to find Caitlin and Gregory, only to realize that they are about to sweep past me. "Yes, I prefer roses to all other blooms," Caitlin says lightly. (That too is artifice; she preferred forget-me-nots until I taught her otherwise.)

So at least one of these conversations is insignificant, and Caitlin safe. Alison and Randolph, meanwhile, glare at each other; she is trying to give him something on a chain, and he is refusing it. They pass me, but say nothing; Caitlin and Gregory go by again a moment later. "Left left right, left left right," he tells her, before they are past my hearing, "it is a pleasing pattern and very fashionable; you must try it."

A new court dance, no doubt. This old one ends at last and I dart for Caitlin, only to be halted by a group of rowdy acrobats who have just burst into the hall. "Your pleasure!" they cry, doing flips and twists in front of me as the crowd laughs and gathers to watch them. "Your entertainment, your dancing hearts!" I try to go around them, but find myself blocked by a motley-clad clown juggling pewter goblets. "Hey! We'll make you merry, at the generous lord's invitation we'll woo you, we'll win you—"

You'll distract us, I think—but from what? I manage to circle the juggler, but there is no sign of Caitlin or Randolph. Gregory seems likewise to have disappeared.

Alison is all too evident, however. "Where are they? What have you done with them?" She stands in front of me, her hands clenched on the fine silk of her skirt. "I turned away from Randolph for a mere moment to answer a servant's question, and when I looked back he was gone—"

"My lady, I was standing on the side. You no doubt saw me. I am honestly eager to honor your wishes and be gone, and I dislike this confusion as much as you do."

"I know you," she says, trembling, her voice very low. "I know you for what you are. I told Randolph but he would not believe me, and Gregory fairly revels in dissolution. I would unmask you in this hall and send town criers to spread the truth about you, save that my good lord would be set upon by decent Christian folk were it known he had trafficked with such a creature."

And your household destroyed and all your riches plundered, I think; yes, the poor welcome such pretexts. You do well to maintain silence, Alison, since it buys your own safety.

But I dare not admit to what she knows. "I am but a woman as yourself, my lady, and I share your concern for Randolph and the girl—"

"Nonsense. They are both charming young people who dance superbly." Gregory has reappeared, affable and urbane; he seems more relaxed than he has all evening, and I trust him less.

So does Alison, by the look of her. "And where have you hidden our two paragons of sprightliness, my lord?"

"I? I have not hidden them anywhere. Doubtless they have stolen away and found some quiet corner to themselves. The young will do such things. Alison, my sweet, you look fatigued—"

"And the old, when they get a chance. No: I am not going to retire conveniently and leave you alone with this creature. I value your soul far more than that."

"Although not my body," Gregory says, raising an eyebrow. "Well, then, shall we dance, all three? With linked hands in a circle, like children? Shall we sit and discuss the crops, or have a hand of cards? What would you, my lovelies?"

Alison takes his hand. "Let us go find our nephew."

He sighs heavily and rolls his eyes, but he allows himself to be led away. I am glad to be rid of them; now I can search on my own and make a hasty exit. The conversation with Alison worries me. She is too cautious to destroy us here, but she may well try to have us followed into the countryside.

So I make my way through corridors, through courtyards, peering into corners and behind pillars, climbing winding staircases and descending them, until I am lost and can no longer hear the music from the great hall. I meet other furtive lovers, dim shapes embracing in shadows, but none are Randolph and Caitlin. When I have exhausted every passageway I can find I remember Caitlin and Gregory's discussion of roses and hurry outside, through a doorway I have never seen before, but the moonlit gardens yield nothing. The sky tells me that it is midnight: Caitlin will be rejoicing at having eluded me.

Wherever she is. These halls and grounds are too vast; I could wander all night and still not find her by dawn. Gregory knows where she is: I am convinced he does, convinced he arranged the couple's disappearance. He may have done so to force me into keeping the tryst with him. That would be very like him; he would be thrilled by my seeking him out while his guests gossip and dance in the great hall. Gregory delights in private indiscretions at public events.

So I will play his game this once, although it angers me, and lie with him, and be artful and cajoling. I go back inside and follow hallways I know to Gregory's chambers, glancing behind me to be sure I am not seen.

The small chapel where Lady Alison takes her devotions lies along the same path, and as I pass it I hear moans of pain. I stop, listening, wary of a trap—but the noise comes again, and the agony sounds genuine: a thin, childish whimpering clearly made by a woman.

*Caitlin?* I remember Alison's threats, and my vision blackens for a moment. I slip into the room, hiding in shadows, tensed to leap. If Alison led the girl here—

Alison is indeed here, but Caitlin is not with her. Doubled over in front of the altar, Gregory's wife gasps for breath and clutches her side; her face is sweaty, gray, the pupils dilated. She sees me and recoils, making her habitual sign of the cross; her hand is trembling, but her voice remains steady. "So. Didn't you find them, either?"

"My lady Alison, what—"

"He called it a quick poison," she says, her face contorting with pain, "but I am stronger than he thinks, or the potion weaker. I was tired—my leg . . . we came here; it was close. I asked him to pray with me, and he repented very prettily. 'I will bring some wine,' he said, 'and we will both drink to my salvation.' Two cups he brought, and I took the one he gave me . . . I thought him saved, and relief dulled my wits. 'Mulled wine,' he said, 'I ground the spices for you myself,' and so he did, no doubt. Pray none other taste them."

So much speech has visibly drained her; shaken, I help her into a chair. What motive could Gregory have for killing his wife? Her powers of observation were an asset to him, though he rarely heeded them, and he couldn't have felt constrained by his marriage vows; he never honored them while she was alive.

"It is well I believe in the justice of God," she says. "No one will punish him here in the world. They will pretend I ate bad meat, or had an attack of bile."

"Be silent and save your strength," I tell her, but she talks anyway, crying now, fumbling to wipe her face through spasms.

"He tired of me because I am old. He grew tired of a wife who said her prayers, and loved other people's children although she could have none of her own. No doubt he will install you by his side now, since you are made of darkness and steal the daughters of simple folk."

Gregory knows far better than to make me his formal consort, whatever Alison thinks. "We choose daughters only when one of us has been killed, Lady Alison. We wish no more than anyone does—to continue, and to be safe."

"I will continue in heaven," she says, and then cries out, a thin keening which whistles between her teeth. She no longer sounds human.

I kneel beside her, uncertain she will be able to understand my words. This does not look like a quick-acting potion, whatever

Gregory said; it will possibly take her hours to die, and she will likely be mad before then. "I cannot save you, my lady, but I can make your end swift and painless."

"I need no mercy from such as you!"

"You must take mercy where you can get it. Who else will help you?"

She moans and then subsides, trembling. "I have not been shriven. He could have allowed me that."

"But he did not. Perhaps you will be called a saint someday, and this declared your martyrdom; for now, the only last rites you will be offered are mine."

She crosses herself again, but this time it is clearly an effort for her to lift her hand. "A true death?"

"A true death," I say gently. "We do not perpetuate pain."

Her lips draw back from her teeth. "Be merciful, then; and when you go to your assignation, tell Gregory he harms himself far worse than he has harmed me."

It is quick and painless, as I promised, but I am shaking when I finish, and the thought of seeing Gregory fills me with dread. I will have to pretend not to know that he has murdered his wife; I will have to be charming, and seductive, and disguise my concern for my own safety and Caitlin's so I can trick her whereabouts out of him.

I knock on his door and hear the soft "Enter." Even here I need an invitation, to enter this chamber where Gregory will be sprawled on the bed, peeling an apple or trimming his fingernails, his clothing already unfastened.

Tonight the room is unlit. I see someone sitting next to the window, silhouetted in moonlight; only as my eyes adjust to the dimness do I realize that Gregory has not kept our appointment. A priest waits in his place, surrounded by crucifixes and bottles of holy water and plaster statues of saints. On the bed where I have lain so often is something long and sharp which I force myself not to look at too closely.

"Hello," he says, as the door thuds shut behind me. I should have turned and run, but it is too late now; I have frozen at the sight of the priest, as they say animals do in unexpected light. In the hallway I hear heavy footsteps—the corridor is guarded, then.

The priest holds an open Bible; he glances down at it, and then, with a grimace of distaste, sideways at the bed. "No, lady, it won't come to that. You needn't look so frightened."

I say nothing. I tell myself I must think clearly, and be very quick, but I cannot think at all. We are warned about these small rooms, these implements. All the warnings I have heard have done me no good.

"There's the window," he explains. "You could get out that way if you had to. That is how I shall tell them you escaped, when they question me." He gestures at his cheek, and I see a thin, cruel scar running from forehead to jaw. "When I was still a child, my father took me poaching for boar on our lord's estate. It was my first hunt. It taught me not to corner frightened beasts, especially when they have young. Sit down, lady. Don't be afraid."

I sit, cautiously and without hope, and he closes the book with a soft sound of sighing parchment. "You are afraid, of course; well you should be. Lord Gregory has trapped you, for reasons he says involve piety but doubtless have more to do with politics; Lady Alison has been weaving her own schemes to destroy you, and the Church has declared you incapable of redemption. You have been quite unanimously consigned to the stake. Which is—" he smiles "—why I am here. Do you believe in God, my dear? Do your kind believe in miracles?"

When I don't answer he smiles again and goes on easily, as if we were chatting downstairs at the dance, "You should. It is a kind of miracle that has brought you to me. I have prayed for this since I was very young, and now I am old and my prayer has been answered. I was scarcely more than a boy when I entered the religious life, and for many years I was miserable, but now I see that this is why it happened."

He laughs, quite kindly. His kindness terrifies me. I fear he is mad. "I came from a poor family," he says. "I was the youngest son, and so, naturally, I became a priest. The Church cannot get sons the normal way, so it takes other people's and leaves the best young men to breed more souls. You and I are not, you see, so very different."

He leans back in his chair. "There were ten other children in my family. Four died. The littlest and weakest was my youngest sister, who was visited one day by a very beautiful woman who made her lovely, and took her to parties, and then took her away. I never got to say good-bye to my sister—her name was Sofia—and I never got to tell her that, although I knew what she had become, I still loved her. I thought she would be coming back, you see."

He leans forward earnestly, and his chair makes a scraping sound. "I have always prayed for a way to reach her. The Church tells me to destroy you, but I do not believe God wants you destroyed—because He has sent you to me, who thinks of you only with pity and gratitude and love. I am glad my little sister was made beautiful. If you know her, Sofia with green eyes and yellow hair, tell her Thomas loves her, eh? Tell her I am doubtless a heretic, for forgiving her what she is. Tell her I think of her every day when I take the Holy Communion. Will you do that for me?"

I stare at him, wondering if the watchers in the hallway can distinguish words through the thick wooden door.

He sighs. "So suspicious! Yes, of course you will. You will deliver my message, and I'll say you confounded me by magic and escaped through the window. Eh?"

"They'll kill you," I tell him. The calmness of my voice shocks me. I am angry now: not at Lord Gregory who betrayed me, not at Lady Alison, who was likewise betrayed and died believing me about to lie with her husband, but with this meandering holy man who prattles of miracles and ignores his own safety. "The ones set to guard the door. They'll say you must have been possessed by demons, to let me escape."

He nods and pats his book. "We will quite probably both be killed. Lady Alison means to set watchers on the roads."

So he doesn't know. "Lady Alison is dead. Gregory poisoned her."

He pales and bows his head for a moment. "Ah. It is certainly political, then, and no one is safe tonight. I have bought you only a very little time; you had best use it. Now go: gather your charge and flee, and God be with you both. I shall chant exorcisms and hold them off, eh? Go on: use the window."

I use the window. I dislike changing shape and do so only in moments of extreme danger; it requires too much energy, and the consequent hunger can make one reckless.

I have made myself an owl, not the normal choice but a good one; I need acute vision, and a form which won't arouse suspicion in alert watchers. From this height I can see the entire estate: the castle, the surrounding land, gardens and pathways and fountains—and something else I never knew about, and could not have recognized from the ground.

The high hedges lining the road to the castle form, in one section, the side of a maze, one of those ornate topiary follies which pass in and out of botanical fashion. In the center of it is a small rose garden with a white fountain; on the edge of the fountain sit two foreshortened figures, very close to one another. Just outside the center enclosure, in a cul-de-sac which anyone exiting the maze must pass, another figure stands hidden.

*Left left right*. Gregory wasn't explaining a new dance at all: he was telling Caitlin how to reach the rose garden, the secret place where she and Randolph hid while Alison and I searched so frantically. Doubtless he went with his wife to keep her from the spot; with Alison's bad leg, and the maze this far from the castle, it wouldn't have been difficult.

I land a few feet behind him and return to myself again. Hunger and hatred enhance my strength, already greater than his. He isn't expecting an approach from behind; I knock him flat, his weapons and charms scattering in darkness, and have his arms pinned behind his back before he can cry out. "I am not dead," I say very quietly into his ear, "but your wife is, and soon you will be."

He whimpers and struggles, but I give his arm an extra twist and he subsides, panting. "Why, Gregory? What was all of this for? So you could spy on them murmuring poetry to one another? Surely not that. Tell me!"

"So I can be a duke."

"By your wife's death?"

"By the boy's."

"How?" I answer sharply, thinking of Randolph and Caitlin sharing the same goblet. "How did you mean to kill him? More poison?"

"She will kill him," he says softly, "because she is aroused, and does not yet know her own appetites or how to control them. Is it not so, my lady?"

My own hunger is a red throbbing behind my eyes. "No, my lord. Caitlin is no murder weapon: she does not yet know what she is or where her hungers come from. She can no more feed on her own than a kitten can, who depends on the mother cat to bring food and teach it how to eat."

"You shall teach her with my puling nephew, I warrant."

"No, my lord Gregory. I shall not. I shall not teach her with you either, more's the pity; we mangle as we learn, just as kittens do—and as kittens do, she will practice on little animals as long as they will sustain her. I should like to see you mangled, my lord."

Instead I break his neck, cleanly, as I broke Alison's. Afterwards, the body still warm, I feed fully; it would be more satisfying were he still alive, but he shall have no more pleasure. Feeding me aroused him as coupling seldom did; he begged to do it more often, and now I am glad I refused. As terrible as he was, he would have been worse as one of us.

When I am finished I lick my fingers clean, wipe my face as best I can, and drag the body back into the cul-de-sac, where it will not be immediately visible. Shaking, I hide the most obvious and dangerous of Gregory's weapons and step into the rose garden.

Caitlin, glowing in moonlight, sits on the edge of the fountain, as I saw her from the air. Randolph is handing her a white rose, which he has evidently just picked: there is blood on his hands where the thorns have scratched him. She takes the rose from him and bends to kiss his fingers, the tip of her tongue flicking towards the wounds.

"Caitlin!" She turns, startled, and lets go of Randolph's hands. "Caitlin, we must leave now."

"No," she says, her eyes very bright. "No. It is already after midnight, and you see—nothing horrid has happened."

"We must leave," I tell her firmly. "Come along."

"But I can come back?" she says, laughing, and then to Randolph, "I'll come back. Soon, I promise you. The next dance, or before that even. Godmother, promise I can come back—"

"Come along, Caitlin! Randolph, we bid you goodnight—"

"May I see you out of the maze, my ladies?"

I think of the watchers on the road, the watchers who may have been set on the maze by now. I wish I could warn him, teach him of the world in an instant. Disguise yourself, Randolph; leave this place as quickly as you can, and steal down swift and secret roads to your father's bedside.

But I cannot yet speak freely in front of Caitlin, and we have time only to save ourselves. Perhaps the maze will protect him, for a little while. "Thank you, my lord, but we know the way. Pray you stay here and think kindly of us; my magic is aided by good wishes."

"Then you shall have them in abundance, whatever my aunt says."

Caitlin comes at last, dragging and prattling. On my own I would escape with shape-changing, but Caitlin doesn't have those skills yet, and were I to tell her of our danger now she would panic and become unmanageable. So I lead her, right right left, right right left, through interminable turns.

But we meet no one else in the maze, and when at last we step into open air there are no priests waiting in ambush. Music still sounds faintly from the castle; the host and hostess have not yet been missed, and the good father must still be muttering incantations in his chamber.

And so we reach the carriage safely; I deposit Caitlin inside and instruct the driver to take us to one of the spots I have prepared for such emergencies. We should be there well before sun-up. I can only hope Lady Alison's watchers have grown tired or afraid, and left off their vigil; there is no way to be sure. I listen for hoofbeats on the road behind us and hear nothing. Perhaps, this time, we have been lucky.

Caitlin doesn't know what I saw, there in the rose garden. She babbles about it in the carriage. "We went into the garden, in the moonlight—he kissed me and held my hands, because he said they were cold. His were so warm! He told me I was beautiful; he said he loved me. And he picked roses for me, and he bled where the thorns had pricked him. He bled for me, godmother—oh, this is the one! This is my prince. How could I not love him?"

I remain silent. She doesn't yet know what she loves. At length she says, "Why aren't we home yet? It's taking so long. I'm hungry. I never had any dinner."

"We aren't going home," I tell her, lighting my lantern and pulling down the shades which cover the carriage's windows. "We have been discovered, Caitlin. It is quite possible we are being followed. I am taking you somewhere safe. There will be food there."

"Discovered?" She laughs. "What have they discovered? That I am poor? That I love Randolph? What could they do to me? He will protect me; he said so. He will marry me."

This is the moment I must tell her. For all the times I have done this, it never hurts any less. "Caitlin, listen to me. You shall never marry Randolph, or anyone else. It was never meant that you should. I am sorry you have to hear this now. I had wanted you to learn some gentler way." She stares at me, bewildered, and, sadly, I smile at her—that expression she has teased me about, asked me for, wondered why I withhold; and when she sees it she understands. The pale eyes go wide, the beautiful hands go to her throat; she backs away from me, crossing herself as if in imitation of Lady Alison.

"Away," she tells me, trembling. "I exorcise thee, demon. In vain dost thou boast of this deed—"

I think of kind Thomas, chanting valiantly in an empty stone chamber as men at arms wait outside the door. "Keep your charms, Caitlin. They'll do you no good. Don't you understand, child? Why do you think everyone has begun to look at you so oddly; why do you think I wouldn't give you a mirror? What do you think was in the soup I gave you?"

The hands go to her mouth now, to the small sharp teeth. She cries out, understanding everything at once—her odd lassitude after the first few balls, the blood I took from her to cure it, her changing hours and changing thirsts—and, as always, this moment of birth rends whatever I have left of a heart. Because for a moment the young creature sitting in front of me is not the apprentice hunter I have made her, but the innocent young girl who stood holding that first invitation to the ball, her heart in her eyes. *I? I have been invited?* I force myself not to turn away as Caitlin cries out, "You tricked me! The story wasn't true!"

She tears at her face with shapely nails, and ribbons of flesh follow her fingers. "You can't weep anymore," I tell her. I would weep for her, if I could. "You can't bleed, either. You're past that. Don't disfigure yourself."

"The story was a lie! None of it was true, ever—"

I make my voice as cold as iron. "The story was perfectly true, Caitlin. You were simply never told all of it before."

"It wasn't supposed to end like this!" All the tears she can't shed are in her voice. "In the story the girl falls in love and marries the prince and—everyone knows that! You lied to me! This isn't the right ending!"

"It's the only ending! The only one there is—Caitlin, surely you see that. Living women have no more protection than we do here. They feed off their men, as we do, and they require permission to enter houses and go to dances, as we do, and they depend on spells of seeming. There is only one difference: you will never, ever look like Lady Alison. You will never look like your mother. You have escaped that."

She stares at me and shrinks against the side of the carriage, holding her hands in front of her—her precious hands which Randolph held, kissed, warmed with his own life. "I love him," she says defiantly. "I love him and he loves me. That part of it is true—"

"You loved his bleeding hands, Caitlin. If I hadn't interrupted, you would have fed from them, and known then, and hated him for it. And he would have hated you, for allowing him to speak of love when all along you had been precisely what his aunt warned him against."

Her mouth quivers. She hates me for having seen, and for telling her the truth. She doesn't understand our danger; she doesn't know how the woman she has scorned all these weeks died, or how close she came to dying herself.

Gregory was a clever man; the plot was a clean one. To sacrifice Randolph to Caitlin, and kill Caitlin as she tried to escape the maze; Gregory would have mourned his nephew in the proper public manner, and been declared a hero for murdering one fiend in person as the other was destroyed in the castle. Any gossip about his own soul would have been effectively stilled; perhaps he had been seduced, but surely he was pure again, to summon the righteousness to kill the beasts?

Oh yes, clever. Alison would have known the truth, and would never have accepted a title won by Randolph's murder. Alison could have ruined the entire plan, but it is easy enough to silence wives.

"Can I pray?" Caitlin demands of me, as we rattle towards daybreak. "If I can't shed tears or blood, if I can't love, can I still pray?"

"We can pray," I tell her gently, thinking again of Thomas who spared me, of those tenuous bonds between the living and the dead. "We must pray, foremost, that someone hear us. Caitlin, it's the same. The same story, with that one difference."

She trembles, huddling against the side of the carriage, her eyes closed. When at last she speaks, her voice is stunned. "I'll never see my mother again."

"I am your mother now. What are mothers and daughters, if not women who share blood?"

She whimpers in her throat then, and I stroke her hair. At last she says, "I'll never grow old."

"You will grow as old as the hills," I tell her, putting my arm around her as one comforts a child who has woken from a nightmare, "but you will never be ugly. You will always be as beautiful as you are now, as beautiful as I am. Your hair and nails will grow and I will trim them for you, to keep them lovely, and you will go to every dance, and wear different gowns to all of them."

She blinks and plucks aimlessly at the poor fabric of her dress, once again a kitchen smock. "I'll never be ugly?"

"Never," I say. "You'll never change." We cannot cry or bleed or age; there are so many things we cannot do. But for her, now, it is a comfort.

She hugs herself, shivering, and I sit beside her and hold her, rocking her towards the certain sleep which will come with dawn. It would be better if Randolph were here, with his human warmth, but at least she doesn't have to be alone. I remember my own shock and despair, although they happened longer ago than anyone who is not one of us can remember; I too tried to pray, and afterwards was thankful that my own godmother had stayed with me.

After a while Caitlin's breathing evens, and I am grateful that she hasn't said, as so many of them do, *Now I will never die*.

We shelter our young, as the mortal mothers shelter theirs—those human women who of necessity are as predatory as we, and as dependent on the invitation to feed—and so there are some truths I have not told her. She will learn them soon enough.

She is more beautiful than Lady Alison or her mother, but no less vulnerable. Her very beauty contains the certainty of her destruction. There is no law protecting women in this kingdom, where wives can be poisoned in their own halls and their murderers never punished. Still less are there laws protecting us.

I have told her she will not grow ugly, but I have not said what a curse beauty can be, how time after time she will be forced to flee the rumors of her perpetual loveliness and all that it implies. Men will arrive to feed her and kiss her and bring her roses; but for all the centuries of gentle princes swearing love, there will inevitably be someone—jealous wife or jaded lord, peasant or priest—who has heard the whispers and believed, and who will come to her resting place, in the light hours when she cannot move, bearing a hammer and a wooden stake.

# MICHAEL FLYNN

## The Forest of Time

Here's a thoughtful and compelling novella by new writer Michael Flynn, which demonstrates that Going Home Again might be even more difficult than Thomas Wolfe thought.

Since his first sale in 1980, Michael Flynn has become a regular contributor to *Analog*, and is at work on a novel. He has a BA in math from La Salle College, an MS for work in topology from Marquette University, and works as an industrial quality engineer and statistician. Born in Easton, Pennsylvania, he now lives in Edison, N.J. His popular story "Eifelheim" was a Hugo Award finalist last year.

# THE FOREST OF TIME

## Michael Flynn

It was the autumn of the year and the trees were already showing their death-colors. Splashes of orange and red and gold rustled in the canopy overhead. Oberleutnant Rudolf Knecht, Chief Scout of the Army of the Kittatinny, wore the same hues mottled for his uniform as he rode through the forest. A scout's badge, carefully rusted to dullness, was pinned to his battered campaign cap.

Knecht swayed easily to the rhythm of his horse's gait as he picked his way up the trail toward Fox Gap Fortress. He kept a wary eye on the surrounding forest. Periodically, he twisted in the saddle and gazed thoughtfully at the trail where it switchbacked below. There had been no sign of pursuit so far. Knecht believed his presence had gone undetected; but even this close to home, it paid to be careful. The list of those who wanted Knecht dead was a long one; and here, north of the Mountain, it was open season on Pennsylvanians.

There were few leaves on the forest floor, but the wind gathered them up and hurled them in mad dances. The brown, dry, crisp leaves of death. Forerunners of what was to be. Knecht bowed his head and pulled the jacket collar tighter about his neck.

Knecht felt the autumn. It was in his heart and in his bones. It was in the news he carried homeward. Bad news even in the best of times, which these were not. Two knick regiments had moved out of the Hudson Valley into the Poconos. They were camped with the yankees. Brothers-in-arms, as if last spring's fighting had never happened. General Schneider's fear: New York and Wyoming had settled their quarrel and made common cause.

Common cause. Knecht chewed on his drooping moustache, now more grey than brown. No need to ask the cause. There was little enough that yanks and knicks could agree on, but killing Pennsylvanians was one.

He remembered that General Schneider was inspecting the fortress line and would probably be waiting for him at Fox Gap. He did not feel the pleasure he usually felt on such occasions. *Na, Konrad, meiner Alt*, he thought. What will you do now? What a burden I must lay upon your shoulders. God help the Commonwealth of Pennsylvania.

He pulled in on the reins. There was a break in the trees here and through it he could see the flank of Kittatinny Mountain. A giant's wall, the ridge ran away, straight and true, becoming bluer and hazier as its forested slopes faded into the distance. Spots of color decorated the sheer face of the Mountain. Fox Gap, directly above him, was hidden by the forest canopy; but Knecht thought he could just make out the fortresses at Wind Gap and Tott Gap.

As always, the view comforted him. There was no way across the Kittatinny, save through the Gaps. And there was no way through the Gaps.

Twenty years since anyone has tried, he thought. He kicked at the horse and they resumed their slow progress up the trail. Twenty years ago; and we blew the knick riverboats off the water.

That had been at Delaware Gap, during the Piney War. Knecht sighed. The Piney War. It seemed such a long time ago. A different world; more innocent, somehow. Or perhaps he had only been younger. He remembered how he had marched away, his uniform new and sharply creased. Adventure was ahead of him, and his father's anger behind. I am too old for such games, he told himself. I should be sitting by the fire, smoking my pipe, telling stories to my grandchildren.

He chewed again on his moustache hairs and spit them out. There had never been any children; and now, there never would be. He felt suddenly alone.

Just as well, he thought. The stories I have to tell are not for the ears of youngsters. What were the stories, really? A crowd of men charged from the trench. Later, some of them came back. What more was there to say? Once, a long time ago, war had been glamorous, with pageantry and uniforms to shame a peacock. Now it was only necessary, and the uniforms were the color of mud.

There was a sudden noise in the forest to his right. Snapping limbs and a muffled grunt. Knecht started, and chastised himself. A surprised scout is often a dead one as well. He pulled a large bore pistol from his holster and dismounted. The horse, well-trained, held still. Knecht stepped into the forest and crouched behind a tall birch tree. He listened.

The noise continued. Too much noise, he decided. Perhaps an animal?

Then he saw the silhouette of a man thrashing through the underbrush, making no attempt at silence. Knecht watched over his gunsight as the man blundered into a stickerbush. Cursing, the other stopped and pulled the burrs from his trousers.

The complete lack of caution puzzled Knecht. The no-man's-land between Pennsylvania and the Wyoming was no place for carelessness. The other was either very foolish or very confident.

The fear ran through him like the rush of an icy mountain stream. Perhaps the bait in a trap; something to hold his attention? He jerked round suddenly, looking behind him, straining for the slightest sign.

But there was nothing save the startled birds and the evening wind.

Knecht blew his breath out in a gust. His heart was pounding. *I am getting too old for this*. He felt foolish and his cheeks burned, even though there was no one to see.

The stranger had reached the trail and stood there brushing himself off. He was short and dark complexioned. On his back he wore a rucksack, connected by wires to a device on his belt. Knecht estimated his age at thirty, but the unkempt hair and beard made him look older.

He watched the man pull a paper from his baggy canvas jacket. Even from where he crouched, Knecht could see it was a map, handsomely done in many colors. A stranger with a map on the trail below Fox Gap. Knecht made a decision and stepped forth, cocking his pistol.

The stranger spun and saw Knecht. Closer up, Knecht could see the eyes bloodshot with fatigue. After a nervous glance at the scout's pistol, the stranger smiled and pointed to the map. "Would you believe it?" he asked in English. "I think I'm lost."

Knecht snorted. "I would not believe it," he answered in the same language. "Put in the air your hands up."

The stranger complied without hesitation. Knecht reached out and snatched the map from his hand.

"That's a Pennsylvania Dutch accent, isn't it?" asked his prisoner. "It sure is good to hear English again."

Knecht looked at him. He did not understand why that should be good. His own policy when north of the Mountain was to shoot at English-speaking voices. He gave quick glances to the map while considering what to do.

"Are you hunting? I didn't know it was hunting season."

The scout saw no reason to answer that, either. In a way, he *was* hunting, but he doubted the prisoner had meant it that way.

"At least you can tell me where in the damn world I am!"

Knecht was surprised at the angry outburst. Considering who held the pistol on whom, it seemed a rash act at best. He grinned and held up the map. "Naturally, you know where in the damn world you are. While you have this map, it gives only one possibility. You are the spy, *nicht wahr?* But, to humor you . . ." He pointed northward with his chin. "Downtrail is the Wyoming, where your Wilkes-Barre masters your report in vain will await. Uptrail is *Festung* Fox Gap . . . and your cell."

The prisoner's shoulders slumped. Knecht looked at the sun. With the prisoner afoot, they should still reach the fort before nightfall. He decided to take the man in for questioning. That would be safer than interrogating him on the spot. Knecht glanced at the map once more. Then he frowned and looked more closely. "United States Geological Survey?" he asked the prisoner. "What are the United States?"

He did not understand why the prisoner wept.

There was a storm brewing in the northwest and the wind whipped through Fox Gap, tearing at the uniform blouses of the sentries, making them grab for their caps. In the dark, amid the rain and lightning, at least one man's grab was too late and his fellows laughed coarsely as he trotted red-faced to retrieve it. It was a small diversion in an otherwise cheerless duty.

What annoyed Festungskommandant Vonderberge was not that Scout Knecht chose to watch the chase also, but that he chose to do so while halfway through the act of entering Vonderberge's office. The wind blew a blizzard of paper around the room and Vonderberge's curses brought Knecht fully into the office, closing the door behind him.

Knecht surveyed the destruction. Vonderberge shook his head. He looked at Knecht. "These bits of paper," he said. "These orders and memoranda and requisitions, they are the nerve messages of the Army. A thousand messages a day cross my desk, Rudi; and not a one of them but deals with matters of the greatest military import." He clucked sadly. "Our enemies need not defeat us in the field. They need only sabotage our filing system and we are lost." He rose from his desk and knelt, gathering up papers. "Come, Rudi, quickly. Let us set things aright, else the Commonwealth is lost!"

Knecht snorted. Vonderberge was mocking him with this elaborate ridicule. In his short time at Fox Gap, Knecht had encountered the Kommandant's strange humor several times. Someone had once told him that Vonderberge had always dreamed of becoming a scientist, but that his father had pressured him into following the family's military tradition. As a result, his command style was, well, unorthodox.

Na, *we all arrive by different paths*, Knecht thought. *I joined to* spite *my father*. It startled him to recall that his father had been dead for many years and that they had never become reconciled.

Knecht stooped and helped collect the scattered documents. Because he was a scout, however, he glanced at their contents as he did so; and as he absorbed their meaning, he read more and collected less.

One sheet in particular held his attention. When he looked up from it, he saw Vonderberge waiting patiently behind his desk. He was leaning back in a swivel chair, his arms crossed over his chest. There was a knowing smile on the Kommandant's thin aristocratic face.

"Is this all . . ." Knecht began.

"*Ach, nein*," the Kommandant answered. "There is much, much more. However," he added pointedly, "it is no longer in order."

"But, this is from the prisoner, Nando Kelly?"

"Hernando is the name; not Herr Nando. It is Spanish, I believe." Vonderberge clucked sadly over the documents and began setting them in order.

Knecht stood over the desk. "But this is crazy stuff!" He waved the sheet in his hand. Vonderberge grabbed for it vainly. Knecht did not notice. "The man must be crazy!" he said.

Vonderberge paused and cocked an eyebrow at him. "Crazy?" he repeated. "So says the Hexmajor. He can support his opinion with many fine words and a degree from Franklin University. I am but a simple soldier, a servant of the Commonwealth, and cannot state my own diagnosis in so impressive a manner. On what basis, Rudi, do *you* say he is crazy?"

Knecht sputtered. "If it is not crazy to believe in countries that do not exist, I do not know what is. I have looked on all our world maps and have found no United States, not even in deepest Asia."

Vonderberge smiled broadly. He leaned back again, clasping his hands behind his neck. "Oh, I know where the United States are," he announced smugly.

Knecht made a face. "Tell me then, O Servant of the Commonwealth. Where are they?"

Vonderberge chuckled. "If you can possibly remember so far back as your childhood history lessons, you may recall something of the Fourth Pennamite War."

Knecht groaned. The Pennamite Wars. He could never remember which was which. Both Connecticut and Pennsylvania had claimed the Wyoming Valley and had fought over it several times, a consequence of the English king's cavalier attitude toward land titles. The fourth one? Let's see . . . 1769, 1771, 1775 . . .

"No," he said finally. "I know nothing at all of the time between

1784 and 1792. I never heard of Brigadier Wadsworth and the Siege of Forty-Fort, or how General Washington and his Virginia militia were mowed down in the crossfire."

"Then you must also be ignorant," continued the Kommandant, "of the fact that the same Congress that sent the General to stop the fighting was also working on a plan to unify the thirteen independent states. Now what do you suppose the name of that union was to be?"

Knecht snorted. "I would be a great fool if I did not say 'The United States.' "

Vonderberge clapped. "Right, indeed, Rudi. Right, indeed. Dickinson was president of the Congress, you know."

Knecht was surprised. "Dickinson? John Dickinson, our first Chancellor?"

"The very same. Being a Pennsylvanian, I suppose the yankee settlers thought he was plotting something by dispatching the supposedly neutral Virginians. . . . Well, of course, with Washington dead, and old Franklin incapacitated by a stroke at the news, the whole thing fell apart. Maryland never did sign the Articles of Confederation; and as the fighting among the states grew worse—over the Wyoming, over Vermont, over Chesapeake fishing rights, over the western lands—the others seceded also. All that Adams and the radicals salvaged was their New England Confederation; and even that was almost lost during Shay's Rebellion and General Lincoln's coup. . . ."

Knecht interrupted. "So this almost-was United States was nothing more than a wartime alliance to throw the English out. It was stillborn in the 1780s. Yet Kelly's map is dated this year."

"*Ja*, the map," mused Vonderberge, as if to himself. "It is finely drawn, is it not? And the physical details—the mountains and streams—are astonishingly accurate. Only the man-made details are bizarre. Roads and dams that are not there. A great open space called an 'airport.' Towns that are three times their actual size. Did you see how large Easton is shown to be?"

Knecht shrugged. "A hoax."

"Such an elaborate hoax? To what purpose?"

"To fool us. He is a spy. If messages can be coded, why not maps?"

"Ah. You say he is a spy. The Hexmajor says he is mad and the map is the complex working out of a system of delusions. I say . . ." He picked up a sheaf of papers from his desk and handed them to Knecht. "I say you should read Kelly's notebook."

The scout glanced at the typewritten pages. "These are transcripts," he pointed out. "They were done on the machine in your office. I recognize the broken stem on the r's." He made it a statement.

Vonderberge threw his head back and laughed, slapping the arm of the chair. "Subtlety does not become you, Rudi," he said looking at him. "Yes, they are transcripts. General Schneider has the originals. When I showed the journal to him, he wanted to read it himself. I made copies of the more interesting entries."

Knecht kept his face neutral. "You, and the General, and the Hexmajor. *Ach!* Kelly is *my* prisoner. I have yet to interview him. I gave you his possessions for safekeeping, not for distribution."

"Oh, don't be so official, Rudi. What are we, Prussians? You were resting, I was bored, and the journal was here. Go ahead. Read it now." Vonderberge waved an inviting hand.

Knecht frowned and picked up the stack. The first few pages were filled with equations. Strange formulae full of inverted A's and backward E's. Knecht formed the words under his breath. ". . . twelve dimensional open manifold . . . Janatpour hypospace . . . oscillatory time . . ." He shook his head. "Nonsense," he muttered.

He turned the page and came to a text:

> "I am embarking on a great adventure. Does that sound grandiose? Very well, let it. Grandiose ideas deserve grandiose expression. Tomorrow, I make my first long range Jump. Sharon claims that it is too soon for such a field test, but she is too cautious. I've engineered the equipment. I know what it can do. Triple redundancy on critical circuits. Molecular foam memory. I *am* a certified reliability engineer, after all. The short Jumps were all successful. So what could go wrong?
>
> "Rosa could answer that. Sweet Rosa. She is not an engineer. She only sees that it is dangerous. And what can I say? It is dangerous. But when has anything perfectly safe been worth doing? The equipment is as safe as I can make it. I tried to explain about probabilities and hazard analysis to Rosa last night, but she only cried and held me tighter.
>
> "She promised to be in the lab a week from tomorrow when I make my return Jump. A week away from Rosa. A week to study a whole new universe. *Madre de Dios!* A week can be both a moment and an eternity."

Knecht chewed his moustache. The next page was titled "Jump #1" followed by a string of twelve "coordinate settings." Then there were many pages which Knecht skimmed, detailing a world that never was. In it, the prehistoric Indians had not exterminated the Ice Age big game. Instead, they had tamed the horse, the elephant, and the camel and used the animal power to keep pace technologically with the Old World. Great civilizations arose in the river valleys of the Colorado and Rio Grande, and mighty empires spread across the Caribbean. Vikings were in Vinland at the same time the Iroquois were discovering Ireland. By the present day there were colonies on Mars.

Knecht shook his head. "Not only do we have a United States," he muttered.

The next entry was briefer and contained the first hint of trouble. It was headed "Jump #2." Except for the reversal of plus and minus signs, the coordinate settings were identical with the first set.

> "A slight miscalculation. I should be back in the lab with Rosa, but I'm in somebody's apartment, instead. It's still Philly out the window—though a shabbier, more run-down Philly than I remember. I must be close to my home timeline because I can recognize most of the University buildings. There's a flag that looks like the stars and stripes on the flagpole in front of College Hall. There's something or other black hanging from the lamppost, but I can't make it out. Well, work first; tourism later. I bet I'll need a vernier control. There must be a slight asymmetry in the coordinates."

Knecht skipped several lines of equations and picked up the narrative once more.

> "I must leave immediately! That black thing on the lamppost kept nagging at the back of my mind. So I got out my binoculars and studied it. It was a nun in a black habit, hanging in a noose. Hanging a long time, too, by the looks of it. Farther along the avenue, I could see bodies on all the lampposts. Then the wind caught the flag by College Hall and I understood. In place of the stars there was a swastika . . .
>
> "Jump #3. Coordinates . . .
>
> "Wrong again. I was too hasty in leaving the Nazi world. The settings were not quite right, but I think I know what went wrong now. The very act of my Jumping has created new branches in time and changed the oscillatory time-distance between them. On the shorter Jumps it didn't matter much, but on the longer ones . . .
>
> "I think I finally have the calculations right. This is a pleasant world where I am, and—thanks to Goodman deVeres and his wife—I've had the time to think the problem through. It seems the Angevin kings still rule in this world and my host has described what seems like scientific magic. Superstition? Mass delusion? I'd like to stay and study this world, but I'm already a week overdue. Darling Rosa must be frantic with worry. I think of her often."

The next page was headed "Jump 4" with settings but no narrative entry. This was followed by . . .

"Jump #5. Coordinates unknown.

"Damn! It didn't work out right and I was almost killed. This isn't an experiment any more. Armored samurai in a medieval Philadelphia? Am I getting closer to or farther from Home? I barely escaped them. I rode north on a stolen horse and Jumped as soon as my charge built up. Just in time, too—my heart is still pounding. No time for calculations. I don't even know what the settings were.

"Note: the horse Jumped with me. The field must be wider than I thought. A clue to my dilemma? I need peace and quiet to think this out. I could find it with Goodman deVeres. I have the coordinates for his world. But his world isn't where I left it. When I jumped, I moved it. Archimedes had nothing on me. Haha. That's a joke. Why am I bothering with this stupid journal?

"I dreamed of Rosa last night. She was looking for me. I was right beside her but she couldn't see me. When I awoke, it was still dark. Off to the north there was a glow behind the crest of the hills. City lights? If that is South Mountain, it would be Allentown or Bethlehem on the other side—or their analogs in this world. I should know by next night. So far I haven't seen anyone; but I must be cautious.

"I've plenty of solitude here-and-now. That slag heap I saw from the mountain must have been Bethlehem, wiped out by a single bomb. The epicenter looked to be about where the steelworks once stood. It happened a long time ago, by the looks of things. Nothing living in the valley but a few scrub plants, insects and birds.

"I rode out as fast as I could to put that awful sight behind me. I didn't dare eat anything. My horse did and is dead for it. Who knows what sort of adaptations have fit the grass for a radio-active environment? I may already have stayed too long. I must Jump, but I daren't materialize inside a big city. I'll hike up into the northern hills before I Jump again."

Knecht turned to the last page. Jump #6. Settings, but no notes. There was a long silence while Knecht digested what he had read. Vonderberge was watching him. Outside, the wind rattled the windows. A nearby lightning strike caused the lights to flicker.

"Herr Festungskommandant . . ."

"His last Jump landed him right in your lap out on the Wyoming Trail."

"Herr Festungskommandant . . ."

"And instead of the solitude he sought, he's gotten solitude of another sort."

"You don't believe . . ."

"Believe?" Vonderberge slammed his palm down on the desk with unexpected violence. He stood abruptly and walked three quick paces to the window, where he gazed out at the storm. His fingers locked tightly behind his back. "Why not believe?" he whispered, his back to the room. "Somewhere there is a world where Heinrich Vonderberge is not trapped in a border fort on the edge of a war with the lives of others heavy on his back. He is in a laboratory, experimenting with electrical science, and he is happy."

He turned and faced Knecht, self-possessed once more.

"What if," he said. "What if the Pennamite Wars had not turned so vicious? If compromise had been possible? Had they lived, might not Washington and Franklin have forged a strong union, with the General as king and the Doctor as prime minister? Might not such a union have spread west, crushing Sequoyah and Tecumseh and their new Indian states before the British had gotten them properly started? Can you imagine a single government ruling the entire continent?"

Knecht said, "No," but Vonderberge continued without hearing him.

"Suppose," he said, pacing the room, "every time an event happens, several worlds are created. One for each outcome." He paused and smiled at Knecht. "Suppose Pennsylvania had not intervened in the Partition of New Jersey? No Piney War. New York and Virginia cut us off from the sea. Konrad Schneider does not become a great General, nor Rudi Knecht a famous spy. Somewhere there is such a world. Somewhere . . . close.

"Now suppose further that on one of these . . . these *moeglichwelten* a man discovers how to cross from one to another. He tests his equipment, makes many notes, then tries to return. But he fails."

A crash of thunder punctuated the Kommandant's words. Knecht jumped.

"He fails," Vonderberge continued, "because in the act of jumping he has somehow changed the 'distance.' So, on his return, he undershoots. At first, he is not worried. He makes a minor adjustment and tries again. And misses again. And again, and again, and again."

Vonderberge perched on the corner of his desk, his face serious. "Even if there is only one event each year, and each event had but two outcomes, why then in ten years do you know how many worlds there would have to be?"

Knecht shook his head dumbly.

"A thousand, Rudi, and more. And in another ten years, a thousand for each of those. Time is like a tree; a forest of trees. Always branching. One event a year? Two possible outcomes? *Ach!* I am a piker! In all of time, how many, many worlds there must be. How to find a single twig in such a forest?"

Knecht could think of nothing to say. In the quiet of the office, the storm without seemed louder and more menacing.

In the morning, of course, with the dark storm only muddy puddles, Knecht could dismiss the Kommandant's remarks as a bad joke. "What if?" was a game for children; a way of regretting the past. Knecht's alert eye had not missed the row of technofiction books in Vonderberge's office. "What if?" was a common theme in that genre, Knecht understood.

When he came to Kelly's cell to interrogate the prisoner, he found that others had preceded him. The guard at the cell door came to attention, but favored Knecht with a conspiratorial wink. From within the cell came the sound of angry voices. Knecht listened closely, his ear to the thick, iron door; but he could make out none of the words. He straightened and looked a question at the guard. The latter rolled his eyes heavenward with a look of resigned suffering. Knecht grinned.

"So, Johann," he said. "How long has this been going on?"

"Since sun-up," was the reply. "The Kommandant came in early to talk to the prisoner. He'd been in there an hour when the Hexmajor arrived. Then there was thunder-weather, believe me, sir." Johann smiled at the thought of two officers bickering.

Knecht pulled two cigars from his pocket humidor and offered one to the guard. "Do you suppose it is safe to leave them both locked in together?" He laughed. "We may as well relax while we wait. That is, if you are permitted . . ."

The guard took the cigar. "The Kommandant is more concerned that we are experts in how to shoot our rifles than in how to sneak a smoke." There was a pause while Knecht lit his cigar. He puffed a moment, then remarked, "This is good leaf. Kingdom of Carolina?"

Knecht nodded. He blew out a great cloud of acrid smoke. "You know you should not have allowed either of them in to see the prisoner before me."

'Well, sir. You know that and I know that; but the Hexmajor and the Kommandant, they make their own rules." The argument in the cell reached a crescendo. Johann flinched. "Unfortunately, they do not make the *same* rules."

"Hmph. Is your Kommandant always so . . . impetuous?" He wanted to know Heinrich Vonderberge better; and one way to do that was to question the men who followed him.

The guard frowned. "Sir, things may be different in the Scout Corps, but the Kommandant is no fool, in spite of his ways. He always has a reason for what he does. Why, no more than two months ago —this was before you were assigned here—he had us counting the number of pigeons flying north. He plotted it on a daily chart." Johann laughed at the memory. "Then he sent us out to intercept a raiding party from the Nations. You see, you know how the sachems still allow private war parties? Well . . ."

There was a banging at the cell door and Johann broke off whatever yarn he had been about to spin and opened it. Vonderberge stalked out.

"We will see about that!" he snapped over his shoulder, and pushed past Knecht without seeing him. Knecht took his cigar from his mouth and looked from the Kommandant to the doorway. Hexmajor Ochsenfuss stood there, glaring at the Kommandant's retreating form. "Fool," the Doctor muttered through clenched teeth. Then he noticed Knecht.

"And what do *you* want? My patient is highly agitated. He cannot undergo another grilling."

Knecht smiled pleasantly. "Why, Herr Doctor. He is not your patient until I say so. Until then, he is my prisoner. I found him north of the Mountain. It is my function to interview him."

"He is a sick man, not one of your spies."

"The men I interview are never *my* spies. I will decide if he is . . . sick."

"That is a medical decision, not a military one. Have you read his journal? It is the product of a deluded mind."

"If it is what it appears to be. It could also be the product of a clever mind. Madness as a cover for espionage? Kelly would not be the first spy with an outrageous cover."

He walked past the doctor into the cell. Ochsenfuss followed him. Kelly looked up from his cot. He sat on the edge, hands clasped tightly, leaning on his knees. A night's sleep had not refreshed him. He pointed at Knecht.

"I remember you," he said. "You're the guy that caught me."

The Hexmajor forestalled Knecht's reply. "*Bitte*, Herr Leutnant," he said in Pennsylvaanish. "You must speak in our own tongue."

"*Warum?*" Knecht answered, with a glance at Kelly. "The prisoner speaks English, *nicht wahr?*"

"Ah, but he must understand German, at least a little. Either our own dialect or the European. Look at him. He is not from the West, despite his Spanish forename. Their skin color is much darker. Nor is he from Columbia, Cumberland, or the Carolina Kingdom. Their accents are most distinctive. And no white man from Virginia on north could be ignorant of the national tongue of Pennsylvania."

"Nor could any European," finished Knecht. "Not since 1917, at any rate. I cannot fault your logic, Herr Doctor; but then, why . . ."

"Because for some reason he has suppressed his knowledge of German. He has retreated from reality, built himself fantasy worlds. If we communicate only in Pennsylvaanish as we are doing now, his own desire to communicate will eventually overcome his 'block' (as we call it); and the process of drawing him back to the real world will have begun."

Knecht glanced again at the prisoner. "On the other hand, it is my duty to obtain information. If the prisoner will speak in English, then so will I."

"But . . ."

"And I must be alone." Knecht tapped his lapel insignia meaningfully. The double-X of the Scout Corps.

Ochsenfuss pursed his lips. Knecht thought he would argue further, but instead, he shrugged. "Have it your way, then; but remember to treat him carefully. If I am right, he could easily fall into complete withdrawal." He nodded curtly to Knecht and left.

Knecht stared at the closed door. He disliked people who "communicated." Nor did he think Vonderberge was a fool like Ochsenfuss had said. Still, he reminded himself, the Hexmajor had an impressive list of cures to his credit. Especially of battle fatigue and torture cases. Ochsenfuss was no fool, either.

He stuck his cigar back between his teeth. Let's get this over with, he thought. But he knew it would not be that easy.

Within an hour Knecht knew why the others had quarreled. Kelly could describe his fantasy world and the branching timelines very convincingly. But he had convinced Vonderberge that he was telling the truth and Ochsenfuss that he was mad. The conclusions were incompatible; the mixture, explosive.

Kelly spoke freely in response to Knecht's questions. He held nothing back. At least, the scout reminded himself, he *appeared* to hold nothing back. But who knew better than Knecht how deceptive such appearances could be?

Knecht tried all the tricks of the interrogator's trade. He came at the same question time after time, from different directions. He hopscotched from question to question. He piled detail on detail. No lie could be perfectly consistent. Contradictions would soon reveal themselves. He was friendly. He was harsh. He put his own words in the prisoner's mouth to see their effect.

None of it worked.

If Kelly's answers were contradictory, Knecht could not say. When the entire story is fantasy, who can find the errors? It was of a piece with the nature of Kelly's cover. If two facts contradict each other, which is true? Answer: both, but in two different worlds.

Frustrated, Knecht decided to let the prisoner simply talk. Silence, too, was an effective tactic. Many a prisoner had said too much simply to fill an awkward silence. He removed fresh cigars from his pocket humidor and offered one to the prisoner, who accepted it gratefully. Knecht clipped the ends and lit them. When they were both burning evenly, he leaned back in the chair. Nothing like a friendly smoke to set the mind at ease. And off-guard.

"So, tell me in your own words, then, how you on the Wyoming Trail were found."

Kelly grunted. "I wouldn't expect the military mind to understand, or even be interested."

Knecht flushed, but he kept his temper under control. "But I am interested, Herr Kelly. You have a strange story to tell. You come from another world. It is not a story I have often encountered."

Kelly looked at him, startled, and unexpectedly laughed. "No, not very often, I would imagine."

"*Ach*, that is the very problem. Just what *would* you imagine? Your story is true, or it is false; and if it is false, it is either deliberately so or not. I must know which, so I can take the proper action."

Kelly ran a hand through his hair. "Look. All I want is to get out of here, away from you . . . military men. Back to Rosa."

"That does not tell me anything. Spy, traveler, or madman, you would say the same."

The prisoner scowled. Knecht waited.

"All right," said Kelly at last. "I got lost. It's that simple. Sharon tried to tell me that a field trip was premature, but I was so much smarter then. Who would think that the distance from B to A was different than the distance from A to B?"

Who indeed? Knecht thought, but he kept the thought to himself. Another contradiction. Except, grant the premise and it wasn't a contradiction at all.

"Sure," the prisoner's voice was bitter. "Action requires a force; and action causes reaction. It's not nice to forget Uncle Isaac." He looked Knecht square in the eye. "You see, when I Jumped, my world moved, too. Action, reaction. I created multiple versions of it. In one, my equipment worked. In others, it malfunctioned in various ways. Each was slightly displaced from the original location." He laughed again. "How many people can say they've misplaced an entire world?"

"I don't understand," said Knecht. "Why not two versions of *all* worlds? When you, ah, Jumped, you could for many different destinations have gone; and in each one, you either arrived, or you did not."

His prisoner looked puzzled. "But that's not topologically relevant.

The Jump occurs in the metacontinuum of the polyverse, so . . . Ah, hell! Why should I try to convince you?"

Knecht sat back and puffed his cigar. Offhand, he could think of several reasons why Kelly should try to convince him.

"You see," the prisoner continued, "there is not an infinity of possible worlds."

Knecht had never thought there was more than one, so he said nothing. Even the idea that there were two would be staggering.

"And they are not all different in the same way. Each moment grows out of the past. Oh, say . . ." He looked at his cigar and smiled. He held it out at arm's length. "Take this cigar, for instance. If I drop it, it'll fall to the floor. That is deterministic. So are the rate, the falling time, and the energy of impact. But, I may or may not choose to drop it. That is probabilistic. It is the choice that creates worlds. We are now at a cusp, a bifurcation point on the Thom manifold." He paused and looked at the cigar. Knecht waited patiently. Then Kelly clamped it firmly between his teeth. "It is far too good a smoke to waste. I chose not to drop it; but there was a small probability that I would have."

Knecht pulled on his moustache, thinking of Vonderberge's speculations of the previous night. Before he had spoken with Kelly. "So you say that . . . somewhere . . . there is a world in which you did?"

"Right. It's a small world, because the probability was small. Temporal cross-section is proportional to *a priori* probability. But it's there, close by. It's a convergent world."

"Convergent."

"Yes. Except for our two memories and some ash on the floor, it is indistinguishable from this world. The differences damp out. Convergent worlds form a 'rope' of intertwined timelines. We can Jump back and forth among them easily, inadvertently. The energy needed is low. We could change places with our alternate selves and never notice. The only difference may be the number of grains of sand on Mars. Tomorrow you may find that I remember dropping the cigar; or I might find that you do. We may even argue the point."

"Unconvincingly," said Knecht sardonically.

Kelly chuckled. "True. How could you *know* what I remember? Still, it happens all the time. The courts are full of people who sincerely remember different versions of reality."

"Or perhaps it is the mind that plays tricks, not the reality."

Kelly flushed and looked away. "That happens, too."

After a moment, Knecht asked, "What has this to do with your becoming lost?"

"What? Oh. Simple, really. The number of possible worlds is large, but it's not infinite. That's important to remember," he continued to himself. "Finite. I haven't checked into Hotel Infinity. I can still find my own room, or at least the right floor." He stood abruptly and paced the room. Knecht followed him with his eyes.

"I don't have to worry about worlds where Washington and Jefferson instituted a pharaonic monarchy with a divine god-king. Every moment grows out of the previous moment, remember? For that to happen, so much previous history would have had to be different that Washington and Jefferson would never have been born." He stopped pacing and faced Knecht.

"And I don't have to worry about convergent worlds. If I find the right 'rope,' I'll be all right. Even a parallel world would be fine, as long as it would have Rosa in it." He frowned. "But it mightn't. And if it did, she mightn't know me."

"Parallel?" asked Knecht.

Kelly walked to the window and gazed through the bars. "Sure. Change can be convergent, parallel, or divergent. Suppose, oh suppose Isabella hadn't funded Columbus, but the other Genoese, Giovanni Caboto, who was also pushing for a voyage west. Or Juan de la Cosa. Or the two brothers who captained the Niña and the Pinta. There was no shortage of bold navigators. What practical difference would it have made? A few names are changed in the history books, is all. The script is the same, but different actors play the parts. The differences stay constant."

He turned around. "You or I may have no counterpart in those worlds. They are different 'ropes.' Even so, we could spontaneously Jump to one nearby. Benjamin Bathurst, the man who walked behind a horse in plain sight and was never seen again. No one took his place. Judge Crater. Ambrose Bierce. Amelia Earhart. Jimmy Hoffa. The Legion II Augusta. Who knows? Some of them may have Jumped."

Kelly inspected his cigar. "Then there are the cascades. For want of a nail, the shoe was lost. The differences accumulate. The worlds diverge. That was my mistake. Jumping to a cascade world." His voice was bitter, self-mocking. "Oh, it'll be simple to find my way back. All I have to do is find the nail."

"The nail?"

"Sure. The snowflake that started the avalanche. What could be simpler?" He took three quick steps along the wall, turned, stepped back, and jammed his cigar out in the ashtray. He sat backward, landing on his cot. He put his face in his hands.

Knecht listened to his harsh breathing. He remembered what Ochsenfuss had said. If I push him too hard, he could crack. A spy cracks one way; a madman, another.

After a while, Kelly looked up again. He smiled. "It's not that hard, really," he said more calmly. "I can approximate it closely enough with history texts and logical calculus. That should be good enough to get me back to my own rope. Or at least a nearby one. As long as Rosa is there, it doesn't matter." He hesitated and glanced at Knecht. "You've confiscated my personal effects," he said, "but I would like to have her photograph. It was in my wallet. Along with my identification papers," he added pointedly.

Knecht smiled. "I have seen your papers, Herr 'Professor Doctor' Kelly. They are very good."

"But . . ."

"But I have drawn others myself just as good."

Kelly shrugged and grinned. "It was worth a try," he said.

Knecht chuckled. He was beginning to like this man. "I suppose it can do no harm," he said, thinking out loud, "to give you a history text. Surely there gives one here in the fortress. If nothing else, it can keep you amused during the long days. And perhaps it can reacquaint you with reality."

"That's what the shrink said before."

"The shrink? What . . . ? Oh, I see. The Hexmajor." He laughed. Then he remembered how Ochsenfuss and Vonderberge had quarreled over this man and he looked at him more soberly. "You understand that you must here stay. Until we know who or what you are. There are three possibilities and only one is to your benefit." He hesitated a moment, then added, "It gives some here who your story believe, and some not."

Kelly nodded. "I know. Do you believe me?"

"Me? I am a scout. I look. I listen. I try to fit pieces together so they make a picture. I take no direct action. No, Herr Kelly. I do not believe you; but neither do I disbelieve you."

Kelly nodded. "Fair enough."

"Do not thank me yet, Herr Kelly. In our first five minutes of talking it is clear to me you know nothing of value of the Wyoming, or the Nations, or anything. In such a case, my official interest in you comes to an end."

"But unofficially . . ." prompted the other.

*"Ja."* Knecht rose and walked to the door. "Others begin to have strong opinions about you, for whatever reasons of their own I do not know. Such are the seeds, and I do not like what may sprout. Perhaps this . . ." He jabbed his cigar at Kelly, suddenly accusing. "You know more than you show. You play-act the hinkle-dreck *Quatschkopf*. And this, the sowing of discord, may be the very reason for your coming."

He stepped back and considered the prisoner. He gestured broadly, his cigar leaving curlicues of smoke. "I see grave philosophical problems with you, Herr Kelly. We Germans, even we Pennsylvaanish Germans, are a very philosophical people. From what you say there are many worlds, some only trivially different. I do not know why we with infinitely many Kellys are not deluged, each coming from a world *almost* like your own!"

Kelly gasped in surprise. He stood abruptly and turned to the wall, his back to Knecht. "Of course," he said. "Stupid, stupid, stupid! The transformation isn't homeomorphic. The topology of the inverse sheaf must not be Hausdorff after all. It may only be a Harris proximity." He turned to Knecht. "Please, may I have my calculator, the small box with the numbered buttons . . . No, damn!" He smacked a fist into his left hand. "I ran the batteries down when I was with Goodman deVeres. Some pencils and paper, then?" He looked eager and excited.

Knecht grunted in satisfaction. Something he had said had set Kelly thinking. It remained to be seen along which lines those thoughts would run.

Rumors flew over the next few days. A small border fort is their natural breeding ground, and Fox Gap was no exception. Knecht heard through the grapevine that Vonderberge had had the Hexmajor barred from Kelly's cell; that Ochsenfuss had telegraphed his superiors in Medical Corps and had Vonderberge overruled. Now there was talk that General Schneider himself had entered the dispute, on which side no one knew; but the General had already postponed his scheduled departure for Wind Gap Fortress and a packet bearing his seal had gone by special courier to Oberkommando Pennsylvaanish in Philadelphia City. A serious matter if the General did not trust the security of the military telegraph.

The General himself was not talking, not even to Knecht. That saddened the scout more than he had realized it could. Since his talk with the prisoner, Knecht had thought more than once how slender was the chain of chance that had brought Schneider and himself together, the team of scout and strategist that had shepherded the Commonwealth through two major wars and countless border skirmishes.

He had dined with the General shortly after submitting his report on Kelly. Dinner was a hearty fare of *shnitz un' knepp*, with *deutch*-baked corn, followed by shoofly pie. Afterward, cigars and brandy wine. Talk had turned, as it often did, to the Piney War. Schneider had deprecated his own role.

"What could I do, Rudi?" he asked. "A stray cannon shot and both Kutz and Rittenhouse were dead. I felt the ball go by me, felt the wind on my face. A foot the other way would have deprived this very brandy of being so thoroughly enjoyed today. Suddenly, I was Commander of the Army of the Delaware, with my forces scattered among the Wachtungs. Rittenhouse had always been the tight-lipped sort. I had no idea what his plans had been. So I studied his dispositions and our intelligence on Enemy's dispositions, and . . ." A shrug. "I improvised."

Knecht lifted his glass in salute. "Brilliantly, as always."

Schneider grinned through his bushy white muttonchop whiskers. "We mustn't forget who secured that intelligence for me. Brilliance cannot improvise on faulty data. You have never failed me."

Knecht flushed. "Once I did."

"Tcha!" The General waved his hand in dismissal. "The nine hundred ninety-nine other times make me forget the once. Only you constantly remember."

Knecht remembered how once he had misplaced an entire regiment of Virginia Foot. It was not where he had left it, but somewhere else entirely. General Schneider, except that he had been Brigadier Schneider, had salvaged the situation and had protected him from Alois Kutz's anger. He had learned something about Konrad Schneider then: The General never let the short-term interfere with the long-term. He would not sacrifice the future on the whim of the moment. It had been such a simple error. He had improperly identified the terrain. The Appalachian Mountains of western Virginia looked much the same from ridge to ridge.

Or was it so simple? He recalled his discussion with the prisoner, Kelly. *Ich biete Ihre Entschuldigung, Herr Brigadier*, he imagined himself saying, but I must have slipped over into a parallel universe. In my timeline, the Rappahannock Guards were on the north side of the river, not the south.

No, it wouldn't work. To believe it meant chaos: A world without facts. A world where lies hid among multiple truths. And what did the General think? What did Konrad Schneider make of Kelly's tale?

Knecht swirled the brandy in his snifter. He watched his reflection dance on the blood-red liquid. "Tell me, Konrad, have you read my report on the prisoner?"

"*Ja*, I have."

"And what did you think?"

"It was a fine report, Rudi. As always."

"No. I meant what did you think of the prisoner's story?"

The General lifted his glass to his lips and sipped his brandy. Knecht had seen many men try to avoid answers and recognized all the tactics. Knecht frowned and waited for an answer he knew he could not trust. For as long as Knecht could remember Schneider had been his leader. From the day he had left his father's house, he had followed Colonel, then Brigadier, then General Schneider, and never before had he been led astray. There was an emptiness in him now. He bit the inside of his cheek so that he could feel something, even pain.

Schneider finished his slow, careful sip and set his glass down. He shrugged broadly, palms up. "How could I know? Vonderberge tells me one thing; Ochsenfuss, another. You, in your report, tell me nothing."

Knecht bristled. "There is not enough data to reach a conclusion," he protested.

Schneider shook his head. "No, no. I meant no criticism. You are correct, as always. Yet, our friends *have* reached conclusions. Different conclusions, to be sure, but we don't know which is correct." He paused. "Of course, he *might* be a spy."

"If he is, he is either a very bad one, or a very, very good one."

"And all we know is . . . What? He loves Rosa and does not love the military. He has some peculiar documents and artifacts and he believes he comes from another world, full of marvelous gadgets. . . ."

"Correction, Herr General. He *says* he believes he came from another world. There is a difference."

"Hmph. *Ja*, you are right again. What is it you always say? The map is not the territory. The testimony is not the fact. Sometimes I envy our friends their ability to reach such strong convictions on so little reflection. You and I, Rudi, we are always beset by doubts, eh?"

Knecht made a face. "If so, Konrad, your doubts have never kept you from acting."

The General stared at him a moment. Then he roared with laughter, slapping his thigh. "Oh, yes, you are right, Rudi. What should I do without you? You know me better than I know myself. There are two kinds of doubts, *nicht wahr?* One says: What is the right thing to do? The other says: Have I done the right thing? But, to command means to decide. I have never fought a battle but that a better strategy has come to mind a day or two later. But where would we be had I waited? Eh, Rudi? The second sort of doubt, Rudi. That is the sort of doubt a commander must have. Never the first sort. And never certainty. Both are disasters."

"And what of Kelly?"

The General reached for his brandy once more. "I will have both the Hexmajor and the Kommandant interview him. Naturally, each will be biased, but in different ways. Between them, we may learn the truth of it." He paused thoughtfully, pursing his lips. "Sooner or later, one will concede the matter. We need not be hasty. No, not hasty at all." He drank the last of his brandy.

"And myself?"

Schneider looked at him. He smiled. "You cannot spend so much time on only one man, one who is almost surely not an enemy agent. You have your spies, scouts, and rangers to supervise. Intelligence to collate. Tell me, Rudi, what those fat knick patroons are planning up in Albany. Have the Iroquois joined them, too? Are they dickering with the Lee brothers to make it a two-front war? I must know these things if I am to . . . improvise. Our situation is grave. Forget Kelly. He is not important."

After he left the General, Knecht took a stroll around the parapet, exchanging greetings with the sentries. Schneider could not have announced more clearly that Kelly was important. But why? And why keep him out of it?

Fox Gap was a star-fort and Knecht's wanderings had taken him to one of the points of the star. From there, defensive fire could enfilade any attacking force. He leaned his elbows on a gun port and gazed out at the nighttime forest farther down the slope of the mountain. The sky was crisp and clear as only autumn skies could be, and the stars were brilliantly close.

The forest was a dark mass, a deeper black against the black of night. The wind soughed through the maple and elm and birch. The sound reached him, a dry whisper, like crumpling paper. Soon it would be the Fall. The leaves were dead; all the life had been sucked out of them.

He sighed. General Schneider had just as clearly ordered him away from Kelly. He had never disobeyed an order. Angrily, he threw a shard of masonry from the parapet wall. It crashed among the treetops below and a sentry turned sharply and shouted a challenge. Embarrassed, Knecht turned and left the parapet.

Once back in his own quarters, Knecht pondered the dilemma of Kelly. His room was spartan. Not much more comfortable, he thought, than Kelly's cell. A simple bed, a desk and chair, a trunk. Woodcuts on the wall: heroic details of long-forgotten battles. An anonymous room, suitable for a roving scout. Next month, maybe, a different room at a different fort.

So what was Kelly? Knecht couldn't see but three possibilities. A clever spy, a madman, or the most pitiful refugee ever. But, as a spy he was not credible; his story was unbelievable, and he simply did not talk like a madman.

*And where does that leave us, Rudi?* Nowhere. Was there a fourth possibility? It didn't seem so.

Knecht decided it was time for a pipe. Cigars were for talk; pipes for reflection. He stepped to the window of his room as he lit it. The pipe was very old. It had belonged to his grandfather, and a century of tobacco had burned its flavor into the bowl. His grandfather had given it to him the night before he had left home forever, when he had confided his plans to the old man, confident of his approval. He had been, Knecht remembered, about Kelly's age at the time. An age steeped in certainties.

Spy, madman, or refugee? If the first, good for me; because I caught him. If the second, good for him; because he will be cared for. He puffed. For two of the three possibilities, custody was the best answer; the only remaining question being what sort of custody. And those two choices were like the two sides of a coin: they used up all probability between them. Heads I win, Herr Kelly, and tails you lose. It is a cell for you either way. That is obvious.

So then, why am I pacing this room in the middle of the night, burning my best leaf and tasting nothing?

*Because, Rudi, there is just the chance that the coin could land on its edge.* If Kelly's outrageous tale were true, custody would not be the best answer. It would be no answer at all.

Ridiculous. It could not be true. He took the pipe from his mouth. The warmth of the bowl in his hand comforted him. Knecht had concluded tentatively that Kelly was no spy. That meant Ochsenfuss was right. Knecht could see that. It had been his own first reaction on reading the notebook. But he could also see why Vonderberge believed otherwise. The man's outlook and Kelly's amiable and sincere demeanor had combined to produce belief.

It was Schneider that bothered him. Schneider had *not* decided. Knecht was certain of that. And that meant . . . What? With madness so obvious, Schneider saw something else. Knecht had decided nothing because he was only interested in spies. Beyond that, what Kelly was or was not meant nothing.

Even if his tale is true, he thought, it is none of my concern. My task is done. I have taken in a suspicious stranger under suspicious circumstances. It is for higher authorities to puzzle it out. Why should I care what the answer is?

*Because, Rudi, it was you who brought him here.*

Knecht learned from Johann the guard that Vonderberge spent the mornings with Kelly, and Ochsenfuss, the afternoons. So when Knecht brought the history book to the cell a few days later, he did so at noon, when no one else was about. He had made it a habit to stop by for a few minutes each day.

He nodded to Johann as he walked down the cell block corridor. "I was never here, soldier," he said. Johann's face took on a look of obligingly amiable unawareness.

Kelly was eating lunch, a bowl of thick rivel soup. He had been provided with a table, which was now littered with scribbled pages. Knecht recognized the odd equations of Kelly's "logical calculus." He handed the prisoner the text: "The History of North America." Kelly seized it eagerly and leafed through it.

"Thanks, lieutenant," he said. "The shrink brought me one, too; but it's in German and I couldn't make sense of it."

"Pennsylvaanish," Knecht corrected him absently. He was looking at the other book. It was thick and scholarly. A good part of each page consisted of footnotes. He shuddered and put it down.

"What?"

"Pennsylvaanish," he repeated. "It is a German dialect, but it is not *Hochdeutsch*. It is Swabian with some English mixed in. The spelling makes it different sometimes. A visitor from the Second Reich would find it nearly unintelligible, but . . ." An elaborate shrug. "What can one expect from a Prussian?"

Kelly laughed. He put his soup bowl aside, finished. "How did that happen?" he asked. "I mean, you folks speaking, ah, Pennsylvaanish?"

Knecht raised an eyebrow. "Because we are Pennsylvanians."

"So were Franklin, Dickinson, and Tom Penn."

"Ah, I see what you are asking. It is simple. Even so far back as the War Against the English the majority of Pennsylvanians were *Deutsch*, German-speakers. So high was the feeling against the English—outside of Philadelphia City, that is—that the Assembly German the official language made. Later, after the Revolution in Europe, many more from Germany came. They were fleeing the Prussians and Austrians."

"And from nowhere else? No Irish? No Poles, Italians, Russian Jews? 'I lift my lamp beside the golden door.' What happened to all of that?"

"I don't understand. *Ja*, some came from other countries. There were Welsh and Scots-Irish here even before the War. Others came later. A few, not many. Ranger Oswoski's grandparents were Polish. But, when they come here, then Pennsylvaanish they must learn."

"I suppose with America so balkanized, it never seemed such a land of opportunity."

"I don't understand that, either. What is 'balkanized'?"

Kelly tapped with his pencil on the table. "No," he said slowly,

"I suppose you wouldn't." He aimed the pencil at the history book. "Let me read this. Maybe I'll be able to explain things better."

"I hope you find in it what you need."

Kelly grinned, all teeth. "An appropriately ambiguous wish, lieutenant, 'What I need.' That could mean anything. But, thank you. I think I will." He hesitated a moment. "And, uh, thanks for the book, too. You've been a big help. You're the only one who comes here and listens to me. I mean, *really* listens."

Knecht smiled. He opened the door, but turned before leaving. "But, Herr Kelly," he said. "It is my job to listen."

Knecht's work absorbed him for several days. Scraps of information filtered in from several quarters. He spent long hours in his office going over them, separating rumor from fact from possible fact. Sometimes, he sent a man out to see for himself and waited in nervous uncertainty until the pigeons flew back. Each night, he threw himself into his rack exhausted. Each morning, there was a new stack of messages.

He moved pins about in his wall map. Formations whose bivouac had been verified. Twice he telegraphed the Southern Command using his personal code to discover what the scouts down along the Monongahela had learned. Slowly, the spaces filled in. The pins told a story. Encirclement.

Schneider came in late one evening. He stood before the map and studied it for long minutes in silence. Knecht sipped his coffee, watching. The General drew his forefinger along the northwestern frontier. There were no pins located in Long House territory. "Curious," he said aloud, as if to himself. Knecht smiled. Five rangers were already out trying to fill in that gap. Schneider would have his answer soon enough.

Knecht had almost forgotten Kelly. There had been no more time for his noontime visits. Then, one morning he heard that Vonderberge and Ochsenfuss had fought in the officers' club. Words had been exchanged, then blows. Not many, because the Chief Engineer had stopped them. It wasn't clear who had started it, or even how it had started. It had gotten as far as it had only because the other officers present had been taken by surprise. Neither man had been known to brawl before.

Knecht was not surprised by the fight. He knew the tension between the two over Kelly. What did surprise him was that Schneider took no official notice of the fight.

Something was happening. Knecht did not know what it was, but he was determined to find out. He decided to do a little intramural spy work of his own.

Knecht found the Hexmajor later that evening. He was sitting alone at a table in the officers' club, sipping an after-dinner liqueur from a thin glass, something Knecht found vaguely effeminate. He realized he was taking a strong personal dislike to the man. Compared to Vonderberge, Ochsenfuss was haughty and cold. Elegant, Knecht thought, watching the man drink. That was the word: elegant. Knecht himself liked plain, blunt-spoken men. But scouts, he told himself firmly, must observe what is, not what they wish to see. The bar orderly handed him a beer stein and he strolled casually to Ochsenfuss' table.

"Ah, Herr Doctor," he said smiling. "How goes it with the prisoner?"

"It goes," said Ochsenfuss, "but slowly."

Knecht sat without awaiting an invitation. He thought he saw a brief glimmer of surprise in the other's face, but the Hexmajor quickly recovered his wooden expression. Knecht was aware that Vonderberge, at a corner table, had paused in his conversation with the Chief Engineer and was watching them narrowly.

"A shame the treatment cannot go speedier," he told Ochsenfuss.

A shrug. "Under such circumstances, the mind must heal itself."

"I remember your work with Ranger Harrison after we rescued him from the Senecas."

Ochsenfuss sipped his drink. "I recall the case. His condition was grave. Torture does things to a man's mind; worse in many ways than what it does to his body."

"May I ask how you are treating Kelly?"

"You may."

There was a long silence. Then Knecht said, "How are you treating him?" He could not detect the slightest hint of a smile on the doctor's face. He was surprised. Ochsenfuss had not seemed inclined to humor of any sort.

"I am mesmerizing him," he said. "Then I allow him to talk about his fantasies. In English," he admitted grudgingly. "I ply him for details. Then, when he is in this highly suggestible state, I point out the contradictions in his thinking."

"Contradictions . . ." Knecht let the word hang in the air.

"Oh, many things. Heavier-than-air flying machines: a mathematical impossibility. Radio, communication without connecting wires: That is action at a distance, also impossible. Then there is his notion that a single government rules the continent, from Columbia to New

England and from Pontiac to Texas. Why, the distances and geographical barriers make the idea laughable.

"I tell him these things while he is mesmerized. My suggestions lodge in what we call the subconscious and gradually make his fantasies less credible to his waking mind. Eventually he will again make contact with reality."

"Tell me something, Herr Doctor."

They both turned at the sound of the new voice. It was Vonderberge. He stood belligerently, his thumbs hooked in his belt. He swayed slightly and Knecht could smell alcohol on his breath. Knecht frowned unhappily.

Ochsenfuss blinked. "Yes, Kommandant," he said blandly. "What is it?"

"I have read that by mesmerization one can also implant false ideas."

Ochsenfuss smiled. "I have heard that at carnival sideshows, the mesmerist may cause members of the audience to believe that they are ducks or some such thing."

"I was thinking of something more subtle than that."

The Hexmajor's smile did not fade, but it seemed to freeze. "Could you be more specific."

Vonderberge leaned toward them. "I mean," he said slowly, "the obliteration of true memories and their replacement with false ones."

Ochsenfuss tensed. "No reputable hexdoctor would do such a thing."

Vonderberge raised a palm. "I never suggested such a thing, either. I only asked if it were possible."

Ochsenfuss paused before answering. "It is. But the false memories would inevitably conflict with a thousand others and, most importantly, with the evidence of the patient's own senses. The end would be psychosis. The obliteration of *false* memories, however . . ."

Vonderberge nodded several times, as if the Hexmajor had confirmed a long-standing belief. "I see. Thank you, Doctor." He turned and looked at Knecht. He touched the bill of his cap. "Rudi," he said in salutation, then turned and left.

Ochsenfuss watched him go. "There is a man who can benefit from therapy. He would reject reality if he could."

Knecht remembered Vonderberge's outburst in his office during the storm. He remembered, too, the map in his own office. "So might we all," he said. "Reality is none too pleasant these days. General Schneider believes . . ."

"General Schneider," interrupted Ochsenfuss, "believes what he wants to believe. But truth is not always what we want, is it?" He looked away, his eyes focused on the far wall. "Nor always what we need." He took another sip of his liqueur and set the glass down. "I am not such a fool as he seems to think. For all that he primes me with questions to put to Kelly, and the interest he shows in my reports, he still has not decided what to do with my patient. He should be in hospital, in Philadelphia."

For the briefest moment, Knecht thought he meant Schneider should be in hospital. When he realized the confusion, he laughed. Ochsenfuss looked at him oddly and Knecht took a pull on his mug to hide his embarrassment.

"If I could use mescal or peyote to heighten his suggestibility," Ochsenfuss continued to no one in particular. "Or if I could keep our friend the Kommandant away from my patient. . . ." He studied his drink in silence, then abruptly tossed it off. He looked at his watch and waved off a hovering orderly. "Well, things cannot go on as they are. Something must break." He laughed and rose from the table. "At least there are a few of us who take a hard-headed and practical view of the world, eh, Leutnant?" He patted Knecht on the arm and left.

Knecht watched him go. He took another drink of beer and wiped the foam from his lips with his sleeve, thinking about what the Hexmajor had said.

A few days later, a carrier pigeon arrived and Knecht rode out to meet its sender at a secret rendezvous deep inside Wyoming. Such meetings were always risky, but his agent had spent many years working her way into a position of trust. It was a mask that would be dropped if she tried to leave the country. Knecht wondered what the information was. Obviously more than could be entrusted to a pigeon.

But she never came to the rendezvous. Knecht waited, then left a sign on a certain tree that he had been there and gone. He wondered what had happened. Perhaps she had not been able to get away after all. Or perhaps she had been unmasked and quietly executed. Like many of the Old-style Quakers, Abigail Fox had learned English at her mother's knee and spoke without an accent; but one never knew what trivial detail would prove fatal.

Knecht chewed on his moustache as he rode homeward. He had not seen Abby for a long time. Now he didn't know if he would ever see her again. The worst part would be never knowing what had happened. Knecht hated not knowing things. That's why he was a good scout. Even bad news was better than no news.

Well, perhaps another pigeon would arrive, explaining everything, arranging another rendezvous. *But how could you be sure, Rudi, that it really came from her?* Spies have been broken before, and codes with them. One day, he knew, he would ride out to a meeting and not come back. He felt cold and empty. He slapped his horse on the rump and she broke into a trot. He was afraid of death, but he would not send others to do what he would not.

It had been two weeks to rendezvous and back and Schneider was still at Fox Gap when Knecht returned. The rumors had grown up thick for harvesting. Between the front gate and the stables five soldiers and two officers asked him if a command shake-up were coming. His friendship with the General was well-known, and why else would Schneider stay on?

Why else, indeed. Kelly. Knecht was certain of it, but the why still eluded him.

Catching up on his paperwork kept Knecht at his desk until well after dark. When he had finished, he made his way to Vonderberge's quarters. Knecht's thought was to pay a "social call" and guide the conversation around to the subject of Kelly. Once he arrived, however, he found himself with some other officers, drinking dark beer and singing badly to the accompaniment of the Chief Engineer's equally bad piano playing. It was, he discovered, a weekly ritual among the permanent fortress staff.

Ochsenfuss was not there, but that did not surprise him.

He was reluctant to bring up the business of the prisoner in front of the other officers, so he planned to be the last to leave. But Vonderberge and the Fortress Staff proved to have a respectable capacity for drinking and singing and Knecht outlasted them only by cleverly passing out in the corner, where he was overlooked when Vonderberge ushered the others out.

"Good morning, Rudi."

Knecht opened his eyes. The light seared his eyes and the top of his head fell off and shattered on the floor. "Ow," he said.

"Very eloquent, Rudi." Vonderberge leaned over him, looking impossibly cheerful. "That must be some hangover."

Knecht winced. "You can't get hangovers from beer."

Vonderberge shrugged. "Have it your way." He held out a tall glass. "Here, drink this."

He sniffed the drink warily. It was dark and red and pungent. "What is it?" he asked suspiciously.

"Grandmother Vonderberge's Perfect Cure for Everything. It never fails."

"But what's in it?"

"If I told you, you wouldn't drink it. Go ahead. Grandmother was a wise old bird. She outlasted three husbands."

Knecht drank. He shuddered and sweat broke out on his forehead. "Small wonder," he gasped. "She probably fed them this."

Vonderberge chuckled and took the glass back. "You were in fine form last night. Fine form. Who is Abby?"

Knecht looked at him. "Why?"

"You kept drinking toasts to her."

He looked away, into the distance. "She was . . . someone I knew."

"Like that, eh?" Vonderberge grinned. Knecht did not bother to correct him.

"You should socialize more often, Rudi," continued the Kommandant. "You'll find we're not such bad sorts. You have a good baritone. It gave the staff a fuller sound." Vonderberge gestured broadly to show how full the sound had been. "We need the higher registers, though. I've thought of having Heinz and Zuckerman gelded. What do you think?"

Knecht considered the question. "Where do they stand on the promotion list?"

Vonderberge looked at him sharply. He grinned. "You are beginning to show a sense of humor, Rudi. A sense of humor."

Knecht snorted. He was easily twenty years the Kommandant's senior. He knew jokes that had been old and wrinkled before Vonderberge had been born. He recalled suddenly that Abigail Fox had been an alto. There were other memories, too; and some empty places where there could have been memories, but weren't. Ach, for what might have been! It wasn't right for spymaster and spy to be too close. He wondered if Kelly had a world somewhere where everything was different.

Vonderberge had his batman serve breakfast in rather than go to the mess. He invited Knecht to stay and they talked over eggs, scrapple, and coffee. Knecht did not have to lead into the subject of Kelly because Vonderberge raised it himself. He unrolled a sheet of paper onto the table after the batman had cleared it, using the salt and pepper mills to hold down the curled ends.

"Let me show you," he said, "what bothers me about Kelly's world."

A great many things about Kelly's world bothered Knecht, not the least of which was the fact that there was no evidence it even existed; but he put on a polite face and listened attentively. Was Vonderberge beginning to have doubts?

The Kommandant pointed to the sheet. Knecht saw that it was a table of inventions, with dates and inventors. Some of the inventions had two dates and two inventors, in parallel columns.

"Next to each invention," said Vonderberge, "I've written when and by whom it was invented. The first column is our world; the second, Kelly's, as nearly as he can remember. Do you notice anything?"

Knecht glanced at the list. "Several things," he replied casually. "There are more entries in the second column, most of the dates are earlier, and a few names appear in both columns."

Vonderberge blinked and looked at him. Knecht kept his face composed.

"You're showing off, aren't you, Rudi?"

"I've spent a lifetime noticing details on documents."

"But do you see the significance? The inventions came earlier and faster in Kelly's world. Look how they *gush* forth after 1870! Why? How could they have been so much more creative? In the early part of the list, many of the same men are mentioned in both columns, so it is not individual genius. Look . . ." His forefinger searched the first column. "The electrical telegraph was invented, when? In 1875, by Edison. In Kelly's world, it was invented in the 1830s, by a man named Morse."

"The painter?"

"Apparently the same man. Why didn't he invent it here? And see what Edison did in Kelly's world: The electrical light, the moving picture projector, dozens of things we never saw until the 1930s."

Knecht pointed to an entry. "Plastics," he said. "We discovered them first." He wondered what "first" meant in this context.

"That is the exception that proves the rule. There are others. Daguerre's photographic camera, Foucault's gyroscope. They are the same in both worlds. But overall there is a pattern. Not an occasional marvel, every now and then; but a multitude, every year! By 1920, in Kelly's world, steamships, *heavier*-than-air craft, railroads, *voice* telegraphy with *and without* wires, horseless carriages, they were an old hat. Here, they are still wonders. Or wondered about."

Inventions and gadgets, decided Knecht. Those were Vonderberge's secret passion, and Kelly had described a technological faerieland. No wonder the Kommandant was entranced. Knecht was less in awe, himself. He had seen the proud ranks of the 18th New York mowed down like corn by the Pennsylvaanish machine guns at the Battle of the Raritan. And he had not forgotten what Kelly had written in his notebook: There were bombs that destroyed whole cities.

Vonderberge sighed and rolled up his list. He tied a cord around it. "It is difficult, Rudi," he said. "Very difficult. Your General, he only wants to hear about the inventions. He does not wonder why there are so many. Yet, I feel that this is an important question."

"Can't Kelly answer it?"

"He might. He has come close to it on several occasions; but he is . . . confused. Ochsenfuss sees to that."

Knecht noticed how Vonderberge's jaw set. The Kommandant's usual bantering tone was missing.

Vonderberge pulled a watch from his right pants pocket and studied its face. "It is time for my appointment with Kelly. Why don't you come with me. I'd like your opinion on something."

"On what?"

"On Kelly."

Knecht sat backward on a chair in the corner of the cell, leaning his arms on the back. A cigar was clamped tightly between his teeth. It had gone out, but he had not bothered to relight it. He watched the proceedings between Kelly and Vonderberge. So far, he did not like what he had seen.

Kelly spoke hesitantly. He seemed distracted and lapsed into frequent, uncomfortable silences. The papers spread out on his table were blank. No new equations. Just doodles of flowers. Roses, they looked like.

"Think, Kelly," Vonderberge pleaded. "We were talking of this only yesterday."

Kelly pursed his lips and frowned. "Were we? *Ja*, you're right. I think we did. I thought it was a dream."

"It was not a dream. It was real. You said you thought the Victorian Age was the key. What was the Victorian Age?"

Kelly looked puzzled. "Victorian Age? Are you sure?"

"Yes. You mentioned Queen Victoria . . ."

"She was never Queen, though."

Vonderberge clucked impatiently. "That was in this world," he said. "In your world it must have been different."

"In my world . . ." It was half a statement, half a question. Kelly closed his eyes, hard. "I have such headaches, these days. It's hard to remember things. It's all confused."

Vonderberge turned to Knecht. "You see the problem?"

Knecht removed his cigar. "The problem," he said judiciously, "is the source of his confusion."

Vonderberge turned back to Kelly. "I think we both know who that is."

Kelly was losing touch, Knecht thought. That was certain. But was he losing touch with reality, or with fantasy?

"Wait!" Kelly's eyes were still closed but his hand shot out and gripped Vonderberge's wrist. "The Victorian Age. That was the time from the War Between the States to World War I." He opened his eyes and looked at Vonderberge. "Am I right?"

Vonderberge threw his hands up. "Tchah! Why are you asking *me?*"

Knecht chewed thoughtfully on his cigar. *World* wars? And they were *numbered?*

"What has this 'Victorian Age' to do with your world's inventiveness?"

Kelly stared at a space in the air between them. He rapped rhythmically on the table with his knuckles. "Don't push it," he said. "I might lose the . . . Yes. I can hear Tom's voice explaining it." The eyes were unfocused. Knecht wondered what sort of mind heard voices talking to it. "What an odd apartment. We were just BS'ing. Sharon, Tom, and . . . a girl, and I. The subject came up, but in a different context."

They waited patiently for Kelly to remember.

"Critical mass!" he said suddenly. "That was it. The rate at which new ideas are generated depends in part on the accumulation of past ideas. The more there are, the more ways they can be combined and modified. Then, boom," he gestured with his hands. "An explosion." He laughed shrilly; sobered instantly. "That's what happened during the Victorian Age. That's what's happening now, but slower."

A slow explosion? The idea amused Knecht. "Why slower?" he asked.

"Because of the barriers! Ideas must circulate freely if they're to trigger new ones. The velocity of ideas is as important to culture and technology as, as the velocity of money is to the economy. The United States would have been the largest free trade zone in the world. The second largest was England. Not even the United Kingdom, just England. Can you imagine? Paying a toll or a tariff every few miles?"

"What has commerce to do with ideas?" asked Vonderberge.

"It's the traveling people who carry ideas from place to place. The merchants, sailors, soldiers. At least until an international postal system is established. And radio. And tourism."

"I see . . ."

"But look at the barriers we have to deal with! The largest nation on the Atlantic seaboard is what? The Carolina Kingdom. Some of the Indian states are larger, but they don't have many people. How far can you travel before you pay a tariff? Or run into a foreign language like English or Choctaw or French? Or into a military patrol that shoots first and asks questions later? No wonder we're so far behind!"

Knecht pulled the cigar from his mouth. "We?" he asked. Vonderberge turned and gave him an anxious glance, so he, too, had noticed the shift in Kelly's personal pronoun.

The prisoner was flustered. "You," he said. "I meant 'you.' Your rate of progress is slower. I . . ."

Knecht forestalled further comment. "No, never mind. A slip of the tongue, *ja?*" He smiled to show he had dismissed the slip. He knew it was important; though in what way he was not yet sure. He took a long puff on his cigar. "Personally, I have never thought our progress slow. The horseless carriage was invented, what? 1920-something, in Dusseldorf. In less than fifty years you could find some in all the major cities. Last year, two nearly collided on the streets of Philadelphia! Soon every well-to-do family will have one."

The prisoner laughed. It was a great belly laugh that shook him and shook him until it turned imperceptibly into a sob. He squeezed his eyes tight.

"There was a man," he said distantly. "Back in my hometown of Longmont, Colorado." He opened his eyes and looked at them. "That would be in Nuevo Aztlan, if it existed, which it doesn't and never has . . ." He paused and shook his head, once, sharply, as if to clear it. "Old Mr. Brand. I was just a kid, but I remember when the newspapers and TV came around. When Old Brand was a youngster, he watched his dad drive a stagecoach. Before he died, he watched his son fly a space shuttle." He looked intently at Knecht. "And you think it is wonderful that a few rich people have hand-built cars after half a century?"

He laughed again; but this time the laugh was brittle. They watched him for a moment, and the laugh went on and on. Then Vonderberge leaned forward and slapped him sharply, twice.

Knecht chewed his moustache. What the prisoner said made some sense. He could see how technological progress—and social change with it—was coupled with free trade and the free exchange of ideas. Yet, he wasn't at all sure that it was necessarily a good thing. There was a lot to be said for stability and continuity. He blew a smoke ring. He wondered if Kelly were a social radical, driven mad by his inability to instigate change, who had built himself a fantasy world in which change ran amok. That made sense, too.

He glanced at his cigar, automatically timing the ash. A good cigar should burn at least five minutes before the ash needed knocking off.

Suddenly, he felt a tingling in his spine. He looked at the cigar as if it had come alive in his hand. It had gone out—he remembered that clearly. Now, it was burning, and he could not recall relighting it. He looked at the ashtray. Yes, a spent match. I relit it, of course. It was such an automatic action that I paid it no mind. That was one explanation. It was his memory playing tricks, not his reality. But the tingling in his spine did not stop.

He looked at Kelly, then he carefully laid his cigar in the ashtray to burn itself out.

"You just wait, though," Kelly was saying to Vonderberge. "Our curve is starting up, too. It took us longer, but we'll be reaching critical mass soon. We're maybe 100 years off the pace. About where the other . . . where my world was just before the world wars."

That simple pronouncement filled Knecht with a formless dread. He watched the smoke from his smoldering cigar and saw how it rose, straight and true, until it reached a breaking point. There, it changed abruptly into a chaos of turbulent streamers, swirling at random in the motionless air. Then we could do the same, he thought. Fight worldwide wars.

Afterward, Knecht and Vonderberge spoke briefly as they crossed the parade ground. The sun was high in the sky, but the air held the coolness of autumn. Knecht was thoughtful, his mind on his cigar, on alternate realities, on the suddenness with which stability could turn to chaos.

"You saw it, didn't you?" asked Vonderberge.

For a moment he thought the Kommandant meant his mysteriously relit cigar. "Saw what?" he replied.

"Kelly. He has difficulty remembering his own world. He becomes confused, disoriented, melancholy."

"Is he always so?"

"Today was better than most. Sometimes I cannot stop his weeping."

"I have never heard him talk so long without mentioning his Rosa."

"Ah, you noticed that, too. But three days ago he was completely lucid and calculated columns of figures. Settings, he said, for his machine. They take into account, ah . . . 'many-valued inverse functions.' " Vonderberge smiled. "Whatever that means. And, if he ever sees his machine again."

"His machine," said Knecht. "Has anyone handled it?"

"No," said Vonderberge. "Ochsenfuss doesn't think it matters. It's just a collection of knobs and wires."

"And you?"

"Me?" Vonderberge looked at him. "I'm afraid to."

"Yet, its study could be most rewarding."

"A true scout. But if we try, four things could happen and none of them good."

Knecht tugged on his moustaches. "We could open it up and find that it is an obvious fake, that it couldn't possibly work."

"Could we? How would it be obvious? We would still wonder whether the science were so advanced that we simply did not understand how it did work. Like a savage with a steam engine." The Kommandant was silent for a moment.

"That's one. You said four things could happen."

"The other three assume the machine works." He held up his fingers to count off his points. "Two: In our ignorance, we damage it irreparably, marooning Kelly forever. Three: We injure ourselves by some sort of shock or explosion."

"And four?"

"Four: We transport ourselves unwittingly to another world."

"A slim possibility, that."

Vonderberge shrugged. "Perhaps. But the penalty for being wrong is . . ."

"Excessive," agreed Knecht dryly.

"I *did* examine his 'calculator,' you know."

Knecht smiled to himself. He had wondered if the Kommandant had done that, too. Knecht had learned little from it, himself.

"It was fine work: the molded plastic, the tiny buttons, the intricate circuits and parts."

"Not beyond the capabilities of any competent electrosmith."

"What! Did you see how small the batteries were? And the, what did he call them? The chips? How can you say that?"

"I didn't mean we could build a calculating engine so small. But, is it a calculating engine? Did you see it function? No. Kelly says the batteries have gone dead. Which is convenient for him. Our regimental electrosmith could easily construct a copy that does the same thing: mainly, nothing."

Vonderberge stopped and held him by the arm. "Tell me, Rudi. Do you believe Kelly or not?"

"I . . ." Well, did he? The business with the cigar was too pat. It seemed important only because of Kelly's toying with another cigar a few weeks before. Otherwise, he would never have noticed, or thought nothing even if he had. Like the prophetic dream: It seems to be more than it is because we only remember them when they come true. "I . . . have no convincing evidence."

"Evidence?" asked Vonderberge harshly. "What more evidence do you need?"

"Something solid," Knecht snapped back. *Something more than that I like the prisoner and the Kommandant and I dislike the Hexmajor*. "Something more than a prisoner's tale," he said. "That becomes more confused as time goes on."

"That is Ochsenfuss' bungling!"

"Or his success! Have you thought that perhaps the Hexmajor is *curing* Kelly of a long-standing delusion?"

Vonderberge turned to go. "No."

Knecht stopped him. "Heinrich," he said.

"What?"

Knecht looked past the Kommandant. He could see the sentries where they paced the walls, and the cannons in their redoubts, and the gangways to the underground tunnels that led to the big guns fortified into the mountainside. "Real or fantasy, you've learned a lot about the prisoner's technology."

"Enough to want to learn more."

"Tell me, Henrich. Do you *want* to learn to make nuclear bombs?"

Vonderberge followed Knecht's gaze. A troubled look crossed his face and he bit his lower lip. "No. I do not. But the same force can produce electricity. And the medical science that produces the miracle drugs can tailor-make horrible plagues. The jets that fly bombs can just as easily fly people or food or trade goods." He sighed. "What can I say, Rudi. It is not the tool, but the tool-user who creates the problems. Nature keeps no secrets. If something can be done, someone will find a way to do it."

Knecht made no reply. He didn't know if a reply was even possible. Certainly none that Vonderberge would understand.

When Ranger O Brien brought the news from the Nations, General Schneider was away from the fortress, inspecting the outposts on the forward slope. Knecht received O Brien's report, ordered the man to take some rest, and decided the General should see it immediately. He telegraphed Outpost Three that he was coming and rode out.

The crest of Kittatinny Mountain and all the forward slope had been clear-cut the distance of a cannon shot. Beyond that was wilderness. Ridge and valley alternated into the distant north, dense with trees, before rising once more into the Pocono range, where Wyoming had her own fortress line. Legally, the border ran somewhere through the no-man's-land between, but the main armies were entrenched in more easily defended terrain.

Knecht reined in at the crest of the Mountain and looked back. The valley of the Lehigh was checkerboarded with broad farms. Farther away, he could discern the smoke plumes of cities at the canal and rail heads. There was a speck in the air, most likely an airship sailing south.

When he turned, the contrast with the land north of the Mountain was jarring. He must have gazed upon that vista thousands of times over the years. Now, for just an instant, it looked *wrong*. It was said to be fertile land. Certainly, enough blood had manured it. And some said there was coal beneath it. He imagined the land filled with farms, mills, and mines.

At that moment of *frisson* he knew, irrationally, that Kelly had been telling the truth all along. Somewhere the barbed wire was used only to keep the *milch* cows safe.

And the bombs and missles? What if it were a rain of death from the other side of the world that we feared, and not a party of Mohawk bucks out to prove themselves to their elders? A slow explosion, Kelly had said. The inventions would come. Nature kept no secrets. The discoveries would be made and be given to the petty rulers of petty, quarreling states. Men with dreams of conquest, or revenge.

Knecht clucked to his horse and started downslope to the picket line. Give Konrad Schneider that, he thought. His only dream is survival, not conquest. Yet he is desperate; and desperate men do desperate things, not always wise things.

"Hah! Rudi!" General Schneider waved to him when he saw him coming. He was standing on the glacis of the outpost along with the Feldwebel and his men. The General's staff was as large as the platoon stationed there, so the area seemed ludicrously crowded. The General stood in their midst, a portly, barrel-chested man with a large curved pipe clenched firmly in his teeth. He pointed.

"Do you think the field of fire is clear enough and wide enough?"

Knecht tethered his horse and walked to where the General stood. He had never known Schneider to ask an idle question. He decided the real question was whether Vonderberge was reliable. He gave the cleared area careful scrutiny. Not so much as a blade of grass. No force large enough to take the outpost could approach unseen. "It seems adequate," he said.

"Hmph. High praise from you, Rudi." The General sucked on his pipe, staring downslope, imagining ranks of yankees and knickerbockers charging up. "It had better be. But you did not ride out here from Fox Gap only to answer an old man's foolish questions."

"No, General."

Schneider stared at him and the smile died on his face. He put his arm around Knecht's shoulder and led him off to the side. The others eyed them nervously. When scouts and generals talked the result was often trouble.

"What is it?"

"Friedrich O Brien has returned from the Nations."

"And?"

"The League has voted six to two to join the alliance against us."

They paced together in silence. Then Schneider said, "So, who held out?"

"Huron and Wyandot."

The General nodded. He released Knecht's shoulder and walked off by himself. He turned and gave a hollow laugh. "Well, at least some of our money was well spent. In the old days, it would have been enough. League votes would have had to be unanimous. Do you think they will fight? The two holdouts, I mean."

"Do you think they will split the League, General, over Pennsylvania?"

"Hmph. No. You are right again. They will go with the majority. But, perhaps, the fighting on the west will be less what? Enthusiastic?"

"At least it is too late in the year for an offensive."

"Perhaps, Rudi. But the crops are in. If they think they can knock us out in a lightning-war before the snows, they may try anyway. How long can they hold their alliance together? It is unnatural. Yankees and knicks and longhousers side-by-side? Pfah! It cannot last. No, they must strike while they have Virginia with them, as well. What do you think? A holding action along the Fortress Line while the Lees strike up the Susquehannah and Shenandoah?"

"Will Virginia bleed for New York's benefit?"

Schneider nodded. "A two-front war, then." He rubbed his hands together briskly. "Well, our strategy is clear. We must stir up problems behind them. In New England or Carolina or Pontiac. And perhaps we have a few surprises of our own."

Knecht looked at him sharply. Schneider was smiling. It was a small smile, but it was a real one, not forced. "What are you talking about?"

Schneider pointed to the wires running from the outpost to the Fortress. "Suppose there were no wires to be cut or tapped. Suppose there were voices in the air, undetectable, sent from anywhere a man could carry an instrument. We would not need messengers or pigeons, either. Think how quickly we could learn of enemy formations and mobilize our own forces to meet them. The right force in the right time and place is worth regiments a mile away and a day late. Or airplanes, darting among the airships with machine guns and bombs. We could carry the fighting all the way to Wilkes Barre and Painted Post."

"Kelly."

*"Ja."* The General chuckled. "Vonderberge tells me of these gadgets, like radio. Crazy notions. But I wonder. What if it were true? Kelly's waking mind does not remember the details of the sort of, hmph, primitive inventions we could hope to copy. And from your report I suspect he would not help us willingly. Oh, he is friendly enough; but he does not like the military and would not help us prepare for war. Especially a war none of his concern. A problem. So, I seize the moment." He clenched his fist and waved it.

"You pass along the information to Ochsenfuss and ask him to find the details by prying in his unconscious mind."

Schneider looked at him. "You knew?"

"I guessed."

"You never guess. You're offended."

"No."

"You are. But I had to leave you out. You would have cut to the truth too quickly. I knew you. If you found that Kelly was mad, well, no harm done; but I was speculating that he was just what he said he was. If that were the case, I could not allow you to prove it."

"Why not?"

"Ochsenfuss, that old plodder. He will not mesmerize except for medical reasons. If you had proven Kelly was, well, Kelly, our friend the Hexmajor would have bowed out and Kelly's secrets would have remained secret. No. I needed Ochsenfuss' skill at mesmerizing. I needed Vonderberge's enthusiasm for technofiction, so he would know what questions to ask. And, for it to work, I needed Kelly's status to remain ambiguous."

"Then the Hexmajor does not know."

"No. He is our protective plumage. I read his reports and send them to a secret team of scientists that OKP has assembled at Franklin University. Only a few people at OKP know anything. Only I, and now you, know everything."

Knecht grunted. Ochsenfuss *did* know. At least he knew something. His remarks at the officers' club had made that clear.

"Vonderberge said we lack the tools to make the tools to make the things Kelly described."

"Then Vonderberge is short-sighted. Pfah! I am no fool. I don't ask for the sophisticated developments. Those are years ahead. Decades. But the original, basic inventions, those are different. As Kelly described it, they came about in a world much like our own. And, Rudi?"

"*Ja*, Herr General?"

"This morning I received word from Franklin. They have sent telegraphic messages *without wires* between Germantown and Philadelphia. They used a special kind of crystal. The pulses travel through the air itself." He grinned like a child with a new toy.

Knecht wondered how much difference such things would make in the coming war. There wasn't time to make enough of them and learn how to use them. He also remembered what Ochsenfuss had said in the officers' club. Something had to break. The question was what. Or who.

Knecht took a deep breath. "It's over, then. You've learned how to make radio messages. Ochsenfuss can stop treating him."

Schneider would not meet his eyes. "The mesmerization must continue. There are other inventions. We need to know about airframes. The details are sketchy yet. And napalm. And . . ."

"Between Ochsenfuss and Vonderberge, Kelly's personality is being destroyed. He hardly remembers who he is, or which world is real."

"This is war. In war there are casualties. Even innocent ones."

"It is not Kelly's war."

"No. But it is yours."

Knecht's mouth set in a grim line. "*Ja*, Herr General."

"You make it look so easy," said Vonderberge.

"Shh," hissed Knecht. He twisted his probe once more and felt the bolt slide back. "These old style locks are easy, and I've had much practice." He pulled the storeroom door open and they stepped inside.

"Schneider will know you did it. Who else has your skill with locks?"

Knecht scowled. "Every scout and ranger in the Corps. But, yes, Schneider will know it was me."

Vonderberge began searching the shelves. "Does that bother you?"

Knecht shrugged. "I don't know. It should. The General has been . . . like a father to me."

"Here it is," said Vonderberge. He stepped back, Kelly's rucksack in his hands. He looked inside. "Yes, the belt controls are here also. I don't think anyone has touched it. Schneider has the only key."

"Do you suppose it still works?"

Vonderberge's hands clenched around the straps. "It must."

They crossed the parade ground to the brig. It was dark. Knecht felt that he should dart from cover to cover; but that was silly. They were officers and they belonged here. They took salutes from three passing soldiers. Everything was normal.

The night guard in the cell block shook his head sadly when he saw them coming. "In the middle of the night, sir?" he said to Vonderberge. "Hasn't that poor bastard spilled his guts yet? Who is he, anyway?"

"As you said, soldier," Vonderberge answered. "Some poor bastard."

While the guard unlocked the cell door, Vonderberge hefted the rucksack, getting a better grip. He stroked the canvas nervously. Knecht could see beads of perspiration on his forehead.

Well, he's risking his career, too, he thought.

"We will never have a better chance, Rudi," Vonderberge whispered. "Kelly was very clear this morning when I told him what we proposed to do. He had already calculated settings several days ago, using his new 'formula.' He only needed to update them. I arranged a diversion to keep Ochsenfuss away from him, so he has not been mesmerized in the meantime. Tomorrow and he may relapse into confusion once more."

"As you say," said Knecht shortly. He was not happy about this. For Knecht, his career was his life. He had been army since his teens. A scout, and a good one; perhaps the best. Now it was on the Line. A scout observes and listens and pieces things together. He does not initiate action. How many times had he said that over the years? He had said it to Kelly. Why should he break his code now, for a man he hardly knew?

Knecht didn't know. He only knew that it would be worse to leave Kelly where he was. An obligation? Because I brought him here? Because of what we might learn from him?

Perhaps I could have argued Konrad into this, he thought. And perhaps not. And if not, there would have been a guard on that storeroom door, and restricted access to the prisoner, and so I have to do this by night and by stealth.

The guard came suddenly to attention. Knecht looked around and saw Ochsenfuss entering the corridor from the guardroom. Vonderberge, already stepping inside the cell, saw him, too. He grabbed Knecht's shoulder. "Talk to him. Keep him out until it's too late."

Knecht nodded and Vonderberge pulled the door shut. Knecht had a momentary glimpse of Kelly, rising from his cot fully dressed. Then the door closed and Ochsenfuss was at his side. The guard looked at them and pretended to be somewhere else. Knecht wondered what he would say to the Hexmajor that would keep him out.

"Up late, *Herr Doctor*," he said. *Clever, Rudi. Very Clever.*

"Insomnia," was the reply. "A common malady, it seems. You might ask who is *not* up late, whiling away the hours in the guardhouse. Do you have a cigar?"

The request caught Knecht by surprise. Dumbly, he took out his pocket humidor. Ochsenfuss made a great show of selecting one of the cigars inside. Knecht took one also and offered one to the guard, who refused.

"Fire?" Ochsenfuss struck a match for Knect, then lit his own. After a moment or two, he blew a perfect smoke ring. "I had an interesting experience today."

"Oh?" Knecht glanced at the guard, who decided this would be a good time to patrol the outside of the building.

"*Ja*. I had a message from Outpost 10. The farthest one. One of the men was behaving oddly. Confinement mania, perhaps. But when I arrived, no one knew about the message. Or, more precisely, no one *acknowledged* knowing about the message. Odd, don't you think?"

"A hoax." Dimly, through the door, Knecht could hear a low pitched hum. The floor seemed to be vibrating, ever so slightly. He thought he could detect a faint whiff of ozone in the air. He studied the doctor's face, but saw no sign of awareness.

"Certainly a hoax. That was obvious. But to what purpose? Simply to laugh at the foolish doctor? Perhaps. But perhaps more. I could see but two possibilities, logically. The message was to make me do something or to prevent me from doing something."

Knecht nodded. "That does seem logical." The night air was cool, but he could feel the sweat running down his back, staining his shirt. The humming rose in pitch.

"Logic is a useful tool," Ochsenfuss agreed inanely. "As nearly as I could tell, the only thing the message made me do was to ride down the Mountain and back up. That did not seem to benefit anyone."

"Is there a point to this, *Herr Doctor?*" Knecht felt jumpy. Abruptly, the humming rose sharply in pitch and dropped in volume, sounding oddly like the whistle of a railroad train approaching and receding at the same time. Then it was gone. Knecht suppressed the urge to turn around. He swallowed a sigh of relief.

"What remains?" Ochsenfuss continued. "What was I prevented from doing? Why treating Kelly, of course. And who has been my opponent in the treatment? The Festungskommandant. So, since my return, I have been watching."

Knecht took the cigar from his mouth and stared. "*You* spied on *me?*"

Ochsenfuss laughed. A great bellow. He slapped Knecht's shoulder. "No, I pay you a high compliment. No one could watch you for long without you becoming aware of the fact. A sense shared by all scouts who survive. No, I followed Vonderberge. When you met him at the storeroom, I retired. It was obvious what you intended to do."

Knecht flushed. "And you told no one?"

Ochsenfuss sucked on his cigar. "No. Should I have?" He paused and pointed the stub of his cigar at the cell door. "He's not coming out, you know."

"What? Who?"

"Your friend, Vonderberge. He's not coming out. He's gone."

Knecht turned and stared at the door. "You mean he took the equipment and left Kelly behind?"

"No, no. They left together. If they stayed close, if they hugged, they would both be inside the field."

"Guard!" bellowed Knecht. "Open this door!" The guard came pounding down the corridor. He unlocked the door and he and Knecht crowded inside. The cell was empty. Knecht saw that Ochsenfuss had not bothered to look. The guard gave a cry of astonishment and ran to fetch the watch-sergeant. Knecht stepped out and looked at the doctor.

The doctor shrugged. "I told you he would reject reality if he could."

"Explain that!" Knecht pointed to the empty cell.

Ochsenfuss blew another smoke ring. "He ran from reality." With a sudden motion, he kicked the cell door. It swung back and banged against the wall. "This is reality," he said harshly. "Vonderberge has fled it. How else can I say it?"

"Obviously, the other worlds are no less real. The evidence is there, now."

"What of it? It is the flight that matters, not the destination. What if the next world fails to please him? Will he reject that reality as well?"

A squad of soldiers came pelting from the guardroom. They pushed past Knecht and Ochsenfuss and crowded into the cell. Their sergeant followed at a more majestic pace.

"How long have you known," Knecht asked Ochsenfuss, "that the other worlds were real?"

Ochsenfuss shrugged. "Long enough." He laughed. "Poor, dull-witted Ochsenfuss! He cannot see a fact if it bit him on the nose." The Hexmajor's lips thinned. "Granted, I am no physical scientist, but what Kelly said went against everything I had ever read or heard. Later, I came to know I was wrong." Another shrug. "Well, we grow too soon old and too late smart. But I ask you, why did Vonderberge believe? He was correct from the beginning, but he believed before he had any real proof. He believed because he *wanted* to believe. And that, too, is madness."

"And Schneider?"

"Schneider never believed. He was making a bet. Just in case it was true. *He was playing games with my patient!*"

Knecht could see genuine anger now. The first real emotion he had ever seen in the Hexmajor. He saw the General for a moment through the Doctor's eyes. It was a side of Konrad he did not care for.

They spoke in an island of calm. Around them soldiers were searching, looking for tunnels. Schneider would be coming soon, Knecht realized. Perhaps it was time to leave, to postpone the inevitable. He and the Doctor walked to the front of the guardhouse but they went no further than the wooden portico facing the parade ground. There was really no point in postponement.

Knecht leaned on the railing, looking out over the parade ground. A squad of soldiers marched past in the dusk: full kit, double-time. Their sergeant barked a cadence at them. Idly, Knecht wondered what infraction they had committed. Across the quadrangle, the Visiting Officers' Quarters were dark.

"So why, after you knew, did you continue to treat him?" He looked over his shoulder at the Doctor.

Ochsenfuss waved his hands. The glowing tip of his cigar wove a complex pattern in the dark. "You read his journal. Do you really suppose he has found his way home this time? No, he goes deeper into the forest of time, hopelessly lost. And Vonderberge with him. Six worlds he had visited already and in what? In three of them, he was in danger. The next world may kill him."

"But . . ."

"Tchah! Isn't it obvious? He was driven to try. He had friends, family. His darling Rosa. Left behind forever. He could not bear the thought that he would never, ever see her again. How could he not try? How could he not fail? With me he had a chance. I saw it and I took it. If I could make him accept *this* world as the only reality, forget the other, then he might have adjusted. It was a daring thing to try."

Knecht looked back out at the parade ground. There had been a fourth possibility, after all. A refugee, but one slowly going mad. Lightning bugs flashed in the evening air. "It was daring," he agreed, "and it failed."

"Yes, it failed. His senses worked for me: everything Kelly saw and heard told him this world was real; but in the end there were too many memories. I could not tie them all off. Some would remain, buried under the false ones, disturbing him, surfacing in his dreams, eventually emerging as psychoses. I restored his memories, then. I could do no more to help him, so I made no effort to stop you."

Knecht's mind was a jumble. Every possible action was wrong. Whether Kelly had been the person he claimed to be, or a madman, Schneider had done the wrong thing. Ochsenfuss had been wrong to try and obliterate the man's true memories. As for himself, all he and Vonderberge had accomplished was to turn him out into a trackless jungle. Oh, we all had our reasons. Schneider wanted defense. Ochsenfuss wanted to heal. Vonderberge wanted escape. And I . . . Knecht wasn't sure what he had wanted.

"We could have kept him here, without your treatment," he told Ochsenfuss. "So the General could have learned more." Knecht was curious why the Doctor had not done that.

As if on cue, the door of the VOQ burst open. Knecht could see Schneider, dressed in pants and undershirt, framed in its light. Schneider strode toward the guardhouse, his face white with rage and astonishment.

Ochsenfuss smiled. "Kelly would have lost what sanity he had left.

If we had not given him the way home, we have at least given him hope. And . . ." He looked in Schneider's direction. "While I am a logical man, I, too, have feelings. Your General thought to make me the fool. So, I made a medical decision in my patient's best interest."

Knecht could not help smiling also. "Perhaps I can buy you a drink tomorrow, in the officers' club. If we are both still in the army by then." His cigar had gone out. He looked at it. "I wonder what world they are in now."

"We will never know," replied Ochsenfuss. "Even if they try to come back and tell us, this world is a twig in an infinite forest. They will never find us again. It will be bad for you, Rudi, if you cannot bear not knowing."

Knecht threw his cigar away. He was a scout. It would be bad for him, not knowing.

# DEAN WHITLOCK

## The Million-Dollar Wound

Here's an unsettling look at an uncomfortably near future society where they've taken the idea of cost-efficiency a bit too far, and given an ugly new meaning to the old slogan, good to the last drop.

This was new writer Dean Whitlock's first published story. He has subsequently sold several more stories to *The Magazine of Fantasy and Science Fiction, Isaac Asimov's Science Fiction Magazine*, and *Aboriginal SF*. You will be hearing a lot more about *him* in the future, too. Whitlock lives in Post Mills, Vermont.

# THE MILLION-DOLLAR WOUND

Dean Whitlock

"Hell," Billy said, "it's only a year. I can make it through a year." He killed his beer and threw the can at the box of empties. "Besides, if I'm lucky, I'll get the million-dollar wound."

He grinned at Frank and me, expecting agreement. We looked at each other and looked back, faces blank. He looked amazed.

"Shit. What the hell do they teach you in medic school? The million-dollar wound is your ticket home. A clean shot through a thigh muscle, a little blood, a little hurt. Keep it clean and it heals right up, but first they give you a Purple Heart and send you Stateside. My grandfather got one in Viet Nam. He was drafted, too, same as us."

He popped open another warm beer, drank the suds off the top, and grimaced. "This pedro beer is real piss."

Frank and I finished ours and took more. "Help if it was cold," Frank said. He went back to his book, and I put a couple of cans in the freezer with the blood.

"Shit, nothing would help this crap," Billy replied. But he kept drinking it.

Billy was the kid of the unit, or looked it. Small, blond, big grin, bright eyes. He took a lot of crap in boot camp and learned to give it back. Drink hard, swear hard, punch a few shoulders to show you're tough. He was a draftee, too, and that didn't help in a platoon full of volunteers. When our medic unit got attached to his group, he started hanging out with us off duty. We drank a lot of that warm Bolivian beer together.

Frank and I weren't really draftees. Frank was premed, as he used to call it. He couldn't afford college, so he was getting his training the hard way. He was thin and dark, with blue growth on his chin two minutes after shaving, and he spent a lot of time reading text-books. I was a CO. I came out of college with an English degree and a choice of immediate employment: war plant, nuke plant, medic, or jail. No Canadian refuge, this war. I took medic, I guess, because I thought somebody had to balance the killing. Anyway, we weren't volunteers, and that suited Billy. We got to be friends, even.

"So Grampa got out whole," Frank said.

"Yeah. Spent the rest of his tour in Germany. Drinking real beer."

"How long was he in 'Nam? Before he got the million-dollar wound, I mean."

"Six months." Billy laughed. "Hell, he was halfway home, anyway, wasn't he? I got eleven months and three days to go, and I haven't even been shot at."

"They had shorter months in 'Nam," I said.

"What do you mean?"

"R and R counted," I told him. "When Gramps went down to Saigon for a week, it was still combat time. He could go for a month to Tahiti and it was still part of the year."

"Shit," Billy threw his can at the box. "Figures the army would nix that one. I gotta spend 365 days on the line."

Frank nodded. "And we've got 730 each."

"With ten sick days," I added.

"Shit. And you guys can't even shoot back."

Patrol was hard work. We were northeast of La Paz, in the foothills near the Mamoré. The terrain was rough and broken, high fields separated by forest and deep ravines. It was hot during the day, cool at night. It rained a lot for weeks and then baked for weeks. The people lived in small houses, raised potatoes, mined copper and tin, and soon enough they started shooting at us. Sometimes it was guerrillas and sometimes it was coke farmers, but the bullets did the same thing. Billy and his unit kept busy shooting back, and Frank and I cleaned up after them.

We were in a quiet area, at least. Short bursts of fire. A few flesh wounds, mostly Band-Aid stuff. One guy tripped, rolled down a hill, and broke his leg. Frank and I slapped on the plaster and carried the dumb ox four miles up to a flat place where a chopper could land.

The first bad one stepped on a blender. That's a spring-mounted trap that closes on your leg and shreds it from the hip down. He screamed, and somebody else shouted "Medic!" and Frank and I went running up to the head of the column. There was a lot of blood and a lot of pain, and the rest of the unit stood around watching with sick looks while four of them held him down and pried the damn thing open. Then the sergeant shouted them into a defensive formation, and Frank and I tried to stop the bleeding. Frank got real businesslike, pumping in morphine and plugging holes like it was a plastic dummy in training. He had good hands, Frank. He would have made a good surgeon. I just poured on gel and handed him staples and tried not to throw up.

We developed that into a pattern. Frank played doctor and I played nurse and the unit played soldier. Frank took it real seriously, treated each man like he was the only patient we had. Then the fighting got serious, and two weeks later, with nine months and thirteen days to go, Billy got his million-dollar wound.

Frank was doctoring at the other end of the line, so I hauled my kit over to Billy. What could I say? He was lying there with a dark stain spreading down his pants and a big grin on his face. I cut the cloth away and wiped off the blood. There was a pair of holes in his thigh, the front one small and tidy, the back one big and ragged. But it had missed the bone and the artery and he knew it.

"Gramps would be proud," I told him. "Do you need morphine?" His smile was getting strained.

He nodded. "Might as well celebrate." I pumped him up and sprayed on some gel, and we sent him off with the rest of the wounded.

Three weeks later he was back, with a Purple Heart and a pair of tiny scars on his leg. No limp, no pain, no Germany. And no more sick days. He had nine months and three days left.

He told us a little bit about it one evening over some beers.

"They took some muscle and skin from my other leg and stuck it in the hole. Then they soaked me in some kind of soup like that shit you guys are always spraying around and shined these big blue lights on my leg."

Frank was real interested. "What did they give you to eat?"

"Mostly crap. And pills. All the time pills. But no morphine. Not even aspirin. Bastards."

"Did they use massage?"

"Shit no. They made me lift weights with my foot."

"What did it feel like under the lights?"

"Hot, I guess." He took another drink. "Mostly it just hurt. Can't feel a damn thing now, though," He rubbed his leg as though he wanted it to hurt. "Shit, it's like it never happened."

I handed him another can. "Looks like you'll have to go for the two-million-dollar wound."

He laughed sharply. "Right. Next time I'll ask the pedros to blow my whole leg off. Then the army can send me home to grow a new one."

We all laughed a little and started making jokes about the wrong size leg, and what else they could grow back. It wasn't all that funny, but all we could do about it was laugh. The soldier who'd stepped on the blender came back a little later, too, and more of the wounded. The once-wounded. They went back out on patrol and they were a lot more careful. And Frank and I got to work on some of them again.

Billy took his second hit about a month later. Just shy of seven months to go. I remember because Frank and I had scraped the big red crosses off our helmets the night before. Frank started carrying a rifle about then, too. The guerrillas had started shooting medics. Maybe they recognized all the rebuilt GIs and thought we were doing the fixing. What did we know? We just poured on gel, pumped them up, and tried to keep them alive until the chopper came.

We had moved farther to the northeast, still near the river, where the hills were less rugged and ravines more forested. We started using napalm on the guerrillas, too, and they started using it back. Probably our own stuff. They didn't have planes and choppers to drop it from, so they canned it and lobbed it in with skeet throwers. The guys called them Frisbees. If you were good, you could hit them in the air, but they splattered fire on anything underneath. If you let them hit, they burned less territory.

Billy was at the front of the line—God knows why, because he never volunteered for that kind of duty. The pedros were above us and started firing down on the trail. Luckily, they started shooting as soon as they saw the lead man. Lucky for the rest of us, at least. Billy hit the bushes and started firing back, while the rest of us went into the trees and gave cover. Then they lobbed in the napalm. Two Frisbees, maybe three, they put a pool of fire right on Billy. We heard him screaming, and then he came running out, the right side of his body and both boots on fire.

You can't stamp out napalm. It sticks to you. We had special blankets and a spray that foamed, and we smothered Billy as fast as we could. His clothes saved most of him from real damage, but his hands weren't covered, and neither was his face. His right hand was charred to the bone, and three fingers gone. His right cheek started to flake away, and the ear, too, and he had third-degree burns from his neck up into his hair. When we took his helmet off, part of his scalp came with it. There wasn't much we could do but give him morphine, cover him with gel, and get him out fast. He kept his eyes shut—they were both still there, thank God—and held his left hand in a fist up under his mouth, muttering to himself and crying. I thought he was praying at first, but he got louder whenever we jolted the stretcher or touched him. I could hear him moaning, "Oh Shit, oh shit, oh shit." over and over again. Even Frank was shaken.

Billy was back in three months, with new pink skin, and a hand that clicked a little when he moved his thumb in a certain way, and white hair in a patch on the right side of his head. And he still had seven months to go. He never talked about the hospital this time, and Frank didn't ask him. We shared a lot more beer and a bottle of vodka Billy had smuggled back, and talked about sports and video and women and everything but war. But Billy kept rubbing his hand through the patch of soft white hair and clicking his thumb.

And finally, after one long time of silence and clicking and Frank turning pages, he seemed to notice his thumb. He stared at his hand curiously and said, "What do you think they can't fix? I mean, what if the suckers had burned off both my legs and my balls, too? Would I be stuck in a wheelchair for the rest of my life? Or would I walk around clicking, with a little pump in my pocket for getting it up?"

"I don't know," Frank said. "We've seen a lot of guys come back."

"So who doesn't come back? I mean, what the hell does it take to get out of this?" I shook my head and offered him the bottle, but he didn't see it. He answered himself. "I'll tell you what—you gotta be a goddamn vegetable, that's what. I mean, you really gotta be maimed. 'Cause they sure aren't gonna let a little mechanical damage get in the way. I mean, shit, that's just a little pain. Just kiss it, make it better." Then he took the bottle. Later that night, Frank and I had to put him to bed.

Billy was real careful for three months. He walked slowly, in camp and on patrol. His eyes moved left to right all the time, scanning. He got thin. Frank and I watched him go from being tense to being scared. It became part of him. He talked and moved and even told jokes scared. He acted calm, but it was fatalism.

Anyway, it was Frank who got hit next, just a month after Billy got back. It was a dumb thing, even for a war. The unit had a bunch of pedros pinned down in a farmhouse, waiting for a chopper to come up and douse them. We were back a ways in some trees tending the casualties. I was putting Band-Aids on a couple of guys who'd gotten nicked, and Frank was trying to stop all the blood from running out of another guy who'd been gut-shot. Suddenly somebody was shooting at us. The two walking wounded started shooting back, and things got real hot.

There wasn't much I could do, so I crawled over to Frank and started working on the other guy with him. Frank kept his usual calm, plugging and stapling, and we were making headway on his stomach when the pedros shot him in the leg. The GI was past feeling, but Frank got mad. He handed me the stapler and picked up his gun and started shooting back.

The extra firepower seemed to help, because it got real quiet. Then four pedros came out of the woods with bayonets and knives. They got one of the GIs before he even heard them, but Frank and the other guy started firing. Two of them went down right then, but the other two took out the second GI and kept coming. Frank kept pulling the trigger and they kept coming, but then one dropped and the last one made a flying lunge and ended up on his face at Frank's feet with the top of his head open. And his gun sticking up out of Frank's foot. The bayonet went straight through six inches into the dirt.

Frank looked down at his foot and up at me. He put down his own gun, wiped his face, and pulled the other gun up out of his foot. Then he sat down and started treating himself for shock. I carried his kit over to him.

"You know," he said. "That was really dumb."

I didn't know if he meant the pedros or his foot. I went over to the first GI and started patching. Billy and some of the other guys showed up just then, and I felt a little better. Billy knelt by Frank and helped him cut the boot away. They took a look at the foot, and Billy squeezed his shoulder.

"You'll be back in a month, Frank," he said.

It was only three weeks. Frank said they were getting better at it. He also said there was one thing they hadn't worked out. Anesthetic. They couldn't give you too much, because it slowed the healing. It was a long three weeks for him.

He smuggled in some more vodka, though, and brought some news from the States.

"No more draft," he told us.

"You're shitting me," Billy said. He clicked his thumb, a nervous habit now.

"No. They say they don't need it anymore. The volunteers are enough."

"They can't be getting that many," I said. Half my graduating class had been against the war.

Frank shook his head. "They don't need as many," he said. "All they have to do is keep the old ones running."

"You sound like a mechanic."

"They gave me a tour of the surgery. They move 'em in, they move 'em out. There's not much they can't fix."

Billy nodded, his eyes hard. Then he had a thought, and he smiled. It looked strange after all that time. "Wait a minute," he said. "What about us suckers that got drafted already? They're gonna have to send us home, aren't they?"

Frank laughed. "Don't bet on it, Billy boy. You've got miles of tread left." He laughed again, but it was pretty flat.

One thing I learned from Frank getting shot: As far as they were concerned, I was a gringo and I had no right to be there. I agreed with them, but I wasn't leaving in a box if I could help it. Nonviolence doesn't preclude self-defense, not when the guy who wants to kill you won't stop to hear your side of it. That's what I told myself, at least. I picked up a .45 in exchange for some pure grain alcohol, practiced a few hours, and started carrying it on patrol. It made me feel a little safer. And it wasn't as blatant as a rifle.

Meanwhile, Billy let his hopes get up about going home. The news came about the draft, and he started waiting for the word. He was still waiting a month later when the pedros got him again.

It was short and dirty, a quick burst of fire from the bushes. Then the pedros took off. The squad went after them and left Frank and me with Billy in the middle of the trail. It was a bad wound. They'd opened his stomach with a shredder and left it and half his intestines lying out on the ground with hundreds of little needles stuck in them. Billy was conscious, beyond pain, watching the organs move as though they were the most interesting thing in the world.

I called for a chopper. Then we clamped the big veins and arteries, pulled out all the needles we could see, poured in some gel, and poured the entrails in with it to move him. Billy stayed awake, watching, and finally I had to walk up the trail to get away from his eyes.

When I looked back, Frank had his rifle up against Billy's head.

I shouted "Frank!" and ran back toward him. He looked up at me and I stopped, kicking up dust that drifted over him and Billy. "Frank, what the hell are you doing?" He looked down at Billy and then back at me. He kept the gun aimed at the white patch in Billy's hair. "Frank?"

He cleared his throat and I waited, sweating. The sun glared. Finally he said. "He asked me to do it."

I looked at Billy. His eyes were closed. "And you were going to?"

He nodded.

"That's murder."

He laughed. "You can't murder a dead man."

"He's not dead." He wasn't. I could see him breathing.

Frank shrugged. "Brain death. That's the only thing that will kill him. That's why he asked me."

"Frank, a doctor's got to save lives, not take them. You don't have the right to make that decision."

"How many times do I have to save them?" But he put down his gun.

The chopper came and took Billy away, and we went back to base.

The next day the Major called me in on the floor to ask what had happened out there. Apparently Frank had come in yelling about zombies and throwing his textbooks at anyone with brass. Somewhere in there he threatened to shoot every wounded soldier on the front. They sent him off, and I heard later that they had him in an institution Stateside. Mentally incompetent. I stayed in the woods with the squad, and eventually Billy came back.

He was down to four months, but he looked like he wasn't going to make it. They all looked like that now, even the lucky ones who'd never been hit. Hell, most of them were volunteers. They'd come in ready to give their lives for their country. Well, they'd done that. And then some.

Two weeks later Billy got it again, another gut wound. I plugged up the holes in his new stomach and looked at the piece of Teflon tubing or whatever it was that ran out of it. My own stomach twisted. The plastic was worse than blood.

His eyes were closed, and he was breathing unevenly. I'd done all I could with my kit, so I took his hand and held it. I thought he was out, but he opened his eyes and looked at me. He squeezed my hand, and I felt his thumb click in my palm.

"How many times are you going to let them kill me?" he said.

Then he went out for good. I checked for a pulse, but it was gone. I closed his eyes and sat back on my heels and thought about how many times I'd sent him off on the chopper. And how many times he'd come back. And then I remembered that he still had three months and two weeks to go.

That's when I took out the .45 and shot him in the head. It's a big bullet, big enough to break your arm with a near miss. No one asked any questions.

I waited for him to come back. I waited three months before I began to believe that Frank was right. And I began to see more head wounds, always in the worst guys, the guys like Billy who'd been hit the most. The guys who had close buddies who'd help them out. Getting out was all they talked about anymore. I did it for one other GI. Like Billy, he asked me to.

And I got a letter from Frank, with a clipping about a peace rally. He was out of the institution and working for some vet agency, writing letters to Congress and to newspapers. He said it was hard, because there was no draft so there was no pressure on anyone at home to save their own butts. But he said it was working. They were going to change things.

I hope to God he's right. I hope they change the regs tomorrow, or end the war so these guys really could get out. Frank's the kind of guy who could make it happen.

Me, I'll do what I can here. I've still got six months to go—six real months. I figure I could still help out a lot of these guys. And you do help out. When they ask you, you do it. They've got a name for it now. They call it the million-dollar wound.

# R. GARCIA Y ROBERTSON

## The Moon of Popping Trees

In the poignant and thoughtful story that follows, new writer R. Garcia y Robertson shows us that the most important journeys of discovery are often undertaken by those who have nothing left to lose.

R. Garcia y Robertson has sold several stories to *Amazing* and has recently completed his first novel, *The Silk Mountain*. He was born in Oakland, California, has a PhD. in the history of science and technology, and currently lives with his family in Mt. Vernon, Washington, in a little cabin just off the Sound, halfway between Seattle and Canada.

# THE MOON OF POPPING TREES

## R. Garcia y Robertson

"This is how the world will end." Stays Behind showed neither fear nor regret. To her, the end of creation was merely a mathematical certainty. She watched through the leather lodge entrance as the storm shook white feathers of snow from a bitter black sky. The wind that drove the snow cut like blade steel, forcing cold fingers through the lacing holes in the tipi. She pulled the warm, woven trade blanket tighter, to completely cover her calico dress. The dress fabric was thin, but bright and red as summer.

Heat from the lodge fire stirred the air. Its living motion made her warm. Heat was motion—she knew it, and felt it. Stays Behind also knew that when all the heat motion in the world was spent, that was how the world would end.

This was not Stays Behind's tipi, but a tiny twelve-skin lodge belonging to a womanless old Shyela named Yellow Legs. An old tipi, it was fashioned from thin, smoke-stained unpainted hides. All tipis were tattered now, and all hides were old and worn. There would be no new ones, now that the great herds were gone. Kiowas claimed that a Snake woman had seen the buffalo disappear into a mountainside. A tall peak in the Wichitas opened wide, inside was a world brimming with clear rivers and wild plum blossoms, the buffalo entered, and the mountain closed behind them. Neither Snakes nor Kiowas could be trusted to see things straight, nor to speak straight about what they had seen. Most Lakota said it was the Wasichu who had killed the buffalo. Either way, they were gone.

"You have seen the world's end?" Yellow Legs was on the far side of the fire, facing the entrance flap and the dawn. He sat in this place of honor, amid hanging parfleches and skin bags pawed by beaded bear claws. Years had hardened his skin, like old leather left in the sun. In the days when buffalo were many, and in the Spirit World, Yellow Legs had seen many strange sights. He accepted that someone one year into womanhood might have seen the world's end.

"No"—Stays Behind stirred the fire—"but the Wasichu say the world will end in snow and ice."

"*Hetchetu aloh*, then it is so, if that is what the Wasichu say." When this Shyela meant to tease her, he spoke like an Ogalala.

Stays Behind called the old Shyela uncle, though she was an Ogalala Lakota and no real relation to him. Long ago, before her parents left for the Spirit World in the Winter of Spotted Sickness, this Shyela had done her family some great service. Now he had no wives or daughters, so Stays Behind cooked his food, cut his wood, tended his fire, and mended those things that weren't too sacred for a woman to touch. His needs were few, so the work was light. Since her sister, Antelope Woman, had married Handsome Dog, neither she nor Yellow Legs cared to stay in her family's cabin. Instead, she slept just inside the entrance to his tipi, wrapped round a shaggy camp dog for warmth.

"No, it is so." Stays Behind jabbed her stick into the ashes, raising sparks and smoke. "Heat is motion. See how the fire leaps towards the smoke hole. Each moon, each day, this motion spreads through the world, like water spreading over the prairie. When all the heat motion has run away, then the world will end."

Yellow Legs looked into the leaping fire. Snow danced past the leather entrance flap, and the rush of warm air drew it into the fire pit. Red embers sputtered, the flakes vanished into rising vapor, and embers burned lower and cooler. "Yes, I see it. The world's fire is always ebbing. Who would think the Wasichu were so wise? Is there anything they do not know?"

"Many things." Stays Behind became excited and authoritative. At one year into womanhood, men never asked her opinion. "The Wasichu wonder about the nature of light, which is like heat, but not like heat."

Leaning back against his buffalo-hide rest, the old Shyela closed his eyes. "Tell me more. I would like to dream of something that even the Wasichu do not understand."

The Red Cloud Agency stood lonely on the prairie. A gray blanket of sky stretched from one end of the world to the other. The wood-frame Agency school was built to army specifications, weather-beaten, and old before its time. Since the Moon of Falling Leaves, none of the boys had come to class. That was the month, November 1890, that the Agent, Lakotas-Scare-This-Lad, had called many soldiers to the Agency. Half of the younger braves had left for the Badlands. The boys took this as a sure sign that school was out.

Teacher Miller could hear them outside, whooping with glee as the girls filed out. Once the boys had feared to defy him openly; now even their skulking was no longer silent. When a Lakota brave-in-training lets an enemy hear him, it isn't clumsiness, but defiance.

Miller was a man of God and science, with sad thoughtful brows and nervous hands. His slender fingers fiddled with the cast iron stove and steel coffeepot. He pretended to ignore the lone girl who remained at her desk. She also looked down, neatly piling papers. Miller knew she could follow his movements without raising her eyes.

Long raven hair framed high earth-brown cheekbones. To Miller, her face was flat and foreign, serious and savage. He had trouble thinking of her as a thirteen-year-old girl. It was easier to picture her as a young animal, or even as a miniature warrior.

Miller banged the lid down on the balky stove, then nudged the coffeepot back over the fire. The stove seldom stayed lit, and the steel pot had a broken handle. Together, they conspired to produce cold coffee and burnt fingers. Today, the stove stayed warm and the coffee was hot. Already it was a special day.

The aroma of burning coffee filled the small schoolroom. The girl lifted her head. "May I have Black Medicine?"

He was already filling her cup, stirring in big crystals of rock sugar. Miller managed to pass the steaming cup, without spilling or touching her hand. She drank and let the hot dark fluid flow through her, feeling the strength of its medicine. The world was brighter, and she became braver.

"Tell me more about Professor Morley, and why the speed of light is . . ." She stumbled on the last word.

"Invariant?" Miller suggested, and she nodded.

The teacher smiled, for it had taken months to convince her that women's questions weren't rude, but now there was no stopping them. "As I said yesterday, Professors Michelson and Morley have done a number of exact experiments. These seem to show that no matter what our movement is, relative to the other, the speed of light appears constant in any given medium. This may imply that the speed of light is a constant which cannot be exceeded."

"Why is that important?"

Miller stopped pacing and pointed to the door. "If you could exceed the speed of light, you could open that door, then race over here and see yourself coming in. Cause could precede effect. Time would appear to run backward. Past and future would both be visible."

Stays Behind studied the dark depths of her cup. Ghost Dancers saw themselves during spirit journeys. Any of the boys outside could have told Miller that Black Elk and Sitting Bull looked into the future. In a Sun Dance on the Rosebud, Sitting Bull had seen "many soldiers falling into camp." Ten days later, Long Hair, who the Crows called Son of the Morning Star, attacked the Lakota and Shyela camped on the Greasy Grass. Long Hair and many soldiers fell.

When a wise man pretends to be more ignorant than any camp child, he must have a reason, though it was often the way with Wasichu that they mixed deep wisdom with childish lies. Out of respect for Teacher Miller, Stays Behind also feigned ignorance.

Instead of speaking, she slid a thoughtfully folded scrap of paper across the unpainted desk top. The paper lay between them, amid the wood grains, till Miller picked it up. He read it, folded it, unfolded it, and reread it, as if the paper were somehow both familiar and out of place.

The paper itself was plain enough. It was torn from a notebook that he himself had handed out. It was the series of equations scrawled across its surface that presented a problem. Their meaning seemed clear. The first dealt with velocity, the second with time, and the third with mass. What Miller couldn't understand was how they'd gotten onto this particular piece of paper.

He looked at the Lakota girl, who seemed to be searching for something in her coffee cup. "Did you write this?"

She shook her head. "Yellow Legs wrote it."

"Yellow Legs? The Cheyenne medicine man that you live with?"

This time she nodded.

"How could he have written these formulas?" The question was not addressed to the girl—any answer she gave would only deepen the mystery.

Stays Behind strove to speak straight. "I told Yellow Legs what you said about light. He listened, and that night he had a vision. Next morning he took my notebook and pencil, and drew what he had seen."

Miller watched heat rise from the stove and waver in the air. Ice was on the windows, beveled bits of frosted crystal that started next to the frames and grew out across the glass. Everything was quite normal, except for the paper in his hand. In a matter of minutes Miller invented and rejected a number of explanations. On his shelf he could see Henry James's new *Principles of Psychology* and two older volumes by Spencer bearing the same name. They gave adequate explanations for dreams and visions, but not for the formulas he was holding.

"What do they mean?"

Miller looked back at the formulas. "The first is a mathematical expression of what I said before. The speed of light will remain the same no matter how fast the observer is moving. The second deals with time and offers a partial explanation for the Michelson-Morley results. It also implies that, if the speed of light were exceeded, time would be reversed. The last formula deals with mass. It says that objects having mass may never reach the speed of light, that objects without mass travel at the speed of light, and that objects with imaginary mass always exceed the speed of light."

Looking up from his hand, he saw that he had lost his audience. "You don't understand any of this, do you?"

She gave polite agreement.

"That's too bad. If you had written this, it would have made me an excellent teacher, and you an even better pupil. Instead, I must deal with a medicine man whose visions make mathematical sense."

The girl looked guilty. "Is that bad?"

Miller paused and lost his chance to answer. The rear door swung open, and a tall, blue-coated Wasichu entered the room.

Stays Behind put down the cup, as though it held poison, and began to back out of the room.

Captain Wallace tipped his hat to the retreating girl, revealing a long lowland Scots face, fair hair, pale eyes, and a sad, drooping moustache. His grin remained fixed on the girl till she was out the door, then he turned it on Miller. "Wasting your time."

It took Miller a moment to harness his Quaker temper. "The government pays me to teach Indians. I was talking mathematics with a pupil. Anything else would have been a waste of time."

Wallace warmed his hands by rubbing them gleefully over the stove. "And exceptional pupils deserve extra instruction? The government pays me to kill Indians, but I make my exceptions, like as not for the same reason you do." His hand went for the coffee. "Since we're almost in the same line of work, can I bum some government coffee off you?"

Miller shrugged and watched Wallace pour with a professional ease that left him envious and irritated.

Captain Wallace added whiskey to the cup from a field canteen. "Take a word from a fellow who's been at his job longer—don't lift her skirt, you'll end up short an arm."

"I don't know what you mean."

"Quaker, if you don't, then you're the only one." Wallace swished his coffee and whiskey together. "Savages ain't got our sense of shame. Every kid on the Agency knows she stays after class. Don't they call her Stays Behind?"

Miller hid behind his own cup. "Children will always—"

"Don't let it shame you. Doesn't shame her. But remember she's spoken for. Like as not she'll marry her brother-in-law, Handsome Dog."

"Brother-in-law?"

"Sure, he's Indian Police, getting enough government money for two women. If taking two sisters at the same time shocks you, then you still got a lot to learn about the Sioux. They figure what's good for one sister is good for the other. Just ain't got our sense of shame."

Wallace sipped from his cup and cocked his head towards the door through which Stays Behind had left. "You probably think of her as some little girl, but she thinks of herself as a Lakota woman."

Miller's hand closed around the paper. "That child is modest to a fault."

"Sure," Wallace said, nodding, "like any Sioux woman should be, but that's a pose. Underneath that modesty, she's a right proper little savage, without a lick of restraint. Decent parents would have taken a stick to her, and done her some good. Instead, her folks let her run wild when they were alive, and now they're gone. You can bet she's played tipi with a bunch of little bucks. She's always had what she wanted, when she wanted it, and she thinks we're the ones who're shameful."

Miller focused on the crumpled paper. "Here, you know savages so well, explain this."

Wallace was an army engineer, so the form was familiar; but the meaning escaped him. "What do they mean?"

"Yellow Legs, the old Cheyenne she lives with, saw these formulas in a vision. Problem is they make mathematical sense, and they represent a plausible solution to an important problem in physics." Miller paused. "But perhaps the Cheyenne are noted for their knowledge of higher mathematics."

"Hell, no proper Cheyenne thinks it's decent to count higher than a thousand." Wallace passed the paper back. "You're making too much of this. The old fellow probably got those figures from some whiskey sutler, then drank enough to get them into his dreams."

The teacher shook his head. "Chances of a whiskey drummer being so deeply involved in theoretical physics are only somewhat less remote than those formulas coming from a Cheyenne medicine man. I'm afraid I'll have to see this old man myself. Do you think Handsome Dog could take me to him?"

Wallace's smile faded. "Perhaps he would, but God knows if he'd get you back. That Cheyenne lives among the worst of the Ghost Dancers, with Burnt Thighs and Ogalalas who'd take a slow and painful interest in your insides. Yellow Legs talks like a medicine man, but in his younger days he was a Dog Soldier who killed more whites than the cholera. Only mathematics he knew then was counting coup."

The Seventh Cavalry tabs on Wallace's uniform caught Miller's eye. "Most people have forgotten those days."

"Not me. I was with Custer, attached to Reno's battalion. When Reno ran for the river, the gunfire was so heavy that half of my troop never heard the recall. My troop commander and most of the men with him didn't make it back across the Little Big Horn. Yellow Legs can tell you all about it when you see him. He was there. Know how he got his name?"

"A certain discoloration of the lower limbs?"

Wallace reached down and ran his thumb up the yellow cavalry stripe on his uniform pants. "It comes from going into battle wearing the breeches of an officer that he'd killed and scalped. While you're looking into higher mathematics, I'd hate for you to find out why there's more hair than heads in Sioux tipis."

The stove had gone out, and Miller felt chilled.

Wallace watched frost gather on a window pane. "Some nights, Quaker, I close my eyes, and I'm right back in that race for the river, with Sioux and Cheyenne riding in among us, yelling, laughing, and knocking men from the saddle."

In winter, the black road between the Agency and the Ghost Dance camps on White Clay Creek became a twisted icy track. When there was school, Stays Behind walked the many miles twice a day, without thinking to complain. This day she rode home in Handsome Dog's buckboard, feeling every frozen rut. Had he not been her brother-in-law, she would have walked.

A red sun crawled towards its grave, bleeding over the land and leaving long shadows behind. Yellow Legs had told her how the Badlands were made from Uncegila, the great mother of water monsters. Her bones had been pressed to stone by the weight of ages. Miller had even shown her smaller creatures trapped in rocks from times gone by, then had told her of huge monsters that had swum in these parts, in the days when the prairies were warm seas. She could hardly imagine how long it took to turn flesh and bone to stone, or seawater into solid land. But today Uncegila seemed freshly slain: the dying light lay in bloody rags upon her bones. This was an omen for sure, but one with no obvious meaning.

She felt something moving under her calico dress, and the Spirit World faded. Stays Behind brought her quirt down hard on Handsome Dog's hand. He jerked it back, sticking it into his mouth and sucking blood off the knuckles.

"Counting coup, little warrior?"

Handsome Dog had a proud feather rising from his wide-brimmed hat. His breast bore a blue coat and an Indian Police badge, but below the belt he wore buckskin breeches, fringed long to drag in the dust. From the waist down, he was all Ogalala.

Stays Behind stayed silent, striving to keep in the spell of the Spirit World.

"You act like Crazy Horse come again, not like a silly girl with rope between her legs. A spirit like that must find the old Shyela cold company."

"I already have a camp dog to keep me warm at night." It made her mad to hear Handsome Dog name the dead so freely, for that was bound to bring bad luck.

Laughing at her answer, he returned to keeping the road between the horse's ears.

The blood on the bones was drying. Red light darkened into purple patches of shadow. Stays Behind cast about for some sign that would give voice to her vision. Growing shadows and stone-strewn snowfields said nothing. Rows of gaunt cottonwoods lined the draws, pointing bare gray fingers at the sky. Stays Behind looked up.

High overhead, a single goose winged its way north and west. Geese seldom go alone, and this deep into winter such birds should be flocking southward. For a time she watched the lone bird, fixing it in her mind, making sure there was no mistaking the sign. Then she asked Handsome Dog, "Do you see that goose headed north and west?"

Her brother-in-law didn't bother to look up. "Silly girl, no goose goes north in the Moon of Popping Trees."

She wished that she had walked the long way alone, then only the Spirit World would have spoken to her.

It was not Handsome Dog, but Stays Behind who took Miller to Yellow Leg's lodge. She explained on the trip out what was proper in the tipi, and what was not. Sucking on rock sugar, she gave her instructions gravely.

Miller knew to turn to his right, and to sit on Yellow Legs's left. He knew not to look directly at his host, not to cross between his host and the fire, and not to speak directly to Stays Behind within the lodge. She entered after Miller, turning the opposite way. The south side of the lodge was for men, the north side for women.

She couldn't prepare him for the sights and smells. Light came only from a dim half-moon fire pit. Miller was lost in a smoky sea of dog smells, human sweat, old leather, and a pleasant aroma rising from a dark carpet of leaves. Snow and cold covered over the camp garbage and animal droppings that lay outside.

As his sight returned, Miller noted that the lodge looked larger on the inside than it had seemed on the outside, a curious illusion. Trade blankets hanging from the lodge poles divided and darkened the tipi. Yellow Legs sat in the darkest recess, wrapped in a buffalo robe. There was a doeskin bundle across his knees. It was tanned white and soft with the hair off; painted blue diamonds chased red triangles across its surface.

From the corner of Miller's eye, Yellow Legs looked older than his sixty winters. Lines lay on his face like dark streaks in old oxblood. His eyes were hidden by a hawk nose, high cheekbones, and sad, heavy lids. Graying hair was held back by a beaded headband.

Miller had manners enough not to speak, since his host's mouth was shut tight as a turtle. Instead, he allowed Stays Behind to serve him a miserable mush made from dried meat and chokecherries. The meal was hard to stomach, but each bite Miller forced down encouraged Yellow Legs. Had Miller meant him harm, he would not have eaten inside the tipi.

"Greetings, Teacher Miller." Yellow Legs stressed *teacher* because Miller was a dead word with no special meaning. Miller had been warned that Yellow Legs spoke English, though no one knew where he had learned it.

The teacher returned the greeting, and there was an awkward pause. Yellow Legs looked past where Stays Behind knelt, speaking to no one in particular. "I knew the teacher would come when she took the paper."

Miller took the words as meant for him, forgot his manners, and began to question as quickly as any Wasichu would. "Yes, I came. Do you know what these formulas mean?"

Yellow Legs drew a red clay pipe from the bundle. He filled it with tobacco and red willow bark. After offering the pipe to the four directions and smoking some himself, he passed the pipe to Miller. It was dangerous to tell power stories in daylight, but smoking together would make it better.

As Miller puffed on the pipe, Yellow Legs observed, "It is often the way with visions that their meaning is not clear. What I wrote was like the words of the Wasichu. Perhaps you can give them meaning."

Miller decided not to attempt an explanation of mass, velocity, and acceleration in the middle of this murky tipi. "They represent a possible solution to a particular problem that interests me."

"Good, then my vision has been of use to you."

"Yes, but what I really want to know is where the vision came from?" Miller was off on another question, without thanking Yellow Legs for the vision gift, but that was often the way with Wasichu.

Yellow Legs drew smoke and power from his pipe. "I have had visions for many winters, and that question has also interested me."

"But, do you always dream in mathematical symbols?"

"My other visions had shown me many strange things, but never such symbols. Perhaps they were meant for you, not for me." He was hinting again that Miller might thank him.

Miller weighed the paper in his hand. "Have your visions always turned out to be true?"

"Truth is not easy to know. I was at the Sun Dance on the Rosebud when Sitting Bull saw many soldiers falling into camp. The world knows what followed. Was it a true vision or not?"

As clear as if Captain Wallace were in the lodge, Miller could see the Seventh Cavalry insignia. He pushed the memory from his mind. "Do you also believe in the Ghost Dance?"

"The Ghost Dance is a thing beyond belief or disbelief." The clay pipe was cold, so Yellow Legs began to repack it. "Wovoka, who gave us the Ghost Dance, once made a vision. He asked each person present to look inside his hat. Many looked inside and saw blue water and a green land where the dead lived again and the buffalo had returned. All saw this except one, who saw only the inside of a hat. Which would one not believe? Would one tell the many that they did not see the Spirit World? Would one tell the one man that he did not see a hat? Visions are real—their meanings remain hidden."

Miller stared straight at the medicine man. "What did you see in the hat?"

"I saw the green land, with the Wasichu gone and the buffalo come back, but I did not see the loved ones I have lost. What that means, I do not know."

He paused, balancing truth and trust against possible betrayal. "Sitting Bull is coming to the Agency. Perhaps he will have an answer. His visions have always been strong."

Letting go of the doeskin bundle, Yellow Legs warmed gnarled fingers over the fire, which had sunk to embers glowing like cracks into the earth's core. "I will tell you my oldest and strongest vision so you may judge its worth." He waited till Miller nodded, then went on. "When I was young, I feared to be brave in battle. I feared to meet a Wasichu's bullet, or to be tortured by the Crows. A medicine man told me that I must seek my own death in a vision, then I could know it and prepare for it in life."

Miller saw the firelight in Yellow Legs's eyes, burning brighter and stronger than his body. "I had a most powerful vision. In this dream I saw my own death. I saw my body laid out for burial—a worn husk, wrapped in wrinkled skins. Overhead, six stars shown down, four were white and two red, yet it was full daylight."

Miller shifted closer to the fire also.

"This dream gave me courage, for I felt that I might never meet death till I saw these six stars shine in daylight. From that day forward I counted many coups, feeling neither fear nor pain in battle. In the Winter of the Hundred Slain, we rode against the Wasichu. When others held back for fear of the bullet storm, I rode right in among them, seizing a Wasichu's many-firing rifle, though he aimed and fired at me as I came up. Every dawn as I saw the stars fade, I knew this was not my day to die."

"Do you expect this charm to always protect you?"

"Protect me?" Yellow Legs stood up, letting slip the buffalo robe. His body was bare to the waist, glowing red in the firelight and filling the rear of the tipi. "Look, I am without a wound. This is not a kill talk, so I won't recount my many battles. Almost all were losing battles. I lost my family, I lost my friends. My people are gone, the buffalo are gone. Even as we speak, Wasichu make ready to cut the tall grass and plow up the prairie. The world I was born with will be no more. Yet still the stars will not shine in daylight. Each dawn I watch them, hoping that this will be the day when they do not fade."

Despite the cold December air, sweat pooled along Miller's spine. Yellow Legs would say no more.

Later, over cards and whiskey, Wallace dragged the story out of him. "So, the old Cheyenne charlatan got to you. I guess that's what makes him a medicine man."

Miller refused to be drawn. "Are we playing straights?"

"Not if you got one." Wallace thumbed broken nails over thick cards. "Dance back the buffalo, and dance us all away. Miller, your head's so full of formulas, you no longer hear plain speech when it's spoken at you."

Cards rose and fell, and money changed hands.

Wallace tapped the bottle before him. "If you drank some, you'd understand Indians better. When my troop was pinned to the wrong bank of the Little Big Horn, with Sioux and Cheyenne crawling up on three sides, what's the first thing Frank Girard and Lonesome Charlie Reynolds did?"

"Begged forgiveness from their maker?"

"Opened a bottle, Quaker. Who'd want to be sober in that spot? A white man drinks to forget his fear and then buckles down to business, but an Indian drinks to get rip-roaring drunk. Wants to start seeing things, visions and whatnot. Which is why they call it 'Holy Water.' We won't give 'em whiskey, so instead they starve and dance themselves into a trance."

Miller combed through his cards. "Where's the harm in that?"

"It'll be more harm to them than us. Those Ghost Dancers are getting ready for one last war party. Don't blame 'em either. I'd want to go down fighting. They figure with visions to guide 'em and ghost shirts to stop our bullets, they just might make it."

"Come, the only weapon I saw was a thirty-year-old rifle, done up with feathers. Looked more like an objet d'art."

The soldier shook his head. "That gun is gonna get Yellow Legs into trouble. Handsome Dog told me about it, an original Henry repeater. Two of Fetterman's men were carrying brand new Henrys."

"Fetterman?"

"Captain, assigned to Fort Phil Kearny, the fort Red Cloud burned down. Fetterman claimed he could ride through the whole Sioux nation with eighty men. He went off without orders to prove it, rode over Lodge Trail Ridge, and ran into a mess of Ogalalas, and into Crazy Horse, Red Cloud, and his Bad Faces, all backed by Cheyenne and Arapaho. They found Fetterman and his command, stripped, scalped, and stuck full of arrows, but they never recovered the rifles."

The sputtering oil lamp cast swaying shadows. "That must have been a long time ago," muttered Miller.

"Too long." Wallace frowned into his cards. "We've gotten lax. Letting them have weapons. Letting hostiles like Yellow Legs stray off their proper reservation. It's gonna stop right here. Ghost Dancers that don't find proper work won't get government rations. Soon it'll be work or starve at this Agency."

A north wind whipped round the cabin, pressing night against the windows. Miller didn't bother to ask where the Ghost Dancers would find work, out on the frozen prairie, in the dead of winter.

The Tachyon rode behind the eyes of a circling hawk, watching the world whirl backwards. The snowbird lost its hunger as it hunted through the frigid air. It remembered a missed kill. When that moment returned, the Tachyon was gone, faster than the hawk's keen eyes could follow.

Then the Tachyon listened with the ears of the hunted, a shaggy mouse scurrying backwards across the snow. Wind whispered, dragging tinkling snow crystals up into the sky. Footfalls froze the mouse in midstep. The Tachyon was gone again, into the lynx that had stalked the mouse, then into the bird the lynx had missed, catching the world in quick wary glances.

Crow, mouse, rabbit, owl—the Tachyon flew from one to the other.

From bird to beast and back again, faster than thought, faster than sight. Finally, the Tachyon rested in a lone wolf, loping out of the hills towards the flats. Fresh in the wolf's memory was the creature that the Tachyon sought. Together, they ran towards that remembered rendezvous. Looking down through the wolf's eyes, the Tachyon saw four fresh legs flashing backwards over the frosted ground.

Behind them, stretching south and east, was a great chain of beings. Many minds that the Tachyon had made use of. Each for a moment had been in the grip of an unseen traveler; now each went its separate and opposite way.

In the half-light of dawn, hunters returned to the lodges empty-handed. The Agent, Lakotas-Scare-This-Lad, had decreed that Ghost Dancers must work six days a week, then cut the rations for those who remained in the dance encampments. Some straggled back to eat at the Agency, but most Ghost Dancers took up guns or bows and went looking for food. The Black Hills still held game, but this sacred hunting ground was gone, pinned behind the iron-fenced flatlands. Hunters scoured the Badlands instead, and found that Uncegila's frozen bones had been picked clean.

Hungry men dispersed through the encampments, finding women to beg food from. Yellow Legs smelled simmering meat as he neared his lodge, the aroma making him think he was dreaming on his feet. Kneeling at the entrance, avoiding the place of honor, he laid his feathered Henry down.

"I have brought nothing for the pot."

"Then you shall feast on what we have here."

Stays Behind had started the cooking fire, then called the camp dog which had warmed her for half of the winter. The cur came wagging its tail, hoping to eat its fill. Stays Behind scratched the beast behind the ears, then bent down and cut its throat. The hound was now cooking in the hide pot from which it had hoped to feed, its paws peeping over the edge.

Dog was a delicacy among the Shyela. A failed hunt would not keep Yellow Legs from eating his fill. Greedy hands scooped dog meat from bowl to mouth. The aroma ate at Yellow Legs's stomach, while biting at his conscience. He noted that Stays Behind had only boiled army beans and bits of rabbit in her bowl. When the buffalo were many, only Snakes and Desert Utes ate rabbit, stealing their meat from the mouths of coyotes. Now nothing with four legs and a tail was safe from Lakota cooking pots. Yellow Legs invited her to have some dog. She declined. He sensed that this meal would have to be paid for later.

The first tasty hunk of dog rolled round his tongue. Yellow Legs closed his eyes, and the smells and sounds from lodge and fire faded. He felt himself in a still dark cabin, smelling cold damp corners and rough-hewn wood. Yellow Legs swallowed slowly and relaxed his lids, and light brought the lodge and fire rushing back.

He took another bite. Voices rang in his head. His brain became clouded, as if just dragged from sleep.

More bites brought chills that prickled like winter wind on naked skin, a wind that wailed with the voices of women.

The last bite made his own voice ring out, though the words were foreign. Rifle fire exploded in his head. Pain passed through his body, back to front, followed by sharp reports, like two pistol shots close at hand. The vision sank into blackness.

Yellow Legs found himself staring into an empty bowl. "What did I say? What speech did I use?"

Stays Behind looked up from her beans. "You spoke like a Hunkpapa Lakota, and you said that you weren't going."

"Like a Hunkpapa?" Yellow Legs sighed, looking back into his bowl. "This was a very small dog."

She laughed. "You brought back no meat; by rights I could have returned to my sister, but I fed you instead."

Her words were straight and strong. "I have had a vision, and you must help me complete it." This soft strength reminded him of Crazy Horse, though Stays Behind could never have heard that voice. Crazy Horse had been murdered in the Moon When Calves Grow Hair, during the Year the Wasichu Chased the Nez Perce. She had been born that next spring, in the Moon of Grass Appearing.

The dog had put him in her debt. He could not say, "Impossible," so he said nothing.

She described the way the day had faded over Uncegila's bones, and how she must follow the lone goose that had gone north and west, follow it into the Black Hills. As she spoke, Stays Behind became bolder, pulling bundles and anything-possible-bags from behind her buffalo-hide rest. She produced a white doeskin dress and several wolfskins. Then she sprinkled sacred sweet grass onto the fire, saying, "We must become wolves and scout into the Spirit World."

"It is not lucky nor lawful for a woman to say that."

She stamped her beaded moccasins and snorted. "Where is your luck old man? Is it waiting here to die, to see stars in the day sky? Is it coming with Sitting Bull? We must make our own luck now, or it will never come."

Yellow Legs fingered the soft, silver wolf fur. "I have been waiting for the Hunkpapa, but now he will never come here."

When Yellow Legs didn't say Sitting Bull's name, Stays Behind knew the Hunkpapa medicine man was dead.

"I felt his death. It was the Hunkpapa you heard, not me, speaking his final words."

Stays Behind lowered her head, hiding sadness behind determination. With Sitting Bull gone, there was even less reason to stay. She heaped more sweet grass on the fire till the tipi steamed like a sweat lodge. Behind this screen of smoke and magic, she stripped off the calico dress, rubbing white clay over limbs and face, donning the white doeskin.

Taking up the white clay, Yellow Legs slowly began to smear it on himself, thinking that the whole time she had shared his tipi, he had never before seen her body. The limbs she whitened were long, almost a woman's. There were young breasts beneath her shirt. Such thoughts were shameful, and he set them aside.

He brought out his ghost shirt, with Moon, Morning Star, and Magpie painted in black on white. "*Hetchetu aloh*, whatever waits to the north and west, it cannot be worse than waiting to see six stars in daylight."

Grinning to hear him talk like an Ogalala again, she painted her hair parting white as well. Taking ashes from the fire, she added black streaks over her nose and eyes. White and black were wolf colors—white for the north, where snow and winter dwell, and black for the west, the direction of death and sunset. She hung a wolfskin over her shoulders, letting the head come up to cover her scalp. She was now more wolf than woman.

The wolf that was Yellow Legs knelt and filled a weaselskin pouch with flint, steel, tobacco, and his most powerful pipe. Then he hefted the Henry rifle. The oiled wood and polished steel felt cold and heavy. Finally, he set the feathered gun aside. The rifle had been in his hands half of his life, but it still bore the power of the people who had fashioned it. On a vision quest, he could not weigh himself down with too much taken from the Wasichu. He selected a bow and several arrows instead.

They cut two horses from the pony herd: a black mare for Stays Behind, and an appaloosa who knew his rider so well that Yellow Legs never bothered with bit or bridle. Silent as a war party, they slipped out of camp, whispering their purpose to their ponies. For food they took the beans and dog meat in their bellies.

Tipi ears poked into the gray sky, between fading stars. Dawn broke as they topped the bluffs above White Clay Creek. A morning wind from off the flats swept snow into drifts and piles, baring patches of dead and dry prairie grass. Above the grassroots, the world was lifeless. An infant sun rested on the horizon, driving back the night, but bringing with it only a bleak half-day.

Keeping White Clay Creek on their right, they went downstream till it ran into the Smoky Earth River. Swinging south, they crossed the frozen Smoky, then they turned north and west again, skirting the edge of the Badlands. By dusk Uncegila's bones were behind them, and the banks of the Good River were before them. They had done a hard day's ride on little water and less food.

An old Minneconjou Lakota, Crooked Corn Woman, had planted herself by the waters of the Good. She farmed the east bank as close as the Wasichu would allow to *Pa Sapa*, the sacred Black Hills. She fed them, rested them, and agreed to care for their horses.

At dawn the next day, they walked dry-shod over the frozen Good, entering the forbidden lands. The west bank was strung with the spiked wire that circled the Wasichu's world. Crossing these fences was a crime, for which some had died, but the Black Hills lay beyond them. After helping each other through the wire, they walked without speaking: white ghosts in a gray world, their breath puffing before them. Stillness was everywhere, the water in the draws was frozen, and sap was sluggish inside the leafless trees. Bird tracks on fresh snow were the only sign of life. Stays Behind was sorry to have shamed Yellow Legs's hunting, but she said nothing. Words were not needed on a vision quest.

As the wane winter sun went to bed, Stays Behind dragged brush into a gully. Yellow Legs lit first the brushwood, then his pipe. He offered the pipe to all four directions, then to Stays Behind. It was the first time she had touched a man's pipe. The black clay and antelope bone felt light and alive with power. Smoke from tobacco, red willow bark, and sumac leaves stung her lungs.

The bushwood burned low. Darkness covered over the Ironlands.

They slept sheltered by this cleft in their Mother's breast, warmed by the wolfskins. Four times they rose in the night, to smoke beneath the dancing blue lights of winter and stars spread like frozen sparks overhead.

A warm young sun climbed over the east edge of the world. They smoked and prayed with it, then set out again. Now the Black Hills stood up before them, bristling with black pines. The land itself rose up under their moccasins. In a day they were through the foothills, and the next morning they turned north towards Vision Peak, where Black Elk's great vision had come. A warm wet wind blew into their white wolf faces. Mist mixed with sweat, cutting channels in the white clay paint.

Though his eyes were older, Yellow Legs was the first to see the thin black fog boiling through the passes ahead. Light lay like water on the slopes around them, but the fog billowed up into a cloud that blotted out Vision Peak. The wet wind grew, turned gray, then began to hurl sleet at them. Sleet became snow, so thick that it whitened the sky. By noon the sun was gone, and they were no longer walking. A white world whirled round them, clinging to their furs, climbing up their high winter moccasins.

"Which way should we go?"

Yellow Legs made no answer. She was the one with the vision.

"I don't want to stand here. I want to keep going." The words left her mouth high-pitched and urgent, but were softened and muffled by the snow.

He studied the white wall around them. To wander blindly in the storm would turn the spirit quest into a death march. Suddenly, Stays Behind was tugging at his buckskins. Standing patiently beside them, with snow clinging to its shaggy hump and long, soft eyelashes, was a full-grown buffalo cow. The beast might have sprung from the soil, for neither of them had seen it emerge from the storm. She was simply there, perfectly still and impossibly solid.

Once their attention was seized, the buffalo turned and started to shuffle off, without bothering to look back. They followed for an almost endless time.

When evening returned, gray was winning over white, and the buffalo became a dark patch in the singing snow. The land turned farther upward, and the snow deepened round their feet. The great beast broke a path for them, beating down the waist-deep drifts with sheer bulk. The two humans floundered forward in her wake.

Suddenly, the buffalo was gone as quickly as she had come. Cold and fear closed round them. At the spot where the beast had been, they came to the edge of a deep canyon. The buffalo had turned down a narrow trail. They followed, descending between canyon walls that curtained off the wind. Small flurries replaced the heavy flakes that had cut like gray flint knives.

Halfway down, the buffalo halted under an overhang, where the trail widened into a spacious sheltered ledge. The buffalo laid herself down on the edge of the ledge. Stays Behind and Yellow Legs wedged themselves between beast and rock. There, they were warm and dry, the buffalo's heavy breathing filling the space around them. This breathing grew rhythmic, and the silky lids shut. As the rhythm lulled them, words formed in their minds, *Sleep, children of my sisters.* Tachyon was talking through the buffalo.

They slept curled against the warm bulk of the buffalo.

When they awoke, the world was new, and wind and storm were

gone. Snow lay on the ledges and filled the canyon floor, each twig of brushwood bending under its white weight. Shining and cruel day flooded down the canyon, forcing back the shadows. Vision Peak reared above them. Lights and colors burned even brighter on empty bellies.

The buffalo rose, shaking snow from her back. As if this were a signal, sharp staccato barks came from farther up the canyon, followed by a howl that shivered over the snow. A coyote was calling. Turning its broad back to the world, the buffalo fixed soft brown eyes on the hungry humans. *If my sisters' children need meat, they may eat of me.* Tachyon turned the buffalo away from the morning sun, into the direction of death.

Yellow Legs packed his pipe, then offered it to the four directions. He prayed to the first buffalo, Slim Walking Woman, and to Yellow-Headed Woman who brought the buffalo, and to Sweet Medicine who taught the People to hunt buffalo with bow and arrow. Then he placed his pipe aside and picked up his bow. He aimed the arrow between the ribs, just behind the hump, where it would go straight to the heart. The buffalo didn't flinch, but as her knees buckled, dimming eyes seemed to reproach him.

Sitting down beside the dead beast, Yellow Legs smoked and studied the zigzag pattern of snow-covered ledges on the far canyon wall. Stays Behind bent over the carcass and was soon elbow-deep in the work of skinning and butchering. The work was new to her, but when she was younger, Stays Behind had spent days watching older women at work. Her keen knife slid through the layers of skin. She peeled these layers back till the skin covered the ground on both sides of the carcass. Blood climbed up the knife's bone handle. Clay-whitened arms were veined with red, but the butchering itself was neat, and no meat touched the ground. When the warm insides were bared, sweet smells steamed up into the canyon air.

Padding footfalls came across the snow, and Yellow Legs looked up. Coyote seated himself boldly at the edge of the ledge. Since he made no move to steal the meat, Yellow Legs was polite. "Greetings, brother coyote."

Coyote ignored him, sniffed the meat, then said to Stays Behind, *Farewell, sister.* Like the buffalo, Coyote didn't say these words aloud, for Tachyon was speaking through him. To Stays Behind, the words were Ogalala; to Yellow Legs, Shyela.

Yellow Legs knew coyotes were lechers and tricksters, but this one was being utterly mannerless. If coyotes could be rude, so could he. "Why do you speak to this woman instead of to me? And are you a Contrary, to greet us with good-byes?"

Coyote cocked his head. *Your world is contrary. First for you is last for me. This is the last I will see of Stays Behind. Yellow Legs and I have met and will meet many times.*

Stays Behind set down her knife, though she had just gotten to the liver. "Coyote, your speech is very confusing."

*To me, I am talking backwards, which is even more confusing.*

Yellow Legs puffed hard on his pipe; neither women nor coyotes seemed to know their places anymore. "I can't recall meeting such a mannerless coyote before."

*Your memories are in my future, so I can't be exact. Perhaps I will learn manners, but we will keep meeting till you dwindle down to a baby and vanish inside your mother.*

Animals had spoken in his visions, even coyotes, though none had looked like this one. Yellow Legs decided to smoke some more on this.

Coyote scratched, then eyed the buffalo meat. *In your past, my future, I will and did bring that buffalo to you. Now is the time to offer me some meat, for this body I inhabit is a hungry one.*

Stays Behind sliced the still warm liver, squeezed gall on it, then offered bits to both man and beast. Yellow Legs refused, but Coyote snapped his down.

*Much better. It's hard to hold a body that is both scared and hungry.*

"Why have you come?" Stays Behind cut more liver for the scruffy beast.

*To bid you good-bye, and to offer you passage to another Earth, which you call the Spirit World, where we spent much time together, where you opened your precious memories many times to me.*

"I don't remember this."

*For you, it hasn't happened yet.*

Yellow Legs set his pipe aside. "You come from the Spirit World?"

The beast licked his lips, begging with its eyes for more. *What you call the Spirit World is merely another Earth, not even far away in this shrinking Universe. It lies beyond the Moon and Morning Star, beside one of the Twin Stars in the winter sky. We offer your people passage there, to thank you for the memories that foretell our future, for the future frightens and fascinates us.*

"Why fear the future?" Stays Behind cut Coyote more liver.

*The Universe shrinks smaller and burns brighter. Entropy decreases, stars burn hotter and burst into gas, and planets melt and break apart. We are all shrinking towards a single fiery implosion. Who wouldn't fear that?*

Stays Behind looked bewildered, but interested. Yellow Legs snorted. "Speak this way to the Wasichu; they would love to argue about such things."

*I have had wonderful conversations with them, and no doubt will again.*

*To them, I am Tachyon because I travel so fast. But at this moment in space-time, speaking to animals or other worldly beings is out of style among them. Those that I approach act very alarmed, weeping and praying, pretending not to hear.*

Yellow Legs agreed. "Not many of my people will wish to leave this world on the word of a rude coyote."

*Yes, yes,* Coyote yawned, *it is very boring to know what will be. I will let you look again at the Spirit World. When you like what you see, bring as many people as you can into the Badlands, in the Moon of Frost in the Tipis.*

Coyote rose, shaking snow from his haunches. *Remember, what you see is only a vision. To move your bodies will be much harder. To move metals is hardest of all. As you measure distance, the Spirit World is far away. Moving only as fast as light, the trip would take almost a lifetime, though it seemed only an instant. Your bodies may never return to this point in space-time. You may take with you only the metal that is in skin and hide, wood and bone.*

Stays Behind looked down at the dissected buffalo. The only metal she saw was the knife in her hand. "I don't understand."

*Never mind, I will send formulas outlining the principles. Take them to Teacher Miller, and he may translate them.*

The contrary coyote turned to Yellow Legs. *When you see the other Earth, you will give up anything to be there. We have seen that it holds everything. Greetings.* Coyote became a coyote, and the Tachyon was gone.

As the beast backed away, Vision Peak seemed to grow. It became a great ghost mountain splitting through the layers of creation. Its roots ran down into the Deep Earth, its slopes thrust through the Air and Near Sky Space, and its peak stretched into the Blue Sky Space that holds the sun and stars. When the mountain reached its full height, a crack opened in the base, and rock and stone peeled apart like a leather lodge entrance. Yellow Legs and Stays Behind saw a brightly lit world within the mountain. They stepped towards it.

Instantly, there was no earth beneath their feet. Their hands reached out to stop them from falling, but instead their arms bit into the air, becoming wings. Feathers sprouted from their bodies, and they became a pair of hawks circling over the vast earth inside Vision Peak.

The land inside the mountain lay like a blanket tossed into a tipi. Much of it was flat, with little folds for hills; other parts were bunched into high mountains that ran in all directions. The plains between were filled to overflowing with herds of wild horses, red deer, antelope, and giant antlered elk. Shaggy brown carpets of buffalo covered the prairie. Even the air felt new.

They flew over many camp circles of tipis. One such circle looked familiar. The hawk that was Yellow Legs glided towards it. The women in the camp circle worked the old way, with stone and bone tools. The men smoked, ate, and danced, taking time to greet the two hawks that settled on a tipi top. They spoke a Shyela tongue, and gray-haired children ran among them. This was the Flexed Leg band of Yellow Legs's people. Everyone had thought them long dead, killed by a stomach sickness when the Wasichu had first poured over the plains.

Yellow Legs wanted to stay, to watch them at work and play, but the hawk that was Stays Behind was eager to fly. He followed her into regions where the air grew chill. Cold breezes blew off white sheets of ice that reared more than a mile into the sky, crushing continents with their weight. Dimly remembered monsters roamed the bases of these white cliffs. Woolly beasts with long horns and ivory tusks, such as stalked through power tales told round fires in the dark of winter.

Green forests, mighty rivers, meat on the hoof—it was a world holding everything that one might want; all things but one. It had no sun. Light rained down from six stars, four white and two red, that shone in full daylight.

The vision ended, and they were back on the cold ledge, beside the still-warm and half-butchered buffalo. Though they had flown as hawks for days, no time had passed at all. Yellow Legs said nothing. He loaded his pipe and smoked, staring again at the far wall of the canyon. Stays Behind went back to her work, cutting meat into strips and setting the strips out to dry. She cleaned and scraped the paunch, filled it with snow, and hung it over a fire.

By evening, the meat that wasn't drying was cooked. The hide had been scraped clean, rubbed with brains and liver, and left to soak overnight. Stays Behind invited Yellow Legs to eat. He barely picked at the roasted flesh, though nothing was sweeter than fresh-killed buffalo meat.

Finally, she broke the silence. "So you have seen stars in daylight."

He nodded. "The land was bountiful; it gives me reason for living. Yet when the coyote said that I would give anything to go there, I did not think he meant the power that has protected me for so many winters."

"In the Spirit World, we would die as we were meant to live."

"You are young, your body is new, and your death is far off. After coming through so many fights, after seeing the world of my dreams, it is hard to say like the Kiowas, *Rocks and mountains, you alone remain*."

She stood up, standing taller in the waning winter moonlight than he had ever seen her. Slipping the white doeskin off, Stays Behind twined arms washed clean with snow round his neck. She rested her young breasts on his chest. "Forget death, and share this young body."

It shocked him, but he did as she said, untying the braided rope that ran between her thighs, the rope that no man should even touch. He did it because it was what Stays Behind had wanted from the start, and because the hawks in whose bodies they had flown were birds mated for life. Coyote had seen to that.

It would have been bad to waste the buffalo, so they camped on the ledge till the robe had time to tan and dry in the weak winter sun. Stays Behind pounded the dried meat and worked the hide into leather. Even after that, they lingered, for the Black Hills dragged at their moccasins, and when they left, it would be forever. Rested and fed, it still took them longer to follow French Creek down into the flats, longer than it had taken them to climb up on empty bellies. Besides, they now had much buffalo meat to carry.

In the iron-wired flatlands they moved faster, anxious to avoid Wasichu and get across the Good. They crossed the Good River at Crooked Corn Woman's camp. There they feasted well, for Crooked Corn Woman was a Christian and the day before had been Christmas. She listened to their vision of the Spirit World, and in return gave them the news among the Minneconjou.

The news they got was bad. Sitting Bull was indeed dead, murdered by Metal Breasts. Fighting had spread to the Good. Hump and his Minneconjou had surrendered to the Wasichu. The last of Sitting Bull's Hunkpapas had come south from Standing Rock. They had joined Big Foot's band on the Good River, then fled into the Badlands. Many Wasichu soldiers were out hunting Big Foot, armed with wagon guns that fired faster than a talkative person could speak.

Stays Behind and Yellow Legs offered to take Crooked Corn Woman with them into the Spirit World, but she said she would rather die where she'd been born. When Jesus raised her, then she promised she would join them.

At dawn they took their horses and rode off across the south face of the Badlands. They rode beneath a great blue bowl of sky. Here, there were no iron fences, and the prairie rose and fell like a living thing, free for as far as eyes could see. Strands of pale grass, slippery with frost, clung to the brown earth.

Late in the day, they came upon a Burnt Thigh. Climbing off their horses, they sat on the frozen prairie, sharing their food with him.

By their wolf faces and the ghost shirt, the Burnt Thigh knew they had been scouting in the Spirit World. Politely, he warned them that the Wasichu were hunting Ghost Dancers. Soldiers said that Bear Coat Miles himself had ordered Sitting Bull and Big Foot arrested.

"We were camped with Black Elk and his Ogalalas on Wounded

Knee Creek. A Black Robe Wasichu found us and tried to bring us back to the Agency. This Wasichu was good, so we listened, but only a few Ogalalas went back with him." The Burnt Thigh pointed his chin towards the Badlands. "We went and hid near Top of the Badlands. The next Wasichu might not be as respectful as this Black Robe. It is not so easy to hide from the Lakota. Two chiefs, American Horse and Fast Thunder, found us and ordered Black Elk's people back to the Agency. They went, though we beat them and told them not to go. Some Burnt Thighs went with them."

There were tears in the Burnt Thigh's eyes, but he said it was from eating buffalo again. "There is no game in the Badlands, so everyone is hungry. Big Foot is so sick his people must carry him. Fasting is fine for visions, but it wastes the body."

As they rode off, Stays Behind asked Yellow Legs, "Will things be as bad as that Burnt Thigh says?"

He kept his face fixed on the line where earth and sky become one. "All Lakota talk like noisy birds, and Burnt Thighs are bossier than blue jays." He was thinking that things had gotten worse since he had taken comfort in this girl's body, and that he should have faced his death alone.

At the Smoky Earth River, they found signs that Ogalalas and Burnt Thighs were a half-day ahead of them, probably Black Elk's people. Atop the pony tracks were ironshod prints, showing that Wasichu were trailing Black Elk, too. Many people were passing like cloud shadows over the prairie. Yellow Legs and Stays Behind waited, letting the Wasichu get well ahead of them, then they camped farther up the Smoky. This would be their last camp alone, under the winter stars.

The new day's sun was high in the sky when they saw the banks of White Clay Creek dip down toward the Ghost Dance camps. Like gathering storm winds, Ogalala Bad Faces were riding up from Red Cloud Agency, bringing with them more bad news. Big Foot's band had been captured by Wasichu soldiers and moved under guard to Wounded Knee. Two Strikes, Kicking Bear, and Short Bull began to gather together Ghost Dancers from among the Burnt Thighs.

The morning after soldiers brought in Big Foot's band, Miller was aboard Handsome Dog's buckboard, headed towards the White Clay Ghost Dance camps. It had been an uneasy evening at the Agency, with Lakota riding in and soldiers marching out. In his mind, Miller went over his last argument with Wallace, putting in every word he should have said. He had let Wallace lord over him, like a High Church Scot preaching to a poor, blind Quaker. The Ghost Dance was going to be broken. Yellow Legs was marked for arrest, just as Sitting Bull and Big Foot had been. Miller couldn't sway Wallace or the army, but he was going to warn Yellow Legs.

The buckboard bounced beneath a bright young winter sun, but even Miller could smell snow in the air. When the first booming came from the east, Miller thought it might be thunder and said as much to Handsome Dog.

The Metal Breast kept his face fixed on the road ahead. "It is wagon guns."

Miller made no reply. He wasn't ready for another argument, though he knew it couldn't be cannon.

As they topped a rise, they saw riders and ponies streaming out of the White Clay camps. Some were headed south, toward the Agency; others were moving east, over the hills. All of them were armed, carrying more guns than Miller thought the Indians owned.

Spinning wheels rolled them right into camp. To Miller, it seemed he was sitting in an open-air theater, watching some strange show. Barren hills appeared ahead and disappeared behind. Armed riders in feathered buckskins flicked past. The camp grew into a tapestry of bare tree limbs, dirty brown tipis, and pine-bough shelters. Blue camp smoke rose from the lodges, where blanketed women worked and talked. Children, skinny dogs, and surly brown faces looked up at him. As long as the buckboard was moving, Miller felt removed and immune. When the buckboard stopped before Yellow Legs's lodge, hard hands seized him and Handsome Dog, pulling them both down to solid ground.

Burnt Thighs pinned their arms. An angry Bad Face began yelling at them in Lakota, waving a razor-edged skinning knife.

The knife flicked out, slicing the metal badge off Handsome Dog's blue uniform jacket. "Metal Breast, you killed Sitting Bull. Your Wasichu friends are killing Big Foot's people."

The Burnt Thighs pulled the jacket back; the next flick of the knife drew blood.

Handsome Dog laughed. "Was that supposed to hurt? Bad Faces and Burnt Thighs are women."

The Bad Face lashed out with his knife, leaving a long strip of flesh hanging from Handsome Dog's chest. "That's for serving the Wasichu so well." He thrust his chin towards Miller. "We're going to skin you and give you a Wasichu skin to wear."

The Burnt Thighs began to strip Miller's clothes off, and Handsome Dog laughed again. "Do it, and you will still be women. I serve the Wasichu, but have the Bad Faces done better? Where was Red Cloud when we rubbed out Long Hair on the Greasy Grass?"

Twisting round, he sneered at the Burnt Thighs who were holding him. "Where was Spotted Tail when we rubbed out Long Hair? Your chiefs were cowering on the agencies, hiding among their women and eating Wasichu cattle."

The Bad Face held his blade in Handsome Dog's face. "You hope to make me mad, make me kill you quickly." He jabbed the blade at Miller. "Your words will be different when you wear this Wasichu's skin."

The tipi entrance opened behind the Bad Face, and Miller barely recognized the man who emerged. It was Yellow Legs, his face covered with paint and half-hidden beneath a war bonnet of black-tipped eagle feathers. He wore his white ghost shirt, with the Moon, Morning Star, and Magpie. Like Wallace had said, his leggings were made from cavalry pants, seat and crotch cut out, a yellow stripe running down each blue leg. His paint repeated those colors—yellow from chin to forehead, a blue band across his eyes. His arms craddled the Henry rifle, hung with still more black-tipped feathers.

He shook this feathered rifle in their faces. "Bad Faces and Burnt Thighs, why are you here? Black Elk has gone to face the Wasichu wagon guns with only his Medicine Bow. Can you be as brave with rifles?"

Silence fell like a heavy snow. They could plainly hear the dull roll of gunfire from Wounded Knee, like far-off pounding on buffalo-hide drums.

He pointed the rifle at Handsome Dog and Miller. "Must you have guns and knives to face one unarmed Metal Breast and the teacher who came only to bring us the wisdom of the Wasichu?"

The Burnt Thighs let go their grip. Handsome Dog's grin turned smug.

"These are my guests." Yellow Legs spoke straight at the Bad Face. "Go count coup at Wounded Knee, and we will all come listen to your kill talk."

Miller hadn't made out a single word, but when Yellow Legs stepped aside, he was delighted to have Handsome Dog hustle him into the gloomy tipi. Stays Behind emerged from the shadows, setting bowls of buffalo meat and chokecherry mush before them. Her calico dress shone like sunset in the firelight, and her hair part was painted to match it. She ignored her brother-in-law and greeted Miller with a shy grin. Both men ate quickly, anxious to make themselves guests in deed as well as word.

Yellow Legs entered and ambled over to the place of honor. Folding his feet beneath him, he sat facing the sunrise. Handsome Dog looked up from his food. "It will be hard for me to return this honor, if you still shun my cabin."

"My sister's cabin," Stays Behind corrected him. "If you wish to do your host a service, honor him as your new brother-in-law."

Handsome Dog rocked back on his heels, laughing. "Such a meal would choke a man. How could my host want a silly girl who jabbers out of turn?"

Yellow Legs packed the red clay pipe and passed it to Handsome Dog. "Things have gone too far. I may no longer refuse her and keep my honor."

Handsome Dog's gaze flicked from host to sister-in-law. "*Hetchetu aloh*, there is something here that needs smoking on."

"If you are insulted, we will not keep you." Stays Behind sat herself at the entrance, untying the tipi flap.

Burnt Thighs stormed back and forth outside, their anger audible through the thin hides. "Look, I'm smoking," Handsome Dog said, putting the pipe to his lips. "May men not smoke without having to hear women?"

When the pipe came back to him, Yellow Legs passed it to Teacher Miller. "I thought badly because you didn't thank me for my vision, but I was wrong. The vision with the Wasichu signs was not meant for you. It was meant for Stays Behind."

Miller was bemused. "How do you know?"

"A coyote told us."

"Coyote?"

"Yes." Yellow Legs sighed. "I know coyotes are hardly to be trusted. But this one sent us past the Moon and Morning Star, to a Spirit World that lies alongside the Twin Stars in the winter sky. Soon, we will all go there for good."

Miller gave polite agreement. Like Handsome Dog, he found it politic to humor his host. They smoked, talked, and ate while snow began to blow down from the sky. As night won out over day, word rode up White Clay Creek that Black Elk's Ogalalas had been driven from the Agency without food or tipis. Few had meat to share, but Stays Behind packed the last of the buffalo meat into anything-possible-bags and lashed them to their ponies.

She also painted Miller's face black and wrapped blankets round his Wasichu suit. Stepping back, she laughed. "You don't look like a Lakota, but neither do you look like a Wasichu. No one will shoot you without asking first what you are."

They set off through the snow, with Yellow Legs leading and Handsome Dog coming along behind, wearing wolfskins over his uniform jacket. It was a good night to be all Ogalala. On the east bank of White Clay Creek, they found red fires on the prairie, flickering through the gray snowfall like broken bits of the setting sun. The dark wind carried a woman's voice, wailing out a death song. As they drew nearer, they could hear that it was Black Elk's mother, singing for her son. He had gone to face the Wasichu with the Sacred Bow of the West, and had not returned. Stays Behind offered her meat, but she wouldn't eat and went on wailing into the wind.

Suddenly, the singing ceased, replaced by the slow beat of tired horses' hooves and by babies crying. Black Elk came riding out of the snow on a weary buckskin, still carrying the Sacred Bow of the West and cradling a crying baby girl. Red Crow was right behind him, with another crying child. Eager hands helped them dismount, and women with milk took the babies. Soon, the only crying round that campfire came from Black Elk's mother, sobbing now that her son was safe.

Black Elk was not the venerable medicine man Miller had expected. Instead, he was a serious young man, with a flaming rainbow and red streaks of lightning on his ghost shirt. When he wasn't having visions, he worked as a clerk in a Wasichu store. His face was red with paint, and eagle feathers hung from his shoulders, wrists, and elbows. These feathers fluttered in the wind, and the red lightning flashed in the firelight. "Big Foot's people have been butchered near Wounded Knee, in the twisted creek that has no name. We scattered the soldiers, saving some women and children. My Medicine Bow protected me, but for many it was too late. These babies have no mothers, and there are many babies lying frozen on the prairie."

Wind and snow whipped between the fires. Everyone talked till dawn. The story of Wounded Knee was told again and again by those who had been there. Yellow Legs and Stays Behind told about their vision. At first light a war party was forming. Men began to rub dirt on themselves, showing that they were nothing without the Earth Mother's help. Black Elk's mother had ceased crying and brought him his rifle. Black Elk set aside his Medicine Bow, mounting his buckskin again. He was still wearing the red war paint. "Yellow Legs, your visions are strong and your buffalo meat good, but I must answer yesterday with bullets. If I do not see you again, seek me in the Spirit World."

The war party crossed White Clay Creek and was gone. Everyone else began the long march into the Badlands. By nightfall they were camped on a high platform in the Badlands, called Sheltering Place. Sheer cliffs fell away at every side. The campsite could only be approached across a narrow neck of land, which was easily swept with rifle fire.

No Wasichu soldiers came to get them, but a Lakota named Little Soldier brought Black Elk back to camp. His rainbow shirt was ripped and bloody, a bullet had torn open his stomach, and his intestines were held in by strips of torn blanket. Old Hollow Horn, a Bear medicine man, was called to heal him. Stays Behind felt strange, for she was no longer able to help Old Hollow Horn with his healing. That was work for virgins. Instead, she sat on the edge of the precipice, watching the cliff fall away beneath her feet cascading into deep shadow.

Miller came and sat beside her, warmed by a blanket, but without his black paint. Everyone here knew he was a Wasichu. During that day's fighting, Black Robes and Sisters from the Mission had worked among the Lakota, helping the wounded and praying for the dead. The Lakota's war was against soldiers. "What will you do?"

Stays Behind looked down, smoothing the creases in her calico dress. "What can I do, besides follow my vision?"

"Medicine visions won't stop machine guns. Look what happened to Black Elk."

She looked towards the Twin Stars, marking where the sun and Morning Star would rise. "Do you still have the paper I gave you?"

Miller fished into his pocket and pulled out the wrinkled scrap of notebook paper. The formulas were smudged and faded. He could no longer read them under the winter stars.

She smoothed the paper against her knee. "Coyote said you could explain them to me."

"These formulas might mean a lot, a new approach to the physics of light, a new way of looking at the world. But first science has to test them. That will take time. No one can say what they really mean. Not right now."

For the first time ever, she looked him straight in the face, her dark eyes deep wells of starlight. "We don't have time. Your science is crushing us with wagon guns and iron wire. Last year, we lost most of the land between the Smoky River and the Good. Now, we are losing the Ghost Dance. By the time you decide what everything means, my people will be gone, gone like the buffalo and the long grass."

Miller nodded. "I told you that everything passes and that one day the whole universe will die the heat death. All science can do is make the best of what is. Study, learn more mathematics, and you can be the one to test these formulas."

Stays Behind folded the paper and fit it into her medicine bag. "There's another way." She pointed away from Sheltering Place, towards the Twin Stars. "Out there is another world, and Coyote is going to take us there. He has collected people and animals from our past and has brought them to a great world, larger than this one. He says that he has already been with me there, talked to me, helped me explore the universe."

She no longer seemed a girl, but a grave and distant young woman.

Miller measured the space between them and found it was only a matter of inches. Wind stirred the stars overhead, and he would have liked to touch her, but the gulf between them was too great. Instead, he pulled the blanket round his knees. "Maybe you can mix mathematics with talking coyotes, but I can't."

When morning came, Yellow Legs led all who would follow away from Sheltering Place, deeper into the Badlands.

The man who finally rescued Miller was a Wasichu, though he wasn't a white man. He was a corporal from the Ninth Cavalry—"colored" as the Wasichu would say. This Black Wasichu had been scouting for hostiles beyond the Smoky, but he found only Miller, resting in a pine-bough lean-to near Top of the Badlands. The Moon of Popping Trees had given way to the Moon of Frost in the Tipis. Miller was exhausted and hungry, but no worse off for his stay among the Lakota.

The corporal explained that the Ninth was searching for Yellow Legs's band. Miller said only that they'd better be ready to go some distance.

The Black Wasichu shook his head. "Don't matter how far, we'll get 'em sure enough. We've got a way with Indians, comes from not being white. No offense meant."

The Quaker said that no offense had been taken.

After helping Miller onto his own mount, the corporal began to lead the lone horse and rider back toward his troop. "Hell, if the old Negro Ninth hadn't shown up, the Seventh would have had another Little Big Horn on White Clay Creek. The Lakota chased them all the way back there from Wounded Knee."

They topped a dun-colored fold in the earth, and the corporal's narrative was cut short. Metal flashed in the frigid morning sun. The corporal pushed back his cap for a better view. "God Almighty, this piece of prairie looks more fit for a church sale than a fight."

From his seat on the horse's back, Miller scanned the litter of abandoned guns, knives, cooking tins, cups, pots, wash buckets, belt buckles, and tent pegs.

The corporal rested his weary arm on the saddle. "Looks like these poor Indians just tried to get rid of everything the white man gave 'em."

He turned a sage eye to the teacher. "You know a lot of them are just crazy with grief, going around seeing things. Back by the Agency, when Red Cloud told his Bad Faces to lay down their guns, a bunch of them ran wild, shooting their own dogs and ponies, just 'cause Red Cloud wouldn't let 'em shoot us no more."

It shook the corporal to see such suffering. He led his horse and Miller through the mess, searching for tracks and stooping to pick up anything that might prove useful. There was a fair amount of silver trinkets to be found, and even a few coins.

Miller watched the cold wind play on a single patch of color—torn, red, and flapping in their path. Even before they reached it, Miller knew what it would be. A crimson calico dress, wrapped round an old Henry rifle from the Fetterman fight.

# NEAL BARRETT, JR.

## Diner

**Here's another story by Neal Barrett, Jr., as different in mood from "Perpetuity Blues" as night is from day, but still strong, surprising, and original.**

# DINER

## Neal Barrett, Jr.

He woke sometime before dawn and brought the dream back with him out of sleep. The four little girls attended Catholic junior high in Corpus Christi. Their hand-painted guitars depicted tropical Cuban nights. They played the same chord again and again, a dull repetition like small wads of paper hitting a drum. The light was still smoky, the furniture unrevealed. He made his way carefully across the room. The screened-in porch enclosed the front side of the house facing the Gulf, allowing the breeze to flow in three directions. He could hear rolling surf, smell the sharp tang of iodine in the air. Yet something was clearly wrong. The water, the sand, the sky had disappeared, lost behind dark coagulation. With sudden understanding he saw the screen was clotted with bugs. Grasshoppers blotted out the morning. They were bouncing off the screen, swarming in drunken legions. He ran outside and down the stairs, knowing what he'd find. The garden was gone. A month before, he'd covered the small plot of ground with old window screens and bricks. The hoppers had collapsed the whole device. His pitiful stands of lettuce were cropped clean, razored on the ground as if he'd clipped them with a mower. Radishes, carrots, the whole bit. Eaten to the stalk. Then it occurred to him he was naked and under attack. Grasshopper socks knitted their way up to his knees. Something considered his crotch. He yelled and struck out blindly, intent on knocking hoppers silly. The fight was next to useless, and he retreated up the stairs.

Jenny woke while he was dressing.

"Something wrong? Did you yell just a minute ago?"

"Hoppers. They're all over the place."

"Oh, Mack."

"Little fuckers ate my salad bar."

"I'm sorry. It was doing so good."

"It isn't doing good now." He started looking for his hat.

"You want something to eat?"

"I'll grab something at Henry's."

She came to him, still unsteady from sleep, awkward and fetching at once. Minnie Mouse T-shirt ragged as a kite. A certain yielding coming against him.

"I got to go to work."

"Your loss, man."

"I dreamed of little Mexican girls."

"Good for you." She stepped back to gather her hair, her eyes somewhere else.

"Nothing happened. They played real bad guitar."

"So you say."

He made his way past the dunes and the ragged stands of sea grass, following the path over soft, dry sand to solid beach, the dark rows of houses on stilts off to his right, the Gulf rolling in, brown as mud, giving schools of mullet a ride. The hoppers had moved on, leaving dead and wounded behind. The sun came up behind dull, anemic clouds. Two skinny boys searched the ocean's morning debris. He found a pack of Agricultural Hero cigarettes in his pocket and cupped his hands against the wind. George Panagopoulos said there wasn't any tobacco in them at all. Said they made them out of half-dried shit and half kelp and that the shit wasn't bad, but he couldn't abide the kelp. Where the sandy road angled into the beach, he cut back and crossed Highway 87, the asphalt cracked and covered with sand, the tough coastal grass crowding in. The highway trailed southwest for two miles, dropping off abruptly where the red-white-and-blue Galveston ferries used to run, the other end stretching northeast up the narrow strip of Bolivar Peninsula past Crystal Beach and Gilchrist, then off the peninsula to High Island and Sabine Pass.

Mack began to find Henry's posters north of the road. They were tacked on telephone poles and fences, on the door of the derelict Texaco station, wherever Henry had wandered in this merchandising adventure. He gathered them in as he walked, snapping them off like paper towels. The sun began to bake, hot wind stinging up sand in tiny storms. The posters said: FOURTH OF JULY PICNIC AT HENRY ORTEGAS DINER. ALL THE BARBECUE PORK YOU CAN EAT. EL DIOS BLESS AMERICA

Henry had drawn the posters on the backs of green accounting forms salvaged from the Sand Palace Motor Home Inn. Even if he'd gotten Rose to help, it was a formidable undertaking.

No easy task to do individually rendered, slightly crazed, and plainly cokeyed fathers of our country. Every George Washington wore a natty clip-on Second Inaugural tie and, for some reason, a sporty little Matamoros pimp mustache. Now and then along the borders, an extra reader bonus, snappy American flags or red cherry bombs going *kapow*.

Mack walked on picking posters. Squinting back east he saw water flat as slate, vanishing farther out with tricks of the eye. Something jumped out there or something didn't.

Jase and Morgan were in the diner, and George Panagopoulos and Fleece. They wore a collection of gimmie caps and patched-up tennis shoes, jeans stiff and sequined with the residue of fish. Mack took the third stool down. Fleece said it might get hotter. Mack agreed it could. Jase leaned down the counter.

"Hoppers get your garden, too?"

"Right down to bedrock is all," Mack said.

"I had this tomato," Panagopoulos said, "this one little asshole tomato 'bout half as big as a plum; I'm taking a piss and hear these hoppers coming and I'm down and out of the house like that. I'm down there in what, maybe ten, twenty seconds flat, and this tomato's a little bugger and a seed. You know? A little bugger hanging down, and that's all." He made a swipe at his nose, held up a finger, and looked startled and goggle-eyed.

Mack pretended to study the menu and ordered KC steak and fries and coffee and three eggs over easy; and all this time Henry's standing over the charcoal stove behind the counter, poking something flat across the grill, concentrating intently on this because he's already seen the posters rolled up and stuffed in Mack's pocket and he knows he'll have to look right at Mack sooner or later.

"Galveston's got trouble," Jase said. "Dutch rowed back from seeing that woman in Clute looks like a frog. Said nobody's seen Mendez for 'bout a week."

"Eddie's a good man for a Mex," Morgan said from down the counter. "He'll stand up for you, he thinks you're in the right."

Mack felt the others waiting. He wondered if he really wanted to get into this or let it go.

Fleece jumped in. "Saw Doc this morning, sneaking up the dunes 'bout daylight. Gotta know if those hoppers eat his dope."

Everyone laughed except Morgan. Mack was silently grateful.

"I seen that dope," Jase said. "What it is there's maybe three tomato plants 'bout high as a baby's dick."

"I don't want to hear nothin' about tomatoes," said Panagopoulos.

"Don't make any difference what it is," Fleece said. "Man determined to get high, he going to do it."

Panagopoulos told Mack that Dutch's woman up in Clute heard

someone had seen a flock of chickens. Right near Umbrella Point. Rhode Island Reds running loose out on the beach.

Mack said fine. There was always a good chicken rumor going around somewhere. That or someone saw a horse or a pack of dogs. Miss Aubrey Gain of Alvin swore on Jesus there was a pride of Siamese cats in Liberty County.

Mack wolfed down his food. He didn't look at his plate. If you didn't look close, you maybe couldn't figure what the hot peppers were covering up.

When he got up to go he said, "Real tasty, Henry," and then, as if the thought had suddenly occurred, "All right if you and me talk for a minute?"

Henry followed him out. Mack saw the misery in his face. He tried on roles like hats. Humble peon. An extra in *Viva Zapata!* Wily tourist guide with gold teeth and connections. Nothing fit. He looked like Cesar Romero, and this was his cross. Nothing could rob him of dignity. No one would pity a man with such bearing.

Mack took out the roll of posters and gave them back. "You know better than that, Henry. It wasn't a real good idea."

"There is no harm in this, Mack. You cannot say that there is."

"Not me I can't, no."

"Well, then."

"Come on. I got Huang Hua coming first thing tomorrow."

"Ah. Of course."

"Jesus, Henry."

"I am afraid that I forgot."

"Fine. Sure. Look, I appreciate the thought, and so does everyone else. This Chink, now, he hasn't got a real great sense of humor."

"I was thinking about a flag."

"What?"

"A flag. You could ask, you know? See what he says. It would not hurt to ask. A very small and insignificant flag in the window of the diner. Just for the one day, you understand?"

Mack looked down the road. "You didn't even listen. You didn't hear anything I said."

"Just for the one day. The Fourth and nothing more."

"Get all the posters down, Henry. Do it before tonight."

"How did you like the George Washington?" Henry asked. "I did all of those myself. Rose did the lettering, but I am totally responsible for the pictures."

"The Washington was great."

"You think so?"

"The eyes kinda follow you around."

"Yes." Henry showed his delight. "I tried for inner vision of the eyes."

"Well, you flat out got it."

Jase and Morgan came out, Jase picking up the rubber fishing boots he'd left at the door. Morgan looked moody and deranged. Mack considered knocking him senseless.

"Look," Mack told him, "I don't want you on my boat. Go with Panagopoulos. Tell him Fleece'll be going with me and Jase."

"Just fine with me," Morgan said.

"Good. It's fine with me, too."

Morgan wasn't through. "You take a nigger fishing on a day with a *r* in it, you goin' to draw sharks certain. I seen it happen."

"You tell that to Fleece," Mack said. "I'll stand out here and watch."

Morgan went in and talked to Panagopoulos. Jase waited for Fleece, leaning against the diner, asleep or maybe not. Mack lit an Agricultural Hero and considered the after-taste of breakfast. Thought of likely antics with Jenny's parts. Wondered how a univalve mollusk with the mental reserve of grass could dream up a wentletrap shell and then wear it. This and other things.

Life has compensations, but there's no way of knowing what they are.

Coming in was the time he liked the best. The water was dark and flat, getting ready for the night. The bow cut green, and no sound at all but a jazzy little counterbeat, the crosswind snapping two fingers in the sails. The sun was down an hour, the sky settling into a shade inducing temporary wisdom. He missed beer and music. Resented the effort of sinking into a shitty evening mood without help.

Swinging in through the channel, Pelican Island off to port, he saw the clutter of Port Bolivar, the rusted-out buildings and the stumps of rotted docks, the shrimpers he used to run heeling drunkenly in the flats. South of that was the chain-link fence and the two-story corrugated building. The bright red letters on its side read SHINING WEALTH OF THE SEA JOYOUS COOPERATIVE 37 WELCOME HOME INDUSTRIOUS CATCHERS OF THE FISH.

This Chinese loony-tune message was clear a good nautical mile away; a catcher of the fish with a double cataract couldn't pretend it wasn't there.

Panagopoulos's big Irwin ketch was in, the other boats as well, the nets up and drying. Fleece brought the sloop in neatly, dropping the sails at precisely the right moment, a skill Mack appreciated all the more because Morgan was scarcely ever able to do it, either rushing in to shore full sail like a Viking bent on pillage or dropping off early and leaving them bobbing in the bay.

The Chinks greatly enjoyed this spectacle, the round-eyes paddling the forty-three-foot Hinckley in to shore.

Mack and Jase secured the lines, and then Jase went forward to help Fleece while the Chinks came aboard to look at the catch. The guards stayed on the dock looking sullen and important, rifles slung carelessly over their shoulders. Fishing Supervisor Lu Ping peered into the big metal hold, clearly disappointed.

"Not much fish," he told Mack.

"Not much," Mack said.

"It's June," Fleece explained. "You got the bad easterlies in June. Yucatan Current kinda edges up north, hits the Amarillo Clap flat on. That goin' to fuck up your fishing real good."

"Oh, yes." Lu Ping made a note. Jase nodded solemn agreement.

Mack told Jase and Fleece to come to the house for supper. He walked past the chain-link fence and the big generator that kept the fish in the corrugated building cooler than anyone in Texas.

The routine was, the boats would come in and tack close to the long rock dike stretching out from the southeast side of the peninsula, out of sight of the Chinks, and the women and kids would wave and make a fuss and the men would toss them fish in canvas bags, flounder or pompano or redfish if they were running or maybe a rare sack of shrimp, keeping enough good fish onboard to keep the Chinese happy but mostly leaving catfish and shark and plenty of mullet in the hold, that and whatever other odd species came up in the nets. It didn't matter at all, since everything they caught was ground up, steamed, pressed, processed, and frozen into brick-size bundles before they shipped it.

Mack thought about cutting through the old part of the port, then remembered about Henry and went back. There were still plenty of posters on fence posts and abandoned bait stands and old houses, and he pulled down all he could find before dark.

They ate in front of the house near the dunes, a good breeze coming in from the Gulf strong enough to keep mosquitoes and gnats at bay, the wind drawing the driftwood fire nearly white. Henry brought a large pot of something dark and heady, announcing it was Acadia Parish shrimp creole Chihuahua style, and nobody said it wasn't. Mack broiled flounder over a grill. Jase attacked guitar. Arnie Mace, Mack's uncle from Sandy Point, brought illegal rice wine. Not enough to count but potent. Fleece drank half a mason jar and started to cry. He said he was thinking about birds. He began to call them off.

Herons and plovers and egrets. Gulls squawking cloud-white thick behind the shrimpers. Jase said he remembered pink flamingos in the tidal flats down by the dike.

"There was an old bastard in Sweeny, you know him, Mack," George Panagopoulos said. "Swears he had the last cardinal bird in Texas. Kept it in a hamster cage long as he could stand it. Started dreaming about it and couldn't sleep, got up in the middle of the night and stir-fried it in a wok. Had a frazzle of red feathers on this hat for some time, but I can't say that's how he got 'em."

"That was Emmett Dodge," Mack said. "I always heard it was a jay."

"Now, I'm near certain it was a cardinal." Panagopoulos looked thoughtfully into his wine. "A jay, now, if Emmett had had a jay, I doubt he could've kept the thing quiet. They make a awful lot of noise."

Mack helped Fleece throw up.

"Georgia won't talk to me," Fleece said miserably. "You the only friend I got."

"I expect you're right."

"You watch out for Morgan. He bad-talkin' you ever chance he get."

"He wants to be pissant mayor, he can run. I sure don't care for the honor."

"He says your eyes beginnin' to slant."

"He said that?"

"Uh-huh."

"Well, fuck him." Fleece was unsteady but intact. Mack looked around for Henry and found him with Rose and Jenny. He liked to stand off somewhere and watch her. A good-looking woman was fine as gold, you caught her sitting by a fire.

He took Henry aside.

"I know what you are going to say," Henry said. "You are angry with me. I can sense these things."

"I'm not angry at all. Just get that stuff taken down before morning."

"I only do what I think is right, *mi compadre*. What is just. What is true." Henry tried for balance. "What I deeply feel in my heart. A voice cries out. It has to speak. This is the tragedy of my race. I feel a great sorrow for my people."

"Okay."

"I shall bow to your wishes, of course."

"Good. Just bow before Huang gets here in the morning."

"I will take them down. I will go and do it now."

"You don't have to do it now."

"I feel I am an intrusion."

"I feel like you've had enough to drink."

"Do you know what I am thinking? What I am thinking at this moment?"

"No, what?"

"I am thinking that I cannot remember tequila."

"Fleece has already done this," Mack said. "I don't want you doing it, too. One crying drunk is enough."

"Forgive me. I cannot help myself. Mack, I don't remember how it tastes. I remember the lime and the salt. I recall a certain warmth. *Nada*. Nothing more."

Tears touched the Cesar Romero eyes, trailed down the Gilbert Roland cheeks. *If Jase plays "La Paloma," I'll flat kill him*, thought Mack. He left to look for Rose.

Jenny told him to come out on the porch and look at the beach. Crickets crawled out of the dunes and made for the water. The sand was black, a bug tide going out to sea. The crickets marched into the water and floated back. In the dark they looked like the ropy strands of a spill.

"The ocean scares me at night," Jenny said.

"Not always. You like it sometimes." He wanted to stop this but didn't know how to do it. She was working up to it a notch at a time.

"It's not you," she said.

"Fine, I'll write that down." He worked his hand up the T-shirt and touched the small of her back. She leaned in comfortably against him.

"Things are still bad, you get too far away from the coast. I don't want you just wandering around somewhere."

"I haven't really decided, Mack. I mean, it's not tomorrow or anything."

"I don't think you're going to find anyone, Jenny." He said it as gently as he could. "Folks are scattered all about."

She didn't answer. They stood a long time on the porch. The house already felt empty.

The chopper came in low out of the south, tilted slightly into the offshore breeze, rotors churning flat, snappy farts as it settled to 87 stirring sand. Soldiers hit the ground. They looked efficient. Counterrevolutionary acts would be dealt with swiftly. Fleece and Panagopoulos leaned against the diner trading butts. Henry came out for a look and ducked inside. The morning was oyster gray with a feeble ribbing of clouds. Major Huang waved at Mack. Then Chen came out of the chopper and started barking at the troops. Mack wasn't pleased. Huang was purely political—fat and happy and not looking for any trouble. Chen was maybe nineteen tops, a cocky little shit with new bars. Mack was glad he didn't speak English, which meant Jase wouldn't try to sell him a shark dick pickled in a jar or something worse.

The Chinese uniforms were gallbladder green to match the chopper. Chen and three troopers stayed behind. The troopers started tossing crates and boxes to the ground. One followed discreetly behind the major.

"Personal hellos," Huang Hua greeted Mack. "It is a precious day we are seeing."

Mack looked at the chopper. "Not many supplies this time."

"Not many fishes," Huang said.

*It's going to be like this, is it?* Mack followed him past the diner down the road to Shining Wealth Cooperative 37. He noticed little things. A real haircut. Starched khakis with creases. He wondered what Huang had eaten for breakfast.

Sergeant Fishing Supervisor Lu Ping greeted the major effusively. He had reports. Huang stuffed them in a folder. The air-conditioning was staggering. Mack forgot what it was like between visits.

"I have reportage of events," Huang began. He sat behind the plain wooden table and folded his hands. "It is a happening of unpleasant nature. Eddie Mendez will not mayor himself in Galveston after today."

"And why's that?"

"Offending abuse. Blameful performance. Defecation of authority." Huang looked meaningfully at Mack. "Retaining back of fishes."

"What'll happen to Eddie?"

"The work you do here is of gravity, Mayor Mack. A task of large importance. Your people in noncoastal places are greatly reliant of fish."

"We're doing the best we can."

"I am hopeful this is true."

Mack looked right at him.

"Major, we're taking all the fish we can net. We got sails and no gas and nothing with an engine to put it into if we did. You're not going to help any shorting us on supplies. I've got forty-one families on this peninsula eating nothing but fish and rice. There's kids here never saw a carrot. We try to grow something, the bugs eat it first 'cause there's no birds left to eat the bugs. The food chain's fucked."

"You are better off than most."

"I'm sure glad to hear it."

"Please to climb down from my back. The Russians did the germing, not us."

"I know who did it."

Huang tried Oriental restraint. "We are engaging to help. You have no grateful at all. The Chinese people have come to fill this empty air."

"Vacuum."

"Yes. Vacuum." Huang considered. "In three, maybe four years, wheat and corn will be achieved in the ground again. Animal and fowl will be brought. This is very restricted stuff. I tell you, Mayor Mack, because I wish your nonopposing. I have ever shown you friendness. You cannot say I haven't."

"I appreciate the effort."

"You will find sweets in this shipment. For the children. Also decorative candles. Toothpaste. Simple magic tricks."

"Jesus Christ."

"I knew this would bring you pleasure."

Huang looked up. Lieutenant Chen entered politely. He handed Huang papers. Gave Mack a sour look. Mack recognized Henry's posters, the menu from the diner. Chen turned and left.

"What is this?" Huang appeared disturbed. "Flags? Counterproductive celebration? Barbecue pork?"

"Doesn't mean a thing," Mack explained. "It's just Henry."

Huang looked quizzically at George Washington, turning the poster in several directions. He glanced at the cardboard menu, at the KC Sirloin Scrambled Eggs Chicken-Fried Steak French Fries Omelet with Cheddar Cheese or Swiss Coffee Refills Free. He looked gravely at Mack.

"I did not think this was a good thing. You said there would be no trouble. One thing leads to a something other. Now it is picnics and flags."

"The poster business, all right," Mack said. "He shouldn't of done that. I figure it's my fault. The diner, now, there's nothing wrong with the diner."

Huang shook his head. "It is fanciment. The path to discontent." He appeared deeply hurt. The poster was an affront. The betrayal of a friend. He walked to the window, hands behind his back. "There is much to have renouncement here, Mayor Mack. Many fences to bend. I have been lenient and foolish. No more Henry Ortega Diner. No picnic. And better fishes, I think."

Mack didn't answer. Whatever he said would be wrong.

Huang recalled something of importance. He looked at Mack again. "You have a black person living here?"

"Two. A man and a woman."

"There is no racing discrimination? They are treated fairly?"

"Long as they keep picking that cotton."

"No textiles. Only fishes."

"I'll see to it."

Mack walked back north, past a rusted Chevy van waiting patiently for tires, past a pickup with windows still intact. Rose hadn't seen Henry. She didn't know where he was. "He didn't mean to cause trouble," she told Mack.

"I know that, Rose."

"He walks. He wanders off. He needs the time to himself. He is a very sensitive man."

"He's all of that," Mack said. He heard children. Smelled rice and fish, strongly seasoned with peppers.

"He respects you greatly. He says you are *muy simpático*. A man of heart. A leader of understanding."

A woman with fine bones and sorrowful eyes. Katy Jurado, *One-Eyed Jacks*. He couldn't remember the year.

"I just want to talk to him, Rose. I have to see him."

"I will tell him. He will come to you. Here, take some chilies to Jenny. It is the only thing I can grow the bugs won't eat. Try it on the fish. Just this much, no more."

"Jenny'll appreciate that." A hesitation in her eyes. As if she might say something more. Mack wouldn't ask. He wasn't mad at Henry. His anger had abated, diluted after a day with Major Hua. He left and walked to the beach. Jase and Fleece were there. Jase had a mason jar of wine he'd maybe conned from Arnie Mace.

"Tell Panagopoulos and some of the others if you see 'em," Mack said, "I want to talk to Henry. He's off roaming around somewhere; I don't want him doing that."

"Your minorities'll do this," Jase reflected. "I'm glad I ain't a ethnic."

"It's a burden," Fleece said. "There going to be any trouble with the Chinks?"

"Not if I can help it."

"Fleece thought of two more birds," Jase said. "A cormorant and a what?"

"Tern."

"Yeah, right."

"Good," Mack said. "Keep your eyes peeled for Henry. He gets into that moon-over-Monterey shit, it'll take Rose a month to get him straight."

"I think I'm going to go," Jenny told him. "I think I got to do that, Mack. It just keeps eatin' away. Papa's likely gone, but Luanne and Mama could be okay."

He put out his cigarette and watched her across the room, watched her as she sat at the kitchen table bringing long wings of hair atop her head, going about this simple task with a quick, unconscious grace. The mirror stood against a white piece of driftwood she'd collected. She collected everything. Sand dollars and angel wings, twisted tritons and bright coquinas that faded in a day. Candle by the mirror in a sand-frosted Dr Pepper bottle, light from this touching the bony hillbilly points of her hips. When she left she would take too much of him with her, and maybe he should figure some way to tell her that.

"I might not be able to get you a pass. I don't know. They don't much like us moving around without a reason."

"Oh, Mack. People do it all the time." Peering at him now past the candle. "Hey, now, I'm going to come on back. I just got to get this done."

He thought about the trip. Saw her walking old highways in his head. Maybe sixty-five miles up to Beaumont, cutting off north before that into the Thicket. He didn't tell her everything he heard. The way people were, things that happened. He knew it wouldn't make a difference if he did.

Jenny settled in beside him. "I said I'm coming back."

"Yeah, well, you'd better."

He decided, maybe at that moment, he wouldn't let her go. He'd figure out a way to stop her. She'd leave him in a minute. Maybe come back and maybe not. He had to know she was all right, and so he'd do it. He listened to the surf. On the porch, luna moths big as English sparrows flung themselves crazily against the screen.

The noise of the chopper brought him out of bed fast, on the floor and poking into jeans before Jase and Panagopoulos made the stairs.

"It's okay," he told Jenny, "just stay inside and I'll see."

She nodded and looked scared, and he opened the screen door and went out. Dawn washed the sky the color of moss. Jase and Panagopoulos started talking both at once.

Then Mack saw the fire, the reflection past the house. "Oh, Jesus H. Christ!"

"Mack, he's got pigs," Panagopoulos said. "I seen 'em. Henry's got pigs."

"He's got what?"

"This is bad shit," Jase moaned, "this is really bad shit."

Mack was down the stairs and past the house. He could see other people. He started running, Jase and Panagopoulos at his heels. The chopper was on the ground, and then Fleece came out of the crowd across the road.

"Henry ain't hurt bad, I don't think," he told Mack.

"Henry's hurt?" Mack was unnerved. "Who hurt him, Fleece? Is someone going to tell me something soon?"

"I figure that Chen likely done a house-to-house," Fleece said, "some asshole trick like that. Come in north and worked down rousting people out for kicks. Stumbled on Henry; shit, I don't know. Just get him out of there, Mack."

Mack wanted to cry or throw up. He pushed through the crowd and saw Chen, maybe half a dozen soldiers, then Henry. Henry looked foolish, contrite, and slightly cockeyed. His hands were tied behind. Someone had hit him in the face. The rotors stirred waves of hot air. The diner went up like a box. Mack tried to look friendly. Chen lurched about yelling and waving his pistol, looking wild-eyed as a dog.

"Let's work this out," Mack said. "We ought to get this settled and go home."

Chen shook his pistol at Mack, danced this way and that in an unfamiliar step. Mack decided he was high on the situation. He'd gotten hold of this and didn't know where to take it, didn't have the sense to know how to stop.

"We can call this off and you don't have to worry about a thing," Mack said, knowing Chen didn't have the slightest notion what he was saying. "That okay with you? We just call it a night right now?"

Chen looked at him or somewhere else entirely. Mack wished he had shoes and a shirt. Dress seemed proper if you were talking to some clown with a gun. He was close enough to see the pigs. The crate was by the chopper. Two pigs, pink and fat, mottled like an old man's hand. They were squealing and going crazy with the rotors and the fire and not helping Chen's nerves or Mack's either. Mack could just see Henry thinking this out, how he'd do it, fattening up the porkers somehow and thinking what everybody'd say when they saw it wasn't a joke, not soyburger KC steak or chicken-fried fish-liver rice and chili peppers. Not seaweed coffee or maybe grasshopper creole crunch. None of that play-food shit they all pretended was something else, not this time, *amigos*, this time honest-to-God pig. Maybe the only pigs this side of Hunan, and only Henry Ortega and Jesus knew where he found them. Mack turned to Chen and gave his best mayoral smile.

"Why don't we just forget the whole thing? Just pack up the pigs there and let Henry be. I'll talk to Major Huang. I'll square all this with the major. That'd be fine with you, now, wouldn't it?"

Chen stopped waving the gun. He looked at Mack. Mack could see wires in his eyes. Chen spoke quickly over his shoulder. Two of the troopers lifted the pigs into the chopper.

"Now, that's good," Mack said. "That's the thing you want to do."

Chen walked off past Henry, his face hot as wax from the fire, moving toward the chopper in this jerky little two-step hop, eyes darting every way at once, granting Mack a lopsided half-wit grin that missed him by a good quarter mile. Mack let out a breath. He'd catch hell from Huang, but it was over. Over and done. He turned away, saw Rose in the crowd and then Fleece. Mack waved. Someone gave a quick and sudden cheer. Chen jerked up straight, just reacting to the sound, not thinking any at all, simply bringing the pistol up like the doctor hit a nerve, the gun making hardly any noise, the whole thing over in a blink and no time to stop it or bring it back. Henry blew over like a leaf, taking his time, collapsing with no skill or imagination, nothing like Anthony Quinn would play the scene.

"Oh, shit, now don't do that." Mack said, knowing this was clearly all a mistake. "Christ, you don't want to do that!"

Someone threw a rock, maybe Jase. Troopers raised their rifles and backed off. A soldier near Chen pushed him roughly toward the chopper. Chen looked deflated. The rotors whined up and blew sand. Mack shut it out, turned it back. It was catching up faster than he liked. He wished Chen had forgotten to take the pigs. The thought seemed less than noble. He considered some gesture of defiance. Burn rice in Galveston harbor. They could all wear Washington masks. He knew what they'd do was nothing at all, and that was fine because Henry would get up in just a minute and they'd all go in the diner and have a laugh. Maybe Jase had another jar of wine. Mack was certain he could put this back together and make it right. He could do it. If he didn't turn around and look at Henry, he could do it. . . .

# GENE WOLFE

## All the Hues of Hell

Here's an unsettling question: If you see a ghost, does the ghost also see *you?*

Gene Wolfe is perceived by many critics as one of the best SF and fantasy writers working today—perhaps *the* best. His tetralogy *The Book of the New Sun*—consisting of *The Shadow of the Torturer. The Claw of the Conciliator, The Sword of the Lictor*, and *The Citadel of the Autarch*—is being hailed as a masterpiece, quite probably the standard against which all subsequent science-fantasy books of the '80s will be judged; ultimately, it may prove to be as influential as J.R.R. Tolkien's *Lord of the Rings* or T.H. White's *The Once and Future King. The Shadow of the Torturer* won the World Fantasy Award. *The Claw of the Conciliator* won the Nebula Award. Wolfe also won a Nebula Award for his story "The Death of Doctor Island." His other books include *Peace, The Fifth Head of Cerberus*, and *The Devil in a Forest*. His short fiction—including some of the best stories of the '70s—has been collected in *The Island of Doctor Death and Other Stories, Gene Wolfe's Book of Days*, and *The Wolfe Archipelago*. His most recent books are *Soldier of the Mist* and *The Urth of the New Sun*. Wolfe lives in Barrington, Illinois, with his family.

# ALL THE HUES OF HELL

## Gene Wolfe

*Three with egg roll,* Kyle thought. *Soon four without—if this shadow world really has (oh, sacred!) life.* The *Egg* was still rolling, still spinning to provide mock gravitation.

Yet the roar of the sharply angled guidance jets now seeped only faintly into the hold, and the roll was slower and slower, the feeling of weight weaker and weaker.

The *Egg* was in orbit . . . around nothing.

Or at least around nothing visible. As its spin decreased, its ports swept the visible universe. Stars that were in fact galaxies flowed down the synthetic quartz, like raindrops down a canopy. Once Kyle caught sight of their mother ship; the *Shadow Show* herself looked dim and ghostly in the faint light. Of the planet they orbited, there was no trace. Polyaris screamed and took off, executing a multicolored barrel-roll with outstretched wings through the empty hold; like all macaws, Polyaris doted on microgravity.

In his earphones Marilyn asked, "Isn't it pretty, Ky?" But she was admiring her computer simulation, not his ecstatic bird: an emerald forest three hundred meters high, sparkling sapphire lakes, suddenly a vagrant strip of beach golden as her hair, and the indigo southern ocean.

One hundred and twenty degrees opposed to them both, Skip answered instead, and not as Kyle himself would have. "No, it isn't." There was a note in Skip's voice that Kyle had noticed, and worried over, before.

Marilyn seemed to shrug. "Okay, darling, it's not really anything to us—less even than ultraviolet. But—"

"I can see it," Skip told her.

Marilyn glanced across the empty hold toward Kyle.

He tried to keep his voice noncommittal as he whispered to his mike: "You can see it, Skip?"

Skip did not reply. Polyaris chuckled to herself. Then silence (the utter, deadly quiet of nothingness, of the void where shadow matter ruled and writhed invisible) filled the *Egg*. For a wild instant, Kyle wondered whether silence itself might not be a manifestation of shadow matter, a dim insubstance felt only in its mass and gravity, its unseen heaviness. Galaxies drifted lazily over the ports, in a white *Egg* robbed of Up and Down. Their screens were solid sheets of deepest blue.

Skip broke the silence. "Just let me show it to you, Kyle. Allow me, Marilyn, to show you what it actually looks like."

"Because you really know, Skip?"

"Yes, because I really know, Kyle. Don't you remember, either of you, what they said?"

Kyle was watching Marilyn across the hold; he saw her shake her head. "Not all of it." Her voice was cautious. "They said so much, darling, after all. They said quite a lot of things."

Skip sounded as though he were talking to a child. "What the Life Support people said. The thing, the only *significant* thing, they did say."

Still more carefully, Marilyn asked, "And what was that, darling?"

"That one of us would die."

An island sailed across her screen, an emerald set in gold and laid upon blue velvet.

Kyle said, "That's my department, Skip. Life Support told us there was a real chance—perhaps as high as one in twenty—that one of you would die, outbound from Earth or on the trip back. They were being conservative; I would have estimated it as one in one hundred."

Marilyn murmured, "I think I'd better inform the Director."

Kyle agreed.

"And they were right," Skip said. "Kyle, I'm the one. I died on the way out. I passed away, but you two followed me."

Ocean and isle vanished from all the screens, replaced by a blinking cursor and the word DIRECTOR.

Marilyn asked, "Respiration monitor, L. Skinner Jansen."

Kyle swiveled to watch his screen. The cursor swept from side to side without any sign of inhalation or exhalation, and for a moment he was taken aback. Then Skip giggled.

Marilyn's sigh filled Kyle's receptors. "The programming wizard. What did you do, Skip? Turn down the gain?"

"That wasn't necessary. It happens automatically." Skip giggled again.

Kyle said slowly, "You're not dead, Skip. Believe me, I've seen many dead men. I've cut up their bodies and examined every organ; I know dead men, and you're not one of them."

"Back on the ship, Kyle. My former physical self is lying in the *Shadow Show*, dead."

Marilyn said, "Your physical self is right here, darling, with Ky and me." And then to the Director: "Sir, is L. Skinner Jansen's module occupied?"

The trace vanished, replaced by NEGATIVE: JANSEN 1'S MODULE IS EMPTY.

"Console," Skip himself ordered.

Kyle did not turn to watch Skip's fingers fly across the keys.

After a moment Skip said, "You see, this place—the formal name of our great republic is Hades, by the way—looks the way it does only because of the color gradations you assigned the gravimeter data. I'm about to show you its true colors, as the expression has it."

A blaze of 4.5, 6, and 7.8 ten-thousandths millimeter light, Polyaris fluttered away to watch Skip. When he made no attempt to shoo her off, she perched on a red emergency lever and cocked an eye like a bright black button toward his keyboard.

Kyle turned his attention back to his screen. The letters faded, leaving only the blue southern ocean. As he watched, it darkened to sable. Tiny flames of ocher, citron, and cinnabar darted from the crests of the waves.

"See what I mean?" Skip asked. "We've been sent to bring a demon back to Earth—or maybe just a damned soul. I don't care. I'm going to stay right here."

Kyle looked across the vacant white hold toward Marilyn.

"I can't," she whispered. "I just can't, Ky. You do it."

"All right, Marilyn." He plugged his index finger into the Exchange socket, so that he sensed rather than saw the letters overlaying the hellish sea on the screens: KAPPA UPSILON LAMBDA 23011 REPORTS JANSEN 1 PSYCHOTIC. CAN YOU CONFIRM, JANSEN 2?

"Confirmed, Marilyn Jansen."

RESTRAINT ADVISED.

Marilyn said, "I'm afraid restraint's impossible as long as we're in the *Egg*, sir."

DO NOT ABORT YOUR MISSION, JANSEN 2. WILL YOU ACCEPT THE RESTRAINT OF JANSEN 1 WHEN RESTRAINT IS PRACTICAL?

"Accepted whenever practical," Marilyn said. "Meanwhile, we'll proceed with the mission."

SATISFACTORY, the Director said, and signed off.

Skip asked, "So you're going to lock me up, honeybone?"

"I hope that by the time we get back it won't be necessary. Ky, haven't you anything to give him?"

"No specifics for psychosis, Marilyn. Not here. I've got some back on the *Shadow Show*."

Skip ruffled his beard. "Sure. You're going to lock up a ghost." Across the wide hold, Kyle could see he was grinning.

Polyaris picked up the word: "Ghost! *Ghost! Ghost!*" She flapped to the vacant center of the *Egg*, posing like a heraldic eagle and watching to make certain they admired her.

The shoreline of a larger island entered their screens from the right. Its beach was ashes and embers, its forest a forest of flames.

"If we're going to make the grab, Marilyn . . ."

"You're right," she said. Courageously, she straightened her shoulders. The new life within her had already fleshed out her cheeks and swollen her breasts; Kyle felt sure she had never been quite so lovely before. When she put on her helmet, he breathed her name (though only to himself) before he plugged into the simulation that seemed so much more real than a screen.

As a score of pink arms, Marilyn's grav beams dipped into the shadow planet's atmosphere, growing dark and heavy as they pulled up shadow fluid and gases from a lake on the island and whatever winds might ruffle it. Kyle reflected that those arms should be blue instead of black, and told the onboard assistant director to revert to the hues Marilyn had originally programmed.

*Rej*, the assistant director snapped.

And nothing happened. The gravs grew darker still, and the big accelerator jets grumbled at the effort required to maintain *Egg* in orbit. When Kyle glanced toward the hold, he discovered it had acquired a twelve-meter yolk as dark as the eggs Chinese bury for centuries. Polyaris was presumably somewhere in that black yolk, unable to see or feel it. He gave a shrill whistle, and she screamed and fluttered out to perch on his shoulder.

The inky simulation doubled and redoubled, swirling to the turbulence of the fresh shadow matter pumped into the *Egg* by the gravs. Generators sang the spell that kept the shadow "air" and "water" from boiling away in what was to them a high vacuum.

The grumbling of the jets rose to an angry roar.

Skip said, "You've brought Hell in here with us, honeybone. You, not me. Remember that."

Marilyn ignored him, and Kyle told him to keep quiet.

Abruptly the gravitors winked out. A hundred tons or more of the shadow-world's water (whatever that might be) fell back to the surface, fully actual to any conscious entity that might be there. "Rains of frogs and fish, Polyaris," Kyle muttered to his bird. "Remember Charlie Fort?"

Polyaris chuckled, nodding.

Skip said, "Then remember too that when Moses struck the Nile with his staff, the Lord God turned the water to blood."

"You're the one who got into the crayon box, Skip. I'll call you

Moses if you like, but I can hardly call you 'I Am,' after you've just assured us you're not." Kyle was following Marilyn's hunt for an example of the dominant life form, less than a tenth of his capacity devoted to Polyaris and Skip.

"You will call me *Master*!"

Kyle grinned, remembering the holovamp of an ancient film. "No, Skip. For as long as you're ill, I am the master. Do you know I've been waiting half my life to use that line?"

Then he saw it, three quarters of a second, perhaps, after Marilyn had: an upright figure striding down a fiery beach. Its bipedal locomotion was not a complete guarantee of dominance and intelligence, to be sure; ostriches had never ruled a world and never would, no matter how big a pest they became on Mars. But—yes—those powerful forelimbs were surely GP manipulators and not mere weapons. *Now, Marilyn! Now!*

As though she had heard him, a pink arm flicked down. For an instant the shadow man floated, struggling wildly to escape, the gravitation of his shadow world countered by their gravitor; then he flashed toward them. Kyle swiveled to watch the black sphere splash (there could be no other word for it) and, under the prodding of the gravs, recoalesce. They were four.

In a moment more, their shadow man bobbed to the surface of the dark and still-trembling yolk. To him, Kyle reflected, they were not there; the *Egg* was not there. To him it must seem that he floated upon a watery sphere suspended in space.

And possibly that was more real than the computer-enhanced vision he himself inhabited, a mere cartoon created from one of the weakest forces known to physics. He unplugged, and at once the *Egg*'s hold was white and empty again.

Marilyn took off her helmet. "All right, Ky, from here on it's up to you—unless you want something more from the surface?"

Kyle congratulated her and shook his head.

"Darling, are you feeling any better?"

Skip said levelly, "I'm okay now. I think that damned machine must have drugged me."

"Ky? That seems pretty unlikely."

"We should de-energize or destroy him, if we can't revise his programming."

Marilyn shook her head. "I doubt that we could reprogram him. Ky, what do you think?"

"A lot of it's hard-wired, Marilyn, and can't be altered without new boards. I imagine Skip could revise my software if he put his mind to it, though it might take him quite a while. He's very good at that sort of thing."

Skip said, "And you're a very dangerous device, Kyle."

Shaking his head, Kyle broke out the pencil-thin cable he had used so often in training exercises. One end jacked into the console, the other into a small socket just above his hips. When both connections were made, he was again in the cybernetic cartoon where true matter and shadow matter looked equally real.

It was still a cartoon with colors by Skip: Marilyn's skin shone snow-white, her lips were burning scarlet, her hair like burnished brass, and her eyes blue fire; Skip himself had become a black-bearded satyr, with a terra-cotta complexion and cruel crimson lips. Kyle tightened both ferrules firmly, tested his jets, released his safety harness, and launched himself toward the center of the *Egg*, making Polyaris crow with delight.

The shadow man drifted into view as they neared the black yolk. He was lying upon what Kyle decided must be his back; on the whole he was oddly anthropomorphic, with recognizable head, neck, and shoulders. Binocular organs of vision seemed to have vanished behind small folds of skin, and Kyle would have called his respiration rapid in a human.

Marilyn asked, "How does he look, Ky?"

"Like hell," Kyle muttered. "I'm afraid he may be in shock. At least, shock's what I'd say if he were one of you. As it is, I . . ." He let the sentence trail away.

There were strange, blunt projections just above the organs that appeared to be the shadow man's ears. Absently, Kyle tried to palpate them; his hand met nothing, and vanished as it passed into the shadow man's cranium.

The shadow man opened his eyes.

Kyle jerked backward, succeeding only in throwing himself into a slow spin that twisted his cable.

Marilyn called, "What's the matter, Ky?"

"Nothing," Kyle told her. "I'm jumpy, that's all."

The shadow man's eyes were closed again. His arms, longer than a human's and more muscled than a body builder's, twitched and were still. Kyle began the minute examination required by the plan.

When it was complete, Skip asked, "How'd it go, Kyle?"

He shrugged. "I couldn't see his back. The way you've got the shadow water keyed, it's like ink."

Marilyn said, "Why don't you change it, Skip? Make it blue but translucent, the way it's supposed to be."

Skip sounded apologetic. "I've been trying to; I've been trying to change everything back. I can't, or anyway not yet. I don't remember just what I did, but I put some kind of block on it."

Kyle shrugged again. "Keep trying, Skip, please."

"Yes, please try, darling. Now buckle up, everybody. Time to rendezvous."

Kyle disconnected his cable and pulled his harness around him. After a moment's indecision, he plugged into the console as well.

If he had been unable to see it, it would have been easy to believe that *Egg*'s acceleration had no effect on the fifty-meter sphere of dark matter at its center; yet that too was mass, and the gravs whimpered like children at the strain of changing its speed and direction, their high wail audible—to Kyle at least—above the roaring of the jets. The black sphere stretched into a sooty tear. Acceleration was agony for Polyaris as well; Kyle cupped her fragile body in his free hand to ease her misery as much as he could.

Somewhere so far above the *Egg* that the gravity well of the shadow planet had almost ceased to make any difference and words like *above* held little meaning, the *Shadow Show* was unfolding to receive them, preparing itself to embed the newly fertilized *Egg* in an inner wall. For a moment Kyle's thoughts soared, drunk on the beauty of the image.

Abruptly the big jets fell silent. The *Egg* had achieved escape velocity.

Marilyn returned control of *Egg* to the assistant director. "That's it, folks, until we start guiding in. Unbuckle if you want."

Kyle tossed Polyaris toward the yolk and watched her make a happy circuit of the *Egg*'s interior.

Skip said, "Marilyn, I seem to have a little problem here."

"What is it?"

Kyle took off his harness and retracted it. He unplugged, and the yolk and its shadow man were gone. Only the chortling Polyaris remained.

"I can't get this Goddamned thing off," Skip complained. "The buckle's jammed or something."

Marilyn took off her own acceleration harness and sailed across to look at it. Kyle joined them.

"Here, let me try it," Marilyn said. Her slender fingers, less nimble but more deft than Skip's, pressed the release and jiggled the locking tab; it would not pull free.

Kyle murmured, "I'm afraid you can't release Skip, Marilyn. Neither can I."

She turned to look at him.

"You accepted restraint for Skip, Marilyn. I want to say that in my opinion you were correct to do so."

She began, "You mean—"

"The Director isn't satisfied yet that Skip has recovered, that's all.

Real recoveries aren't usually so quick or so . . ." Kyle paused, searching his dictionary file for the best word. "Convenient. This may be no more than a lucid interval. That happens, quite often. It may be no more than a stratagem."

Skip cursed and tore at the straps.

"Do you mean you can lock us . . . ?"

"No," Kyle said. "I can't. But the Director can, if in his judgment it is indicated."

He waited for Marilyn to speak, but she did not.

"You see, Marilyn, Skip, we tried very hard to prepare for every foreseeable eventuality, and mental illness was certainly one of those. About ten percent of the human population suffers from it at some point in their lives, and so with both of you on board and under a great deal of stress, that sort of problem was certainly something we had to be ready for."

Marilyn looked pale and drained. Kyle added, as gently as he could, "I hope this hasn't been too much of a shock to you."

Skip had opened the cutting blade of his utility knife and was hacking futilely at his straps. Kyle took it from him, closed it, and dropped it into one of his own storage areas.

Marilyn pushed off. He watched her as she flew gracefully across the hold, caught the pilot's-chair grab bar, and buckled herself into the seat; her eyes were shining with tears. As if sensing her distress, Polyaris perched on the bar and rubbed her ear with the side of her feathered head.

Skip muttered, "Go look at your demon, Kyle. Go anyplace but here."

Kyle asked, "Do you still think it's a demon, Skip?"

"You've seen it a lot closer up than I have. What do you think?"

"I don't believe in demons, Skip."

Skip looked calm now, but his fingers picked mechanically at his straps. "What *do* you believe in, Kyle? Do you believe in God? Do you worship Man?"

"I believe in life. Life is my God, Skip, if you want to put it like that."

"Any life? What about a mosquito?"

"Yes, any life. The mosquito won't bite me." Kyle smiled his metal smile.

"Mosquitoes spread disease."

"Sometimes," Kyle admitted. "Then they must be destroyed, the lower life sacrificed to the higher. Skip, your Marilyn is especially sacred to me now. Do you understand that?"

"Marilyn's doomed."

"Why do you say that?"

"Because of the demon, of course. I tried to tell her that she had doomed herself, but it was actually you that doomed her. You were the one who wanted him. You had to have him, you and the Director; and if it hadn't been for you, we could have gone home with a hold full of dark matter and some excuse."

"But you aren't doomed, Skip? Only Marilyn?"

"I'm dead and damned, Kyle. My doom has caught up with me. I've hit bottom. You know that expression?"

Kyle nodded.

"People talk about hitting bottom and bouncing back up. If you can bounce, that isn't the bottom. When somebody gets where I am, there's no bouncing back, not ever."

"If you're really dead, Skip, how can the straps hold you? I wouldn't think that an acceleration harness could hold a lost soul, or even a ghost."

"They're not holding me," Skip told him. "It was just that at the last moment I didn't have guts enough to let Marilyn see I was really gone. I'd loved her. I don't anymore—you can't love anything or anyone except yourself where I am. But—"

"Can you get out of your seat, Skip? Is that what you're saying, that you can get out without unfastening the buckle?"

Skip nodded slowly, his dark eyes (inscrutable eyes, Kyle thought) never leaving Kyle's face. "And I can see your demon, Kyle. I know you can't see him because you're not hooked up. But I can."

"You can see him now, Skip?"

"Not now—he's on the far side of the black ball. But I'll be able to see him when he floats around to this side again."

Kyle returned to his seat and connected the cable as he had before. The black yolk sprang into being again; the shadow man was facing him—in fact glaring at him with burning yellow eyes. He asked the Director to release Skip.

Together they drifted toward the center of the *Egg*. Kyle made sure their trajectory carried them to the side of the yolk away from the shadow man; and when the shadow man was no longer in view, he held Skip's arm and stopped them both with a tug at the cable. "Now that I know you can see him, too, Skip, I'd like you to point him out to me."

Skip glanced toward the watery miniature planet over which they hovered like flies—or perhaps merely toward the center of the hold. "Is this a joke? I've told you, I can see him." A joyous blue and yellow comet, Polyaris erupted from the midnight surface, braking on flapping wings to examine them sidelong.

"That's why I need your input, Skip," Kyle said carefully. "I'm not certain the feed I'm getting is accurate. If you can apprehend shadow matter directly, I can use your information to check the simulation. Can you still see the demon? Indicate his position, please."

Skip hesitated. "He's not here, Kyle. He must be on the other side. Shall we go around and have a look?"

"The water's still swirling quite a bit. It should bring him to us before long."

Skip shrugged. "Okay, Kyle, you're the boss. I guess you always were."

"The Director's our captain, Skip. That's why we call him what we do. Can you see the demon yet?" A hand and part of one arm had floated into view around the curve of the yolk.

"No. Not yet. Do you have a soul, Kyle?"

Kyle nodded. "It's called my original monitor. I've seen a printout, though of course I didn't read it all; it was very long."

"Then when you're destroyed it may be sent here. Here comes your demon, by the way."

Kyle nodded.

"I suppose it may be put into one of these horrors. They seem more machine than human, at least to me."

"No," Kyle told him. "They're truly alive. They're shadow life, Skip, and since this one is the only example we have, just now it must be the most precious life in the universe to you, to Marilyn, and to me. Do you think he sees us?"

"He sees me," Skip said grimly.

"When I put my fingers into his brain, he opened his eyes." Kyle mused. "It was as though he felt them there."

"Maybe he did."

Kyle nodded. "Yes, possibly he did. The brain is such a sensitive mechanism that perhaps a gravitational disturbance as weak as that results in stimulation, if it is uneven. Put your hand into his head, please. I want to watch. You say he's a demon—pretend you're going to gouge out his eyes."

"You think I'm crazy!" Skip shouted. "Well, I'm telling you, you're crazy!"

Startled, Marilyn twisted in her pilot's chair to look at them.

"I've explained to you that he *sees* me," Skip said a little more calmly. "I'm not getting within his reach!"

"Touch his nose for me, Skip. Like this." Kyle lengthened one arm until his fingers seemed to brush the dark water several meters from the drifting shadow man's hideous face. "Look here, Skip. I'm not afraid."

Skip screamed.

* * *

"Have I time?" Kyle asked. He was holding the grab bar of Marilyn's control chair. In the forward port, the *Shadow Show* was distinctly visible.

"We've a few minutes yet," Marilyn told him. "And I want to know. I have to, Ky. He's the father of my child. Can you cure him?"

"I think so, Marilyn, though your correcting the simulator hues has probably helped Skip more than anything I've done thus far."

Kyle glanced appreciatively in the direction of the yolk. It was a translucent blue, as it should have been all along, and the shadow man who floated there looked more like a good-natured caricature of a human being than a demon. His skin was a dusty pinkish brown, his eyes the cheerful bright-yellow of daffodils. It seemed to Kyle that they flickered for a moment, as though to follow Polyaris in her flight across the hold. Perhaps a living entity of shadow matter could apprehend true matter after all—that would require a thorough investigation as soon as they were safely moored in the *Shadow Show*.

"And he can't really see shadow matter, Ky?"

Kyle shook his head. "No more than you or I can, Marilyn. He thought he could, you understand, at least on some level. On another he knew he couldn't and was faking it quite cleverly." Kyle paused, then added, "Freud did psychology a considerable disservice when he convinced people that the human mind thinks on only three levels. There are really a great many more than that, and there's no question but that the exact number varies between individuals."

"But for a while you really believed he might be able to, from what you've told me."

"At least I was willing to entertain the thought, Marilyn. Occasionally you can help people like Skip just by allowing them to test their delusional systems. What I found was that he had been taking cues from me—mostly from the direction of my eyes, no doubt. It would be wrong for you to think of that as lying. He honestly believed that when you human beings died, your souls came here, to this shadow planet of a shadow system, in a shadow galaxy. And that he himself was dead."

Marilyn shook her head in dismay. "But that's insane, Ky. Just crazy."

*She has never looked this lovely*, Kyle thought. Aloud he said, "Mental illness is often a way of escaping responsibility, Marilyn. You may wish to consider that. Death is another, and you may wish to consider that also."

For a second Marilyn hesitated, biting her lip. "You love me, don't you, Ky?"

"Yes, I do, Marilyn. Very much."

"And so does Skip, Ky." She gave him a small, sad smile. "I suppose I'm the luckiest woman alive, or the unluckiest. The men I like most both love me, but one's having a breakdown. . . . I shouldn't have started this, should I?"

"While the other is largely inorganic," Kyle finished for her. "But it's really not such a terrible thing to be loved by someone like me, Marilyn. We—"

Polyaris shrieked and shrieked again—not her shrill cry of pleasure or even her outraged squawk of pain, but the uncanny, piercing screech that signaled a prowling ocelot: Danger! *Fire!* Flood! INVASION and *CATASTROPHE!*

She was fluttering about the shadow man, and the shadow man was no longer a dusty pinkish brown. As Kyle stared, he faded to gray, then to white. His mouth opened. He crumpled, slowly and convulsively, into a fetal ball.

Horrified, Kyle turned to Marilyn. But Marilyn was self-absorbed, her hands clasping her belly. "It moved, Ky! It just moved. *I felt life!*"

# MICHAEL MCDOWELL

## Halley's Passing

Here's a closely observed (and very scary) study of a very methodical man of a *very* unusual sort.

Michael McDowell is the author of more than thirty books, including *Cold Moon over Babylon, The Amulet*, and the six-volume serial novel *Blackwater*. McDowell has also worked extensively in television, and recently co-scripted his first feature film, *Beetlejuice*.

# HALLEY'S PASSING

## Michael McDowell

"Would you like to keep that on your credit card?" asked the woman on the desk. Her name was Donna and she was dressed like Snow White because it was Halloween.

"No," said Mr. Farley, "I think I'll pay cash." Mr. Farley counted out twelve ten-dollar bills and laid them on the counter. Donna made sure there were twelve, then gave Mr. Farley change of three dollars and twenty-six cents. He watched to make certain she tore up the charge slips he had filled out two days before. She ripped them into thirds. Original copy, Customer's Receipt, Bank Copy, two intervening carbons—all bearing the impress of Mr. Farley's Visa card and his signature—they went into a trash basket that was invisible beneath the counter.

"Good-bye," said Mr. Farley. He took up his one small suitcase and walked out the front door of the hotel. His suitcase was light blue Samsonite with an X of tape underneath the handle to make it recognizable at an airport baggage claim.

It was seven o'clock. Mr. Farley took a taxi from the hotel to the airport. In the back of the taxi, he opened his case and took out a black loose-leaf notebook and wrote in it:

10385 *Double Tree Inn*
*Dallas, Texas*
*Checkout 1900/$116.74/*
*Donna*

The taxi took Mr. Farley to the airport and cost him $12.50 with a tip that was generous but not too generous.

Mr. Farley went to the PSA counter and picked up an airline schedule and put it into the pocket of his jacket. Then he went to the Eastern counter and picked up another schedule. In a bar called the Range Room he sat at a small round table. He ordered a vodka martini from a waitress named Alyce. When she had brought it to him, and he had paid her and she had gone away, he opened his suitcase, pulled out his black loose-leaf notebook and added the notations:

*Taxi $10.20 + 2.30/#1718*
*Drink at Airport Bar*
*$2.75 + .75/Alyce*

He leafed backwards through the notebook and discovered that he had flown PSA three times in the past two months. Therefore he looked into the Eastern Schedule first. He looked on page 23 first because $2.30 had been the amount of the tip to the taxi driver. On page 23 of the Eastern airline schedule were flights from Dallas to Milwaukee, Wisconsin, and Mobile, Alabama. All of the flights to Milwaukee changed in Cincinnati or St. Louis. A direct flight to Mobile left at 9:10 p.m. arriving 10:50 p.m. Mr. Farley returned the black loose-leaf notebook to his case and got up from the table, spilling his drink in the process.

"I'm very sorry," he said to Alyce, and left another dollar bill for her inconvenience.

"That's all right," said Alyce.

Mr. Farley went to the Eastern ticket counter and bought a coach ticket to Mobile, Alabama. He asked for an aisle seat in the nonsmoking section. He paid in cash and after taking out his black loose-leaf notebook, he checked his blue Samsonite bag. He went through security, momentarily surrendering a ringful of keys. The flight to Mobile departed Gate 15 but Mr. Farley sat in the seats allotted to Gate 13, directly across the way. He read through a copy of *USA Today* and he gave a Snickers bar to a child in a pumpkin costume who trick-or-treated him. He smiled at the child, not because he liked costumes or Halloween or children, but because he was pleased with himself for having been foresightful enough to buy three Snickers bars just in case he ran into trick-or-treating children on Halloween night. He opened his black loose-leaf notebook and amended the notation of his most recent bar tab:

*Drink at Airport Bar*
*$2.75 + 1.75/Alyce*

The flight for Mobile began boarding at 8:55. As the announcement was made for the early accommodation of those with young children or other difficulties, Mr. Farley went into the men's room.

A Latino man in his twenties with a blue shirt and a lock of hair dangling down his neck stood at a urinal, looking at the ceiling and softly farting. His urine splashed against the porcelain wall of the urinal. Mr. Farley went past the urinals and stood in front of the two stalls and peered under them. He saw no legs or feet or shoes but he took the precaution of opening the doors. The stalls were empty, as he suspected, but Mr. Farley did not like to leave such matters to chance. The Latino man, looking downwards, flushed the urinal, zipping his trousers and backing away at the same time. Mr. Farley leaned down and took the Latino man by the waist. He swung the Latino man around so that he was facing the mirrors and the two sinks in the restroom and could see Mr. Farley's face.

"Man—" protested the Latino man.

Mr. Farley rolled his left arm around the Latino man's belt and put his right hand on the Latino man's head. Mr. Farley pushed forward very swiftly with his right hand. The Latino man's head went straight down towards the sink in such a way that the cold-water faucet, shaped like a Maltese Cross, shattered the bone above the Latino man's right eye. Mr. Farley had gauged the strength of his attack so that the single blow served to press the Latino's head all the way down to the porcelain. The chilled aluminum faucet was buried deeply in the Latino man's brain. Mr. Farley took the Latino man's wallet from his back pocket, removed the cash and his Social Security card. He gently dropped the wallet into the sink beneath the Latino man's head and turned on the hot water. Mr. Farley peered into the sink, and saw blood, blackish and brackish swirling into the rusting drain. Retrieving his black loose-leaf notebook from the edge of the left-hand sink where he'd left it, Mr. Farley walked out of the rest room. The Eastern flight to Mobile was boarding all seats and Mr. Farley walked on directly behind a young woman with brown hair and a green scarf and directly in front of a young woman with slightly darker brown hair in a yellow sweater-dress. Mr. Farley sat in Seat 4-C and next to him, in Seat 4-A, was a bearded man in a blue corduroy jacket who fell asleep before take-off. Mr. Farley reached into his pocket and pulled out the bills he'd taken from the Latino man's wallet. There were five five-dollar bills and nine one-dollar bills. Mr. Farley pulled out his own wallet and interleaved the Latino man's bills with his own, mixing them up. Mr. Farley reached into his shirt pocket and pulled out the Latino man's Social Security card, cupping it from sight and slipping it into the Eastern Airlines In-Flight Magazine. He turned on the reading light and opened the magazine. The Social Security card read:

Ignazios Lazo
424-70-4063

Mr. Farley slipped the Social Security card back into his shirt pocket. He exchanged the in-flight magazine for the black loose-leaf notebook in the seat back pocket. He held the notebook in his lap for several minutes while he watched the man in the blue corduroy jacket next to him, timing his breaths by the sweep second hand on his watch. The man seemed genuinely to be asleep. Mr. Farley declined a beverage from the stewardess, who did not wear a name tag, and put his finger to his lips with a smile to indicate that the man in the blue corduroy jacket was sleeping and probably wouldn't want to be disturbed. When the beverage cart was one row behind and conveniently blocking the aisle so that no one could look over his shoulder as he wrote, Mr. Farley opened the black loose-leaf notebook on his lap, and completed the entry for Halloween:

*2155/Ignazios Lazo/c*
*27/Dallas Texas/ Airport/*
*RR/38/Head onto Faucet*

RR meant Rest Room, and Mr. Farley stared at the abbreviation for a few moments, wondering whether he shouldn't write out the words. There was a time when he had been a good deal given to abbreviations, but once, in looking over his book for a distant year, he had come across the notation CRB, and had had no idea what that stood for. Mr. Farley since that time had been careful about his notations. It didn't do to forget things. If you forgot things, you might repeat them. And if you inadvertently fell into a repetitious pattern—well then, you just might get into trouble.

Mr. Farley got up and went into the rest room at the forward end of the passenger cabin. He burned Ignazios Lazo's Social Security card, igniting it with a match torn from a book he had picked up at the casino at the MGM Grand Hotel in Las Vegas. He waited in the rest room till he could no longer smell the nitrate in the air from the burned match, then flushed the toilet, washed his hands, and returned to his seat.

The flight arrived in Mobile at three minutes past eleven. While waiting for his blue Samsonite bag, Mr. Farley went to a Yellow Pages telephone directory for Mobile. His flight from Dallas had been Eastern Flight No. 71, but Mr. Farley was not certain there would be that many hotels and motels in Mobile, Alabama, so he decided on number 36, which was half of 72 (the closest even number to 71). Mr. Farley turned to the pages advertising hotels and counted down thirty-six to the Oasis Hotel. He telephoned and found a room was available for fifty-six dollars. He asked what the cab fare from the airport would be and discovered it would be about twelve dollars, with tip. The reservations clerk asked for Mr. Farley's name, and Mr. Farley, looking down at the credit card in his hand, said, "Mr. T.L. Rachman." He spelled it for the clerk.

Mr. Rachman claimed his bag, and went outside for a taxi. He was first in line, and by 11:30 he had arrived at the Oasis Hotel, downtown in Mobile. In the hotel's Shore Room Lounge, a band was playing in Halloween costume. The clerk on the hotel desk was made up to look like a mummy.

"You go to a lot of trouble here for holidays, I guess," said Mr. Rachman pleasantly.

"Anything for a little change," said the clerk as he pressed Mr. Rachman's MasterCard against three copies of a voucher. Mr. Rachman signed his name on the topmost voucher and took back the card. Clerks never checked signatures at this point, and they never checked them later either, but Mr. Rachman had a practiced hand, at least when it came to imitating a signature.

Mr. Rachman's room was on the fifth and topmost floor, and enjoyed a view down to the street. Mr. Rachman unpacked his small bag, carefully hanging his extra pair of trousers and his extra jacket. He set his extra pair of shoes, with trees inside, into the closet beneath the trousers and jacket. He placed his two laundered shirts inside the topmost bureau drawer, set his little carved box containing an extra watch and two pairs of cufflinks and a tie clip and extra pairs of brown and black shoelaces on top of the bureau, and set his toiletries case next to the sink in the bathroom. He opened his black loose-leaf notebook and though it was not yet midnight, he began the entry for 110185, beneath which he noted:

*110185 Eastern 71 Dallas-Mobile*
*Taxi $9.80 + 1.70*
*Oasis Hotel/4th St*
*T.L. Rachman*

In the bathroom, Mr. Rachman took scissors and cut up the Visa card bearing the name Thomas Farley, and flushed away the pieces. He went down to the lobby and went into the Shore Room Lounge and sat at the bar. He ordered a vodka martini and listened to the band. When the bartender went away to the rest room, Mr. Rachman poured his vodka martini into a basin of ice behind the bar. When the bartender returned, Mr. Rachman ordered another vodka martini.

The cocktail lounge—and every other bar in Mobile—closed at 1 a.m. Mr. Rachman returned to his room, and without ever turning on the light, he sat at his window and looked out into the street. After the laundry truck had arrived, unloaded, and driven off from the service entrance of the Hotel Oasis, Mr. Rachman retreated from the window. It was 4:37 on the morning of the first of November, 1985. Mr. Rachman pulled the shade and drew the curtains. Towards noon, when the maid came to make up the room, Mr. Rachman called out from the bathroom, "I'm taking a bath."

"I'll come back later," the maid called back.

"That's all right," Mr. Rachman said loudly. "Just leave a couple of fresh towels on the bed." He sat on the tile floor and ran his unsleeved arm up and down through the filled tub, making splashing noises.

Mr. Rachman counted his money at sundown. He had four hundred fifty-eight dollars in cash. With all of it in his pocket, Mr. Rachman walked around the block to get his bearings. He had been in Mobile before, but he didn't remember exactly when. Mr. Rachman had his shoes shined in the lobby of a hotel that wasn't the one he was staying in. When he was done, he paid the shoeshine boy seventy-five cents and a quarter tip, and got into the elevator behind a businessman who was carrying a briefcase. The businessman with the briefcase got off on the fourth floor, and just as the doors of the elevator were closing Mr. Rachman startled and said, "Oh this is my floor, too," and jumped off behind the businessman with the briefcase. Mr. Rachman put his hand into his pocket, and jingled his loose change as if he were looking for his room key. The businessman with the briefcase put down his briefcase beside Room 419 and fumbled in his pocket for his own room key. Mr. Rachman stopped and patted all the pockets of his jacket and trousers. "Did I leave it at the desk?" he murmured to himself. The businessman with the briefcase put the key into the lock of Room 419, and smiled a smile that said to Mr. Rachman, *It happens to me all the time, too*. Mr. Rachman smiled a small embarrassed smile, and said, "I sure hope I left it at the desk," and turned and started back down the hall past the businessman with the briefcase.

The businessman and his briefcase were already inside of Room 419 and the door was beginning to shut when Mr. Rachman suddenly changed direction in the hallway and pushed the door open.

"Hey," said the businessman. He held his briefcase up protectively before him. Mr. Rachman shut the door quietly behind him. Room 419 was a much nicer room than his own, though he didn't care for the painting above the bed. Mr. Rachman smiled, though, for the businessman was alone and that was always easier. Mr. Rachman pushed the businessman down on the bed and grabbed the briefcase away from him. The businessman reached for the telephone. The red light was blinking on the telephone telling the businessman he had a message at the desk. Mr. Rachman held the briefcase high above his head and then brought it down hard, giving a little twist to his wrist just at the last so that a corner of the rugged leather case smashed against the bridge of the businessman's nose, breaking it. The businessman gaped, and fell sideways on the bed. Mr. Rachman raised the case again and brought the side of it down against the businessman's cheek with such force that the handle of the case broke off in his hand and the businessman's cheekbones were splintered and shoved up into his right eye. Mr. Rachman took the case in both hands and swung it hard along the length of the businessman's body and caught him square beneath his chin in the midst of a choking scream so that the businessman's lower jaw was shattered, detached, and then embedded in the roof of his mouth. In the businessman's remaining eye was one second more of consciousness and then he was dead. Mr. Rachman turned over the businessman's corpse and took out his wallet, discovering that his name was Edward P. Maguire, and that he was from Sudbury, Massachusetts. He had one hundred and thirty-three dollars in cash, which Mr. Rachman put into his pocket. Mr. Rachman glanced through the credit cards, but took only the New England Bell telephone credit card. Mr. Maguire's briefcase, though battered and bloody, had remained locked, secured by an unknown combination. Mr. Rachman would have taken the time to break it open and examine its contents but the telephone on the bedside table rang. The hotel desk might not have noticed Mr. Maguire's entrance into the hotel, but Mr. Rachman did not want to take a chance that Mr. Maguire's failure to answer the telephone would lead to an investigation. Mr. Rachman went quickly through the dead man's pockets, spilling his change onto the bedspread. He found the key of a Hertz rental car with the tag number indicated on a plastic ring. Mr. Rachman pocketed it. He turned the dead man over once more and pried open his shattered mouth. A thick broth of clotting blood and broken teeth spilled out over the knot of Mr. Maguire's tie. With the tips of two fingers, Mr. Rachman picked out a pointed fragment of incisor, and put it into his mouth, licking the blood from his fingers as he did so. As he peered out into the hallway, Mr. Rachman rolled the broken tooth around the roof of his mouth, and then pressed it there with his tongue till its jagged edge drew blood and he could taste it. No one was in the hall, and Mr. Rachman walked out of Room 419, drawing it closed behind him. He took the elevator down to the basement garage, and walked slowly about till he found Mr. Maguire's rented car. He drove out of the hotel garage and slowly circled several streets till he found a stationery store that was still open. Inside he bought a detailed street map of Mobile. He studied it by the interior roof light of the rented car. For two hours he drove through the outlying suburbs of the city, stopping now and then before a likely house, and noting its number on the map with a black felt-tip marker. At half-past eleven he returned to the Oasis Hotel and parked the rental car so that it would be visible from his window. He went up to his room, and noted in his diary, under 110185:

> *1910/Edward P Maguire/c*
> *43/Mobile Alabama/Hotel*
> *Palafox 419/1133/Jaw and*
> *Briefcase*

On a separate page in the back of the loose-leaf notebook, he added:

> *Edward P Maguire*
> *(110185)/9 Farmer's*
> *Road/Sudbury MA 01776/*
> *617 392 3690*

That was just in case. Sometimes Mr. Rachman liked to visit widows. It added to the complexity of the pattern, and so far as Mr. Rachman was concerned, the one important thing was to maintain a pattern that couldn't be analyzed, that was arbitrary in every point. That was why he sometimes made use of the page of notations in the back of the book—because too much randomness was a pattern in itself. If he sometimes visited a widow after he had met her husband, he broke up the pattern of entirely unconnected deaths. Mr. Rachman, who was methodical to the very core of his being, spent a great percentage of his waking time in devising methods to make each night's work seem entirely apart from the last's. Mr. Rachman, when he was young, had lived in a great city and had simply thought that its very size would hide him. But even in a great city, his very pattern of randomness had become apparent, and he had very nearly been uncovered. Mr. Rachman judged that he would have to do better, and he began to travel. In the time since then, he had merely refined his technique. He varied the length of his stays, he varied his acquaintance. That's what he called them, and it wasn't a euphemism—he simply had no other word for them, and really, they were the people he got to know best, if only for a short time. He varied his methods, he varied the time of the evening, and he even varied his variety. Sometimes he would arrange to meet three old woman in a row, three old women who lived in similar circumstances in a small geographical area, and then he would move on, and his next acquaintance would be a young man who exchanged his favors for cash. Mr. Rachman imagined a perfect pursuer, and expended a great deal of energy in evading and tricking this imaginary hound. Increasingly, over the years Mr. Rachman's greatest satisfaction lay in evading this nonexistent, dogged detective. His only fear was that there was a pattern in the carpet he wove which was invisible to him, but perfectly apparent to anyone who looked at it from a certain angle.

No one took notice of Mr. Maguire's rented car that night. Next morning Mr. Rachman told the chambermaid he wasn't feeling well and would spend the day in bed, so she needn't make it up. But he let her clean the bathroom as she hadn't been able to do the day before. He lay with his arm over his eyes. "I hope you feel better," said the chambermaid. "Do you have any aspirin?"

"I've already taken some," said Mr. Rachman, "but thank you. I think I'll just try to sleep."

That night, Mr. Rachman got up and watched the rented car. It had two parking tickets on the windshield. At 11:30 p.m. he went downstairs, got into the car, and drove around three blocks slowly, just in case he was being followed. He was not, so far as he could tell. He opened his map of Mobile, and picked the house he'd marked that was nearest a crease. It was 117 Shadyglade Lane in a suburb called Spring Hill. Mr. Rachman drove on, to the nearest of the other places he'd marked. He stopped in front of a house on Live Oak Street, about a mile away. No lights burned. He turned into the driveway and waited for fifteen minutes. He saw no movement in the house. He got out of his car, closing the door loudly, and walked around to the back door, not making any effort to be quiet.

There was no door bell so he pulled open the screen door and knocked loudly. He stood back and looked up at the back of the house. No lights came on that he could see. He knocked more loudly, then without waiting for a response he kicked at the base of the door, splintering it in its frame. He went into the kitchen, but did not turn on the light.

"Anybody home?" Mr. Rachman called out as he went from the kitchen into the dining room. He picked up a round glass bowl from the sideboard and hurled it at a picture. The bowl shattered noisily. No one came. Mr. Rachman looked in the other two rooms on the ground floor, then went upstairs, calling again, "It's Mr. Rachman!"

He went into the first bedroom, and saw that it belonged to a teenaged boy. He closed the door. He went into another bedroom and saw that it belonged to the parents of the teenaged boy. He went through the bureau drawers, but found no cash. The father's shirts, however, were in Mr. Rachman size—16½ × 33—and he took two that still bore the paper bands from the laundry. Mr. Rachman checked the other rooms of the second floor just in case, but the house was empty. Mr. Rachman went out the back door again, crossed the backyard of the house, and pressed through the dense ligustrum thicket there. He found himself in the backyard of a ranch house with a patio and a brick barbeque. Mr. Rachman walked to the patio and picked up a pot of geraniums and hurled it through the sliding glass doors of the den. Then he walked quickly inside the house, searching for a light switch. A man in pajamas suddenly lurched through a doorway, and he too was reaching for the light switch. Mr. Rachman put one hand on the man's shoulder, and with his other he grabbed the man's wrist. Then Mr. Rachman gave a twist, and smashed the back of the man's elbow against the edge of a television set with such force that all the bones there shattered at once. Mr. Rachman then took the man by the waist, lifted him up and carried him over to the broken glass door. He turned him sideways and then pushed him against the long line of broken glass, only making sure that the shattered glass was embedded deep into his face and neck. When Mr. Rachman let the man go, he remained standing, so deep had the edge of broken door penetrated his head and chest. Just in case, Mr. Rachman pressed harder. Blood poured out over Mr. Rachman's hands. With a nod of satisfaction, Mr. Rachman released the man in pajamas and walked quickly back across the patio and disappeared into the shrubbery again. On the other side, he looked back, and could see the lights going on in the house. He heard a woman scream. He took out a handkerchief to cover his bloody hands and picked up the shirts which he'd left on the back porch of the first house. Then he got into his car and drove around till he came to a shopping mall. He parked near half a dozen other cars—probably belonging to night watchmen—and took off his blood-stained jacket. He tossed it out the window. He took off his shirt, and wiped off the blood that covered his hands. He threw that out of the window, too. He put on a fresh shirt and drove back to the Oasis Hotel. He parked the car around the block, threw the keys into an alleyway, and went back up to his room. In his black looseleaf notebook he wrote, under 110285:

*1205/unk./mc 35/Spring*
*Hill (Mobile) Alabama/*
*$0/Broken glass*

Mr. Rachman spent the rest of the night simply reading through his black loose-leaf notebook, not trying to remember what he could not easily bring to mind, but merely playing the part of the tireless investigator trying to discern a pattern. Mr. Rachman did not think he was fooling himself when he decided that he could not.

When the chambermaid came the next day, Mr. Rachman sat on a chair with the telephone cradled between his ear and his shoulder, now and then saying, "Yes" or "No, not at all" or "Once more and let me check those numbers", as he made notations on a pad of paper headed up with a silhouette cartouche of palm trees.

Mr. Rachman checked out of the Oasis Hotel a few minutes after sundown, and smiled a polite smile when the young woman on the desk apologized for having to charge him for an extra day. The bill came to $131.70 and Mr. Rachman paid in cash. As he watched the young woman on the desk tear up the credit card receipt, he remarked, "I don't like to get near my limit," and the young woman on the desk replied, "I won't even apply for one."

"But they sometimes come in handy, Marsha," said Mr. Rachman, employing her name aloud as a reminder to note it later in his diary. Nametags were a great help to Mr. Rachman in his travels, and he had been pleased to watch the rapid spread of their use. Before 1960 or thereabouts, hardly anyone had worn a nametag.

Mr. Rachman drove around downtown Mobile for an hour or so, just in case something turned up. Once, driving slowly down an alleyway that was scarcely wider than his car, a prostitute on yellow heels lurched at him out of a recessed doorway, plunging a painted hand through his rolled-down window. Mr. Rachman said, "Wrong sex," and drove on.

"Faggot!" the prostitute called after him.

Mr. Rachman didn't employ prostitutes except in emergencies, that is to say, when it was nearly dawn and he had not managed to make anyone's acquaintance for the night. Then he resorted to prostitutes, but not otherwise. Too easy to make that sort of thing a habit.

And habits were what Mr. Rachman had to avoid.

He drove to the airport, and took a ticket from a mechanized gate. He drove slowly around the parking lot, which was out of doors, and to one side of the airport buildings. He might have taken any of several spaces near the terminal, but Mr. Rachman drove slowly about the farther lanes. He could not drive very long, for fear of drawing the attention of a guard.

A blue Buick Skylark pulled into a space directly beneath a burning sodium lamp. Mr. Rachman made a sudden decision. He parked his car six vehicles down, and quickly climbed out with his blue Samsonite suitcase. He strode towards the terminal with purpose, coming abreast of the blue Buick Skylark. A woman, about thirty-five years old, was pulling a dark leather bag out of the backseat of the car. Mr. Rachman stopped suddenly, put down his case and patted the pockets of his trousers in alarm.

"My keys . . ." he said aloud.

Then he checked the pockets of his suit jacket. He often used the forgotten keys ploy. It didn't really constitute a habit, for it was an action that would never appear later as evidence.

The woman with the suitcase came between her car and the recreational vehicle that was parked next to it. She had a handbag over her shoulder. Mr. Rachman suddenly wanted very badly to make this one work for him. For one thing, this was a woman, and he hadn't made the acquaintance of a female since he'd been in Mobile. That would disrupt the pattern a bit. She had a purse, which might contain money. He liked the shape and size of her luggage, too.

"Excuse me," she said politely, trying to squeeze by him. "I think I locked my keys in my car," said Mr. Rachman, moving aside for her.

She smiled a smile which suggested that she was sorry but that there was nothing she could do about it.

She had taken a single step towards the terminal when Mr. Rachman lifted his right leg and took a long stride forward. He caught the sole of his shoe against her right calf, and pushed her down to the pavement. The woman crashed to her knees on the pavement with such force that the bones of her knees shattered. She started to fall forward, but Mr. Rachman spryly caught one arm around her waist and placed his other hand on the back of her head. In his clutching fingers, he could feel the scream building in her mouth. He swiftly turned her head and smashed her face into the high-beam headlight of the blue Buick Skylark. He jerked her head out again, and even before the broken glass had spilled down the front of her suit jacket, Mr. Rachman plunged her head into the low-beam headlight. He jerked her head out, and awkwardly straddling her body, he pushed her between her Buick and the next car in the lane, a silver VW GTI. He pushed her head hard down against the pavement four times, though he was sure she was dead already. He let go her head, and peered at his fingers in the light of the sodium lamp. He smelled the splotches of blood on his third finger and his palm and his thumb. He tasted the blood, and then wiped it off on the back of the woman's bare leg. Another car turned down the lane, and Mr. Rachman threw himself onto the pavement, reaching for the woman's suitcase before the automobile lights played over it. He pulled it into the darkness between the cars. The automobile drove past. Mr. Rachman pulled the woman's handbag off her shoulder, and then rolled her beneath her car. Fishing inside the purse for her car keys, he opened the driver's door and unlocked the back door. He climbed into the car and pulled in her bag with him. He emptied its contents onto the floor, then crawled across the back seat and opened the opposite door. He retrieved his blue Samsonite suitcase from beneath the recreational vehicle where he'd kicked it as he struck up his acquaintance with the woman. The occupants of the car that had passed a few moments before walked in front of the Buick. Mr. Rachman ducked behind the back seat for a moment till he could no longer hear the voices—a man and a woman. He opened his Samsonite case and repacked all his belongings into the woman's black leather case. He reached into the woman's bag and pulled out her wallet. He took her Alabama driver's license and a Carte Blanche credit card that read A. B. Frost rather than Aileen Frost. He put the ticket in his pocket. Mr. Rachman was mostly indifferent to the matter of fingerprints, but he had a superstition against carbon paper of any sort.

Mr. Rachman surreptitiously checked the terminal display and found that a plane was leaving for Birmingham, Alabama, in twenty minutes. It would probably begin to board in five minutes. Mr. Rachman rushed to the Delta ticket counter, and said breathlessly, "Am I too late to get on the plane to Birmingham? I haven't bought my ticket yet."

Mark, the airline employee said, "You're in plenty of time—the plane's been delayed."

This was not pleasant news. Mr. Rachman was anxious to leave Mobile. Aileen Frost was hidden beneath her car, it was true, and might not be found for a day or so—but there was always a chance that someone would find her quickly. Mr. Rachman didn't want to be around for any part of the investigation. Also, he couldn't now say, "Well, I think I'll go to Atlanta instead." That would draw dangerous attention to himself. Perhaps he should just return to Mr. Maguire's car and drive away. The evening was still early. He could find a house in the country, make the acquaintance of anyone who lived there, sit out quietly the daylight hours, and leave early the following evening.

"How long a delay?" Mr. Rachman asked Mark.

"Fifteen minutes," said Mark pleasantly, already making out the ticket. "What name?"

Not Frost, of course. And Rachman was already several days old.

"Como," he said, not knowing why.

"Perry?" asked Mark with a laugh.

"Peter," said Mr. Como.

Mr. Como sighed. He was already half enamoured of his alternative plan. But he couldn't leave now. Mark might remember a man who had rushed in, then rushed out again because he couldn't brook a fifteen-minute delay. The ticket from Mobile to Birmingham was $89, five dollars more than Mr. Como had predicted in his mind. Putting his ticket into the inside pocket of his jacket that did not contain Aileen Frost's ticket to Wilmington, Mr. Como went into the men's room and locked himself into a stall. Under the noise of the flushing toilet, he quickly tore up Aileen Frost's ticket, and stuffed the fragments into his jacket pocket. When he left the stall he washed his hands at the sink until the only other man in the rest room left. Then he wrapped the fragments in a paper towel and stuffed that deep into the waste paper basket. Aileen Frost's license and credit card he slipped into a knitting bag of a woman waiting for a plane to Houston.

Mr. Como had been given a window seat near the front of the plane. The seat beside him was empty. After figuring his expenses for the day, Mr. Como wrote in his black loose-leaf notebook:

*0745/Aileen Frost/fc*
*35/Mobile Airport Parking*
*Lot/$212/Car headlights*

Mr. Como was angry with himself. Two airport killings within a week. That was laziness. Mr. Como had fallen into the lazy, despicable habit of working as early in the evening as possible. This, even though Mr. Como had *never* failed, not a single night, not even when only minutes had remained till dawn. But he tended to fret, and he didn't rest easy till he had got the evening's business out of the way. That was the problem of course. He had no other business. So if he worked early, he was left with a long stretch of hours till he could sleep with the dawn. If he put off till late, he only spent the long hours fretting, wondering if he'd be put to trouble. *Trouble* to Mr. Como meant witnesses (whose acquaintance he had to make as well), or falling back on easy marks—prostitutes, nightwatchmen, hotel workers. Or, worst of all, pursuit and flight, and then some sudden, uncomfortable place to wait out the daylight hours.

On every plane trip, Mr. Como made promises to himself: he'd use even more ingenuity, he'd rely on his expertise and work at late hours as well as early hours, he'd try to develop other interests. Yet he was at the extremity of his ingenuity, late hours fretted him beyond any pleasure he took in making a new acquaintance, and he had long since lost his interest in any pleasure but that moment he saw the blood of each night's new friend. And even that was only a febrile memory of what had once been a hot true necessity of desire.

Before the plane landed, Mr. Como invariably decided that he did too much thinking. For, finally, instinct had never failed him, though everything else—Mr. Como, the world Mr. Como inhabited, and Mr. Como's tastes—everything else changed.

"Ladies and gentlemen," said the captain's voice, "we have a special treat for you tonight. If you'll look out the left side of the plane, and up—towards the Pleiades—you'll see Halley's Comet. You'll see it better from up here than from down below. And I'd advise you to look now, because it won't be back in our lifetimes."

Mr. Como looked out of the window. Most of the other passengers didn't know which stars were the Pleiades, but Mr. Como did. Halley's Comet was a small blur to the right of the small constellation. Mr. Como gladly gave his seat to a young couple who wanted to see the comet. Mr. Como remembered the 1910 visitation quite clearly, and that time the comet had been spectacular. He'd been living in Canada, he thought, somewhere near Halifax. It was high in the sky then, brighter than Venus, with a real tail, and no one had to point it out to you. He tried to remember the time before—1834, he determined with a calculation of his fingernail on the glossy cover of the Delta In-Flight Magazine. But 1834 was beyond his power of recollection. The Comet was surely even brighter then, but where had he been at that time? Before airports, and hotels, and credit cards, and the convenience of nametags. He'd lived in one place then for long periods of time, and hadn't even kept proper records. There'd been a lust then, too, for the blood, and every night he'd done more than merely place an incrimsoned finger to his lips.

But everything had changed, evolved slowly and immeasurably, and he was not what once he'd been. Mr. Como knew he'd change again. The brightness of comets deteriorated with every pass. Perhaps on its next journey around the sun, Mr. Como wouldn't be able to see it at all.

# ORSON SCOTT CARD

## America

Orson Scott Card began publishing in 1977, and by 1978 had won the John W. Campbell Award as best new writer of the year. His short fiction has appeared in *Omni, Isaac Asimov's Science Fiction Magazine, Analog, The Magazine of Fantasy and Science Fiction,* and elsewhere. His novels include *Hot Sleep, A Planet Called Treason, Songmaster,* and *Hart's Hope*. In 1986 his novel *Ender's Game* won both the Hugo and the Nebula Award; his novel *Speaker for the Dead* won both awards in 1987. His most recent novels are *Wyrms* and *Seventh Son*. Upcoming are two more novels in the "Seventh Son" series, *Red Prophet* and *Prentice Alvin*, from Tor, and two collections *Cardography,* from Hypatia Press, and *Tales from the Mormon Sea*, from Phantasia Press. Card's story "Hatrack River" a recent World Fantasy Award Winner, was in our Fourth Annual Collection; his story "The Fringe" was in our Third Annual Collection. Card lives in Greensboro, North Carolina, with his family.

In the story that follows, he spins an engrossing tale of a young boy's obsession with a mysterious Indian woman, and the stunning consequences for the whole world that unfold from it.

# AMERICA

## Orson Scott Card

Sam Monson and Anamari Boagente had two encounters in their lives, forty years apart. The first encounter lasted for several weeks in the high Amazon jungle, the village of Agualinda. The second was for only an hour near the ruins of the Glen Canyon Dam, on the border between Navaho country and the State of Deseret.

When they met the first time, Sam was a scrawny teenager from Utah and Anamari was a middle-aged spinster Indian from Brazil. When they met the second time, he was governor of Deseret, the last European state in America, and she was, to some people's way of thinking, the mother of God. It never occurred to anyone that they had ever met before, except me. I saw it plain as day, and pestered Sam until he told me the whole story. Now Sam is dead, and she's long gone, and I'm the only one who knows the truth. I thought for a long time that I'd take this story untold to my grave, but I see now that I can't do that. The way I see it, I won't be allowed to die until I write this down. All my real work was done long since, so why else am I alive? I figure the land has kept me breathing so I can tell the story of its victory, and it has kept *you* alive so you can hear it. Gods are like that. It isn't enough for them to run everything. They want to be famous, too.

### Agualinda, Amazonas

Passengers were nothing to her. Anamari only cared about helicopters when they brought medical supplies. This chopper carried a precious packet of benaxidene; Anamari barely noticed the skinny, awkward boy who sat by the crates, looking hostile. Another Yanqui who doesn't want to be stuck out in the jungle. Nothing new about that. Norteamericanos were almost invisible to Anamari by now. They came and went.

It was the Brazilian government people she had to worry about, the petty bureaucrats suffering through years of virtual exile in Manaus, working out their frustrations by being petty tyrants over the helpless Indians. No I'm sorry we don't have any more penicillin, no more syringes, what did you do with the AIDS vaccine we gave you three years ago? Do you think we're made of money here? Let them come to town if they want to get well. There's a hospital in São Paulo de Olivença, send them there, we're not going to turn you into a second hospital out there in the middle of nowhere, not for a village of a hundred filthy Baniwas, it's not as if you're a doctor, you're just an old withered up Indian woman yourself, you never graduated from the medical schools, we can't spare medicines for you. It made them feel so important, to decide whether or not an Indian child would live or die. As often as not they passed sentence of death by refusing to send supplies. It made them feel powerful as God.

Anamari knew better than to protest or argue—it would only make that bureaucrat likelier to kill again in the future. But sometimes, when the need was great and the medicine was common, Anamari would go to the Yanqui geologists and ask if they had this or that. Sometimes they did. What she knew about Yanquis was that if they had some extra, they would share, but if they didn't, they wouldn't lift a finger to get any. They were not tyrants like the Brazilian bureaucrats. They just didn't give a damn. They were there to make money.

That was what Anamari saw when she looked at the sullen light-haired boy in the helicopter—another Norteamericano, just like all the other Norteamericanos, only younger.

She had the benaxidene, and so she immediately began spreading word that all the Baniwas should come for injections. It was a disease that had been introduced during the war between Guyana and Venezuela two years ago; as usual, most of the victims were not citizens of either country, just the Indios of the jungle, waking up one morning with their joints stiffening, hardening until no movement was possible. Benaxidene was the antidote, but you had to have it every few months or your joints would stiffen up again. As usual, the bureaucrats had diverted a shipment and there were a dozen Baniwas bedridden in the village. As usual, one or two of the Indians would be too far gone for the cure; one or two of their joints would be stiff for the rest of their lives. As usual, Anamari said little as she gave the injections, and the Baniwas said less to her.

It was not until the next day that Anamari had time to notice the young Yanqui boy wandering around the village. He was wearing rumpled white clothing, already somewhat soiled with the greens and browns of life along the rivers of the Amazon jungle. He showed no sign of being interested in anything, but an hour into her rounds, checking on the results of yesterday's benaxidene treatments, she became aware that he was following her.

She turned around in the doorway of the government-built hovel and faced him. "O que é?" she demanded. What do you want?

To her surprise, he answered in halting Portuguese. Most of these Yanquis never bothered to learn the language at all, expecting her and everybody else to speak English. "Posso ajudar?" he asked. Can I help?

"Não," she said. "Mas pode olhar." You can watch.

He looked at her in bafflement.

She repeated her sentence slowly, enunciating clearly. "Pode olhar."

"Eu?" Me?

"Você, sim. And I can speak English."

"I don't want to speak English."

"Tanto faz," she said. Makes no difference.

He followed her into the hut. It was a little girl, lying naked in her own feces. She had palsy from a bout with meningitis years ago, when she was an infant, and Anamari figured that the girl would probably be one of the ones for whom the benaxidene came too late. That's how things usually worked—the weak suffer most. But no, her joints were flexing again, and the girl smiled at them, that heartbreakingly happy smile that made palsy victims so beautiful at times.

So. Some luck after all, the benaxidene had been in time for her. Anamari took the lid off the clay waterjar that stood on the one table in the room, and dipped one of her clean rags in it. She used it to wipe the girl, then lifted her frail, atrophied body and pulled the soiled sheet out from under her. On impulse, she handed the sheet to the boy.

"Leva fora," she said. And, when he didn't understand, "Take it outside."

He did not hesitate to take it, which surprised her. "Do you want me to wash it?"

"You could shake off the worst of it," she said. "Out over the garden in back. I'll wash it later."

He came back in, carrying the wadded-up sheet, just as she was leaving. "All done here," she said. "We'll stop by my house to start that soaking. I'll carry it now."

He didn't hand it to her. "I've got it," he said. "Aren't you going to give her a clean sheet?"

"There are only four sheets in the village," she said. "Two of them are on my bed. She won't mind lying on the mat. I'm the only one in the village who cares about linens. I'm also the only one who cares about this girl."

"She likes you," he said.

"She smiles like that at everybody."

"So maybe she likes everybody."

Anamari grunted and led the way to her house. It was two government hovels pushed together. The one served as her clinic, the other as her home. Out back she had two metal washtubs. She handed one of them to the Yanqui boy, pointed at the rainwater tank, and told him to fill it. He did. It made her furious.

"What do you want!" she demanded.

"Nothing," he said.

"Why do you keep hanging around!"

"I thought I was helping." His voice was full of injured pride.

"I don't need your help." She forgot that she had meant to leave the sheet to soak. She began rubbing it on the washboard.

"Then why did you ask me to . . ."

She did not answer him, and he did not complete the question.

After a long time he said, "You were trying to get rid of me, weren't you?"

"What do you want here?" she said. "Don't I have enough to do, without a Norteamericano *boy* to look after?"

Anger flashed in his eyes, but he did not answer until the anger was gone. "If you're tired of scrubbing, I can take over."

She reached out and took his hand, examined it for a moment. "Soft hands," she said. "Lady hands. You'd scrape your knuckles on the washboard and bleed all over the sheet."

Ashamed, he put his hands in his pockets. A parrot flew past him, dazzling green and red; he turned in surprise to look at it. It landed on the rainwater tank. "Those sell for a thousand dollars in the States," he said.

Of course the Yanqui boy evaluates everything by price. "Here they're free," she said. "The Baniwas eat them. And wear the feathers."

He looked around at the other huts, the scraggly gardens. "The people are very poor here," he said. "The jungle life must be hard."

"Do you think so?" she snapped. "The jungle is very kind to these people. It has plenty for them to eat, all year. The Indians of the Amazon did not know they were poor until Europeans came and made them buy pants, which they couldn't afford, and build houses, which they couldn't keep up, and plant gardens. Plant gardens! In the midst of this magnificent Eden. The jungle life was good. The Europeans made them poor."

"Europeans?" asked the boy.

"Brazilians. They're all Europeans. Even the black ones have turned European. Brazil is just another European country, speaking a European language. Just like you Norteamericanos. You're Europeans too."

"I was born in America," he said. "So were my parents and grandparents and great-grandparents."

"But your bis-bis-avós, they came on a boat."

"That was a long time ago," he said.

"A long time!" She laughed. "I am a pure Indian. For ten thousand generations I belong to this land. You are a stranger here. A fourth-generation stranger."

"But I'm a stranger who isn't afraid to touch a dirty sheet," he said. He was grinning defiantly.

That was when she started to like him. "How old are you?" she asked.

"Fifteen," he said.

"Your father's a geologist?"

"No. He heads up the drilling team. They're going to sink a test well here. He doesn't think they'll find anything, though."

"They will find plenty of oil," she said.

"How do you know?"

"Because I dreamed it," she said. "Bulldozers cutting down the trees, making an airstrip, and planes coming and going. They'd never do that, unless they found oil. Lots of oil."

She waited for him to make fun of the idea of dreaming true dreams. But he didn't. He just looked at her.

So she was the one who broke the silence. "You came to this village to kill time while your father is away from you, on the job, right?"

"No," he said. "I came here because he hasn't started to work yet. The choppers start bringing in equipment tomorrow."

"You would rather be away from your father?"

He looked away. "I'd rather see him in hell."

"This *is* hell," she said, and the boy laughed. "Why did you come here with him?"

"Because I'm only fifteen years old, and he has custody of me this summer."

"Custody," she said. "Like a criminal."

"He's the criminal," he said bitterly.

"And his crime?"

He waited a moment, as if deciding whether to answer. When he spoke, he spoke quietly and looked away. Ashamed. Of his father's crime. "Adultery," he said. The word hung in the air. The boy turned back and looked her in the face again. His face was tinged with red.

Europeans have such transparent skin, she thought. All their emotions show through. She guessed a whole story from his word—a beloved mother betrayed, and now he had to spend the summer with her betrayer. "Is that a *crime*?"

He shrugged. "Maybe not to Catholics."

"You're Protestant?"

He shook his head. "Mormon. But I'm a heretic."

She laughed. "You're a heretic, and your father is an adulterer."

He didn't like her laughter. "And you're a virgin," he said. His words seemed calculated to hurt her.

She stopped scrubbing, stood there looking at her hands. "Also a crime?" she murmured.

"I had a dream last night," he said. "In my dream your name was Anna Marie, but when I tried to call you that, I couldn't. I could only call you by another name."

"What name?" she asked.

"What does it matter? It was only a dream." He was taunting her. He knew she trusted in dreams.

"You dreamed of me, and in the dream my name was Anamari?"

"It's true, isn't it? That *is* your name, isn't it?" He didn't have to add the other half of the question: You *are* a virgin, aren't you?

She lifted the sheet from the water, wrung it out and tossed it to him. He caught it, vile water spattering his face. He grimaced. She poured the washwater onto the dirt. It spattered mud all over his trousers. He did not step back. Then she carried the tub to the water tank and began to fill it with clean water. "Time to rinse," she said.

"You dreamed about an airstrip," he said. "And I dreamed about you."

"In your dreams you better start to mind your own business," she said.

"I didn't ask for it, you know," he said. "But I followed the dream out to this village, and you turned out to be a dreamer, too."

"That doesn't mean you're going to end up with your pinto between my legs, so you can forget it," she said.

He looked genuinely horrified. "Geez, what are you talking about! That would be fornication! Plus you've got to be old enough to be my mother!"

"I'm forty-two," she said. "If it's any of your business."

"You're *older* than my mother," he said. "I couldn't possibly think of you sexually. I'm sorry if I gave that impression."

She giggled. "You are a very funny boy, Yanqui. First you say I'm a virgin—"

"That was in the dream," he said.

"And then you tell me I'm older than your mother and too ugly to think of me sexually."

He looked ashen with shame. "I'm sorry, I was just trying to make sure you knew that I would never—"

"You're trying to tell me that you're a good boy."

"Yes," he said.

She giggled again. "You probably don't even play with yourself," she said.

His face went red. He struggled to find something to say. Then he threw the wet sheet back at her and walked furiously away. She laughed and laughed. She liked this boy very much.

The next morning he came back and helped her in the clinic all day. His name was Sam Monson, and he was the first European she ever knew who dreamed true dreams. She had thought only Indios could do that. Whatever god it was that gave her dreams to her, perhaps it was the same god giving dreams to Sam. Perhaps that god brought them together here in the jungle. Perhaps it was that god who would lead the drill to oil, so that Sam's father would have to keep him here long enough to accomplish whatever the god had in mind.

It annoyed her that the god had mentioned she was a virgin. That was nobody's business but her own.

Life in the jungle was better than Sam ever expected. Back in Utah, when Mother first told him that he had to go to the Amazon with the old bastard, he had feared the worst. Hacking through thick viney jungles with a machete, crossing rivers of piranha in tick-infested dugouts, and always sweat and mosquitos and thick, heavy air. Instead the American oilmen lived in a pretty decent camp, with a generator for electric light. Even though it rained all the time and when it didn't it was so hot you wished it would, it wasn't constant danger as he had feared, and he never had to hack through jungle at all. There were paths, sometimes almost roads, and the thick, vivid green of the jungle was more beautiful than he had ever imagined. He had not realized that the American West was such a desert. Even California, where the old bastard lived when he wasn't traveling to drill wells, even those wooded hills and mountains were grey compared to the jungle green.

The Indians were quiet little people, not headhunters. Instead of avoiding them, like the adult Americans did, Sam found that he could be with them, come to know them, even help them by working with Anamari. The old bastard could sit around and drink his beer with the guys—adultery *and* beer, as if one contemptible sin of the flesh weren't enough—but Sam was actually doing some good here. If there was anything Sam could do to prove he was the opposite of his father, he would do it; and because his father was a weak, carnal, earthy man with no self-control, then Sam had to be a strong, spiritual, intellectual man who did not let any passions of the body rule him. Watching his father succumb to alcohol, remembering how his father could not even last a month away from Mother without having to get some whore into his bed, Sam was proud of his self-discipline. He ruled his body; his body did not rule him.

He was also proud to have passed Anamari's test on the first day. What did he care if human excrement touched his body? He was not afraid to breathe the hot stink of suffering, he was not afraid of the innocent dirt of a crippled child. Didn't Jesus touch lepers? Dirt of the body did not disgust him. Only dirt of the soul.

Which was why his dreams of Anamari troubled him. During the day they were friends. They talked about important ideas, and she told him stories of the Indians of the Amazon, and about her education as a teacher in São Paulo. She listened when he talked about history and religion and evolution and all the theories and ideas that danced in his head. Even Mother never had time for that, always taking care of the younger kids or doing her endless jobs for the church. Anamari treated him like his ideas mattered.

But at night, when he dreamed, it was something else entirely. In those dreams he kept seeing her naked, and the voice kept calling her "Virgem America." What her virginity had to do with America he had no idea—even true dreams didn't always make sense—but he knew this much: when he dreamed of Anamari naked, she was always reaching out to him, and he was filled with such strong passions that more than once he awoke from the dream to find himself throbbing with imaginary pleasure, like Onan in the Bible, Judah's son, who spilled his seed upon the ground and was struck dead for it.

Sam lay awake for a long time each time this happened, trembling, fearful. Not because he thought God would strike him down—he knew that if God hadn't struck his father dead for adultery, Sam was certainly in no danger because of an erotic dream. He was afraid because he knew that in these dreams he revealed himself to be exactly as lustful and evil as his father. He did not want to feel any sexual desire for Anamari. She was old and lean and tough, and he was afraid of her, but most of all Sam didn't want to desire her because he was not like his father, he would never have sexual intercourse with a woman who was not his wife.

Yet when he walked into the village of Agualinda, he felt eager to see her again, and when he found her—the village was small, it never took long—he could not erase from his mind the vivid memory of how she looked in the dreams, reaching out to him, her breasts loose and jostling, her slim hips rolling toward him—and he would bite his cheek for the pain of it, to distract him from desire.

It was because he was living with Father; the old bastard's goatishness was rubbing off on him, that's all. So he spent as little time with his father as possible, going home only to sleep at night.

The harder he worked at the jobs Anamari gave him to do, the easier it was to keep himself from remembering his dream of her kneeling over him, touching him, sliding along his body. Hoe the weeds out of the corn until your back is on fire with pain! Wash the Baniwa hunter's wound and replace the bandage! Sterilize the instruments in the alcohol! Above all, do not, even accidentally, let any part of your body brush against hers; pull away when she is near you, turn away so you don't feel her warm breath as she leans over your shoulder, start a bright conversation whenever there is a silence filled only with the sound of insects and the sight of a bead of sweat slowly etching its way from her neck down her chest to disappear between her breasts where she only tied her shirt instead of buttoning it.

How could she possibly be a virgin, after the way she acted in his dreams?

"Where do you think the dreams come from?" she asked.

He blushed, even though she could not have guessed what he was thinking. Could she?

"The dreams," she said. "Why do you think we have dreams that come true?"

It was nearly dark. "I have to get home," he said. She was holding his hand. When had she taken his hand like that, and why?

"I have the strangest dream," she said. "I dream of a huge snake, covered with bright green and red feathers."

"Not all the dreams come true," he said.

"I hope not," she answered. "Because this snake comes out of—I give birth to this snake."

"Quetzal," he said.

"What does that mean?"

"The feathered serpent god of the Aztecs. Or maybe the Mayas. Mexican, anyway. I have to go home."

"But what does it mean?"

"It's almost dark," he said.

"Stay and talk to me!" she demanded. "I have room, you can stay the night."

But Sam had to get back. Much as he hated staying with his father, he dared not spend a night in this place. Even her invitation aroused him. He would never last a night in the same house with her. The dream would be too strong for him. So he left her and headed back along the path through the jungle. All during the walk he couldn't get Anamari out of his mind. It was as if the plants were sending him the vision of her, so his desire was even stronger than when he was with her.

The leaves gradually turned from green to black in the seeping dark. The hot darkness did not frighten him; it seemed to invite him to step away from the path into the shadows, where he would find the moist relief, the cool release of all his tension. He stayed on the path, and hurried faster.

He came at last to the oilmen's town. The generator was loud, but the insects were louder, swarming around the huge area light, casting shadows of their demonic dance. He and his father shared a large one-room house on the far edge of the compound. The oil company provided much nicer hovels than the Brazilian government.

A few men called out to greet him. He waved, even answered once or twice, but hurried on. His groin felt so hot and tight with desire that he was sure that only the shadows and his quick stride kept everyone from seeing. It was maddening: the more he thought of trying to calm himself, the more visions of Anamari slipped in and out of his waking mind, almost to the point of hallucination. His body would not relax. He was almost running when he burst into the house.

Inside, Father was washing his dinner plate. He glanced up, but Sam was already past him. "I'll heat up your dinner."

Sam flopped down on his bed. "Not hungry."

"Why are you so late?" asked his father.

"We got to talking."

"It's dangerous in the jungle at night. You think it's safe because nothing bad ever happens to you in the daytime, but it's dangerous."

"Sure, Dad. I know." Sam got up, turned his back to take off his pants. Maddeningly, he was still aroused; he didn't want his father to see.

But with the unerring instinct of prying parents, the old bastard must have sensed that Sam was hiding something. When Sam was buck naked, Father walked around and *looked*, just as if he never heard of privacy. Sam blushed in spite of himself. His father's eyes went small and hard. I hope I don't ever look like that, thought Sam. I hope my face doesn't get that ugly suspicious expression on it. I'd rather die than look like that.

"Well, put on your pajamas," Father said. "I don't want to look at that forever."

Sam pulled on his sleeping shorts.

"What's going on over there?" asked Father.

"Nothing," said Sam.

"You must do *something* all day."

"I told you, I help her. She runs a clinic, and she also tends a garden. She's got no electricity, so it takes a lot of work."

"I've done a lot of work in my time, Sam, but I don't come home like *that*."

"No, you always stopped and got it off with some whore along the way."

The old bastard whipped out his hand and slapped Sam across the face. It stung, and the surprise of it wrung tears from Sam before he had time to decide not to cry.

"I never slept with a whore in my life," said the old bastard.

"You only slept with one woman who wasn't," said Sam.

Father slapped him again, only this time Sam was ready, and he bore the slap stoically, almost without flinching.

"I had one affair," said Father.

"You got caught once," said Sam. "There were dozens of women."

Father laughed derisively. "What did you do, hire a detective? There was only the one."

But Sam knew better. He had dreamed these women for years. Laughing, lascivious women. It wasn't until he was twelve years old that he found out enough about sex to know what it all meant. By then he had long since learned that any dream he had more than once was true. So when he had a dream of Father with one of the laughing women, he woke up, holding the dream in his memory. He thought through it from beginning to end, remembering all the details he could. The name of the motel. The room number. It was midnight, but Father was in California, so it was an hour earlier. Sam got out of bed and walked quietly into the kitchen and dialed directory assistance. There was such a motel. He wrote down the number. Then Mother was there, asking him what he was doing.

"This is the number of the Seaview Motor Inn," he said. "Call this number and ask for room twenty-one twelve and then ask for Dad."

Mother looked at him strangely, like she was about to scream or cry or hit him or throw up. "Your father is at the Hilton," she said.

But he just looked right back at her and said, "No matter who answers the phone, ask for Dad."

So she did. A woman answered, and Mom asked for Dad by name, and he was there. "I wonder how we can afford to pay for two motel rooms on the same night," Mom said coldly. "Or are you splitting the cost with your friend?" Then she hung up the phone and burst into tears.

She cried all night as she packed up everything the old bastard owned. By the time Dad got home two days later, all his things were in storage. Mom moved fast when she made up her mind. Dad found himself divorced and excommunicated all in the same week, not two months later.

Mother never asked Sam how he knew where Dad was that night. Never even hinted at wanting to know. Dad never asked him how Mom knew to call that number, either. An amazing lack of curiosity, Sam thought sometimes. Perhaps they just took it as fate. For a while it was secret, then it stopped being secret, and it didn't matter how the change happened. But one thing Sam knew for sure—the woman at the Seaview Motor Inn was not the first woman, and the Seaview was not the first motel. Dad had been an adulterer for years, and it was ridiculous for him to lie about it now.

But there was no point in arguing with him, especially when he was in the mood to slap Sam around.

"I don't like the idea of you spending so much time with an older woman," said Father.

"She's the closest thing to a doctor these people have. She needs my help and I'm going to keep helping her," said Sam.

"Don't talk to me like that, little boy."

"You don't know anything about this, so just mind your own business."

Another slap. "You're going to get tired of this before I do, Sammy."

"I love it when you slap me, Dad. It confirms my moral superiority."

Another slap, this time so hard that Sam stumbled under the blow, and he tasted blood inside his mouth. "How hard next time, Dad?" he said. "You going to knock me down? Kick me around a little? Show me who's boss?"

"You've been asking for a beating ever since we got here."

"I've been asking to be left alone."

"I know women, Sam. You have no business getting involved with an older woman like that."

"I help her wash a little girl who has bowel movements in bed, Father. I empty pails of vomit. I wash clothes and help patch leaking roofs and while I'm doing all these things we talk. Just talk. I don't imagine you have much experience with that, Dad. You probably never talk at all with the women *you* know, at least not after the price is set."

It was going to be the biggest slap of all, enough to knock him down, enough to bruise his face and black his eye. But the old bastard held it in. Didn't hit him. Just stood there, breathing hard, his face red, his eyes tight and piggish.

"You're not as pure as you think," the old bastard finally whispered. "You've got every desire you despise in me."

"I don't despise you for *desire*," said Sam.

"The guys on the crew have been talking about you and this Indian bitch, Sammy. You may not like it, but I'm your father and it's my job to warn you. These Indian women are easy, and they'll give you a disease."

"The guys on the crew," said Sam. "What do they know about Indian women? They're all fags or jerk-offs."

"I hope someday you say that where they can hear you, Sam. And I hope when it happens I'm not there to stop what they do to you."

"I would never *be* around men like that, Daddy, if the court hadn't given you shared custody. A no-fault divorce. What a joke."

More than anything else, those words stung the old bastard. Hurt him enough to shut him up. He walked out of the house and didn't come back until Sam was long since asleep.

Asleep and dreaming.

Anamari knew what was on Sam's mind, and to her surprise she found it vaguely flattering. She had never known the shy affection of a boy. When she was a teenager, she was the one Indian girl in the schools in São Paulo. Indians were so rare in the Europeanized parts of Brazil that she might have seemed exotic, but in those days she was still so frightened. The city was sterile, all concrete and harsh light, not at all like the deep soft meadows and woods of Xingu Park. Her tribe, the Kuikuru, were much more Europeanized than the jungle Indians—she had seen cars all her life, and spoke Portuguese before she went to school. But the city made her hungry for the land, the cobblestones hurt her feet, and these intense, competitive children made her afraid. Worst of all, true dreams stopped in the city. She hardly knew who she was, if she was not a true dreamer. So if any boy desired her then, she would not have known it. She would have rebuffed him inadvertently. And then the time for such things had passed. Until now.

"Last night I dreamed of a great bird, flying west, away from land. Only its right wing was twice as large as its left wing. It had great bleeding wounds along the edges of its wings, and the right wing was the sickest of all, rotting in the air, the feathers dropping off."

"Very pretty dream," said Sam. Then he translated, to keep in practice. "Que sonho lindo."

"Ah, but what does it mean?"

"What happened next?"

"I was riding on the bird. I was very small, and I held a small snake in my hands—"

"The feathered snake."

"Yes. And I turned it loose, and it went and ate up all the corruption, and the bird was clean. And that's all. You've got a bubble in that syringe. The idea is to inject medicine, not air. What does the dream mean?"

"What, you think I'm a Joseph? A Daniel?"

"How about a Sam?"

"Actually, your dream is easy. Piece of cake."

"What?"

"Piece of cake. Easy as pie. That's how the cookie crumbles. Man shall not live by bread alone. All I can think of are bakery sayings. I must be hungry."

"Tell me the dream or I'll poke this needle into your eye."

"That's what I like about you Indians. Always you have torture on your mind."

She planted her foot against him and knocked him off his stool onto the packed dirt floor. A beetle skittered away. Sam held up the syringe he had been working with; it was undamaged. He got up, set it aside. "The bird," he said, "is North and South America. Like wings, flying west. Only the right wing is bigger." He sketched out a rough map with his toe on the floor.

"That's the shape, maybe," she said. "It could be."

"And the corruption—show me where it was."

With her toe, she smeared the map here, there.

"It's obvious," said Sam.

"Yes," she said. "Once you think of it as a map. The corruption is all the Europeanized land. And the only healthy places are where the Indians still live."

"Indians or half-Indians," said Sam. "All your dreams are about the same thing, Anamari. Removing the Europeans from North and South America. Let's face it. You're an Indian chauvinist. You give birth to the resurrection god of the Aztecs, and then you send it out to destroy the Europeans."

"But why do I dream this?"

"Because you hate Europeans."

"No," she said. "That isn't true."

"Sure it is."

"I don't hate *you*."

"Because you know me. I'm not a European anymore, I'm a person. Obviously you've got to keep that from happening anymore, so you can keep your bigotry alive."

"You're making fun of me, Sam."

He shook his head. "No, I'm not. These are true dreams, Anamari. They tell you your destiny."

She giggled. "If I give birth to a feathered snake, I'll know the dream was true."

"To drive the Europeans out of America."

"No," she said. "I don't care what the dream says. I won't do that. Besides, what about the dream of the flowering weed?"

"Little weed in the garden, almost dead, and then you water it and it grows larger and larger and more beautiful—"

"And something else," she said. "At the very end of the dream, all the other flowers in the garden have changed. To be just like the flowering weed." She reached out and rested her hand on his arm. "Tell me *that* dream."

His arm became still, lifeless under her hand. "Black is beautiful," he said.

"What does *that* mean?"

"In America. The U.S., I mean. For the longest time, the blacks, the former slaves, they were ashamed to be black. The whiter you were, the more status you had—the more honor. But when they had their revolution in the sixties—"

"You don't remember the sixties, little boy."

"Heck, I barely remember the seventies. But I read books. One of the big changes, and it made a huge difference, was that slogan. Black is beautiful. The blacker the better. They said it over and over. Be proud of blackness, not ashamed of it. And in just a few years, they turned the whole status system upside down."

She nodded. "The weed came into flower."

"So. All through Latin America, Indians are very low status. If you want a Bolivian to pull a knife on you, just call him an Indian. Everybody who possibly can, pretends to be of pure Spanish blood. Pure-blooded Indians are slaughtered wherever there's the slightest excuse. Only in Mexico is it a little bit different."

"What you tell me from my dreams, Sam, this is no small job to do. I'm one middle-aged Indian woman, living in the jungle. I'm supposed to tell all the Indians of America to be proud? When they're the poorest of the poor and the lowest of the low?"

"When you give them a name, you create them. Benjamin Franklin did it, when he coined the name *American* for the people of the English colonies. They weren't New Yorkers or Virginians, they were Americans. Same thing for you. It isn't Latin Americans against Norteamericanos. It's Indians and Europeans. Somos todos indios. We're all Indians. Think that would work as a slogan?"

"Me. A revolutionary."

"Nós somos os americanos. Vai fora, Europa! America p'ra americanos! All kinds of slogans."

"I'd have to translate them into Spanish."

"Indios moram na India. Americanos moram na America. America nossa! No, better still: Nossa America! Nuestra America! It translates. Our America."

"You're a very fine slogan maker."

He shivered as she traced her finger along his shoulder and down the sensitive skin of his chest. She made a circle on his nipple and it shriveled and hardened, as if he were cold.

"Why are you silent now?" She laid her hand flat on his abdomen, just above his shorts, just below his navel. "You never tell me your own dreams," she said. "But I know what they are."

He blushed.

"See? Your skin tells me, even when your mouth says nothing. I have dreamed these dreams all my life, and they troubled me, all the time, but now you tell me what they mean, a white-skinned dream-teller, you tell me that I must go among the Indians and make them proud, make them strong, so that everyone with a drop of Indian blood will call himself an Indian, and Europeans will lie and claim native ancestors, until America is all Indian. You tell me that I will give birth to the new Quetzalcoatl, and he will unify and heal the land of its sickness. But what you never tell me is this: Who will be the father of my feathered snake?"

Abruptly he got up and walked stiffly away. To the door, keeping his back to her, so she couldn't see how alert his body was. But she knew.

"I'm fifteen," said Sam, finally.

"And I'm very old. The land is older. Twenty million years. What does it care of the quarter-century between us?"

"I should never have come to this place."

"You never had a choice," she said. "My people have always known the god of the land. Once there was a perfect balance in this place. All the people loved the land and tended it. Like the garden of Eden. And the land fed them. It gave them maize and bananas. They took only what they needed to eat, and they did not kill animals for sport or humans for hate. But then the Incas turned away from the land and worshipped gold and the bright golden sun. The Aztecs soaked the ground in the blood of their human sacrifices. The Pueblos cut down the forests of Utah and Arizona and turned them into red-rock deserts. The Iroquois tortured their enemies and filled the forests with their screams of agony. We found tobacco and coca and peyote and coffee and forgot the dreams the land gave us in our sleep. And so the land rejected us. The land called to Columbus and told him lies and seduced him and he never had a chance, did he? Never had a choice. The land brought the Europeans to punish us. Disease and slavery and warfare killed most of us, and the rest of us tried to pretend we were Europeans rather than endure any more of the punishment. The land was our jealous lover, and it hated us for a while."

"Some Catholic you are," said Sam. "I don't believe in your Indian gods."

"Say *Deus* or *Cristo* instead of *the land* and the story is the same," she said. "But now the Europeans are worse than we Indians ever were. The land is suffering from a thousand different poisons, and you threaten to kill all of life with your weapons of war. We Indians have been punished enough, and now it's our turn to have the land again. The land chose Columbus exactly five centuries ago. Now you and I dream our dreams, the way he dreamed."

"That's a good story," Sam said, still looking out the door. It sounded so close to what the old prophets in the Book of Mormon said would happen to America; close, but dangerously different. As if there were no hope for the Europeans anymore. As if their chance had already been lost, as if no repentance would be allowed. They would not be able to pass the land on to the next generation. Someone else would inherit. It made him sick at heart, to realize what the white man had lost, had thrown away, had torn up and destroyed.

"But what should I do with my story?" she asked. He could hear her coming closer, walking up behind him. He could almost feel her breath on his shoulder. "How can I fulfill it?"

By yourself. Or at least without me. "Tell it to the Indians. You can cross all these borders in a thousand different places, and you speak Portuguese and Spanish and Arawak and Carib, and you'll be able to tell your story in Quechua, too, no doubt, crossing back and forth between Brazil and Colombia and Bolivia and Peru and Venezuela, all close together here, until every Indian knows about you and calls you by the name you were given in my dream."

"Tell me my name."

"Virgem America. See? The land or god or whatever it is wants you to be a virgin."

She giggled. "Nossa senhora," she said. "Don't you see? I'm the new Virgin *Mother*. It wants me to be a *mother*, all the old legends of the Holy Mother will transfer to me; they'll call me virgin no matter what the truth is. How the priests will hate me. How they'll try to kill my son. But he will live and become Quetzalcoatl, and he will restore America to the true Americans. That is the meaning of my dreams. My dreams and yours."

"Not me," he said. "Not for any dream or any god." He turned to face her. His fist was pressed against his groin, as if to crush out all rebellion there. "My body doesn't rule me," he said. "Nobody controls me but myself."

"That's very sick," she said cheerfully. "All because you hate your father. Forget that hate, and love me instead."

His face became a mask of anguish, and then he turned and fled.

He even thought of castrating himself, that's the kind of madness that drove him through the jungle. He could hear the bulldozers carving out the airstrip, the screams of falling timbers, the calls of birds and cries of animals displaced. It was the terror of the tortured land, and it maddened him even more as he ran between thick walls of green. The rig was sucking oil like heartblood from the forest floor. The ground was wan and trembling under his feet. And when he got home he was grateful to lift his feet off the ground and lie on his mattress, clutching his pillow, panting or perhaps sobbing from the exertion of his run.

He slept, soaking his pillow in afternoon sweat, and in his sleep the voice of the land came to him like whispered lullabies. I did not choose you, said the land. I cannot speak except to those who hear me, and because it is in your nature to hear and listen, I spoke to you and led you here to save me, save me, save me. Do you know the desert they will make of me? Encased in burning dust or layers of ice, either way I'll be dead. My whole purpose is to thrust life upward out of my soils, and feel the press of living feet, and hear the songs of birds and the low music of the animals, growling, lowing, chittering, whatever voice they choose. That's what I ask of you, the dance of life, just once to make the man whose mother will teach him to be Quetzalcoatl and save me, save me, save me.

He heard that whisper and he dreamed a dream. In his dream he got up and walked back to Agualinda, not along the path, but through the deep jungle itself. A longer way, but the leaves touched his face, the spiders climbed on him, the tree lizards tangled in his hair, the monkeys dunged him and pinched him and jabbered in his ear, the snakes entwined around his feet; he waded streams and fish caressed his naked ankles, and all the way they sang to him, songs that celebrants might sing at the wedding of a king. Somehow, in the way of dreams, he lost his clothing without removing it, so that he emerged from the jungle naked, and walked through Agualinda as the sun was setting, all the Baniwas peering at him from their doorways, making clicking noises with their teeth.

He awoke in darkness. He heard his father breathing. He must have slept through the afternoon. What a dream, what a dream. He was exhausted.

He moved, thinking of getting up to use the toilet. Only then did he realize that he was not alone on the bed, and it was not his bed. She stirred and nestled against him, and he cried out in fear and anger.

It startled her awake. "What is it?" she asked.

"It was a dream," he insisted. "All a dream."

"Ah yes," she said, "it was. But last night, Sam, we dreamed the same dream." She giggled. "All night long."

In his sleep. It happened in his sleep. And it did not fade like common dreams, the memory was clear, pouring himself into her again and again, her fingers gripping him, her breath against his cheek, whispering the same thing, over and over: "Aceito, aceito-te, aceito." Not love, no, not when he came with the land controlling him, she did not love him, she merely accepted the burden he placed within her. Before tonight she had been a virgin, and so had he. Now she was even purer than before, Virgem America, but his purity was hopelessly, irredeemably gone, wasted, poured out into this old woman who had haunted his dreams. "I hate you," he said. "What you stole from me."

He got up, looking for his clothing, ashamed that she was watching him.

"No one can blame you," she said. "The land married us, gave us to each other. There's no sin in that."

"Yeah," he said.

"One time. Now I am whole. Now I can begin."

"And now I'm finished."

"I didn't mean to rob you," she said. "I didn't know you were dreaming."

"I thought I was dreaming," he said, "but I loved the dream. I dreamed I was fornicating and it made me glad." He spoke the words with all the poison in his heart. "Where are my clothes?"

"You arrived without them," she said. "It was my first hint that you wanted me."

There was a moon outside. Not yet dawn. "I did what you wanted," he said. "Now can I go home?"

"Do what you want," she said. "I didn't plan this."

"I know. I wasn't talking to you." And when he spoke of home, he didn't mean the shack where his father would be snoring and the air would stink of beer.

"When you woke me, I was dreaming," she said.

"I don't want to hear it."

"I have him now," she said, "a boy inside me. A lovely boy. But you will never see him in all your life, I think."

"Will you tell him? Who I am?"

She giggled. "Tell Quetzalcoatl that his father is a European? A man who blushes? A man who burns in the sun? No, I won't tell him. Unless someday he becomes cruel, and wants to punish the Europeans even after they are defeated. Then I will tell him that the first European he must punish is himself. Here, write your name. On this paper write your name, and give me your fingerprint, and write the date."

"I don't know what day it is."

"October twelfth," she said.

"It's August."

"Write October twelfth," she said. "I'm in the legend business now."

"August twenty-fourth," he murmured, but he wrote the date she asked for.

"The helicopter comes this morning," she said.

"Good-bye," he said. He started for the door.

Her hands caught at him, held his arm, pulled him back. She embraced him, this time not in a dream, cool bodies together in the doorway of the house. The geis was off him now, or else he was worn out; her body had no power over his anymore.

"I did love you," she murmured. "It was not just the god that brought you."

Suddenly he felt very young, even younger than fifteen, and he broke away from her and walked quickly away through the sleeping village. He did not try to retrace his wandering route through the jungle; he stayed on the moonlit path and soon was at his father's hut. The old bastard woke up as Sam came in.

"I knew it'd happen," Father said.

Sam rummaged for underwear and pulled it on.

"There's no man born who can keep his zipper up when a woman wants it." Father laughed. A laugh of malice and triumph. "You're no better than I am, boy."

Sam walked to where his father sat on the bed and imagined hitting him across the face. Once, twice, three times.

"Go ahead, boy, hit me. It won't make you a virgin again."

"I'm not like you," Sam whispered.

"No?" asked Father. "For you it's a sacrament or something? As my daddy used to say, it don't matter who squeezes the toothpaste, boy, it all squirts out the same."

"Then your daddy must have been as dumb a jackass as mine." Sam went back to the chest they shared, began packing his clothes and books into one big suitcase. "I'm going out with the chopper today. Mom will wire me the money to come home from Manaus."

"She doesn't have to. I'll give you a check."

"I don't want your money. I just want my passport."

"It's in the top drawer." Father laughed again. "At least I always wore my clothes home."

In a few minutes Sam had finished packing. He picked up the bag, started for the door.

"Son," said Father, and because his voice was quiet, not derisive, Sam stopped and listened. "Son," he said, "once is once. It doesn't mean you're evil, it doesn't even mean you're weak. It just means you're human." He was breathing deeply. Sam hadn't heard him so emotional in a long time. "You aren't a thing like me, son," he said. "That should make you glad."

Years later Sam would think of all kinds of things he should have said. Forgiveness. Apology. Affection. Something. But he said nothing, just left and went out to the clearing and waited for the helicopter. Father didn't come to try to say good-bye. The chopper pilot came, unloaded, left the chopper to talk to some people. He must have talked to Father because when he came back he handed Sam a check. Plenty to fly home, and stay in good places during the layovers, and buy some new clothes that didn't have jungle stains on them. The check was the last thing Sam had from his father. Before he came home from that rig, the Venezuelans bought a hardy and virulent strain of syphilis on the black market, one that could be passed by casual contact, and released it in Guyana. Sam's father was one of the first million to die, so fast that he didn't even write.

## Page, Arizona

The State of Deseret had only sixteen helicopters, all desperately needed for surveying, spraying, and medical emergencies. So Governor Sam Monson rarely risked them on government business. This time, though, he had no choice. He was only fifty-five, and in good shape, so maybe he could have made the climb down into Glen Canyon and back up the other side. But Carpenter wouldn't have made it, not in a wheelchair, and Carpenter had a right to be here. He had a right to see what the red-rock Navaho desert had become.

Deciduous forest, as far as the eye could see.

They stood on the bluff where the old town of Page had once been, before the dam was blown up. The Navahos hadn't tried to reforest here. It was their standard practice. They left all the old European towns unplanted, like pink scars in the green of the forest. Still, the Navahos weren't stupid. They had come to the last stronghold of

European science, the University of Deseret at Zarahemla, to find out how to use the heavy rainfalls to give them something better than perpetual floods and erosion. It was Carpenter who gave them the plan for these forests, just as it was Carpenter whose program had turned the old Utah deserts into the richest farmland in America. The Navahos filled their forests with bison, deer, and bears. The Mormons raised crops enough to feed five times their population. That was the European mindset, still in place: enough is never enough. Plant more, grow more, you'll need it tomorrow.

"They say he has two hundred thousand soldiers," said Carpenter's computer voice. Carpenter *could* speak, Sam had heard, but he never did. Preferred the synthesized voice. "They could all be right down there, and we'd never see them."

"They're much farther south and east. Strung out from Phoenix to Santa Fe, so they aren't too much of a burden on the Navahos."

"Do you think they'll buy supplies from us? Or send an army in to take them?"

"Neither," said Sam. "We'll give our surplus grain as a gift."

"He rules all of Latin America, and he needs *gifts* from a little remnant of the U.S. in the Rockies?"

"We'll give it as a gift, and be grateful if he takes it that way."

"How else might he take it?"

"As tribute. As taxes. As ransom. The land is his now, not ours."

"We made the desert live, Sam. That makes it ours."

"There they are."

They watched in silence as four horses walked slowly from the edge of the woods, out onto the open ground of an ancient gas station. They bore a litter between them, and were led by two—not Indians—Americans. Sam had schooled himself long ago to use the word *American* to refer only to what had once been known as Indians, and to call himself and his own people Europeans. But in his heart he had never forgiven them for stealing his identity, even though he remembered very clearly where and when that change began.

It took fifteen minutes for the horses to bring the litter to him, but Sam made no move to meet them, no sign that he was in a hurry. That was also the American way now, to take time, never to hurry, never to rush. Let the Europeans wear their watches. Americans told time by the sun and stars.

Finally the litter stopped, and the men opened the litter door and helped her out. She was smaller than before, and her face was tightly wrinkled, her hair steel-white.

She gave no sign that she knew him, though he said his name. The Americans introduced her as Nuestra Señora. Our Lady. Never speaking her most sacred name: Virgem America.

The negotiations were delicate but simple. Sam had authority to speak for Deseret, and she obviously had authority to speak for her son. The grain was refused as a gift, but accepted as taxes from a federated state. Deseret would be allowed to keep its own government, and the borders negotiated between the Navahos and the Mormons eleven years before were allowed to stand.

Sam went further. He praised Quetzalcoatl for coming to pacify the chaotic lands that had been ruined by the Europeans. He gave her maps that his scouts had prepared, showing strongholds of the prairie raiders, decommissioned nuclear missiles, and the few places where stable governments had been formed. He offered, and she accepted, a hundred experienced scouts to travel with Quetzalcoatl at Deseret's expense, and promised that when he chose the site of his North American capital, Deseret would provide architects and engineers and builders to teach his American workmen how to build the place themselves.

She was generous in return. She granted all citizens of Deseret conditional status as adopted Americans, and she promised that Quetzalcoatl's armies would stick to the roads through the northwest Texas panhandle, where the grasslands of the newest New Lands project were still so fragile that an army could destroy five years of labor just by marching through. Carpenter printed out two copies of the agreement in English and Spanish, and Sam and Virgem America signed both.

Only then, when their official work was done, did the old woman look up into Sam's eyes and smile. "Are you still a heretic, Sam?"

"No," he said. "I grew up. Are you still a virgin?"

She giggled, and even though it was an old lady's broken voice, he remembered the laughter he had heard so often in the village of Agualinda, and his heart ached for the boy he was then, and the girl she was. He remembered thinking then that forty-two was old.

"Yes, I'm still a virgin," she said. "God gave me my child. God sent me an angel, to put the child in my womb. I thought you would have heard the story by now."

"I heard it," he said.

She leaned closer to him, her voice a whisper. "Do you dream, these days?"

"Many dreams. But the only ones that come true are the ones I dream in daylight."

"Ah," she sighed. "My sleep is also silent."

She seemed distant, sad, distracted. Sam also; then, as if by conscious decision, he brightened, smiled, spoke cheerfully. "I have grandchildren now."

"And a wife you love," she said, reflecting his brightening mood.

"I have grandchildren, too." Then she became wistful again. "But no husband. Just memories of an angel."

"Will I see Quetzalcoatl?"

"No," she said, very quickly. A decision she had long since made and would not reconsider. "It would not be good for you to meet face to face, or stand side by side. Quetzalcoatl also asks that in the next election, you refuse to be a candidate."

"Have I displeased him?" asked Sam.

"He asks this at my advice," she said. "It is better, now that his face will be seen in this land, that your face stay behind closed doors."

Sam nodded. "Tell me," he said. "Does he look like the angel?"

"He is as beautiful," she said. "But not as pure."

They embraced each other and wept. Only for a moment. Then her men lifted her back into her litter, and Sam returned with Carpenter to the helicopter. They never met again.

In retirement, I came to visit Sam, full of questions lingering from his meeting with Virgem America. "You knew each other," I insisted. "You had met before." He told me all this story then.

That was thirty years ago. She is dead now, he is dead, and I am old, my fingers slapping these keys with all the grace of wooden blocks. But I write this sitting in the shade of a tree on the brow of a hill, looking out across woodlands and orchards, fields and rivers and roads, where once the land was rock and grit and sagebrush. This is what America wanted, what it bent our lives to accomplish. Even if we took twisted roads and got lost or injured on the way, even if we came limping to this place, it is a good place, it is worth the journey, it is the promised, the promising land.

# MICHAEL BISHOP

## For Thus Do I Remember Carthage

Michael Bishop is one of the most acclaimed and respected members of that highly talented generation of writers who entered SF in the 1970s. His short fiction has appeared in almost all the major magazines and anthologies, and has been gathered in three collections: *Blooded on Arachne, One Winter in Eden*, and the recent *Close Encounters with the Deity*. In 1983, he won the Nebula Award for his novel *No Enemy but Time*. His other novels include *Transfigurations, Stolen Faces, Ancient of Days, Catacomb Years*, and *Eyes of Fire*. His most recent novel is *The Secret Ascension*. Upcoming is a new novel, *Unicorn Mountain*. Bishop and his family live in Pine Mountain, Georgia.

# FOR THUS DO I REMEMBER CARTHAGE

## Michael Bishop

### 1

Augustine wants no company, and the last person whom he expects to intrude is a troublesome astronomer from Far Cathay.

A fever has besieged the old man. In the bishop's house next to the basilica of Hippo Regius, he mulls the imminence of his own death and the portentous events of this past year.

An army of 20,000 Vandals has besieged Hippo. Under their wily king Genseric, they seem inevitable occupiers. Boniface, Count of Africa, has held them at bay throughout the summer with a force of Gothic mercenaries and a few ragtag volunteers from among the male population of upper Numidia—but Genseric's fleet has blockaded the harbor and Vandal soldiers have disabled the power plant providing Hippo with electricity. Augustine must read the psalms copied out and affixed to his bedchamber walls by the flicker of an olive-oil lamp rather than by the steady incandescence of one of Seneca the Illuminator's clever glass globes.

"This earthly city cannot last," the bishop tells himself, "but the City of God . . . the City of God endures."

Possidius appears inside the door of his bedchamber with a tray of pears, bread, and marinated chick-peas.

Bishop of Calama, a town twenty leagues to the south, Possidius fled to Hippo last October to escape the oncoming barbarians. (Two Numidian bishops less wise than he were tortured to death outside the walls of their cities.) He has lived in Augustine's episcopal quarters ten months now, but has been fussily nursing the brilliant old man for only these past two weeks.

"Go away, Possidius," murmurs Augustine.

"A modest *convivium*. Excellency, you must eat."

"Sometimes, Christ forgive me, it's hard to remember why."

"To maintain your strength, sir. And, this evening, you have a visitor."

"But I've forbidden visitors. Especially physicians."

"This isn't a physician. Vindicianus has almost lost patience with you, Excellency."

The old man in the loose black *birrus* says, "Whoever it is, is sadly unwelcome. Not for his shortcomings, but for mine."

Tears streak Augustine's face. He has been reading the Davidic psalm beginning "*Blessed is he whose transgression is forgiven*," and the balm of its verse "*Thou shalt preserve me from trouble*" has surely induced these tears. Frequently, of late, he weeps, and Possidius cannot tell if he does so from pity for the plight of Roman Africa, or from an unspeakable gratitude to God, or from some ancient shame for which only he of all men would scruple to indict himself. Undoubtedly, he weeps for many reasons, but the bishop of Calama is unable to sort them out.

"He's a stargazer, Excellency, who hails—he declares—from the capital of Africa." Possidius places the food tray on Augustine's writing desk.

"Carthage?"

"So he says. But he's spent the past thirty years looking at the stars from various high escarpments in Northern Wei."

"Ah, yes. Flying machines and dragons aren't the only miracles from that mythic land, are they?"

"Telescopes, Excellency. Horseless chariots. Boxes that talk, and others in which pictures dance like living people. Seneca the Illuminator says they've perfected machines in Cathay a *century* in advance of any made by the Daedaluses of Rome or Constantinople.

"But the greatest miracle, Excellency, may be that your visitor has returned to Numidia exactly when Genseric's Vandals have come bearing down on us from Gibraltar and Mauretania. The astronomer sneaked through their siege lines to enter the city. Morally, sir, I think you should grant him the interview he desires."

"Morally," the old man mutters. On his feet for the first time since Possidius came in, he totters to his desk, picks up a pear, burnishes it on his robe. He lifts it to his face, sniffing it for submerged memories. He has lived three quarters of a century, and a year besides, and that Possidius should be defining morality for him—fabled Defender of the Faith against the errors of Manichees, Donatists, and Pelagians—stings. But God knows that he sometimes needs chastening, and perhaps Possidius is God's flail.

"Does my would-be visitor have a name?"

"Iatanbaal, sir."

"Christ save us. A pagan name. Does this man have any Latin, Possidius, or am I to talk to him in my execrable Neo-Punic?"

Possidius smiles. "Latin is Iatanbaal's first language. But for three decades he has spoken in the tongues of Babel."

" 'Given of God,' " Augustine muses.

"Excellency?"

"In Neo-Punic, *Iatanbaal* means 'given of God.' " He places the pear back on his desk and lapses into reverie.

"Father Augustine," Possidius prompts.

The old apostle stirs. "Oh, yes. Our visitor. Iatanbaal. 'Given of God.' In that case, let him come in."

## 2

It startles Augustine to find that Iatanbaal—why did he expect a younger man?—is hard on sixty. The astronomer, who drops to his knees to kiss the bishop's hand, is as gray as he is.

The stargazer wears a tight tunic in decadent late-Roman style, but a pair of leggings—*trousers*—favored by Hsiung-nu horsemen in the service of the Wei Cathayans among whom he has lived since the turn of the fifth Christian century. Over one shoulder Iatanbaal carries a long leathern bag, and on his left wrist he wears a thin strap bearing on it an oblong jewel, very like obsidian.

This jewel is featureless, but when the astronomer stands, it strikes the edge of Augustine's desk. Suddenly, a row of crimson characters ignites atop the black stone. However, the gleam dies quickly, and Augustine crosses his hands on his breast to stare at the enigmatic bracelet.

"Pardon me, Excellency," the astronomer says, and their eyes lock. "This device is a miniature time-gem."

The bishop realizes that he and his guest are the same height, with irises the same slaty Berber gray. In other circumstances—the besieging Vandals elsewhere, his own death a decade rather than days away—they might have been friends. Augustine lets his gaze fall again to the "time-gem."

Each time that Iatanbaal depresses a metal stem on the device, tiny crimson characters appear. At first they say *VII:XXXVIII*. A moment later: *VII:XXXIX*. The astronomer explains that these numerals signify the hour and the minute, and that the horological artisans of Loyang made him a device with Roman digits—a feeble thrust at his homesickness. He reveals that the time-gem takes its power from a coinlike disc, or *energon*, within the jewel.

"Seven-forty," says the bishop when new numerals—*VII:XL*—wink into view. "By what criteria do you establish the hour?"

"In Northern Wei, Father Augustine, scientifically. But while traveling, by sun and simple intuition."

Augustine tacks about. "Why have you come, Master Iatanbaal?" His guest, he knows, wants to give him the time-gem, and he has no wish to accept it, either as token of esteem or as bribe. Death's specter has carried him beyond flattery, beyond manipulation.

"Because in your *Confessions*—a copy of which the former bishop of Alexandria let me see—I found you have an unusual philosophy of time, rivaling in sophistication the theories of our most learned Cathayan astronomers." Iatanbaal refastens his time-gem's strap. "It leads me to suspect that you alone of all Romanized westerners may be able to comprehend the startling cosmogony of the Wei genius Sung Hsi-chien. Comprehend and so appreciate."

"I wrote my *Confessions* a long time ago." Augustine eyes the astronomer warily. What he had penned about time in that book was that before God made heaven and earth, neither they nor time itself had any existence. Time did not begin until God spoke the word that inaugurated creation. Before time, there was no time, and what God did then (the conjecture that He was readying Hell for pryers into mysteries being a jesting canard), no mortal mind may reckon. Is that so amazing a theory of time? Is it powerful enough to call a Carthaginian astronomer home from Cathay to praise him? Augustine can scarcely credit such a motive.

"But, Excellency, you repeat and extend your discussion of time in the eleventh and twelfth books of *The City of God*. I read that masterpiece in Alexandria, too, but this time during a brief stop on my trip home from the Orient. In the eleventh book, you write—I've memorized the words—'*the world was made, not in time, but simultaneously with time*,' while in the twelfth you argue against those who hold that history is cyclic and that this world is born but to die and rise again. Sung Hsi-chien has discovered empirical proof of your positions in his astronomical observations, and this, I think, is a brave coincidence of minds."

"Empirical proof?" Augustine's fever has made him woozy. He sits down at his desk. "Master Iatanbaal, what need of empirical proof has a faith predicated on reason?"

"Why, none, I suppose, but Sung Hsi-chien and five generations of Cathayan lens-grinders, astronomers, cosmogonists, and sky-ray readers have still provided it. Since I was lucky enough to help Sung with his researches, I can outline these proofs for you."

"I don't require them."

"No, of course you don't. But you of all philosophers should wish to learn Sung's 'New Cosmogony.' "

"Ague grips me. I'm dying, Master Iatanbaal."

"Here, eat."

The astronomer pushes Possidius's tray toward the bishop, then hefts his long bag onto the opposite end of the desk. From it he pulls a tube of ivory and silver; an ebony box with a small glass port on its upper face; and two enameled packets, which Augustine decides are accessories to the ebony box. How he knows this, he cannot guess. But, sipping thoughtfully at his chick-pea marinade, he waits for Master Iatanbaal to explain.

"A telescope," the astronomer obliges, pointing to the tube. "Outside Lunghsi, in a tower on the Great Wall, the Wei Cathayans have a telescope so much larger than this one, Father Augustine, that it dwarfs the pillars of the Parthenon. An instrument even bigger dominates a hill near Lo-yang, while the grandest device of all stares skyward from a dome outside Ching-chao. Such far-seers, manned by imperial astronomers and scientists, have altered most of our old notions of the heavens."

Augustine dunks his bread in the piquant marinade. Telescopes larger than temple pillars? he thinks, working his bad teeth. This importunate scoundrel is lying.

"The Wei have also invented a type of colossal telescope that gathers and focuses invisible sky-rays from distant stars. The best is beyond Ku-shih, in the Takla Makan Desert, and Sung and his helpers visit it several times a year in a pterodrac—a mechanical flying dragon—commissioned by the Emperor. I myself have flown in this pterodrac, Father Augustine."

A madman, the bishop thinks. Colossal telescopes and draconoid flying machines. Fantasies that he presents as Holy Writ . . .

Iatanbaal lays the telescope aside and seizes on his ebony box, shifting it so that its tiny eye points directly at Augustine. "A luminotype chamber," he says, fingering a lever on its side. "With this, one can save the image of any object or person as it exists at the instant the operator depresses this lever. The Cathayans call such images—" the word worse than Greek to Augustine—"but I say *luminopicts*, 'light pictures,' and in Northern Wei scarcely a household is without a wall of such images in the family shrine."

"Why do you regale me with lies?"

Iatanbaal, heretofore the mildest of guests, bristles at this, but remains civil. "Lies? No lies, Excellency. The opposite. Your entire life has been a quest for truth, your whole career as a bishop a battle for truth against pagans and heretics. My prime motive in coming here—in traveling such distance; in risking my life to defy the Vandal blockade—was to bring you the cosmogonic truths that I learned in Cathay. To instruct you in them so that you may append them—before you die—to *The City of God*, the most glorious philosophy of history ever conceived."

"*Magnum opus et arduum*," Augustine murmurs. But aloud he says, "That book is finished. I can add nothing to it."

"I speak of *The City of God* in your mind, Excellency, not of dry words on paper. This grander *City of God*, the Platonic one you revise with every breath . . . unless I misjudge you terribly, *that* book will never be finished until your soul departs your body."

This approach nearly disarms Augustine. But he concludes that Iatanbaal is patronizing him and says, "I fear my soul is soon to do that. Please, sir, precede it in departing. I tire."

"By Christ, old man, I've not come all these years and all this distance to have you spurn my message!"

"Away, astronomer."

"God does not will it!"

"*Possidius*!" Augustine cries. "*Possidius, this man is*—"

"You don't believe me? Here, look!" Iatanbaal opens one of the packets beside his luminotype chamber. He thrusts at Augustine a smooth square of parchment: an image of five robed Cathayans.

These men are rendered monochromatically, in palpable light and shadow, their faces sharp but alien, the image of their robes as silken as the imaged garments. Augustine slides his thumb across the surface of this provocative square.

"A luminopict," Iatanbaal says. "The older man, at center, is Sung Hsi-chien. The rest are students—gifted disciples."

"A clever painting under an equally clever glaze."

"This isn't a hand-drawn artifact!" Iatanbaal says. "This is a luminopictic image from life, caught on a light-sensitive substance by the rapid opening and closing of this mechanical eye!"

"Do you destroy the box to remove the image? And must you make a second box to catch a second image?"

Possidius enters the bedchamber. Augustine wordlessly signals his fatigue to his fellow bishop, and Possidius, a wraith in black, approaches the astronomer.

"It's time for you to go."

The violence with which Iatanbaal shrugs aside Possidius's hand alarms Augustine. "Even the prodigal son received a warmer welcome than the one you hypocrites have tendered me!" Tears of resentment and frustration squeeze glistening from his lower lids.

"The basilica of Hippo Regius has a hostel for visitors," says Possidius. "Many now staying in it are refugees, but you, too, may shelter there. So why defame our hospitality?"

"Your flea-ridden hostel be damned!"

"Sir," says Possidius. "Sir, you try our—"

"I have no intention of deserting Father Augustine—not until death itself abstracts him from history!"

The old bishop, stunned by the astronomer's presumption, pounds his fist on the desk. "What gives you the right to impose yourself on a dying man in this unconscionable way?"

"One thing only: I'm your son, old man. I'm your son."

The fever in Augustine makes his head feel like the inflating hood of a cobra. He can think of nothing to say.

"Once, Father, you wrote of me, praising my virtues but taking no credit for them: 'I had no part in that boy, but the sin.' More recently, supposing me dead and quoting Cicero, you declared, 'You are the only man of all men whom I would wish to surpass me in all things.' A most poignant declaration."

"But you *are* dead," the bishop manages, woozier than ever with both brain heat and the fever of incomprehension.

"Iatanbaal means 'given of God,' Father. Adeodatus does, too, and my name—my true name—is Adeodatus."

## 3

Augustine remembers Carthage. There he acquired a concubine, a woman not of his class. The happiest issue of that union was the boy whom they named Adeodatus, 'given of God.' In those days—Christ be merciful—Augustine was a Manichee, a dualist proclaiming his belief in two contending gods, one benevolent and caring, one so malign and cruel that you could fix on it every sort of calamity plaguing the world. That was sixty years ago. Recently, a letter from Paulinus, bishop of Nola, has accused Augustine (facetiously, of course) of championing dualism again:

"What is *The City of God* but a manifesto dividing Creation into two camps? It seems, Aurelius Augustinius, you'll never completely elude the ghosts of your wayward past."

One such ghost has just popped up. Adeodatus—the boy he thought had died with the noble Nebridius in the undertow off the beach at Ostia—has reentered his life. He has done so only days before a mortal fever will—how did "Iatanbaal" put it?—oh, yes, *abstract him from history*. A reunion that renders mundane even the Gospel parable of the prodigal son.

How did Adeodatus survive those currents? And did Nebridius, Augustine's dearest companion after Alypius, also survive?

A single oil-burning lamp hisses in the bedchamber. Possidius has retreated to his own room. Genseric's soldiers shout obscene challenges along the inland walls of the city: shouts that clash, echo, fade, resurge.

Augustine's son—a "boy" of sixty—sits cross-legged on the floor, recounting in a monotone the story of his and Nebridius's adventure off the Italian coast. Adeodatus had been sixteen and his father's friend thirty-five.

"Nebridius, Father, had no adventure. I'm certain he drowned. I, though, was whipped out to sea. Prayer kept me afloat. Libyan pirates picked me up west of Naples. For the next nine years I was a helpless witness to their raids around the coastal towns of the Mediterranean. Finally, unwisely trusted to carry out a theft on my own, I escaped into the arms of some Greek mariners. These kind Greeks transported me to Alexandria. . . ."

Heavy-lidded and hot, Augustine listens to Adeodatus with half his attention. The details of his story are not important; vitally important, however, is the fact that after venturing to Cathay from Alexandria and living there an adult lifetime, his son has returned to Numidia. To keep filial vigil at his deathbed and to bring him . . . well, the Truth.

The old man feels his son's dry lips kissing his forehead; his own papery eyelids flutter open.

"Sleep, Father. In the morning you'll easily comprehend all the miraculous things I intend to tell you."

"Adeodatus—"

"Sleep. I've come home to stay."

Augustine remembers Carthage. He dreams of it. There he met his son's low-born mother. There he deceived the blessed Monica, his own mother, by boarding a ship to Italy while she supposed him awaiting a fairer wind. City of rowdy "scholars," pagan shrines, vain theatrics, and vulgar circus shows. In his dream—his fevered memory—Carthage rises again, raucous with trade and pageantry. He sees it as it was then, four decades before the globes of Seneca the Illuminator set its streets and windows ablaze even at deepest midnight. His memory, carried into dream, quickens every emotion—the four great perturbations of the mind—that he experienced as a self-conscious youth in Carthage.

Desire, joy, fear, and sorrow.

I knew them all there, the dreaming Augustine reflects. I know them all again every time I reenvision the city.

God, too, he discovers and rediscovers in memory and dream, as he inwardly quests for the One Thing to fill the emptiness created by his own temporary amnesia. That One Thing is God. If he ever forgets God, he finds Him again in memory, a fact that seems to the bishop a rational proof of His existence. For you cannot remember what you have wholly forgotten. God, however, resides within; and when you trip over That Which refurnishes the emptiness, you say to yourself, "This is it," and you know that the processes of your own mind have led you ineluctably back to Him.

As memory can resurrect the Carthage of old, Augustine dreamily reasons, so can it reacquaint us with our changeless Father. . . .

Adeodatus has made a pallet for himself in the bedchamber. He is using his doubled-up telescope bag for a pillow.

The cries of the barbarian heretics beyond Hippo's walls—Arian Christians who deny that Father and Son share the same substance—buzz in Augustine's head like evil flies. When he moans, his own son touches a wet cloth to his brow.

And another thing, Augustine thinks: As my memory holds every unforgotten moment of my life, God contains every possible reality, but without possessing either a past or a future. Everything that has ever happened, is happening now, or will happen tomorrow abides in Him. He foreknew—*knows*, rather—that Adeodatus would return as I lay on death's threshold, and He has ever known what he will tell me tomorrow about Sung Hsi-chien's "New Cosmogony."

Dear God, you are indeed an unpredictable dramaturge.

## 4

Morning. Augustine's fever has broken. He offers a prayer of thanksgiving and another for deliverance. Then he and Adeodatus eat the pears that Possidius brought to him last night.

"The universe is far vaster than any Greek or Roman astronomer has ever told us," Adeodatus says.

It would not surprise Augustine if the universe were *infinite* in size. Can the omnipotence of the Creator have limits?

"And far older," Adeodatus continues. "And far stranger than even Ptolemy himself supposed."

Augustine has read—long ago—Claudius Ptolemaeus's great book on astronomy. Once, in Milan, he even perused a Latin translation of a star catalogue compiled by Hipparchus, much of whose original work, in Greek, Ptolemy summarized and supplemented in his own book.

But Adeodatus has already begun his recitation:

"First, the Earth circles the Sun, just as Aristarchus of Samos posited. Second, beyond Saturn are three planets that no Western observer has ever beheld. Third, there is a force that I can best call *attractiveness* that governs the movements of both planetary bodies and stars. Fourth, the Sun is but an unprepossessing minnow of a star in an enormous school of stars that the Cathayans call the Silver Whirlpool. Fifth, as many of these 'schools' of stars swim through the universe as do solitary stars in our local Silver Whirlpool. The Cathayans have their own picturesque word for these enormous stellar families, but let me simply call them *lactastrons*, for they resemble whirlpools of curdled milk. Sixth, light travels at a speed—accurately determined a century ago by an Eastern Chin astronomer named Wang Mi—that is a universal constant. Seventh, this speed, altogether peculiarly, does not increase if you add any other velocity to it. Eighth—"

Just as I first supposed, Augustine thinks. My visitor—*my son*—is a madman. Flesh of my flesh, a lunatic.

Aloud he protests: "How can you add something to something else without making it larger?"

Adeodatus hesitates. "I don't know. But Wang Mi conclusively determined that nothing exceeds the speed of light, and from this discovery eventually sprang Sung Hsi-chien's . . . well, I can only translate these remarkable constructs as his 'Postulatum of Temporal Comparativity' and his 'Postulatum of Attractive Comparativity.' From them, Father, Sung and his best students were able to go on to the formulation of a 'New Cosmogony,' and it is *that* great truth—with its implications for faith and eschatology—into which I want to initiate you."

"Add one to ten," Augustine growls. "It sums to eleven. You *cannot* add something to something else without enlarging it."

Adeodatus puts a hand on his father's forearm. "Add Christ to God, Father. Have you made the Almighty greater?"

The old man is stymied. "No" is the only orthodox answer. To say "Yes" would be to embrace a heresy akin to Arianism, the chief spiritual error of Hippo's besiegers.

Adeodatus resumes his lecture. He talks of lactastrons—milky clans of stars—thousands of *annilumes* away. The Cathayans, he says, have so refined the arts of lens- and mirror-making that they can see the microworlds at their fingertips as profitably as they can the cosmos annilumes beyond our own whirl of planets. Indeed, they have discovered the basic units of matter (*atoms*, to follow Democritus) and ordered the various earthly elements on a graph now used as a vital pedagogic tool in their science academies.

Yet another device—Adeodatus, with a Greek twist, translates it as *chromoscope*—enables Cathayan astronomers to deduce the physical composition of celestial bodies and so to classify them. What they know about the creation of the heavens and the Earth beggars the imagination; not even the poetry of Genesis is grand enough to hymn the boldness of their discoveries.

"You're insane," Augustine says. "These outlandish lies reveal your contempt for me. They blaspheme the Creator."

"Father Augustine, I'm not asking you to deny God or to betray Christ. Once, Catholicism struck you as ridiculous. You were a Manichee who dismissed the faith of your mother, Monica, as beneath the consideration of the educated. Yet today, caught in orthodoxy, you spurn the knowledge I bring from Cathay because it seems—at first—contrary to your current thinking. When, Father, did your mind petrify? Don't you see that not one item in my catalogue of wonders sabotages your faith at any *essential* level?"

Where does this graybeard boy get the audacity to prate of the petrification of my mind? Augustine asks himself. Why, from me, of course. He inherited it. . . .

Later that day, three men try to pay Augustine their respects: Possidius, who brings the *prandium*, a midday meal of cheese, fruit, and wine; Eraclius, the priest who succeeded Augustine in the basilica's pulpit; and Vindicianus, a physician who wants to apply a poultice of grape hulls and olive oil to Augustine's forehead.

Following his father's wishes, Adeodatus allows the *prandium* to enter, but not the man who brought it. He also turns away Eraclius and Vindicianus. On departing, the latter announces that Augustine probably won't live to regret declining his poultice.

The bishop eats another pear—forbidden fruit, it seems to him, and therefore gloriously sweet—while his son takes the cheese and most of the watered wine. As they refuel themselves, Adeodatus continues his recitation:

In addition to planets, stars, nebular bodies, and lactastrons of all shapes, sizes, and degrees of energy production, the cosmos contains such perplexing phenomena as "invisible abysses" (dying stars whose own terrible "attractiveness" has led them to collapse into colossal stellar deadfalls) and "quasistrons" ("almost-stars" which a Northern Wei observer, Hong-yi Chiu, detected twenty-five years ago with the sky-ray-gathering telescopes in the Takla Makan Desert). These latter phenomena, Adeodatus tells Augustine, appear to be the most distant objects in all the created universe. That they should even be detectable suggests that they are pouring into the void more candlepower and invisible-ray emissions than all the suns in the entire Silver Whirlpool. Perhaps each quasistron is a battlefield in the war between the fallen angels in Lucifer's camp and the seraphic host still loyal to God.

"Those battles occurred near time's nativity," says Augustine. "Even if they continue today in every human breast, they began long before God made Adam."

"Exactly. The light from quasistrons has been en route to us from five to ten billion years; we are peering not only to the far periphery of the universe but also to its temporal infancy. We are retro-observing the pangs of Creation."

Augustine's temples throb. He cannot say if he is exhilarated or demoralized by this news. Or even whether he believes it.

"Undoubtedly, most of the quasistrons Hong-yi Chiu has found and indexed don't even exist anymore." Adeodatus shows his father the luminopict again. "Look. This is Hong-yi. This stout, youthful fellow standing next to Sung. It was in his household that I lived for the last six years of my sojourn in Cathay. He believes that quasistrons—the term *almost-stars* was his coinage, and even Sung came to approve it—are the hearts of forming lactastrons, and that quasistrons derive their power from invisible abysses—'attraction pits'—eating all the interstellar matter around them. If angelic war preceded the generation of lactastrons, Father, it was a war of unholy violence. But, on the macrocosmic level at least, that war has been over for billions of years."

"More mendaciousness," Augustine counters. "Reckoning by our sacred scriptures, we know that not six thousand years have passed since Creation." But the authority with which Adeodatus states his case has sabotaged the old man's certitude.

"The scriptures are often metaphorical, Father, and Sung's New Cosmogony invalidates their chronology."

Augustine refrains from crying blasphemy; he has already done that. "Stop temporizing, then. Tell me Sung's theory."

Relieved, the graybeard boy talks of sky-ray transmission, the ongoing sibilance of the void, and a law whose discovery he credits to Hong-yi Chiu's father, Hong-yi Pang, who stated it thus: "All lactastrons but the nearest are fleeing from our Silver Whirlpool at velocities in harmony with their distances."

The "Formula of Hong-yi Pang," as Adeodatus terms it, implies that every lactastron in the cosmos had its beginning in a compact central locale. Time and matter alike were frozen together in a lump in this primeval place. Presumably, upon God's command they exploded like a many-vented volcano, flinging the ingredients of Creation out into the virgin dark.

But it was old Sung Hsi-chien who formed this idea from his own theories of comparativity, the observations of four generations of Cathayan stargazers, the hypotheses of a forward-looking school of microtheoreticians, and the lactastron law of the elder Hong-yi. Sung called his simple but startling explanation of the origin of the cosmos the "Earliest Eruption Postulatum."

Adeodatus, Augustine senses, places more faith in Sung's theory than in the opening verses of Genesis. Oddly, however, his son's enthusiasm for the Cathayan's cosmogony excites him, too. Excites and frightens . . .

He gropes for a response: "Billions of leagues, billions of years. Adeodatus, you play among these enormous figures like a boy stirring a stick in an anthill. How did Hong-yi Chiu, this friend of yours, arrive at the absurd conclusion that his 'almost-stars'—his *quasistrons*—are so preposterously far away?" The bishop has realized that the vast stretches of time in Sung's cosmogony depend for their validity—granting the accuracy of Wang Mi's calculation of the speed of light—on the reliability of Cathayan assessments of interstellar distances; and so he seeks, halfheartedly perhaps, to attack the postulatum at this point.

A strategy that fails to disconcert his son. Adeodatus speaks of measuring the distance to stars by noting their differences in observed direction when viewed at different times in the Earth's orbit about the Sun. Again translating from the Cathayan, he calls this difference the *transprox* of the star. He goes on to talk of the *chromolume patterns* of heavenly bodies and of how those of his friend Chiu's quasistrons disclose a *sanguineous conversion* typical of celestial bodies receding at high speeds. The evidence for the existence of great distances and of vast stretches of time in the constitution of the universe, he implies, is overwhelming; only an illiterate reversionary would question it.

"Now when I set out for home from Ku-shih, Father," Adeodatus concedes, "a dispute was raging between my friend Chiu and another of Sung's disciples, An Hopeh, about the *meaning* of the sanguineous conversions shown by Chiu's quasistrons. Did the lengthening—the reddening—of the light rays from these almost-stars result from their rapid recession from us or from curious attractional effects that would permit us to think them much nearer our own lactastron, possibly even within it?

"This was an important dispute. If the reddening derived from recession, it would confirm Sung's Earliest Eruption Postulatum: the universe is ever inflating. If, on the other hand, it results from a discordant attractiveness in Chiu's quasistrons, the enemies of Sung's postulatum—those who believe that something other than a primeval eruption began the universe—could rightfully take heart. Further, they wouldn't have to explain from where the quasistrons gather all the 'fuel' to burn so brightly for so long. Because the almost-stars would be *nearer* than Chiu believes, they wouldn't be as perplexingly bright as he has always claimed.

"In any event, Father, An Hopeh had many allies, astronomers jealous of old Sung or simply unhappy with the notion of a universe forever expanding. Not long before I left, however, the dispute seemed to be resolving itself in Hong-yi Chiu's favor. Two of his pupils at the Lo-yang Academy of Sky Studies found some quasistrons surrounded by a faint, glowing pilosity. A luminous hairiness. It had the precise look of very distant lactastrons, and chromoscopic surveys of the light from this pilosity show it to exhibit the same sanguineous conversion—reddening—as the almost-stars embedded in it. This seems to prove that Chiu's quasistrons are truly billions of annilumes away and that Sung is right in crediting the origin of the universe to a primordial eruption."

"Enough of this," Augustine murmurs, clutching his head in his gnarled hands. "Please, Adeodatus, no more today."

"Forgive me, Father. I've spoken in such detail only because I wanted you to see that your theory of time coincides with Sung's. So does your belief in the linearity of history. You reject the Greek notion of cycles; so do Sung and his disciples, who believe the universe will die of cold, a plethora of icy, black lactastrons wobbling out into the darkness forever."

"That *isn't* what I believe!" Augustine rages. "We'll have our end not in ice, but in judgment and transformation!"

"You speak of the soul, Father, but I of the palpable world all about us. And Sung has found too little attractive force among the lactastrons to halt the universal expansion and to draw all matter back into a lump that may again erupt, to begin this cosmic vanity anew. *His* position coincides with *yours*—a 'No!' to the periodic rebirth of worlds. In that, you're kindred thinkers."

"We're brothers only in our shared humanity!" Augustine says. "What religion does he have?"

Adeodatus thinks. "I'm not sure. His work, perhaps."

"I've listened to you for as long as I can, Master Iatanbaal. Harangue me no more. Have mercy upon me and go."

The astronomer—his son—reluctantly obeys, and Augustine notes with wary surprise that darkness has fallen and that he himself is chill-ridden as well as feverish. Genseric's soldiers rattle their weaponry outside the city gates, and both the Roman Empire and the bishop's careworn body seem destined for the charnel heap. . . .

## 5

An uproar in the corridor. Possidius is arguing with somebody who speaks Latin with a peculiar accent. Augustine, his intellect a scatter of crimson coals, sits up to see a tall black man pushing into his bedchamber past the flustered Possidius. The black man wears only a soiled tunic and sandals. Over his shoulder, a large woven bag as filthy as his tunic.

"You can't do this! The bishop is gravely ill!"

"I had a dream," the black man keeps saying, dancing with the frantic Possidius. "My dream told me to come to Augustine."

Augustine gathers the coals of his mind into a single glowing pile and looks at the Ethiop. This business of the dream touches him: He has never been able to dismiss the requests of those who have dreamed that he could help them. Indeed, Monica, his mother, envisioned his own salvation in a dream.

"Let him stay, Possidius."

The black man bows his head respectfully and says, "My name, Excellency, is Khoinata. Thank you."

"Where's my son?" Augustine asks Possidius.

"In the hostel, Excellency. He has assured me that he won't intrude on you again without your direct summons."

"A policy that I urge you, too, to adopt, Possidius."

As soon as Possidius, visibly wounded, has left, Augustine asks the Ethiop what distance he has traveled and why he thinks that the bishop of Hippo can help him. Like Adeodatus, Khoinata has sneaked through Vandal lines to enter the city, and he has come all the way from the farthest Kush, a great African kingdom, for the privilege of this interview. He believes that what he has brought with him will prove to the imperious Romans that the Kushites are a people with an admirable history and a civilization deserving of the prose of a Tacitus or a Suetonius.

"What do you have?" Augustine asks him.

Instantly, Khoinata gets down on all fours, opens his bag, and begins assembling with impressive dexterity and speed the skeleton of a creature that seems—to Augustine's untutored eye—a troubling conflation of human being and ape.

"My brothers and I found these bones far south of Meroe. They belong to an early kind of man, a kind almost certainly ancestral to you and me. Notice: the curve of these foot bones—the way they fit with these other bones from the lower legs—*that* shows that the creature walked erect. And the skull—look here, Excellency—its skull is larger than those of apes and yet not quite so large as an adult Roman's. One of our wisest chieftains, Khoboshama, shaped a theory to explain such strangeness. He calls it the 'Unfolding of Animal Types,' and I believe it should greatly interest teachers of natural history from Carthage to Milan."

Augustine merely stares at Khoinata.

Khoinata says, "We know these bones are old—very, very old—because Khoboshama counted the rock layers in the declivity where we found them. In addition, he . . ."

Augustine spreads out the coals of his mind. He cannot keep them burning under Khoinata's discourse. He both sees and does not see the skeleton that his guest has arranged—as if from dry, brown coals—on the floor of his bedchamber. The creature has been dead for almost two million years—yes, that's the figure that the man cites—but it lives in Khoinata's imagination, and Augustine has no idea how to drive it from thence.

"Excellency, are you listening?"

"No," the bishop replies.

"But, Excellency, only you of all Romanized westerners are wise enough to grasp the far-ranging implications of . . ."

The old man feels a foreign excrescence on his arm. He glances down and finds that Adeodatus has strapped his Cathayan time-gem to his wrist.

Heedless of Khoinata, he depresses the stem on the side of its obsidian jewel, and these characters manifest on the black face of the tiny engine: *XII:I*.

The hour is one minute past midnight.

Something old is ending. Something new is beginning.

# KIM STANLEY ROBINSON

## Mother Goddess of the World

Kim Stanley Robinson sold his first story in 1976, and quickly established himself as one of the most respected and critically acclaimed writers of his generation. He is a frequent contributor to such markets as *Isaac Asimov's Science Fiction Magazine, The Magazine of Fantasy and Science Fiction, Universe*, and *Omni*. Robinson's books include the acclaimed novel *The Wild Shore, Icehenge*, and *The Memory of Whiteness*, and the critical book *The Novels of Philip K. Dick*. His most recent books are *The Planet on the Table,* a collection, and a new novel, *The Gold Coast.* His World Fantasy Award–winning story "Black Air" was in our in our First Annual Collection; his story "The Lucky Strike" was in our Second Annual Collection; "Green Mars" was in our Third Annual Collection; and "Down and Out in the Year 2000" was in our Fourth Annual Collection. Robinson and his wife, Lisa, are back in the United States after several years in Switzerland.

Robinson is known for his use of exotic locales, having given us stories set on Mars, on a ship of the Spanish Armada, in a sinking future Venice, and on the molten surface of Mercury. Here he takes us deep into the Himalayas, and up Chomolunga, Mother Goddess of the World, the tallest mountain on Earth (you probably know it better as Mt. Everest), for a delightful screwball comedy featuring an oddly assorted cast of characters on a risky, improbable, and decidedly *strange* quest.

# MOTHER GODDESS OF THE WORLD

## Kim Stanley Robinson

### 1

My life started to get weird again the night I ran into Freds Fredericks, near Chimoa, in the gorge of the Dudh Kosi. I was guiding a trek at the time, and was very happy to see Freds. He was traveling with another climber, a Tibetan by the name of Kunga Norbu, who appeared to speak little English except for "Good morning," which he said to me as Fred introduced us, even though it was just after sunset. My trekking group was settled into their tents for the night, so Freds and Kunga and I headed for the cluster of teahouses tucked into the forest by the trail. We looked in them; two had been cleaned up for trekkers, and the third was a teahouse in the old style, frequented only by porters. We ducked into that one.

It was a single low room; we had to stoop not only under the beams that held up the slate roof, but also under the smoke layer. Old style country buildings in Nepal do not have chimneys, and the smoke from their wood stoves just goes up to the roof and collects there in a very thick layer, which lowers until it begins to seep out under the eaves. Why the Nepalis don't use chimneys, which I would have thought a fairly basic invention, is a question no one can answer; it is yet another Great Mystery of Nepal.

Five wooden tables were occupied by Rawang and Sherpa porters, sprawled on the benches. At one end of the room the stove was crackling away. Flames from the stove and a hissing Coleman lantern provided the light. We said Namaste to all the staring Nepalis, and ducked under the smoke to sit at the table nearest the stove, which was empty.

We let Kunga Norbu take care of the ordering, as he had more Nepali than Freds or me. When he was done the Rawang stove keepers giggled and went to the stove, and came back with three huge cups of Tibetan tea.

I complained to Freds about this in no uncertain terms. "Damn it, I thought he was ordering chang!"

Tibetan tea, you see, is not your ordinary Lipton's. To make it they start with a black liquid that is not made from tea leaves at all but from some kind of root, and it is so bitter you could use it for suturing. They pour a lot of salt into this brew, and stir it up, and then they dose it liberally with rancid yak butter, which melts and floats to the top.

Actually it tastes worse than it sounds. I have developed a strategy for dealing with the stuff whenever I am offered a cup; I look out the nearest window, and water the plants with it. As long as I don't do it too fast and get poured a second cup, I'm fine. But here I couldn't do that, because twenty-odd pairs of laughing eyes were staring at us.

Kunga Norbu was hunched over the table, slurping from his cup and going "ooh," and "ahh," and saying complimentary things to the stove keepers. They nodded and looked closely at Freds and me, big grins on their faces.

Freds grabbed his cup and took a big gulp of the tea. He smacked his lips like a wine taster. "Right on," he said, and drained the cup down. He held it up to our host. "More?" he said, pointing into the cup.

The porters howled. Our host refilled Freds's cup and he slurped it down again, smacking his lips after every swallow. I held my nose to get down a sip, and they thought that was funny too.

So we were in tight with the teahouse crowd, and when I asked for chang they brought over a whole bucket of it. We poured it into the little chipped teahouse glasses and went to work on it.

"So what are you and Kunga Norbu up to?" I asked Freds.

"Well," he said, and a funny expression crossed his face. "That's kind of a long story, actually."

"So tell it to me."

He looked uncertain. "It's too long to tell tonight."

"What's this? A story too long for Freds Fredericks to tell? Impossible, man, why I once heard you summarize the Bible to Laure, and it only took you a minute."

Freds shook his head. "It's longer than that."

"I see." I let it go, and the three of us kept on drinking the chang, which is a white beer made from rice or barley. We drank a lot of it, which is a dangerous proposition on several counts, but we didn't care. As we drank we kept slumping lower over the table to try and get under the smoke layer, and besides we just naturally felt like slumping at that point. Eventually we were laid out like mud in a puddle.

Freds kept conferring with Kunga Norbu in Tibetan, and I got curious. "Freds, you hardly speak a word of Nepali, how is it you know so much Tibetan?"

"I spent a couple years in Tibet, a long time ago. I was studying in one of the Buddhist lamaseries there."

"*You* studied in a Buddhist lamasery in Tibet?"

"Yeah sure! Can't you tell?"

"Well . . ." I waved a hand. "I guess that might explain it."

"That was where I met Kunga Norbu, in fact. He was my teacher."

"I thought he was a climbing buddy."

"Oh he is! He's a climbing lama. Actually there's quite a number of them. See when the Chinese invaded Tibet they closed down all the lamaseries, destroyed most of them in fact. The monks had to go to work, and the lamas either slipped over to Nepal, or moved up into mountain caves. Then later the Chinese wanted to start climbing mountains as propaganda efforts, to show the rightness of the thoughts of Chairman Mao. The altitude in the Himalayas was a little bit much for them, though, so they mostly used Tibetans, and called them Chinese. And the Tibetans with the most actual mountain experience turned out to be Buddhist lamas, who had spent a lot of time in really high, isolated retreats. Eight of the nine so-called Chinese to reach the top of Everest in 1975 were actually Tibetans."

"Was Kunga Norbu one of them?"

"No. Although he wishes he was, let me tell you. But he did go pretty high on the North Ridge in the Chinese expedition of 1980. He's a really strong climber. And a great guru too, a really holy guy."

Kunga Norbu looked across the table at me, aware that we were talking about him. He was short and skinny, very tough looking, with long black hair. Like a lot of Tibetans, he looked almost exactly like a Navaho or Apache Indian. When he looked at me I got a funny feeling; it was as if he was staring right through me to infinity. Or somewhere equally distant. No doubt lamas cultivate that look.

"So what are you two doing up here?" I asked, a bit uncomfortable.

"We're going to join my Brit buddies, and climb Lingtren. Should be great. And then Kunga and I might try a little something on our own."

We found we had finished off the bucket of chang, and we ordered another. More of that and we became even lower than mud in a puddle.

Suddenly Kunga Norbu spoke to Freds, gesturing at me. "Really?" Freds said, and they talked some more. Finally Freds turned to me. "Well, this is a pretty big honor, George. Kunga wants me to tell you who he really is."

"Very nice of him," I said. I found that with my chin on the table I had to move my whole head to speak.

Freds lowered his voice, which seemed to me unnecessary as we were the only two people in the room who spoke English. "Do you know what a tulku is, George?"

"I think so," I said. "Some of the Buddhist lamas up here are supposed to be reincarnated from earlier lamas, and they're called tulkus, right? The abbot at Tengboche is supposed to be one."

Freds nodded. "That's right." He patted Kunga Norbu on the shoulder. "Well, Kunga here is also a tulku."

"I see." I considered the etiquette of such a situation, but couldn't really figure it, so finally I just scraped my chin off the table and stuck my hand across it. Kunga Norbu took it and shook, with a brief, modest smile.

"I'm serious," Freds said.

"Hey!" I said. "Did I say you weren't serious?"

"No. But you don't believe it, do you."

"I believe that you believe it, Freds."

"He really is a tulku! I mean I've seen proof of it, I really have. His *ku kongma*, which means his first incarnation, was as Naropa, a very important Tibetan lama born in 1555. The monastery at Kum-Bum is located on the site of his birth."

I nodded, at a loss for words. Finally I filled up our little cups, and we toasted Kunga Norbu's age. He could definitely put down the chang like he had had lifetimes of practice. "So," I said, calculating. "He's about four hundred and thirty-one."

"That's right. And he's had a hard time of it, I'll tell you. The Chinese tore down Kum-Bum as soon as they took over, and unless the monastery there is functioning again, Naropa can never escape being a disciple. See, even though he is a major tulku—"

"A major tulku," I repeated, liking the sound of it.

"Yeah, even though he's a major tulku, he's still always been the disciple of an even bigger one, named Tilopa. Tilopa Lama is about as important as they come—only the Dalai Lama tops him—and Tilopa is one hard, hard guru."

I noticed that the mention of Tilopa's name made Kunga Norbu scowl, and refill his glass.

"Tilopa is so tough that the only disciple who has ever stuck with him has been Kunga here. Tilopa—when you want to become his student and you go ask him, he beats you with a stick. He'll do that for a couple of years to make sure you really want him as a teacher. And then he really puts you through the wringer. Apparently he uses the methods of the Ts'an sect in China, which are tough. To teach you the Short Path to Enlightenment he pounds you in the head with his shoe."

"Now that you mention it, he does look a little like a guy who has been pounded in the head with a shoe."

"How can he help it? He's been a disciple of Tilopa's for four hundred years, and it's always the same thing. So he asked Tilopa when he would be a guru in his own right, and Tilopa said it couldn't happen until the monastery built on Kunga's birth site was rebuilt. And he said that *that* would never happen until Kunga managed to accomplish—well, a certain task. I can't tell you exactly what the task is yet, but believe me it's tough. And Kunga used to be *my* guru, see, so he's come to ask me for some help. So that's what I'm here to do."

"I thought you said you were going to climb Lingtren with your British friends?"

"That too."

I wasn't sure if it was the chang or the smoke, but I was getting a little confused. "Well, whatever. It sounds like a real adventure."

"You're not kidding."

Freds spoke in Tibetan to Kunga Norbu, explaining what he had said to me, I assumed. Finally Kunga replied, at length.

Freds said to me, "Kunga says you can help him too."

"I think I'll pass," I said. "I've got my trekking group and all, you know."

"Oh I know, I know. Besides, it's going to be tough. But Kunga likes you—he says you have the spirit of Milarespa."

Kunga nodded vigorously when he heard the name Milarespa, staring through me with that spacy look of his.

"I'm glad to hear it," I said. "But I still think I'll pass."

"We'll see what happens," Freds said, looking thoughtful.

## 2

Many glasses of chang later we staggered out into the night. Freds and Kunga Norbu slipped on their down jackets, and with a "Good night" and a "Good morning" they wandered off to their tent. I made my way back to my group. It felt really late, and was maybe 8:30.

As I stood looking at our tent village, I saw a light bouncing down the trail from Lukla. The man carrying the flashlight approached—it was Laure, the sirdhar for my group. He was just getting back from escorting clients back to Lukla. "Laure!" I called softly.

"Hello George," he said. "Why late now?"

"I've been drinking."

"Ah." With his flashlight pointed at the ground I could easily make out his big smile. "Good idea."

"Yeah, you should go have some chang yourself. You've had a long day."

"Not long."

"Sure." He had been escorting disgruntled clients back to Lukla all day, so he must have hiked five times as far as the rest of us. And here he was coming in by flashlight. Still, I suppose for Laure Tenzing Sherpa that did not represent a particularly tough day. As guide and yakboy he had been walking in these mountains all his life, and his calves were as big around as my thighs. Once, for a lark, he and three friends had set a record by hiking from Everest Base Camp to Kathmandu in four days; that's about two hundred miles, across the grain of some seriously uneven countryside. Compared to that today's work had been like a walk to the mailbox, I guess.

The worst part had no doubt been the clients. I asked him about them and he frowned. "People go co-op hotel, not happy. Very, very not happy. They fly back Kathmandu."

"Good riddance," I said. "Why don't you go get some chang."

He smiled and disappeared into the dark.

I looked over the tents holding my sleeping clients and sighed.

So far it had been a typical videotrek. We had flown in to Lukla from Kathmandu, and my clients, enticed to Nepal by glossy ads promising them video Ansel Adamshood, had gone wild in the plane, rushing about banging zoom lenses together in an attempt to film everything. They were irrepressible until they saw the Lukla strip, which from the air looks like a toy model of a ski jump. Pretty quickly they were strapped in and looking like they were reconsidering their wills—all except for one tubby little guy named Arnold, who continued to roll up and down the aisle like a bowling ball, finally inserting himself into the cockpit so he could shoot over the pilots' shoulders. "We are landing at Lukla," he announced to his camera's mike in a deep fakey voice, like the narrator of a bad travelogue. "Looks impossible, but our pilots are calm."

Despite him we landed safely. Unfortunately one of our group then tried to film his own descent from the plane, and fell heavily down the steps. As I ascertained the damage—a sprained ankle—there was Arnold again, leaning over to immortalize the victim's every writhe and howl.

A second plane brought in the rest of our group, led by Laure and my assistant Heather. We started down the trail, and for a couple of hours everything went well—the trail serves as the Interstate Five of the region, and is as easy as they come. And the view is awesome—

the Dudh Kosi valley is like a forested Grand Canyon, only bigger. Our group was impressed, and several of them filmed a real-time record of the day.

Then the trail descended to the banks of the Dudh Kosi river, and we got a surprise. Apparently in the last monsoon a glacial lake upstream had burst its ice dam, and rushed down in a devastating flood, tearing out the bridges, trail, trees, everything. Thus our fine interstate ended abruptly in a cliff overhanging the torn-to-shreds riverbed, and what came next was the seat-of-the-pants invention of the local porters, for whom the trail was a daily necessity. They had been clever indeed, but there really was no good alternative to the old route; so the new trail wound over strewn white boulders, traversed unstable new sand cliffs, and veered wildly up and down muddy slides that had been hacked out of dense forested walls. It was radical stuff, and even experienced trekkers were having trouble.

Our group was appalled. The ads had not mentioned this.

The porters ran ahead barefoot to reach the next tea break, and the clients began to bog down. People slipped and fell. People sat down and cried. Altitude sickness was mentioned more than once, though as a matter of fact we were not much higher than Denver. Heather and I ran around encouraging the weary. I found myself carrying three videocameras. Laure was carrying nine.

It was looking like the retreat from Moscow when we came to the first of the new bridges. These are pretty neat pieces of backwoods engineering; there aren't any logs in the area long enough to span the river, so they take four logs and stick them out over the river, and weigh them down with a huge pile of round stones. Then four more logs are pushed out from the other side, until their ends rest on the ends of the first four. Instant bridge. They work, but they are not confidence builders.

Our group stared at the first one apprehensively. Arnold appeared behind us and chomped an unlit cigar as he filmed the scene. "The *Death Bridge*," he announced into his camera's mike.

"Arnold, please," I said. "Mellow out."

He walked down to the glacial gray rush of the river. "Hey, George, do you think I could take a step in to get a better shot of the crossing?"

"NO!" I stood up fast. "One step in and you'd drown, I mean look at it!"

"Well, okay."

Now the rest of the group were staring at me in horror, as if it weren't clear at first glance that to fall into the Dudh Kosi would be a very fatal error indeed. A good number of them ended up crawling across the bridge on hands and knees. Arnold got them all for posterity, and filmed his own crossing by walking in circles that made me cringe. Silently I cursed him; I was pretty sure he had known perfectly well how dangerous the river was, and only wanted to make sure everyone else did too. And very soon after that—at the next bridge, in fact—people began to demand to be taken back to Lukla. To Kathmandu. To San Francisco.

I sighed, remembering it. And remembering it was only the beginning. Just your typical Want to Take You Higher Ltd. videotrek. Plus Arnold.

## 3

I got another bit of Arnold in action early the next morning when I was in the rough outhouse behind the trekkers' teahouses, very hung over, crouched over the unhealthily damp hole in the floor. I had just completed my business in there when I looked up to see the big glass eye of a zoom lens, staring over the top of the wooden door at me.

"No, Arnold!" I cried, struggling to put my hand over the lens while I pulled up my pants.

"Hey, just getting some local color," Arnold said, backing away. "You know, people like to see what it's really like, the details and all, and these outhouses are really something else. Exotic."

I growled at him. "You should have trekked in from Jiri, then. The lowland villages don't have outhouses at all."

His eyes got round, and he shifted an unlit cigar to the other side of his mouth. "What do you do, then?"

"Well, you just go outside and have a look around. Pick a spot. They usually have a shitting field down by the river. Real exotic."

He laughed. "You mean, turds everywhere?"

"Well, something like that."

"That sounds great! Maybe I'd better walk back out instead of flying."

I stared at him, wrinkling my nose. "Serious filmmaker, eh Arnold?"

"Oh, yeah. Haven't you heard of me? Arnold McConnell? I make adventure films for PBS. And sometimes for the ski resort circuit, video rentals, that kind of thing. Skiing, hang gliding, kayaking, parachuting, climbing, skateboarding—I've done them all. Didn't you ever see *The Man Who Swam Down the Zambesi?* No? Ah, that's a bit of a classic, now. One of my best."

So he had known how dangerous the Dudh Kosi was. I stared at him reproachfully. It was hard to believe he made adventure films;

he looked more like the kind of Hollywood producer you'd tell couch jokes about. "So you're making a real film of this trip?" I asked.

"Yeah, sure. Always working, never stop working. Workaholic."

"Don't you need a bigger crew?"

"Well sure, usually, but this is a different kind of thing, one of my 'personal diary' films I call them. I've sold a couple to PBS. Do all the work myself. It's kind of like my version of solo climbing."

"Fine. But cut the part about me taking a crap, okay?"

"Sure, sure, don't worry about it. Just got to get everything I can, you know, so I've got good tape to choose from later on. All grist for the mill. That's why I got this lens. All the latest in equipment for me. I got stuff you wouldn't believe."

"I believe."

He chomped his cigar. "Just call me Mr. Adventure."

"I will."

## 4

I didn't run into Freds and Kunga Norbu in Namche Bazaar, the Sherpas' dramatically placed little capital town, and I figured they had left already with Freds's British friends. Then I kept my group there a couple of days to acclimatize, and enjoy the town, and I figured that if I caught up with them at all, it'd be up at their base camp.

So I was quite surprised to run across the whole group in Pheriche, one of the Sherpas' high mountain villages.

Most of these villages are occupied only in the summer, to grow potatoes and pasture yaks. Pheriche, however, lies on the trekking route to Everest, so it's occupied almost year-round, and a couple of lodges have been built, along with the Himalayan Rescue Association's only aid station. It still looks like a summer pasturage: low rock walls separate potato fields, and a few slate-roofed stone huts, plus the lodges and the tin-roofed aid station. All of it is clustered at the end of a flat-bottomed glacial valley, against the side of a lateral moraine five hundred feet high. A stream meanders by and the ground is carpeted with grasses and the bright autumn red of berberi bushes. On all sides tower the fantastic white spikes of some of the world's most dramatic peaks—Ama Dablam, Taboche, Tramserku, Kang Taiga—and all in all, it's quite a place. My clients were making themselves dizzy trying to film it.

We set up our tent village in an unused potato field, and after dinner Laure and I slipped off to the Himalaya Hotel to have some chang. I entered the lodge's little kitchen and heard Freds cry, "Hey George!" He was sitting with Kunga Norbu and four Westerners; we joined them, crowding in around a little table. "These are the friends we're climbing with."

He introduced them, and we all shook hands. Trevor was a tall slender guy, with round glasses and a somewhat crazed grin. "Mad Tom," as Freds called him, was short and curly-headed, and didn't look mad at all, although something in his mild manner made me believe that he could be. John was short and compact, with a salt-and-pepper beard, and a crusher handshake. And Marion was a tall and rather attractive woman—though I suspected she might have blushed or punched you if you said so—she was attractive in a tough, wild way, with a stark strong face, and thick brown hair pulled back and braided. They were British, with the accents to prove it: Marion and Trevor quite posh and public school, and John and Mad Tom very thick and North country.

We started drinking chang, and they told me about their climb. Lingtren, a sharp peak between Pumori and Everest's West Shoulder, is serious work from any approach, and they were clearly excited about it, in their own way: "Bit of a slog, to tell the truth," Trevor said cheerfully.

When British climbers talk about climbing, you have to learn to translate it into English. "Bit of a slog" means don't go there.

"I think we ought to get lost and climb Pumori instead," said Marion. "Lingtren is a perfect *hill*."

"Marion, really."

"Can't beat Lingtren's price, anyway," said John.

He was referring to the fee that the Nepali government makes climbers pay for the right to climb its peaks. These fees are determined by the height of the peak to be climbed—the really big peaks are super expensive. They charge you over five thousand dollars to climb Everest, for instance, and still competition to get on its long waiting list is fierce. But some of the toughest climbs in Nepal aren't very high, relative to the biggies, and they come pretty cheap. Apparently Lingtren was one of these.

We watched the Sherpani who runs the lodge cook dinner for fifty, under the fixed gazes of the diners, who sat staring hungrily at her every move. To accomplish this she had at her command a small woodburning stove (with chimney, thank God), a pile of potatoes, noodles, rice, some eggs and cabbage, and several chang-happy porter assistants, who alternated washing dishes with breaking up chunks of yak dung for the fire. A difficult situation on the face of it, but the Sherpani was cool: she cooked the whole list of orders by memory, slicing and tossing potatoes into one pan, stuffing wood in the fire, flipping twenty pounds of noodles in mid-air like they were a single hotcake—all with the sureness and panache of an expert juggler. It was a kind of genius.

Two hours later those who had ordered the meals that came last in her strict sequence got their cabbage omelets on French fries, and the kitchen emptied out as many people went to bed. The rest of us settled down to more chang and chatter.

Then a trekker came back into the kitchen, so he could listen to his shortwave radio without bothering sleepers in the lodge's single dorm room. He said he wanted to catch the news. We all stared at him in disbelief. "I need to find out how the dollar's doing," he explained. "Did you know it dropped *eight percent* last week?"

You meet all kinds in Nepal.

Actually it's interesting to hear what you get on shortwave in the Himal, because depending on how the ionosphere is acting, almost anything will bounce in. That night we listened to the People's Voice of Syria, for instance, and some female pop singer from Bombay, which perked up the porters. Then the operator ran across the BBC world news, which was not unusual—it could have been coming from Hong Kong, Singapore, Cairo, even London itself.

Through the hissing of the static the public-school voice of the reporter could barely be made out ". . . British Everest Expedition of 1987 is now on the Rongbuk Glacier in Tibet, and over the next two months they expect to repeat the historic route of the attempts made in the twenties and thirties. Our correspondent to the expedition reports—" and then the voice changed to one even more staccato and drowned in static: "—the expedition's principal goal of recovering the bodies of George Mallory and Andrew Irvine, who were last seen near the summit in 1924, *crackle, buzz*. . . .chances considerably improved by conversations with a partner of the Chinese climber who reported seeing a body on the North Face in 1980 *bzzzzkrkrk!*—description of the site of the finding *sssssssss* . . . snow levels very low this year, and all concerned feel chances for success are *ssssskrkssss*." The voice faded away in a roar of static.

Trevor looked around at us, eyebrows lifted. "Did I understand them to say that they are going to search for Mallory and Irvine's *bodies*?"

A look of deep horror creased Mad Tom's face. Marion wrinkled her nose as if her chang had turned to Tibetan tea. "I can't believe it."

I didn't know it at the time, but this was an unexpected opportunity for Freds to put his plan into action ahead of schedule. He said,

"Haven't you heard about that? Why Kunga Norbu here is precisely the climber they're talking about, the one who spotted a body on the North Face in 1980."

"He *is*?" we all said.

"Yeah, you bet. Kunga was part of the Chinese expedition to the North Ridge in 1980, and he was up there doing reconnaissance for a direct route on the North Face when he saw a body." Freds spoke to Kinga Norbu in Tibetan, and Kunga nodded and replied at some length. Freds translated for him: "He says it was a Westerner, wearing old-fashioned clothing, and it had clearly been there a long time. Here, he says he can mark it on a photo—" Freds got out his wallet and pulled a wad of paper from it. Unfolded, it revealed itself as a battered black-and-white photo of Everest as seen from the Tibetan side. Kunga Norbu studied it for long time, talked it over with Freds, and then took a pencil from Freds and carefully made a circle on the photo.

"Why he's circled half the North Face," John pointed out. "It's fooking useless."

"Nah," Freds said. "Look, it's a little circle."

"It's a little photo, innit."

"Well, he can describe the spot exactly—it's up there on top of the Black Band. Anyway, someone has managed to get together an expedition to go looking for the bodies, or the body, whatever. Now Kunga slipped over to Nepal last year, so this expedition is going on second-hand information from his climbing buds. But that might be enough."

"And if they find the bodies?"

"Well, I think they're planning to take them down and ship them to London and bury them in Winchester Cathedral."

The Brits stared at him. "You mean Westminster Abbey?" Trevor ventured.

"Oh that's right, I always get those two mixed up. Anyway that's what they're going to do, and they're going to make a movie out of it."

I groaned at the thought. More video.

The four Brits groaned louder than I did. "That is rilly dis-gusting," Marion said.

"Sickening," John and Mad Tom agreed.

"It is a travesty, isn't it?" Trevor said. "I mean those chaps belong up there if anybody does. It's nothing less than grave robbing!"

And his three companions nodded. On one level they were joking, making a pretense of their outrage; but underneath that, they were dead serious. They meant it.

## 5

To understand why they would care so much, you have to understand what the story of Mallory and Irvine means to the British soul. Climbing has always been more important there than in America—you could say that the British invented the sport in Victorian times, and they've continued to excel in it since then, even after World War Two when much else there fell apart. You could say that climbing is the Rolls Royce of British sport. Whymper, Hillary, the brilliant crowd that climbed with Bonnington in the Seventies: they're all national heroes.

But none more so than Mallory and Irvine. Back in the twenties and thirties, you see, the British had a lock on Everest, because Nepal was closed to foreigners, and Tibet was closed to all but the British, who had barged in on them with Younghusband's campaign back in 1904. So the mountain was their private playground, and during those years they made four or five attempts, all of them failures, which is understandable: they were equipped like Boy Scouts, they had to learn high altitude technique on the spot, and they had terrible luck with weather.

The try that came closest was in 1924. Mallory was its lead climber, already famous from two previous attempts. As you may know, he was the guy who replied "Because it's there" when asked why anyone would want to climb the thing. This is either a very deep or a very stupid answer, depending on what you think of Mallory. You can take your pick of interpretations; the guy has been psychoanalyzed into the ground. Anyway, he and his partner Irvine were last glimpsed, by another expedition member, just eight hundred feet and less than a quarter of a mile from the summit—and at one P.M., on a day that had good weather except for a brief storm, and mist that obscured the peak from the observers below. So they either made it or they didn't; but something went wrong somewhere along the line, and they were never seen again.

A glorious defeat, a deep mystery: this is the kind of story that the English just love, as don't we all. All the public school virtues wrapped into one heroic tale—you couldn't write it better. To this day the story commands tremendous interest in England, and this is doubly true among people in the climbing community, who grew up on the story, and who still indulge in a lot of speculation about the two men's fate, in journal articles and pub debates and the like. They love that story.

Thus to go up there, and find the bodies, and end the mystery, and cart the bodies off to England . . . You can see why it struck my drinking buddies that night as a kind of sacrilege. It was yet another modern PR stunt—a money-grubbing plan made by some publicity hound—a Profaning of the Mystery. It was, in fact, a bit like video-trekking. Only worse. So I could sympathize, in a way.

6

I tried to think of a change of subject, to distract the Brits. But Freds seemed determined to fire up their distress. He poked his finger onto the folded wreck of a photo. "You know what y'all oughta do," he told them in a low voice. "You mentioned getting lost and climbing Pumori? Well shit, what you oughta do instead is get lost in the other direction, and beat that expedition to the spot, and hide old Mallory. I mean here you've got the actual eyewitness right here to lead you to him! Incredible! You could bury Mallory in rocks and snow and then sneak back down. If you did that, they'd never find him!"

All the Brits stared at Freds, eyes wide. Then they looked at each other, and their heads kind of lowered together over the table. Their voices got soft. "He's a genius," Trevor breathed.

"Uh, no," I warned them. "He's not a genius." Laure was shaking his head. Even Kunga Norbu was looking doubtful.

Freds looked over the Brits at me and waggled his eyebrows vigorously, as if to say: this is a great idea! Don't foul it up!

"What about the Lho La?" John asked. "Won't we have to climb that?"

"Piece of cake," Freds said promptly.

"No," Laure protested. "Not piece cake! Pass! Very steep pass!"

"Piece of cake," Freds insisted. "I climbed it with those West Ridge direct guys a couple years ago. And once you top it you just slog onto the West Shoulder and there you are with the whole North Face, sitting right off to your left."

"Freds," I said, trying to indicate that he shouldn't incite his companions to such a dangerous, not to mention illegal, climb. "You'd need a lot more support for high camps than you've got. That circle there is pretty damn high on the mountain."

"True," Freds said immediately. "It's pretty high. Pretty damn high. You can't get much higher."

Of course to climbers this was only another incitement, as I should have known.

"You'd have to do it like Woody Sayres did back in '62," Freds went on. "They got Sherpas to help them up the Nup La over by

Cho Oyo, then bolted to Everest when they were supposed to be climbing Gyachung Kang. They moved a single camp with them all the way to Everest, and got back the same way. Just four of them, and they almost climbed it. And the Nup La is twenty miles further away from Everest than the Lho La. The Lho La's right there under it."

Mad Tom knocked his glasses up his nose, pulled out a pencil and began to do calculations on the table. Marion was nodding. Trevor was refilling all our glasses with chang. John was looking over Mad Tom's shoulder and muttering to him; apparently they were in charge of supplies.

Trevor raised his glass. "Right then," he said. "Are we for it?"

They all raised their glasses. "We're for it."

They were toasting the plan, and I was staring at them in dismay, when I heard the door creak and saw who was leaving the kitchen. "Hey!"

I reached out and dragged Arnold McConnell back into the room. "What're you doing here?"

Arnold shifted something behind his back. "Nothing, really. Just my nightly glass of milktea, you know . . ."

"It's him!" Marion exclaimed. She reached behind Arnold and snatched his camera from behind his back; he tried to hold onto it, but Marion was too strong for him. "Spying on me again, were you? Filming us from some dark corner?"

"No no," Arnold said. "Can't film in the dark, you know."

"Film in tent," Laure said promptly. "Night."

Arnold glared at him.

"Listen, Arnold," I said. "We were just shooting the bull here you know, a little private conversation over the chang. Nothing serious."

"Oh I know," Arnold assured me. "I know."

Marion stood and stared down at Arnold. They made a funny pair—her so long and rangy, him so short and tubby. Marion pushed buttons on the camera until the video cassette popped out, never taking her eye from him. She could really glare. "I suppose this is the same film you used this morning, when you filmed me taking my shower, is that right?" She looked at us. "I was in the little shower box they've got across the way, and the tin with the hot water in it got plugged at the bottom somehow. I had the door open a bit so I could stretch up and fiddle with it, when suddenly I noticed this pervert filming me!" She laughed angrily.

"I bet you were quite pleased with that footage, weren't you, you peeping Tom!"

"I was just leaving to shoot yaks," Arnold explained rapidly, staring up at Marion with an admiring gaze. "Then there you were, and what was I supposed to do? I'm a filmmaker, I film beautiful things. I could make you a star in the States," he told her earnestly. "You're probably the most beautiful climber in the world."

"And all that competition," Mad Tom put in.

I was right about Marion's reaction to a compliment of that sort —she blushed to the roots, and considered punching him too—she might have, if they'd been alone.

"—adventure films back in the States, for PBS and the ski resort circuit," Arnold was going on, chewing his cigar and rolling his eyes as Marion took the cartridge over toward the stove.

The Sherpani waved her off. "Smell," she said.

Marion nodded and took the video cassette in her hands. Her forearms tensed, and suddenly you could see every muscle. And there were a lot of them, too, looking like thin bunched wires under the skin. We all stared, and instinctively Arnold raised his camera to his shoulder before remembering it was empty. That fact made him whimper, and he was fumbling at his jacket pocket for a spare when the cassette snapped diagonally and the videotape spilled out. Marion handed it all to the Sherpani, who dumped it in a box of potato peels, grinning.

We all looked at Arnold. He chomped his cigar, shrugged. "Can't make you a star that way," he said, and gave Marion a soulful leer. "Really, you oughta give me a chance, you'd be great. Such *presence*."

"I would appreciate it if you would now leave," Marion told him, and pointed at the door.

Arnold left.

"That guy could be trouble," Freds said.

## 7

Freds was right about that.

But Arnold was not the only source of trouble. Freds himself was acting a bit peculiar, I judged. Still, when I thought of the various oddities in his recent behavior—his announcement that his friend Kunga Norbu was a tulku, and now this sudden advocacy of a Save Mallory's Body campaign—I couldn't put it all together. Why did he just happen to have a photo of the North Face of Everest in his wallet, for instance? It didn't make sense.

So when Freds's party and my trekking group took off upvalley from Pheriche on the same morning, I walked with Freds for a while. I wanted to ask him some questions. But there were a lot of people on the trail, and it was hard to get a moment to ourselves.

As an opener I said, "So, you've got a woman on your team."

"Yeah, Marion's great. She's probably the best climber of us all. And incredibly strong. You know those indoor walls they have in England, for practicing?"

"No."

"Well, the weather is so bad there, and the climbers are such fanatics, that they've built these thirty and forty foot walls inside gyms, and covered them with concrete and made little handholds." He laughed. "It looks dismal—scuzzy old gym with bad light and no heating, and all these guys stretched out on a concrete wall like some new kinda torture . . . Anyway I visited one of these, and they set me up in a race with Marion, up the two hardest pitches. Maybe 5.13 in places, impossible stuff. And there was a leak too. Everyone started betting on us, and the rule was someone had to top out for anyone to collect on the bets. I did my best, but I was hurrying and I came off about halfway up. So she won, but to collect the bets she had to top out. With the leak it really was impossible, but everyone who had bet on her was yelling at her to do it, so she just grit her teeth and started making these *moves*, man—" Freds illustrated in the air between us as we hiked—"And she was doing them in slow motion so she wouldn't come off. Just hanging there by her fingertips and toes, and I swear to God she hung on that wall for must've been *three hours*. Everyone else stopped climbing to watch. Guys were going home—guys were begging her to come off—guys had tears in their eyes. Finally she topped out and crawled over to the ladder and came down, and they mobbed her. They were ready to make her queen. In fact she pretty much is queen, as far as English climbers are concerned—you could bring the real one in, and if Marion were there they wouldn't even notice."

Then Arnold slipped between us, looking conspiratorial. "I think this Save Mallory scheme is a great idea," he whispered through clenched teeth. "I'm totally behind you, and it'll make a *great movie*."

"You miss the point," I said to him.

"We ain't doing nothing but climb Lingtren," Freds said to him.

Arnold frowned, tucked his chin onto his chest, chewed his cigar. Frowning, Freds left to catch up with his group, and they soon disappeared ahead. So I lost my chance to talk to him.

We came to the upper end of Pheriche's valley, turned right and climbed to get into an even higher one. This was the valley of the Khumbu glacier, a massive road of ice covered with a chaos of gray rubble and milky blue melt ponds. We skirted the glacier and followed a trail up its lateral moraine to Lobuche, which consists of three teahouses and a tenting ground. The next day we hiked on upvalley to Gorak Shep.

Now Gorak Shep ("Dead Crow") is not the kind of place you see on posters in travel agencies. It's just above 17,000 feet, and up there the plant life has about given up. It's just two ragged little teahouses under a monstrous rubble hill, next to a gray glacial pond, and all in all it looks like the tailings of a very big gravel mine.

But what Gorak Shep does have is mountains. Big snowy mountains, on all sides. How big? Well, the wall of Nuptse, for instance, stands a full seven thousand feet over Gorak Shep. An avalanche we saw, sliding down a fraction of this wall and sounding like thunder, covered about two World Trade Centers' worth of height, and still looked tiny. And Nuptse is not as big as some of the peaks around it. So you get the idea.

Cameras can never capture this kind of scale, but you can't help trying, and my crowd tried for all they were worth in the days we were camped there. The ones handling the altitude well slogged up to the top of Kala Pattar ("Black Hill"), a local walker's peak which has a fine view of the Southwest Face of Everest. The day after that, Heather and Laure led most of the same people up the glacier to Everest Base Camp, while the rest of us relaxed. Everest Base Camp, set by the Indian Army this season, was basically a tent village like ours, but there are some fine seracs and ice towers to be seen along the way, and when they returned the clients seemed satisfied.

So I was satisfied too. No one had gotten any bad altitude sickness, and we would be starting back the next morning. I was feeling fine, sitting up on the hill above our tents in the late afternoon, doing nothing.

But then Laure came zipping down the trail from Base Camp, and when he saw me he came right over. "George George," he called out as he approached.

I stood as he reached me. "What's up?"

"I stay talk friends porter Indian Army base camp, Freds find me Freds say his base camp come please you. Climb Lho La find man camera come hire Sherpas finish with Freds, very bad follow Freds."

Now Laure's English is not very good, as you may have noticed. But after all we were in his country speaking my language—and for him English came after Sherpa, Nepali, and some Japanese and German, and how many languages do you speak?

Besides, I find I always get the gist of what Laure says, which is not something you can always say of all our fellow native speakers. So I cried out, "No! Arnold is *following* them?"

"Yes," Laure said. "Very bad. Freds say come please get."

"Arnold hired their Sherpas?"

Laure nodded. "Sherpas finish porter, Arnold hire."

"Damn him! We'll have to climb up there and get him!"

"Yes. Very bad."

"Will you come with me?"

"Whatever you like."

I hustled to our tents to get together my climbing gear and tell Heather what had happened. "How did he get up there?" she asked. "I thought he was with you all day!"

"He told me he was going with you! He probably followed you guys all the way up, and kept on going. Don't worry about it, it's not your fault. Take the group back to Namche starting tomorrow, and we'll catch up with you." She nodded, looking worried.

Laure and I took off. Even going at Laure's pace we didn't reach Freds's base camp until the moon had risen.

Their camp was now only a single tent in a bunch of trampled snow, just under the steep headwall of the Khumbu Valley—the ridge that divides Nepal from Tibet. We zipped open the tent and woke Freds and Kunga Norbu.

"All right!" Freds said. "I'm glad you're here! Real glad!"

"Give me the story," I said.

"Well, that Arnold snuck up here, apparently."

"That's right."

"And our Sherpas were done and we had paid them, and I guess he hired them on the spot. They have a bunch of climbing gear, and we left fixed ropes up to the Lho La, so up they came. I tell you I was pretty blown away when they showed up in the pass! The Brits got furious and told Arnold to go back down, but he refused and, well, how do you make someone do something they don't want to up there? If you punch him out he's likely to have trouble getting down! So Kunga and I came back to get you and found Laure at Base Camp, and he said he'd get you while we held the fort."

"Arnold climbed the Lho La?" I said, amazed.

"Well, he's a pretty tough guy, I reckon. Didn't you ever see that movie he made of the kayak run down the Baltoro? Radical film, man, really it's up there with *The Man Who Skied Down Everest* for radicalness. And he's done some other crazy things too, like flying a hang glider off the Grand Teton, filming all the way. He's tougher than he looks. I think he just does the Hollywood sleaze routine so he can get away with things. Anyway those are some excellent climbing Sherpas he's got, and with them and the fixed ropes he just had to gut it out. And I guess he acclimatizes well, because he was walking around up there like he was at the beach."

I sighed. "That is one determined filmmaker."

Freds shook his head. "The guy is a leech. He's gonna drive the Brits bats if we don't haul his ass back down here."

## 8

So the next day the four of us started the ascent of the Lho La, and were quickly engaged in some of the most dangerous climbing I've ever done. Not the most technically difficult—the Brits had left fixed rope in the toughest sections, so our progress was considerably aided. But it was still dangerous, because we were climbing an icefall, which is to say a glacier on a serious tilt.

Now a glacier as you know is a river of ice, and like its liquid counterparts it is always flowing downstream. Its rate of flow is much slower than a river's, but it isn't negligible, especially when you're standing on it. Then you often hear creaks, groans, sudden cracks and booms, and you feel like you're on the back of a living creature.

Put that glacier on a hillside and everything is accelerated; the living creature becomes a dragon. The ice of the glacier breaks up into immense blocks and shards, and these shift regularly, then balance on a point or edge, then fall and smash to fragments, or crack open to reveal deep fissures. As we threaded our way up through the maze of the Lho La's icefall, we were constantly moving underneath blocks of ice that looked eternal but were actually precarious—they were certain to fall sometime in the next month or two. I'm not expert at probability theory, but I still didn't like it.

"Freds," I complained. "You said this was a piece of cake."

"It is," he said. "Check out how fast we're going."

"That's because we're scared to death."

"Are we? Hey, it must be only 45 degrees or so."

This is as steep as an icefall can get before the ice all falls downhill at once. Even the famous Khumbu Icefall, which we now had a fantastic view of over to our right, fell at only about 30 degrees. The Khumbu Icefall is an unavoidable part of the standard route on Everest, and it is by far the most feared section; more people have died there than anywhere else on the mountain. And the Lho La is worse than the Khumbu!

So I had some choice words for our situation as we climbed very quickly indeed, and most of them left Laure mystified. "Great, Freds," I shouted at him. "Real piece of cake all right!"

"Lot of icing, anyway," he said, and giggled. This under a wall that would flatten him like Wile E. Coyote if it fell. I shook my head.

"What do you think?" I said to Laure.

"Very bad," Laure said. "Very bad, very dangerous."

"What do you think we should do?"

"Whatever you like."

We hurried.

Now I like climbing as much as anybody, almost, but I am not going to try to claim to you that it is an exceptionally sane activity. That day in particular I would not have been inclined to argue the point. The thing is, there is danger and there is danger. In fact climbers make a distinction, between objective danger and subjective danger. Objective dangers are things like avalanches and rockfall and storms, that you can't do anything about. Subjective dangers are those incurred by human error—putting in a bad hold, forgetting to fasten a harness, that sort of thing. See, if you are perfectly careful, then you can eliminate all the subjective dangers. And when you've eliminated the subjective dangers, you have only the objective dangers to face. So you can see it's very rational.

On this day, however, we were in the midst of a whole wall of objective danger, and it made me nervous. We pursued the usual course in such a case, which is to go like hell. The four of us were practically running up the Lho La. Freds, Kunga, and Laure were extremely fast and strong, and I am in reasonable shape myself; plus I get the benefits of more adrenalin than less imaginative types. So we were hauling buns.

Then it happened. Freds was next to me, on a rope with Kunga Norbu, and Kunga was the full rope length ahead of us—about twenty yards—leading the way around a traverse that went under a giant serac, which is what they call the fangs of blue ice that protrude out of an icefall, often in clusters. Kunga was right underneath this serac when without the slightest warning it sheered off and collapsed, shattering into a thousand pieces.

I had reflexively sucked in a gasp and was about to scream when Kunga Norbu jostled my elbow, nearly knocking me down. He was wedged in between Freds and me, and the rope tying them together was flapping between our legs.

Trying to revise my scream I choked, gasped for breath, choked again. Freds slapped me on the back to help. Kunga was definitely there, standing before us, solid and corporeal. And yet he had been under the serac! The broken pieces of the ice block were scattered before us, fresh and gleaming in the afternoon sun. The block had sheered off and collapsed without the slightest quiver or warning—there simply hadn't been time to get out from under it!

Freds saw the look on my face, and he grinned feebly. "Old Kunga Norbu is pretty fast when he has to be."

But that wasn't going to do. "Gah . . ." I said—and then Freds and Kunga were holding me up. Laure hurried to join us, round-eyed with apprehension.

"Very bad," he said.

"Gah," I attempted again, and couldn't go on.

"All right, all right," Freds said, soothing me with his gloved hands. "Hey, George. Relax."

"He," I got out, and pointed at the remains of the serac, then at Kunga.

"I know," Freds said, frowning. He exchanged a glance with Kunga, who was watching me impassively. They spoke to each other in Tibetan. "Listen," Freds said to me. "Let's top the pass and then I'll explain it to you. It'll take a while, and we don't have that much day left. Plus we've got to find a way around these ice cubes so we can stick to the fixed ropes. Come on, buddy." He slapped my arm. "Concentrate. Let's do it."

So we started up again, Kunga leading as fast as before. I was still in shock, however, and I kept seeing the collapse of the serac, with Kunga under it. He just couldn't have escaped it! And yet there he was up above us, jumaring up the fixed ropes like a monkey scurrying up a palm.

It was a miracle. And I had seen it. I had a hell of a time concentrating on the rest of that day's climb.

## 9

In the late afternoon we topped the Lho La, and set our tent on the pass's flat expanse of deep hard snow. It was one of the spacier campsites I had ever occupied: on the crest of the Himalaya, in a broad saddle between the tallest mountain on earth, and the very spiky and beautiful Lingtren. Below us to one side was the Khumbu Glacier; on the other was the Rongbuk Glacier in Tibet. We were at about 20,000 feet, and so Freds and his friends had a long way to go before reaching old Mallory. But nothing above would be quite as arbitrarily dangerous as the icefall. As long as the weather held, that is. So far they had been lucky; it was turning out to be the driest October in years.

There was no sign of either the British team or Arnold's crew, except for tracks in the snow leading up the side of the West Shoulder and disappearing. So they were on their way up. "Damn!" I said. "Why didn't they wait?" Now we had more climbing to do, to catch Arnold.

I sat on my groundpad on the snow outside the tent. I was tired. I was also very troubled. Laure was getting the stove to start. Kunga

Norbu was off by himself, sitting in the snow, apparently meditating on the sight of Tibet. Freds was walking around singing "Wooden Ships," clearly in heaven. "I mean, is this a great campsite or *what*," he cried to me. "Look at the view! It's too much, too much. I wish we'd brought some chang with us. I do have some hash, though. George, time to break out the pipe, hey?"

"Not yet, Freds. You get over here and tell me what the hell happened down there with your buddy Kunga Norbu. You promised you would."

Freds stood looking at me. We were in shadow—it was cold, but windless—the sky above was clear, and a very deep dark blue. The airy roar of the stove starting was the only sound.

Freds sighed, and his expression got as serious as it ever got: one eye squinted shut entirely, forehead furrowed, and lips squeezed tightly together. He looked over at Kunga, and saw he was watching us. "Well," he said after a while. "You remember a couple of weeks ago when we were down at Chimoa getting drunk?"

"Yeah?"

"And I told you Kunga Norbu was a tulku."

I gulped. "Freds, don't give me that again."

"Well," he said. "It's either that or tell you some kind of a lie. And I ain't so good at lying, my face gives me away or something."

"Freds, get serious!" But looking over at Kunga Norbu, sitting in the snow with that blank expression, and those weird black eyes, I couldn't help but wonder.

Freds said, "I'm sorry, man, I really am. I don't mean to blow your mind like this. But I did try to tell you before, you have to admit. And it's the simple truth. He's an honest-to-God tulku. First incarnation the famous Naropa, born in 1555. And he's been around ever since."

"So he met George Washington and like that?"

"Well, Washington didn't go to Tibet, so far as I know."

I stared at him. He shuffled about uncomfortably. "I know it's hard to take, George. Believe me. I had trouble with it myself, at first. But when you study under Kunga Norbu for a while, you see him do so many miraculous things, you can't help but believe."

I stared at him some more, speechless.

"I know," Freds said. "The first time he pulls one of his moves on you, it's a shock. I remember my first time real well. I was hiking with him from the hidden Rongbuk to Namche, we went right over Lho La like we did today only in the opposite direction, and right around Everest Base Camp we came across this Indian trekker who was turning blue. He was clearly set to die of altitude sickness, so

Kunga and I carried him down between us to Pheriche, which was already a long day's work as you know. We took him to the Rescue Station and I figured they'd put him in the pressure tank they've got there, have you seen it? They've got a tank like a miniature submarine in their back room, and the idea is you stick a guy with altitude sickness in it and pressurize it down to sea level pressure, and he gets better. It's a neat idea, but it turns out that this tank was donated to the station by a hospital in Tokyo, and all the instructions for it are in Japanese, and no one at the station reads Japanese. Besides as far as anyone there knows it's an experimental technique only, no one is quite sure if it will work or not, and nobody there is inclined to do any experimenting on sick trekkers. So we're back to square one and this guy was sicker than ever, so Kunga and I started down towards Namche, but I was getting exhausted and it was really slow going, and all of a sudden Kunga Norbu picked him up and slung him across his shoulders, which was already quite a feat of strength as this Indian was kind of pear-shaped, a heavy guy—and then Kunga just took off running down the trail with him! I hollered at him and ran after him trying to keep up, and I tell you I was *zooming* down that trail, and still Kunga ran right out of sight! Big long steps like he was about to fly! I couldn't believe it!"

Freds shook his head. "That was the first time I saw Kunga Norbu going into *lung-gom* mode. Means magic long-distance running, and it was real popular in Tibet at one time. An adept like Kunga is called a *lung-gom-pa*, and when you get it down you can run really far really fast. Even levitate a little. You saw him today—that was a *lung-gom* move he laid on that iceblock."

"I see," I said, in a kind of daze. I called out to Laure, still at the stove: "Hey Laure! Freds says Kunga Norbu is a tulku!"

Laure smiled, nodded. "Yes, Kunga Norbu Lama very fine tulku!"

I took a deep breath. Over in the snow Kunga Norbu sat cross-legged, looking out at his country. Or somewhere. "I think I'm ready for that hash pipe," I told Freds.

## 10

It took us two days to catch up to Arnold and the Brits, two days of miserable slogging up the West Shoulder of Everest. Nothing complicated here: the slope was a regular expanse of hard snow, and we just put on the crampons and ground on up it. It was murderous work. Not that I could tell with Freds and Laure and Kunga Norbu. There may be advantages to climbing on Everest with a tulku, a

Sherpa long-distance champion, and an American space cadet, but longer rest stops are not among them. Those three marched uphill as if paced by Sousa marches, and I trailed behind huffing and puffing, damning Arnold with every step.

Late on the second day I struggled onto the top of the West Shoulder, a long snowy divide under the West Ridge proper. By the time I got there Freds and Laure already had the tent up, and they were securing it to the snow with a network of climbing rope, while Kunga Norbu sat to one side doing his meditation.

Further down the Shoulder were the two camps of the other teams, placed fairly close together as there wasn't a whole lot of extra flat ground up there to choose from. After I had rested and drunk several cups of hot lemon drink, I said, "Let's go find out how things stand." Freds walked over with me.

As it turned out, things were not standing so well. The Brits were in their tent, waist deep in their sleeping bags and drinking tea. And they were not amused. "The man is utterly daft," Marion said. She had a mild case of high-altitude throat, and any syllable she tried to emphasize disappeared entirely. "We've *oyd* outrunning him, but the Sherpas are good, and he *oyy* be strong."

"A fooking leech he is," John said.

Trevor grinned ferociously. His lower face was pretty sunburned, and his lips were beginning to break up. "We're counting on you to get him back down, George."

"I'll see what I can do."

Marion shook her head. "God knows we've tried, but it does no good whatever, he won't listen, he just rattles on about making me a *stee*, I don't know how to *dee* with that." She turned red. "And none of these brave chaps will agree that we should just go over there and seize his bloody camera and throw it into Ti*bee*!"

The guys shook their heads. "We'd have to deal with the Sherpas," Mad Tom said to Marion patiently. "What are we going to do, fight with them? I can't even imagine it."

"And if Mad Tom can't imagine it," Trevor said.

Marion just growled.

"I'll go talk to him," I said.

But I didn't have to go anywhere, because Arnold had come over to greet us. "Hello!" he called out cheerily. "George, what a surprise! What brings you up here?"

I got out of the tent. Arnold stood before me, looking sunburned but otherwise all right. "You know what brings me up here, Arnold. Here, let's move away a bit, I'm sure these folks don't want to talk to you."

"Oh, no, I've been talking to them every day! We've been having lots of good talks. And today I've got some real news." He spoke into the tent. "I was looking through my zoom over at the North Col, and I see they've set up a camp over there! Do you suppose it's that expedition looking for Mallory's body?"

Curses came from the tent.

"I know!" Arnold exclaimed. "Kind of puts the pressure on to get going, don't you think? Not much time to spare."

"Bugger off!"

Arnold shrugged. "Well, I've got it on tape if you want to see. Looked like they were wearing Helly-Hansen jackets, if that tells you anything."

"Don't tell me you can read labels from this distance," I said.

Arnold grinned. "It's a hell of a zoom lens. I could read their lips if I wanted to."

I studied him curiously. He really seemed to be doing fine, even after four days of intense climbing. He looked a touch thinner, and his voice had an altitude rasp to it, and he was pretty badly sunburned under the stubble of his beard—but he was still chewing a whitened cigar between zinc-oxided lips, and he still had the same wide-eyed look of wonder that his filming should bother anybody. I was impressed; he was definitely a lot tougher than I had expected. He reminded me of Dick Bass, the American millionaire who took a notion to climb the highest mountain on each continent. Like Bass, Arnold was a middle-aged guy paying pros to take him up; and like Bass, he acclimatized well, and had a hell of a nerve.

So, there he was, and he wasn't falling apart. I had to try something else. "Arnold, come over here a little with me, let's leave these people in peace."

"Good *reee*!" Marion shouted from inside the tent.

"That Marion," Arnold said admiringly when we were out of earshot. "She's really beautiful, I mean I really, really, really like her." He struck his chest to show how smitten he was.

I glared at him. "Arnold, it doesn't matter if you're falling for her or *what*, because they *definitely* do not want you along for this climb. Filming them destroys the whole point of what they're trying to do up there."

Arnold seized my arm. "No it doesn't! I keep trying to explain that to them. I can edit the film so that no one will know where Mallory's body is. They'll just know it's up here safe, because four young English climbers took incredible risks to keep it free from the publicity hounds threatening to tear it away to London. It's great,

George. I'm a filmmaker, and I know when something will make a great movie, and this will make a great movie."

I frowned. "Maybe it would, but the problem is this climb is illegal, and if you make the film, then the illegal part becomes known and these folks will be banned by the Nepali authorities. They'll never be let into Nepal again."

"So? Aren't they willing to make that sacrifice for Mallory?"

I frowned. "For your movie, you mean. Without that they could do it and no one would be the wiser."

"Well, okay, but I can leave their names off it or something. Give them stage names. Marion Davies, how about that?"

"I think that one's been used before." I thought. "Listen, Arnold, you'd be in the same kind of trouble, you know. They might not ever let you back, either."

He waved a hand. "I can get around that kind of thing. Get a lawyer. Or baksheesh, a lot of baksheesh."

"These guys don't have that kind of money, though. Really, you'd better watch it. If you press them too hard they might do something drastic. At the least they'll stop you, higher up. When they find the body a couple of them will come back and stop you, and the other two bury the body, and you won't get any footage at all."

He shook his head. "I got lenses, haven't I been telling you? Why I've been shooting what these four eat for breakfast every morning. I've got hours of Marion on film for instance," he sighed, "and my God could I make her a star. Anyway I could film the burial from here if I had to, so I'll take my chances. Don't you worry about me."

"I am *not* worrying about you," I said. "Take my word for it. But I do wish you'd come back down with me. They don't want you up here, and I don't want you up here. It's dangerous, especially if we lose this weather. Besides, you're breaking your contract with our agency, which said you'd follow my instructions on the trek."

"Sue me."

I took a deep breath.

Arnold put a friendly hand to my arm. "Don't worry so much, George. They'll love me when they're stars." He saw the look on my face and stepped away. "And don't you try anything funny with me, or I'll slap some kind of kidnapping charge on you, and you'll never guide a trek again."

"Don't tempt me like that," I told him, and stalked back to the Brits' camp.

I dropped into their tent. Laure and Kunga Norbu had joined them, and we were jammed in there. "No luck," I said. They weren't surprised.

"Superleech," Freds commented cheerfully.

We sat around and stared at the blue flames of the stove.

Then, as usually happens in these predicaments, I said, "I've got a plan."

It was relatively simple, as we didn't have many options. We would all descend back to the Lho La, and maybe even down to Base Camp, giving Arnold the idea we had given up. Once down there the Brits and Freds and Kunga Norbu could restock at the Gorak Shep teahouses, and Laure and I would undertake to stop Arnold, by stealing his boots for instance. Then they could go back up the fixed ropes and try again.

Trevor looked dubious. "It's difficult getting up here, and we don't have much time, if that other expedition is already on the North Col."

"I've got a better plan," Freds announced. "Looky here, Arnold's following you Brits, but not us. If we four pretended to go down, while you four took the West Ridge direct, then Arnold would follow you. Then we four could sneak off into the Diagonal Ditch, and pass you by going up the Hornbein Couloir, which is actually faster than the West Ridge direct. You wouldn't see us and we'd be up there where the body is, lickety-split."

Well, no one was overjoyed at this plan. The Brits would have liked to find Mallory themselves, I could see. And I didn't have any inclination to go any higher than we already had. In fact I was dead set against it.

But by now the Brits were absolutely locked onto the idea of saving Mallory from TV and Westminster Abbey. "It would do the job," Marion conceded.

"And we might lose the leech on the ridge," Mad Tom added. "It's a right piece of work or so I'm told."

"That's right!" Freds said happily. "Laure, are you up for it?"

"Whatever you like," Laure said, and grinned. He thought it was a fine idea. Freds then asked Kunga Norbu, in Tibetan, and reported to us that Kunga gave the plan his mystic blessing.

"George?"

"Oh, man, no. I'd rather just get him down some other way."

"Ah come on!" Freds cried. "We don't have another way, and you don't want to let down the side, do you? Sticky wicket and all that?"

"He's your fooking client," John pointed out.

"Geez. Oh, man . . . Well . . . All right."

I walked back to our tent feeling that things were really getting out of control. In fact I was running around in the grip of other people's plans, plans I by no means approved of, made by people whose mental balance I doubted. And all this on the side of a mountain that had killed over fifty people. It was a bummer.

## 11

But I went along with the plan. Next morning we broke camp and made as if to go back down. The Brits started up the West Ridge, snarling dire threats at Arnold as they passed him. Arnold and his Sherpas were already packed, and after giving the Brits a short lead they took off after them. Arnold was roped up to their leader Ang Rita, raring to go, his camera in a chest pack. I had to hand it to him—he was one tenacious peeping Tom.

We waved good-bye and stayed on the shoulder until they were above us, and momentarily out of sight. Then we hustled after them, and took a left into the so-called Diagonal Ditch, which led out onto the North Face.

We were now following the route first taken by Tom Hornbein and Willi Unsoeld, in 1963. A real mountaineering classic, actually, which goes up what is now called the Hornbein Couloir. Get out any good photo of the North Face of Everest and you'll see it—a big vertical crack on the right side. It's a steep gully, but quite a bit faster than the West Ridge.

So we climbed. It was hard climbing, but not as scary as the Lho La. My main problem on this day was paranoia about the weather. Weather is no common concern on the side of Everest. You don't say, "Why snow would really ruin the day." Quite a number of people have been caught by storms on Everest and killed by them, including the guys we were going to look for. So whenever I saw wisps of cloud streaming out from the peak, I tended to freak. And the wind whips a banner of cloud from the peak of Everest almost continuously. I kept looking up and seeing that banner, and groaning. Freds heard me.

"Gee, George, you sound like you're really hurting on this pitch."

"Hurry up, will you?"

"You want to go faster? Well, okay, but I gotta tell you I'm going about as fast as I can. I don't think I want to tell Kunga to hurry more, because he might do it."

I believed that. Kunga Norbu was using ice axe and crampons to fire up the packed snow in the middle of the couloir, and Freds was right behind him; they looked like roofers on a ladder. I did my best to follow, and Laure brought up the rear. Both Freds and Kunga had grins so wide and fixed that you'd have thought they were on acid.

Their teeth were going to get sunburned they were loving it so much. Meanwhile I was gasping for air, and worrying about that summit banner . . . it was one of the greatest climbing days of my life.

How's that, you ask? Well . . . it's hard to explain. But it's something like this: when you get on a mountain wall with a few thousand feet of empty air below you, it catches your attention. Of course part of you says oh my God, it's all over. Whyever did I do this! But another part sees that in order not to die you must pretend you are quite calm, and engaged in a semi-theoretical gymnastics exercise intended to move you higher. You *pay attention* to the exercise like no one has ever paid attention before. Eventually you find yourself on a flat spot of some sort—three feet by five feet will do. You look around and realize that you did not die, that you are still alive. And at that point this fact becomes really exhilarating. You really *appreciate* being alive. It's a sort of power, or a privilege granted you, in any case it feels quite special, like a flash of higher consciousness. Just to be alive! And in retrospect, that *paying attention* when you were climbing—your remember that as a higher consciousness too.

You can get hooked on feelings like those; they are the ultimate altered state. Drugs can't touch them. I'm not saying this is real healthy behavior, you understand. I'm just saying it happens.

For instance, at the end of this particular intense day in the Hornbein Couloir, the four of us emerged at its top, having completed an Alpine-style blitz of it due in large part to Kunga Norbu's inspired leads. We made camp on top of a small flat knob just big enough for our tent. And looking around—what a feeling! It really was something. There were only four or five mountains in the world taller than we were in that campsite, and you could tell. We could see all the way across Tibet, it seemed. Now Tibet, as Galen Rowell once said, tends mostly to look like a freeze-dried Nevada—but from our height it was range after range of snowy peaks, white on black forever, all tinted sepia by the afternoon sun. It seemed the world was nothing but mountains.

Freds plopped down beside me, idiot grin still fixed on his face. He had a steaming cup of lemon drink in one hand, his hash pipe in the other and he was singing "Truckin'." He took a hit from the pipe and handed it to me.

"Are you sure we should be smoking up here?"

"Sure, it helps you breathe."

"Come on."

"No, really. The nerve center that controls your involuntary breathing shuts down in the absence of carbon dioxide, and there's hardly any of that up here, so the smoke provides it."

I decided that on medical grounds I'd better join him. We passed the pipe back and forth. Behind us Laure was in the tent, humming to himself and getting his sleeping bag out. Kunga Norbu sat in the lotus position on the other side of the tent, intent on realms of his own. The world, all mountains, turned under the sun.

Freds exhaled happily. "This must be the greatest place on earth, don't you think?"

That's the feeling I'm talking about.

## 12

We had a long and restless night of it, because it's harder than hell to sleep at that altitude. But the next day dawned clear and windless once again, and after breakfasting we headed along the top of the Black Band.

Our route was unusual, perhaps unique. The Black Band, harder than the layers of rock above and below it, sticks out from the generally smooth slope of the face in a crumbly rampart. So in effect we had a sort of road to walk on. Although it was uneven and busted up, it was still twenty feet wide in places, and an easier place for a traverse couldn't be imagined. There were potential campsites all over it.

Of course usually when people are at 28,000 feet on Everest, they're interested in getting either higher or lower pretty quick. Since this rampway was level and didn't facilitate any route whatsoever, it wasn't much traveled. We might have been the first on it, since Freds said that Kunga Norbu had only looked down on it from above.

So we walked this high road, and made our search. Freds knocked a rock off the edge, and we watched it bounce down toward the Rongbuk Glacier until it became invisible, though we could still hear it. After that we trod a little more carefully. Still, it wasn't long before we had traversed the face and were looking down the huge clean chute of the Great Couloir. Here the rampart ended, and to continue the traverse to the fabled North Ridge, where Mallory and Irvine were last seen, would have been ugly work. Besides, that wasn't where Kunga Norbu had seen the body.

"We must have missed it," Freds said. "Let's spread out side to side, and check every little nook and cranny on the way back." So we did, taking it very slowly, and ranging out to the edge of the rampart as far as we dared.

We were about halfway back to the Hornbein Couloir when Laure found it. He called out, and we approached.

"Well dog my cats," Freds said, looking astonished.

The body was wedged in a crack, chest deep in a hard pack of snow. He was on his side, and curled over so that he was level with the rock on each side of the crack. His clothing was frayed, and rotting away on him; it looked like knit wool. The kind of thing you'd wear golfing in Scotland. His eyes were closed, and under a fraying hood his skin looked papery. Sixty years out in sun and storm, but always in below-freezing air, had preserved him strangely. I had the odd feeling that he was only sleeping, and might wake and stand.

Freds knelt beside him and dug in the snow a bit. "Look here—he's roped up, but the rope broke."

He held up an inch or two of unraveled rope—natural fibers, horribly thin—it made me shudder to see it. "Such primitive gear!" I cried.

Freds nodded briefly. "They were nuts. I don't think he's got an oxygen pack on either. They had it available, but he didn't like to use it." He shook his head. "They probably fell together. Stepped through a cornice maybe. Then fell down to here, and this one jammed in the crack while the other one went over the edge, and the rope broke."

"So the other one is down in the glacier," I said.

Freds nodded slowly. "And look—" he pointed above. "We're almost directly under the summit. So they must have made the top. Or fallen when damned close to it." He shook his head. "And wearing nothing but a jacket like that! Amazing."

"So they made it," I breathed.

"Well, maybe. Looks like it, anyway. So . . . which one is this?"

I shook my head. "I can't tell. Early twenties, or mid-thirties?"

Uneasily we looked at the mummified features.

"Thirties," Laure said. "Not young."

Freds nodded. "I agree."

"So it's Mallory," I said.

"Hmph." Freds stood and stepped back. "Well, that's that. The mystery solved." He looked at us, spoke briefly with Kunga Norbu. "He must be under snow most years. But let's hide him under rock, for the Brits."

This was easier said than done. All we needed were stones to lay over him, as he was tucked down in the crack. But we quickly found that loose stones of any size were not plentiful; they had been blown off. So we had to work in pairs, and pick up big flat plates that were heavy enough to hold against the winds.

We were still collecting these when Freds suddenly jerked back and sat behind an outcropping of the rampart. "Hey, the Brits are over there on the West Ridge! They're almost level with us!"

"Arnold can't be far behind," I said.

"We've still got an hour's work here," Freds exclaimed. "Here—Laure, listen—go back to our campsite and pack our stuff, will you? Then go meet the Brits and tell them to slow down. Got that?"

"Slow down," Laure repeated.

"Exactly. Explain we found Mallory and they should avoid this area. Give us time. You stay with them, go back down with them. George and Kunga and I will follow you guys down, and we'll meet you at Gorak Shep."

Gorak Shep? That seemed farther down than necessary.

Laure nodded. "Slow down, go back, we meet you Gorak Shep."

"You got it, buddy. See you down there."

Laure nodded and was off.

"Okay," Freds said. "Let's get this guy covered."

We built a low wall around him, and then used the biggest plate of all as a keystone to cover his face. It took all three of us to pick it up, and we staggered around to get it into position without disturbing him; it really knocked the wind out of us.

When we were done the body was covered, and most of the time snow would cover our burial cairn, and it would be just one lump among thousands. So he was hidden. "Shouldn't we say something?" Freds asked. "You know, an epitaph or whatever?"

"Hey, Kunga's the holy man," I said. "Tell him to do it."

Freds spoke to Kunga. In his snow goggles I could see little images of Kunga, looking like a Martian in his dirty red down jacket, hood and goggles. Quite a change in gear since old Mallory!

Kunga Norbu stood at the end of our cairn and stuck out his mittened hands; he spoke in Tibetan for a while.

Afterwards Freds translated for me: "Spirit of Chomolungma, Mother Goddess of the World, we're here to bury the body of George Leigh Mallory, the first person to climb your sacred slopes. He was a climber with a lot of heart and he always went for it, and we love him for that—he showed very purely something that we all treasure in ourselves. I'd like to add that it's also clear from his clothing and gear that he was a total loon to be up here at all, and I in particular would like to salute that quality as well. So here we are, four disciples of your holy spirit, and we take this moment to honor that spirit here and in us, and everywhere in the world." Kunga bowed his head, and Freds and I followed suit, and we were silent; and all we heard was the wind, whistling over the Mother Goddess into Tibet.

## 13

Fine. Our mission was accomplished, Mallory was safely hidden on Everest for all time, we had given him what I had found a surprisingly moving burial ceremony, and I for one was pretty pleased. But back at our campsite, Freds and Kunga started acting oddly. Laure had packed up the tent and our packs and left them for us, and now Freds and Kunga were hurrying around repacking them.

I said something to the effect that you couldn't beat the view from Mallory's final resting place, and Freds looked up at me, and said, "Well, you could beat it by a *little*." And he continued repacking feverishly. "In fact I've been meaning to talk to you about that," he said as he worked. "I mean, here we are, right? I mean here we are."

"Yes," I said. "We are here."

"I mean to say, here we are at almost twenty-eight thou, on Mount Everest. And it's only noon, and it's a perfect day. I mean a *perfect* day. Couldn't ask for a nicer day."

I began to see what he was driving at. "No way, Freds."

"Ah come on! Don't be hasty about this, George! We're above all the hard parts, it's just a walk from here to the top!"

"No," I said firmly. "We don't have time. And we don't have much food. And we can't trust the weather. It's too dangerous."

"Too dangerous! All climbing is too dangerous, George, but I don't notice that that ever stopped you before. Think about it, man! This ain't just some ordinary mountain, this ain't no Rainier or Denali, this is *Everest*. Sargaramantha! Chomo*lun*gma! The BIG E! Hasn't it always been your secret fantasy to climb Everest?"

"Well, no. It hasn't."

"I don't believe you! It sure is mine, I'll tell you that. It's gotta be yours too."

All the time we argued Kunga Norbu was ignoring us, while he rooted through his pack tossing out various inessential items.

Freds sat down beside me and began to show me the contents of his pack. "I got our butt pads, the stove, a pot, some soup and lemon mix, a good supply of food, and here's my snow shovel so we can bivvy somewhere. Everything we need."

"No."

"Looky here, George." Freds pulled off his goggles and stared me in the eye. "It was nice to bury Mallory and all, but I have to tell you that Kunga Norbu Lama and I have had what you'd call an *ulterior motive* all along here. We joined the Brits on the Lingtren climb because I had heard about this Mallory expedition from the north side, and I was planning all along to tell them about it, and show them our photo, and tell them that Kunga was the guy who saw Mallory's body back in 1980, and suggest that they go hide him."

"You mean Kunga *wasn't* the one who saw Mallory's body?" I said.

"No, he wasn't. I made that up. The Chinese climber who saw a body up here was killed a couple years later. So I just had Kunga circle the general area where I heard the Chinese saw him. That's why I was so surprised when we actually ran across the guy! Although it stands to reason when you look at the North Face—there isn't anywhere else but the Black Band that would have stopped him.

"Anyway I lied about that, and I also suggested we slip up the Hornbein Couloir and find the body when Arnold started tailing the Brits—and all of that was because I was just hoping we'd get into this situation, where we got the time and the weather to shoot for the top, we were both just *hoping* for it man and here we are. We got everything planned, Kunga and I have worked it all out—we've got all the stuff we need, and if we have to bivvy on the South Summit after we bag the peak, then we can descend by way of the Southeast Ridge and meet the Indian Army team in the South Col, and get escorted back to Base Camp, that's the yak route and won't be any problem."

He took a few deep breaths. "Plus, well, listen. Kunga Lama has got *mystic reasons* for wanting to go up there, having to do with his longtime guru Tilopa Lama. Remember I told you back in Chimoa how Tilopa had set a task for Kunga Norbu, that Kunga had to accomplish before the monastery at Kum-Bum would be rebuilt, and Kunga set free to be his own lama at last? Well—the task was to *climb Chomolungma*! That old son of a gun said to Kunga, you just climb Chomolungma and everything'll be fine! Figuring that meant that he would have a disciple for just as many re-incarnations as he would ever go through this side of nirvana. But he didn't count on Kunga Norbu teaming up with his old student Freds Fredericks, and his buddy George Fergusson!"

"Wait a minute," I said. "I can see you feel very deeply about this, Freds, and I respect that, but I'm not going."

"We need you along, George! Besides, we're going to do it, and we can't really leave you to go back down the West Ridge by yourself—that'd be more dangerous than coming along with us! And we're going to the peak, so you have to come along, it's that simple!"

Freds had been talking so fast and hard that he was completely out of breath; he waved a hand at Kunga Norbu. "You talk to him," he said to Kunga, then switched to Tibetan, no doubt to repeat the message.

Kunga Norbu pulled up his snow goggles, and very serenely he looked at me. He looked just a little sad; it was the sort of expression you might get if you refused to give to the United Way. His black eyes looked right through me just as they always did, and in that high-altitude glare his pupils kind of pulsed in and out, in and out, in and out. And damned if that old bastard didn't hypnotize me. I think.

But I struggled against it. I found myself putting on my pack, and checking my crampons to make sure they were really, really, really tight, and at the same time I was shouting at Freds. "Freds, be reasonable! No one climbs Everest unsupported like this! It's too dangerous!"

"Hey, Messner did it. Messner climbed it in two days from North Colby himself, all he had was his girlfriend waiting down at base camp."

"You can't use Reinhold Messner as an example," I cried. "Messner is cuckoo."

"Nah. He's just tough and fast. And so are we. It won't be a problem."

"Freds, climbing Everest is generally considered a problem." But Kunga Norbu had put on his pack and was starting up the slope above our campsite, and Freds was following him, and I was following Freds. "For one big problem," I yelled, "we don't have any oxygen!"

"People climb it without oxygen all the time now."

"Yeah, but you pay the price. You don't get enough oxygen up there, and it kills brain cells like you can't believe! If we go up there we're certain to lose *millions* of brain cells."

"So?" He couldn't see the basis of the objection.

I groaned. We continued up the slope.

## 14

And that is how I found myself climbing Mount Everest with a Tibetan tulku and the wild man of Arkansas. It was not a position that a reasonable person could defend to himself, and indeed as I trudged after Freds and Kunga I could scarcely believe it was happening. But every labored breath told me it was. And since it was, I decided I had better psych myself into the proper frame of mind for it, or else it would only be that much more dangerous. "Always wanted to do this," I said, banishing the powerful impression that I had been hypnotized into the whole deal. "We're climbing Everest, and I really want to."

"That's the attitude," Freds said.

I ignored him and kept thinking the phrase "I want to do this," once for every two steps. After a few hundred steps, I had to admit that I had myself somewhat convinced. I mean, Everest! Think about it! I suppose that like anyone else, I had the fantasy in there somewhere.

I won't bother you with the details of our route; if you want them you can consult my anonymous article in the *American Alpine Journal*, 1986 issue. Actually it was fairly straightforward; we contoured up from the Hornbein Couloir to the upper West Ridge, and continued from there.

I did this in bursts of ten steps at a time; the altitude was finally beginning to hammer me. I acclimatize as well as anyone I know, but nobody acclimatizes over 26,000 feet. It's just a matter of how fast you wind down.

"Try to go as slow as you need to, and avoid rests," Freds advised.

"I'm going as slow as I can already."

"No you're not. Try to just flow uphill. Really put it into first gear. You fall into a certain rhythm."

"All right. I'll try."

We were seated at this point to take off our crampons, which were unnecessary. Freds had been right about the ease of the climb up here. The ridge was wide, it wasn't very steep, and it was all broken up, so that irregular rock staircases were everywhere on it. If it were at sea level you could run up it, literally. It was so easy that I could try Freds's suggestion, and I followed him and Kunga up the ridge in slow-slow motion. At that rate I could go about five or ten minutes between rests—it's hard to be sure how long, as each interval seemed like an afternoon on its own.

But with each stop we were a little higher. There was no denying the West Ridge had a first-class view: to our right all the mountains of Nepal, to our left all the mountains of Tibet, and you could throw in Sikkim and Bhutan for change. Mountains everywhere: and all of them below us. The only thing still above us was the pyramid of Everest's final summit, standing brilliant white against a black blue sky.

At each rest stop I found Kunga Norbu was humming a strange Buddhist chant; he was looking happier and happier in a subtle sort of way, while Fred's grin got wider and wider. "Can you believe how perfect the day is? Beautiful, huh?"

"Uh huh." It was nice, all right. But I was too tired to enjoy it. Some of their energy poured into me at each stop, and that was a good thing, because they were really going strong, and I needed the help.

Finally the ridge became snow-covered again, and we had to sit down and put our crampons back on. I found this usually simple process almost more than I could handle. My hands left pink after-images in the air, and I hissed and grunted at each pull on the straps. When I finished and stood, I almost keeled over. The rocks swam, and even with my goggles on the snow was painfully white.

"Last bit," Freds said as we looked up the slope. We crunched into it, and our crampons spiked down into firm snow. Kunga took off at an unbelievable pace. Freds and I marched up side by side, sharing a pace to take some of the mental effort out of it.

Freds wanted to talk, even though he had no breath to spare. "Old Tilopa Lama. Going to be. Mighty surprised. When they start re-building Kum-Bum. Ha!"

I nodded as if I believed in the whole story. This was an exaggeration, but it didn't matter. Nothing mattered but to put one foot in front of the other, in blazing white snow.

I have read that Everest stands just at the edge of the possible, as far as climbing it without oxygen goes. The scientific team that concluded this, after a climb in which air and breath samples were taken, actually decided that theoretically it wasn't possible at all. Sort of a bumblebee's flight situation. One scientist speculated that if Everest were just a couple hundred feet taller, then it really couldn't be done.

I believe that. Certainly the last few steps up that snow pyramid were the toughest I ever took. My breath heaved in and out of me in useless gasps, and I could hear the brain cells popping off by the thousands, *snap crackle pop*. We were nearing the peak, a triangular dome of pure snow; but I had to slow down.

Kunga forged on ahead of us, picking up speed in the last approach. Looking down at the snow, I lost sight of him. Then his boots came into my field of vision, and I realized we were there, just a couple steps below the top.

The actual summit was a ridged mound of snow about eight feet long and four feet wide. It wasn't a pinnacle, but it wasn't a broad hilltop either; you wouldn't have wanted to dance on it.

"Well," I said. "Here we are." I couldn't get excited about it. "Too bad I didn't bring a camera." The truth was, I didn't feel a thing.

Beside me Freds stirred. He tapped my arm, gestured up at Kunga Norbu. We were still below him, with our heads at about the level of his boots. He was humming, and had his arms extended up and out, as if conducting a symphony out to the east. I looked in that direction. By this time it was late afternoon, and Everest's shadow extended to the horizon, even above. There must have been ice particles in the air to the east, because all of a sudden above the darkness of

Everest's shadow I saw a big icebow. It was almost a complete circle of color, much more diaphanous than a rainbow, cut off at the bottom by the mountain's triangular shadow.

Inside this round bow of faint color, on the top of the dark air of the shadow peak, there was a cross of light-haloed shadow. It was a Spectre of the Brocken phenomenon, caused when low sunlight throws the shadows of peaks and climbers onto moisture-filled air, creating a glory of light around the shadows. I had seen one before.

Then Kunga Norbu flicked his hands to the sides, and the whole vision disappeared, instantly.

"Whoah," I said.

"Right on," Freds murmured, and led me the last painful steps onto the peak itself, so that we stood beside Kunga Norbu. His head was thrown back, and on his face was a smile of pure, child-like bliss.

Now, I don't know what really happened up there. Maybe I went faint and saw colors for a moment, thought it was an icebow, and then blinked things clear. But I know that at that moment, looking at Kunga Norbu's transfigured face, I was quite sure that I had seen him gain his freedom, and paint it out there in the sky. The task was fulfilled, the arms thrown wide with joy . . . I believed all of it. I swallowed, a sudden lump in my throat.

Now I felt it too; I felt where we were. We had climbed Chomolungma. We were standing on the peak of the world.

Freds heaved his breath in and out a few times. "Well!" he said, and shook mittened hands with Kunga and me. "We did it!" And then we pounded each other on the back until we almost knocked ourselves off the mountain.

## 15

We hadn't been up there long when I began to consider the problem of getting down. There wasn't much left of the day, and we were a long way from anywhere homey. "What now?"

"I think we'd better go down to the South Summit and dig a snow cave for the night. That's the closest place we can do it, and that's what Haston and Scott did in '75. It worked for them, and a couple other groups too."

"Fine," I said. "Let's do it."

Freds said something to Kunga, and we started down. Immediately I found that the Southeast Ridge was not as broad or as gradual as the West Ridge. In fact we were descending a kind of snow-covered knife edge, with ugly gray rocks sticking out of it. So this was the yak route! It was a tough hour's work to get down to the South Summit, and the only thing that made it possible was the fact that we were going downhill all the way.

The South Summit is a big jog in the Southeast Ridge, which makes for a lump of a subsidiary peak, and a flat area. Here we had a broad sloping expanse of very deep, packed snow—perfect conditions for a snow cave.

Freds got his little aluminum shovel out of his pack and went to it, digging like a dog after a bone. I was content to sit and consult. Kunga Norbu stood staring around at the infinite expanse of peaks, looking a little dazed. Once or twice I summoned up the energy to spell Freds. After a body-sized entryway, we only wanted a cave big enough for the three of us to fit in. It looked a bit like a coffin for triplets.

The sun set, stars came out, the twilight turned midnight blue; then it was night. And seriously, seriously cold. Freds declared the cave ready and I crawled in after him and Kunga, feeling granules of snow crunch under me. We banged heads and got arranged on our butt pads so that we were sitting in a little circle, on a rough shelf above our entrance tunnel, in a roughly spherical chamber. By slouching I got an inch's clearance above. "All right," Freds said wearily. "Let's party." He took the stove from his pack, held it in his mittens for a while to warm the gas inside, then set it on the snow in the middle of the three of us, and lit it with his lighter. The blue glare was blinding, the roar deafening. We took off our mitts and cupped our hands so there was no gap between flame and flesh. Our cave began to warm up a little.

You may think it odd that a snow cave can warm up at all, but remember we are speaking relatively here. Outside it was dropping to about 10 below 0, Fahrenheit. Add any kind of wind and at that altitude, where oxygen is so scarce, you'll die. Inside the cave, however, there was no wind. Snow itself is not that cold, and it's a great insulator: it will warm up, even begin to get slick on its surface, and that water also holds heat very well. Add a stove raging away, and three bodies struggling to pump out their 98.6, and even with a hole connecting you to outside air, you can get the temperature well up into the 30s. That's colder than a refrigerator, but compared to 10 below it's beach weather.

So we were happy in our little cave, at first. Freds scraped some of the wall into his pot and cooked some hot lemon drink. He offered me some almonds, but I had no appetite whatsoever; eating an almond was the same as eating a coffee table to me. We were all dying for drink, though, and we drank the lemon mix when it was boiling, which at this elevation was just about bath temperature. It tasted like heaven.

We kept melting snow and drinking it until the stove sputtered and ran out of fuel. Only a couple of hours had passed, at most. I sat there in the pitch dark, feeling the temperature drop. My spirits dropped with it.

But Freds was by no means done with the party. His lighter scraped and by its light I saw him punch a hole in the wall and set a candle in it. He lit the candle, and its light reflected off the slick white sides of our home. He had a brief discussion with Kunga Norbu.

"Okay," he said to me at the end of it, breath cascading whitely into the air. "Kunga is going to do some *tumo* now."

"Tumo?"

"Means, the art of warming oneself without fire up in the snows."

That caught my interest. "Another lama talent?"

"You bet. It comes in handy for naked hermits in the winter."

"I can see that. Tell him to lay it on us."

With some crashing about Kunga got in the lotus position, an impressive feat with his big snow boots still on.

He took his mitts off, and we did the same. Then he began breathing in a regular, deep rhythm, staring at nothing. This went on for almost half an hour, and I was beginning to think we would all freeze before he warmed up, when he held his hands out toward Freds and me. We took them in our own.

They were as hot as if he had a terrible fever. Fearfully I reached up to touch his face—it was warm, but nothing like his hands. "My Lord," I said.

"We can help him now," Freds said softly. "You have to concentrate, harness the energy that's always inside you. Every breath out you push away pride, anger, hatred, envy, sloth, stupidity. Every breath in, you take in Buddha's spirit, the five wisdoms, everything good. When you've gotten clear and calm, imagine a golden lotus in your belly button . . . Okay? In that lotus you imagine the syllable *ram*, which means fire. Then you have to see a little seed of flame, the size of a goat dropping, appearing in the *ram*. Every breath after that is like a bellows, fanning that flame, which travels through the *tsas* in the body, the mystic nerves. Imagine this process in five stages. First, the *uma tsa* is seen as a hair of fire, up your spine more or less . . . Two, the nerve is as big around as your little finger . . . Three, it's the size of an arm . . . Four, the body becomes the *tsa* itself and is perceived as a tube of fire . . . Five, the *tsa* engulfs the world, and you're just one flame in a sea of fire."

"My Lord."

We sat there holding Kunga Norbu's fiery hands, and I imagined myself a tube of fire: and the warmth poured into me—up my arms, through my torso—it even thawed my frozen butt, and my feet. I stared at Kunga Norbu, and he stared right though the wall of our cave to eternity, or wherever, his eyes glowing faintly in the candlelight. It was weird.

I don't know how long this went on—it seemed endless, although I suppose it was no more than an hour or so. But then it broke off—Kunga's hand cooled, and so did the rest of us. He blinked several times and shook his head.

He spoke to Freds.

"Well," Freds said. "That's about as long as he can hold it, these days."

"What?"

"Well . . ." He clucked his tongue regretfully. "It's like this. Tulkus tend to lose their powers, over the course of several incarnations. It's like they lose something in the process, every time, like when you keep making a tape from copies or whatever. There's a name for it."

"Transmission error," I said.

"Right. Well, it gets them too. In fact you run into a lot of tulkus in Tibet who are complete morons. Kunga is better than that, but he is a bit like Paul Revere. A little light in the belfry, you know. A great lama, and a super guy, but not tremendously powerful at any of the mystic disciplines, any more."

"Too bad."

"I know."

I recalled Kunga's fiery hands, their heat pronging into me. "So . . . he really is a tulku, isn't he."

"Oh yeah! Of course! And now he's free of old Tilopa, too—a lama in his own right, and nobody's disciple. It must be a great feeling."

"I bet. So how does it work again, exactly?"

"Becoming a tulku?"

"Yeah."

"Well, it's a matter of concentrating your mental powers. Tibetans believe that none of this is supernatural, but just a focusing of natural powers that we all have. Tulkus have gotten their psychic energies incredibly focused, and when you're at that stage, you can leave your body whenever you want. Why if Kunga wanted to, he could die in about ten seconds."

"Useful."

"Yeah. So when they decide to go, they hop off into the Bardo. The Bardo is the other world, the world of spirit, and it's a confusing place—talk about hallucinations! First a light like God's camera flash goes off in your face. Then it's just a bunch of colored paths, apparitions, everything. When Kunga describes it it's really scary. Now if you're just an ordinary spirit, then you can get disoriented, and be reborn as a slug or a game show host or *anything*. But if you stay focused, you're reborn in the body you choose, and you go on from there."

I nodded dully. I was tired, and cold, and the lack of oxygen was making me stupid and spacy; I couldn't make sense of Freds's explanations, although it may be that that would have happened anywhere.

We sat there. Kunga hummed to himself. It got colder.

The candle guttered, then went out.

It was dark. It continued to get colder.

After a while there was nothing but the darkness, our breathing, and the cold. I couldn't feel my butt or my legs below the knee. I knew I was waiting for something, but I had forgotten what it was. Freds stirred, started speaking Tibetan with Kunga. They seemed a long way away. They spoke to people I couldn't see. For a while Freds jostled about, punching the sides of the cave. Kunga shouted out hoarsely, things like "Hak!" and "Phut!"

"What are you doing?" I roused myself to say.

"We're fighting off demons," Freds explained.

I was ready to conclude, by watching my companions, that lack of oxygen drove one nuts; but what was my basis for comparison? My sample was skewed.

Some indeterminate time later Freds started shoveling snow out of the tunnel. "Casting out demons?" I inquired.

"No, trying to get warm. Want to try it?"

I didn't have the energy to move.

Then he shook me from side to side, switched to English, told me stories. Story after story, in a dry, hoarse, frog's voice. I didn't understand any of them. I had to concentrate on fighting the cold. On breathing. Freds became agitated, he told me a story of Kunga's, something about running across Tibet with a friend, a *lung-gom-pa* test of some kind, and the friend was wearing chains to keep from floating away entirely. Then something about running into a young husband at night, dropping the chains in a campfire . . . "The porters knew about *lung-gom*, and the next morning they must have tried to explain it to the British. Can you imagine it? Porters trying to explain these chains come out of nowhere . . . explaining they were used by people running across Tibet, to keep from going orbital? Man, those Brits must've thought they were invading Oz. Don't you think so? Hey, George? George? . . . George?"

## 16

But finally the night passed, and I was still there.

We crawled out of our cave in the pre-dawn light, and stamped our feet until some sensation came back into them, feeling pretty pleased with ourselves. "Good morning!" Kunga Norbu said to me politely. He was right about that. There were high cirrus clouds going pink above us, and an ocean of blue cloud far below in Nepal, with all the higher white peaks poking out of it like islands, and slowly turning pink themselves. I've never seen a more otherwordly sight; it was as if we had climbed out of our cave onto the side of another planet.

"Maybe we should just shoot down to the South Col and join those Indian Army guys," Freds croaked. "I don't much feel like going back up to the peak to get to the West Ridge."

"You aren't kidding," I said.

So down the Southeast Ridge we went.

Now Peter Habeler, Messner's partner on the first oxygenless ascent of Everest in 1979, plunged down this ridge from the summit to the South Col in *one hour*. He was worried about brain damage; my feeling is that the speed of his descent is evidence it had already occurred. We went as fast as we could, which was pretty alarmingly fast, and it still took us almost three hours. One step after another, down a steep snowy ridge. I refused to look at the severe drops to right and left. The clouds below were swelling up like the tide in the Bay of Fundy; our good weather was about to end.

I felt completely disconnected from my body, I just watched it do its thing. Below Freds kept singing "Close to the Edge." We came to a big snow-filled gully and glissaded down it carelessly, sliding twenty or thirty feet with each dreamy step. All three of us were staggering by this point. Cloud poured up the Western Cwm, and mist magically appeared all around us, but we were just above the South Col by this time, and it didn't matter.

I saw there was a camp in the col, and breathed a sigh of relief. We would have been goners without it.

The Indians were still securing their tents as we walked up. A week's perfect weather, and they had just gotten into the South Col. Very slow, I thought as we approached. Siege-style assault, logistical pyramid, play it safe—slow as building the other kind of pyramid.

As we crossed the col and closed on the tents, navigating between piles of junk from previous expeditions, I began to worry. You see, the Indian Army has had incredible bad luck on Everest. They have tried to climb it several times, and so far as I know, they've never succeeded. Mostly this is because of storms, but people tend to ignore that, and the Indians have come in for a bit of criticism from the climbing community in Nepal. In fact they've been called terrible climbers. So they are a little touchy about this, and it was occurring to me, very slowly, that they might not be too amused to be greeted in the South Col by three individuals who had just bagged the peak on an overnighter from the north side.

Then one of them saw us. He dropped the mallet in his hand.

"Hi there!" Freds croaked.

A group of them quickly gathered around us. The wind was beginning to blow hard, and we all stood at an angle into it. The oldest Indian there, probably a major, shouted gruffly, "Who are you!"

"We're lost," Freds said. "We need help."

Ah, good, I thought. Freds has also thought of this problem. He won't tell them where we've been. Freds is still thinking. He will take care of this situation for us.

"Where did you come from?" the major boomed.

Freds gestured down the Western Cwm. Good, I thought. "Our Sherpas told us to keep turning right. So ever since Jomosom we have been."

"Where did you say!"

"Jomosom!"

The major drew himself up. "Jomosom," he said sharply, "is in *western* Nepal."

"Oh," Freds said.

And we all stood there. Apparently that was it for Freds's explanation.

I elbowed him aside. "The truth is, we thought it would be fun to help you. We didn't know what we were getting into."

"Yeah!" Freds said, accepting this new tack thankfully. "Can we carry a load down for you, maybe?"

"We are still climbing the mountain!" the major barked. "We don't need loads carried down!" He gestured at the ridge behind us, which was disappearing in mist. "This is Everest!"

Freds squinted at him. "You're kidding."

I elbowed him. "We need help," I said.

The major looked at us closely. "Get in the tent," he said at last.

## 17

Well, eventually I concocted a semi-consistent story about us idealistically wanting to porter loads for an Everest expedition, although who would be so stupid as to want to do that I don't know. Freds was no help at all—he kept forgetting and going back to his first story, saying things like, "We must have gotten on the wrong plane." And neither of us could fit Kunga Norbu into our story very well; I claimed he was our guide, but we didn't understand his language. He very wisely stayed mute.

Despite all that, the Indian team fed us and gave us water to slake our raging thirst, and they escorted us back down their fixed ropes to the camps below, to make sure they got us out of there. Over the next couple of days they led us all the way down the Western Cwm and the Khumbu Icefall to Base Camp. I wish I could give you a blow-by-blow account of the fabled Khumbu Icefall, but the truth is I barely remember it. It was big and white and scary; I was tired. That's all I know. And then we were in their base camp, and I knew it was over. First illegal ascent of Everest.

## 18

Well, after what we had been through, Gorak Shep looked like Ireland, and Pheriche looked like Hawaii. And the air was oxygen soup.

We kept asking after the Brits and Arnold and Laure, and kept hearing that they were a day or so below us. From the sound of it the Brits were chasing Arnold, who was managing by extreme efforts to stay ahead of them. So we hurried after them.

On our way down, however, we stopped at the Pengboche Monastery, a dark brooding old place in a little nest of black pine trees, supposed to be the chin whiskers of the first abbot. There we left Kunga Norbu, who was looking pretty beat. The monks at the monastery made a big to-do over him. He and Freds had an emotional parting, and he gave me a big grin as he bored me through one last time with that spacy black gaze. "Good morning!" he said, and we were off.

So Freds and I tromped down to Namche, which reminded me strongly of Manhattan, and found our friends had just left for Lukla, still chasing Arnold. Below Namche we really hustled to catch up with them, but we didn't succeed until we reached Lukla itself. And then we only caught the Brits—because they were standing there by the Lukla airstrip, watching the last plane of the day hum down the tilted grass and ski jump out over the deep gorge of the Dudh Kosi—while Arnold McConnell, we quickly found out, was on that plane, having paid a legitimate passenger a fat stack of rupees to replace him. Arnold's Sherpa companions were lining the strip and waving good-bye to him; they had all earned about a year's wages in this one climb, it turned out, and they were pretty fond of old Arnold.

The Brits were not. In fact they were fuming.

"Where have you been?" Trevor demanded.

"Well . . ." we said.

"We went to the top," Freds said apologetically. "Kunga had to for religious reasons."

"Well," Trevor said huffily. "We considered it ourselves, but *we* had to chase *your* client back down the mountain to try and get his film. The film that will get us all kicked out of Nepal for good if it's ever shown."

"Better get used to it," Mad Tom said gloomily. "He's off to Kathmandu, and we're not. We'll never catch him now."

Now the view from Lukla is nothing extraordinary, compared to what you can see higher up; but there are the giant green walls of the gorge, and to the north you can see a single scrap of the tall white peaks beyond; and to look at all that, and think you might never be allowed to see it again. . . .

I pointed to the south. "Maybe we just got lucky."

"What?"

Freds laughed. "Choppers! Incoming! Some trekking outfit has hired helicopters to bring its group in."

It was true. This is fairly common practice, I've done it myself many times. RNAC's daily flights to Lukla can't fulfill the need during the peak trekking season, so the Nepali Air Force kindly rents out its helicopters, at exorbitant fees. Naturally they prefer not to go back empty, and they'll take whoever will pay. Often, as on this day, there is a whole crowd clamoring to pay to go back, and the competition is fierce, although I for one am unable to understand what people are so anxious to get back to.

Anyway, this day was like most of them, and there was a whole crowd of trekkers sitting around on the unloading field by the airstrip, negotiating with the various Sherpa and Sherpani power brokers who run the airport and get people onto flights. The hierarchy among these half-dozen power brokers is completely obscure, even to them, and on this day as always each of them had a list of people who had paid up to a hundred dollars for a lift out; and until the brokers discussed it with the helicopter crew, no one knew who was going to be the privileged broker given the go-ahead to march his clients on board. The crowd found this protocol ambiguous at best, and they were milling about and shouting ugly things at their brokers as the helicopters were sighted.

So this was not a good situation for us, because although we were desperate, everyone else wanting a lift claimed to be desperate also, and no one was going to volunteer to give up their places. Just before the two Puma choppers made their loud and windy landing, however, I saw Heather on the unloading field, and I ran over and discovered that she had gotten our expedition booked in with Pemba Sherpa, one of the most powerful brokers there. "Good work, Heather!" I cried. Quickly I explained to her some aspects of the situation, and looking wide-eyed at us—we were considerably filthier and more sunburnt than when we last saw her—she nodded her understanding.

And sure enough, in the chaos of trekkers milling about the choppers, in all that moaning and groaning and screaming and shouting to be let on board, it was Pemba who prevailed over the other brokers. And Want To Take You Higher Ltd.'s "Video Expedition to Everest Base Camp"—with the addition of four British climbers and an American—climbed on board the two vehicles, cheering all the way. With a *thukka thukka thukka* we were off.

"Now how will we find him in Kathmandu?" Marion said over the noise.

"He won't be expecting you," I said. "He thinks he's on the last flight of the day. So I'd start at the Kathmandu Guest House, where we were staying, and see if you can find him there."

The Brits nodded, looking grim as commandos. Arnold was in trouble.

## 19

We landed at the Kathmandu airport an hour later, and the Brits zipped out and hired a taxi immediately. Freds and I hired another one and tried to keep up, but the Brits must have been paying their driver triple, because that little Toyota took off over the dirt roads between the airport and the city like it was in a motorcross race. So we fell behind, and by the time we were let off in the courtyard of the Kathmandu Guest House, their taxi was already gone. We paid our driver and walked in and asked one of the snooty clerks for Arnold's room number, and when he gave it to us we hustled on up to the room, on the third floor overlooking the back garden.

We got there in the middle of the action. John and Mad Tom and Trevor had Arnold trapped on a bed in the corner, and they were standing over him not letting him go anywhere. Marion was on the other side of the room doing the actual demolition, taking up video cassettes one at a time and stomping them under her boot. There was a lot of yelling going on, mostly from Marion and Arnold. "*That's* the one of me taking my bath," Marion said. "And *that's* the one of me changing my shirt in my tent. And *that's* the one of me taking a pee at eight thousand meters!" and so on, while Arnold was shouting "No, no!" and "Not that one, my God!" and "I'll sue you in every court in Nepal!"

"Foreign nationals can't sue each other in Nepal," Mad Tom told him.

But Arnold continued to shout and threaten and moan, his sun-torched face going incandescent, his much-reduced body bouncing up and down on the bed, his big round eyes popping out till I was afraid they would burst, or fall down on springs. He picked up the fresh cigar that had fallen from his mouth and threw it between Trevor and John, hitting Marion in the chest.

"Molester," she said, dusting her hands with satisfaction. "That's all of them, then." She began to stuff the wreckage of plastic and videotape into a daypack. "And we'll take this along, too, thank you very much."

"Thief," Arnold croaked.

The three guys moved away from him. Arnold sat there on the bed, frozen, staring at Marion with a stricken, bug-eyed expression. He looked like a ballon with a pinprick in it.

"Sorry, Arnold," Trevor said. "But you brought this on yourself, as you must admit. We told you all along we didn't want to be filmed."

Arnold stared at them speechlessly.

"Well, then," Trevor said. "That's that." And they left.

Freds and I watched Arnold sit there. Slowly his eyes receded back to their usual pop-eyed position, but he still looked disconsolate.

"Them Brits are tough," Freds offered. "They're not real sentimental people."

"Come on, Arnold," I said. Now that he was no longer my responsibility, now that we were back, and I'd never have to see him again—now that it was certain his videotape, which could have had Freds and me in as much hot water as the Brits, was destroyed—I felt a little bit sorry for him. Just a little bit. It was clear from his appearance that he had really gone through a lot to get that tape. Besides, I was starving. "Come on, let's all get showered and shaved and cleaned up, and then I'll take you out to dinner."

"Me too," said Freds.

Arnold nodded mutely.

## 20

Kathmandu is a funny city. When you first arrive there from the West, it seems like the most ramshackle and unsanitary place imaginable: the buildings are poorly constructed of old brick, and there are weed patches growing out of the roofs; the hotel rooms are bare pits; all the food you can find tastes like cardboard, and often makes you sick; and there are sewage heaps here and there in the mud streets, where dogs and cows are scavenging. It really seems primitive.

Then you go out for a month or two in the mountains, or a trek or a climb. And when you return to Kathmandu, the place is utterly transformed. The only likely explanation is that while you were gone they took the city away and replaced it with one that looks the same on the outside, but is completely different in substance. The accommodations are luxurious beyond belief; the food is superb; the people look prosperous, and their city seems a marvel of architectural sophistication. Kathmandu! What a metropolis!

So it seemed to Freds and me, as we checked into my home away from home, the Hotel Star. As I sat on the floor under the waist-high tap of steaming hot water that emerged from my shower, I found myself giggling in mindless rapture, and from the next room I could hear Freds bellowing the old 50s rocker, "Going to Katmandu."

An hour later, hair wet, faces chopped up, skin all prune-shriveled, we met Arnold out in the street and walked through the Thamel evening. "We look like coatracks!" Freds observed. Our city clothes were hanging on us. Freds and I had each lost about twenty pounds, Arnold about thirty. And it wasn't just fat, either. Everything wastes away at altitude. "We'd better get to the Old Vienna and put some of it back on."

I started salivating at the very thought of it.

So we went to the Old Vienna Inn, and relaxed in the warm steamy atmosphere of the Austro-Hungarian Empire. After big servings of goulash, schnitzel Parisienne, and apple strudel with whipped cream, we sat back sated. Sensory overload. Even Arnold was looking up a little. He had been quiet through the meal, but then again we all had, being busy.

We ordered a bottle of rakshi, which is a potent local beverage of indeterminate origin. When it came we began drinking.

Freds said, "Hey, Arnold, you're looking better."

"Yeah, I don't feel so bad." He wiped his mouth with a napkin streaked all red; we had all split our sun-destroyed lips more than once, trying to shovel the food in too fast. He got set to start the slow process of eating another cigar, unwrapping one very slowly.

"Not so bad at all." And then he grinned; he couldn't help himself; he grinned so wide that he had to grab the napkin and staunch the flow from his lips again.

"Well, it's a shame those guys stomped your movie," Freds said.

"Yeah, well." Arnold waved an arm expansively. "That's life."

I was amazed. "Arnold, I can't believe this is you talking. Here those guys took your videotape of all that *suffering* you just put us through, and they *stomp* it, and you say, "That's life?"

He took a long hit of the rakshi. "Well," he said, waggling his eyebrows up and down fiendishly. He leaned over the table toward us. "They got one copy of it, anyway."

Freds and I looked at each other.

"Couple hundred dollars of tape there that they crunched. I suppose I ought to bill them for it. But I'm a generous guy; I let it pass."

"One copy?" I said.

"Yeah." He tipped his head. "Did you see that box, kind of like a suitcase, there in the corner of my room at the Guesthouse?"

We shook our heads.

"Neither did the Brits. Not that they would have recognized it. It's a video splicer, mainly. But a copier too. You stick a cassette in there and push a button and it copies the cassette for storage, and then you can do all your splicing off the master. You make your final tape that way. Great machine. Most freelance video people have them now, and these portable babies are really the latest. Saved my ass, in this case."

"Arnold," I said. "You're going to get those guys in trouble! And us too!"

"Hey," he warned, "I've got the splicer under lock and key, so don't get any ideas."

"Well you're going to get us banned from Nepal for good!"

"Nah. I'll give you all stage names. You got any preferences along those lines?"

"Arnold!" I protested.

"Hey, listen," he said, and drank more rakshi. "Most of that climb was in Tibet, right? Chinese aren't going to be worrying about it. Besides, you know the Nepali Ministry of Tourism—can you really tell me they'll ever get it together to even see my film, much less take names from it and track those folks down when they next apply for a visa? Get serious!"

"Hmm," I said, consulting with my rakshi.

"So what'd you get?" Freds asked.

"*Everything*. I got some good long-distance work of you guys finding the body up there—ha!—you thought I didn't get that, right? I tell you I was filming your *thoughts* up there! I got that, and then the Brits climbing on the ridge—everything. I'm gonna make stars of you all."

Freds and I exchanged a relieved glance. "Remember about the stage names," I said.

"Sure. And after I edit it you won't be able to tell where on the mountain the body was, and with the names and all, I really think Marion and the rest will love it. Don't you? They were just being shy. Old fashioned! I'm going to send them all prints of the final product, and they're gonna love it. Marion in particular. She's gonna look beautiful." He waved the cigar and a look of cowlike yearning disfigured his face. "In fact, tell you a little secret, I'm gonna accompany that particular print in person, and make it part of my proposal to her. I think she's kind of fond of me, and I bet you anything she'll agree to marry me when she sees it, don't you think?"

"Sure," Freds said. "Why not?" He considered it. "Or if not in this life, then in the next."

Arnold gave him an odd look. "I'm going to ask her along on my next trip, which looks like it'll be China and Tibet. You know how the Chinese have been easing up on the Tibetan religions lately? Well, the clerk at the Guest House gave me a telegram on my way out—my agent tells me that the authorities in Lhasa have decided they're going to rebuild a whole bunch of Buddhist monasteries that they tore down during the Cultural Revolution, and it looks like I'll be allowed to film some of it. That should make for a real heart-string basher, and I bet Marion would love to see it, don't you?"

Freds and I grinned at each other. "*I'd* love to see it," Freds declared. "Here's to the monasteries, and a free Tibet!"

We toasted the idea, and ordered another bottle.

Arnold waved his cigar. "Meanwhile, this Mallory stuff is dynamite. It's gonna make a hell of a movie."

## 21

Which is why I can tell you about this one—the need for secrecy is going to be blown right out the window as soon as they air Arnold's film, *Nine Against Everest: Seven Men, One Woman, and a Corpse*. I hear both PBS and the BBC have gone for it, and it should be on any day now. Check local listings for times in your area.

# HONORABLE MENTIONS

## 1987

Vance Aandahl, "Deathmarch in Disneyland," *F & SF*, July.
Poul Anderson, "Letter from Tomorrow," *Analog*, August.
Isaac Asimov, "Galatea," *IASFM*, mid-December.
Iain Banks, "Descendant," *Tales from the Forbidden Planet*.
John Barnes, "Digressions from the Second Person Future," *IASFM*, January.
Neal Barrett, Jr., "Class of '61," *IASFM*, October.
———, "Highbrow," *IASFM*, July.
Greg Bear, "The Visitation," *Omni*, June.
Gregory Benford, "As Big as the Ritz," *Interzone 18*.
———, "The Mandikini," *The Universe*.
Michael Bishop, "God's Hour," *Omni*, June.
James P. Blaylock, "Myron Chester and the Toads," *IASFM*, February.
Bruce Boston, "One-Trick Dog," *IASFM*, May.
Ben Bova, "Silent Night," *IASFM*, December.
J. P. Boyd, "The Anger of Time," *F & SF*, February.
Eric Brown, "Krash-Bangg Joe and the Pineal-Zen Equation," *Interzone 21*.
Edward Bryant, "The Baku," *Night Visions 4*.
———, "Doing Colfax," *Night Visions 4*.
William S. Burroughs, "Ghost Lemurs of Madagascar," *Omni*, April.
Pat Cadigan, "The Boys in the Rain," *Twilight Zone*, June.
———, "Lunatic Bridge," *The Book of Omni Science Fiction #5*.
Orson Scott Card, "Carthage City," *IASFM*, September.
———, "Eye for Eye," *IASFM*, March.
———, "Runaway," *IASFM*, June.
Lillian Stewart Carl, "Out of Darkness," *IASFM*, April.
Jonathan Carroll, "Friend's Best Man," *IASFM*, January.
Susan Casper, "Covenant with a Dragon," *In the Field of Fire*.
———, "Under Her Skin," *Amazing*, March.
Kathryn Cramer, "Forbidden Knowledge," *Mathenauts*.

Jack Dann, "Visitors," *IASFM*, October.
——— and Jeanne Van Buren Dann, "The Apotheosis of Isaac Rosen," *Omni*, June.
Avram Davidson, "The Engine of Samoset Erastus Hale and One Other, Unknown," *Amazing*, July.
———, "Mountaineers Are Always Free," *F & SF*, October.
Charles de Lint, "Uncle Dobbin's Parrot Fair," *IASFM*, November.
Paul DiFilippo, "Conspiracy of Noise," *F & SF*, November.
David Drake, "The Fool," *Whispers VI*.
George Alec Effinger, "Another Dead Grandfather," *F & SF*, December.
———, "King of the Cyber Rifles," *IASFM*, mid-December.
M. J. Engh, "Aurin Tree," *IASFM*, February.
George M. Ewing, "A Little Further up the Fox," *IASFM*, April.
Sharon N. Farber, "Ice Dreams," *IASFM*, March.
Brad Ferguson, "The World Next Door," *IASFM*, September.
Michael Flynn, "In the Country of the Blind," *Analog*, Oct.-Nov.
John M. Ford, "Fugue State," *Under the Wheel*.
Karen Joy Fowler, "Letters from Home," *In the Field of Fire*.
Robert Frazier, "Across those Endless Skies," *In the Field of Fire*.
Stephen Gallagher, "Like Shadows in the Dark," *Shadows 10*.
William Gibson, "The Silver Walks," *High Times*, November.
Lisa Goldstein, "Cassandra's Photographs," *IASFM*, August.
Charles L. Grant, "Everything to Live For," *Whispers VI*.
Peni Griffin, "Nereid," *Twilight Zone*, April.
Russell Griffin, "Saving Time," *F & SF*, February.
Philip C. Jennings, "The Castaway," *Amazing*, March.
———, "Moondo Bizarro," *New Destinies II*, Fall.
Gwyneth Jones, "The Snow Apples," *Tales from the Forbidden Planet*.
Richard Kadrey, "Goodbye Houston Street, Goodbye," *Interzone 19*.
James Patrick Kelly, "Heroics," *IASFM*, November.
John Kessel, "Credibility," *In the Field of Fire*.
Garry Kilworth, "Hogfoot Right and Bird-Hands," *Other Edens*.
———, "Paper Moon," *Omni*, January.
Dean R. Koontz, "Hardshell," *Night Visions 4*.
Nancy Kress, "Cannibals," *IASFM*, May.
———, "Glass," *IASFM*, September.
Marc Laidlaw, "Nutrimancer," *IASFM*, August.
———, "Shalamari," *IASFM*, December.
Tanith Lee, "Crying in the Rain," *Other Edens*.
Justin Leiber, "Tit for Tat," *Amazing*, July.
Bruce McAllister, "Kingdom Come," *Omni*, February.
Jack McDevitt, "Dutchman," *IASFM*, February.
———, "In the Tower," *Universe 17*.

———, "To Hell with the Stars," *IASFM*, December.
Cooper McLaughlin, "The Order of the Peacock Angel," *F & SF*, January.
Tom Maddox, "Spirit of the Night," *IASFM*, September.
Barry N. Maltzberg, "The Queen of Lower Saigon," *In the Field of Fire*.
George R. R. Martin, "The Pear-Shaped Man," *Omni*, October.
Lisa Mason, "Arachne," *Omni*, November.
Pat Murphy, "Clay Devils," *Twilight Zone*, April.
Susan Palwick, "The Visitation," *Amazing*, September.
Frederik Pohl, "My Life as a Born-Again Pig," *Synergy 1*.
———, "The View from Mars Hill," *IASFM*, May.
Steven Popkes, "The Rose Garden," *IASFM*, August.
———, "Stovelighter," *IASFM*, mid-December.
Keith Roberts, "Equivalent for Giles," *Tales from the Forbidden Planet*.
———, "Piper's Wait," *Other Edens*.
———, "The Tiger Sweater," *F & SF*, October.
R. Garcia y Robertson, "The Flying Mountain," *Amazing*, May.
Kim Stanley Robinson, "The Blind Geometer," *IASFM*, August.
———, "The Return from Rainbow Bridge," *F & SF*, August.
Rudy Rucker, "Bringing in the Sheaves," *IASFM*, January.
———, "The Man Who Was a Cosmic String," *The Universe*.
Richard Paul Russo, "Prayers of a Rain God," *F & SF*, May.
Geoff Ryman, "Love Sickness," *Interzone 20–21*.
Al Sarrantonio, "Pigs," *Shadows 10*.
Charles Sheffield, "Guilt Trip," *Analog*, August.
———, "Trapalanda" *IASFM*, June.
Lucius Shepard, "The Black Clay Boy," *Whispers VI*.
———, "The Glassblower's Dragon," *F & SF*, April.
———, "On the Border," *IASFM*, August.
———, "The Sun Spider," *IASFM*, April.
Lewis Shiner, "Dancers," *Night Cry*, Summer.
———, "Rebels," *Omni*, November.
——— and Edith Shiner, "Six Flags over Jesus," *IASFM*, November.
John Shirley, "Ticket to Heaven," *F & SF*, December.
Robert Silverberg, "The Fascination of the Abomination," *IASFM*, July.
———, "The Secret Sharer," *IASFM*, September.
Dave Smeds, "Goats," *In the Field of Fire*.
———, "Termites," *IASFM*, May.
Dean Wesley Smith, "The Jukebox Man," *Night Cry*, Fall.
Brian Stableford, "Layers of Meaning," *Interzone 21*.
———, "Sexual Chemistry," *Interzone 20*.

Bruce Sterling, "The Little Magic Shop," *IASFM*, October.
Tim Sullivan, "Dinosaur on a Bicycle," *IASFM*, March.
Michael Swanwick, "Foresight," *Interzone 20*.
Steve Rasnic Tem, "Dinosaur," *IASFM*, May.
James Tiptree, Jr. "Yanqui Doodle," *IASFM*, July.
Larry Tritten, "In Video Veritas," *F & SF*, December.
Harry Turtledove, "Images," *IASFM*, March.
———, "Last Favor," *Analog*, mid-December.
———, "Superwine," *IASFM*, April.
Eric Vinicoff, "Independents," *Analog*, April.
Howard Waldrop, "He-We-Await," *All About Strange Monsters of the Recent Past*.
———, "Thirty Minutes over Broadway!," *Wild Cards 1*.
Ian Watson, "Jewels in an Angel's Wings," *Synergy 1*.
———, "The Moon and Michelangelo," *IASFM*, October.
———, "When Jesus Comes down the Chimney," *Interzone 18*.
Lawrence Watt-Evans, "Why I Left Harry's All-Night Hamburgers," *IASFM*, July.
Andrew Weiner, "The Alien in the Lake," *IASFM*, September.
———, "Rider," *IASFM*, July.
———, "Waves," *IASFM*, March.
Dean Whitlock, "Roadkill," *IASFM*, November.
Cherie Wilkerson, "The Moment of the Rose," *IASFM*, February.
Walter Jon Williams, "Wolf Time," *IASFM*, January.
Connie Willis, "Lord of Hosts," *Omni*, June.
———, "Winter's Tale," *IASFM*, December.
Robert Charles Wilson, "Ballads in ¾ Time," *F & SF*, April.
———, "Extras," *F & SF*, December.
Robley Wilson, Jr., "Flaggers," *IASFM*, June.
Ken Wisman, "The Finder-Keeper," *Shadows 10*.
———, "The Philosophical Stone," *Interzone 21*.
Gene Wolfe, "In the House of Gingerbread," *Architecture of Fear*.
———, "The Peace Spy," *IASFM*, January.
Jane Yolen, "The White Babe," *IASFM*, June.
———, "Wolf/Child," *Twilight Zone*, June.
Robert F. Young, "What Bleak Land," *F & SF*, January.